READER'S
DIGEST
CONDENSED
BOOKS

READER'S DIGEST ASSOCIATION (CANADA) LTD.
CONDENSED BOOKS DIVISION

215 Redfern Ave., Montreal, Que. H3Z 2V9
Editor: Deirdre Gilbert
Assistant Editor: Anita Winterberg
Design: Andrée Payette
Production Manager: Holger Lorenzen

FIRST EDITION
PRINTED IN THE U.S.A.

READER'S DIGEST CONDENSED BOOKS

In this volume

COMEBACK
by Dick Francis

Peter Darwin is a diplomat, not
a detective. But when he visits
his boyhood home in England
and befriends a local veterinarian,
he is drawn into a mystery that
baffles everyone, including the
police. Prize thoroughbred horses
are dying from causes no one can
explain. Pure coincidence? Or is
some malicious scheme behind
these sudden deaths? Peter's search
for the answer leads toward a
scandal buried deep in the past–
but there is even more danger
in the present when the killer
starts claiming human victims.
A fine mix of medicine and murder
by the bestselling author of
Longshot. / Page 7

SCARLETT
**The Sequel to
Margaret Mitchell's
GONE WITH THE WIND**
by Alexandra Ripley

Scarlett O'Hara — she stood up
against Sherman's rampage through
Georgia; she held on to Tara against
all odds, and she became one of
the most unforgettable heroines of
all time. But at the end of *Gone
With the Wind* she had lost what
she cherished most–the heart of
Rhett Butler. Now, in the eagerly
awaited sequel, she is determined
to win him back. In a sprawling
novel of adventure and romance
that sweeps from the elegant

THE DECEIVER
by Frederick Forsyth

drawing rooms of Charleston and Savannah, to the ancient castles and farmlands of strife-torn Ireland, Scarlett O'Hara and Rhett Butler are vividly brought to life once again — along with a host of other fascinating characters, both new and familiar. A satisfyingly rich conclusion to an epic story. / Page 129

He is called The Deceiver — the most cunning espionage player in the British Secret Intelligence Service. Sam McCready is the master when it comes to dirty tricks. But now the Cold War is over, and McCready's superiors want to put him out to pasture. Sam knows the danger is still there, and he sets out to make his point. But will a dazzling display of his exploits prove his value? Or will it show that he's a dangerous maverick, better shuffled off to an obscure desk job? In the balance hangs not only McCready's fate–but the future of British Intelligence. First-rate suspense fiction from the internationally acclaimed author of *The Day of the Jackal* and *The Negotiator.* / Page 407

BACK

Dick Francis

Something is desperately
wrong at Ken McClure's veterinary
practice. Eight horses have died,
all under suspicious
circumstances. A fire in
the night has destroyed
any evidence that might lead to
an answer. Coincidence? Or
careful planning? The answer
seems clear when the next
victim is a human one. . . .

CHAPTER 1

I'M PETER Darwin.

    Everyone asks, so I may as well say at once that no, I'm not related to Charles.

I was in fact born Peter Perry, but John Darwin, marrying my widowed mother when I was twelve, gave me, among many other things, a new life, a new name, and a new identity. Twenty years rolled like mist over the memories of my distant childhood in Gloucestershire, and now I, Peter Darwin, was thirty-two, adopted son of a diplomat, in the diplomatic service myself.

As my stepfather's postings and later my own were all at the whim of the Foreign Office, I'd mostly lived those twenty years abroad, from Caracas to Lima, from Moscow to Cairo to Madrid, housed in Foreign Office lodgings, counting nowhere home.

Friendships were transitory. Locals, left behind. Other diplomats and their children came and went. I was rootless and nomadic, well used to it and content.

"Look us up if you're ever in Florida," Fred Hutchings said casually, leaving Tokyo to be consul in Miami. "Stay for a day or so if you're passing through."

"Thanks," I said. We'd worked together for months in Tokyo without friction. He half meant the invitation. He was trained in politeness, as we all were.

My own new posting, when it came through nearly a year later, was, surprisingly, to England, to the Foreign and Commonwealth Office, in Whitehall.

"What?" My stepfather, in Mexico City, chuckled with pleasure on the phone when I told him. "Private secretary! Well done! The pay's rotten. You'll have some leave first, though. Come and see us. Your mother misses you."

So I spent nearly a month with them and then set off to England via Miami, which was why, after a delayed flight and a missed connection, I found myself with twenty-four hours to kill and the echo of Fred Hutchings' invitation in my head. Why not? I thought, and phoned him.

His voice sounded genuinely welcoming, and I pictured him on the other end of the line—forty, plump, freckled, eager, with a forehead that perspired under the slightest nervous pressure.

"Great, great," he was saying heartily. "I'd ask you here for the night, but the children aren't well. How about dinner? Get a taxi to The Diving Pelican, on A Hundred and Eighty-sixth Street, North Miami Beach. I'll meet you there at eight. Come to think of it, two friends are going to England tomorrow too. You'll like them. Maybe you'll all be on the same plane. I'll introduce you."

"Thank you," I said faintly.

"A pleasure. See you, then."

With a sigh I replaced the receiver, booked myself and my bags into the airport hotel for the night, and in due course taxied as instructed to the rendezvous.

The Diving Pelican, less striking than its name, glowed dimly at one end of a dark row of shops. I pulled open the door and stepped into a small entrance hall. Fred was sitting alone at a round table. Not very large over all, the place was pleasantly packed. Not a pelican in sight, diving or otherwise.

Fred rose to his feet to pump my hand. "Sorry I'm alone, but Meg didn't want to leave the children. They've got chicken pox."

I made sympathetic noises.

"Covered in spots, poor little buggers," Fred said.

He recommended the house speciality, a seafood fettuccine. At my prompting, he told me about life in his consulate, mostly a matter, he said, of British tourists complaining of lost documents, stolen money, and decamping boyfriends.

Midway through our meal there was a small burst of clapping, and Fred exuded pleasure. "Ah," he said proprietorially. "Vicky Larch and Greg Wayfield. They're the friends I told you about, who are going to the U.K. tomorrow."

Vicky Larch and Greg Wayfield were more than friends; they were also singers. They had come into the restaurant without fanfare, through curtains at the far end, she dressed in a white sequined tunic, he in a madras checked jacket, both in light-colored trousers. The only thing really surprising about them was their age. They were mature, one might say, and no longer slim.

They fiddled around with amplifying equipment and tapped microphones, got the equipment going and ran a tape: soft, sweet music from old stage shows. Greg Wayfield then began to sing with a good, true voice—gentle, virile, and full of timbre.

The song ended, and the diners applauded. Then the woman smoothed into a love song, the words a touch sad, moody. They're pros, I thought with relief. Good old pros, having a ball.

They sang six songs alternately and finished with a duet, and then, to enthusiastic clapping, they threaded their way around the tables and sat down with Fred and me.

Fred made introductions. Half standing, I shook the singers' hands and said how much I'd enjoyed their performance.

At close quarters they looked as wholesome and old-fashioned as their act—he still handsome, she with the air of a young chanteuse trapped in a grandmotherly body.

"Did you sing in nightclubs?" I asked her.

Her blue eyes widened. "How did you know?"

"Something about your phrasing. Intimate. Designed for shadowy late-night spaces."

"Well, yes, I did clubs for years." She was amused. "But I retired ages ago. We sing here just for fun."

Her hair was white—a fluffy, well-cut helmet. She had good skin, lightly made up, and her only real concession to theatricality lay in the silky dark upcurling false eyelashes. Her accent was English. She seemed serene, secure, and sensible.

Fred checked that we all were in fact booked on the same flight. No doubt about it. British Airways' jumbo to Heathrow.

"Great. Great," Fred said.

Greg, I thought, was American, though it was hard to tell. A mid-Atlantic man: halfway accent, American clothes, English facial bones. He had presence, but not his wife's natural stage charisma. He hadn't been a soloist, I thought.

Greg said they'd better get back to work. They sang another three songs each, and returned to our table, accepting plaudits on the way. They drank wine and talked with animation, scattering information about themselves—including the fact that Greg had been trained for opera—and further proving that they were solidly good, well-intentioned people.

Greg said they were going to England for a month. One of Vicky's daughters was getting married.

Vicky's daughter?

Yes, she said, the children were all hers. Two boys, two girls. She'd divorced their father long ago. She and Greg were new together: eighteen months married, still on honeymoon.

"Belinda—she's my youngest. She's marrying a veterinary surgeon," Vicky said. "She's worked for him for ages, but this came on suddenly a few weeks ago. So anyway, we're off to horse country. He acts as a vet at Cheltenham races."

I made a small noise in my throat, and they looked at me inquiringly. I said, "My father and mother met at Cheltenham races."

They exclaimed over it, of course, and it seemed a bit late to say that my mother and *stepfather* met at Cheltenham races, so I let it pass. My real father, I thought, was anyway John Darwin—the only father I could remember, since my natural father had died when I was a baby.

"Peter's father is an ambassador," Fred said. Then, reflecting, he added, "Didn't your father spend his entire youth at the races? Didn't you say so in Tokyo, when you went to the Japan Cup?"

"I expect I said it," I agreed, "though it was a bit of an exaggeration. Still, he says he learns more about a country faster at the races than in a month of diplomatic handshaking."

Greg asked a few things about our time in Japan. Fred had been a first secretary in the commercial department, oiling the wheels of trade. My own job had been to learn the political scene. The customs and cadences of Japan still flowed strongly in my head. It was always an odd feeling of deprivation, leaving behind a culture one had striven intensely to understand.

The diners in the restaurant had gradually drifted away, leaving the four of us as the last to leave. Vicky and Greg went off to pack up their equipment, and Fred and I divided the bill between us.

Vicky and Greg returned, she carrying a large white handbag aglitter with multicolored stones, and he following. We all four left the restaurant and stood for a while outside the door, Vicky and Greg making plans to find me the following day.

Final good-nights. "Our car's down there," Vicky said, pointing to the distance.

"Mine's over there," Fred said, pointing the other way.

We all nodded and moved apart, the evening over.

"They're nice people," Fred said contentedly.

"Yes," I agreed.

We climbed into his car. He started the engine, switched on the lights, backed out of the parking space, and turned the car to the general direction of the airport.

"Stop!" I yelled abruptly, struggling to undo the seat belt.

"What's wrong?" Fred said, jamming his foot on the brake.

I didn't answer him. I swung open the car door and scrambled out, running almost before I had both feet on the ground.

In the passing beam of Fred's headlights I'd seen the distant sparkle of Vicky's sequined tunic and seen also that she was struggling, falling, with a dark figure crowding her . . . attacking.

I sprinted, hearing her cry out shrilly.

I myself yelled, "Vicky, Vicky," in an attempt to frighten off the mugger, but he seemed glued to her like a leech, she on the ground and kicking, he close on her, hunched and intent.

I reached the man, cannoning into him to knock him away. He was heavier than I'd thought and not easily deterred, and far from running from me, he seemed to view me as merely another mug to be robbed. He jabbed a strong fist at my face. I ducked. He then connected with a fist to my chest, which left me breathless.

Vicky suddenly rose to her feet and came up behind our assailant. I saw her eyes momentarily over his shoulder, stretched wide with fear and full of determination. She took aim and kicked at him hard. He hissed fiercely with pain and turned towards her.

Vicky had her long scarlet nails up, her fingers bent like a witch. Her mouth was stretched open, and out of it came a shriek that rose to a scream. It raised the hairs on my own neck, and it broke the nerve of the thief. He took a stumbling step to go around her and then departed at a shambling run.

Vicky fell weakly into my arms, her voice roughened. "Oh, God. . . . There were two of them. . . . Greg . . ."

Headlights blazed at us, fast advancing. Vicky and I clutched each other, like dazzled rabbits; then tires squealed to a stop, and the black figure emerging like a silhouette through the bright beam resolved itself into the solid familiarity of Fred.

"Is she all right?" Fred asked anxiously. "Where's Greg?"

He wasn't hard to find. He was lying in a tumbled, unconscious heap near the rear wheel on the far side of what turned out to be his and Vicky's dark blue BMW.

I squatted down and felt around his neck for his pulse. "He's alive," I said, relieved, straightening.

Before we could do anything, a police car wailed with its siren down the road and drew up beside us. A big man in midnight-blue trousers and shirt with insignia stepped out, bringing his notebook to the ready and telling us someone had just reported a woman screaming. He had been cruising nearby, he said.

Greg began moaning and struggled to sit up, appearing dazed and disoriented. Vicky supported him around the shoulders.

The policeman unclipped a hand-held radio from his belt and called for an ambulance and then, with notable kindness, asked Vicky just what had occurred.

She tried to answer, but the phrases came out unconnectedly, as if from splintered thoughts. "He was trying to take my *rings*— the plane tickets— It's my daughter's wedding. . . ." She took a visibly deep breath and tried again. "They were waiting behind the car. . . . They jumped on Greg when he went round. . . . They stole my handbag. My passport . . . What are we going to *do?*"

The distress-filled plea was answered pragmatically by Fred, who said he wasn't consul for nothing and he'd get her to her daughter's wedding willy-nilly.

The urgent, whipping siren of an ambulance split the night, and paramedics spilled out purposefully, taking charge. The policeman told Vicky he would be following them to the hospital, asked Greg for his car keys, and handed them to Fred.

Two more police cars arrived fast, with flashing lights and wailing sirens, disgorging enough figures to arrest half the neighborhood. Vicky and Greg were helped into the ambulance, which at once departed, followed immediately by the first policeman.

One of the new bunch wrote down my name under Fred's and paused over the address I gave him: the Foreign and Commonwealth Office, Whitehall, London, England. He asked what I'd observed. I made my guesses at the mugger's age, height, weight, and so on, but I couldn't remember his face well enough to be sure I'd recognize him in other clothes, in daylight.

The officer shut his notebook. He would be grateful, he indicated, if we would present ourselves at his police station the following morning at ten a.m.

The scattered searchers returned without a mugger. There was no sign either, it seemed, of a capacious white bejeweled handbag or Greg's wallet.

As fast as they'd arrived, the midnight blues departed, leaving a sudden deafening silence in which Fred and I stood and looked at each other a touch dazedly, deciding what to do next.

"You'd better drive the BMW to the hospital," Fred said, "and collect them and take them home. I can't do it. I promised Meg I wouldn't be late. She's got her hands full with the children."

"All right. Where's the hospital?"

He began to give me directions but shrugged finally and said I'd better follow him. He led me to the entrance, pointed to it emphatically through his open window, and, without pausing for more speech, zoomed away towards the chicken pox.

I found Greg and the friendly policeman sitting glumly side by side in the hospital waiting area, Greg looking drained and gray. "How are you feeling?" I asked Greg—an unnecessary question.

"Tired," he said, "but my head's all right. They say there's only a bruise. Got to rest a bit, that's all."

I nodded. "I brought your car," I said. "I'll drive you home."

He said limply, "Thanks."

Conversation lapsed. After a time Vicky reappeared, accompanied by a young doctor. Her face, cleaned of makeup, seemed lined and pudgy. The false eyelashes had been removed. The young doctor told Greg that his wife was fine.

I glanced at my watch; it was nearly two o'clock. The doctor departed, and the policeman gently asked Vicky questions, which she answered in a low voice, without emotion. After a while he asked her and Greg to go to the police station at ten in the morning to complete their statements. He said good night to us and left.

I fetched the car to the door. Greg and Vicky chose to sit together in the back, and I asked for the most elementary instructions on how to get to their home.

I drove with care and at last pulled up in a semicircular drive outside their front door. Telling the couple to stay where they were for a moment, I got Greg to give me the key, and fed it into the lock. All was dark and quiet inside, and I felt around and found the light switch. I tried to hurry Greg and Vicky into the house, but they were agonizingly slow. It wasn't until we were all safely inside that I began in any way to relax.

They lived in a one-story house, most of the rooms flowing into one another without doors. I went around checking that all the curtains were drawn. Returning to find them both sitting in the chairs nearest the front door, as if their legs could take them no farther, I suggested that they make themselves a hot drink before they went to bed. I said I would phone for a taxi.

"Oh no," Vicky said, near to tears. "Stay here. Please do. I feel so shaky. And I'm scared."

Greg reached across for her hand and squeezed it. He didn't actually say he was scared, but he too begged me to stay.

I thought with longing of a quiet bed in the airport hotel, but saw I couldn't abandon them to a panic-filled night. I'd known them for less than six hours—felt I'd been with them forever.

"I'll stay," I said.

CHAPTER 2

Two nights later I flew to England. Across the aisle Vicky and Greg slumbered peacefully, blanketed to their chins, heads together, babes in the wood.

"Peter, it wouldn't hurt you to put your journey off for one more day," Fred Hutchings had said. We were in his office at the time, in the consulate in Miami, on the day after the mugging. "It isn't as if you've got anything to go *to*, especially. And Greg and Vicky are badly shaken by all this. You know they are."

Fred was at his most earnest, almost evangelical in his desire to do good. He had persuaded me not only to travel to England with his distressed friends but to deliver them safely to their daughter in Gloucestershire. I was aware that if they'd been going to somewhere like Northumberland, my response might have been different, but there had been a tug of curiosity about returning to the county of my childhood. Several weeks remained of my leave, and I hadn't planned to do anything in them except find somewhere in London to live. So to Gloucestershire. . . . Why not?

I rented a car at Heathrow Airport when we arrived in the morning and drove westward in the general direction of Cheltenham and the racecourse, Vicky having said that her daughter lived close to the track itself. We arrived in the area at about noon and drew up at a garage to ask for final directions.

"The vets' place? Turn right, go past the fire station . . ."

The road ran through an uneasy mix of centuries, the mellow and old elbowed by aggressive shopfronts and modernized pubs. Not a village, more a suburb: no cohesive character.

"The vets' place" was a substantial brick building set back from the road. I parked the car and helped Vicky unwind to her feet. She was suffering from jet lag and overall exhaustion. And the weather hardly helped. Straight from the warmth of Florida to a cold, windy late February day in England was a shiversome transition.

Vicky wore a dark green trouser suit with a white blouse, inadequate for the English out-of-doors, and had had no energy for brightening things with jewelry or gold chains. Greg did his best to be her mainstay, but despite his protestations, it was clear that being knocked unconscious had shaken him to the foundations. Moreover, back in Florida the police had depressed us all by their opinion that the muggers would not be caught.

Outside the vets' place, Greg extricated himself from the car, and all three of us went over to the brick building and in through a glassed entrance door to a lobby. This brown-carpeted space was furnished with two chairs, and a counter for leaning on while one talked with the young woman in an office on the far side of it.

She was sitting at a desk, speaking on a telephone. Eventually she disconnected and turned in our direction and said, "Yes?"

"Belinda Larch. . . ." Vicky said tentatively.

I said to the young woman, "This is her mother, just arrived from America."

She wasn't moved to any show of excessive welcome. "Well, she's in the hospital section assisting the vets. They're operating on a horse. I'm sorry, but you'll have to wait."

"Can you phone her?"

She started to say no, then looked at me and with raised eyebrows picked up the receiver. The conversation was short but produced results. The girl put down the phone and drew a labeled bunch of keys out of a drawer.

"Belinda says these are the keys to the cottage where her mother will be staying. She'll come as soon as she can."

"And where's the cottage?"

"I don't know. The address is on that label on the key ring."

I escorted Greg and Vicky back to the car and sought directions from passersby. Finally I got a reliable pointer from a telephone repairman up a pole, and I drove away up a hill, around a bend, and down the first turning on the left. "It's the first house along there on the right," I'd been told from aloft. "You can't miss it."

I did in fact nearly miss it, because it wasn't my idea of a cottage. No thatched roof and roses around the door. Thetford Cottage was a full-blown house, a weathered gray three-story edifice built of stone from the local Cotswold Hills.

Vicky got out of the car uncertainly, holding on to my arm, blown by the wind. "Is this the place?" she said doubtfully.

She looked at the bare flower beds, the leafless trees and bedraggled grass, her shoulders sagging ever more forlornly.

"If the key fits, it is," I said, trying to sound encouraging; and indeed the key did fit, and turned easily in the lock.

The house was cold inside, with a deep chill speaking of no recent heating. We stood in a wood-floored hall looking around at a lot of closed doors and a polished wood staircase.

"Well," I said, shivering myself, "let's see what we've got."

A pair of double doors led into a large drawing room, another door into a dining room, a third into a small sitting room with armchairs, television, and a fire that lit with switches, not paper, wood, and coal. Turned on, it warmed up nicely and put on a show of flickering flames. Vicky subsided speechlessly into an armchair near it and sat huddled, looking ill.

"Back in a moment," I said, and made tracks up the staircase, looking for blankets. All the doors upstairs were closed. The first I opened revealed a bathroom. The second held twin beds, unmade, the bedclothes neatly stacked on each.

Better than blankets: duvets. Royal blue, scattered with white daisies. I gathered the pair of them into my arms and negotiated the bare polished wooden stairs downwards.

Vicky hadn't moved. Greg stood over her, looking helpless.

"Right," I said, handing them the duvets. "You tuck these round you, and I'll see what's in the kitchen."

I'd left all the hall doors open. One led to a cold, antiseptic kitchen of white fitments around a black-and-white tiled floor. On a central table stood the first signs of recent human life: an unopened box of tea bags, some artificial sweeteners, and a packet of shortbread. The refrigerator was empty except for a carton of milk.

I made tea for both of them and carried it, along with the shortbread, to the little sitting room. Vicky drank her tea holding the cup with both hands, as if to warm them. The room itself by then was perceptibly warmer than the rest of the house, and I began to think of roaming around, switching on every heater I could find.

Action was frustrated by the arrival of a car outside, the slam of a door, and the rapid entrance into the house of a young woman in a hurry. Belinda, one supposed.

We heard her voice calling, "Mother?" followed by her appearance in the doorway. She was slim, in stonewashed jeans topped by a padded olive-green jacket. Pretty in a fine-boned, scrubbed sort of way. Maybe thirty, I thought. Her light brown hair was drawn up into a utilitarian ponytail.

"Mother? Oh, good, you got here. Hello, Greg," Belinda said briefly, going over to him and giving him a dutiful peck. Her mother got the same treatment in turn: a kiss on the cheek, but no deeply loving welcoming hug.

"Well, Mother, I'm sorry, but I can't stay," she said. "I'd arranged to have yesterday free, but you being a day late . . ." She shrugged. "I have to go back. The horse died. They have to do a postmortem. I'm so worried. . . ." She stared hard at her mother. "What's the matter with you? You look awful."

"I told you on the phone—"

"Oh yes, so you did. By the way, we're getting married in church instead of the registrar's office, and we're having the reception here in this house. I'll tell you about it later. I have to go back to the hospital now. Make yourselves comfortable, won't you?" Her gaze sharpened from vague to center upon me. "Sorry, didn't catch your name."

"Peter Darwin," I obliged.

"Peter," Vicky said forcefully, "has been our lifeline."

"Oh? Well, good. Nice of you to have helped them." Her gaze slid away, encompassing the room in general. "The Sandersons, who own the house, have gone to Australia for a couple of months. They're renting it to you quite cheaply, Mother, and I've engaged the caterers. . . . You always said you wanted me to have a proper wedding, and I decided it would be a good idea, after all."

"Yes, dear," Vicky said, accepting it meekly.

"Three weeks tomorrow," Belinda told her. "And now, Mother, I really have to run. I'll phone you later."

She gave a brief wave, turned, and departed.

After a short silence Vicky said valiantly, "She was a really sweet baby. But . . ." She paused and sighed. "We get on quite well really, as long as we don't see each other too much."

Greg gave me a sideways look and made no comment.

"Right," I said cheerfully. "We may as well get your cases in, and if you like, I'll go to the shops."

Vicky said apathetically that she would unpack later; meanwhile, she was going to sleep at once, in her clothes, upstairs.

I left Greg fussing over her, drove to the straggly suburb, and bought all the essentials. I collected some Scotch, a newspaper, and other comforts and headed back to Thetford Cottage, finding things as I'd left them. Greg, dozing, woke up when I went in, and followed me into the kitchen to watch me stow the provisions.

"You should be all right now," I said, closing the fridge.

He was alarmed. "But surely you're staying. Just one more night? For Vicky's sake. *Please.*"

For his sake too, I saw. I supposed I could stay one night there and start my rediscovery of Gloucestershire in the morning, so against my gut reaction, I said yes.

VICKY woke at six thirty in the evening and came tottering down the stairs. Greg and I had by that time lowered the Scotch level, read the newspapers, and found out how the television worked.

Belinda had not telephoned.

At seven, however, a car arrived outside, and the daughter herself came in as before, managerial rather than loving. This time she had brought her affianced.

"Mother, you met Ken two or three years ago, you remember."

"Yes, dear," Vicky said kindly. She offered him her cheek for a kiss and after the fleetest of pauses received one.

"And this is Greg," Belinda said. "He's my stepfather."

"How do you do," Ken said politely, shaking Greg's hand.

Greg gave him a smile and said he was sure pleased to be in England for the happy occasion.

Ken, at the moment, looked a long way from happy. Anxiety vibrated in his every gesture—not a simple nervousness at meeting his future in-laws but a much deeper, overriding bunch of worries, too intense to be covered. He was tall, thin, sandy, and wiry-looking, like a long-distance runner. A touch of Norwegian, perhaps, about the shape of his head and the light blue of his eyes. Fair hair on the point of thinning. I guessed his age at nearing forty and his dedication to his job as absolute.

"Sorry," Belinda said to me. "Can't remember your name."

"Peter Darwin."

"Oh yes." She glanced towards Ken. "Mother's helper."

He shook my hand perfunctorily. "Ken McClure," he said.

It sounded very familiar. "Kenny?" I said doubtfully.

"No, Ken. Kenny was my father."

"Oh."

None of them paid any attention, but I felt as if I'd been kicked in the subconscious by sleeping memory. I knew about Kenny McClure—but what did I know?—from a long time ago.

He'd killed himself.

The knowledge came back abruptly, accompanied by the curiosity I'd felt about it as a child. Kenny McClure had acted as veterinary surgeon at Cheltenham races. I knew I'd driven round the track with him in his Land-Rover a few times, but I couldn't now recall what he looked like.

Ken had made an attempt at dressing for the occasion in a suit, shirt, and tie, but he wore one black shoe and one brown. Belinda had come in a blue woolen dress under the olive jacket and, having made the effort herself, was critical of Vicky, who hadn't.

"Mother, honestly, you look as if you'd slept in those clothes."

"Yes, dear, I did."

Belinda impatiently swept her upstairs to find something less crumpled, and Greg offered Ken some Scotch.

Ken eyed the bottle with regret. "Better not," he said. "Driving, and all that."

"Belinda told us," Greg said, "that you've had some trouble with a horse today."

"It died." Ken had clamped a lid tight over his troubles, and the strain came out in staccato speech. "Couldn't save it."

"I'm real sorry."

Ken nodded. "Rotten for you too—the mugging, I mean." His pale eyes turned my way. "Not at my best this evening." He spoke with a recognizable Gloucestershire accent.

Vicky and Belinda reappeared, Vicky in red this time, and Ken and Belinda led the way in his car—Vicky, Greg, and I following in the rented car—to a small country inn with a restaurant attached. We sat around a small dark table in a corner of a room heavily raftered and furnished in oak. We ordered drinks, and Belinda stared at me from over her glass. "Mother says you're a secretary. I can't understand why she needs one."

"No, dear," Vicky began, but Belinda made a shushing movement with her hand.

"Secretary, chauffeur, general helper, what does it matter?" she said. "Mother, I'm sorry to be frank, but I don't see how you justify the expense of someone else."

Greg and Vicky both looked deeply embarrassed.

"I'm a civil servant," I said peacefully to Belinda. "A private secretary in the Foreign Office. Your mother isn't paying me. I'm literally here just to help them over the few sticky days since they were attacked. I was coming to England in any case, so we traveled together. Perhaps I should have explained sooner."

Belinda gave a shrug. Ken made a visible effort to retrieve the evening from gloom, and to some extent succeeded.

"What wine do you like with dinner . . . um . . . Mother?"

"Don't call me Mother. Call me Vicky."

He called her Vicky easily, without the "um." She said she preferred red wine. Any. He could choose.

Vicky and Ken were going to be all right, I thought, and was glad for Vicky's sake. Belinda softened enough over dinner to put a glow on the thin beauty that had to be attracting Ken, and Greg offered a toast to their marriage.

By the time coffee arrived, Vicky, like a rose given water, had revived to the point of flirting very mildly with Ken. Ken and Greg remained outwardly cordial but inwardly stiff. Belinda bossed her mother, was reserved with Greg, and took Ken for granted. A pretty normal setup, all in all.

Ken retreated every five minutes or so, for brief seconds, into his consuming troubles, but made no attempt to share them. He talked instead about a horse he'd bought two years earlier—for peanuts—to save it from being put down.

"Nice horse," he said. "It cracked a cannon bone. The owner wanted it put down. I told him I could save the horse if he'd pay for the operation, but he didn't want the expense. So I offered him a bit more than he would have got from the dog-food people, and he took it. I did the operation and put the horse in training, and it won a nice race the other day. And now Ronnie Upjohn, that's the owner, won't speak to me except to say he'll sue me."

"What a pig," Vicky said indignantly.

Ken nodded. "Luckily, I got him to sign a paper at the time, so he hasn't a chance of winning. He won't sue in the end. But I guess I've lost a client."

Ronnie Upjohn, I thought. I knew that name too. Couldn't attach any immediate information to it except that it was linked in my vague memory with another name: Travers.

Upjohn and Travers.

Who or what was Upjohn and Travers?

"We're running the horse here at Cheltenham in a couple of weeks," Ken said. "I'm giving it to Belinda, and it'll run in her name. If it wins, it'll be a nice wedding present for both of us."

"What sort of race?" I asked, making conversation.

"A two-mile hurdle. Are you a racing man?"

"I go sometimes. It's years since I went to Cheltenham."

"Peter's parents met on Cheltenham racecourse," Vicky said, and after Belinda's and Ken's exclamations of interest I gave them all a version of the facts that was not the whole truth, but enough for the casual chat of a dinner party.

"My mother was helping out with some secretarial work," I said. "My father blew into her office with a question, and bingo, love at first sight."

"It wasn't at first sight with us," Belinda said, briefly touching Ken's hand. "Fiftieth or sixtieth sight, more like."

Ken nodded. "I had her under my feet for months and never really saw her."

"You were getting over that frightful Eaglewood girl," Belinda said, teasing him.

"Izzy Eaglewood isn't frightful," Ken protested.

Izzy Eaglewood, I thought. A familiar name, but out of sync. Something different. What else? Russet! I almost laughed aloud. *Russet* Eaglewood had been the name to giggle over in extremely juvenile smutty jokes. We had been ignorant about what she actually did. We called it *it*. Giggle, giggle. One day—one unimaginable day—we would find out about *it* ourselves.

The knowledge came crowding back. Russet Eaglewood's father had been one of the leading trainers of steeplechasers. The Eaglewoods had their stables at the end of our village, half a mile from our little house. Their horses clattered through the village at dawn on their way up to the gallops, and I'd played in the stable yard often with Jimmy Eaglewood, until he got hit by a lorry and died after three hushed weeks in a coma. I could remember the drama well, but not Jimmy's face. I couldn't clearly remember any of the faces.

Ken called for the bill and settled it with a credit card, but before we could rise to go, a buzzer sounded insistently somewhere in his clothes.

"Damn," he said, feeling under his jacket and unclipping a small portable telephone from his belt. "I'm on call. Sorry."

He flipped open the phone, said his name, and listened. It was obviously no routine summons to a sick animal, because the blood left his face and he stood up clumsily and fast, literally swaying on his feet, tall and toppling.

He looked wildly at all of us sitting around the table.

"The hospital's on fire," he said.

CHAPTER 3

THE vets' place was on fire, but actually not, as it turned out, the new hospital itself, which lay separately to the rear. All one could see from the road, though, was the entrance and office block of the single-story building totally in flames.

Ken had raced off from the restaurant, driving like the Furies, leaving the rest of us to follow. I broke the speed limit into town.

We couldn't get the car near the vets' place. Fire apparatus, police cars, and sightseers crowded the edges of the parking area and wholly blocked the roadway. Spotlights, streetlights, headlights threw deep black shadows behind the milling helpers, and the flames lent orange halos to the firemen's helmets.

Belinda, leaving us at a run as soon as our car came to a halt, pushed and snaked a path through to the front. Ken was out of sight. There were the thuds of two explosions somewhere inside the walls, each causing huge spurts of flame to fly outwards through the front windows. Acrid smoke swirled after them.

"Back, back," voices yelled.

Two more thuds. Through the windows sharp, brilliant tongues of flame licked across the parking space towards the spectators.

Another thud. Another fierce jet-burst of flames. The whole roof fell in, like a clap of thunder, and then, dramatically, the roaring inferno turned to black, billowing smoke and the pyrotechnics petered out into a wet and dirty mess, smelling sour.

Ash drifted in the wind. One could hear the hiss of water dousing hot embers. In time the crowd slowly began to leave, allowing the three of us to get closer to the ruined building.

"Do you think it's safe?" Vicky asked doubtfully, stopping well short.

"Why don't you go back to the car," I said. "I'll find the other two. I'll tell them I'm driving you back to the house."

They both looked relieved, and went away slowly with the dispersing throng. I ducked a few officials, saw no immediate sign of Belinda and Ken, but found on the right of the burned building an extension of the parking area that led back into a widening space at the rear. Movement, lights, and more people.

Seeing Ken briefly and distantly as he hurried in and out of a patch of light, I set off despite warning shouts from behind. The heat radiating from the brick wall on my left proved to be of roasting capacity. Ken saw me as I hurried towards him, and he stood still, looking back where I'd come from.

"Can I do anything?" I said.

"The horses are all right," Ken said. "But I need . . . I need—"
He stopped suddenly and began shaking, as if the enormity of the disaster had abruptly overwhelmed him once the need for urgent

action had diminished. His mouth twisted, his whole face quivering.

"I'll take Vicky and Greg to the house and then come back," I said. "Just hold on."

I left by the rear gate, hurrying back to the main road. Vicky and Greg made no objections to being taken home. They hoped Belinda would forgive them, but they were going to bed to sleep for a week, and please would I ask her not to wake them. I glanced at them affectionately as they stood drooping in the polished hall of Thetford Cottage, then left them to shut the door behind me.

I returned to the vets' place from the rear and took brief stock of what lay in the unburned area: a new-looking one-story building; a row of stable boxes set back under an overhanging roof, all empty, with their doors open; and a glass-walled thirty-yard passage connecting the burned and unburned buildings.

As Ken was nowhere to be seen and a door to the new building stood open, I went inside to look for him and found myself in an entrance hall furnished as a waiting room. Everything, including the tiled floor and a coffee machine in a corner, was soaking wet. A man trying to get sustenance from that machine gave it a smart kick of frustration, as if its demise, after all else, was insupportable.

"Where's Ken?" I asked him.

He pointed through an open door and attacked the machine again, and I went where directed. I found Ken in a smallish office, a functional room already occupied by more people than the architect had intended.

Ken was standing by the uncurtained window, still trembling. A gray-haired man sat gloomily behind a metal desk. A woman with a dirt-smudged face stood beside him. Two more men and another woman perched on office furniture or leaned against walls. The room smelled of smoke, and it was chilly enough to make Ken's shivers reasonably physical in origin.

The heads all turned my way when I appeared in the doorway. "Come in," Ken said, and to the others added, "He's a helper."

They nodded. They all looked exhausted. The man who had been kicking the coffee machine came into the office, passed me, and slid down to sit on the floor, with his spine against the wall. His eyes were red-rimmed, his hands and face dirty, his age anywhere from thirty to fifty.

The gray-haired man behind the desk seemed to be the senior

in rank as well as years. He looked around at the others and wearily said, "Suggestions?"

"We go to bed," the coffee-machine man said.

"Buy a better computer," one of the other men offered. "When the records are saved on backup disks, store them in a vault."

"A bit late for that," said one of the women, "since all the records are burned."

"The new records, then."

"If we have a practice," Ken said with violence.

"How did the fire start?" I asked.

The gray-haired man answered with deep tiredness. "We were having the place painted. We ourselves have a no-smoking rule, but workmen with cigarettes . . ."

"Not arson, then," I said.

"Are you a journalist?" one of the women demanded.

Ken shook his head. "He's a diplomat. He fixes things."

None of them looked impressed. The gray-haired man said that if I had any practical suggestions, I should give them.

I said with hesitation, "I would leave someone here all night with all the lights on. Just in case it was arson."

"It couldn't have been arson," the man said. "Why would anyone want to burn our building?"

One of the other men said, "They wouldn't get far trying to burn this hospital. It's supposed to be fireproof."

"And it didn't burn," the woman said. "The fire doors held in the passage."

"So we still have our hospital," the gray-haired man told me, "but we've lost the pharmacy, the lab, the small-animal surgeries, and, as you heard, every record we possessed." He stopped, shaking his head hopelessly. "I think the going-to-bed suggestion was a good one, and I propose we adopt it. Also, if anyone will stay here all night, please volunteer."

After a pause Ken said jerkily, "I'll stay if Peter will."

I'd let myself in for it, I thought. Oh, well. "Okay," I said.

"Who's on call?" the gray-haired man asked.

"I am," Ken said.

"And I am," a dark-haired young woman added.

The senior man nodded. "Right. Ken stays. Everyone else sleep." He rose to his feet, pushing himself up tiredly with hands flat on the desk. "Council of war here at nine in the morning." He came around the desk and paused in front of me. "Whoever you are, thanks." He briefly shook my hand. "Carey Hewett," he said.

"Peter Darwin."

"Oh. Any relation to . . ."

I shook my head.

"No. Of course not." He led the way out of the office, and the rest drifted after him, yawning and nodding to me briefly.

"Where's Belinda?" I asked as the last of them disappeared.

"Belinda?" Ken looked temporarily lost. "Belinda . . . went with the horses." He paused, then explained. "We had three horses out in the boxes. Patients. We've sent them to a trainer who had room in his yard. Belinda went to look after them."

He was still faintly trembling. "Sit down," I said. I pointed to the gray-haired man's padded chair behind the desk.

Ken groped his way to it and sat, as if his legs had given way.

"Apart from the fire," I said, "what's the problem?"

He put his elbows on the desk and his head in his hands and didn't answer for at least a minute. When he finally spoke, his voice was low and painfully controlled.

"I operate on horses about five times a week. Normally, you'll lose less than one out of every two hundred on the table. For me, that means maybe one or at most two deaths a year. You can't help it; horses are difficult under anesthetic. Anyway"—he swallowed—"I've had four die that way in the last two months."

It seemed more like bad luck to me than utter tragedy, but I said, "Is that excessive?"

"You don't understand!" The pressure rose briefly in his voice. "The word goes round like wildfire in the profession. Then the public hears it, and no one's sending horses to you anymore. You can lose it like *that*." He snapped his long fingers. "I *know* I'm a good surgeon. Carey knows it; they all know it. But they've got themselves to consider. We're all in it together."

I swept a hand around the empty office.

"The people who were here . . ."

Ken nodded. "Six vets in partnership, including me, and also Scott, the anesthetist. And before you ask, no, I can't blame him. He's a good technician and a trained veterinary nurse, like Belinda."

"What happened this morning?" I asked.

"Same thing," Ken said miserably. "I was putting some screws in a split cannon bone. Routine. But the horse's heart slowed and his blood pressure dropped, and we couldn't get it back."

"We?"

"Usually it would have been just Scott, Belinda, and me, but today we had Oliver Quincy assisting as well. The owner insisted because he'd heard the rumors. And still the horse died. . . ."

After an interval I said, "I suppose you've checked all the equipment and the drugs you use."

"Of *course* we have. Over and over."

"Who checked last?"

"I did." He said it automatically, then understood the significance of what I was asking. He said again, more slowly, "Maybe I shouldn't have. But I wanted to be sure."

The remark and action, I thought, of an innocent man.

I said, "Mightn't it have been more prudent to let one of the other vets see to the cannon bone?"

"What?" He looked at me blankly, then explained. "We're partners in a big general practice. We're all interchangeable to some extent, but we all have our own specialities. Carey and the two women are small-animal vets, though Lucy Amhurst does sheep and ponies as well. Jay Jardine does cattle. I do horses. Oliver Quincy is a general large-animal man working with both Jay and me, though he does mostly medical work and only minor surgery. Castrations, things like that, on-site."

I reflected a bit and asked, "Have there been any over-the-top calamities in the dog and cat departments?"

Ken shook his head in depression. "Only horses."

"Racehorses?"

"Mostly. But a couple of weeks ago there was an Olympic show jumper—and that didn't die during an operation. I had to put it down." He looked into tormented space. "A week earlier I'd done a big repair job here on its near hind, where it had staked itself breaking a jump, and it was healing fine back at home. Then the whole leg swelled like a balloon, and the tendon was shot to hell. I opened the leg up, but it was hopeless. . . . The tendon had disintegrated. There wasn't anything to repair."

"Does that happen often?" I asked.

"No. The owner was furious. They'd insured the horse; otherwise we would have had another lawsuit on our hands."

I asked Ken to show me around the rest of the hospital. Lethargically he rose and told me that the office we were in was used by whoever was operating in the theater for writing notes of the procedures used together with drugs prescribed. The notes, he added, with a despairing shake of his head, were then taken to the secretarial section and stored in files.

"Not in the computer?" I asked, flicking a finger at a monitor that stood on a table near the desk.

"In the main computer in the office, yes, but our secretary enters only the date, the name of the animal, owner, type of surgery, and a file number. If anyone wants to refer back, they just call up the file number and go and find their actual notes." He gestured helplessly. "Now all the files are bound to have gone. So has the computer itself, I suppose. This terminal is dead, anyway. So there will be no records anymore to prove that all the operations when the horses died were normal procedures."

I reflected that, on the other hand, if in fact there had been any departure from regular procedures, all records of that too had conveniently vanished.

He led the way out of the office and into the central passage. The floors throughout were of gray-streaked black vinyl tiles, the walls an unrelenting white. Nothing was made of wood. Doors were metal everywhere, painted brown. A row of three on the left-hand side were storerooms, Ken said. All the doors were locked. Ken opened them, and we checked inside: all quiet.

On the right, past the office, lay another, bigger, room, housing X-ray developing equipment and a movable X-ray machine on wheels. There was also a simple bed, with folded blankets, and a closed door giving access from the car park for patients.

"We have to keep all these doors locked, including the office," Ken said grimly. "We've found things walking out of here when we're all busy in the theater."

Beyond the X-ray room there was an extra-wide door straight ahead. The passage itself turned right.

"That door," Ken said, pointing ahead, "is the entry to the theater area from this side." He unlocked the theater door, pressed rows of switches to light our path, and led the way into a vestibule, with doors on either side and another across the end.

"Changing rooms right and left," Ken said. "Then we go ahead into the central supply of gowns and gloves and so on. We'd better put gowns and shoe covers on, if you don't mind, in the interest of cleanliness in the operating room."

In the supply room, he handed me a pair of plastic disposable shoe covers and a cotton overall, dressing in similar style himself, and then supplied us also with hats, like shower caps, and masks. "Instruments and drugs are in here too," he went on, showing me locked glass-fronted cupboards. "This cupboard here opens both ways, from this side and from inside the operating room. The drug cupboard has two locks and unbreakable glass."

"A fortress," I commented.

Ken pointed to a door on the right. "You can go through the scrub room into the operating room," he said, "but we'll go straight in from here." He pushed open double swing doors ahead and walked into the scene of his disasters.

It was unmistakably an operating theater, though the wide central table must have been almost nine feet long, with an upward-pointing leg at each corner, like a four-poster bed. There were trolleys, carts, and wheeled tables around the walls, all of metal. I had an impression of more space than I'd expected.

Without ado Ken skirted the table, went to the far wall, inserted a key, and a whole section slid away to reveal another room beyond. I followed Ken into this space and found that the floor was spongy underfoot. I remarked on it, surprised.

Ken, nodding, said, "The walls are padded too," and punched his fist against one of the gray plastic-coated panels that lined the whole room. "This stuff is like the mats they put down for gymnasts. We anesthetize the horses in here, and the padding stops them from hurting themselves when they go down."

Ken pointed upwards. "See those rails in the ceiling and those chains hanging down? We fasten the horse's legs into padded cuffs, attach the cuffs to the chains, winch up the horse, and he travels along the rails into the theater." He pointed back through the sliding door. "The rails guide the horse right over the table. Then we lower him into position. The table is mobile too."

He rolled the wall-door into place again and relocked it, then went into a short corridor, which we crossed to enter wh Ken called the preparation room. There was a clutter of treatment carts around the walls there, and more cupboards.

"Emergency equipment," he explained briefly. "This is reception, where the horses arrive." He stepped out of the shoe covers and gestured to me to do the same, throwing them casually into a discard bin. "From here we go back into the corridor and down there into the outside world."

Each of Ken's keys had a colored tag with a stick-on label identifying its purpose in the general scheme of things. Ken clanked like an old-time jailer.

A gust of wind blew specks of ash in through the widening opening of the outside door, and Ken motioned to me to hurry through after him, relocking as usual behind us.

Outside, we were still under a wide roof, which covered a good-sized area in front of a row of four new-looking boxes. All the box doors stood open, the patients having left.

"That's about it," Ken said, looking around. "We unload the sick animals just here and usually take them straight into reception. There's often not much time to lose."

"Nearly always horses?" I asked.

He nodded. "Occasionally cattle. But mostly horses."

Reflecting, I asked, "How many horses are there in your area?"

"Between us we're the regular vets of, say, half a dozen or more racing stables, five riding schools, a bunch of pony clubs, countless hunting people, showing people. . . ." He smiled. "There are a whole lot of horses in Gloucestershire. It keeps us going." The smile faded. "Up to now."

I listened to the hopelessness and also the fear, and wondered if either of those emotions sprang from facts he hadn't told me.

"That's it, then," Ken said, turning back.

He closed and bolted the empty boxes as we passed them and, at the end, made for a door that led to an offshoot of the central passage. A long line of pegs on the wall held an anorak or two, a couple of cloth caps, and a horse's head-collar. Ken took the gowns back to the changing room and returned to comment on the silence everywhere in a building usually full of bustle.

I agreed that we could relax on the score of ill-intentioned intruders for the moment, and I rather regretted having offered an all-night service. Cold was a problem I hadn't given much thought to, and although it was by then nearing three o'clock, it would presumably get colder still before dawn.

"How about us borrowing those anoraks," I suggested, "and wrapping ourselves in blankets."

"Yes, we could—" he began to say, but was forestalled by the same muffled noise as in the restaurant, the chirp of his telephone on his belt. He pulled it out and flipped it open.

"Hewett and Partners," he said. "Yes. . . . Ken speaking."

I wouldn't have thought he could grow much paler, but he did. "Yes," he said. "Well . . . I'll come straightaway."

He clipped the phone back onto his belt with fumbling fingers and tried with three or four deep breaths to get himself back into control, but the pale blue eyes were halfway to panic.

"It's the Vernonside Stud," he said. "They've a broodmare with colic. I'll have to go."

Unhesitatingly he went down the passage and into the drug room, where he rapidly gathered equipment to take out to his car.

"I'll be gone an hour at least," he said. He gave me a brief glance. "Do you mind staying here? It's a bit of an imposition. . . . I hardly know you, really."

"I'll stay," I said.

"Phone the police if anything happens," he said. "You'd better have my keys." He threw me the heavy bunch. "See you." He sped out the far door, and within seconds I heard his car start up and drive away.

I took a blanket from the X-ray room and, wrapped to the chin, sat on the padded chair in the office, put my feet up on the desk, and read an article in a veterinary journal about oocyte transfers from infertile mares into other mares for gestation. This was not, one might say, riveting entertainment.

I dozed over an account of 3-D computer scanning of bone-stress factors in hocks and awoke with a start to hear someone rapping on the window with something hard, like a coin.

A face accompanied the hand, and a voice shouted, "Let me in." He pointed vigorously in the direction of the rear door, and as I went along the passage I remembered that he was the one who'd been kicking the coffee machine. He came in, stamping his feet and complaining of the cold. He held two large thermos flasks and explained that in the rush he'd forgotten his keys.

33

"But not to worry—Ken said you were here. He's on his way back here with the mare." He thrust the thermos flasks into my grasp and kicked off his boots, reaching up for a pair of indoor shoes on a shelf above the pegs. Slipping his feet into those, he took off his padded jacket. Then he said, "It's freezing in here," and put it on again. "Ken's phoning Belinda, and I'm to get the theater ready." He was moving as he talked. "I hate these middle-of-the-night emergencies." He reached the central passage and marched into the office. "I take it you know nothing about anesthetizing horses."

"Nothing."

"Can't be helped. Are these Ken's keys? Good."

He picked up the bunch and exited rapidly. He was tall, wide-shouldered, dark-haired, and he moved jerkily, as if there was far more explosive power available in his muscles than he needed. I followed him into the passage and found him unlocking one of the storerooms. He went in and reappeared with several large plastic bags full of clear liquid. "Do you mind carrying these?" He pushed them into my care, and setting off down the passage at a great rate, he unlocked the wide door leading to the vestibule and the theater. "Do you mind putting on a gown and shoe covers?" he said, stacking the bags of fluid on a shelf that was accessible from the operating room.

We donned the whole paraphernalia, and when we were clad, he went backwards through the double swing doors into the theater itself and held one open for me to follow.

"Good." He bustled about. "Ventilator." He rolled one of the metal carts from against the wall to the head of the operating table. "Horses can't breathe very well on their own when they're under anesthetic," he said. "Most animals can't."

He expertly linked together the tubes of the ventilator and plugged an electric lead into a socket in the floor.

"We went through all this ad infinitum yesterday morning," he said. "Checked every valve, checked the pump, checked the oxygen, which comes in from outside cylinders when we turn on this tap." He showed me. "Sometimes the heart starts failing and there's not a damn thing one can do about it. We've had our fair share of those recently. Anyway, I'm checking everything twice."

There was the sound of a car door slamming outside. Scott—it

34

had to be Scott, the anesthetist—lifted his head at the sound and rolled enough wall to one side to allow us access to the padded room. He crossed the spongy floor and unlocked the door to the corridor. With myself still at his heels (snapping off the shoe covers) we went down there and emerged into the brisk air and found Ken letting down the rear ramp of a small horse trailer that had been towed there by a Land-Rover.

"Scott. Good," Ken said, letting the ramp fall with a clang. "I had to drive the damn thing myself. They've two mares foaling at this moment at Vernonside and no staff to spare. They're stressed beyond sense. This mare is dying on her feet, and she's carrying a foal, worth God knows what, by Rainbow Quest."

He sped into the trailer to fetch his patient, who came lumbering backwards down the ramp. Heavy with foal, she was bloatedly fat. Her head hung low; her eyes were dull.

Ken saw me standing there and in black distress said, "Her heart's laboring, and there's feedback up from her stomach. That means her gut's obstructed. It means she'll die probably within an hour if I don't operate on her, and quite likely if I do."

"You'd be safer with a second opinion," I said.

"Yes. I phoned Carey on my way back here, asking him to get someone or come himself. He said to trust my own ability."

"So you'll go ahead," I said.

"Got no choice, have I? Just look at her."

He handed the mare's leading rein to Scott, who said, "Belinda's not here yet."

"She's not coming," Ken said. "Couldn't reach her at the stable."

"But . . ." Scott said, and fell silent.

"Yes. But." Ken looked directly at me. "What I want *you* to do is watch and make notes. A witness."

CHAPTER 4

IN THE padded room, while Scott held the mare by the head-collar Ken found her jugular vein and pushed into it what looked like a long hypodermic needle covered with plastic, and an end connector that remained outside on the skin.

"Catheter," he said, removing the needle and leaving the plastic sleeve in the vein.

I nodded.

"Intravenous drip," he enlarged, fastening to the catheter a tube from one of the bags of fluid that Scott was busily suspending from the ceiling. "You have to keep the body fluids up."

He went briefly to the operating room, returning with a small syringe full of liquid, which he injected into the mare's neck via the catheter.

"Half a cc of Domosedan," he said, spelling it for me as I wrote on a pad on a clipboard. "It's a sedative to make her manageably dozy. Mind you, don't get within reach of her feet. Horses kick like lightning, even in this state. Go behind that half wall."

I stood obediently behind a freestanding section of padded wall that allowed one to see while being shielded from trouble.

"What do you do with the syringe now?" I asked.

"Throw it away. It's disposable."

"Keep it," I said.

Ken considered things and nodded. "Right."

He took the syringe into the operating room and put it in a dish on one of the tables. He wore what I did: his own shoes covered with disposable covers, green cotton trousers, a short-sleeved green shirt, a lab coat, a surgical mask dangling around his neck, a soft white cap over his hair.

Scott, in similar clothes, rubbed a hand down the mare's nose, fondling her ears and making soothing noises until she was quiet and semiconscious on her feet.

Ken, watching her closely, had come back carrying a larger syringe in another dish. "Antibiotic," he said, injecting. He went away to pick up a third.

"This is ketamine hydrochloride," he said, returning and spelling it again for me. "Sends her to sleep."

Ken temporarily disconnected the drip and with smooth skill injected the mare again through the catheter in her neck. Almost immediately the great body swung around, staggered, and collapsed slowly sideways, the head flopping with a thump onto the spongy floor.

"Intubation," Ken said to Scott.

Scott nodded and passed an impressively large tube into the mare's mouth and down her throat.

"For oxygen and halothane," Ken told me briefly.

Scott opened the sliding door to the operating room, went in, and returned with the padded cuffs for the mare's legs and also bags to cover her feet. Both men buckled these on, then pulled down the chains from the ceiling and linked them to the cuffs. Scott fetched a sort of canvas sling, with handles, for carrying the mare's head, and Ken without waste of time pressed buttons on a panel in the theater wall to activate the winch.

The chains wound back and hoisted the half-ton horse effortlessly into the air. Scott supported her head in the sling while Ken reconnected the drip. Then Ken pressed another button, and a rolling trolley moved slowly along the ceiling rails, taking the dangling body, intravenous fluid and all, into the theater.

The rails themselves positioned the patient directly over the table. Ken pressed buttons. The chains lengthened, letting down their burden until the mare was lying on her back, with all four legs in the air, her distended belly a brown, rounded hump. Scott then helped Ken hitch the leg cuffs to the four posts at the corners of the table so that her legs were comfortably bent.

"Ventilator on," Ken said. "Gas on."

Scott fixed the tube in the horse's mouth to a tube from the ventilator, and the oxygen-halothane mixture began pumping with slow, insistent rhythm into the mare's lungs.

"Good," Ken said. "Now I'm going to slide another catheter into her facial artery. It will directly monitor her blood pressure."

I nodded and watched his deft fingers push a small tube into the mare's jaw and connect it to a machine. Both he and Scott watched the two lines that appeared on a monitoring screen.

"Final scrub," Ken said at length.

I followed him into the scrub room, where he scrubbed his hands clean and dried them on a sterile towel. Then I helped him put on a fresh sterile gown, and he pushed his hands into sterile latex gloves.

"If this mare dies," Ken said, "I'm finished."

"Stop thinking about it."

He stood for a moment with all the strain showing in his eyes; then he blinked a few times and took a deep breath.

"Come on, then." He turned away and went towards the theater. Scott stood in front of the blood pressure screen, watching it.

Ken said to me, "I need Scott to assist me. Will you stand by

37

this screen? Watch it all the time. A horse's blood pressure is about the same as humans', ideally one twenty over eighty, but like humans', it drops under anesthesia. If it drops below seventy, an alarm will go off. Watch that line there. And that counter— that's the heart rate. If there's any change, tell me immediately."

"Right."

He went around to the other side of the table, where Scott brought forward instruments on rolling carts.

"All set?" Ken asked Scott, and Scott nodded.

It was the last moment that Ken could have drawn back, but the commitment in his mind had been made long before.

"Incision," he said, dictating to me while he picked up a scalpel and with precision suited the deed to the word. "Ten inches, beside the umbilicus."

I wrote fast what he'd said and switched my gaze back to what he was doing.

"Watch the blood pressure," Ken said fiercely. "Don't watch me; watch the monitor between writing."

Working calmly, methodically, Ken cut into the abdominal cavity, then slowly felt his way around the internal organs, his eyes in his fingertips.

"The mare's less than a month from foaling," he said. "It's a good-sized foal." He was silent for a moment or two, then said unemotionally, "If she collapses and I can't save her, I'll deliver the foal here and now by caesarean section."

Scott glanced at him quickly and away, knowing, I thought, a good deal more than I did about the risks of such a procedure.

"Ah," Ken said finally. "Here we are. What a twist." He brought up some part I couldn't see and made an instantaneous decision to cut out the tangled obstruction altogether.

"Eyes on the screen *all the time*," he instructed me sharply.

I obeyed him, seeing his actions only in peripheral vision.

Supplied with instruments by Scott, he worked steadily, attaching clamps, removing tissue, swabbing, stitching. Time passed.

He murmured to himself and finally looked up. "All right. The obstruction's excised and the gut repaired. Ready to close up."

He did a quick, half-audible checklist on the abdomen, almost like a pilot coming in to land, and, still with deftness and care, fastened the incision together in three layers, finally closing the skin with a row of small steel staples. When he'd finished, he pulled his mask down and gave me a look of shaky triumph.

"She's made it so far," he said. "Scott, gas off."

"Ventilator off," Scott said. "Disconnect the catheter?"

Ken nodded. "She's got a strong heart. Write down the time," he said to me, and I added the time to my notes.

"Ninety-one minutes from incision to finish," I said.

Ken smiled with professional satisfaction, the doubts and shakes in abeyance. He and Scott unclipped the mare's legs from the posts. Then the hoist, with Scott supporting her head, lifted her up off the table. She rolled along the rails and through the sliding door into the padded room. The hoist lowered the mare onto an extra panel of floor padding until she lay on her side. Scott removed the cuffs from her legs and put a rope halter on her head, leading the rope through a ring on top of the half wall so that someone standing behind the wall could partly control her.

"She'll take twenty minutes or so to wake up slowly," Ken said. "Maybe in half an hour she'll be on her feet, but she'll be woozy for a good while. We'll leave her here for an hour after she's standing, then put her in the stable."

He spoke with earnest dedication, a doctor who cared. I followed him back to the vestibule, where he stripped off all the disposable garments. Scott and I did the same, Ken walking back immediately to take a continuing look at his patient.

"He won't leave her," Scott said. "He always wants to see them wake up. How about that coffee?"

He strode off towards the office to return with the thermoses he'd brought, and all three of us drank the contents, watching the mare until movement began to come back, first into her head and neck, then into her forelegs, until, with a sudden heave, she was sitting sideways. The mare rested in the same position for another ten minutes, and then, as if impelled by instinct, staggered onto all four feet. She was clearly free of the terrible pain of the colic.

Ken handed Scott the rope and left him watching the mare. He then jerked his head for me to follow him back into the operating room.

"I want to look at something," he said. He went over to the table where the three dishes lay with the spent syringes in them. Another dish contained a large bit of convoluted tissue.

"That's what I took out of the mare," Ken said.

I stared at it. "It's huge. What is it?"

"A twisted bit of intestine, but there's something odd about it. Wait while I get some gloves, and I'll find out."

He went and returned with clean gloves, and then he slightly loosened the knot in which one loop of intestine had tightened around another. Incredibly, there seemed to be a thread wound in among the tissue: pale, strong thread, like nylon.

"Just look at this," Ken said disbelievingly. I peered into his hands and saw a three-inch-diameter semicircular needle, the strong sort used for stitching carpet. The needle was threaded with the nylon. The needle, passing round and round in the intestine, had effectively stitched it into the knot.

"We have this happen from time to time with cats and dogs," Ken said. "They swallow sewing needles that have fallen to the floor, and literally stitch themselves together. I've never known it in a horse. It's a real curiosity."

I SLEPT at Thetford Cottage for four hours, as if drugged, and was awakened by a gentle, persistent tapping on the bedroom door. Rousing reluctantly, I managed a hoarse croak. "Yes?"

Vicky opened the door with apology and said Ken had phoned to ask if I would go down to the hospital. "It's some sort of meeting," she said.

She was looking altogether more like herself this morning. "Are you feeling better?" I asked.

"Much," she said, "though still not right, and Greg's the same. It's going to take us days."

She went away, and I tottered into some clothes, jet-lagged myself if the truth were told. The face in the bathroom mirror, even when newly shaved, had tired brownish green eyes below the usual dark hair and eyebrows.

At the hospital, chaotic activity filled the rear car park. A tow truck was trying to maneuver a Portakabin into a space. There were animals weaving in and out, mostly on leads, and people with anxious expressions or open mouths, or both.

I backed out of the melee and left the rented car in the road outside. From the rear, the main visible legacy of the flames was great black licks of soot above the frames where the windows had been. There was still a lingering smell of doused ash, sour and acrid, leaving a taste in the mouth.

I went into the entrance hall, which had a chaotic quality all its own, with cats and barking dogs sitting on people's laps all around the walls, and the center filled by Carey Hewett in a white medical coat arguing with a fire officer, one of the women vets trying to sort out patient priority, and a large man in a tweed suit demanding Carey Hewett's attention.

I threaded a way along to a rear entrance and let myself out into the stable area. I found Ken leaning on the half door of the first of the boxes, looking in at his patient. He was drooping with tiredness.

"How's she doing?" I asked, reaching him.

He knew my voice without turning his head.

"Oh, hallo. Thanks for coming. She's doing fine."

She looked, of course, anything but fine to me. The intravenous drip led into her neck from a bag at the ceiling, and another tube led out of one nostril.

"Her owner's coming," Ken said. "Carey says he's upset."

"Understandable."

Ken shook his head wearily. "Not about her colic. About me. He'd heard the rumors. Apparently he told Carey he should have got a different surgeon. He demanded I be here to talk to him, so I wanted you along for backup. Hope you don't mind."

"A witness you wanted, and a witness you've got."

"You've no obligation," he said.

"I'm interested," I said truthfully. "How old are you?"

"Thirty-four, just," he answered, surprised. "Why?"

I'd thought him a good deal older. It was the elongated bone structure and the intimations of thinning hair.

"I'm thirty-three, almost," I said as a quid pro quo, and after a moment he held out his hand to be shaken. The bond of mutual age was an odd one, but it definitely existed. From that moment Ken and I, though not yet close friends, all the same became a team.

A good deal of bustle appeared to be going on behind us across the car park. The Portakabin had finally been positioned to everyone's satisfaction and the tow truck disconnected.

"Instant office," Ken said, but it was more like instant clinic, as it was the animals with their owners who presently straggled across from the hospital, not the administrators.

41

Belinda appeared at that moment, giving me an irritated glance. "Peter doesn't belong here," she said.

"I asked him to come," Ken said.

Belinda bit off whatever rose into her mind and said to Ken, "Carey wants to see you in the entrance hall more or less five minutes ago."

Ken gave her a fonder smile than I could have managed and set off around the outside of the building, taking it for granted that I would go with him.

Emptied of the cats, dogs, and assorted owners, the entrance hall now held only Carey Hewett himself and the bulky man in the tweed suit, who swung around to stare hard at Ken.

"Are you Ken McClure?"

Ken said he was.

Carey Hewett made no comment about my presence. He forestalled the large man as he drew breath, and said to Ken, "This is the mare's owner, Wynn Lees."

Wynn Lees. Again the extraordinary fizz of memory. I knew a lot about Wynn Lees, if it was the same person. The Wynn Lees of twenty-five years ago had been a cautionary tale freely used by my mother to scare me into good behavior. "If you smoke at your age . . . If you're cruel to insects . . . If you steal . . . If you play truant . . . you'll grow up like Wynn Lees."

The present-day Wynn Lees had a fleshy, obstinate look on his heavy face, the cheeks broken-veined from wind and weather. A bull of a man, with no razor brains, he was saying belligerently to Ken, "You had no right to operate without my say-so."

Ken explained. "The stud groom had your phone number. He stood beside me while I tried it. Your wife answered."

"When was that?" Lees interrupted.

"About a quarter past three this morning."

"She couldn't have answered. She takes sleeping pills."

"Well, she did answer. She said you weren't at home and she didn't know where you were. I explained the mare had colic and needed an emergency operation. She said to go ahead."

Wynn Lees looked more shaken by his wife's wakefulness than seemed sensible, and he belatedly came around to acknowledging his debt to Ken. "Well, if my wife said . . . and the mare's apparently all right. . . . Well then, no hard feelings."

I didn't think the half apology anywhere near good enough, nor, I sensed, did Ken, though Carey Hewett definitely relaxed inwardly. He took the owner out the front door, into the car park, and turned left towards the stable. Ken and I followed, but halfway there I put my hand briefly on his arm to slow him down a pace or two for privacy.

"What is it?" Ken asked.

"Don't trust Wynn Lees. And don't tell him what you found in the horse's gut."

"Whyever not?"

"In case he already knows."

Ken gave me a stare of total astonishment, but by then we were approaching the mare's box and within earshot of Lees himself.

Lees was shocked by the mare's appearance, but Carey tried to reassure him, and Belinda, who was still there, told him the old girl was doing fine.

"Will the foal be born normally?" Lees asked.

Ken gave his opinion that he couldn't see any reason why not.

"Only a very skillful surgeon," Carey said, "could have performed such an operation successfully so late in the gestation period."

"I expect the mare's insured," I said neutrally.

I got swift glances from all three men, but it was Lees's attention that sharpened on my presence. "It's none of your business."

"No, of course not," I agreed. "Just a random thought."

Lees said to Ken, "Did you find any reason for the colic?"

After the briefest of pauses Ken said, "Colic's usually caused by a kink in the gut. If it persists, as it did in this case, you have to operate to straighten it. Sometimes, like in your mare, the gut's so badly knotted that you have to cut out the twisted piece."

Wynn Lees turned from the box and, in what I interpreted as acceptance of things as they were, marched away to drive off in a polished Rolls-Royce. Carey watched the departure with an unreadable expression of his own and, thanking Ken for his forbearance, took Belinda off towards the Portakabin.

Ken said, "Why don't you trust Mr. Lees?"

"He acts as if he wanted the mare dead."

Ken said slowly, "Do you mean . . . for the insurance? He doesn't need the money; he was driving a Rolls. I can't believe

43

anyone would deliberately scheme to kill a horse by feeding it something to block its gut— That's what you're saying, isn't it?"

"Could you get a horse to swallow anything if it didn't want to?"

"Oh yes. Pack it in something round and slippery, then practically throw it down the horse's gullet. Horses can't vomit. Once they've swallowed something, it's for keeps."

"Our Mr. Lees," I said, "never dreamed that his wife would wake up and okay the operation."

"No." Ken smiled. "That was a shock, wasn't it? She sounded far from having taken a sleeping pill. I'm pretty sure she had a man with her. I heard his voice."

We enjoyed the thought of Lees the cuckold. Serve him right.

Ken yawned and said that as he was technically off duty, he would go home for food and sleep. "On call tonight, free tomorrow afternoon. I've promised to take Belinda to the races tomorrow. Stratford-upon-Avon. Care to come?"

"Belinda wouldn't want me."

"What? Rubbish. See if Vicky and Greg would come too. We could all go in my car. Why not? It's settled." He smiled and yawned again. "I like Vicky. Great old girl. I've drawn a winner in the mother-in-law stakes, don't you think?"

"You have," I agreed.

Just then a fireman appeared and asked if the boss was around, as they wanted to show him something "out front." Ken fetched Carey from the Portakabin, and the three of us trudged after the fireman, back up the driveway.

The scene out front was reasonably orderly. There were six firemen in fireproof suits and three or four policemen.

Seeing Carey Hewett arrive, one of the firemen came to meet him, followed immediately by a policeman. A small amount of handshaking took place, followed by the news that in the firemen's professional opinion, the fire had been set. Arson.

"I can't believe it," Carey said. "What makes you think so?"

The fireman explained that they had found some big bottles of cleaning fluid. Spot remover, that sort of thing. "Highly inflammable," the fireman said.

"I expect we'd have spot remover," Carey said dazedly, "but I've no idea what's in the cleaning cupboard."

"Ah, but this was three bottles, all empty. And you know what?

These bottles had no caps on. Firebugs are always in such a hurry they forget the caps. And the bottles weren't in any cupboard. We found them in the big front room, where the two secretaries worked. Then there's the paint. You were having the place painted inside, right?"

Carey nodded.

"Well, sir, there's paint tins in there with the lids off. Good workmen don't leave lids off pots that've got paint in still."

Carey said forlornly, "Is there any chance of anything being left in there to salvage?"

The fireman shook his head. "Not a lot."

"We're insured against arson," Carey said dully. "But no insurance can bring back my records. All those years of work . . ."

He broke off. Carey, the elder statesman of the practice, looked gray, spent, and sad, standing dispiritedly in the small, chilly breeze that had sprung up to ruffle our hair and sting our noses.

CHAPTER 5

THE journey to Stratford-upon-Avon races was short enough for Belinda to remain civil, even if not cordial, in my direction. She seemed to have accepted that I would be part of the scenery for as long as I stayed around, and I'd been at pains to mention that I'd have to be reporting for work in London soon.

"When?" Ken asked bluntly.

"Three weeks from Monday."

"I was hoping . . ." He stopped, glanced at me over his shoulder, and went on. "How about a spot of detective work?"

"Ken!" Belinda was reasonably exasperated. "If you mean the things that have been going wrong in the practice— Well, Peter can't begin to understand them in veterinary terms, can he? Far less explain them."

"There was the fire, dear," Vicky murmured.

"Yes, Mother, but the police will see to that."

Belinda, sitting in front next to Ken, had come dressed in a chestnut leather skirt, a big white sweater, knee-high boots, and a leather overcoat. She looked slender and pretty, her hair falling free to her shoulders. I sat between Vicky and Greg in a bit of a crush in the back. Vicky wore intense red to dramatize her white hair

45

and seemed back to normal in vitality. Ken himself looked slightly less haunted, as if he'd put the worst of the anxieties on hold.

Inside the racecourse, the five of us split apart, Greg and Vicky going off in search of lunch, leaving me on my own to enjoy the first steeplechase meeting I'd been to in years.

Cheltenham racecourse had been my childhood playground, my familiar backyard. My mother's secretarial work had been in the racecourse manager's office. During school holidays, while she labored at her desk, I was allowed by the manager to go almost everywhere on the course and in the buildings.

Race days had been magic, and until John Darwin came along, I had taken it for granted that one day I would be one of the jockeys rocketing over the jumps. I read sporting newspapers; knew the names and fortunes of every steeplechase horse, trainer, and jockey in the business; fantasized eternally about being top jockey and winning all the top races.

Two minor impediments damped the prospects. First, I had no pony of my own and could only snatch infrequent opportunities to ride at all. Second, I faced the implacable determination of my mother that I shouldn't achieve my aim.

It had got my father into his grave. The man who'd sired me, whom I knew only from photographs, was a jockey over jumps for one short year. Four winners to the good, Paul Perry, age twenty-one, had ridden out as usual one morning. His mount, they said, had shied at a bird flying out of a hedge; he himself was flung into the path of a passing car and was already dead when the other lads dismounted to help him.

The widow, barely twenty herself, was sustained through the months to come by the charitable Injured Jockeys' Fund, a marvelous organization that eventually found for her, a trained secretary, the job at Cheltenham racecourse.

Coming back to my long-dead father's world after a gap of twenty years, it seemed in some ways as if time itself had stood still. The jockeys' names were as they'd always been, yet these had to be the sons and daughters of the pack I'd idolized. The same thing with trainers, though in this case, as I progressively discovered, many were indeed the same old brigade.

J. Rolls Eaglewood, for instance, identified as he stood with his runner in the parade ring before the first race, was an old man with a walking stick, on which he leaned heavily. J. Rolls Eagle-wood, father of Russet, was undoubtedly the same man.

Many owners, also, were recognizably the same. I looked through the race card for Ronnie Upjohn, the owner threatening to sue Ken for daring to win with an Upjohn castoff, but he had no runner that day. Upjohn . . . and Travers. Upjohn and Travers. They ran together in my mind, like Abbott and Costello, but definitely without the laughs.

I turned away from the parade ring and began to thread a way through the throng to a good watching place on the stands and, not looking where I was going, almost cannoned into two short men in navy overcoats, who happened to be Japanese.

I apologized in English. They bowed to me, unspeaking. I went on up to the stands.

The two Japanese, standing below and to the left of me in the area outside the weighing room, looked bewildered and lost. They were joined by a young woman, who was trying to talk to them by signs. The two men consulted each other earnestly and bowed a few times to their companion, but it was obvious that no one was understanding anything much.

The impulse to help was ingrained, I supposed. I strolled down from the stands and stopped a pace or two from the young woman, who, at close quarters, looked impatient as well as harassed.

"Can I perhaps be of service?" Good old Foreign Office lingo.

She flicked me a glance. "Not unless you speak Japanese."

"Well, yes, I do. That's why I asked."

She turned her full attention my way and metaphorically clutched the offered life buoy, as one seeing escape from drowning.

"Then please," she said, "ask them what they want. They want something, and they can't seem to be able to tell me what."

I bowed to the Japanese and asked them the question. The extent of their relief at hearing their own language was almost comical, and so was their answer. I bowed and pointed out to them what they wanted, and they hurried away.

The young woman watched openmouthed, crossly.

"They wanted the loo," I said.

She stared at me, then melted inside and began to laugh.

"Thanks," she said easily. "I've been showing them round London for three days, and this morning their translator was sick,

47

and he couldn't come. They're part of the Japanese Jockey Club."

"Ah," I said. "I think I've met one of them before."

"Really. Where?"

"In Japan. I used to work there."

She gave me a bright, assessing look, and I in turn noted the small mouth, the huge blue eyes, and the thick, frizzed blond-streaked brown hair chopped off straight and round at earlobe level, except for an eyebrow-length fringe. The overall effect was slightly zany doll, but the mind inside was no toy.

"I work for the British Jockey Club," she said. "I arrange things for visiting bigwigs. Transport, hotels, that sort of thing."

I could think of worse things than having my path smoothed by her. "I'm Peter," I said.

"Annabel."

She said casually, "What did you do in Japan?"

"Worked for the Foreign Office."

The Japanese Jockey Club came back and bowed, expressing especial pleasure when I said I recognized one of them.

Annabel took her charges into the betting enclosure, and I watched them from the stands. They moved slowly from book-maker to bookmaker until one of the men produced some money. The bet was struck, the ticket given. The trio then went up into the stands behind the bookmakers and watched the race from there.

Greg and Vicky appeared at my side. I diagnosed a slight case of boredom. I didn't see Ken and Belinda at all and found later they'd walked down the course to be nearer the jumps. Annabel brought the Japanese to stand by the parade-ring rails to watch the next lot of runners walk around, and far more for enjoyment than obligation, I joined them.

They were all pleased, the men almost effusively so. I'd be-come their dearest buddy in the West. They hoped I could tell them which of the horses in front of us would win the next race.

I watched the parade and pointed to a load of lean, glossy muscle striding around phlegmatically with its head down. The Japanese bowed their thanks and hurried back to the bookies.

"So you know about horses?" Annabel asked.

"I wanted to be a jockey, once."

She looked up at my height. "There have been six-foot jockeys, I suppose."

She wore black and white all over: black boots, checked skirt, white turtleneck, black short coat, and huge fluffy white scarf with black pom-pom fringes. She looked at times sixteen and at times double that, and had an overall air of competence.

"Do you live in London?" I asked.

"Fulham Road, if you can call that London. And you?"

"Homeless, for now," I said.

The Japanese came back, happily waving tickets, and we all went up on the stands to watch. Their horse survived to the last hurdle and there turned end over end in a flurry of legs.

I apologized. The Japanese put their useless tickets in their pockets along with their dashed hopes and decided that for the next race they would like to walk down to the fences. I was ready to say I'd go with them, when I spotted Ken walking alone.

"I have to speak to someone," I said hastily in two languages. "Please, please excuse me."

I left them in mid-bow and reached Ken before he moved off. "I want to talk to you," I said. "Alone and uninterrupted."

"All right." He made up his mind. "How about the bar?"

The bar turned out to be worse than useless because as we reached the door we came face to face with J. Rolls Eaglewood, who was on his way out, limping along with his walking stick.

"Afternoon, sir," Ken said.

J. Rolls stopped dead, fixing a dire glare on Ken's face.

"You killed my horse," he said.

Ken shook his head weakly. "He died. We couldn't save him."

"Sheer bloody incompetence."

Eaglewood at close quarters, though thin, gray-haired, and with age-freckled skin, still generated the power and threat I associated with his name. His voice held the rasp of one long used to instant obedience. "You're never to attend my horses again, or I'll be transferring my business to another firm of vets."

Ken miserably made no attempt at defense. Eaglewood gave him a brief, fierce nod and stumped off out of earshot.

"You see?" Ken said, shaking and as pale as ever. "I can't even blame him. The horse that died on Thursday morning—with the split cannon bone—came from his stable. Another of his died on the table about a month ago while I was doing respiratory-tract surgery. And one died in its own box. . . ." His voice took the by now familiar note of desperation. "I don't do anything wrong. I'm always careful. They just *died*."

"Mm. Well, why don't you give me a complete chronological list of all the things that have ended badly. Also the names of all the owners and trainers and anything special about them."

"I'd need my notes—" He broke off. "All my notes are *burned*."

We'd moved away from the door to the bar, and we stood in the area outside the weighing room. "What you've got to do," I told Ken, "is start wondering how you would have set about killing the horses that died. Think about how to commit equine murder."

"But I . . ." His voice tailed off indecisively.

"Knowledge isn't guilt," I said. "It doesn't mean you've done it."

I looked at his unhappy face and understood his unwillingness to part with information that might sound like confession. Looking over his shoulder, I saw Belinda making her way towards us.

"Think out the list," I urged Ken. "Meet me early tomorrow at the hospital. Alone."

"How early?"

"Eight?"

"All right," he said. "Eight."

"Eight what?" Belinda asked, overhearing.

"Number eight in the next race," I explained.

I left them and made tracks for Annabel as she brought her retinue back to the paddock. After twenty minutes apart we greeted each other as old friends. The two Japanese talked animatedly between themselves about the next race, and Annabel and I looked at each other with a lot of unspoken questions.

"Who," she said, "were you talking to when we came back? A tall, thin man with fair hair, and a tetchity girl."

"Ken McClure and Belinda Larch."

She frowned. "Is he a vet?"

"Yes, he is. I met him the day before yesterday."

"They were talking about him upstairs."

"Who upstairs?"

"The directors and stewards. One of them was, anyway. He said your friend was killing horses left, right, and center."

"Really?" I was interested. "Who was he?"

"I was introduced to about eight people, so I can't remember his name, but I think he might have been one of the stewards."

"Let's see," I said, and turned my race card back to page one, and there to my confusion found in the list of stewards the name I'd searched all the inner pages for in vain: R. D. Upjohn, Esq.

"Ronnie!" Annabel exclaimed. "They called him Ronnie." She studied my face. "Mean something to you?"

I told her about the preserved castoff that went on to win. "Ken made him look a fool. Some men can't bear it."

She looked at her watch. "I really ought to take these two back upstairs to the directors' room. Would you mind suggesting it?"

The Japanese went, and for me, unexpectedly, the fizz went out of the hour with their departure. I said to myself, Peter, my boy, you know nothing about her. . . . But everything had to begin *somewhere*.

I rejoined Greg and Vicky on the stands. Annabel stayed out of sight until after the last race, when she came down from above and shepherded her charges towards the exit. She saw me hovering there (I was already keeping Ken and the others waiting) and came to my side with a small-mouthed grin.

"Ronnie Upjohn is that man ahead of us—with the woman in the orange coat." We walked on together out into the car park, followed by the two Japanese. "He seems fairly ordinary."

We arrived at a big car, with a chauffeur waiting to carry away the very important Japanese. I bowed in farewell to the two men, keeping an eye on the departing orange coat.

"Go chase him," Annabel said, "if you must."

I smiled at her blue eyes. "I'll phone you," I said, and hurried after the orange coat as fast as I could.

The coat stopped beside a large gray car, and Ronnie Upjohn unlocked the car doors. I had time to see him clearly before he folded himself into the front passenger seat. The lady was driving.

Ronnie Upjohn was sixtyish and basically unremarkable. I had to tick off features mentally to have any chance of knowing him elsewhere. Hair, gray. Eyebrows, medium bushy. Eyes, slightly drooping at outside edges. Nose, large, a bit bulbous. Mustache, brownish. . . . I gave up. He was by then inside the car.

I turned away and started walking across the main car park towards Ken's car and found him standing with his arms folded, watching my antics with astonishment.

"Did you know who you were following?" he asked incredulously. "That was Ronnie Upjohn."

"I certainly hope so." I paused. "Apart from acting as a steward, what does he do?"

"Owns a few horses." Ken thought it over. "He's something in finance. I don't exactly know. He's semiretired, I think."

"He's doing you no good just now," I said.

Ken sighed. "No one is."

THAT evening, when they'd all gone out, I ate cheese on toast and drank some wine and telephoned my mother in Mexico City.

I pictured her on the other end of the line, as beautiful as ever. I listened with a familiar sense of security to her light voice, elegant and very young, ageless.

"Wynn Lees?" she repeated in disbelief. "You seriously don't want to get mixed up with Wynn Lees, darling."

"What did he do that was so awful?" I asked. "All I can dredge up about him is a vague impression that he went to prison."

"Yes, he certainly did. For cruelty to horses."

"For *what?*" I was stunned.

"The first time, it was for cruelty to horses. He and another youth cut off a horse's tongue. I didn't know about it until we moved to Cheltenham, and by that time Wynn Lees was over thirty and had been to prison again, but the second time was for fighting. He was a horrible man. He went off to somewhere like Australia afterwards."

"Who did he fight?" I asked.

"What? Oh. . . . It wasn't just for fighting. He'd attacked some man with a rivet gun and shot staples into him through his jeans. Stapled the jeans to the man. I think he'd accused the man of playing round with his girlfriend behind his back."

"Okay," I said. "Let me try you with some more names. How about Ronnie Upjohn?"

"Upjohn. . . ." Her voice was negative, without recognition.

"Upjohn and Travers," I said. "Who were Upjohn and Travers?"

"My darling, I haven't a clue. Anyone else?"

"J. Rolls Eaglewood. Old, and with a walking stick."

"J. Rolls!" She laughed. "Ruled his yard like iron, and our village too. So the old monster's still training. . . . What happened to his daughter, Russet? He would never hear a word against her."

"I don't know yet. There's a granddaughter now, called Izzy. She was Ken McClure's girlfriend for a while." I paused. "Mum, did you ever know why Kenny McClure killed himself?"

After a brief silence she said, "Depression, I suppose. It was a dreadful shock at the time. I never believed the rumors."

"What rumors?"

"Something to do with drugs. With ordering the wrong drugs. People trying to explain why he would kill himself when he was so well liked and a good vet. It was really upsetting."

"How did he kill himself?"

"Shotgun. Blew his head to pieces. Darling, don't make me remember. It made me feel ill for days at a time. Just thinking about it now brings it all back."

The strength of her reaction surprised me. I'd never speculated about her love life between husbands. But at twenty something, she must have been at least ready and available for love.

Always alarmingly able to interpret my silences, my mother said, "Kenny was married. It wasn't right for him to leave his wife and children. We both agreed on that. So it didn't last very long. It was over years before he killed himself. I saw him often, but we were just friends. Is that what you wanted to know?"

"I think so, yes."

"You know," she said tentatively, "if you can help your friend Ken in his troubles, it would be sort of fitting. Don't let him do what his father did. I would have given anything to know what was troubling Kenny . . . to have stopped him. So help his son for me and Kenny, will you?"

I was extraordinarily moved. Parents were full of the most amazing surprises.

"I will help him," I promised, "if I can."

I WENT along to the hospital at eight the next day, determined to dig everything I could out of Ken, but there was no chance for a quiet private chat early on a Sunday morning. I found the whole place seething with activity.

A police barrier denied entry to the rear car park, which was itself full of police cars. Across the tarmac I could see Carey Hewett in his by now familiar state of distress. I'd never seen him otherwise. Ken, in the same group, waved to me and walked over.

"The fire service were apparently here all day yesterday with the insurance people," he said, "sifting through the mess, looking for absolute proof of arson."

"And did they find it?"

"They didn't say. But what they did find was a *body*."

CHAPTER 6

"**W**HOSE body?" I asked automatically.

"No one knows," Ken said.

We went across the tarmac to join the group around Carey Hewett. He wore Sunday morning casual clothes—checked shirt and maroon sweater. On top of that he looked a bewildered and worried man. This last shock had noticeably aged him.

"I don't understand how anyone could have been in the building so late on Thursday," he was saying. "Everything was locked."

"Could have been the arsonist," one of the men in the group said. He was a plainclothes policeman, I gradually discovered. I also gathered gradually that the body had been found in the general area of what had been the pharmacy, and had been burned beyond recognition. Even its sex hadn't yet been determined.

"They apparently found the body last night," Ken told me as an aside. "What a bloody *mess!*"

"It could be worse," I said. "It might have been one of you in there. One of you might have disturbed the arsonist and been bumped off for your pains."

"I suppose so." The thought didn't especially alarm him. "There's often one of us around here at night when we've got patients in the boxes. Scott was in and out all day yesterday looking after the mare, and I came three times to check on her."

"So the mare's doing all right?"

"Fingers crossed."

We left the group and went over to look at the mare and another horse. They both seemed half asleep, standing quietly.

"What's wrong with this one?" I asked.

"He had wind troubles. Couldn't get air down to his lungs under pressure because one side of his larynx is paralyzed. Quite

55

common in big horses. I put in a suture to hold that side of his larynx open so he can breathe better. He's been no problem."

"You operated on him here in the hospital?"

"Yes. Wednesday morning. It's a fairly long procedure. He'd been scheduled for a couple of weeks. It wasn't an emergency."

"Have the horses that died all been emergencies?"

Ken thought briefly and shook his head. "One died out here of heart failure after a successful operation to remove a knee chip. Scott stayed here all night after the op, checking him regularly. One minute he was all right. Next minute dead."

"Did Scott actually see him fall?"

"No, I don't think so. To be honest, I think Scott went to sleep, though he swore he didn't. We did an autopsy, but"—he shrugged—"we found nothing amiss. His heart had just stopped."

"Is that common?"

"Not really. More common after a hard race."

"Did you make out that list?"

"Haven't had a minute." He was as ambivalent as ever.

"What did you do wrong?" I said.

"Nothing," he said unconvincingly.

"*Something* must have been wrong. Why don't you just tell me?"

He gave me an unhappy look and shrugged his shoulders.

"The first one—" he began tentatively, his long face miserable. "I thought afterwards maybe I'd missed . . . but it seemed so illogical— And it would have worn off anyway in the end. . . ."

"What, Ken? What would have worn off?"

"Atropine," he said.

"Is that a poison?" I asked.

He said patiently, "It's poisonous. It's belladonna. But it relaxes things. Stops spasms."

"Stops the heart?"

He shook his head. "It could stop movement in the gut, which would become distended, and you'd have to take the horse to surgery. But the gut would start working again normally when the atropine wore off. Only that's not what happened. They both died under anesthesia."

"*Both?*"

"I can't be sure. . . ."

Irritatingly, at that point Scott arrived with two other vets, Oliver Quincy and Lucy Amhurst.

"You know Peter, don't you?" Ken asked his colleagues, and they nodded to me uninterestedly. Almost immediately another two arrived, Jay Jardine and Yvonne Floyd; they were followed closely by Belinda.

They moved by consensus in through the main door, Scott, Belinda, and I following, and came to form a conference in the office, fetching along the chairs from the entrance hall. Carey Hewett alone remained outside with the police.

Lucy Amhurst demanded to know what was going on, which no one, of course, could tell her. "We've enough dead horses for a glue factory, we've arson, and we've a body. It's not funny."

She was a positive, middle-aged, no-nonsense person, with a stocky countrywoman's body. She sat in the desk chair and fixed a rather headmistressy gaze on me and said, "Excuse me, we know you're a friend of Ken's, but I think you might explain a bit more who you are."

"He's a civil servant," Belinda said. "Some sort of secretary."

"A snoop," Jay Jardine said disapprovingly.

Lucy Amhurst gave me a judicial inspection. "Well, we do need some answers. If he doesn't come up with anything, we'll be no worse off."

There were shrugs. No one had passionate views. I quietly stayed, and no one raised the subject again.

Jay Jardine, the cattle man, was thin, short, self-assertive, and a fairly recent graduate from veterinary college. He was the youngest of the group and, it seemed to me, the least liked.

"Carey's dragging his feet," he complained. "You know we have to have lab space. I phoned him yesterday evening again, but he's still done nothing. He's too old to cope with this, that's obvious."

The others protested up and down the scale, from outrage (Lucy) to anxiety (Yvonne Floyd).

"He's sixty, isn't he?" Yvonne said worriedly.

She was young enough to think sixty unimaginably ancient.

Yvonne Floyd, thirtyish, wore a wedding ring and emphasized her femininity with a luxuriant mass of almost black hair. Even so early, she wore lipstick and eyeliner, and a skirt with a black lace-edged underslip that showed when she crossed her legs.

57

Oliver Quincy hardly took his eyes off the legs, though whether from lust or absentmindedness I wasn't quite sure. He was a brown-haired, roly-poly sort of man in early middle age, with a more comforting, relaxed aura than the others.

Yvonne said anxiously, "What will happen if the whole partnership falls to pieces?"

"If it does," Oliver said easily, "I'm hiring."

"What do you mean?" Lucy asked.

"*Quincy* and Partners," he said. "If Carey bows out, we go on as before, but without him. With me, instead, as senior partner."

"He won't bow out," Lucy said, upset.

Young Jay Jardine said, "We can bow him out. Tell him he's too old, he's lost our confidence."

"Carey built up this practice," Ken protested. "It's *his*."

"It's normal," Oliver said. "The young herd always gets rid of the old bull."

"The old man won't stand for it," Scott said forcefully. "You'll see. We're all staying with Carey."

Oliver's mild-seeming gaze moved from Scott's face to Ken's. "Quincy and Partners," he said, "can't be doing with a discredited surgeon. Sorry, and all that."

There was a blank silence.

"Who owns the hospital?" I asked. The heads all turned my way. "Who owns the burned building?" I added. "Who gets the insurance money?"

"The bank," Ken said. "They hold the mortgage."

"Why do you ask?" Lucy said.

"I just wondered if anyone benefitted especially if the whole place burned down."

They thought about it, but one could see that it was basically caring for sick animals they were interested in, not finance.

"We'll have to ask Carey," Lucy said. "He's still in charge." The seeds of doubt had been sown, though.

Ken's prospects looked appalling. Carey's loyalty to him couldn't last forever, and the others of necessity would ditch him. With such an ignominious departure hanging over him, no one at all reputable would take him on.

Into the silence in which his five partners variously reviewed their futures, Carey himself put his gray head.

"Oh, there you all are," he said, unreceptive to the atmosphere. "The police want to see you over in the Portakabin." His voice sounded tired. His manner looked defeated.

He, his partners, and his nurses traipsed across the tarmac, Ken last. I walked beside Ken. We went into the Portakabin, where a constable was taking names. I gave my name and sat down like everyone else.

The senior policeman in charge, middle-aged, local accent, air of sober reliability, said he was interested in knowing who had left the main veterinary building last on Thursday, before the fire.

Yvonne Floyd said that when she left at seven, only Carey had remained. "We hold small-animal clinics on Mondays and Thursdays from five to seven. I do Thursdays."

The policeman reluctantly slid his eyes away from the lace-edged slip and sought confirmation from Carey.

Yes, Carey agreed wearily. Thursday had been a long, bothersome day. He hadn't left until after eight. At that time he'd let himself out and locked the front door from the outside. He'd then gone on along to the stable boxes, where he found Scott. He'd said good night to Scott and driven home.

The policeman nodded and asked which of us was Scott.

Scott identified himself, broad-shouldered, lean, the power machine. "Scott Sylvester, qualified veterinary nurse."

The policeman then asked how many people had keys to the burned building.

"We all do," Carey said.

"Can you tell me if the internal doors were locked, sir?"

"When I left on Thursday," Carey said, "only the pharmacy and path-lab doors were locked."

The policeman asked who had a key to the pharmacy.

"We all do," Carey said again. "Including the senior secretary and the cleaners. And each cabinet has its own lock, of course. The secretary and cleaners don't have keys to those."

"Glass-fronted cabinets, sir?"

Carey nodded.

"The investigators say there was a great deal of melted glass in the pharmacy area. There seems to be no chance of identifying if anything is missing. We just ask you—all of you—to make a list of what you know was in the pharmacy so that if any of it turns up in other hands, we can proceed further with our inquiries."

The policeman turned to a fresh page in his spiral-bound note-book. "I'd like to make a list of where you all were during the evening. Starting with Mr. Hewett, please, sir."

"I told you, I left after eight and went home."

"How far away is home, sir?"

"Are all these questions necessary?" Carey protested. "You surely can't think one of *us* started the fire."

"We can't tell who started it, sir, but we'd like to eliminate as many people as possible."

"Oh, I see. Well, I live five minutes away."

"And you spent the evening with your wife?"

"My wife's dead. I got some supper, played some music, read the newspaper."

The policeman nodded, made a note, and continued to the next name on his list. "Mrs. Amhurst?"

"Miss," Lucy said.

"Thursday evening, madam?" he asked economically.

"Same as Carey, I suppose, though in my case, instead of music I watched some television."

"How far away from here do you live, madam?"

"A mile and a quarter. In Riddlescombe."

I looked at her. Riddlescombe was the village where I'd lived with my mother, where the Eaglewoods still held sway.

The policeman consulted his list. "Mrs. Floyd?"

"Like I told you," Yvonne said, "I went home at seven."

"And home is?"

"Painswick Road. About a couple of miles from here. My hus-band was away on business, but the kids were in."

"Er . . . how old are your children?"

"They're my husband's. Fifteen and sixteen. Boys."

"And could they vouch for you, madam?"

"They were doing their homework. They have a room each. I always go up and tell them when I get in. We get on pretty well."

"So you went downstairs, madam, I'm guessing, and cooked some food and spent the evening more or less alone?"

"I suppose so. Read the day's letters and a magazine. Watched the news. Then Oliver phoned and said this place was on fire."

The policeman made the briefest of notes.

"Oliver Quincy, large animals?" he asked next.

"That's me," Oliver said.

"Sir, your evening?"

"Oh, well, I was bloody tired. So I drove out to a pub and had a couple of pints and some bar food."

"Are you married, sir?"

"My wife goes where she likes, and so do I."

"How did you hear the building was on fire, sir?"

"I phoned him," Carey said. "He was a long time answering, but he was the first I'd tried to reach. I think of Oliver as my second-in-command. It was natural to get to him first and ask him to phone everyone else."

"The phone was ringing when I got home," Oliver confirmed. "I phoned Yvonne, Lucy, and Jay and told them, but got no answer from the others."

"I was in the Red Lion pub, just along the road," Scott said.

"Mr. McClure?" the policeman asked.

"I took my fiancée, Belinda here, and her parents out to dinner. Peter was with us too."

The policeman again reviewed his list. "Belinda Larch, qualified veterinary nurse? Peter Darwin, general assistant?"

"Right," Ken said. "We were just about to leave the restaurant when Lucy phoned me there."

Lucy nodded. "He was on call, so I phoned his portable phone from the hospital office. Does all this matter?"

"Some things matter; some don't," said our "philosopher" policeman. "We can't tell yet." He consulted the list. "Mr. Jay Jardine?"

With unsuppressed irritation Jay said he'd gone home and had a row with his live-in girlfriend. She'd stormed out. So what.

So nothing, it seemed. His answer got written down without comment, and it appeared the present session of questions had come to an end. The constable and his senior officer stood up to leave, and Carey went with them.

Oliver stood up, stretching. "There's no point in waiting about here. I'm off to play golf. Who's on call?"

"Carey is," Lucy told him, "and Ken."

Oliver said, "Then let's hope it is a quiet Sunday." He walked purposefully out of the Portakabin, followed immediately by Jay.

Everyone else stood and moved in their wake. Scott announced he was spending the day by the lake, stripping down the engines of his speedboat, and marched briskly out of the car park. We heard the roar of his engine starting, and presently saw his strong figure riding a motorbike past the entrance.

Lucy said, "He pumps iron; he's got pectorals you'd hardly believe; he's as physical as they come."

"He's a good nurse," Ken said to me. "You saw him."

"Loyal to Carey too," Lucy went on approvingly.

"We may as well all go home," Yvonne said. "Oliver was right; we can't do any more here."

"I suppose not," Lucy agreed reluctantly.

The two women walked together to the gate. Belinda urged Ken to come with her to Thetford Cottage for lunch.

"You go on, darling," Ken said. "I just want to go over a few things with Peter." He walked ahead of me into the office.

"Right," he said, settling into the chair behind the desk and stretching for a notepad to write on. "No secrets, no reservations, and don't use what I tell you against me."

"Not a chance," I agreed, and thought about his father and my mother, and the promises I'd made her.

CHAPTER 7

"CHRONOLOGICALLY," Ken said, "if we're counting horses that've died when I wouldn't expect them to, the first one was months ago, last year, September maybe. Without my notes I can't be certain."

"What happened?" I said.

"I got called out to Eaglewood's at six one morning. Old man Eaglewood was away, and the head lad was in charge. He said one of the horses was extremely ill, so I went over. It was a three-year-old colt that I'd been treating for a strained tendon, but otherwise he'd been perfectly healthy. But he was lying on his side in his box in a coma, with occasional spasms in his muscles, obviously dying. I asked how long he'd been like that, but the lad didn't know."

"What did you do?" I asked.

"He was too far gone to be helped. I just took some blood samples for analysis and put him out of his misery."

"And what was wrong with him?"

Ken shook his head. "Everything in his blood was just about within normal limits, though the blood sugar was low, but . . ."

"But what?"

"Before he died, the colt's heart rate was very high and there was swelling round his eyes. I began to think about poisons—about what would cause spasms, high heart rate, and coma. I asked the head lad if he'd been insured, because you can't help wondering, but he didn't know. I talked it over with Carey several times, and in the end he asked Eaglewood himself about the insurance, but it seemed the owner actually hadn't insured the colt at all."

"But you weren't really satisfied?"

"Well, I mean, it was a mystery. I'm certain that colt was deliberately killed, even if there wasn't an obvious reason for it."

"What killed him?" I asked, fascinated.

"Insulin," he said, "though I can't prove it."

"*Insulin?*"

"Yes. Well horses don't get diabetes, except so rarely it's almost never. You wouldn't give horses insulin for anything. If you gave a horse a big overdose, his blood sugar would fall catastrophically and he would go into hypoglycemic shock. It fitted the symptoms of the colt."

"It *must* have been for the insurance," I said, pondering.

"But Mr. Eaglewood said the colt wasn't insured."

"Did he own the colt himself?"

"No. As a matter of fact he belonged to the same man who owns the mare. Wynn Lees."

I drew in a breath sharply. "How much do you know about Wynn Lees?" I asked.

"Nothing much. Why did you tell me not to trust him?"

I thought briefly about letting him know, but decided not to. Not yet. "Instinct," I said. "He gave me the shivers."

Ken nodded. The man had had much the same effect on him.

After a moment I said, "Is your mother still alive?"

"Yes, she is. Why do you ask?"

"I don't know. I just wondered if she'd had a chance yet of enjoying Greg and Vicky being here. They'd have a lot to talk about, with the wedding just ahead. And I'd like to meet her too."

He looked at me in dawning dismay. "Why haven't I arranged it? But there's been so much on my mind. How about today for lunch?" He stretched a hand out to the phone. "I'll ask at once."

It was Vicky who answered, received the suggestion with enthusiasm, and said it was a lovely idea and that she would tell Belinda it was fixed. Ken disconnected with a smile and redialed, reaching his own parent and evoking a more moderate response. Ken was persuasive; he would pick her up, he promised, and take her home afterwards.

"My mother's not like Vicky," he said, putting down the receiver. "She likes things planned well in advance. She thinks we're hurrying the wedding, but the truth is, she's against me marrying *anyone*." He sighed. "Parents!"

"Do you remember your father?"

"Only vaguely. I was ten when he died. I wish . . ." He paused. "I wish I knew why he died. The older I get, the more I want to know why." I waited without movement, and he said, "He killed himself." It was clearly still a painful thought.

I looked down at his notepad, on which he'd written the single word insulin. "How about if you let me write the notes?"

He pushed the pad and pen across gladly. I turned to a new page, and after a bit of thought he began again on the saga.

"The next one I can't explain was soon after Christmas. That was the one I thought had been given atropine. Racehorse. A hurdler. Trained by Zoe Mackintosh."

"*Zoe* Mackintosh? Is she a trainer's daughter?" I asked. Mackintosh, in my shadowy memory, was a man.

Ken nodded. "Her father, old Mac. He's still there, but his memory's going. He's a cantankerous old man, and he's always breathing over her shoulder. She still employs Hewett and Partners because she's known Carey all her life—he and Mac are great buddies—but she's been huffy to me about the dead horses."

"More than one?"

"Two. And I'd swear they were both given atropine."

"Were both these horses owned by the same person?" I asked.

"No idea."

"And were they insured?"

"I don't think so. You'd have to ask Zoe or the owners, and frankly, I'm not going to."

"You're scared of her!"

"You haven't met her."

"Describe the atropine horses."

"The first one, a bay four-year-old gelding, large white blaze down its nose. The second one, a five-year-old gelding, chestnut."

"Okay." I wrote down the descriptions. "How did they die?"

"Colic cases, both times the same. Without warning, their heart started to fail, their blood pressure dropped disastrously, and we'd lost them on the operating table."

"How many have died like that now?"

"Four in eight weeks." He swallowed. "Like I told you, the last one was putting screws in a split cannon bone, and before that there was the respiratory tieback, like the one here now. Those two were both Eaglewood's."

"After the respiratory tieback, what next?"

He thought for a good while. "I suppose the next one was Nagrebb's show jumper. The horse splintered one of the jumps, and when I went there, it was still in the field, with a sharp piece of wood a foot long driven into its near hind above the hock. The girl who rode it was in tears, which didn't help the horse. Horses react to fear with fear. In the end I got old man Nagrebb to take his daughter into the house. After that I pulled the stake out of the leg and inspected the damage, which was mainly muscular. I did a clean-and-repair job and closed the skin."

He paused, thinking back. "Well, the leg was healing okay. I went out there several times. I took out the sutures. End of case. Then a day or two later I got a panic call and went and found its lower leg and fetlock up like a balloon and the horse unable to put its foot to the ground. So we brought it here and I opened the leg, and the tendon had literally disintegrated. There was nothing to repair. Of course we had to put the horse down, and it was this famous show jumper. Nagrebb had insured it, so we told the insurers the horse couldn't be saved."

He stopped again and looked at me earnestly. "There is something that would make that happen."

"What?" I asked.

"Some stuff called collagenase. It's an enzyme that dissolves collagen, which is what tendons and ligaments are made of. If you injected, say, two cc's of collagenase into a tendon, you would get that result. Still, you can't just go out and *buy* it. It's supplied by chemical companies, but it's only used in research laboratories.

It's pretty dicey stuff. It would dissolve human tendons too."

"Go on to the next one."

"Okay. The next one that died was the one out in the intensive care box. The one I told you about this morning."

"Who owned it?"

"Chap called Fitzwalter. Decent sort. He didn't blame me. The blood tests were negative for any unexplained substance."

I studied his pale, worried face.

"And straight after that the second Mackintosh horse came in, and it died on the table exactly like the first one." He shook his head. "Then last Thursday, the day you came, we lost the Eagle-wood horse with the cannon bone. Just the same. Failing heart and diving blood pressure."

"Was there anything—anything at all—different in the two Mackintosh operations from the one I saw you do on the mare? Apart from not finding any physical obstructions, I mean?"

"Nothing, except naturally that it was Scott and Belinda who were with me, not you. Belinda runs the room; Scott does the anesthetic. We always work that way."

"Just the three of you?"

"Not always. Any of the others might come in."

"Go back to last Thursday morning," I said. "You checked everything twice. You had Oliver there. Go through it all in your mind, right from when the horse arrived. Don't skip anything."

I watched him think, watched the small movements in his facial muscles as he passed from procedure to procedure. Watched him shake his head and frown.

"Absolutely nothing," he burst out. "Nothing except—"

"Except *what?*" I asked.

"Well, Oliver was watching the screen. I glanced over a couple of times. I can't swear to it, but I think now that the heartbeat line on the electrocardiograph had changed slightly." He frowned heavily. "I'll have to look a few things up."

"Here?" I asked, looking around the bare office.

"No, at home. All my books are at home. Carey kept all his in his office." He shook his head. "Some of those books are irreplaceable."

"Very bad luck," I said.

"There's no saying the troubles are over either."

"Particularly not with an unknown body lying around."

66

He rubbed a hand tiredly over his face. "Let's go along to Thetford Cottage."

"Okay. But Ken . . . Until they find out whose body it is, well, don't go down any dark alleys."

He stared. He didn't seem to have worried in the least about the body or seen it as any warning to be careful.

"It was the arsonist," he protested.

"Maybe. Just take care."

"You scare me, you know."

"Good."

AT LUNCH at Thetford Cottage, Vicky did her best to charm Ken's mother—Josephine—but in truth they were incompatible spirits. Vicky, spontaneous, rounded, generous, was having to break through to a defensive, plainly dressed, angular woman in whom disapproval was a habit.

Eventually we all sat down to roast lamb with potatoes, peas, carrots, and gravy. Once everyone had passed, poured, and was safely munching, it wasn't very difficult to introduce the subject of Ken's brilliant work on the colicky mare being met with suspicion and ingratitude from its owner.

"A most extraordinary man," I said. "Wynn Lees, his name is. I didn't like him at all."

Josephine McClure, sitting next to me, raised her head. "Ken," she said severely, "you didn't tell me you'd done any work for Wynn Lees. Stay away from him."

Ken said, bemused, "I didn't know you knew him."

"I don't know him. I know *of* him. That's not the same."

"What do you know of him?" I asked. "Do tell us."

She sniffed. "He tortured some horses and went to jail. It was a frightful scandal. I haven't heard his name for years."

"Ken's also been having a spot of trouble with Ronnie Upjohn," I said. "Do you know any scandal about *him?*"

"Upjohn?" She frowned. "He used to know my husband."

I said tentatively, "Is he in business? Does he by chance have a partner?"

"Oh, you mean old Mr. Travers? No, that was Ronnie's father's partner. A frightful lecher."

"Upjohn and Travers," I said. I held my breath.

"That's right." She went on eating unemotionally.

"What sort of business was it?" I asked.

"I don't know. Something to do with finance. Ronnie Upjohn's never done a day's work in his life, as far as I know."

"You know so much about all these people," I said admiringly. "How about the Eaglewoods?"

"Oh no, not the Eaglewoods," Belinda said.

Josephine gave her future daughter-in-law a sharp glance and made a breathtaking statement. "I suppose you're an advance on that Izzy girl."

"What was wrong with Izzy Eaglewood?" I asked Josephine.

"Her mother." Josephine compressed her lips, but couldn't resist imparting knowledge. Now wound up, she would run and run. "Izzy's mother was and is a tart."

"How about Zoe Mackintosh? Are there any nice scandals about her or her family?"

"Her old father's going gaga, if you call that a scandal. He always was a villain. But very slippery. I heard he lost a lot of his money a few months back in a property crash."

"How about the Nagrebb family?" I asked her.

"She's the show jumper, isn't she? Ken looks after their horses." She finished her plateful, put her knife and fork tidily together, and turned to Ken. "Isn't that man Nagrebb," she asked, "the one who got into trouble for training show jumpers cruelly?"

Ken nodded.

"What did he do?" I asked.

"Rapped their shins with a pole, while they were jumping, to teach them to lift their legs higher," Ken said. "Nagrebb's horses always had lumps and contusions on their shins."

Belinda said, "Nagrebb's daughter swore he didn't do it."

Ken smiled. "She does everything he tells her. She rode the horses while he hit their legs. She wants to win, and Daddy provides the wherewithal, and there's no way she's going to blow the whistle on him."

"A wicked world," Vicky said sadly.

WHEN the lunch party broke up, I left Thetford Cottage and drove to Riddlescombe village to see how much I remembered. I'd had only vague pictures in my mind, but it was a revelation how much was vividly familiar as I drove down the long, straggly main street. The post office, the garage, the pubs—all were still there. Time hadn't swept away the cottages or changed the stone houses. I parked the car and walked, and remembered who had lived where and who had died and who had run away.

It was like walking back into a lost land that had existed for twenty years in mothballs. Untouched by centuries, there stood the tiny ancient church to which I'd gone. Surrounded still by a low stone wall, a patch of grass, haphazard yews, and weathered gray anonymous gravestones, it remained as always an expression of hope against hope for the life everlasting.

The old latch clicked up with a familiar hollow cluck under my thumb, and I pushed open the heavy wooden door to smell the musty mixture of hymnbooks, hassocks, and altar flowers. I wandered to the rear of the church and read again the small brass plaque still fixed high up inconspicuously.

PAUL PERRY. Years of birth and death. REST IN PEACE.

My mother had blown a kiss to the plaque every Christmas Day, and although on this return I didn't do that, I did wish him well, that very young horseman who'd given me life.

I walked on down the road to the bungalow where we had lived. It looked small, of course. The paint was old, the garden bare but tidy, the front gate, which I'd swung on, missing altogether. I paused outside and wondered whether or not to try to go in, but in the end I turned back with the old memories undisturbed, and strolled again to the car.

I decided, before I left, that I'd go up to the end of the village, to the Eaglewood stables. I left the car outside and wandered in, hoping to look like a lost tourist, harmless.

I got no more than six paces into the yard before being challenged with an authoritative, "Yes? Can I help you?"

I swiveled. The voice came from a thin, fortyish woman in jeans and sweater who was up a stepladder fixing onto a stable wall a painted sign saying DON'T FEED THE HORSES.

"Er," I said, improvising, "I'd been hoping to talk to Mr. Eaglewood."

"What about?"

I cleared my throat. "About insurance." The first thing that came into my head.

She regarded the sign, nodded to herself, and came down the ladder. A chilly little breeze cooled the thin February sunshine and swirled her thick tawny hair across her face. Her vitality and natural magnetism generated a force field all of their own.

She gave me a head-to-toe glance that felt like a moving X ray through flesh and spirit. "What sort of insurance?"

"Insuring the horses against death."

She shook her head. "That's a matter for the owners."

"Perhaps Mr. Eaglewood—"

"I'm the business manager," she interrupted. "I run the finances. When the owners want to insure their horses, we put them in touch with an agent. It's no use you talking to Mr. Eaglewood."

"Then . . . you couldn't tell me if Mr. Wynn Lees insured the colt that died here in a coma last September?"

"What?"

"Or," I said, "did the owner of the horse that died during a respiratory operation insure him beforehand? And—er—how long before the operation in which he died last Thursday did that horse split its cannon bone?"

She stared at me speechlessly.

"Ken McClure is in a lot of trouble," I said, "and I don't think it's of his own making."

"Just who are you?" she said. "A policeman?"

"No. Just a friend of Ken's."

"What's your name?"

"Peter Darwin."

"Any relation to Charles?"

"No."

"Do you know who I am?" she asked.

I suggested slowly, "Mr. Eaglewood's daughter?"

"If you know Ken, you know he had a fling with my daughter," said Russet Eaglewood.

"He's fond of her," I said.

She shrugged philosophically. "Izzy threw herself at him, poor little thing. He treated her decently enough. She just grew out of it." She paused, then said, "It's windy out here, and the lads will be along any minute for evening stables. Why don't you and I go inside, where we can talk quietly."

Without waiting for my assent, she set off, not to the big, looming main house, but to a small, separate two-story wing, where she lived alone, she said.

Her taste in interiors ran to antique woods and classic fashions. On the walls, original oils, mostly of horses. Over all, a relaxed prosperity. She offered me an armchair and sat in another, on the opposite side of the fireplace, her blue-clad legs crossed, a telephone and an address book on a small table at her elbow.

"There's no way I'm going to talk to Wynn Lees if I don't have to," she said. "I can't understand why my father agreed to train the colt for him in the first place. But the colt died of seizures, didn't it? Or at least Ken had to put it down."

"Ken said that colt wasn't insured. Were the other two?"

"I never heard so." She lifted the telephone receiver, looked up a number, and then spoke to the owner of the respiratory-tract horse. The horse was not insured. She repeated the conversation with the cannon-bone owner, with the same results.

"There were three days between the horse's splitting its cannon bone and the operation," she said. "It was a stress fracture. Ken and Carey both thought the horse could be saved. The owner agreed to go ahead because the horse could be sent to stud if he didn't get back his racing form. So those two horses just simply died in the hospital. They weren't insured. My father, and everyone else, believes Ken was careless, if not plain negligent."

I shook my head. "I've watched him. I know he couldn't be careless or negligent."

"Are you *seriously* saying," she asked, "that someone somehow engineered these two deaths?"

"Trying to find out."

"But if it wasn't for insurance, what was the purpose?"

I sighed. "To discredit Ken perhaps."

"But *why?*"

"He doesn't know."

She looked at me broodingly. "Of course," she said finally, "someone else besides the owner could have insured those horses. We had an owner once who wasn't doing well in his business, and he owed us a worrying amount. His best asset was the horse we were training for him. The horse was due to run in a preliminary race, and I was uneasy, so the day before the race I insured him for more than enough to cover what the owner owed us. . . . And this is the point—I didn't tell the owner I'd done it."

"And did the horse die?"

"Not in the race. He won it. He was killed in a motorway crash coming home."

I made a sound of sympathy.

She nodded. "The owner was astounded when I told him I'd done the insurance. I did it in his name, and he gave us what he owed. But I *could* have insured the horse and never told him and pocketed all the money myself."

I took a slow, deep breath. "Thank you," I said.

"The insurers," she said, "might possibly check that the name on the policy was the name of the registered owner, but even that's not certain. And they would never phone every owner to make sure the owner knew about and intended the insurance."

"Well," I said, stirring, "I can't thank you enough."

"Like a drink?"

"That would be great," I said.

She rose fluidly, went over to a tray of bottles on a table, and returned with two glasses full of deep, rich Bordeaux.

I drank some wine. "Ken mentioned something about a boy who lived here long ago. Jimmy, wasn't it?"

Her face softened, and she spoke with regret. "My little brother." She nodded. "A proper little tearaway he was."

I willed her in silence to go on, and after a moment she did. "Always larking around with a boy from the village." She smiled. "Funny how some things still seem like yesterday."

I was tempted to tell her I was the boy from the village, but I still thought the anonymity of Peter Darwin, diplomat, might give me more chance of unraveling Ken's troubles, so I let the moment go by.

CHAPTER 8

THE next morning, Monday, I went down to the hospital to meet Ken and found he'd been called out to deal with an acute laminitis. After that he was scheduled to do two operations. This information came from Oliver Quincy, who had taken up the position he most coveted, the padded chair behind the desk. He wasn't especially friendly to the declared ally of the man he intended to oust.

"What's your gripe against Ken, actually?" I asked.

"You know perfectly well. He screws it up."

"He's a good surgeon."

"Was." He stared at me judiciously. "He shouldn't have let the cannon bone die last Thursday."

"Why do you think the horse died?"

He went on staring and didn't answer. If he knew, he wasn't telling. If he'd known how to stop it, he hadn't told Ken.

I didn't much like his company, so I wandered back into the car park. The police had put a barrier across the back of the burned building, warning off foolhardy sightseers. Far away down the side drive I could see the unceasing activity of serious officialdom still pecking away in search of guilt.

Over by the stable boxes, Scott was seeing to the unloading from a horse trailer of a skittish horse, full of vigor, looking not in the least ill. A groom with him led him into one of the empty boxes, bolting him in but leaving the top half of the door open.

I strolled over as the trailer plus groom drove out of the car park, and asked Scott if the broodmare was still progressing.

"Doing well," he said. "Her owner's with her at this moment."

"He's not!" I said, alarmed.

Shrugging, seeing no danger, Scott said, "He has every right. She's his property."

The top half of the mare's box was also bolted back, and I went to it without delay. Wynn Lees was standing there, looking critically at the mare's big belly. He turned inquiringly my way, his fleshy face already set in a scowl. He barely remembered me from Friday morning except as some sort of assistant.

"Get Carey to come here," he said truculently. "I'm not satisfied with this."

I turned away and asked Scott for Carey's whereabouts. Over in the Portakabin for the clinic, Scott said, so I went over there and delivered the message.

Carey walked back to the stable with me and went into the mare's box. From outside, all I could hear of the conversation were remarks concerning the approaching birth of the foal. After a short while both men came out, not looking overly fond of each other, the one to leave in his Rolls, the other to go back to his invalids.

Scott decided to move the mare along the row to the far-end box, to leave the intensive care box free for the new patients. I walked along with him as he led the great pregnant creature.

"Last Thursday," I said, "when the cannon-bone horse died, did you notice anything you wouldn't expect in the trace on the screen? The electrocardiograph trace, I mean."

"Look—" He sounded aggrieved. "Is Ken trying to say it was my fault the horse died? Because I'll tell you straight, it wasn't."

I said soothingly, "Ken says you're a very good anesthetist."

"And anyway, Oliver was watching the screen as well as me."

Scott led the mare into the box and bolted the bottom half of her door, and before I could think of anything else to ask him, a small plain white van swirled into the car park and pulled up with a jerk. Scott gave it a glance and strode over to greet the driver.

Carey in his white lab coat hurried out of the Portakabin. "Take it all into the office in the hospital," he said. "We'll unpack and distribute from there."

The van, it appeared, contained replacements for essentials destroyed in the burned pharmacy. I went a few paces and offered Carey a suggestion for making the "lost" list that the policeman had wanted the previous morning. "I just thought," I said diffidently, "that if you asked all your suppliers to send duplicate invoices going back over, say, six months, you'd have a pretty accurate inventory."

He looked at me vaguely, but then his gaze sharpened and came alive with understanding. "Good idea. Yes. A comprehensive list from the wholesalers and no need for us to rack our brains. Get Ken to see to it, will you?"

He bustled off after the driver, who was carrying armfuls of boxes into the hospital. I followed him into the office and found Scott there, carefully checking off each arriving box against a delivery note running to several pages.

Oliver Quincy's contribution to the activity was nil. He took what he needed and departed on his morning's first errand.

Ken himself returned at that point, blowing in with a gale of enthusiasm for the renewed supplies.

"Did the wind-op horse come?" he asked.

"Out in a box." Scott nodded.

"I thought they might cry off."

Carey cleared his throat. "I'm afraid I told him . . . I had to promise the owner I would—er—attend the procedure."

Ken swallowed the insult to his ability as just another bitter pill and asked me to be there as well to take notes. Scott looked surprised. Carey said it wasn't necessary, but Ken stuck his toes in, and it was fixed.

Lucy Amhurst came in on a search for the new drugs and gave me a nod of friendly acceptance. "How's the sleuthing?" she asked.

"What sleuthing?" Carey asked.

"Surely you remember," Lucy said. "We gave him the go-ahead yesterday morning to see what he could do for Ken. Oh no!" she exclaimed. "You weren't there, of course." I guessed she was herself remembering the anti-Carey conversation, as her cheeks went slowly red. "We didn't see any harm in letting Peter find out whatever he could if it would help Ken."

"No. That's fine." Carey nodded. "I agree." He went back to his dogs and cats.

Lucy suggested Ken and Scott store the drugs somewhere safe, then took what she herself needed and followed Carey.

"Do you keep a list of who takes what?" I asked.

"We do normally," Ken said. "We have a book. Had." He sighed. He decided to put everything on the shelves in one of the storerooms, and I helped him and Scott carry the boxes.

I wanted Ken's undivided attention for an hour, but didn't get it. He sat in the padded chair and insisted on writing his notes on the steeplechaser with laminitis that he'd just visited.

"Funny thing," he said, pausing and looking up at me. "They say the horse was quite all right yesterday."

"What about it?" I asked.

"It reminded me . . ." He stopped, frowning, and went on slowly. "One of Nagrebb's show jumpers had laminitis. . . . That's an inflammation of the layer of tissue between the hoof wall and the bone of the foot. One of Nagrebb's horses developed it, and Nagrebb was annoyed I couldn't cure it. Then one day last autumn he called me out, and there was this same jumper in the field, literally unable to move. It wasn't just in his two forefeet, as it had been, but in all four. I said we could try to save the horse, though frankly it was a very poor prognosis. Nagrebb decided to put him out of his misery. I wonder. . . ."

"*Ken!*" I said.

"Well, you could *give* a horse laminitis pretty easily. All you'd need to do is put a tube down into its esophagus and pour a gallon or so of sugar solution into its stomach. A huge amount of sugar all at once would result in very severe laminitis."

"If Nagrebb did it," I said, "there's no way of finding out."

Ken nodded gloomily. "And what would be the point?"

"Insurance," I said.

"You keep on about insurance."

I brought a couple of folded sheets of paper out of my pocket and said I wanted to show him some lists.

"No. Not now. I simply want to do these notes before the op. Show me the lists later, okay?"

"Okay." I watched him scribble for a bit and asked if I could use the telephone. He pointed to it. I lifted it, asked directory assistance for the Jockey Club, and then asked the Jockey Club for Annabel, in public relations. Remarkably, she was there.

"It's Peter," I said. "How are the Japanese?"

"They leave today."

"How about dinner tomorrow in London?"

"Can't do tomorrow. How about tonight?"

"Where will I find you?"

She sounded amused. "Daphne's, Draycott Avenue."

"Eight o'clock?"

"See you," she said. "Got to rush." The phone disconnected before I could even say good-bye.

Ken looked at my expression. "You're not leaving, are you?"

"Not yet. Not if there's anything I can do."

"I rely on you," he said.

I thought he wouldn't have minded much if his patient hadn't turned up that morning, because in spite of his success with the broodmare, he was again looking pale and apprehensive.

The operation, however, went smoothly from start to finish. Carey watched intently. I watched and took notes. Scott and Belinda moved expertly as Ken's satellites, and the prancing horse, fast asleep, got his larynx widened to improve his breathing.

From behind the safe section of wall we watched him wake in

the recovery room. He staggered to his feet, looking miserable but most decisively alive.

"Good," Carey said, going off to the office. "I promised to phone the owner."

Ken and I stripped off our gowns and went into the office, where Carey was giving his thumbs-up report. After Carey had gone, Ken finally said it was time for my list.

I brought it out of my trouser pocket. We sat in the chairs side by side, and I explained what he was seeing.

"The list on the left-hand page," I said, "is of the owners and trainers whose horses have died with question marks, to say the least, the various ways they may or may not have died, and where. The list on the next page is . . . well . . ."

Ken looked at the second list and protested immediately, as it named all his partners plus Belinda and Scott.

"They're not involved," he insisted.

"All right. Look at the first list, then."

I'd written in table form:

Wynn Lees/ Eaglewood	Colt with insulin	Put down in stable
Mackintosh	Colic from atropine?	Died on table
Mackintosh	Colic from atropine?	Died on table
Eaglewood	Respiratory tract	Died on table
Eaglewood	Cannon bone	Died on table
Fitzwalter	Chipped knee	Died in intensive care
Nagrebb	Show jumper/dissolved tendon	Put down on table
Nagrebb	Show jumper/laminitis	Put down in field

"Whew," Ken said thoughtfully, reading to the end.

"All the horses that died on the table," I pointed out, "could have been there by appointment. If two were given atropine, their time was chosen. They weren't random emergencies."

"No, I suppose not."

"So the deaths on the table very likely had a common premeditated cause, and it's up to you to work out what."

"But I've thought and thought." His despair surfaced again.

"Mm. That's where the second list comes in."

"No."

"It has to," I said. "Do Lees, Eaglewood, Mackintosh, Fitzwalter, or Nagrebb have the veterinary knowledge to accomplish all this? Has any of them had the opportunity?"

He shook his head. "But they're my friends. My partners."

Partners aren't always friends, I thought.

"Incidentally," I said, "you know the pharmacy list the police want? Carey agrees it would be a good idea for you to ask your suppliers for copies of their invoices for six months back."

"One of the secretaries can do it."

"I just thought," I said diffidently, "that if you did it yourself, you could get the invoices sent back to you personally. Just suppose someone here had ordered something like . . . collagenase."

The pale eyes stared as if they would never blink. After a long pause he said, "That would have to come from the chemical companies that supply us with research reagents for laboratory use only." He sighed. "All right. I'll write to them. I'll write to all I can think of. I'm sure they'll all come back negative."

"Quite likely," I agreed, and hoped not.

THE afternoon's operation, with Carey coming in tired but vigilant and me taking notes, passed off without crisis. The more accustomed I became to the general theater routine, the more impressed I was by Ken in action. Once he had a scalpel in his hand, his self-doubts seemed to evaporate.

He closed the incision with a row of staples, and the hoist once again lifted the big inert body by its feet to transport it to the padded recovery room. Everyone followed and waited in safety while the patient staggered and lunged back to consciousness.

"Good. Good," Carey said, sighing nevertheless. He still looked overtired, I thought. He seemed to be functioning in irregular spurts of energy—not, like Scott, with inexhaustible stamina.

As if to confirm my impression, he rubbed a hand over his face and said, "I've asked Lucy to be on call instead of me. That makes Lucy and Jay tonight. Let's hope it's quiet. I'm going home."

Ken and I went with him along to the office, where he phoned the referring vets to tell them their horse was recovering normally. Oliver Quincy, who'd been writing notes all afternoon while monitoring the well-being of the morning's patient, said grumpily it was about time he was relieved.

"This isn't my job," he protested. "It's Scott's or Belinda's."

"We must all muck in," Carey said, seeing no difficulty.

Oliver gave him an unfriendly glance and said that he'd better be going. Jay put his head in briefly with much the same message, and they left together, thick as thieves.

Ken began writing his own professional notes to supplement those I'd taken. I borrowed the phone again and got through to Vicky, telling her I was going to London and might be back in the early hours or even later.

Ken looked up and grinned. "Is Annabel the girl at Stratford?"

"She is."

"You don't waste time."

I smiled and prepared to go. "See you tomorrow."

I left the hospital and walked across the car park to the car. Belinda came out of the hospital and went into the intensive care box briefly to get it ready for the new incumbent. She then took a look in the next box, where the morning's patient stood, and after that went along for a routine peek at the mare. I watched her trim, capable figure and wondered if time and motherhood would soften or harden her caring instincts. Some nurses grew gentle, some unsympathetic. A toss-up, I thought.

She unbolted the mare's door and went in, and came tearing out at high speed, yelling, "Ken! Ken!" She ran into the hospital, and I thought, Oh, no, and went over to the end box to see.

The big mare lay on her side. The head lay floppily. The liquid eye looked gray, opaque, unseeing.

The mare was dead.

Ken came at a run, stricken. He fell to his knees beside her and put his ear to her brown body behind the shoulder, but one could see from his face that there was nothing to hear. He sat back on his heels, as moved and devastated as if she'd been a child.

I thought of the courage he'd dredged up to operate on that mare. Thought of the extreme skill he'd summoned to save her life while believing he was risking his own future. Felt impotently angry that so much holy nerve, so much artistry had gone to waste. But it was no longer just for Ken and to please my mother that I'd do my utmost to pierce the fog. Now, too, I felt personally engaged in avenging the horses themselves—the silent, splendid victims with no defense against predatory man.

"She shouldn't have died," Ken said. "She was out of danger."

It was a fraction too soon, I judged, to say I disagreed. Danger, in that place, wore many faces.

He smoothed his hand over the brown flank, then rose.

"She's been dead for some time," he said. He stood up wearily, trembling. "We'll never survive this. It's the absolute end."

Belinda said defensively, "She was all right at lunchtime. When I came along and checked, she was eating hay."

Ken was only half listening. "We'll have to have a postmortem," he said dully. "I'll see if I can get any blood." He walked away disjointedly towards his car and after a while returned with a case containing syringes and bottles.

"I'll have to get Carey and any number of outside vets to be there," he said. "And as for what Wynn Lees will say . . ." His voice stopped; the shakes didn't.

"He was here this morning," I said.

"Dear God."

I described what I'd seen of Wynn Lees's visit. "The mare was all right when he left. Scott moved her along to the end box afterwards, and she was fine. You ask Carey."

Ken looked down at the corpse. "No telling what Carey will say about this."

"If he's got any sense, he'll start thinking about poison."

"But last time," Ken said, "when the Fitzwalter horse dropped dead out here, all the tests were negative. No poison."

"Try again."

Without answering, he began to draw blood from the mare.

"How did you say you would give a horse atropine?" I asked.

"Inject it or scatter it on its feed. But this isn't atropine."

"No, but test its feed anyway."

He nodded. "Makes sense. Water too. Belinda, see if you can find two glass jars with tight lids."

Belinda went off without question, accustomed to being given orders in the line of duty. Ken shook his head over his task. "And the foal," he said with a deep sigh. "Such a *waste*."

He began to label the phials containing the samples of blood.

"I'll divide each sample into two and send them to two different labs," he said. "Double-check."

Belinda returned with two jars, into which she put samples of

water and hay. Scott came fast on her heels and couldn't contain his feelings, a mixture of disbelief, rage, and fear of being held responsible, as far as I could see.

"I put her in the box. I even gave her new water and fresh hay, and she was right as rain. Peter will tell you. There's just no way she could be dead."

No one bothered to say that, one way or another, she was.

Ken finished packing the samples, snapped the case shut, and stood up to his six feet four. "Who's looking after this afternoon's patient?" he said. "Scott, go and check at once. He's not to be left alone, even if I have to sit on a chair all night outside his door." He gave me a wild look. "I'll have to tell Carey."

I went with him into the office and listened to the fateful phone call. Carey, on the other end, received the news not with screeching fury, but with silence.

Ken told him he wanted an outside vet to do the postmortem, and he told him Peter suggested they look for poison.

That last sentence produced a sharp reaction that I couldn't quite hear but which surprised and embarrassed Ken. Finally Ken said, "Yes. Yes, okay," and slowly put down the receiver.

"He won't believe anyone deliberately killed the mare. He says you're panicking."

"Is he coming here?"

He shook his head. "He's going to fix the postmortem for tomorrow morning, and he's going to tell Wynn Lees."

"Wynn Lees might know already."

I SCORCHED the tires on my way to London. Annabel efficiently had arrived on time at Daphne's restaurant. I was seventeen minutes late. She was sitting primly at a table for two, a single glass of wine before her.

"Sorry," I said, taking the opposite chair.

"Excuses?"

"A dead horse. A hundred miles. Traffic."

"I suppose that will do." The small mouth curved. "What dead horse?"

I told her in some detail and no doubt with heat.

"You care," she said when I'd finished.

"Yes, I do. Did the Oriental chums get off all right?"

She said they had. We consulted menus and chose, and I took stock of the surroundings and of her.

She'd come dressed again in black and white: black skirt, loose harlequin black-and-white top, with big black pom-poms for buttons down the front. The cropped frizzy hair looked fluffy, and she wore gentle eye makeup and pale pink lipstick.

The narrow restaurant was packed and noisy, the waiters hurrying, precariously holding big trays head-high.

"Lucky to get a table," I commented, looking around.

"I booked," she said.

I smiled. Effective public relations.

She considered me, her head on one side. "Are you looking for somewhere to live in London?"

"Three weeks today," I said, nodding, "I start work in Whitehall. So I need somewhere to lay my head."

"I could put out a few feelers."

"I'd be grateful."

She ate snails, adept with the tongs. I had settled for safe old pâté and toast.

"Do you have a last name?" I asked, eating.

"Nutbourne. Do you?"

"Darwin. As in, but not descended."

"You must always be asked."

"Pretty often."

"And, um, is your father, say, a bus driver?"

"He's another diplomat. And yours?"

She chewed the last snail and put down the fork.

"A clergyman," she said. She looked at me carefully, waiting for a response.

I said judicially, "Some perfectly good people are clergymen's daughters."

She smiled, the eyes crinkling. "He's a bishop, actually."

"My father's an ambassador," I said, "to be fair."

"Thanks," she said.

"It doesn't mean we can't turn cartwheels naked in Hyde Park."

"It does," she said. "The virtues of the fathers are visited on the children, just like sins. Millstones aren't in it."

We progressed to Dover soles, and I asked her if there was

anyone in the Jockey Club who was a specialist in fraudulent insurance claims on dead horses.

She looked at me soberly. "Is that what's been happening?"

"Almost certainly, unless we have a psychopath on the loose."

She thought it over. "I'm friends with the deputy director of the security service," she said. "I could ask him to meet you."

"Could you? When?"

"If you'll wait until I've finished my dinner, I'll phone him."

Sleuthing took a step back while Annabel Nutbourne carefully cleared every particle from the fish bones and left a skeleton as bare as an anatomy lesson. There were fewer insecurities, I thought, beneath that confident exterior, than one met normally.

She chose cappuccino coffee with nutmeg on top for us both, and after that, while I paid the bill, she made the phone call.

"He says," she reported, "no time like the present."

The deputy director of the security service of the Jockey Club met us in the entrance hall of a gaming club and signed us in as guests. He was big in a useful way, and the watchful eyes of his trade made me speculate on a police past, upper ranks.

"Brose," Annabel said, rubbing his arm in greeting, "this is Peter Darwin." To me she said, "John Ambrose. Call him Brose."

He shook my hand; nothing indecisive about that either. He led us into a wide gaming room, where life was lived on green baize under bright low-slung lights.

"Brose goes round the clubs keeping tabs on seamy characters from the racecourse, and they hate it. He says anyone sweating over losing is ripe for trouble, and besides that, he gets told things on the quiet that put crooks out of business and keep racing at least halfway honest."

We went to a railed-off corner section, with small tables. A waitress, without being asked, brought Brose a glass of *citron pressé*, which he dispatched in a long, smooth swallow.

"What is it exactly you want to know?" he said.

I explained about Hewett and Partners' troubles with horses, though not in great detail except for the mare.

"She was carrying a foal by Rainbow Quest," I said. "Her owner's a weird man—"

"Name?" Brose interrupted.

"The owner? Wynn Lees."

Brose grunted, and his attention sharpened.

I explained about the colic operation and the needle, and I described the circumstance of the mare's death that afternoon.

He looked at me. "You think Wynn Lees did it?"

"He was there in the morning, but she was alive when he left."

He summoned a refill lemon with a raised finger.

"I'll tell you," he said at length. "I'd lay you odds the foal was not by Rainbow Quest."

"Why?" Annabel said.

"Because the mare's died the way she has." He paused. "Look, you own a decent broodmare, you send her to Rainbow Quest. She seems to be in foal, and you take her home very pleased, but somewhere along the line she slips it. All you have now is a barren year. But suppose you go out and buy some other unknown mare in foal to some obscure stallion. Well, now you have a mare in foal at about the right stage of gestation, and you insure it as if it's your mare in foal to Rainbow Quest. Then you ship the decent mare to some of your shady mates in Australia." He paused to drink. "These days paternity can be proved without doubt. If I were the insurance company, I'd make sure. Pity your vets didn't take tissue from the foal."

"They still could," I said. "The postmortem's tomorrow."

"What's your priority in all of this?" Brose asked.

"Um . . . to stitch Ken McClure's reputation together again and prove the horses' deaths weren't his doing."

"Difficult," he said.

"Is it impossible?" Annabel asked.

"Never say anything's impossible. Unlikely's better."

"We also," I said, "have the vets' main building destroyed by arson, with an unknown body in it."

Brose listened impassively, Annabel openmouthed, to the extent of Hewett and Partners' problems.

"Carey Hewett, the senior partner, looks older by the hour. The partners are falling apart in loyalties. All their records were burned. Their chief remaining asset, the hospital, is gradually being boycotted by clients frightened by Ken operating on their horses."

Brose pursed his lips. "I take it back. Impossible is the right word."

"It would be really helpful," I said, "if you could give me a list of unidentifiable poisons."

"If you can't identify them," Brose said, "you can't prove they were administered. What's more, all poisons are hard to find and identify if you have no general idea of what to look for."

He stood up. "Keep me posted on Wynn Lees. It's not strictly a racing matter as such, but I might be able to suggest a few things." He patted Annabel on her rag-doll hair, nodded to me amiably, and ambled off.

Annabel and I went back to the outer world, to the house she shared in Fulham.

She thanked me for the dinner. I thanked her for Brose. We stood on the pavement for a few moments. I kissed her cheek.

"Good luck with everything," she said. "It sounds as if you and the vets need a miracle."

"A miracle would be fine."

Instead, we got a nightmare.

CHAPTER 9

VICKY had left a note on my pillow: "Ken asks you to go to the hospital at nine a.m."

With a groan, as the night had already half gone, I set my alarm, crawled under the daisy duvet, and fell into sleep.

I awakened with a feeling of unease and returned to the hospital. At first sight everything seemed relatively normal, even if gloomy under a scurrying cloudy sky. I went in through the rear door and found Ken in the office, pale and seething.

"What's the matter?" I said.

"Three referrals have canceled for later this week. They've all heard about the mare, and they're now in a full-scale panic. On top of that, I sat here until three this morning checking on yesterday's patients; then Scott took over. So I came back ten minutes ago, and guess what? No Scott. He must have gone off somewhere for breakfast."

"How are the patients?"

"All right," he said grudgingly, "but that's not the point."

"No," I agreed. "When's the postmortem on the mare?"

He looked at his watch. "Carey said at ten. I suppose I'd better be there. I wondered if you would mind finishing these letters to the pharmaceutical companies so that they can go out today. I was doing them last night. I wrote a general letter, and I've made enough copies for every firm I could think of." He pushed them across the desk towards me, along with another sheet of paper with the names and addresses. "I know it's a ghastly chore, but it was you who suggested it."

"I've got another suggestion," I said. "Take a tissue sample from the dead foal to do a test for paternity." I told him Brose's theory. "To activate the insurance, the mare had to die. You inconveniently saved her life, so someone had another go. If Brose is right, he, she, or they couldn't afford to have the foal born. You'd have to get a tissue sample from Rainbow Quest as well."

"Not difficult. Tissue matching is expensive, though. So is searching for poison, incidentally."

"So you do think it was poison?"

"She shouldn't have died. . . . Something stopped her heart."

Yvonne Floyd, coming into the office, said she had an emergency dog case on its way and had come over to ready things for the small-animal theater. "I'll need both Scott and Belinda."

"Yes," Ken said. "They're around."

"Great." And she looked great herself in her white lab coat: white, gleaming teeth, bright eyes, cloud of black hair. She went out of the office and turned in the direction of the theater.

"Terrific surgeon," Ken said.

"Terrific legs."

After a pause, there was a crash of a door slamming back against a wall, a clatter in the corridor, and a groan.

"What's that?" Ken said, alarmed, rising to his feet.

I, being nearest to the door, was first through it, Ken on my heels. Yvonne was coming towards us, weaving and stumbling, her eyes stretched wide, one hand clamped over her mouth. We went towards her to help her, and she shook her head violently.

"Yvonne!" Ken exclaimed. "What's the matter?"

She leaned weakly against the wall, tears coming into her eyes, looking as if she would pass out. Ken and I moved instantly, one to each side of her to give her support. She shook us off and, unable to speak, pointed with a wild sweep of an arm towards the theater. Ken gave me a frightened glance, and we went fearfully along there to see what had caused such an extreme reaction. It was the door to the vestibule that had crashed against the wall; it was still open. We went into the supply room and tried the door to the small-animal section, but it was locked. We pushed on through the swing doors leading to the big main operating room.

What we saw there brought me perilously near fainting myself.

Scott lay on the long equine operating table, on his back, his arms and legs in the air. Around each ankle and each wrist was buckled a padded cuff. Each cuff was attached to a chain from the hoist. He had been lifted onto the table like a horse. He was dressed, as always, in blue jeans and sweater. There was about that energetic, hard-muscled body an unaccustomed, absolute stillness, a silence as lonely as the cosmos.

Ken and I stood one on each side of him, looking down on his face. His head was tipped back, his jaw jutting up. His eyes were unnervingly half open, as if he were watching and waiting for our help. Scott's mouth had been securely fastened shut by a neat row of staples. Small silvery tacks. Nine of them.

Ken turned towards the controls of the hoist.

"Don't touch it," I said.

He stopped and turned back. "We must get the police."

"Yes. And make sure no one else comes in here."

A stapler was lying on the floor near my feet. I left it alone. We went back into the corridor and along to Yvonne, who was kneeling on the floor, her head against the wall. Ken squatted down beside her. She turned to him and clung, sobbing.

I went on past them into the office. I found a large piece of paper, wrote "Do not enter" on it, grabbed a roll of sticky tape, and went out into the fresh air to stick the paper onto the outside door leading to the large-animal reception room.

I returned to the office, wrote a second notice, and stuck it onto the vestibule door. Then Ken came back from the entrance hall and joined me in the office. He sat in the chair behind the desk, looking at the telephone.

"You do it." He gave me the receiver.

I did it at dictation speed. Someone would come, they said.

In the pause before the police arrived, Carey himself turned up, wanting to know why the notice was on the outside door.

I found it difficult to tell him. While I did, he went even grayer.

The telephone rang, and because it was next to my hand, I answered it.

"This is Lucy. Is Yvonne there?"

"Er . . . where are you?" I asked.

"In the Portakabin, of course."

I remembered that the old building's number had been re-routed to a swaying wire connected to the temporary accommodation. "Lucy, when you can, come over here."

"I can't possibly. Belinda and I are knee-deep in distemper jabs. Anyway, will you tell Yvonne to come?"

"She can't come," I said.

She heard the calamity note in my voice. "What's the matter?" she asked, her own alarm awakening.

"I'm not telling you on the phone, but it's catastrophic."

After a brief silence she simply replaced her receiver, and a moment later she appeared in the office doorway prepared to be annoyed with me for frightening her. But one look at Carey's bent head, at Ken's extra pallor, at my own signs of strain convinced her that fear was reasonable.

I said, as the other two were mute, "Scott's dead."

"Oh no!" She was horrified. "On his motorbike?"

"It wasn't his bike," I said. "He's here, in the theater, and it looks . . . Well, it looks as if someone's killed him."

She sat down abruptly on one of the chairs.

Through the window I saw Oliver Quincy arrive in his mud-spattered white car, which he parked next to mine. My glance fell on the folder of letters Ken had pushed my way in a long-ago different time zone, and on impulse I picked it up and took it out to my car, meeting Oliver as he locked his own.

"I'd better warn you—" I said slowly.

He interrupted brusquely. "Not *another* dead horse?"

I shook my head. He shrugged, turned away, and went into the office through the rear door. I stowed the folder of letters in the trunk of my car and locked it just as a police car drove in.

It stopped outside the entrance hall, and the same plainclothes policeman as before emerged from it, followed by the same constable. They went in through the hospital's front door, and I decided to go back that way myself.

Lucy and Yvonne were coming out of the washroom together,

both looking sick and shaky. They sat unhappily on two of the chairs, each with a tissue to her face.

"I left Belinda coping with the whole Portakabin," Lucy said, sniffing. "I'll have to go back." She went out to the car park.

"I ought to help her," Yvonne said with difficulty. "But I can't."

"Much better to sit here for a bit," I said.

Jay Jardine in his self-assertive way strode into the entrance hall and came to a halt at the sight of us. "What's going on?" he demanded. "That bloody rude policeman in the office told me to come along here and wait. Why is he here? What's the matter?"

I told him.

He stared. Then he sat down, leaving a chair between him and Yvonne. He said only, "Too bad."

The understatement of the day, I thought.

Eventually two more police cars came to a halt outside the entrance door. A thickset man, with the broken-veined complexion of a farmer, ambled without great speed into the entrance hall, followed by an elderly man with heavy black-rimmed glasses and the black, top-opening bag of an old-fashioned doctor.

The farmer type asked briefly, "The office?" Jay told him. He nodded and went down there. The second police car contained a photographer and other specialists, who after a while followed their master under Jay's direction.

Ken came the other way, disjointed. "They've gone into the operating room," he said. "Come outside, Peter. I need air."

I went with him, looking at my watch. Nine fifty. The morning had seemed a week long already. The air was brisk and cold.

"Did you remember the postmortem?" I asked.

"Carey did. He phoned them to go ahead without us."

I said, "Did you, um, ask him to get some foal tissue?"

He raised his eyebrows. "I forgot it. Does it matter now?"

"Maybe more than before. You never know."

He pulled his portable phone off his belt, looked up the number in a small pocket address book, and got through to someone who seemed to have no problem understanding that he wanted properly labeled tissue samples.

I asked Ken if he owned a typewriter of any sort.

"Whatever for?"

"The letters. The envelopes. I can't use the office now."

He thought briefly. "I've an old battered portable at home. Would that do?"

"Sooner the better," I said, nodding. "Where do you live? I'll pick up the typewriter and come back. Then I can get on with the letters as soon as possible. If anyone complains, say I went out for pastries."

Ken gave me directions and his house keys, and I found the typewriter, along with a packet of large envelopes and a sheet of stamps. On the way back I stopped at a bakery.

When I returned to the hospital, they had taken away Scott's body, and the vets had scattered about their business. Ken and Belinda were alone at the stables checking on their horse patients. Yvonne was in the office, with the door closed. When she came out, she was crying awkwardly.

"They want to see you next," she said, wiping her eyes.

I went where required.

The farmer look-alike was standing by the window. He turned at my arrival and announced himself as Detective Superintendent Ramsey of the Gloucestershire police.

He checked a list. "You are Peter Darwin, employed here as a general assistant?"

"Not employed," I said. "Unpaid helper. I'm on leave from the Foreign Office."

He wrote that down and asked me what sort of unpaid help I'd been giving. I told him that several horses had died in the hospital, that Ken McClure, my friend, was worried about it, and that I was trying to help him find out why they'd died.

"And, sir, have you succeeded?"

I said regretfully, "No."

He pursed his lips and made another note, then looked up. "You saw Scott Sylvester's body, I understand."

"Yes." I swallowed. "How did he die?"

"All in good time," he said blandly. "When you were in the theater, did you see anything of note? Except Sylvester, of course."

"There was a surgical stapler on the floor."

He made another note.

"Also," I said, "I think all the doors were unlocked, which isn't usual." I paused. "When Ken and I went into the theater, the door to the padded room was open, and so was the one from there to the corridor and the reception room."

He made a note. "And was it you who put up the notices?"

I nodded.

"Where were you, sir, between nine last night and nine this morning?"

I said calmly, "In London, at a private dinner, after which I was in the company of the Jockey Club's deputy director of security. Then I drove back here to Cheltenham and went to bed. I'm staying with Ken McClure's fiancée's parents, about a mile from here."

Ramsey asked how long I would be staying there.

"Several more days, I should think."

VICKY and Greg were out when I reached Thetford Cottage. I let myself in, took Ken's typewriter and the folder of letters up to my bedroom, and set to work.

Ken's letters explained the police's need-to-know request for the pharmacy's burned contents and asked for the firm's cooperation. The letter was all right as far as it went, I thought, but below Ken's signature I added an extra paragraph.

"This matter is of extreme urgency," I wrote. "Certain dangerous, unusual, and/or illegal substances may have been stolen prior to the arson and may have passed into the general community. Please treat this request *with the utmost urgency* and send copies of all relevant invoices back by return post in the stamped addressed envelope provided."

I lavishly stamped page-size envelopes for the return information, addressing them to Hewett and Partners at Thetford Cottage (temporary office). Then I folded the letters and return envelopes together, enclosing them in business envelopes addressed to the pharmaceutical firms. It took me a fair while to complete the task, but when they were done, I drove to the post office and sent the whole bunch on its way.

Back in Thetford Cottage, I phoned Ken's portable number. He answered at once.

"Where are you?" I asked. "It's Peter."

"On my way to a dickey tendon. What do you need?"

"I thought we might go and see the Mackintoshes . . . or the Nagrebbs."

He drew in an audible breath. "You do think of vicious ways of passing the afternoon. No, thanks."

"Do you or don't you want your reputation back?"

After a silence he gave me directions. "Zoe Mackintosh is a tigress, and her old man's in dreamland. I'll meet you outside there in, say, fifteen minutes."

"Fine."

I drove through Riddlescombe and stopped on a hillside looking down on the Mackintoshes' village. Slate roofs, yellow-gray Cotswold stone walls. Sleeping fields waiting for spring. The sense of déjà vu was immensely strong. I'd seen these roofs. I'd run down the road where I now sat in the car. Jimmy Eaglewood and I, laughing, had splashed in the stream going down to the valley. I couldn't see the stream from where I sat, but I knew it was there.

Near the appointed time for meeting Ken I started the engine, released the brake, and rolled down the hill. Ken met me at the entrance to the drive to a long gray house with gables and ivy.

"Hi," I said prosaically, getting out of my car.

"I hope you know what you're doing," he said with resignation. "Zoe knows my car. She'll attack me."

"Get in mine, then."

He climbed out of his car and folded his length in with me. "Carey's resigning," he said. "I thought I'd better tell you."

"That's unthinkable. When did he say this?"

"In the office, after you left. When I went in, Carey was there with that superintendent. He had more or less collapsed. I told him we needed him, but he didn't answer properly. If Carey disbands the partnership, we'll have to start again."

"And to start again," I pointed out, "you need a clean slate."

I started the car, drove in through the gates, and stopped in a graveled area short of the house. Then, alone, I got out of the car and walked along the last piece of driveway to the house.

The woman who opened the door was sandy-colored, of indeterminate age, with dry, curly hair and fair eyelashes. She was thin and strong, dressed in jeans, checked shirt, and faded sweater. She looked me up and down and waited.

"Miss Zoe Mackintosh? I'm from Hewett and Partners."

"I didn't send for anyone."

"We're . . . er . . . working on the question of why two of your horses died in our hospital."

"Bit late for that," she said crisply.

"Could we possibly ask you a few questions?"

She put her head to one side. "I suppose so. Who's we?"

I looked back to the car. "Ken McClure's with me."

"Oh no. He killed them."

"I don't think so," I said. "Couldn't you please listen?"

She hesitated. "He told me some rubbish about atropine."

"What if it wasn't rubbish?"

She gave me a straight, uncompromising inspection, then made up her mind at least to hear the case for the defense.

"Come in, then," she said, stepping back. She looked across to the car and said grudgingly, "I told Ken he'd never set foot in here again, but he can come too."

"Thank you," I said. I made a beckoning arm movement to Ken, but he approached warily and stopped a full pace behind me.

"Zoe . . ." he said tentatively.

"Come in and get on with it."

We stepped in, and she closed the door behind us, then led the way into a square room crowded with office paraphernalia, racing colors, photographs, sagging armchairs, and six assorted dogs. Zoe scooped several dogs off the chairs and invited us to sit.

"So what about these horses?" she said.

"I think they and others died as a result of insurance swindles."

She shook her head decisively. "Our two weren't insured. Their owners don't let us forget it."

I said, "Horses can be insured without the owner knowing."

Her eyes widened in memory. "Russet Eaglewood did that once."

"Yes. She told me. Yours and theirs died in the same way."

Zoe looked at Ken.

I shook my head. "Not his fault."

"Whose, then?"

"We're trying to find out." I paused. "The horses all died in the hospital, except perhaps one—"

"How many died?" she interrupted.

"Eight or nine," I said.

"You're kidding!"

95

"You shouldn't have told her," Ken protested.

"One death could be put down to your carelessness," I said. "Perhaps even two. But *eight* unexplained deaths? Eight, when you are an expert surgeon? You've been carrying the can for someone else, Ken, and sensible people like Miss Mackintosh will realize it."

The sensible Miss Mackintosh gave me an ironic glance, but all the same looked on Ken as victim, not villain, from then on.

"To get the horses to the hospital—after they'd been insured, of course—" I said, "they had to be made ill. Which is why we'd like you to concentrate hard on who had any opportunity to give your horses emergency-size colic by feeding them atropine."

"To be frank, any of our lads would have fed their mothers to the horses for a tenner. Too easy. Sorry." A buzzer rasped loudly. "My father," Zoe said briefly, rising. "I'll have to go."

"I'd very much like to meet your father," I said.

She raised fair, bushy eyebrows. "You're five years too late. But come if you like."

We followed her through double doors to a large, splendid drawing room whose far wall was glass from floor to ceiling. Just outside the glass was a huge wooden mill wheel, more than half of it visible. It was decoration only; there was no movement.

"Where's the stream?" I said.

"There isn't one. It dried up years ago," Zoe said, crossing the floor. "Dad," she finished, coming to a halt by a high-backed chair, "you've got some visitors."

The chair made no reply. Ken and I walked around to the front of it and met the man who had been Mac Mackintosh.

CHAPTER 10

MACKINTOSH was small and wrinkled, an old dried apple of a horseman. Set in the weather-beaten face, his deep blue eyes looked intelligent enough, and it was only gradually one realized that the thoughts behind them were out of sequence.

He said in a high, scratchy voice, "Who's that with you?"

"It's Ken McClure," Zoe informed him, "and a friend of his."

"I'm Peter," I said.

"You said," he told Zoe, "that only Carey would come."

"Yes, I know I did. Carey will still come to play cards with you, but Ken is back looking after the horses." To us she quietly added, "They've played cards together for years, but it's a farce these days. Carey just pretends now, which is good of him."

Ken and I were standing between Mackintosh and the window. Ken turned sideways, and the backlight from the window fell on half of his bony face, the rest being still in shadow. Mackintosh sat up sharply in his chair and stared at him joyfully.

"Kenny," he said, "did you bring the stuff? I thought you were—" He broke off, fearfully confused. "Dead," he said faintly.

"I'm not Kenny," Ken said, moved.

Mackintosh flopped back in the chair. "We lost the money."

"What money?" I asked.

Zoe said, "You won't get a sensible answer. He's talking about the money he lost in a bad property investment. It preys on his mind. Every time anything worries him or he doesn't understand something, he goes back to it."

I asked Ken, "Is that what your mother was talking about?"

"Josephine?" Zoe involuntarily made a face. "She always enjoys a good disaster. Sorry, Ken." To me she added, "Dad lost a small fortune, but he wasn't alone. The scheme looked all right on paper. Dozens of people guaranteed slices of a huge loan to build an entertainment-and-leisure center between Cheltenham and Tewkesbury, and it did get built, but the location and the design of it were all wrong and so no one would use it or buy it, and the bank called in all the loans. I can't bear to look at the damn thing."

"What was it called?" I asked.

"Porphyry Place," Zoe said.

Ken nodded. "A great white elephant, except a lot of it's dark red. I pass it sometimes. Rotten luck."

"Ronnie Upjohn," Mackintosh said gleefully, "finally got his comeuppance."

"What does he mean?" I asked.

"Ronnie Upjohn is a steward," Zoe explained. "For years he kept reporting Dad to the Jockey Club and accusing him of taking bribes from the bookies, which of course Dad never did."

Mackintosh shrieked with laughter, his guilt plainly a satisfaction.

"Dad!" Zoe protested, knowing, I saw, the charges were true.

"Ronnie Upjohn lost a packet," Mackintosh said, and relapsed into puzzlement. "Steinbeck laid it off at a hundred to six."

"What does he mean?" I asked Zoe again.

She shrugged. "Old bets. Steinbeck was a bookie, died years ago. Dad remembers things but muddles them up." She gave her father a look compounded of affection, exasperation, and fear.

"As you're here," Zoe said to Ken, "would you like to look round at evening stables?"

Ken's pleased acceptance pleased Zoe equally.

"Come on, Dad," Zoe said, helping her father to his feet. "Time for stables."

The old man was physically much stronger than I'd somehow expected. Short, and with slightly bowed legs, he moved without hesitation and headed straight down the big room in evident eagerness. The three of us followed him out into the tiled hall and passage and down past the open door of Zoe's room. She put her head in there and whistled, and the six dogs came bounding out.

Outside, this enlarged party crammed into a dusty Land-Rover and set off down a rear roadway. The head lad joined us in the yard of a brick-built white-painted stable, and we slowly progressed from box to box. Ken discussed the horses' old injuries with Zoe, and old man Mackintosh gave the head lad an unending stream of instructions, which were gravely acknowledged but which sounded to me contradictory.

At one point I asked Zoe which boxes had been occupied by the two atropine colics.

"Reg," she said to the head lad, "talk to my friend here, will you? Answer any question. He's on the side of the angels."

Reg, small and whippy, like Mackintosh himself, gave me a suspicious inspection. Reg, I thought, might be on the side of the devil. I asked him about the boxes. Reluctantly he pointed and identified them—numbers 6 and 16. The numbers were painted in black on the white wall above the door of each box.

"Do you know anyone called Wynn Lees?" I asked him.

"No, I don't." The answer was immediate.

Old Mackintosh had also heard the question, and gave a different answer. "Wynn Lees?" he said cheerfully. "He tacked a man's trousers to his crotch. With a rivet gun."

I glanced at Ken. He was going rigid with shock.

"Dad!" Zoe protested automatically.

"Do you know Wynn Lees, sir?" I asked.

The blue eyes sparkled at me. "He went away. . . . I expect he's dead. Six is Vinderman."

"Come on, Dad," Zoe said, moving along the row of boxes.

He said mischievously, as if reciting a nursery rhyme, "Revised Edition, Wishywashy, Pennycracker, Glue."

Zoe said, "They don't want to be bothered with all that, Dad."

I asked him lazily, "What comes after Glue?"

"Faldy, Vinderman, Kodak, Boy Blue."

I smiled broadly. He laughed happily, pleased.

"They're the names of horses he used to train long ago," Zoe said. "He forgets the names of today's." She took his arm. "Let's get on; the lads are all waiting."

He went amenably, and we came to a horse that Zoe said had been much stronger since he'd been cut. For cut, read castrated, I thought. Most male steeplechasers were geldings.

"Oliver Quincy did it," Zoe said. "He came out several times. Dad likes him."

We came to the last box. "Poverty," Mackintosh said, feeding a carrot to a chestnut horse. "How's he doing, Reg?"

"Coming along fine, sir."

"Well, thanks, Reg," Zoe said. "That's all. I'll be down later."

Reg nodded, and Zoe invited us halfheartedly to go in for a drink and didn't mind when we declined.

"Come again," Mackintosh said warmly.

"Thank you, sir," Ken said.

I looked along the sweep of the fine, mellow frontage, the mill wheel out of sight around the far end, the old stream gone forever.

"Splendid house," I said. "A piece of history. I wonder who lived here before."

"As it's been here two centuries, I can't tell you everyone," Zoe said, "but Dad bought it from a family called Travers."

KEN wanted to talk, not about the Mackintoshes, but about his session with the superintendent. When we reached his car, we sat on for a while in mine and he told me what had gone on in the office after I'd left.

"Superintendent Ramsey wanted to know if there were any

surgical gloves missing. How could we know? We buy them by the hundred pairs. Carey told him to stop asking, no one knew."

"You and Carey were both there?"

"Yes, for a while."

"What else did they ask?"

"They asked if I thought Scott had killed the horses."

"Mm."

"What do you mean, mm. He couldn't have. He was a *nurse*."

"Maybe he found out who killed them," I said.

Ken swallowed. "I didn't believe you when you said things were dangerous. I mean, killing horses is one thing, but killing a man is different."

"If you have the means to kill without trace, that's dangerous."

"Yes, I see."

"And Scott is the second person dead here."

"The second? Oh, you mean the arsonist?"

"Everyone forgets him," I said. "Or her, of course. How about us going to see Nagrebb?"

He hated the idea. "Nagrebb's bad enough, but his son's worse."

"I thought you said he had a daughter."

"He has. Two sons and a daughter. One son is also a show jumper, and the meanest bastard who ever sat in a saddle."

"That's saying something, with Wynn Lees about."

"You'll be wanting to see *him* next!"

"Actually, no, I don't think so," I said. "Who trained the Fitzwalter horse?"

"He trained it himself. He holds a permit."

"What's he like?"

"Fitzwalter? Opinionated, but if you're thinking of going to see *him,* I don't mind coming with you. He took it quite well when his horse died. He hasn't stopped employing me."

"Where does he live?"

"Five miles or so."

"We might as well."

He removed himself from my car to his own and led the way through country lanes to a bare upland and a gray stone house. The house, unremarkable, stood next to about three acres of smashed and rotting cars. We turned off the road into a straight drive that led past the house and ended by a small open-ended stable yard constructed from old sheds, a garage or two, and a henhouse.

"Fitzwalter's a scrap metal merchant," Ken said unnecessarily as we got out of the cars. "Makes a fortune."

"An odd mixture, scrap metal and horses," I said.

In the yard, evening stables were in full swing. Fitzwalter, whom Ken introduced simply as Fitz, came out of a garagelike stall and greeted us with a wave. He wore patched corduroys and a big checked rough wool shirt. He had straight black hair, dark eyes, and tanned skin, and was thin, energetic, and perhaps sixty.

"You should see him at the races," Ken said under his breath. "He has his suits made. Looks like a city gent."

He looked more like a Gypsy at that moment, but his voice was standard English and his manner businesslike. He seemed pleased to see Ken, nodded to include me, and we headed for the barn. In there, I discovered, were two roomy stalls, each containing a good-looking narrow bay horse. Ken ran his hand down the legs of each horse. A good deal of nodding went on.

"How many horses do you train?" I asked Fitzwalter.

"Six at present," he said. "I've room for seven, but we lost one a while back. Good little colt. Pity he had a chipped bone."

"Did you have him insured?" I asked sympathetically.

"Yes, but not for enough." He shrugged easily. "Some I insure, some I don't. Most times the premium's too high, so I don't insure. I risk it. With him, well, he was expensive when I bought him, so I took some cover. Not enough, though. Win some, lose some."

I smiled noncommittally. He was perhaps lying, I thought. He led the way out of the barn.

Fitzwalter offered drinks, but we again declined. He looked at Ken speculatively and came to a decision.

"One of my lads," he said, "told me a rumor I can't believe."

Ken said, "What rumor?"

"That one of your people was murdered this morning." He inspected Ken's face and got his answer. "Who was it? Not Carey!"

"Scott Sylvester, our anesthetist," Ken said reluctantly.

"What happened?"

"We don't know," Ken said. "The police are trying to find out. We're trying to go on as normal, but frankly I don't know how long we'll be able to. It'll be in the papers. . . . It's devastating."

Fitzwalter's dark eyes looked into the distance, considering. "Well, I'm sorry."

"Thanks." Ken sighed deeply. "When it was just dead horses, life was simpler."

"Yes. I heard you had an epidemic."

"Everyone's heard," Ken said despondently.

"And a fire and another body. I don't see how Hewett and Partners can survive."

Ken didn't answer.

"Time to go," I said, and Ken nodded.

Fitzwalter gave a pitying shake of the head and turned away. Ken and I were both supposed to be returning to Thetford Cottage, but it seemed he had as little eagerness as I.

"How about a pint?" he said. "I haven't eaten all day, and I feel queasy."

"I'll follow you," I said, and he nodded.

As the day darkened, we went through the country lanes and ended in a quiet old pub. I settled for brandy in a lot of water.

"It's hopeless, isn't it?" Ken said, staring into his glass. "Talking to Fitz, I could see it."

"How old is Nagrebb?" I asked. "Is he sixty or more?"

"He doesn't look it, but his son's over thirty. What does it matter?"

"All the owners or trainers of the dead horses have been men of sixty or more."

He stared. "So what?"

"So I don't really know. I'm just looking for similarities," I said. "We have a cruel-to-horses pervert, a gaga old man, a scrap metal dealer, an unscrupulous show-jumping trainer, the old tyrant father of Russet Eaglewood, and a steward."

"What steward?"

"Ronnie Upjohn."

"But his horse *lived*."

"He's the right age." I paused, then said, "Did they all know your father?"

He gave me a slightly wild look, but didn't shirk the question.

"Old Mackintosh obviously did," he said. "My father was a vet in this area, so I expect he knew most of them."

"Do they all know each other?"

He frowned. "Eaglewood knows Lees and Mackintosh and Fitzwalter and Upjohn. The three trainers all know each other well, of course. Nagrebb's in a different world."

"And all this started since Wynn Lees came back from Australia."

"I suppose it did."

Wholly depressed, we finished our drinks and drove to Thetford Cottage. We passed a subdued evening, without cheer.

IN THE morning I went back to the hospital. The car park, usually overfilled, was half empty. I parked near the police cars by the front entrance and went in and found Ken, Oliver, Jay, and Lucy all sitting glumly silent in the office.

"Carey's closed the practice," Ken said.

"I didn't think he would do this to us!" Lucy exclaimed. "He didn't even ask us."

"He hasn't the right," Oliver said. "It's a partnership."

"Is Carey here?" I asked.

They shook their heads. "He came. He told us. He left."

"And the police?"

As if on cue, the police constable appeared in the doorway and asked the vets to go with him to join the superintendent. They trooped out and followed him. I might have tried to tack on, but the telephone on the desk gave me a better idea, and I phoned Annabel at the Jockey Club instead.

"Oh, good," she said when I announced myself. "I didn't know how to reach you. Some people I know need a new sharer in their flat. Are you interested?"

"Fervently," I said.

"Can you come this evening? My house at six?"

"I'll be there, and I'm highly grateful."

"Have to go now. Bye."

I put down the receiver, thinking that life wasn't all doom and gloom after all. Almost immediately the phone rang again, and I picked it up and said, "Hewett and Partners."

A voice on the other end said, "This is the Parkway Chemical Company. We need to speak to Kenneth McClure about a letter we received from him this morning."

I said, "I'm Kenneth McClure."

"Fine. Then I'm answering your query. I'm the sales manager. Will you be needing replacements for what you've lost?"

"Yes, we will," I said. "If you can send us the past invoices, we can make up a new shopping list."

"Splendid," he said. "You will remember, though, won't you, that there are some substances we can't put in the post? Like last time, you'll have to send someone to collect it."

"Okay," I said.

"Last time, according to our records, your messenger was a Mr. Scott Sylvester. He's been vouched for. But if you send anyone else, he'll need full identification and a covering letter from your laboratory. Sorry, but we have to be careful, as you know."

"Yes," I said. "Could you give us the copies of the invoices as soon as possible? Also a copy of the delivery note that I'm sure you gave Scott Sylvester when he collected from you? It would help us restore our records."

"Of course. I'll assemble it straightaway. Glad to help." He put the phone down gently, and I stood thinking of the possible significance of what he'd told me.

Scott had personally collected at least one substance that couldn't be sent through the mail. I'd wanted to ask the sales manager exactly what Scott had carried, but I hadn't wanted to make him suspicious. Whenever the reply fell through the letter box at Thetford Cottage, we would find out.

I reached Annabel's house on time at six. Her clothes this time were baggy black silk trousers and a big top that looked as if it were made of soft white feathers. She'd added silver boots, a wide silver belt, and silver earrings, and she carried a black, swinging cape to put on to keep warm. I kissed her cheek.

"We may as well go straight on in your car," she said. "The people are expecting us."

The flat itself was on the fourth of six floors and approached by a creaky old lift. The inhabitants were a bearded professor and his intimidated wife. The room they offered was large and old-fashioned, with a view of nearby roofs and fire escapes. I didn't like it much, but it was at least a foothold. We agreed on terms and I gave them a deposit, and Annabel and I descended to the car.

The flat had the virtue at least of being within two miles of

Annabel's house, and I hoped I might be crossing those two miles frequently. The bishop's daughter already had me thinking in such heavy, unaccustomed words as permanent, forever, and commitment; and common sense told me it was far too soon for that. Common sense had never come to grips with an Annabel.

"Six forty," she said, looking at her watch. "Brose has fixed up someone for you to meet, if you want. It's about insuring horses."

"Yes, please," I said with interest.

I drove while she gave directions to a hotel near the Jockey Club's London quarters. Brose himself was in the bar, talking to a short, bald man with a paunch and gold-rimmed glasses.

"Meet Mr. Higgins," he said, indicating the paunch. "His company insures horses."

We shook hands, completing the introductions. I bought drinks for everyone.

"Brose suggested," Higgins said in a fruity bass voice, "that I just talk, and if you want to ask anything, fire away."

"Great," I said.

"Insuring horses," he began, "is risk business. Premiums are high because the risks are high, understand?"

I nodded. "What about a broodmare in foal to a top stallion?"

"Mm. We'd write a policy, as long as the pregnancy was definitely established and proceeding normally. How old a mare?"

"I can tell you," Brose said. "She was nine and had been barren one year but had borne two healthy foals—one colt, one filly."

Higgins raised his eyebrows above the gold rims of his glasses. I could feel my own eyebrows going up in unison.

"How do you know?" I asked.

"Peter, really. I'm a detective. I obtained the list of mares covered by Rainbow Quest last season and checked them. I phoned the former owner of that mare you were supposed to have in the hospital and asked him how come he had sold her to Wynn Lees. He said his business was going bad and he needed to sell things."

"Was the mare in foal when he sold her?" I asked.

"He says so. Maybe she was, maybe she wasn't. Either way, he sold her to Wynn Lees." He paused. "Did you get tissue samples from the foal?"

I nodded. "They need some of Rainbow Quest's too."

"I'll get that for you," Brose said.

I thanked him profoundly. He didn't like fraud, he said.

Higgins nodded. "The temptation to kill an insured horse is one reason for the high premiums. Fraud is a major problem."

"Did your company," I asked, "insure any horses that died during or after surgical operations?"

"Not recently," he said.

"Would you ever insure a horse specifically against dying during an operation?" I asked.

Higgins pursed his lips. "I would if it was already insured. I would charge an extra one percent premium and pay up if the horse died."

"It's all wicked," Annabel said.

Brose and Higgins smilingly agreed with her. Higgins after a while said his good-byes and left.

Brose then stood up to his full height, patted Annabel's hair, and told me he'd keep in touch. When he'd gone, Annabel and I sat on, constantly talking, though with many things unspoken.

She asked about my future in the service, and I thought I heard a distant echo of an inquisition desired by her father.

"Did you tell your parents about me?" I asked curiously.

"Just in passing. I was telling them about the Japanese."

"In Japan," I said, "all the men carry things around in bright carrier bags rather than in pockets or briefcases."

"What on earth has that got to do with anything?"

"Nothing," I said. "I thought you might like to know. In Japan every native person has straight black hair. All the women's names end in *ko*. Yuriko, Mitsuko, Yoko."

"And did you sleep on the floor and eat raw fish?"

"Routine," I agreed. "But I never ate fugu."

"What on earth is fugu?"

"It's the fish that's the chief cause of death from food poisoning in Japan. Fugu restaurants prepare it with enormous precautions, but people still die—" My voice stopped, as if of its own accord. I sat like stone.

"What is it?" Annabel asked. "What have you thought of?"

"Fugu," I said, unclamping my throat, "is one of the deadliest of poisonous fish. It kills fast because it paralyzes the neuro-muscular system and stops a person breathing. Its more common name is the puffer fish. I think someone told me it takes so little to be lethal that it's virtually undetectable in a postmortem."

She sat with her mouth open.

"The problem is," I said, "you can't exactly go out and buy a puffer fish in Cheltenham."

CHAPTER 11

THE evening with Annabel ended like the earlier one, with a kiss. A brief kiss, but on the lips. She stood a pace away after it and looked at me doubtfully.

"How about Friday?" I said.

"You must be tired of driving."

"Soon it'll be two miles, not a hundred."

"Friday," she agreed, nodding. "Same time, same place."

Wishing I didn't have to go, I drove back to Thetford Cottage and there slept fitfully, with unhappy, disconcerting dreams. I awoke thinking there was something in the dreams that I should remember, but the phantom movies slid quickly away.

I bathed and dressed, and breakfasted with Vicky and Greg. Then I hung around impatiently for the postman, but he brought only one of the reply envelopes and that not the one from Parkway Chemicals. It contained a whole bunch of invoices for things I'd never heard of. I tried Ken's portable phone number. He said to give him half an hour and he would come to Thetford Cottage.

When he arrived, Ken took the invoices and looked through them. "They've sent a whole year's," he observed. "Let's see. . . . Sodium, potassium, calcium, chlorine. . . . Mm, these are the ingredients of Ringer's solution."

"What's Ringer's solution?"

"An all-purpose maintenance fluid. The stuff in the drips. I use commercially prepared sterile bags for operations," he said, "but we make our own in-house fluid for the drips out in the stable, as it's much cheaper. In the pharmacy Scott weighed out these ingredients, which are white powders, and stored them in plastic bags. When we need some fluid, we add distilled water."

He went on looking through the invoices, frowning.

"We've certainly used a lot of potassium," he said.

He sat staring into space, hit much as I had been by fugu.

"I should have seen it," he said.

"Seen what?"

"Potassium chloride." He looked at me with horror. "I think the four that died on the table died of excess potassium, which is called hyperkalemia, and I should have seen it at the time."

"You weren't expecting the fluids to be wrong."

"Even so . . ." He frowned. "The waves on the EKG that I told you about, that looked different? The heart was slowing down."

"Wasn't it Scott's job to tell you?"

"The captain's responsible for the ship. I simply never gave a thought that the slowing was due to excess potassium. I hadn't given them extra potassium."

"Exactly," I said. "Who fetched the bags, and who changed them when they were empty in all those four operations?"

After a moment he said, "Scott."

"Always Scott?"

He searched his memory. "Oliver assisted once. He took Scott's place. It *can't* have been Scott who killed them."

"All right," I said. "You think there was too much potassium in the bags of fluid. How did it get there? How did it get there for those four specific horses and for no others?"

He looked blank. "It can't have been Scott. I won't believe it."

"On the night of the mare's operation," I said, "I saw Scott collect the bags of fluid, and I helped him carry them along into the pharmacy room. He stacked them on the shelf there that can be reached from inside the theater by opening the glass door. Did he have any routine for which bags he took?"

"Yes. Always the nearest or uppermost."

"So if you wanted to add potassium, you could do it in the storeroom, knowing which bags would be used next."

Ken said with relief, "Then it could have been anybody."

"I think we ought to talk to Superintendent Ramsey," I said.

I got busy on the phone and ended with an invitation to meet the policeman in the hospital office later that morning.

Ramsey, the farmer type, listened patiently. He came with us into the storeroom to see how the bags of fluid were kept. He followed us to the small pharmacy section, where the bags were stacked on the shelf, and he came into the operating room and saw how they could be reached when needed by opening the glass door.

No one actually mentioned the possibility that Scott had discovered who had doctored the bags; it hardly needed to be said.

Back in the office, Ramsey said ruminatively, "The horses are long gone. There's no way of proving your theory." He looked thoughtfully at each of us in turn, then picked up the envelope containing the invoices. "This wasn't a bad idea. Let me have the other answers when they come."

We said we would, and I asked him if he knew yet what had killed Scott. And if he yet knew who had been burned in the fire.

"We're proceeding," he said, "with our inquiries."

I WENT to see Nagrebb.

Ken wouldn't come with me, but I wanted to see the man who'd almost certainly killed two horses—one with laminitis, the other with a dissolved tendon. He and Wynn Lees hadn't cared if their horses died in agony. I'd seen Wynn Lees's mare suffering, and I'd felt bitterness when she died. I couldn't prove her owner had fed her a carpet needle. I couldn't prove he'd injected his Eagle-wood horse with insulin. I *believed* he had, with a revulsion so strong that I wanted never to be near him again.

Nagrebb instantly gave me the same feeling.

I'd imagined him large, bullish, and unintelligent, like Wynn Lees, so his physical appearance was a surprise. He was out in a paddock behind his house. The paddock was fenced with once white horizontal railings. Inside it, on well-worn grass, a man and an auburn-haired woman stood beside a bright red-and-white show jump, like a length of imitation brick wall, exhorting an-other man, on a dark, muscly horse, to launch himself over it. The horse ran out sideways to avoid jumping and received a couple of vicious slashes of a whip to remind him not to do it again.

At that point all three noticed my arrival and offered only scowls as greeting. The man on the horse and the woman were young, I saw. The older man, noticeably top-heavy, with legs too short for the depth of torso, strode grimly towards the paddock railings. Bald, sharp-eyed, pugnacious, a rottweiler of a man. I got out of the car and went close to the fence.

"Mr. Nagrebb?" I asked.

"What do you want?" He stopped a few feet short of the fence, raising his voice. "Who are you? I'm busy."

"It won't take long. I'm writing an article on causes of equine deaths. You're so knowledgeable, I thought you might help me."

"You thought wrong. Clear off."

"I heard you might tell me about acute overnight laminitis."

His reaction in its way was proof enough. The sudden stillness, the involuntary contraction of muscles around the eyes.

"What are you talking about?" he demanded.

There must have been something about him that transmitted anxiety to the other two, as the young woman came running over and the man trotted across on the horse. She was fierce-eyed, a harpy; he was as dark and well muscled as his horse.

"What is it, Dad?" he asked.

"Man wants to know about sudden acute laminitis."

"Does he, indeed." He knew, too, what I was talking about. I wasn't sure about the girl.

"I need firsthand accounts," I said. "It's for general public readership. Just your own words describing how you felt when you found your horse fatally crippled."

"Tripe," the son said, bringing the horse right up to the fence and warningly raising his effective whip.

I began to make a placatory retreat, but at that moment another car swept around and came to a halt beside mine.

The driver climbed out. Oliver Quincy, to my dismay.

"Hello," he said to me in surprise. "What the hell are you doing here?" His displeasure was evident.

"Do you know him?" Nagrebb demanded.

"Of course. Friend of Ken McClure's. Has his nose into everything in the hospital."

The atmosphere took a chilly turn for the worse.

"I'm writing an article about the hospital," I said. "What are you doing here yourself?"

"None of your bloody business," Nagrebb said, and Oliver answered simultaneously, "Usual thing. Strained tendon." He was eyeing me with antagonism.

"Are you still in the partnership?" I asked.

"The partnership may dissolve," Oliver replied, "but horses still need attention."

Nagrebb's son suddenly slid from his horse, handed the reins to his father, then bent down and ducked under the paddock railings to join Oliver and me. The aggression poured out of him.

"You're trouble," he said to me, hitting me very fast and hard in the stomach with his fist.

I might as well have been kicked by a horse. I went down and doubled over in virtual paralysis. Then Nagrebb's son put his booted foot on my bent shoulder and toppled me over.

No one protested.

Breath slowly returned. There was no point in trying to attack Nagrebb junior in turn. Words were my weapons, not arms. I got to my knees and to my feet. Nagrebb looked watchful and his son insufferably superior. Oliver was impassive. The girl was smiling.

I found enough breath to speak. Fought to keep my temper.

"Illuminating," I said.

I turned my back on them and walked the few steps to my car.

"Don't come back," Nagrebb said.

Not on your life, I thought. Not for my own life either.

I opened the car door and eased painfully into the driver's seat in ignominious defeat. When I got back to Thetford Cottage, I sat for a while in the car, and Ken came out to see why.

"What's the matter?" he asked.

I winced. "Nagrebb's son upset my solar plexus."

He was exasperated. "Why did he hit you?"

"I asked about acute overnight laminitis."

He looked shocked. "That was a damn silly thing to do."

"By the way, Oliver was there, looking at strained tendons."

"Was Nagrebb himself there?"

"He was. Also a fierce red-haired girl, who found it amusing that Nagrebb's son had knocked me down."

Ken nodded. "That was Nagrebb's daughter. I warned you the son was poison."

Poison, I thought. I was on the point of telling Ken about fugu, but the more I thought about it, the more it seemed farfetched. But if one nontraceable poison existed, then so might others. Wait, I thought, for the delivery note from Parkway Chemicals.

On Friday morning two more reply envelopes arrived, but still not the one from Parkway Chemicals. Ken read the invoices.

"Nothing out of the ordinary," was his comment on the first lot.

The second stack excited him. He pushed the papers across the kitchen table, pointing to one line with a jabbing finger.

"Insulin! We ordered insulin! I can't believe it."

"*Who* exactly ordered it?"

"Heaven knows." He frowned.

"When the orders arrive, who handles them?"

"One of the secretaries puts the parcels in the pharmacy. Any one of us opens them and puts the contents on the shelves. Anything unusual or risky is in a special section. Was, of course. I keep seeing the pharmacy as it was, and forgetting it's gone."

"So if anyone unpacked a parcel containing insulin, that's where it would be put—the special section, available for the person who ordered it to pick it up?"

"Dead easy," he said.

He went on reading the invoices, finding something that almost stopped his breathing. "We ordered collagenase," he said hollowly.

"Who ordered it?"

"There's no way of telling." He shook his head. "Insulin was ordered six months ago. That figures. Wynn Lees's horse died last September, just after the insulin would have reached here."

"And the collagenase?"

He looked up the date. "Same thing. It was delivered here a few days after Nagrebb's horse staked itself."

I sighed. We weren't much further forward, except that with every step it became more and more certain that someone had been using the partnership's own methods as a pathway to fraud.

"What about atropine?" I asked.

"We use that all the time after eye surgery, to dilate the pupil. It would naturally appear in small quantities on the invoices."

I telephoned Superintendent Ramsey.

"What is it?" he said a touch impatiently.

"Answers from pharmaceutical companies."

A short pause, then, "Hospital office, three o'clock."

As Ken had been called out by a regular client, I met the superintendent alone in the office. We sat by the desk, and I gave him the invoices and explained the significance of insulin and collagenase. For good measure I told him about the carpet needle and mentioned Brose's theory about the paternity of the dead foal.

"And you're telling me all this now," he said, "because if I discover who killed the horses, I'll know who killed Sylvester?"

"Yes."

"Anything else?"

I hesitated, then said, "I've seen or been to visit the owners or trainers of all the suspiciously dead horses. I wanted to try to find out if they themselves were involved with their horses' deaths."

"And?"

"Two are villains; one definitely isn't. One probably is; one may be, but doesn't know it."

He asked me about the last one, and I told him about old Mackintosh and his fade-in, fade-out memory.

"He remembers," I said, "the order in which racehorses in a far-back time stood in the loose boxes in his stable yard. He recited them for me like an incantation. Six, he said, was Vinderman. Well, one of the horses that was probably given colic through atropine was stabled in box number six. I thought perhaps that if Mackintosh were provided with an apple, say, or a carrot—he gives his horses carrots every day—to feed especially to Vinderman, he would trot down to his stable and give it to the horse in box number six.

"I think it's also possible that the head lad knows who visited box six—and box sixteen—bearing gifts. The head lad knows more than he's saying." I then added, "Mackintosh lives in an old millhouse that used to belong to some people called Travers."

Even experienced policemen don't have total control of their muscles. I had really surprised him.

"Travers," I repeated. "What does it mean to you?"

He didn't answer directly. "Do *you* know anyone called Travers?" he asked.

I shook my head.

He thought for a good time, but told me nothing. Then he indicated by standing up that the interview was over.

"Where can I reach you tomorrow?" I asked. "We found out that Scott went to a chemical company personally to collect something not allowed to be sent through the post. By tomorrow we should know what it was. I could call you."

"Do it." He nodded. Without waste of time he sat down again, wrote a number on a piece of memo paper, and handed it to me.

"About Travers," I said. "There was a financial firm of some sort long ago called Upjohn and Travers. The present Upjohn, Ronnie, acts as a race steward. Anyway, Ronnie Upjohn's father had a partner called Travers. He would be at least ninety now, I should think, if he's still alive."

"Anything else?" Ramsey said.

"Um . . . Porphyry Place."

"That red monstrosity? What about it?"

"Old Mackintosh lost money in it. So did Ronnie Upjohn and a lot of other people round here."

He nodded a shade grimly, and I wondered fleetingly if he'd been among the unfortunates.

I went on conversationally. "You don't have to be the owner of a horse to insure it. It can be insured without the owner knowing. The payout, sent in good faith by the company, never reaches the owner, who remains in ignorance from start to finish. It's a big maybe," I said, "but maybe someone came up with a way of recovering their losses in Porphyry Place. Could you get a list of the people who lost money guaranteeing those loans?"

"Don't tell me," he said, ironic despite his training, "that you haven't managed that yourself."

A smile glimmered briefly. He came with me out to the car park and waited until I had driven to the exit, almost as if shepherding me out. He needn't have worried that I'd go back. There was barely time to scorch the miles to the Fulham Road by six o'clock.

ANNABEL, relatively conservative in the silver cowboy boots below a straight black dress, suggested dinner in a bistro. The bistro had candles, red-checked tablecloths, and a male Gypsy singer with a flower behind his ear. I told Annabel about Vicky and Greg's singing. She would like to hear them, she said.

"Come down on Sunday," I said on impulse.

"Sunday I see the bishop and his wife." She looked down at her pasta, her eyes in shadow, considering. "I only miss Sundays with them if it's important."

"This is important."

She raised her eyes. "I'll come on the train."

"For country pub lunch?"

She nodded.

"And stay for the evening, and I'll drive you home."

"I can go back on the train. I can look after myself."

"All the same, I'll drive you."

She smiled. "The bishop will have to approve of you."

"I tremble to meet him. So . . . does the bishop have any other daughters or sons?"

"Two of each," she said. "I'd guess that you're an only child."

"How do you know?"

"You don't need roots."

"How strong are yours?" I asked.

"I've never tried to pull them up."

We looked at each other.

"I'll be in England for four years," I said. "After that, a month or so every two years." She listened carefully. "The Foreign Office pays for children to come home from foreign postings and go to boarding schools."

"Did you do that?"

"Only for my last two years. I wanted to stay with my parents. I like them, and it's a multi-everything life."

A job description, I thought, was an odd sort of way to tell her I was more than ordinarily interested in her future. She seemed to have no trouble understanding. It was also plain that Annabel wanted to be sure of her footing.

I drove her home and kissed her good-bye, as before. This time the kiss lasted longer. She said she would take whichever train on Sunday reached Cheltenham nearest to noon.

ON SATURDAY morning the letter from Parkway Chemicals finally arrived. While I waited for Ken I read the few intelligible pieces of information supplied with the invoices. The delivery note given to Scott had warnings stamped all over it: EXTREMELY HAZARDOUS MATERIAL. FOR THE USE OF QUALIFIED PERSONNEL. LABORATORY ONLY. HAND DELIVERED.

Scott had signed his name in acceptance.

The fuss, it seemed, was over three small ampoules of something called tetrodotoxin.

When Ken saw it, he said immediately, "Anything with the suffix toxin is poisonous." He frowned over the details and read them aloud. " 'Three ampoules one milligram tetrodotoxin with sodium citrate buffer. Soluble in water. Read safety sheet.' "

"What is it?" I asked.

"I'll have to look it up," Ken said.

The owners of Thetford Cottage had a dictionary and a small encyclopedia. Ken and I searched in vain for tetrodotoxin.

As I had the dictionary in my hands, I looked up puffer fish:

Puffer, also called blowfish or globefish, capable of inflating the body with water or air until it resembles a globe, the spines in the skin becoming erected . . .

So far, so good. It was the sting in the tail that had me gasping:

. . . of the fish family Tetraodontidae.

Puffer fish. It was my old friend fugu after all.

CHAPTER 12

"**P**UFFER fish?" Ramsey said.

The superintendent had met us alone again in the empty hospital. Ken had gone home to get his book on poisons.

" 'Tetrodotoxin,' " Ken read aloud, " 'is one of the most potent poisons known. It comes from the puffer fish and causes respiratory and cardiovascular failure through paralysis of the neuromuscular system. A fatal dose is extremely small. It is very unlikely to be detected by forensic examination.' "

There was a dismayed pause while we each worked out that there might still be a good deal of the stuff lying around.

"Scott," I said, "must have known who asked him to travel that distance to fetch the package. Must have known who he gave it to. He didn't necessarily know what was in it." I paused and added, "I guess he found out the hard way."

"Jeez," Ken said under his breath.

"Tell us," I begged Ramsey. "Just say yes or no. Did you find any needle puncture mark on Scott?"

He pursed his mouth. "The answer is yes," he said finally.

The symbolic closing of Scott's mouth, I thought, had been an unconscious declaration of motive, an obsession sweeping all decency away. Scott might have been an accomplice who finally objected. He might have discovered irregularities and threatened to reveal them. He might have tried a little dangerous blackmail. The brutality of the staples had been the violent response.

Ramsey, having once begun to divulge, continued. "I see no

116

harm in telling you what will be released to the press later today. We've identified the person burned in your fire. It was a man, thirty-two years old. An insurance agent." He paused. "His name was Travers. Theodore Travers."

"Upjohn and Travers," I said.

Ramsey nodded. "We looked them up after you spoke of them yesterday. The firm no longer exists and hasn't for many years, but in the days of old Travers it was an insurance agency. It broke up when both Travers and Upjohn died."

"Why," I said, "should an insurance agent be present in the veterinary building late in the evening?"

"Well, why?" Ramsey asked, as if knowing the answer.

"Someone let him in to discuss insurance schemes," I said. "Maybe illicit insurance of horses. Maybe they had an argument that ended either in the accidental or intentional death of Travers. Maybe the place was set on fire to cover it up."

"That's a lot of maybes," Ramsey observed, "though I'm not saying you're wrong."

Ramsey ushered us out again. Ken and I stood together by our cars in the car park, and Ken said, "What next?"

What happened next was one of those extraordinary flashes of ancient memory, incomplete but blindingly clear. I knew I'd once heard my mother say more than she'd told me on the phone.

"Um," I said, "how about if we go to see Josephine? To talk about your father."

"No," he protested, "you can't."

"I think we must," I said, and told him in part what I wanted.

He looked upset but went back inside, called her, and then drove to Josephine's home while I followed.

Josephine lived on the top two floors of a fine, big Edwardian house situated in a graceful semicircular terrace in Cheltenham. Ken having forewarned her, she was pleased enough to see us. She wore a gray skirt, a prim cream shirt, and a green cardigan.

We sat down. Beginning was difficult. "Was Ken's father a good sportsman?" I asked. "Er . . . did he like fishing?"

"No, he didn't," Josephine said. "Why do you ask?"

"Shooting?" I said.

Josephine looked at Ken, who said, "Tell him. We've never really known why Dad killed himself. Peter has a theory."

"Kenny," she said, "used to shoot pheasants with the crowd. Mac Mackintosh. Rolls Eaglewood. Ronnie Upjohn. Those people. I don't like thinking about it."

"I know," I said placatingly. "Where was he when he shot himself?"

"Oh, dear. Oh, dear." She gulped.

If the flash in my memory was right, I knew the answer, but for Ken's sake, it had to come from his mother.

"You've never told me where he died," Ken said. "No one would talk to me about him. I was too young, everyone said. Now I have to know where and why."

Tears streamed from her eyes. Bit by bit she told him.

"He died . . . He shot himself . . . standing in the stream . . . somewhere below the mill wheel . . . on the Mackintosh place."

The revelation rocked Ken and confirmed my vision. In memory I heard clearly my weeping mother's voice, sometime soon after she'd heard the news, talking to a visitor while I hid out of sight. She'd said, "He fell into the millstream."

"Was his gun in the stream with him?" I asked gently.

"Of course it was. Otherwise he couldn't have shot himself."

She stood up abruptly and went over to a mahogany bureau. From the lowest drawer she produced a large polished wooden box. The box contained newspapers, typewritten sheets, and letters.

I flipped through the papers. The letters, on top, were expressions of sympathy. The newspapers varied from factual to garish and bore many identical pictures of the dead man. "Well liked." "Respected." Verdict at the inquest: "Not enough evidence to prove he intended to take his own life." No suicide notes. Doubts and questions: "If he hadn't meant to kill himself, what was he doing standing in a stream in January with his shoes and socks on?"

"I can't bear to read them," Josephine said wretchedly.

"I thought there was a fuss about a drug he shouldn't have ordered," I said. "There's nothing about it here."

"Yes, there is," Ken said faintly. He'd been reading one of the typewritten sheets with his mouth open. "You'll *never* believe this. And who on earth told you?"

"Can't remember," I said erroneously.

He handed me the paper, looking pale and shattered. "I don't understand it."

118

I read. It seemed to be a letter of opinion, but had no heading and no signature. It was shocking and in a way inevitable.

It said baldly:

Kenneth McClure, shortly before his death, had ordered and obtained a small supply, ostensibly for research purposes, of the organic compound tetrodotoxin. A horse in his care subsequently died suddenly without apparent cause, consistent with tetrodotoxin poisoning. While not accusing him of having himself administered this extremely dangerous material, one had to consider whether the acquisition or dispensing of it could have engendered a remorse strong enough to lead to suicide.

In a shaking voice Ken asked his mother, "Do you know about this tetrodotoxin?"

"There was an awful commotion, but I didn't want to hear it," she said vaguely. "I didn't want people knowing that Kenny had done wrong, don't you see?"

What I saw quite clearly was that somewhere among the old crowd the knowledge of the deadliness of tetrodotoxin had been slumbering in abeyance all these years, and something—perhaps the Porphyry fiasco—had awakened it to virulence.

"Kenny!" old Mackintosh had said joyfully when we'd visited him. "Did you bring the stuff?"

Kenny had, I judged. And then presumably had repented and shot himself—or had decided to blow the whistle and had been silenced.

Scott, the messenger, with his mouth shut. Travers, the insurance agent, burned. Kenny, the vet, in the water, and his gun with him, washed clean of prints. Tetrodotoxin, arguably, had been too much for any of them to stomach.

"Oh, God," Ken said miserably. "So that was why. I wish now that I didn't know."

"You know where," I said, "but not whether. He left no note. So the question is, Did he kill himself in the stream or did someone shoot him on the bank so that he fell backwards into the water?"

Ken protested. "Why should anyone kill him?"

"Why was Scott killed?" I asked.

He was silent.

KEN STAYED WITH JOSEPHINE, and I spent the afternoon aimlessly driving around the countryside, thinking. I drove past the ugly red lump of Porphyry Place. The conviction that gradually emerged seemed to have been staring me in the face all along, saying, Here I am. Look at me. It was theory, though, more than substance. Matching the foal's DNA might be helpful. Porphyry Place might cough up a name. Villainous old Mackintosh essentially knew, as I did, things he couldn't always call to mind.

I drove back to Thetford Cottage in the dark. A short while after, Ken telephoned.

"Look"—he sounded awkward—"my mother's been crying buckets. You let loose a logjam of grief. But I thank you. I don't know how you know the things you know, but as far as I'm concerned, my father can rest in peace."

"I'm glad."

"Since I got home," he said, "Carey phoned. He sounded pretty depressed. I honestly think he's stopped caring. Anyway, I told him about the invoices and what we'd been doing."

"What did he say?"

"Nothing much. Just that we'd done well. I think Oliver's right. We'll have to work something out for ourselves. Anyway, thanks again. See you tomorrow, no doubt."

Maybe, I thought as he disconnected. But tomorrow Annabel would be coming, and I wanted a private, not a family, lunch.

SHE came on the train nearest noon, and we kissed familiarly. She wore a vast sweater of white stars on black over tight black stretchy trousers. Pink lipstick. Huge eyes.

"I've found a super pub for lunch," I said, "but we've got to make a short stop on the way. A tiny bit of sleuthing."

"And I've brought you," she said, smiling, "a present from Brose's friend Higgins to help you along."

She took an envelope from a shiny black handbag and gave it to me. It contained, I found, a list of three insurance companies that had paid out on horses that died off the racecourse during the past year. Alongside each company was a name and number for me to get in touch with.

"Wonderful," I said, very pleased.

We climbed into my car and set off to the horse hospital.

I said, "Vicky took a message from the superintendent who's in charge of Scott's death, saying he wants to see me briefly late this morning. Ken and I have talked to him at the hospital every day lately. It's getting to be a habit."

"How are things going in general?" she asked.

"I'll tell you over lunch. How's the bishop?"

"Cautious."

I smiled. I was growing less cautious every time I saw her.

There was only one car by the front entrance of the hospital when we got there. Not Ramsey's usual car, not a car I knew.

We went into the entrance hall and down to the office, which was empty, and continued to the door of the theater vestibule. It opened to the touch, and we went through, with me pointing out the changing rooms and pharmacy cupboard to Annabel.

We went into the theater and looked around. Annabel was enthusiastic about the hoist. The sliding door to the padded recovery room was wide open to every passing germ. We went through there, Annabel exclaiming over the resilient floor and bouncing up and down a couple of times.

There seemed to be no one about. We went on across the corridor and into the reception room, with its array of equipment around the walls, all quiet and ready for use.

"Usually they're so careful about locking everything," I said. I tried the door leading outside. That at least was secure.

I began to feel vaguely uneasy. The entire theater area felt wrong, though I couldn't analyze why. Perhaps it was because I was pretty sure who had murdered Scott. Perhaps it wasn't such a good idea to be here on a Sunday morning.

"Let's go back to the office," I said abruptly. I turned and led the way back through the padded room, heading for the passage.

I went through into the theater, looked back over my shoulder, and was flooded with horror. Annabel was down on her knees, her arms making uncoordinated movements, her head hanging low. Even as I sprinted back to her she fell forward, unconscious, onto the spongy floor.

"Annabel!" I was agonized, kneeling beside her, turning her, not knowing what help to get her, frenzied with worry.

I heard only at the last minute the rustle of clothes behind me and turned my head too late, too late.

A figure advanced from a bare yard away, a figure in surgical gown, surgical gloves, surgical cap and mask. He carried a syringe, which he jabbed like a dagger at my neck.

I felt the deep sting of the needle. I grabbed towards his clothes, and he skipped back, the eyes like gray pebbles over the mask.

I knew too late that he'd been hiding behind the half wall, that he'd darted out to inject Annabel, that he'd hidden again and come out of the other end to creep up behind me as I bent over her.

I knew, while clouds swiftly gathered in my brain— I knew, as I went to inexorable sleep, that I'd been right.

The man in surgeon's clothes had murdered Scott.

An old gray man with all the veterinary knowledge in the world.

Carey Hewett.

I WAS lying on the floor, my nose pressed to the padding. Awareness was partial. My limbs wouldn't work, nor my voice. The fact of being alive was in itself amazing.

Annabel!

The thought of her stormed through my half-consciousness. With an enormous effort I tried to move, seeming to myself to fail.

I must have stirred. There was a fast exclamation above me. I realized that someone was moving my hands, hastening roughly.

Instinctive fear swamped me. There was a clank of chains, and I knew that sound. The chains of the hoist.

No, I protested numbly. No. Not that. Not like Scott.

Flight was impossible. My limbs still had no strength. Equine padded cuffs had been strapped around my wrists. He clipped the chains onto the cuffs. My eyes came open.

Annabel lay on the floor a few feet away, fast asleep. I couldn't bear it. I'd brought her into appalling danger. I'd taken the message to meet Ramsey to be genuine. I should have been more careful, knowing that Ken had told Carey how much we'd discovered.

Muscles recovered faster. I stretched the fingers of one hand towards the buckles on the other wrist. The chains clinked.

Another exclamation from across the room.

The hoist whined, reeling in the chains, tugging my wrists, lifting my arms, pulling me up until I dangled in the air. Carey stood inside the theater and pressed the hoist's buttons. Raging and helpless, I began to travel along the rails towards the operating table. Carey's mercilessness and lack of emotion were unnerving.

"I've told Ramsey it was you who murdered Scott!" I yelled it, all at once without control.

He paid no attention. He stopped the hoist when I was still short of the table and put his head to one side, considering. It was as if he hadn't intended or expected me to be awake at that point. The syringeful of what I hoped against hope had been simple anesthetic had been at least half used on Annabel, and he hadn't been able to put me out for as long as he'd meant.

He made a decision and crossed to one of the wall tables, upon which lay a kidney dish. He picked up a syringe that had been lying there, and held it up to the light.

I didn't need telling that I was meeting the puffer fish.

Imminent extinction gave me powers I would have said were impossible. As he started towards me I bent my arms to raise myself and jackknife my body, bringing my knees to my chin, trying by straightening fiercely to get my feet to the edge of the operating table, which gave me purchase to swing out and try to knock away the syringe with my shoes.

Carey skipped backwards, carefully holding the syringe high. I swung futilely in the air, feeling wrenched and furious.

He pressed a hoist button and moved me a yard farther from the table, towards him. Instantly I repeated the jackknife, aiming this time straight at him. He retreated rapidly. My feet hit the wall where he had been, and I pushed off from it violently, turning in the air, scything with my legs at the syringe.

I connected with Carey's head, by some chance with one foot each side of it. I tried to grip his head tight, but all that happened was that his surgical cap and mask were pulled off.

In an extraordinary way it seemed to fluster him. He bent down to retrieve the fallen cap, and I, still swinging, launched my feet with total desperation at Carey's backside.

The force of the connection was hard enough to overbalance him, hard enough to send him staggering forward, and hard enough for him to crash his forehead against the sharp metal corner of one of the cabinets before he could straighten up.

He collapsed in a heap, stunned.

Feverishly I fought to undo the buckles of the constricting cuffs. I sweated. Struggled. Made my fingers overcome the opposing force of my weight. My hands slid free at last, and I fell, landing awkwardly, thinking immediately of a weapon.

The solution was fitting and blindingly simple. I pushed the hoist buttons, lengthening the chains to their full extent. Then, very carefully, I bent Carey's arms behind his back and fastened the cuffs to his wrists.

I went to the controls and shortened the chains until they were just tight enough to lift Carey's glove-covered hands two or three inches clear of his back. When he woke in that position, he'd scarcely be able to pick his head off the floor.

Suffocating with anxiety, I ran into the padded room and over to Annabel. I felt her pulse. Alive.

I stumbled unsteadily back to the office and sent a telephoned SOS to Ramsey to arrive with reinforcements. Went back to Annabel, sitting down beside her weakly, watching Carey through the sliding door for signs of murderous consciousness.

Between intuition and probability I'd come to see that it had to be Carey I was looking for. Carey was the grand old man, the one respected and trusted above all others by the clients.

All those old men. His generation. All knowing each other for half a lifetime. All knowing the secrets.

Long ago Ronnie Upjohn's father and Theodore Travers' grandfather had been insurance agents who'd made a fortune.

Long ago Kenny McClure had ordered tetrodotoxin in order to pass it to the iniquitous Mackintosh, who everlastingly played cards with Carey. It was Carey, I judged, who'd persuaded Kenny—a vet, but not his partner—to acquire the poison, and Kenny, balking at what he'd done, had got shot for his pains.

Long ago Wynn Lees had stapled an enemy's pants to his body, had done his time, and had gone to Australia.

The present troubles had begun after Wynn Lees's return, and perhaps he'd been the trigger that restarted the engine.

Carey had to have needed money. Not impossible that in the Porphyry crash he'd lost the savings that were to see him through old age. Not impossible to suppose he'd tried to get them back by using his professional knowledge. Not impossible to guess that he'd somehow persuaded the third-generation insurance man Travers to join him in growing rich, nor that Travers had wanted out, like Kenny, and found that out meant dead.

Carey, I thought, had burned the building not just to postpone or avoid identification of Travers but also to cover all his own tracks. Orders, invoices, all the telltale paperwork had conveniently gone up in smoke, and particularly the blood samples taken that day when the cannon-bone horse was dying on the table. Those samples would have shown excessive potassium.

No one would ever have questioned Carey's going in and out of the storeroom where the intravenous drip fluids were kept. No one would ever question what chemicals Carey ordered. No one would worry if he was seen at Eaglewood's one night, checking on his patients while surreptitiously taking insulin with him.

Carey, I thought, had meant to make his money and go. Events had hurried him: Travers had precipitated the fire. Ken had saved the colicky mare from what should have been curtains. It had been necessary, from Carey's point of view, only to finish off the mare and close the mouth of the man who'd carried the poison. After that there was nothing to keep him, and he'd smartly announced the end of the partnership. If Ken hadn't told him how much we'd found out, he would quite likely have been peacefully packing at the moment, rich again and ready to emigrate.

Annabel stirred.

I felt enormous, heart-swelling, thankful relief. "Don't worry," I said. "You're going to be all right very soon, I promise you."

She opened her eyes and used them for smiling.

By the time Ramsey arrived, she was sitting, snuggled in my arms but shivering with apprehension that the still prostrate figure in the surgical gown would come to life. He had jumped out from behind the wall, she said. She'd caught a horrified glimpse of him before he jabbed her with the needle.

The burly superintendent appeared inquiringly through the door and stared in astonishment at the man on the floor.

"I think," I said, "that that's your murderer. And be careful, because under him or nearby there's a hypodermic syringe oozing something that may be very detrimental to your health."

A WEEK later I phoned my mother and told her most of what had happened. At the end she exclaimed, "I can't believe a vet would kill horses! He must have been warped!"

"Oh yes," I said.

I thought of Carey as I'd seen him last, lying securely strapped to a stretcher. Eyes closed. Harmless-looking. I heard later that he'd woken up concussed and been bewilderingly calm ever since.

The syringe, whose needle Carey had tried to stick into me in the theater, had rolled under a nearby table. Wary analysis proved the contents to be indubitably tetrodotoxin.

"Smoking gun," Ramsey said with satisfaction.

Ramsey's list obtained from Porphyry Place showed Carey to have lost a sum that made me wince.

Higgins' insurance friends came up with every dead horse on our list: agent each time, Theodore Travers; recipients mostly fictitious but also Wynn Lees, Fitzwalter, and Nagrebb.

The expedited report on the DNA matching of the mare and foal with Rainbow Quest came back negative; nowhere near a match, he wasn't the sire, positively not. Wynn Lees, certain to be charged with fraud, had cannily skipped the country.

My mother said, "What about Ken?"

"I had to tell him I'd lived here as a boy."

"You didn't tell him about me and his father?" she asked.

"No, not a word."

I told her that Ken and Belinda's wedding was going ahead as planned, and that Ken would emerge with his reputation restored.

"And Mum," I said, "your Kenny.... I found out why he died."

There was a silence on the line. Then she said, "Tell me," and I told her the theories, and that Josephine believed them and was comforted.

"Are your theories right?"

"Yes, I think so."

A little pause. A voice gentle on a breath. "Thanks, darling."

I smiled. "Do you want a daughter-in-law?" I asked.

"Yes! You know I do."

"Her name is Annabel," I said.

When Dick Francis is asked how he finds the ideas for his mystery novels, he cheerfully confesses, "I begin thinking about evil deeds." The evil deeds that were the inspiration for *Comeback* followed a

visit the former jockey and his wife, Mary, made to England in September 1990. While there, Francis met Dr. Jenny Hall, a veterinarian, whose practice is near the racing stables owned by the Francises' elder son, Merrick. "Dr. Hall suggested I write a book in which the central character was a veterinarian," Francis says. "So I did." She also provided him with a number of medical details and later checked the manuscript for accuracy.

Francis' knowledge of Japanese customs, which he imparted to his diplomat hero, Peter Darwin, was gained on another trip

Dick Francis

he and Mary made, to the Orient in 1988. But Francis admits he has never eaten the deadly fugu fish as a delicacy, even after it has been detoxified. Would he care to if he had the opportunity? "No, thank you very much," he says, laughing.

Comeback is Dick Francis' thirtieth mystery, and his thirteenth to appear in Condensed Books. (The first was *Nerve,* in volume 57, back in 1964; the most recent was *Longshot,* in March 1991.) He and his wife have been permanent residents of Florida for the past six years, although they still travel a great deal, and always return to their native England to attend the Grand National steeplechase races each April. Concerning his next novel, Dick Francis says he is still gathering ideas. But it's a sure bet that eventually more evil deeds will come to mind.

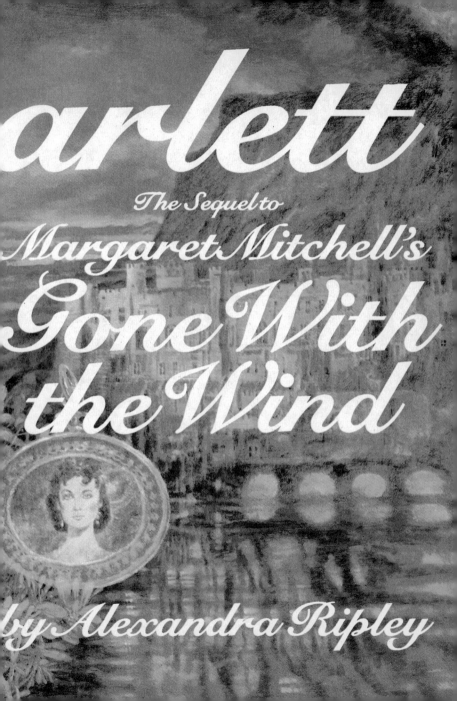

arlett

The Sequel to

Margaret Mitchell's

Gone With the Wind

by Alexandra Ripley

1

*T*HIS will be over soon, and then I can go home to Tara.

Scarlett O'Hara Hamilton Kennedy Butler stood alone, a few steps away from the other mourners at Melanie Wilkes's burial. It was raining, and the black-clad men and women held black umbrellas over their heads. They leaned on one another, the women weeping, sharing shelter and grief.

Scarlett shared her umbrella with no one, nor her grief. The gusts of wind blew stinging cold wet rivulets under the umbrella, down her neck, but she was unaware of them. She felt nothing, she was numbed by loss. She would mourn later, when she could stand the pain. She held it away from her—all pain, all feeling, all thinking. Except for the words that repeated again and again in her mind, the words that promised healing from the pain to come and strength to survive until she was healed.

This will be over soon, and then I can go home to Tara.

"Ashes to ashes, dust to dust . . ."

The minister's voice penetrated the shell of numbness, the words registered. No! Scarlett cried silently. Not Melly. That's not Melly's grave, it's too big, she's so tiny, her bones no bigger than a bird's. No! She can't be dead, she can't be.

Scarlett's head jerked to one side, denying the open grave, the plain pine box being lowered into it, the lid nailed closed above Melanie's gentle, loving, heart-shaped face.

No! You mustn't do this, it's raining. She mustn't be left in the cold rain. I can't bear it, I won't believe she's gone. She loves me, she is my friend, my only true friend. Melly loves me, she wouldn't leave me now, just when I need her most.

Scarlett looked at the people surrounding the grave, and hot anger surged through her. None of them care as much as I do. No one knows how much I love her. Melly knows, though, doesn't she? She knows, I've got to believe she knows.

They'll never believe it, though. Not Mrs. Merriwether or the Meades or the Whitings or the Elsings. Look at them bunched up around India Wilkes and Ashley, like a flock of wet crows in their mourning clothes. It wouldn't enter their heads that I might be needing some comforting, that I was closer to Melanie than any of them. They act as if I wasn't even here. Nobody has paid any attention to me at all. Not even Ashley. He knew I was there those awful two days after Melly died, when he needed me to manage things: The coffin. The cemetery plot. The notice in the paper. Now they're leaning all over each other, weeping and wailing. Well, I won't give them the satisfaction of seeing me cry all by myself with nobody to lean on. I mustn't cry. Not here.

This will be over soon, and then I can go home to Tara.

THE jagged pieces of Scarlett's shattered life were all around her there in Atlanta's Oakland Cemetery. A tall spire of granite, gray stone streaked with gray rain, was somber memorial to the world that was gone forever, the carefree world of her youth before the War. It was the Confederate memorial, symbol of the proud, heedless courage that had plunged the South, with bright banners flying, into destruction. It stood for so many lives lost— the friends of her childhood, the gallants who had begged for waltzes and kisses in the days when she had no problems greater than which wide-skirted ball gown to wear. It stood for her first husband, Charles Hamilton, Melanie's brother. It stood for the sons, brothers, husbands, fathers of all the rain-wet mourners on the small knoll where Melanie Wilkes was being buried.

There were other graves, other markers. Frank Kennedy, Scarlett's second husband. And the small, terribly small, grave with the headstone that read EUGENIE VICTORIA BUTLER, and under it BONNIE. Scarlett's last child, and the most loved.

The living, as well as the dead, were all around her. The front row of mourners held those who'd been closest to Melanie. White and black, their faces all streaked with tears, except Scarlett's. The old coachman, Uncle Peter, stood with Dilcey and Cookie in a protective black triangle around Beau, Melanie's bewildered little boy.

The older generation of Atlanta were there, with the tragically few descendants that remained to them. The Meades, the Whitings, the Merriwethers, the Elsings; Aunt Pittypat Hamilton and her brother, Uncle Henry Hamilton, their feud forgotten in mutual grief for their niece. Younger, but looking as old as the others, India Wilkes sheltered herself within the group and watched her brother, Ashley, from grief-shadowed eyes. He was bareheaded in the rain, unconscious of the cold wetness, unable to accept the finality of the minister's words or the coffin being lowered into the grave.

Ashley. Tall and thin and colorless, his pale gilt hair now almost gray, his pale, stricken face as empty as his staring, unseeing gray eyes. He stood erect, his stance a salute, the inheritance of his years as a gray-uniformed officer.

Ashley. He was the center and the symbol of Scarlett's ruined life. For love of him she'd ignored the happiness that had been hers for the taking. She'd turned her back on her husband, not seeing his love for her, not admitting her love for him, because wanting Ashley was always in the way. And now Rhett was gone, his only presence here a spray of golden flowers among all the others. She'd betrayed her only friend, scorned Melanie's loyalty and love. And now Melanie was gone. And even Scarlett's love for Ashley was gone, for she'd realized—too late—that the habit of loving him had long since replaced love itself.

She did not love him, and she never would again. But now, when she didn't want him, Ashley was hers, her legacy from Melanie. She had promised Melly she'd take care of him and of Beau, their child.

Ashley was the cause of her life's destruction. And the only thing left to her from it.

Scarlett stood apart and alone. There was only cold gray space between her and the people she knew in Atlanta, space that once

133

Melanie had filled, keeping her from isolation and ostracism. There was only the cold, wet wind beneath the umbrella in the place where Rhett should have been to shelter her with his strong, broad shoulders and his love.

She held her chin high into the wind, accepting its assault without feeling it.

This will be over soon, and then I can go home to Tara.

"LOOK at her," whispered a black-veiled lady to the companion sharing her umbrella. "Hard as nails. No heart at all."

"You know what folks say" was the answering whisper. "She has heart aplenty for Ashley Wilkes. Do you think they—"

Everyone was thinking the same thing.

The awful, hollow thud of earth on wood made Scarlett clench her fists. She wanted to scream, to shout—anything to shut out the terrible sound of the grave closing over Melanie.

But the cry that shattered the solemnity was Ashley's. "Melly. Mell—eee!" It was the cry of a soul in torment.

He stumbled toward the deep muddy pit, like a man newly struck blind, his hands searching for the small, quiet creature who was all his strength. But there was nothing to hold, only the streaming silver streaks of cold rain.

Scarlett looked at Dr. Meade, India, Henry Hamilton. Why don't they do something? Why don't they stop him?

"Mell—eee . . ."

For the love of God! He's going to break his neck, and they're all just standing there watching, gawping at him teetering on the edge of the grave.

"Ashley, stop!" she shouted. "Ashley!" She threw aside her umbrella and began to run, slipping and sliding on the wet grass. She grabbed Ashley around the waist, but he fought her.

"Ashley, don't! Melly can't help you now." Scarlett's voice was harsh, to cut through Ashley's unhearing, demented grief.

He halted. He moaned softly, and then his whole body crumpled in Scarlett's supporting arms. Just when her grasp was breaking from the weight of him, Dr. Meade and India caught Ashley's limp arms and lifted him erect.

"You can go now, Scarlett," said the doctor. "There's no more damage left for you to do."

"But, I—" She looked at the faces around her, the eyes avid for more sensation. Then she turned and walked away. The crowd drew back, as if a brush of her skirts might soil them.

Scarlett wouldn't let them see that they could hurt her. She raised her chin defiantly, letting the rain pour down over her face. Her back was straight, her shoulders square until she reached the gates of the cemetery and was out of sight. Then she grabbed one of the iron palings. She felt dizzy from exhaustion.

Her coachman, Elias, ran to her, but Scarlett walked to her carriage, ignoring the hand held out to help her. Inside the plush-upholstered box, she sank into a corner. She was chilled to the bone, horrified by what she had done. How could she have shamed Ashley like that in front of everybody when only a few nights ago she had promised Melanie that she would take care of him, protect him as Melly had always done? But what else could she have done? Let him throw himself into the grave?

She had to get to Tara, she had to. Mammy was there. Mammy would put her brown arms around her, Mammy would hold her close. She could cry in Mammy's arms, cry herself empty of pain; she could rest her head on Mammy's breast, rest her wounded heart on Mammy's love. Mammy would hold her and love her, would share her pain and help her bear it.

"HELP me out of these wet things, Pansy," Scarlett ordered her maid when she got to her house on Peachtree Street. "Hurry. If you make me miss my train, I'll take a strap to you."

Pansy knew she couldn't do that. The slavery days were over, Miss Scarlett didn't own her, she could quit anytime she wanted to. But there was a desperate, feverish glint in Scarlett's green eyes. She looked capable of anything.

"Pack the black wool merino, it's going to be colder," said Scarlett. She stared at the open wardrobe. Black wool, black silk, black velvet. She could go on mourning for the rest of her days. Mourning for her little Bonnie still, and now mourning for Melanie. I should find something darker than black, something more mournful to wear to mourn for myself.

I won't think about that, not now. I'll go mad if I do. I'll think about it when I get to Tara. I can bear it there. I've got to get to Mammy and Tara.

THERE WAS A LOUD BURST OF steam. The train was moving, she was on her way at last. Everything was going to be all right. She was going home to Tara. Scarlett pictured it, sunny and bright, the white house gleaming, glistening green leaves of cape jasmine bushes studded with perfect white blossoms. She imagined the entrance drive, the dark cedars that bordered it, then the wide green lawn and the beloved house on top of the low hill.

Scarlett sighed heavily. Her sister Suellen was the lady of the house at Tara now. Ha! Crybaby of the house was more like it. All Suellen had ever done was whine. And she had her own children now, whiny little girls just like she used to be.

Scarlett's children were at Tara, too. Wade Hampton Hamilton and Ella Kennedy. She'd sent them with Prissy, their nursemaid, when she got the news that Melanie was dying. She couldn't have gotten through those terrible days and nights after Melly's death if she'd had Wade and Ella to cope with, too. She was so tired. . . . Her head dropped, and her eyes closed in sleep.

"JONESBORO, ma'am," said the conductor.

Scarlett blinked. "Thank you." Only five miles to Tara now. Soon I'll be home. Home! "Pansy, get the valises off the rack. We're here."

Will Benteen, Suellen's husband, was waiting on the platform. Scarlett genuinely loved and respected Will. If she could have had a brother, she'd wish he could be just like Will. Except for the wooden peg leg, and, of course, not a cracker. It was just that there was no mistaking Will for a gentleman; he was unmistakably lower class. She forgot it after she was with him for a minute, because he was such a good, kind man.

"Will!" He walked toward her in his special swinging gait. She threw her arms around his neck and hugged him fiercely. "Oh, Will, I'm so glad to see you."

Will accepted her embrace without emotion. "I'm glad to see you, too, Scarlett. It's been a long time. Almost two years."

Scarlett was dumbfounded. Had it been that long? No wonder her life had come to such a sorry state. Tara had always given her new life, new strength when she needed it. How could she have gone so long without it?

Will gestured to Pansy and walked toward the wagon outside

the station. "Hope you don't mind riding rough, Scarlett. As long as I was coming to town, I figured I might as well get some supplies." The wagon was piled high with sacks and parcels.

"I don't mind at all," said Scarlett truthfully. She was going home, and anything that would take her there was fine. "Climb up on those feed sacks, Pansy."

Scarlett was silent on the long drive to Tara, drinking in the remembered quiet of the countryside. The air was new-washed, and the afternoon sun was warm on her shoulders. She'd been right to come home. Tara would give her the sanctuary she needed, and with Mammy she'd be able to find a way to repair her ruined world. She smiled as they turned onto the familiar drive.

But when the house came in sight, she let out a cry of despair. "Will, what happened?" Tara was covered by vines, ugly cords hung with dead leaves, and the windows had sagging shutters.

"Nothing happened except summer, Scarlett. I do the fixing up for the house in winter, when there's no crops to tend. I'll be starting on those shutters in a few weeks. It's not October yet."

"Oh, Will, why won't you let me give you some money? You could hire some help."

Will's reply was patient. "There's no help to be had for love nor money. Besides, we make out all right, Big Sam and me. Your money ain't needed."

Scarlett had run up against Will's pride before, and she knew that he was unbendable. He was right that the crops and the stock had to come first. Their demands couldn't be put off.

"You're right," she said to Will.

The door to the house flew open, and the porch filled with people. Suellen stood in front, holding her youngest child in her arms above the swollen belly that strained the seams of her faded cotton dress. Scarlett forced a gaiety she didn't feel. "Good Lord, Will, is Suellen having another baby?"

Will chuckled. "We're still trying for a boy." He lifted a hand in greeting to his wife and three daughters.

Scarlett waved, too, her eyes searching out the black faces. Prissy was there; Wade Hampton and Ella were hiding behind her skirts. . . . And Big Sam and his wife, Delilah . . . There was—what was her name?—oh, yes, Lutie, the Tara children's mammy. But where was Mammy? Scarlett called out to her children. "Hello, darlings, Mother's here." Then she turned back to Will. "Where's Mammy, Will?"

"She's sick in bed, Scarlett."

Scarlett jumped down from the still moving wagon, stumbled, caught herself and ran to the house. "Where's Mammy?" she said to Suellen, deaf to the excited greetings of the children.

"A fine hello that is, Scarlett, but no worse than I'd expect from you. What did you think you were doing, sending Prissy and your children here without so much as a by-your-leave, when you know that I've got my hands full and then some?"

"Suellen, if you don't tell me where Mammy is, I'll scream."

Prissy pulled on Scarlett's sleeve. "I knows where Mammy is, Miss Scarlett. She's powerful sick, so we fixed up that little room next the kitchen for her. It's nice and warm there. . . ."

Prissy was talking to air. Scarlett was at the door to Mammy's sickroom, holding on to the framework for support.

That—that—wasn't her Mammy in the bed. Mammy was a big woman, strong and fleshy, with warm brown skin. This creature was gray and shriveled, hardly making a rise under the faded patchwork quilts that covered her. It had been hardly more than six months since Mammy left Atlanta, not long enough to have wasted away like this. It couldn't be.

Then she heard Mammy's voice. Thin and halting, but Mammy's beloved, loving voice. "Now, Missy, ain't I done tole you and tole you not to set foot outside without you wears a bonnet and carries a sunshade. . . . Tole you and tole you."

"Mammy!" Scarlett fell to her knees beside the bed. "Mammy, it's Scarlett. Your Scarlett. Please don't be sick, Mammy, I can't bear it, not you." She put her head down on the bed beside the bony, thin shoulders and wept stormily, like a child.

A weightless hand smoothed her bent head. "Don't cry, chile. Ain't nothing so bad that it can't be fixed."

"Everything," Scarlett wailed. "Everything's gone wrong."

"Hush, now, it's only one cup. And you got another tea set. You kin still have your tea party just like Mammy promised you."

Scarlett drew back, horrified. She stared at Mammy's face and saw the shining love in the sunken eyes, eyes that did not see her.

"No," she whispered. She couldn't stand it. "Mammy," she said loudly. "Look at me, Mammy," she sobbed. "It's me, Scarlett."

Will's big hands closed around her wrists. "You don't want to do that," he said. "She's happy when she's like that, Scarlett. She's back in Savannah taking care of your mother when she was a little girl. Those were happy times for her. She was young and strong; she wasn't in pain. Let her be."

"But I want her to know me, Will. I never told her how much she means to me. I have to tell her."

"You'll have your chance. Lots of times she's different, knows everybody. Knows she's dying, too. These times are better. Now you come on with me. Everybody's waiting for you."

Scarlett allowed Will to help her to her feet. She followed him silently to the living room. Suellen started immediately to berate her again, but Will hushed her. "Scarlett's suffered a deep blow, Sue, leave her alone." He poured whiskey into a glass and placed it in Scarlett's hand.

The whiskey helped. It burned the familiar path through her body, dulling her pain.

"Hello, darlings," she said to her children, "come give Mother a hug." Her voice sounded as if it belonged to someone else.

SCARLETT spent all the time she could in Mammy's room, at Mammy's side. She had fastened all her hopes on the comfort of Mammy's arms around her, but now it was her strong young arms that held the dying old black woman. She sang the lullabies Mammy had so often sung to her, and when Mammy talked in delirium to Scarlett's dead mother, Scarlett answered with the words she thought her mother might have said.

Sometimes Mammy recognized her, and she smiled at the sight of her favorite. Then her quavering voice would scold Scarlett, as she had scolded her since Scarlett was a baby. "Your hair looks purely a mess, Miss Scarlett. Now you go brush a hundred strokes, like Mammy taught you." But then Mammy would slide back into that other world where Scarlett did not exist.

During the day Suellen or Dilcey would share the work of the sickroom, and Scarlett could snatch a half hour's sleep. But at night Scarlett kept solitary vigil, holding Mammy's thin hand in hers. While the house slept and Mammy slept, she was able at last to cry, and her heartbroken tears eased her pain a little.

Once, in the small quiet hour before dawn, Mammy woke.

"What for is you weeping, honey?" she whispered. She stroked Scarlett's bent head. "Old Mammy is ready to lay down her load and rest in the arms of the Lord. There ain't no call to take on so."

"I'm sorry," Scarlett sobbed. "I just can't stop crying."

"Tell old Mammy what's troubling her lamb."

Scarlett looked into the wise, loving eyes and felt the most profound pain she had ever known. "I've done everything wrong, Mammy. I don't know how I could have made so many mistakes."

"Miss Scarlett, you done what you had to do. Can't nobody do more than that. The good Lord sent you some heavy burdens, and you carried them. Don't fret yourself now." Mammy's heavy eyelids closed over tears that glistened in the dim light.

How can I not fret? Scarlett wanted to shout. My life is ruined, and I don't know what to do. I need Rhett, and he's gone. I need you, and you're leaving me, too.

Scarlett lifted her head, wiped her tears away on her sleeve and squared her shoulders. Never in all her life had she been beaten, not by old Sherman's army, not by the worst the carpetbaggers could do. Nobody, nothing could beat her unless she let them. If I messed up my life, she decided, I'll clean up the mess. I won't lie in it. Scarlett kissed the old woman's forehead. "I love you, Mammy."

"No need to tell me what I knows already." Mammy slid into sleep, escaping from pain.

"Yes, there is a need," Scarlett told her. She knew Mammy couldn't hear her, but she spoke aloud anyhow. "I never told Melanie I loved her, and I didn't tell Rhett until it was too late. At least with you I won't make the mistake I did with them."

Scarlett stared down at the dying old woman. "I love you, Mammy," she whispered. "What's going to become of me when I don't have you to love me?"

2

*P*RISSY's head poked sideways around the cracked-open door to the sickroom. "Miss Scarlett, Mister Will he say for me to come sit with Mammy whilst you eat some breakfast."

Mammy was sleeping. Scarlett felt ravenously hungry. She

washed her hands hastily in the kitchen and entered the dining room. Will was just getting up from the table.

"Can I help you, Uncle Will?" Wade asked hopefully. He jumped up. Then he saw his mother, and his face lost its eagerness. He'd have to stay at the table and use his best manners, or she'd be cross. He walked slowly to hold Scarlett's chair for her.

"What lovely manners you have, Wade," Suellen cooed. "Good morning, Scarlett. Aren't you proud of your young gentleman?"

Scarlett looked blankly at Suellen, then at Wade. He was a nice-looking boy, Scarlett realized with surprise. Big for his age, too—more like thirteen than not yet twelve. She sat in the chair Wade was holding. "Thank you, Wade Hampton," she said.

"Mother," Wade said cautiously, "may I please go help Uncle Will in the fields?"

"Yes, yes, go on." Scarlett picked up her knife and fork.

"Me, too," Ella piped up.

"Me, too," echoed Suellen's Susie.

"You're not invited," said Wade. "Fields are man's business." Susie began to cry.

"Now look what you've done!" Suellen said to Scarlett.

"Me? It's not my child making all that noise." Scarlett always meant to avoid quarrels with Suellen when she came to Tara, but the habits of a lifetime were too strong. They had begun fighting as babies and had never really stopped.

But I'm not going to let her ruin the first meal I've been hungry for in who knows how long, Scarlett said to herself, and she concentrated on her breakfast. She didn't even lift her eyes when Wade followed Will out the door and Ella's wails joined Susie's.

"Uncle Rhett would let me go, too," Ella sobbed.

I won't listen, thought Scarlett, I'll just close my ears and enjoy my breakfast.

"Mother—Mother, when is Uncle Rhett coming to Tara?" Scarlett heard Ella's words in spite of herself. What could she say to Ella? "Never." Was that the answer? She couldn't, wouldn't believe it herself. She looked at her red-faced daughter with loathing.

Ella had the ginger-colored, curly hair of her father, Frank Kennedy. It stuck out around her tear-blotched face like rusted coils of wire, always escaping from the tight braids Prissy plaited. Ella's body was like wire, too—skinny and angular. She was older than Susie, almost seven compared to Susie's six and a half, but Susie was so much taller that she could bully Ella with impunity. No wonder Ella wants Rhett to come, Scarlett thought. He really cares for her, and I don't. She gets on my nerves just like Frank did, and no matter how hard I try, I just can't love her.

"When's Uncle Rhett coming, Mother?" Ella asked again. Scarlett pushed her chair away from the table and stood up.

"That's grown-ups' business," she said. She couldn't bear to think about Rhett now, she'd think about all that later.

"JUST one more little spoonful of broth, Mammy darling, it'll make me happy."

The old woman turned her head away from the spoon. "Tired."

"I know," said Scarlett. "Go to sleep, then." She looked down at the almost full bowl. Mammy was eating less every day.

"Miss Ellen . . ." Mammy called weakly.

"I'm here, Mammy," Scarlett replied. It always hurt when Mammy didn't know her, when she thought the hands that tended her were the hands of Scarlett's mother. I shouldn't let it bother me, Scarlett told herself every time. It was always Mother who took care of the sick, not me. Mother was kind to everyone, she was an angel, she was a perfect lady. I should take it as praise to be mistaken for her.

"Miss Ellen." The old, old eyes opened halfway. "You ain't Miss Ellen."

"It's Scarlett, Mammy, your very own Scarlett."

"Miss Scarlett, I wants Mist' Rhett. Something to say . . ."

Scarlett's teeth cut into her lip. I want him, too, she was crying silently. So much. But he's gone, Mammy.

She saw that Mammy had slipped into a near-coma again, and she was fiercely grateful. At least Mammy was free of pain. Her own heart was aching, as if it were full of knives. How she needed Rhett. If he could just be here with me, feeling the same sorrow I feel. For Rhett loved Mammy, too, and Mammy loved him. He'd never worked so hard to win anyone over, and he'd never cared as much for anyone's opinion as he did Mammy's. He'd be broken-hearted when he learned that she was gone, he'd wish so much that he'd been able to say good-bye to her.

Scarlett's head lifted. Of course. What a fool she was being. She looked at the wizened old woman. "Oh, Mammy, darling, thank you," she breathed. "I came to you for help, for you to make everything all right again, and you will."

SHE found Will in the stable rubbing down the horse.

"Oh, I'm so glad to find you, Will," Scarlett said. Her green eyes were sparkling. "Can I use the horse and buggy? I need to go to Jonesboro. Unless maybe— You weren't fixing to go to Jonesboro yourself for anything, were you?"

Will looked at her calmly. He understood Scarlett better than she realized. "Is there something I can do for you? If I was planning to go to Jonesboro, that is."

"Oh, Will, you are a dear, sweet thing. I'd so much rather stay with Mammy, yet I really need to let Rhett know about her. She's asking for him." Scarlett fiddled with the horse's mane, then looked up at Will. "He's in Charleston on family business. So if you'll just send a telegram. And you'd better make it from you, Will. Rhett knows how I adore Mammy. He's liable to think I was exaggerating how sick she is." She smiled brilliantly. "He thinks I haven't any more sense than a june bug."

Will knew that was the biggest lie of all. "You're right," he said. "Rhett should come as soon as he can. I'll ride over now."

Scarlett relaxed. "Thank you," she said.

She was sure Rhett would come. He could be at Tara in two days if he left Charleston as soon as he got the wire.

BUT Rhett didn't come in two days. Or three or four or five. Scarlett stopped listening for the sound of hoofbeats on the drive. Now there was another sound that took all her attention—the horrible rasping noise that was Mammy's effort to breathe.

Suellen joined Scarlett's vigil, the lifelong jealousies between them forgotten in their joint need to help the old black woman. They brought pillows to prop her up, they kept the croup kettle steaming constantly. They spooned sips of water between her cracked lips. But nothing eased Mammy's struggles.

Scarlett read aloud to Mammy from the worn Bible on the nightstand by the bed. She read the Psalms, and her voice gave no sign of the pain in her heart. When night came, Suellen lit the lamp and took over from Scarlett, reading until Will sent her to get some rest.

"You, too, Scarlett," he said. "I'll sit with Mammy. I'm not much of a reader, but I know a lot of the Bible by heart."

"You recite, then. But I'm not leaving Mammy. I can't." She sat and leaned her tired back against the wall.

When the first thin light of day showed at the windows, the sounds suddenly became different, each breath more noisy, longer silences between them. Scarlett scrambled to her feet. Will rose from the chair. "I'll get Suellen," he said.

Scarlett took his place by the bed. Mammy's forehead creased with effort. "Wanted . . . to wait for . . . Mist' Rhett. But so . . . tired."

Scarlett swallowed. "You don't need to hang on, Mammy. You can rest. He couldn't come." She heard hurried footsteps in the kitchen. "Suellen's on her way. And Mister Will. We'll all be here with you, darling. We all love you."

A shadow fell across the bed, and Mammy smiled.

"She wants me," said Rhett. Scarlett looked up at him, unbelieving. "Move over," he said gently. "Let me get near Mammy."

Scarlett stood, feeling the nearness of him, the bigness, the strength, the maleness, and her knees were weak.

Rhett knelt by Mammy and Scarlett knelt beside him, her shoulder touching his arm, and she was happy in the midst of her heartbreak. *Rhett's here. What a fool I was to give up hope like that. Rhett had come. Everything was going to be all right.*

"I wants you to do something for me." Mammy's voice sounded strong, as if she had saved her strength for this moment.

"Anything, Mammy," Rhett said. "I'll do anything you want."

"Bury me in my fine red silk petticoat what you gived me. See to it. I know that Lutie got her eye on it."

Rhett laughed. Scarlett was shocked. *Laughter at a deathbed.* Then she realized that Mammy was laughing, too.

Rhett put his hand on his heart. "Lutie won't even get a look at it, Mammy. I'll make sure it goes with you to heaven."

Mammy's hand reached for him, gesturing his ear closer to her lips. "You take care of Miss Scarlett," she said. "She needs caring, and I can't do no more."

Scarlett held her breath.

"I will, Mammy," Rhett said.

"You swear it." The command was faint but stern.

"I swear it," said Rhett. Mammy sighed quietly.

Scarlett let her breath out with a sob. "Oh, Mammy darling, thank you," she cried. "Mammy . . ."

"She can't hear you, Scarlett." Rhett's hand moved gently across Mammy's face, closing her eyes. "That's a whole world gone, an era ended," he said softly. "May she rest in peace."

"Amen," said Will from the doorway.

Rhett stood, turned. "Hello, Will, Suellen."

"Her last thought was for you, Scarlett," Suellen cried. "You always were her favorite." She began to weep loudly. Will took her in his arms.

Scarlett ran to Rhett and held her arms up to embrace him. "I've missed you so," she said.

Rhett circled her wrists with his hands and lowered her arms to her sides. "Don't, Scarlett," he said. "Nothing's changed." His voice was quiet.

"What do you mean?" Scarlett cried.

"You know full well what I mean."

"Oh, Rhett, you can't be leaving me, not really. Why don't you put your arms around me and comfort me? You promised Mammy."

Rhett shook his head, a faint smile on his lips. "You've known me all these years, Scarlett, and yet, when you want to, you can forget all you've learned. It was a lie. I lied to make a dear old woman's last moments happy. Remember, my pet, I'm a scoundrel, not a gentleman." He walked toward the door.

"Don't go, Rhett, please," Scarlett sobbed. Then she put both hands over her mouth to stop herself. She'd never be able to respect herself if she begged him again. She turned her head sharply, unable to bear the sight of him leaving. She saw the triumph in Suellen's eyes and the pity in Will's.

"He'll be back," she said. "He always comes back. Always." She took a deep breath. "Where's Mammy's petticoat, Suellen? I intend to see that she's buried in it."

SCARLETT was able to stay in control of herself until Will brought in the coffin. Then she began to shake. I need air, she thought. I need to get out of this house. She picked up her skirts and ran.

Outside, the morning air was fresh and cool. Scarlett stumbled through the tall grasses of the pasture, down the hill to the woods that bordered the river. The high-topped pines smelled sharply sweet; they shaded a soft, thick mat of bleached needles, shed over hundreds of years. Scarlett crumpled wearily onto the cushioned ground, then settled herself in a sitting position, with a tree trunk at her back. She had to think; there must be some way to salvage her life from the ruins.

But she was so confused, so tired.

She'd been tired before. Worse tired than this. When she had to get to Tara from Atlanta with the Yankee army on all sides, she hadn't let tiredness stop her. When she had to forage for food all over the countryside, when she had to pick cotton or hitch herself to the plow, she hadn't given up because she was tired. She had found strength to keep going in spite of everything. She wasn't going to give up now. It wasn't in her to give up.

She stared ahead, facing all her demons. Melanie's death . . . Mammy's death . . . Rhett's leaving her, saying that their marriage was dead. That was the worst. Rhett's going away.

She had to find a way to get him back. She'd always been able to get any man she wanted, and Rhett was a man like any other man, wasn't he?

No, he wasn't like any other man, and that's why she wanted him. She shivered, suddenly afraid. She'd always gotten what she wanted, somehow. Until now.

She had to think, to remember what Rhett had said. Not last night, or whenever it was that Mammy died. What did he say at our house, the night he left Atlanta? He talked on and on, explaining things. He was so calm, so horribly patient, the way you can be with people you don't care enough about to get mad at them.

She found what she needed. Yes, she remembered it clearly. Rhett had offered her a divorce. Then, after her furious rejection of the offer, he had said it. "I'll come back often enough to keep gossip down." Scarlett smiled. She hadn't won yet, but there was a chance. A chance was enough to go on with. She stood up.

The muddy yellow Flint River ran slowly and deeply below the ledge that held the pine woods. Scarlett looked down at the current. "Moving on," she murmured. "Just like me. Don't look back, what's done is done. Move on." She squinted up at the bright sky. A line of brilliant white clouds was running across it.

They looked full of wind. It's going to get colder, she thought automatically. I'd better find something warm to wear this afternoon at the burial. She turned toward home.

THE graveyard at Tara was not very large. Mammy's grave looked big, ever so much bigger than Melly's, Scarlett thought.

The wind had a bite in it, and for all that, the sky was so blue and the sun so bright. Yellowed leaves skittered across the burial ground. Autumn's coming, she thought. I used to love the fall. Riding through the woods, the air tasting like cider. So long ago. There hasn't been a proper riding horse at Tara since Pa died.

She looked at the gravestones. Her father—GERALD O'HARA, BORN COUNTY MEATH, IRELAND. Her mother—ELLEN ROBILLARD O'HARA, BORN SAVANNAH, GEORGIA. At least Mammy was being buried here, next to Miss Ellen, and not in the slaves' burial plot.

The graveyard looks terrible, Scarlett thought. Weeds all over the place, it's downright shabby. This whole funeral is downright shabby, Mammy would have hated it. That black preacher is going on and on, and he didn't even know her. Mammy was a Roman Catholic, everybody in the Robillard house was except Grandfather. We should have gotten a priest, but the closest one is in Atlanta, it would have taken days. Poor Mammy.

Scarlett looked again at the unkempt graveyard. It would break Mother's heart to see this, she thought. Scarlett could—for a moment—see the tall, graceful form of her mother, Ellen O'Hara. Always impeccably groomed, always soft-voiced, always occupied with the perpetual work required to produce the orderly perfection that was life at Tara under her guidance. How did she do it? Scarlett cried silently. How did she make the world so wonderful? We were all so happy then. How I wish she was still here!

No, no, I don't want her to be here. It would make her so sad to see what's happened to Tara, what's happened to me. She'd be disappointed in me, and I couldn't bear that.

Scarlett looked at the mourners. Suellen and Will and me and the children and the servants. At least we all really loved Mammy, she thought. Big Sam's eyes are red from crying. Look at poor old Pork, he's crying, too. Why, his hair's almost white; I never think of him as old. Dilcey sure doesn't look her age, she hasn't changed a bit since she first came to Tara. . . .

Scarlett's exhausted, rambling mind suddenly sharpened. What were Pork and Dilcey doing here at all? They hadn't worked at Tara for years. Not since Pork became Rhett's valet and Dilcey, Pork's wife, went to Melanie's house, in Atlanta, as Beau's mammy. There was no way they could have learned about Mammy's death. Unless Rhett told them.

Scarlett looked over her shoulder. Had Rhett come back? There was no sign of him.

As soon as the service was over, she made a beeline for Pork.

"It's a sad day, Miss Scarlett." His eyes were still wet with tears.

"Yes, it is, Pork," she said. She walked slowly beside the old black servant, listening to his reminiscences of the early days at Tara. He'd come to Tara with her father when there was nothing there except a burned-out old building and fields gone to brush.

Little by little, Scarlett extracted the information she wanted. Rhett had gone back to Charleston to stay. Pork had packed all of Rhett's clothes and sent them to the depot for shipping. It was his final duty as Rhett's valet; he was retired now, with a parting bonus that was big enough for him to have a place of his own. "I can do for my family, too," Pork said proudly. Dilcey would never need to work again, and their daughter, Prissy, would have something to offer any man who wanted to marry her.

Scarlett smiled and agreed with Pork that Mist' Rhett was a fine gentleman. Inside, she was raging. That fine gentleman's generosity was making a real hash of things for her. Who was going to take care of Wade and Ella with Prissy gone? And how was she to find a good nursemaid for Beau? He'd just lost his mother, and his father was half crazy with grief, and now Dilcey—the only one in that house with any sense—was leaving, too. I came to Tara to get some rest, to straighten out my life, and all I found was more problems. Can't I ever get any peace?

Will Benteen quietly and firmly provided Scarlett with that respite. He sent her to bed. She slept for almost eighteen hours, and she woke with a clear plan of where to begin.

"I HOPE you slept well," said Suellen when Scarlett came down to the dining room for breakfast. Her voice was sickeningly honeyed. "You must have been awfully tired, after all you've been through." The truce was over, now that Mammy was dead.

When Scarlett answered, her words were equally sweet. "I hardly felt my head touch the pillow, and I was gone. The country air is so refreshing." She needed to stay on good terms with Suellen if she was going to carry out her plan. She smiled at her sister.

"What's so funny, Scarlett? Do I have a spot on my nose?"

Suellen's voice set Scarlett's teeth on edge, but she held on to her smile. "I'm sorry, Sue. I was just remembering when we were all children. I was such a horrid little girl. I don't know how you and Carreen put up with me." She buttered a biscuit as if it were her only concern.

Suellen looked suspicious. "You did torment us, Scarlett."

"I know. Even when we got older. I drove you and Carreen like mules when we had to pick the cotton after the Yankees stole everything."

"You nearly killed us. There we were, half dead from the typhoid, and you dragged us out of bed and into the hot sun. . . ."

Scarlett nodded encouragement, making little noises of contrition. How Suellen does love to complain, she thought. She waited until Suellen began to run down before she spoke.

"I feel so mean, and there's just nothing I can do to make up for all the bad times I put you through. I do think Will is wicked not to let me give you-all any money. After all, it is for Tara."

"I've told him the same thing a hundred times," Suellen said.

I'll just bet you have, thought Scarlett. "Men are so bullheaded," she said. Then, "Oh, Suellen, I just thought of something. Do say yes, Will couldn't possibly fuss about it. What if I left Ella and Wade here and sent money to you for their keep? They're so peaked from living in the city, and the country air would do them a world of good."

"I don't know, Scarlett. We're going to be awfully crowded when the baby comes." Suellen's expression was greedy but wary.

"I know," Scarlett crooned sympathetically. "Wade Hampton eats like a horse, too. I guess it would run about a hundred dollars a month just to feed the children and buy them shoes."

She doubted that Will had a hundred dollars a year in cash money from his hard work at Tara. Suellen was speechless, she noted with satisfaction. She was sure her sister's voice would return in no time to accept. I'll write a nice fat bank draft after breakfast, she thought. "These are the best biscuits I ever tasted," Scarlett said. "Could I have another?"

With the children taken care of, she was beginning to feel much better. She knew she should go back to Atlanta—she still had to do something about Beau. Ashley, too; she'd promised Melanie. But she'd come to Tara for country peace and quiet, and she was determined to have some before she left.

After breakfast Suellen went out to the kitchen. It gave Scarlett a chance to be alone and peaceful.

She poured herself another cup of coffee and drank it, not caring that it was only lukewarm. Then she left the dining room.

The sitting room showed the signs of poverty and constant use by a young family; Scarlett hardly recognized the velvet-covered settee where she had posed herself prettily when beaux proposed. And Suellen had rearranged everything, too. It wasn't really Tara this way.

She grew more and more despondent as she went from room to room. Nothing was the same. Every time she came home, there were more changes, more shabbiness. All the furniture needed recovering, the curtains were practically rags, and you could see the floor right through the carpets. Oh, why did Will have to be so stubborn! She could get new things for Tara if he would let her.

It should be mine! I'd take better care of it. Pa always said he'd leave Tara to me. But he never made a will. That's just like Pa, he never thought of tomorrow. Scarlett frowned, but she couldn't really be angry at her father. No one had ever stayed angry at Gerald O'Hara, he was like a lovable naughty child.

The one I'm mad at—still—is Carreen. Baby sister or not, she was wrong to do what she did, and I'll never forgive her, never. She made up her mind to go into the convent, and I accepted it. But she never told me she was going to use her third share of Tara as her dowry for the convent.

She should have told me! I would have found the money somehow. Then I'd have two-thirds ownership. Not the whole thing, like it should be, but at least clear control. It's not fair. I'm the one who saved Tara from the Yankees and the carpetbaggers. It is mine, no matter what the law says, and it'll be Wade's someday. I'll see to that, no matter what it takes.

Scarlett rested her head against the split-leather covering on the old sofa in the small room from which Ellen O'Hara had quietly ruled the plantation. There seemed to be a lingering trace of her mother's lemon verbena toilet water, even after all these years. This was the peacefulness she had come to find. Never mind the changes, the shabbiness. Tara was still Tara, still home. And the heart of it was here, in Ellen's room.

The only sound she could hear was the slow ticking of the clock in the hall beyond the closed door. But the quiet that she'd longed for so much was now, suddenly, driving her crazy. She stood up abruptly. I'd better write that bank draft for Suellen, she thought.

Her signature on the check was characteristic of Scarlett. Clear, unembellished and businesslike. She looked at it for a moment. The check was dated October 11, 1873. More than three weeks since Melly's death. She'd been at Tara for twenty-two days, taking care of Mammy.

The date had other meanings, too. It was more than six months ago now that Bonnie died. Scarlett could leave off the unrelieved dull black of deep mourning. She could accept social invitations. She could reenter the world.

I want to go back to Atlanta, she thought. I want some gaiety. There's been too much grieving, too much death. I need life.

She folded the check for Suellen. I miss the store, too.

And Rhett will be coming to Atlanta "to keep gossip down." I've got to be there.

I'll pack my things, and then I'll give Suellen her check. I'll take the train after dinner today. Will can drive me to the depot and be back in plenty of time to milk his nasty old cows.

Home to Atlanta. Tara's not home for me anymore, no matter how much I love it. It's time for me to go.

HALFWAY to Jonesboro, Scarlett blurted out what was preying on her mind. "Will, about Rhett— The way he left so fast . . . I hope Suellen's not going to go blabbing all over the county."

Will looked at her with his pale blue eyes. "Now, Scarlett. Family don't bad-mouth family. You can take my word on it. Suellen'll never tell your troubles to anybody. She don't want folks talking loose about the O'Haras any more than you do."

Scarlett relaxed a little. She trusted Will completely. And he was wise, too. She'd never known him to be wrong.

"You do believe he'll be back, don't you, Will?"

Will chewed quietly on a straw in the corner of his mouth. At last he said, "I can't say I do, Scarlett, but I ain't the one to know."

She felt as if he had struck her. Then quick anger erased the pain. "You just don't understand anything at all, Will Benteen! Rhett's upset right now, but he'll get over it. He'd never do anything as low as go off and leave his wife stranded."

Will nodded. Scarlett could take it for agreement if she wanted to. But he hadn't forgotten Rhett's sardonic description of himself. He was a scoundrel. Always had been and likely always would be.

Scarlett stared at the familiar red clay road in front of her. Her jaw was set, her mind working furiously. Rhett would come back. He had to because she wanted him to, and she always got what she wanted. All she had to do was set her mind to it.

3

FIVE Points was the Atlanta that Scarlett loved. The streets that met at Five Points were turbulent with life, with energy. There was shouting and the sound of whips cracking, of people hurrying, arguing, laughing. The noise and push were a tonic to Scarlett's spirit. So was the disorder on her desk at the house. She needed life and action around her after the numbing succession of deaths, and she needed work to do.

There were stacks of newspapers to be read, piles of daily business accounts from the general store she owned in the very center of Five Points and mounds of bills to be paid. Scarlett sighed with pleasure and pulled her chair up close to the desk.

She lit the lamp and reached eagerly for the store accounts. Then her hands stopped in midair when a square envelope on top of the newspapers caught her eye. It was addressed simply "Scarlett," and the handwriting was Rhett's.

Her fingers tore the sealed envelope open.

"Believe me," Rhett's letter began, "when I say that you have my deepest sympathy in your bereavement. Mammy's death is a great loss. I am grateful that you notified me in time for me to see her before she went."

Scarlett looked up in a rage and spoke aloud. "Grateful, my foot! So you could lie to her and to me, you varmint." Oh, she'd get even with him for shaming her in front of Suellen and Will. No matter how long she had to wait and plan, she'd find a way.

She lowered her head to read on.

She would find her life unaltered, Rhett stated. The household bills would be paid by his lawyers—an arrangement he had made years before—and all monies drawn from Scarlett's bank account by check would be replaced automatically. She might want to instruct any new shops where she opened accounts to send their bills directly to his lawyers.

Scarlett read all this with fascination. Money always interested her, always had, since the day when she was forced by the Union Army to discover what poverty was. Money was safety, she believed. She hoarded the money she earned herself, and now, viewing Rhett's openhanded generosity, she was shocked. I knew he was rich. But not this rich.

Then—he does still love me, this proves it. No man would ever spoil a woman the way Rhett has spoiled me all these years unless he loved her to distraction, and he's going to keep on giving me everything I want. He must still feel the same, or he'd rein in. Oh, I knew it! He didn't mean all those things he said. He just didn't believe me when I told him I know now that I love him.

Scarlett held Rhett's letter to her cheek. She'd prove it to him, prove she loved him with all her heart, and then they'd be so happy—the happiest people in the whole world!

She slept extremely well that night. It was good to be home, especially with Rhett's letter safely under her pillow.

SHE woke and stretched luxuriously. The crackle of paper beneath her pillow made her smile. After she rang for her breakfast tray, she began to plan her day. First to the store. No, the store would have to wait. She had other obligations to see to first.

Whatever possessed me to promise Melly that I'd take care of Ashley and Beau?

But I promised. I'd best go there first.

WHEN her carriage pulled up in front of Ashley and Melanie's tiny house on Ivy Street, Scarlett saw that the mourning wreath was gone from the door and the windows were all shuttered. India, she thought at once. Of course. She's taken Ashley and

Beau to live at Aunt Pittypat's house. She must be mighty pleased with herself.

Ashley's sister was, and always had been, Scarlett's implacable enemy. Scarlett bit her lip and considered her dilemma. She was sure that Ashley must have moved to Aunt Pitty's with Beau; it was the most sensible thing for him to do. Without Melanie and now with Dilcey gone, there was no one to run Ashley's house or mother his son. At Pittypat's there was comfort, an orderly household and constant affection for the little boy from women who had loved him all his life.

If only India didn't live with Aunt Pitty, Scarlett thought. She could manage timid Aunt Pitty. But Ashley's sister was another matter. India would just love to have a confrontation, to show Scarlett the door.

If only she hadn't promised Melanie—but she had. "Drive me to Miss Pittypat Hamilton's," Scarlett ordered Elias.

INDIA answered her knock. She looked at Scarlett's fashionable fur-trimmed mourning costume, and a tight, satisfied smile moved her lips.

Smile all you like, you old crow, thought Scarlett. "I've come to see how Ashley is," she said.

"You're not welcome here." India began to close the door.

Scarlett pushed against it. "India Wilkes, don't you dare slam that door in my face. I made a promise to Melly, and I'll keep it if I have to kill you to do it."

India answered by putting her shoulder to the door. The undignified struggle lasted for only a few seconds. Then Scarlett heard Ashley's voice. "Is that Scarlett, India? I'd like to talk with her."

The door swung open, and Scarlett marched in, noting with pleasure that India's face was mottled with anger.

Ashley came forward into the hallway to greet her, and Scarlett's brisk steps faltered. He looked desperately ill. Dark circles ringed his pale eyes, and his clothes hung from his sagging frame, like broken wings on a blackbird. Scarlett's heart turned over. She no longer loved Ashley the way she had for all those years, but he was still part of her life. There were so many shared memories, she couldn't bear to see him in such pain. "Dear Ashley," she said gently, "come and sit down. You look tired."

They sat on a settee in Aunt Pitty's small, fussy, cluttered parlor for more than an hour, and Scarlett listened while Ashley talked. He recounted stories of his dead wife's kindness, nobility, her love for Scarlett, for Beau, for him. His voice was low and without expression, bleached by grief and hopelessness. His hand groped blindly for Scarlett's, and he grasped it with despairing strength. She let him hold on to her.

India stood in the arched doorway—a dark, still spectator.

Finally, Ashley turned his head from side to side. "Scarlett, I can't go on without her. I can't."

Scarlett pulled her hand away. She had to break through the shell of despair that bound him, or it would kill him, she was sure. She stood and leaned down over him. "Listen to me, Ashley Wilkes," she said. "Do you think you're the only person who loved Melly and depended on her? I did, more than I knew. I expect a lot of other people did, too. But we're not going to curl up and die for it. That's what you're doing. And I'm ashamed of you.

"Melly is, too, if she's looking down from heaven. Do you have any idea what she went through to have Beau? Well, I know what she suffered; it would have killed the strongest man God ever made. Now you're all he's got. Is that what you want Melly to see? That her boy is practically an orphan because his pa feels too sorry for himself to care about him? Do you want to break her heart, Ashley Wilkes? Because that's what you're doing." She caught his chin in her hand and forced him to look at her.

"You pull yourself together, do you hear me, Ashley? You find your boy and take him in your arms and tell him not to be scared, that he has a father to take care of him."

Scarlett walked from the room, pushing India out of the way.

As she opened the door to the porch she could hear India. "My poor, darling Ashley. Don't pay any attention to the horrible things Scarlett said. She's a monster."

Scarlett slammed the door behind her.

"Just drive, Elias," she told her coachman. "Anywhere at all." Had she gotten through to Ashley? She'd been so mean— Well, she had to be, he was being drowned in sympathy. But had it done any good? Ashley adored his son, maybe he'd pull himself together for Beau's sake. "Maybe" wasn't good enough. He had to. She had to make him do it.

"Take me to Mr. Henry Hamilton's law office," she told Elias.

Uncle Henry was terrifying to most women, but not to Scarlett. She knew he rather liked her. He was her lawyer and knew how shrewd she was in her business dealings.

When she walked into his office without waiting to be announced, he put down the letter he was reading and chuckled. "Do come in, Scarlett." He offered her a chair.

She paced forward and back, ignoring the chair beside his desk. "Isn't it true," she said, "that when Charles died, he left me all his property?"

"You know it is. Stop that fidgeting and sit down. He left the warehouses near the depot that the Yankees burned. And he left some farmland outside of town that will be in town before too long, the way Atlanta has been growing."

Scarlett perched on the edge of the chair. "And half of Aunt Pitty's house on Peachtree Street. Didn't he leave me that, too?"

"Now, Scarlett, don't tell me you want to move in there."

"Of course not. But I want Ashley out of there. India and Aunt Pitty are going to sympathize him into his grave. He can go back to his own house. I'll find him a housekeeper."

"Are you sure that's why you want him back in his own house?"

Scarlett bridled. "God's nightgown, Uncle Henry!" she said. "Are you turning into a scandalmonger in your old age?"

"Don't show your claws to me, young lady. Settle back in that chair and listen to some hard truths. You've got maybe the best business head I ever met, but otherwise you're about as dim-witted as the village idiot.

"Now, about Ashley's house," the old lawyer said slowly. "It's been sold. I advised him to move into Pitty's and sell it. I advised him to move because he needed the money from the sale to keep his lumber business from going under."

"What do you mean? Ashley doesn't know tootle about making money, but he can't go under. Builders always need lumber."

"If they're building, Scarlett. But there was a big financial scandal in New York a couple of weeks ago. A speculator named Jay Cooke miscalculated, and he crashed. He took a bunch of other speculators with him. In New York they're calling it the panic. It's already spreading. Atlanta hasn't felt the panic yet, but I expect it'll get here soon."

Scarlett felt a stab of terror. "What about my store?" she cried. "And my money? Are the banks safe?"

"The one you bank in is. Fact is, Atlanta's not likely to get hurt much. But business is at a standstill. That means building, too. And if nobody's building, nobody needs lumber."

Scarlett frowned. "So Ashley won't be making any money from the sawmills."

"No. And now Ashley's with his sister and his aunt, according to my advice. And that doesn't suit you."

"No, sir, it doesn't suit at all. He's like a dead man walking, and they're making him worse. I gave him a good talking-to. But I know it won't stick. Not as long as he's in that house."

She looked at Uncle Henry's skeptical expression. "I don't care what you think. I'm not after Ashley. I made a deathbed promise to Melanie that I'd take care of him and Beau."

Her outburst made Henry uncomfortable. "You're the last person who can help Ashley right now," he said. "I told you I was going to deliver some hard truths, and that's one of them. Right or wrong, there was a lot of speculation about you and Ashley at one time. India thought the worst and said it. Miss Melly stood up for you, and most people followed her lead—for love of her, mind you, not because they were especially fond of you.

"But you couldn't leave well enough alone. You had to make a spectacle of yourself at Melanie's graveside. Throwing your arms around her husband—"

He held up one hand. "I know what you're about to say, Scarlett. I was there. I saw it. Ashley was about to throw himself in the grave, maybe break his neck. That's not the point. What you did broke all the rules. You made a scene in public. You laid hands on a man who wasn't your husband. You interrupted a burial. There's not a lady in town that isn't on India's side right now. That means against you. You don't have a friend to your name, Scarlett. You've made a mess of things, and I don't know how you can ever put it right."

The old lawyer stood up. "Leave Ashley where he is. Some sweet-talking little lady will come along one of these days and snap him up. Then she'll take care of him. You leave Pittypat's house the way it is, including your half. And keep sending money through me to pay for its upkeep, the way you've always done. That'll satisfy your promise to Melanie.

"Come on. I'll escort you to your carriage."

Scarlett took his arm and walked meekly beside him. But inside, she was seething.

"PANIC," Henry Hamilton had called it. Scarlett was terrified that she'd lose the money she had earned and hoarded. When she left the lawyer's office, she went immediately to her bank and converted all the cash in her lockbox to gold. She could still remember the elegantly engraved, worthless Confederate bonds her father had depended on. She had no faith at all in paper.

Scarlett's next stop was her store, Kennedy's Emporium. It was her inheritance from her brief marriage to Frank Kennedy. That and Ella. Her pleasure in the store more than offset her disappointment in the child.

Willie Kershaw, the head clerk, had done well when she was away. She'd add an extra dollar when she paid him for this week.

Also, she was planning to add to his duties. "Willie," she told him privately, "I want you to open a credit account."

Kershaw's protuberant eyes bulged. There had never been credit extended in the store after Scarlett took over its management. He listened carefully to her instructions, then swore he wouldn't tell a living soul.

At midday Scarlett left the store and went home. During dinner she thought about the errand she'd planned for the afternoon, wished fervently that the idea had never crossed her mind and decided that it had to be done.

THERE was no answer to her ring at Aunt Pittypat's front door. Scarlett was sure she saw one of the lace curtains twitch at a parlor window. She rang again and waited.

If anybody saw me standing here locked out, I'd perish with shame, she thought. Uncle Henry was right. She wasn't being received. All her life she had heard of people who were so scandalous that no decent person would open the door to them. But she was Scarlett O'Hara, daughter of Ellen Robillard, of the Savannah Robillards. This couldn't be happening to her.

Her eyes felt hot, a warning of tears. Then, as so often happened, she was swept by a tide of anger. Half this house belonged to her! How dare anybody lock the door against her!

She banged on the door with her fist and rattled the doorknob. "I know you're in there, India Wilkes," she shouted through the keyhole. "I came to talk to you, and I'm not leaving until I do."

Scarlett heard the bolts rattle. "For the love of heaven, come in," India whispered hoarsely. "You'll make us the talk of the town."

How Rhett would love this! Scarlett thought all of a sudden. In the good days of their marriage she had always told him about her triumphs in business and in the small social world of Atlanta. It made him laugh and call her his never-ending source of delight. Maybe he'd laugh again when she told him how India was puffing like a dragon that had to back down.

India stationed herself against the door to the parlor. "What do you want?" Her voice was icy.

"I don't know if you're aware of it," Scarlett said, "but Melly asked me on her deathbed to watch out for Beau and Ashley."

India's body jerked as if she'd been shot. "I won't have you hanging around here after him. You'll ruin Ashley's name just like you've ruined your own."

"The last thing I want to do, India Wilkes, is spend one more minute in this house than I have to. I came to tell you that I've made arrangements at my store for you to get anything you need."

"The Wilkeses don't take charity, Scarlett."

"You simpleton, I'm not talking charity. I'm talking about my promise to Melanie. You don't have any idea how quick a boy Beau's age goes through breeches. Or how much they cost. Do you want Ashley to be burdened with worries like that?

"I know just how small an income Aunt Pitty gets. There's a little thing called the panic, too. Businesses are folding. Ashley's likely to have less money coming in than ever.

"'Take care of Ashley, but don't let him know it.' That's what Melly said to me. How can I not let him know it if you won't help?"

India hesitated, and Scarlett knew she was winning. "You don't have to go to the store yourself," she said. "You can send a list by somebody else."

"Only for Beau's school clothes," India said grudgingly.

Scarlett kept herself from smiling. Once India saw how pleasant it was to get things for free, she'd do a lot more shopping than that.

"I'll say good day, then, India. Mr. Kershaw is the head clerk. Put his name on your list, and he'll take care of everything."

SCARLETT COULDN'T GET TO sleep that night. Every time she closed her eyes, she saw the wide front door of Aunt Pitty's house, closed and bolted against her.

The next morning, as Scarlett crossed the sidewalk to her carriage, she saw Mrs. Elsing and her daughter approaching on foot. Scarlett paused, ready to smile and say hello. The two Elsing ladies stopped dead when they saw her, then, without a word, turned and walked away. Scarlett was paralyzed for a moment. Then she scurried into her carriage and hid her face in its shadowy corner. Could Uncle Henry possibly be right that *every* door in Atlanta was going to be closed to her?

Scarlett stayed in the sanctuary of her carriage, sending Elias into her store with the clerks' pay envelopes. If she got out, she might see someone she knew, someone who would cut her dead. It was unbearable even to think of it.

India Wilkes must be behind this. I won't let her get away with it. "Go to the lumberyard," she ordered Elias when he returned. She'd tell Ashley. He'd do something to stop India's poison.

Her already heavy heart sank even lower when she saw the lumberyard. There were stacks and stacks of pine boards and not a wagon to be seen, or a loader. Nobody was buying.

Scarlett wanted to cry. She would never understand how she'd let Rhett trick her into selling the lumber business to Ashley. If she were still running it, this would never have happened. She would have sold the lumber somehow to someone. Things were awful all around, but she mustn't fuss at Ashley. She wanted him to help her.

"The yard looks wonderful!" she said brightly, entering the office. "You must have the sawmill running day and night to keep such a good stock up, Ashley."

He looked up from the account books on his desk, and Scarlett knew that cheerfulness would be wasted on him. He looked no better than when she'd given him the talking-to. He stood, tried to smile. His ingrained courtesy was stronger than his exhaustion, but his despair was greater than both.

I can't tell him anything about India, Scarlett thought, or about the business, either. He's got all he can bear just making himself draw the next breath.

"Scarlett, dear, how kind of you to stop by. Won't you sit down?"

"Kind" is it? God's nightgown! Ashley sounds like he doesn't know what's coming out of his mouth. Why should he care that I'm chancing whatever's left of my reputation by coming here without a chaperone? He doesn't care anything about himself— any fool could see that—why should he care anything about me? I can't sit down and make polite conversation. I can't stand it. But I have to.

"Thank you, Ashley," she said, and sat on the chair he was holding. "I've been down to Tara—"

"Why did you stop me, Scarlett?" said Ashley. Now there was emotion in the words—anger, betrayal, pain. "I wanted to be in the grave. Any grave, not just Melanie's. It's the only thing I'm fit for. . . . No, don't say whatever you were going to say, Scarlett. Say what you must be thinking—that I'm letting the lumber business die. Your lumber business that you invested all your heart in. I'm a miserable failure, Scarlett. You know it. I know it. The whole world knows it. Blame me, why don't you?"

Ashley shook his head with slow, heavy swings from side to side. From his throat burst one tearing sob. "Forgive me, Scarlett, I beg you. I had no right to burden you with my troubles. Now I have the shame of this outburst to add to my other shames. Be merciful, my dear, and go now."

Scarlett fled without a word.

Later she sat at her desk with all her legal records neatly stacked in front of her. It was going to be even harder to keep her promise to Melly than she'd expected. Clothing and household goods weren't nearly enough. And Ashley wouldn't lift a finger to help himself. She was going to have to make him successful whether he cooperated or not. She'd promised Melanie.

Scarlett made a list of her assets. She had the store, but the profits would certainly go down some when the panic got to Atlanta. She had the saloon near the depot. She didn't own it, she leased the land and building to the man who did. She could raise the rent, but a few more dollars a month wouldn't be enough to bail out Ashley. She needed real money.

The gold in her safe box. She had more than twenty-five thousand dollars of real money. By most people's reckoning, she was wealthy. But not by hers. She still didn't feel safe.

I could buy the lumber business back from Ashley, she thought, and for a moment her mind hummed with excitement. Then she sighed. That wouldn't solve anything. When she made a success of the business, he'd feel like more of a failure than ever. No, somehow she had to make Ashley a success at the business.

I just don't believe that there's no market for lumber. Panic or no panic, people have got to be building something. Scarlett riffled through the stack of papers. She'd had an idea.

There it was, the plot of the farmland Charles Hamilton had left her. The hundred acres were right on the edge of Atlanta now, the way things were growing. If she could find a good builder—and they must all be feeling mighty hungry for work—she could put up maybe a hundred gimcrack houses. Everybody who was losing money was going to have to live closer to the bone. Their big houses would be the first thing to go, and they'd have to find someplace they could afford to live.

I won't make any money, but I won't lose much. And I'll see to it that the builder uses only lumber from Ashley—the best he's got. He'll make a good income, and he'll never know it came from me. I can manage that. All I need is a builder who can keep his mouth shut.

"YES, ma'am, Mrs. Butler, I'm hungry for work all right," said Joe Colleton. The builder was a short, lean man in his forties, with dark eyes and a face leathered by long exposure to the sun. "I need work, but not bad enough to work for you."

He was the only honest-to-the-bone builder in Atlanta; Scarlett had learned that when she was selling lumber in the boom years of rebuilding after the War. Since Ashley mustn't know she was helping him, she couldn't oversee the work herself. She couldn't be seen to be involved.

"I don't know what I'll do if you turn me down."

"Mrs. Butler, you sold me green lumber once, after you told me it was cured. I don't do business twice with someone who cheats me once." Colleton's direct, knowing gaze was disconcerting.

"Mr. Colleton, I need somebody very special to help me," she said. "I made a deathbed promise to my dearest friend, Mrs. Wilkes. She asked me to help, and now I'm asking you." The whole story tumbled out—how Melanie had always sheltered Ashley . . . Ashley's ineptness . . . the unsold lumber . . . the need for secrecy. . . .

Colleton held up his hand to stop her. "All right, Mrs. Butler. If it's for Mrs. Wilkes, I'll take the job. You'll get the best-built houses with the best materials in them."

Scarlett put her hand in his. "Thank you," she said. She felt as if she'd scored the triumph of her life.

It was only some hours later, at home, that she remembered that she hadn't intended to use the best of everything, only the best lumber. What difference did it make what the houses looked like?

Then Scarlett's shoulders slumped. Melanie. She missed the gentle, loving friend who had been so much more important to her than she had ever realized; the world was colder and darker without Melanie. And so lonely. Scarlett had been back from the country for only two days, but she had known enough loneliness in that time to strike fear deep into her heart.

She could have told Melanie about Rhett leaving; Melanie was the only person she could ever confide in about such a disgraceful thing. Right before she died, Melly had told her what she most needed to hear. "Be kind to Captain Butler, he loves you so." Those were her very words, and just the thought of those words made Scarlett feel better. If Melly said that Rhett loved her, then he did, it wasn't only her own wishful thinking.

SCARLETT couldn't sleep that night. Insomnia was no stranger to her; she'd learned years before that two or three brandies would calm her down and help her sleep. She left her bed and padded downstairs to the dining room.

She lit the candles in the six-armed candelabra on the dining-room table and blew out her lamp. Then she went to the sideboard. She selected a glass, took it and the brandy decanter to the table and sat in the armchair at the head of the table.

The brandy sent a relaxing warmth through her body. Scarlett sighed. She filled the elegant little cordial glass again, tossed the brandy down her throat with a deft twist of the wrist. Mustn't hurry, she thought, pouring. It's not ladylike.

The candles burned low, and the decanter slowly emptied, and Scarlett's usual control over her mind and memory was loosened. This was the room where it had all begun. The table had been bare like this, with only candles on it and the silver tray that held the brandy decanter and glasses. Rhett was drunk. She'd never seen him really drunk like that, he could always hold his liquor. He was drunk that night, though, and cruel. He said such horrible, hurting things to her, and he twisted her arm so that she cried out in pain.

But then . . . then he carried her up to her room and forced himself on her. Except that he didn't have to force her to accept him. She came alive when he kissed her lips and throat and body. She burned at his touch. . . .

No lady would ever feel the wild wanting she had felt. Scarlett tried to push her thoughts back into the crowded dark corner of her mind where she kept the unbearable and unthinkable. But she'd had too much to drink.

She dropped her arms onto the table in front of her, her head onto her arms. And she abandoned herself to the waves of desire and pain that made her call out brokenly into the empty, silent, candlelit room.

"Rhett, oh, Rhett, I need you."

4

*W*INTER was approaching, and Scarlett grew more frantic with every passing day. Joe Colleton had dug the hole for the cellar of the first house, but repeated rains made it impossible to pour the concrete foundations. "Mr. Wilkes would smell a rat if I bought lumber before I'm ready to frame," he said reasonably, and Scarlett knew he was right. But it made the delay no less frustrating. If only the cold rain would stop. . . . If only the days would stop getting shorter. She could keep busy in the daytime, but darkness closed her in the empty house with only her thoughts for companions as she walked from room to room in the big house, like a dried pea rattling around in an empty washtub.

She'd be glad to have Wade and Ella come home, but Suellen had written that they were all under quarantine with the long, itchy torture of chicken pox. *Things will get better when the rain stops . . . when winter's over . . . when Rhett comes home. . . .*

At last the weather turned to bright, cold, sunny days. Colleton ordered concrete then, and the lumber from Ashley.

Scarlett plunged into a celebration of shopping for gifts. It was nearly Christmas. She bought presents for Ella and each of

Suellen's girls. And for Wade, Suellen and Will. She decided not to get a present for Beau. She wouldn't put it past India to send it back unopened. Besides, Beau wasn't lacking for anything. The Wilkes account at her store was mounting up every week.

She bought a gold cigar cutter for Rhett, but she lacked the nerve to send it. Instead, she made her gifts to her two aunts in Charleston much nicer than usual. They might tell Rhett's mother how thoughtful she was, and Mrs. Butler might tell Rhett.

I wonder if he'll send me anything. Or maybe he'll come home for Christmas to keep gossip down. The possibility was real enough to send Scarlett into a happy frenzy of decorating the house. When it was a bower of pine branches, holly and ivy, she took the leftovers down to the store.

The day's newspaper was on the seat of her carriage. A front-page headline caught her eye: CARNIVAL TO CONCLUDE WITH MASQUERADE BALL. She snatched the paper up and read the article.

Atlanta would be graced on January 6, it said, with a carnival sure to rival the magnificence of New Orleans' famous Mardi Gras. The Twelfth Night Revelers, a body lately formed by the city's leading figures, were the instigators of this fabulous event. The king of carnival would reign over Atlanta, attended by a court of noblemen. He'd enter the city and traverse it on a float in a parade, and all the city's citizens were invited. The daylong revels would conclude with a masked ball at DeGives Opera House.

"The Revelers," Scarlett read, "have distributed three hundred invitations to Atlanta's finest knights and fairest ladies."

"Damn!" she said. It wasn't fair. Rhett would surely be dancing in Charleston, and all her enemies in Atlanta would be having a good time, while she was stuck by herself in her huge, silent house.

Well, she wasn't going to wallow in misery, she told herself. She was going to go to the ball; somehow she'd find a way.

It was not difficult to get an invitation to the ball. Scarlett learned that the vaunted parade would be made up largely of floats—decorated wagons advertising products and stores. There was a fee for participants, of course, but all those businesses in the parade received two invitations to the ball. She entered Kennedy's Emporium in the parade.

Now she had to think about her costume. She was still in ordinary mourning, but surely that didn't mean she had to wear black for a masquerade ball. The whole idea was to fool people, wasn't it? To be disguised. The ball was sounding better every minute.

She'd wear a wonderful costume, with a long train trimmed with white fur, and all the jewelry she wanted. Her costume and mask would protect her from India Wilkes and the other women. She intended to have a wonderful time, to dance every dance, to be part of things again.

ON THE night of the ball Scarlett was costumed as the queen of hearts. She would have preferred to have been the queen of diamonds, with a glittering paste crown and dog collar and brooches. However, then she wouldn't have been able to wear her pearls, which the jeweler had told her were "fine enough for the queen herself." And besides, she had found nice, big imitation rubies to sew all around the low neck of her red velvet gown. It was so good to be wearing color!

She had a mysterious red satin eye mask that covered her face down to the tip of her nose, and her lips were reddened to match it. She felt very daring and quite safe. Tonight she could dance to her heart's content without anyone knowing who she was.

With her mask in place Scarlett stepped out of her carriage and entered the ballroom. She looked around with astonishment. DeGives Opera House had been transformed. The handsome theater was now truly a king's palace.

A dance floor had been built over the lower half of the auditorium, extending the large stage into a mammoth ballroom. Dr. Meade was Rex, king of carnival. He was seated on his throne at the far end of the room, with uniformed attendants on each side. In the center of the dress circle was the biggest orchestra Scarlett had ever seen, and on the floor were masses of dancers, watchers, wanderers. As soon as she entered the room, a mandarin in Chinese robes put his silken arm around her waist and whirled her onto the dance floor. The tune was a waltz, her partner a dizzying dancer. As they spun, Scarlett caught glimpses of masked Hindus, harlequins, pirates and nymphs, all dancing as madly as she.

When the music stopped, she was breathless. "Wonderful," she gasped. Then the mandarin was gone, elbowed aside by a monk. Without a word he took Scarlett's hand, then circled her waist with his arm.

She danced as she hadn't danced in years. She was giddy, infected by the thrilling madness of masquerade, intoxicated by the delight of being at a party again, by her unquestionable success.

She recognized Ashley. He was masked, but she knew him as soon as she saw him. He wore a mourning band around the sleeve of his black-and-white harlequin outfit. India must have dragged him here so she'd have an escort, Scarlett thought. Of course, a man in mourning doesn't have to give up going out the way a woman does. He can put an armband on his best suit and start courting his next love before his wife's hardly cold in her grave. But anybody could tell poor Ashley hates being here. Look at the way he's all droopy in his fancy dress.

The evening wore on. A portly cavalier released Scarlett's hand to the mandarin, who was back for the third time, and Scarlett begged for a chair and a glass of Champagne.

But when her escort led her toward the sitting-out side of the room, her eyes brushed a tall, bearded pirate who was leaning against a doorjamb. He bowed to her, and her breath caught in her throat. There was something . . . the air of insolence. . . .

The pirate was wearing a white shirt and dark evening trousers. Not a costume at all, except for the red silk sash tied around his waist, with two pistols tucked into it. And blue bows tied to the ends of his thick beard. His mask was a simple black cloth over his eyes. He seemed to be staring at her right through the mask.

Then he smiled, his teeth very white against his dark beard and swarthy skin. Scarlett felt faint. It was Rhett.

"Excuse me, I must go. No, really, I mean it." She pushed away from the mandarin and ran to her husband.

Rhett bowed again. "Edward Teach at your service, ma'am."

"Who?" Did he think she hadn't recognized him?

"Edward Teach, Scarlett, commonly known as Blackbeard, the greatest villain that ever plowed the waters of the Atlantic." Rhett twirled a ribboned lock of the beard.

Scarlett's heart leaped. He's having fun, she thought, just the way he used to before—before things went bad, before I loved him so much. I mustn't put my foot wrong now. I mustn't.

"How did you know it was me?" she said. "I have a mask on."

"I only had to look for the most ostentatiously dressed woman, Scarlett. It was bound to be you."

"Oh, you . . . you skunk." She forgot that she was trying to amuse him. "Why did you come? Not just to insult me."

"I promised you I'd make myself visible often enough to keep down gossip, Scarlett. This was a perfect occasion."

"A masked ball? Nobody knows who anybody is."

"At midnight the masks come off. That's about four minutes from now. We'll waltz to visibility, then leave." Rhett took her in his arms, and Scarlett forgot her anger, forgot the peril of unmasking before her enemies, forgot the world. Nothing was important but that he was here and holding her.

SCARLETT lay awake most of the night, struggling to understand what had happened. Everything was fine at the ball. When twelve o'clock came, Dr. Meade said that everyone should take off their masks, and Rhett was laughing when he yanked off his beard, too. I'd take an oath he was enjoying himself. He kind of saluted the doctor and bowed to Mrs. Meade, and then he whisked me out of there as easy as a greased pig. He didn't even seem to notice the way people turned their backs on me.

And in the carriage coming home, he asked how things were at Tara and if his lawyer was paying my bills on time, and by the time I answered, we were home. That's when it happened. He was here, right downstairs in the hallway. He said good night and went up to his dressing room.

He wasn't hateful or cold, he just said good night and went upstairs. What does that mean? Why did he bother to come all the way to Atlanta? Not just to go to a party when it's party time in Charleston. Not because it was a masquerade—he could go to Mardi Gras if he wanted to. After all, he has lots of friends in New Orleans.

He'd said, "To keep down gossip." In a pig's eye.

Sleep, when it came, was brief and restless. Nevertheless, Scarlett woke in good time to go down to breakfast in her most becoming dressing gown.

"Up so early, my dear?" Rhett said. "How thoughtful of you. I won't have to write a note of farewell." He tossed his napkin onto the table. "I've packed some things Pork overlooked. I'll be by for them later, on my way to the train."

Don't leave me, Scarlett's heart begged. She looked away lest he see the pleading in her eyes. "For heaven's sake finish your coffee, Rhett," she said. "I'm not going to make a scene." She must be calm. Maybe then he'd stay.

He was standing, his watch open in his hand. "No time," he said. "There are people I have to see while I'm here. I'm going to be very busy until summer. I'll drop the word that I'm going to South America on business so no one will gossip about my absence. You see, my dear, I'm keeping my promise to preserve the purity of your reputation." Rhett grinned malevolently and closed the watch. "Good-bye, Scarlett."

"Why don't you go on to South America and get lost there forever!"

When the door closed behind him, Scarlett's hand reached for the decanter of brandy. Why had she carried on like that? That wasn't how she felt at all. But he'd always done that to her, goaded her into saying things she didn't mean.

She'd never been so unhappy in her whole life.

Later Scarlett was ashamed of herself. Drinking in the morning! Only low-life drunks did such a thing. Things weren't so bad, really, she told herself. At least she knew now when Rhett would be coming back. It was much too far in the future, but it was definite. Now she wouldn't waste time wondering if it might be today. Or tomorrow. Or the day after that.

FEBRUARY . . . March . . . April . . .

I only have to hold out until summer—the words were her litany and her lifeline—then Rhett will come. I can tell him, Rhett's the only one I can tell, he's the only one who cares about me. He won't make me live like this, outcast and unhappy, once he knows how awful everything is. What went wrong? I was so sure that if I could just have enough money, I'd be safe. Now I'm rich, and I feel more afraid than ever before.

But when summer came, there was no visit by Rhett, no word from him. It was then that Scarlett began to drink steadily—to shut out the silence while she listened for his footsteps.

She didn't think anything of it when she began having sherry in the afternoon. And she hardly noticed when she changed from sherry to whiskey . . . or when she began to take a glass of brandy as soon as she got up in the morning.

She hardly even noticed when summer became fall.

PANSY BROUGHT THE AFTERNOON mail to the bedroom on a tray. Lately Scarlett had tried sleeping for a while after dinner. It filled up part of the empty afternoon, and it gave her some rest, a relief denied to her at night.

Scarlett took the topmost letter and opened it. It was from Aunt Eulalie. She always hated the preachy missives from her dead mother's sister. But Aunt Eulalie lived in Charleston. She might mention Rhett. His mother was her closest friend.

Scarlett's eyes moved rapidly. Aunt Pauline having trouble with her knee . . . a visit to Sister Mary Joseph . . . At this, Scarlett made a face. She couldn't think of her baby sister Carreen by her religious name, even though she'd been in the convent in Charleston for eight years. Scarlett turned the page over, frowning.

Rhett's name leaped from the tangle of words:

> It does one's heart good to see a cherished friend like Eleanor Butler find happiness after so many sorrows. Rhett is quite his mother's gallant, and his devotion has done much to redeem him in the eyes of all those who deplored the wild ways of his younger days. It is beyond my comprehension, and also that of your aunt Pauline, why you insist on maintaining your unaccountable preoccupation with trade when it is keeping you from your proper place by the side of your husband.

Scarlett threw the letter on the floor. So that was Rhett's story! That she wouldn't leave the store and go to Charleston with him. How dare he spread such slander? She'd have some choice words to say to Mr. Rhett Butler when he came home. He'd probably deny it, the skunk. Well, she'd shake Aunt Eulalie's letter in his face. Let's see him call his mother's best friend a liar!

Suddenly Scarlett felt cold. She knew what he'd say. "Would you rather I told the truth? That I left you because living with you was intolerable?"

The shame of it. Anything was better than that. I need a drink, she thought. I'll just sip a small brandy.

She hurried downstairs to the dining room and poured brandy into a glass at the sideboard. Her hand lifted the glass to her lips, and she drank deep.

The movement caught her eye, reflected in the mirror above the sideboard. Slowly Scarlett lowered her hand and set the glass down. She looked into her own eyes. She couldn't believe what they saw—a pale, thin, sunken-eyed woman.

What had happened to her?

Her hand reached automatically for the decanter, providing the answer. Scarlett pulled her hand away, and she saw that it was shaking. She clutched the sideboard for support and stared at her reflection. "Fool!" she said, and tears slid slowly down her cheeks.

She wanted a drink more than she'd ever wanted anything in her life. Her right hand closed around the neck of the glittering glass. Scarlett looked at her hand as if it belonged to a stranger, at the heavy crystal decanter and the promise of escape that lay within it. Slowly, watching her movements in the mirror, she lifted the decanter and backed away from her frightening reflection.

Then she drew in a long breath and swung her arm with all the strength she could find. The decanter sparkled blue and red and violet in the sunlight as it crashed into the huge mirror. For an instant Scarlett saw her face cracking into pieces, saw her twisted smile of victory. Then the silvered glass fragmented, and tiny shards spattered onto the sideboard. The top of the mirror seemed to lean forward from its frame, and huge jagged pieces fell crashing like cannon fire onto the sideboard, onto the floor.

Scarlett was crying and laughing and shouting at the destruction of her own image. "Coward! Coward! Coward!"

The servants had rushed to the door when they heard the noise. "Go away," Scarlett said. "I want to be by myself."

But she was by herself whether she wanted to be or not. Rhett wasn't coming home. She'd known that for a long time, but she'd refused to face it. No wonder she hadn't known that woman in the mirror. That cowardly fool wasn't Scarlett O'Hara. Scarlett O'Hara didn't drown her sorrows. Scarlett O'Hara didn't hide and hope. She faced the worst the world could hand her. And she went out into the danger to take what she wanted.

Scarlett shuddered. She had come so close to defeating herself.

No more. It was time—long past time—to take her life in her own hands. No more brandy. She had flung away that crutch.

It shouldn't take more than a few weeks to get back to looking her best. She had no time to waste.

Rhett hadn't come back to her, so she'd have to go to him.

To Charleston.

5

ONCE her mind was made up, Scarlett's life changed radically. She had a goal now, and all her energy poured into achieving it. She got Mrs. Marie, the dressmaker, to make a wardrobe for her in only a few weeks. By November, Uncle Henry Hamilton had taken over the financial management of the store and saloon, with a guarantee that the money would go to Joe Colleton for the houses.

Scarlett's normal appetite for food had returned, and her face was already filled out enough so that a dimple flickered when she smiled. She looked almost like a girl again, she was sure.

It was time to go.

DON'T look back, she'd always told herself. Now she truly meant it. Her whole life was behind her. All the demands of her businesses were in Uncle Henry's hands, her responsibilities to Melanie were taken care of, her children were settled at Tara. She was free to do anything she wanted to do, and she knew what that was. She'd go to Charleston and have a wonderful time. It didn't mean a thing that she had hated it when she was last there. That was over twelve years ago, and she'd been so young then, only seventeen, and a new widow with a baby. Wade Hampton hadn't even cut his teeth yet. Everything would be completely different now. It was all going to work out just fine. She'd prove to Rhett that she loved him. She'd show him that she did. He'd see. And then he'd be sorry he'd left her. He'd put his arms around her and kiss her, and they'd be happy forever after.

SCARLETT'S aunts, Pauline and Eulalie, lived on the Battery, the most fashionable address in Charleston. They threw open the door of their house the moment her buggy from the train station stopped. Golden light streamed out onto the path from the sidewalk, and Scarlett ran through it to the sanctuary it promised.

But they look so old! she thought when she was close to her aunts. I don't remember Aunt Pauline being skinny as a stick and all wrinkled like that. And when did Aunt Eulalie get so fat? She looks like a balloon with gray hair on top.

"Look at you!" Eulalie exclaimed. "You've changed so, Scarlett, why I'd hardly know you."

Scarlett quailed as she accepted her aunts' embraces. Surely she hadn't got old, too.

"Look at Scarlett, sister," Eulalie burbled. "She's grown up to be the image of Ellen."

Pauline sniffed. "There is a clear resemblance. I will say that."

Scarlett smiled happily. There was no greater compliment in the world that anyone could pay her.

The aunts fluttered and argued about settling Pansy in the servants' quarters and getting the trunks upstairs to Scarlett's bedroom. "Don't you lift a finger, honey," Eulalie said to Scarlett. "You must be worn out." Scarlett settled herself on a settee in the drawing room. Now that she was finally here, the feverish energy that had gotten her through the preparations seemed to have evaporated, and she realized that her aunt was right. She was worn out.

She all but dozed off during supper. Both her aunts had soft voices, and even though their conversation consisted largely of polite disagreement on everything, the sound of it was lulling. Also, they weren't saying anything that interested her. She had already learned what she wanted to know. Rhett was living at his mother's house, but he was out of town.

"Gone north," Pauline said.

"But for good reason, sister," Eulalie reminded her. "He's in Philadelphia buying back some of the family silver that the Yankees stole."

Scarlett wondered how soon she could go up to bed. No sleeplessness would plague her tonight, she was sure of it.

And she was right. Now that she'd taken her life in her own hands, she could sleep like a baby. She woke in the morning with a sense of well-being that she hadn't felt for years.

Her aunt Eulalie punctured Scarlett's bubble before she'd finished her first cup of breakfast coffee. "We've planned something for today," she said. "We sent our maid, Susie, with a note to Eleanor Butler. We'll call on her this morning."

Rhett's mother! She'd only met Eleanor Butler once, at Bonnie's funeral, and she had almost no memory of her except that Mrs. Butler was very tall and dignified. I know I'll have to see her, Scarlett thought, but not now. I'm not ready.

Scarlett's heart pounded. Suppose Rhett had told his mother the truth about why he'd left Atlanta, that he had walked out on the marriage. "I'd better go look at my clothes," Scarlett said. "Pansy'll have to press the wrinkles out of whatever I'm going to wear." She fled to her room.

"You won't need that heavy fur cape, Scarlett," said Pauline.

"Indeed not," said Eulalie, eyeing the fashionable garment.

Scarlett knew why they didn't want her to wear her cape. They were just like the old-guard dowagers in Atlanta. A person had to be shabby like them to be respectable. She undid the cape and handed it to Pansy. Then she followed her aunts out into the bright day.

She gasped when she stepped down from the entrance. It was like May, not November, and the sun's warmth settled on her shoulders like a weightless blanket. "Oh, Aunties, this feels wonderful," she said. "I hope your carriage has a fold-down top."

The aunts laughed. "Dear child," Eulalie said, "there's not a living soul in Charleston with a carriage anymore, except for Sally Brewton. We'll walk. Everyone does."

"The carpetbaggers have carriages," Pauline corrected.

"You could hardly call the carpetbaggers 'living souls,' sister."

"They're vultures," Pauline agreed with a sniff.

"Buzzards," said Eulalie. The sisters laughed again. Scarlett laughed with them. The beautiful day was making her feel almost giddy with delight. Suddenly she felt a great fondness for her aunts. She followed them across the wide, empty street in front of the house and up a short stairway to an elevated promenade on the other side of it. At the top of the stairway a breeze touched her lips with a taste of salt.

"Oh, my goodness," she said. On the far side of the promenade the green-brown waters of Charleston harbor stretched before her to the horizon. To her left, flags fluttered on the tall masts of ships along the wharves. To her right, the trees of a long, low island glowed a bright green in the sunlight. The salt-sweet light breeze caressed her neck. She knew now that she'd been right to come.

The promenade was so wide, they walked three abreast along it. Twice they met other people—first an elderly gentleman in an old-fashioned frock coat, then a lady accompanied by her grandson. Each time they stopped, the aunts would introduce Scarlett,

"Our niece from Atlanta. She's married to Eleanor Butler's boy Rhett." To Scarlett the day was getting better with every passing minute. Then she saw that the next walkers approaching them were Yankee soldiers.

Her step faltered, she grabbed Pauline's arm. "Keep walking," said Pauline clearly. "They'll have to get out of our way."

Scarlett looked at Pauline with shock. Who would have thought that her skinny old aunt could be so brave?

When only three paces separated them, the soldiers drew aside. Pauline and Eulalie sailed past them as if they were not there. Scarlett lifted her chin to equal the tilt of her aunts' and kept pace.

"Why are there Yankee soldiers in Charleston?" she asked. "The War's been over for practically ten years."

"My goodness, Scarlett," said Eulalie, "didn't you know? Charleston is still under military occupation. They hate us because we threw them out of Fort Sumter."

"Come along," said Pauline. "We cross here. The Butler house is the one with the fresh paint."

"Lucky Eleanor," said Eulalie, "to have such a devoted son. Rhett positively worships his mother."

Scarlett stared at the house. Not a house, a mansion. Shining white columns soared a hundred feet to support the roof overhang above the deep porches along the side of the tall, imposing brick house. Scarlett had never seen any place as grand.

Pauline had her by the arm, hurrying her across the street. In time Scarlett found herself standing inside a door, looking at a tall, elegant woman, with shining white hair crowning a lined, lovely face.

"Dear Eleanor," said Eulalie.

"You've brought Scarlett," said Mrs. Butler. "My dear child," she said to Scarlett, and bent to kiss her cheek.

Scarlett closed her eyes. The faint scent of lemon verbena surrounded her, floating gently from Eleanor Butler's silk gown and silken hair. It was the fragrance that had always been part of Ellen O'Hara, the scent for Scarlett of comfort, of safety, of love, of life before the War. Scarlett felt her eyes spilling uncontrollable tears.

"There, there," Rhett's mother said. "It's all right, my dear. Whatever it is, it's all right now. You've come home at last. I've been longing for you to come." She put her arms around her daughter-in-law and held her close.

ELEANOR BUTLER WAS A southern lady. Her slow, soft voice and indolent, graceful movements disguised a formidable energy and efficiency. Ladies were trained from birth to be decorative, to be appealingly helpless. They were also trained to manage huge houses and large staffs of servants—always making it seem that the house, the garden, the kitchen, the servants ran themselves, while the lady of the house sat at leisure in the drawing room.

Eleanor soothed Scarlett with gentle words and fragrant tea, she flattered Pauline and diverted Eulalie. She also murmured to Manigo, her manservant, that her maid, Celie, would help him transfer Scarlett's things from her aunts' house to the big bedroom overlooking the garden where Mister Rhett slept.

In under ten minutes everything had been accomplished to move Scarlett, without opposition or injured feelings, to the tranquil life under Eleanor Butler's roof. Scarlett felt like a girl again, safe from all harm, sheltered by a mother's all-powerful love.

She gazed at Eleanor through misted, admiring eyes. This was what she wanted to be, had always meant to be—a lady like her mother, like Eleanor Butler. Ellen O'Hara had instructed her to be a lady, had planned for it and wanted it. I can do it now, Scarlett told herself. I can make up for all the mistakes I made. I can make Mother proud of me.

Scarlett felt safe and loved and invincible. She could do anything, everything. And she would. She would win Rhett's love again. She would be admired and respected and adored by everyone. And she would never, ever, be lonely again.

When Pauline and Eulalie had swallowed the last of the tea, Eleanor Butler stood, pulling Scarlett up with her. "I have to pick up my boots from the cobbler this morning," she said, "so I'll take Scarlett along and introduce her to King Street. No woman can possibly feel at home until she knows where the shops are. Will you-all join us?"

To Scarlett's immense relief her aunts declined. She wanted Mrs. Butler all to herself.

King Street was a delight. Stores lined it for block after block—everything and anything could be bought on King Street. There were crowds of shoppers, too, and dozens of smart carriages. Scarlett remembered what her aunts had told her: there wasn't a carriage to be had in Charleston except those owned by Yankees, carpetbaggers and the scalawags that were fattening on the defeated South. When she followed Mrs. Butler into one of the boot shops, it did her heart good to see the proprietor turn over his richly dressed customer to a young assistant so that he could hurry forward to Rhett's mother. It was a pleasure to be with a member of the old guard in Charleston.

Scarlett decided to get a pair of boots for herself. She raised her skirt a few inches to display her fragile leather shoes. "Something more suitable for city walking," she said proudly. No one was going to take her for a carriage-riding scalawag.

When the proprietor disappeared behind a curtain in the rear of the shop, Eleanor whispered to Scarlett, "Look closely at his hair when he kneels to fit your boots. He colors it with boot polish."

It took all of Scarlett's self-control not to laugh when she saw that Mrs. Butler was right, especially when Eleanor was looking at her with such a conspiratorial twinkle in her dark eyes. She didn't blame Rhett one bit for adoring his mother.

Scarlett was sorely disappointed when Eleanor Butler said it was time to go home. She couldn't remember ever having had such fun.

They took the horsecar back downtown. As it moved slowly along its tracks Eleanor said, "We'll go to the Market tomorrow. You'll meet everyone you should know there."

A sudden noise made Scarlett jump. Then she realized that it was the chime of a great clock. "That's every Charlestonian's timekeeper," Eleanor Butler said, "the bells in Saint Michael's steeple. One o'clock. No wonder I'm tired, it was a long morning."

Scarlett helped Mrs. Butler down at the last stop, the end of Meeting Street. In front of them was a park, and small children were running, rolling hoops, tossing balls on the grass.

"Scarlett, I hope you'll forgive me; I know I shouldn't, but I have to ask." Mrs. Butler's cheeks had splotches of bright color. "I just can't stand not knowing. . . . Have you and Rhett ever thought of another child? I understand that you'd be afraid to repeat the heartbreak you felt when Bonnie died."

"A baby . . . " Scarlett's voice trailed off. Had Mrs. Butler read her mind? She was counting on getting pregnant as soon as possible. Rhett was crazy about children, and he'd love her forever if she gave him one. "Miss Eleanor, I want a baby more than anything else in the whole world."

"I do so long to be a grandmother again," said Mrs. Butler. "When Rhett brought Bonnie to visit me, I could hardly keep from smothering her with hugging. You see, Margaret—that's my other son's wife, you'll meet her today—poor Margaret is barren. And Rosemary—Rhett's sister . . . I'm very much afraid that there'll never be anyone for Rosemary to marry."

Scarlett kissed Mrs. Butler on the cheek. "I'm just longing for a baby, Miss Eleanor. We'll convince Rhett, the two of us."

"You've made me very happy, Scarlett. We'll go home now, it's only around the corner there. Then I think I'll have a little rest before dinner. My committee is meeting at the house this afternoon, and I need to have my wits about me. I hope you'll join us. We raise money with cake sales and bazaars for the Confederate Home for Widows and Orphans."

God's nightgown! Were they all the same, these southern ladies? It was just like Atlanta, Scarlett thought. Always Confederate this and Confederate that. Couldn't they admit the War was over and get on with their lives? She'd have a headache. . . . No, she'd go to the committee meeting. She was never going to make the mistakes here she'd made in Atlanta. She was never going to be shut out and lonely again.

"That sounds mighty nice," she said. "I never did have time for extra work in Atlanta. My former husband, Frank Kennedy, left a fine business as an inheritance for our little girl. I felt it was my duty to watch over it for her." That should take care of that story Rhett was telling.

Eleanor Butler nodded comprehension. Scarlett lowered her lashes to hide the delight in her eyes.

"Would you like to take coffee on the piazza, Scarlett?" asked Eleanor Butler when she and Scarlett were finishing dessert.

"Oh, yes, I'd like that very much." Scarlett followed Mrs. Butler to the second-floor porch.

She drank the first cup and was about to ask for another when Eleanor Butler gestured toward the street. "Here comes my committee," she said. "I'd recognize that sound anywhere."

Scarlett heard it, too, a tinkling of tiny bells. She ran to the railing above the street to look.

A pair of horses was racing toward her, pulling a handsome dark green brougham with yellow-spoked wheels. When the carriage stopped in front of the house, Scarlett could see that sleigh bells were attached to the yellow spokes. She'd never seen such a thing. The driver was a woman, wearing a dark brown riding habit and yellow gloves. She was half standing, pulling on the traces with all her might, her ugly face screwed up with determination; she looked for all the world like a dressed-up monkey.

The brougham's door opened, and a laughing young man stepped out. He handed down a stout lady, then a younger woman with a broad smile on her face. "Come inside, Scarlett," Mrs. Butler said, "and help me with the tea things." Scarlett followed her eagerly. What a peculiar turnout of people. Where did they find that monkey-woman driver? And who could the man be? Men didn't bake cakes for charity. He looked rather handsome, too. Scarlett paused to smooth her hair.

"You look a bit shaken, Emma," Mrs. Butler was saying. She and the stout woman touched cheeks. "Have a restful cup of tea, but first let me present Rhett's wife, Scarlett."

"It'll take more than a cup of tea to repair my nerves after that ride." The woman held out her hand. "How do you do, Scarlett. I'm Emma Anson, or rather what remains of Emma Anson."

Eleanor embraced the younger woman and led her to Scarlett. "This is Margaret, dear, Ross's wife. Margaret, meet Scarlett."

Margaret Butler was pale and fair-haired, with sapphire-blue eyes. She took Scarlett's hands and kissed her cheek. "I always wanted a sister, and a sister-in-law is practically the same thing."

Scarlett returned Margaret's kiss. Miss Eleanor and now Margaret were on her side.

"Scarlett," said Mrs. Butler, "do come meet Sally Brewton."

"And Edward Cooper," added a male voice. "Don't deprive me of the chance to kiss Mrs. Butler's hand, Eleanor. I'm already smitten."

"You must wait your turn, Edward," Mrs. Butler said.

Scarlett hardly looked at Edward Cooper. She was staring at Sally Brewton, the monkey-faced driver of the carriage.

Sally Brewton was a tiny woman in her forties. She was shaped like a thin, active young boy, and her face did, in fact, greatly resemble a monkey's. She wasn't in the least upset by Scarlett's rude stare. Sally had adapted long ago to people's reaction to her remarkable ugliness. She walked over to Scarlett now. "My dear Mrs. Butler, you must think us as mad as March hares. The truth is that there's a perfectly rational explanation for our—shall we say?—dramatic arrival. I am the only surviving carriage possessor in town, and I find it impossible to keep a coachman. So if my husband is otherwise occupied, I do the driving myself." Sally grinned. "But I am an appallingly bad driver. So whenever I take the carriage out, it is bedecked in bells, as advance warning to people to get out of my way."

"Rather like a leper," offered Mrs. Anson.

"I shall ignore that," Sally said with an air of injured dignity. She smiled at Scarlett, a smile of such genuine goodwill that Scarlett felt warmed by it. "Do call on me whenever you need the brougham. The fact is, I adore careening through the streets, scattering scalawags and carpetbaggers to the four winds."

"Miss Eleanor, please forgive me," Scarlett heard a new voice say. She turned and drew in a sharp breath. There was a girl in the doorway, a young girl with shining brown hair that grew in a widow's peak above her soft brown eyes. "I'm so sorry to be late," the girl continued. Her voice was a little breathless. She was wearing a brown dress, with white linen collar and cuffs, and an old-fashioned bonnet. She looks for all the world like Melanie, Scarlett thought. Like a soft little brown bird.

"You're not late at all, Anne," said Eleanor Butler. "Come meet Scarlett and have some tea. Anne Hampton—Scarlett Butler."

Anne Hampton was their expert on the Confederate Orphan Home and the school that had sort of grown by itself because there was no place else for the orphans to go. She had graduated from the school last year and now was teaching there.

"How do you do, Mrs. Butler." Anne extended a cold little hand. Scarlett felt it quiver in her own warm one when she shook it.

"Please call me Scarlett," she said.

She's Melly to the life, Scarlett thought. Just as frail, just as mousy, just as sweet—I can tell that already.

The sky was darkening outside the windows, and Eleanor Butler asked Scarlett to draw the curtains. As Scarlett did so, she heard a rumbling of thunder in the distance and then a spattering of rain on the glass.

"Let's come to order," said Miss Eleanor. "We've got a lot of business to do. Everyone take a seat. Emma, will you pour, please? And, Scarlett, we'll need more hot water. Just pull that bell rope, please, my dear. Now, ladies and gentleman, the first order of business is very exciting. I've received a large check from a lady in Boston. What shall we do with it?"

"Tear it up and send the pieces back to her."

"Emma!" said Mrs. Butler. "We need all the money we can get."

Anne Hampton's eyes were glowing with emotion. "I've got nine little girls who I'm teaching to read," she said, "and only one book to teach from. If the ghost of Abe Lincoln came and offered to buy us some books, I'd—I'd kiss him!"

Scarlett saw astonishment on the faces of the other women. But Edward Cooper's expression was something quite different. Why, he's in love with her, she thought. He's really quite attractive if you like the type, sort of slender and dreamy-looking. Not all that different from Ashley, come to think of it.

"We're agreed, then, are we?" said Eleanor. "Emma?"

"We're agreed. Books are more important than rancor. Now, is anyone ever going to bring that hot water?"

Scarlett rang again from her corner, then saw the door opening.

"Did you ring for tea, Mrs. Butler?" Rhett pushed the door wider with his foot. His hands were holding a huge silver tray laden with gleaming teapot, urn, sugar bowl, milk pitcher, strainer and three tea caddies. "India, China or chamomile?" He was smiling with delight at his surprise.

Rhett! Scarlett couldn't breathe. How handsome he was. He'd been in the sun somewhere, he was brown as an Indian. Oh, how she loved him.

"Rhett! Oh, darling." Mrs. Butler grabbed a napkin and wiped her eyes. "You said 'some silver' in Philadelphia. I had no idea it was the tea service. It's a miracle."

"It's also very heavy. Miss Emma, will you please push that makeshift china to one side? I'd be honored if you'd brew your heart's desire. Sally, my beloved, when are you going to let me duel your husband to the death and abduct you?" He placed the tray on the table, leaned across it and kissed the three women sitting on the settee behind it. Then he looked around.

Look at me, Scarlett begged silently from the shadowy corner. Kiss me. But he didn't see her. "Anne," he said, "it's a pleasure to see you. Edward, I can't say the same for you. I don't approve of your organizing yourself a harem in my house." Then Rhett smiled at his mother. "Stop that crying, now, Mama dear, or I'll think you don't like your surprise."

Eleanor looked up at him, her face shining with love. "Bless you, my son. You make me very happy."

Scarlett couldn't stand another minute of it. She ran forward. "Rhett, darling—"

His head turned toward her, and she stopped. His face was rigid, all emotion withheld. They faced one another for a breathless moment. Then his lips turned downward at one corner in the sardonic smile she knew so well and feared so much. "It's a fortunate man," he said slowly, "who receives a greater surprise than he gives." He held his hands out for hers, his outstretched arms keeping a distance between them. His mustache brushed her cheek. He'd like to kill me, she thought.

Rhett's hand clamped like a vise around her upper arm. "I'm sure you ladies—and Edward—will excuse us if we leave you," he said. There was an appealing roguishness in his voice. "It's been much too long since I've had a chance to talk to my wife."

He propelled Scarlett out the door without giving her an opportunity to make her good-byes.

6

*R*HETT didn't speak while he rushed her upstairs and into his bedroom. He closed the door and stood with his back against it. "What the hell are you doing here, Scarlett?"

She wanted to hold out her arms to him, but the hot rage in his eyes warned her not to. Scarlett made her eyes widen in innocence, her voice charmingly breathless. "Aunt Eulalie wrote and told me what you were saying, Rhett—about how you longed for me to be here with you, but I wouldn't leave the store. Oh, darling, why didn't you tell me? I don't care two pins for the store, not compared to you." She watched his eyes warily.

"It won't work, Scarlett. You know you could never lie to me."

It was true, and she did know it. She had to be honest.

"I came because I wanted to be with you." Her quiet statement had a simple dignity.

Rhett looked at her straight back and proudly lifted head, and his voice softened. "My dear Scarlett," he said, "we might have been friends in time, when the memories had softened to bitter-sweet nostalgia. Perhaps we might arrive at that yet, if we are both patient. But nothing more. Go back to Atlanta, Scarlett, leave me be. I no longer love you. I can speak no more clearly than that."

The blood had drained from Scarlett's face. "I can speak clearly, too, Rhett. I am your wife, and you are my husband."

"An unfortunate circumstance that I offered to correct." His words were like a whiplash. Scarlett forgot that she had to control herself.

"Divorce you? Never! And I'll never give you cause to divorce me. I'm your wife, and like a dutiful wife, I've come to your side." Then she played her trump card. "Your mother is overjoyed that I'm here. What are you going to tell her if you throw me out? Because I'll tell her the truth, and it'll break her heart."

Rhett paced heavily from end to end of the big room, muttering curses, profanity and vulgarity such as Scarlett had never heard. This was the Rhett that was only hearsay to her. This was Rhett the rumrunner, habitué of the lowest taverns in Havana, Rhett the lawless adventurer. She watched, shocked and fascinated, until suddenly his pacing stopped and he turned to face her. His black eyes glittered, but no longer with rage. They held humor, dark and bitter. He was Rhett Butler, Charleston gentleman.

"Check," he said with a wry, twisted smile. "But not mate, Scarlett." He held out his opened palms in momentary surrender. "You'll stay here until you want to go. I don't expect it to be very long. You were driven out of Atlanta—miraculously minus tar and feathers." He laughed at the look on her face. "Oh, yes, I know all about your ostracism in Atlanta. But what matters now is that you are here, and I cannot for the moment do anything about it. However, I don't really have to. You'll soon reveal yourself for what you are; then everyone will feel pity for me and compassion for my mother. And I'll pack you up and ship you back to Atlanta to the genteelly silent cheers of the entire community. You think you can pass yourself off as a lady, don't you?"

"I am a lady, damn you. I'll thank you to remember that my mother was a Robillard from Savannah and that the O'Haras descend from the kings of Ireland!"

Rhett grinned. "Leave it alone, Scarlett. Show me the clothes you brought with you." He sat in the chair nearest him, stretched out his long legs and took a cigar from his pocket. "You don't object if I smoke in my room, I hope," he said.

She stared at him, frustrated. "Of course not."

"Thank you. Now show me your clothes. You'd never attempt to win back my favors without an arsenal of new frocks, all in execrable taste. I won't have you making my mother a laughing-stock. So show them to me, and I'll see what can be salvaged."

Scarlett stalked into the dressing room to collect her things. Maybe this was a good thing. She'd try the clothes on for him. That way he'd see her in her shimmy. She quickly unhooked the dress she was wearing and stepped out of the pile of rich fabric. Then she gathered up her new dresses and walked slowly into the bedroom, her bosom half revealed, her legs silk-stockinged.

"Dump them on the bed," said Rhett, "and put on a wrapper before you freeze. It's gotten colder with the rain, or haven't you noticed?" He blew a stream of smoke to his left, turning his head away from her. "Don't catch cold trying to be alluring, Scarlett. You're wasting your time." Scarlett's face became livid with anger, her eyes like green fire. But Rhett was not looking at her. He was examining the finery on the bed. "Rip off all the lace and bows," he said about the first gown. "This one is hopeless. . . . This will do if you replace the gold buttons with black ones." It took only a few minutes for him to go through them all.

"And you'll need some sturdy boots, plain black," he added.

"I bought some this morning," Scarlett said with ice in her voice, "when your mother and I went shopping. I don't see why you don't buy her a carriage, since you love her so much."

"You don't understand Charleston. That's why you'll be miserable here in no time at all. I could buy her this house because ours was destroyed by the Yankees, and everyone she knows still has a house just as grand. But I cannot set her apart from her friends by buying her luxuries that they cannot afford."

"Sally Brewton has a carriage."

"Sally Brewton is unlike anyone else. She always has been. Sally's an original. Charleston has respect—even fondness—for eccentricity. But no tolerance for ostentation. And you, my dear Scarlett, have never been able to resist ostentation."

"I hope you're enjoying insulting me, Rhett Butler!"

Rhett laughed. "As a matter of fact, I am. Now start making one of those dresses decent to wear for this evening."

After he was gone, Scarlett put on Rhett's dressing gown. It was warmer than hers, and she was shivering. She stroked the soft foulard that enveloped her. Strange to think of Rhett choosing such a light, almost fragile-feeling wrapper when he was so solid and strong himself. But then so many things about him mystified her. She didn't know him at all, never had. Scarlett felt a moment of dreadful hopelessness. She shook it off hurriedly and rang sharply for Pansy. The bows and lace had to be picked off the pink gown so she could wear it tonight. She wanted to look especially pretty for Rhett. . . . Scarlett looked at the wide expanse of counterpane on the big bed, and her thoughts made her blush.

RHETT took command of the conversation at supper that night. He recounted his search for the tea service in Philadelphia, transforming it into an adventure, painting deft word portraits of the succession of people he talked to, mimicking their accents and idiosyncrasies with such skill that his mother and Scarlett found themselves laughing until their sides ached.

"And after following that long trail to get him," Rhett concluded with a theatrical gesture of dismay, "just imagine my horror when the new owner seemed to be too honest to sell the tea service for the twenty times its value I offered. For a minute I was afraid I'd have to steal it back, but, fortunately, he was receptive to the suggestion that we amuse ourselves with a friendly game of cards."

Eleanor Butler tried to look disapproving. "I do hope you didn't do anything dishonest, Rhett," she said.

"Mama! You shock me. I only deal from the bottom when I'm playing with professionals. This miserable Yankee was such an amateur I had to cheat to let him win a few hundred dollars to ease his pain."

Scarlett glanced at Rhett often as he talked. She'd never seen him so relaxed and happy and totally at home. I never made a home for him, she realized. He never even liked the house. It was mine, done the way I wanted, not his at all. Scarlett wanted to tell Rhett that she was sorry for the past, that she'd make up for all her mistakes. But she kept silent. She mustn't break his mood.

The candles in their tall silver holders bathed the table and the three of them in a warm, still light, making an island of soft brilliance in the shadows of the long room. The world outside was closed off by the thick folds of curtains at the windows and by the intimacy of the small candlelit island. Love made an airy yet unbreakable web between mother and son. Scarlett had a sudden consuming yearning to be enclosed in that web.

Rhett dropped his napkin on the table and stood. He stepped to Scarlett's side and kissed the top of her head, then moved on to take his mother's hand in his and kiss it. "I'm off now, Mama," he said.

Oh, Rhett, no! Scarlett wanted to shout. But she was too stunned to say anything, even to ask where he was going.

"I wish you wouldn't go out in the rainy pitch-dark, Rhett," his mother protested. "And Scarlett's here. You've barely had a chance to say hello to her."

"It's stopped raining," Rhett said. "I can't waste the chance to ride the tide upriver to the plantation. Scarlett understands that you've got to check up on your workers if you've been away—she's a businesswoman. Aren't you, my pet?" His eyes glittered when he looked at her. Then he walked into the hall.

She pushed back from the table and, without a word to Mrs. Butler, ran frantically after him. He was in the vestibule, buttoning his coat. "Rhett, wait!" Scarlett cried. She ignored the warning in his look when he turned to face her. "Everything was so nice at supper," she said. "Why do you want to go?"

Rhett stepped past her and pushed the door from the vestibule to the hallway. It closed with a click of the latch, shutting off the rest of the house. "Don't make a scene, Scarlett. They're wasted on me." Then, as if he could see inside her skull, he drawled his final words, "Don't count on sharing my bed, either, Scarlett."

He opened the door to the street. Before she could say a word, he was gone. The door swung closed behind him.

Scarlett grimaced—half anger, half unwilling laughter—in grudging acknowledgment of Rhett's cleverness. He'd known what she was planning. Well then, she'd have to give up the idea of having a baby right away, think of something else. Her brow was furrowed when she went back to join Rhett's mother.

"There now, dear, don't be upset," Eleanor Butler said. "He'll be all right. Rhett knows the river like the back of his hand." She had been standing near the mantel, unwilling to go into the hall and risk intruding on Rhett's farewell to his wife. "Let's go into the library—it's cozy there—and let the servants clear the table."

Scarlett settled into a high-back chair, protected from drafts. Mrs. Butler sat with a shawl on her knees, talking about Charleston before the War. Scarlett closed her eyes and inhaled the faint whisper of lemon verbena. She half dozed, lulled by the soft reminiscences of a gentler time. When a disturbance erupted in the hall beyond the door, she was jerked back to consciousness, and she blinked, confused, at the man in the doorway. Rhett? No, it couldn't be Rhett unless he'd shaved off his mustache.

The big man stepped unevenly across the doorsill. "I came to meet my sister," he said. The words slurred together.

Margaret Butler ran toward Eleanor. "I tried to stop him," she cried, "but he was in one of those moods."

Mrs. Butler stood up. "Hush, Margaret," she said with quiet urgency. "Ross, I'm waiting for a proper greeting."

Scarlett's mind was clear now. So this was Rhett's brother. And drunk, too, by the look of him.

Ross staggered toward her. His eyes raked her body, then fastened on her tousled curls and rouged face. "So this is Scarlett," he said thickly. "I might have known Rhett would end up with a fancy piece like her. Come on, Scarlett, give your new brother a friendly kiss. You know how to please a man, I'm sure." His big hands ran up her arms like huge spiders and fastened on her bare throat. Then his open mouth was over hers. Scarlett tried to shove him away, but Ross was too strong.

She could hear Eleanor Butler's voice and Margaret's, but she couldn't make out what they were saying. All her attention was focused on the need to break free of the repulsive embrace and on the shame of Ross's insulting words.

"Ross!" Mrs. Butler hurled the name like a knife. "Ross!" He turned with a clumsy lurch, thrusting Scarlett away.

"I have rung for Manigo," his mother said. "He will help you home. You have disgraced yourself and Margaret and me, and you will not be received in this house until I have recovered from the shame you've caused me."

"I'm so sorry, Miss Eleanor," Margaret wept.

Mrs. Butler put her hands on Margaret's shoulders. "Go home now, Margaret. You will, of course, always be welcome here."

Manigo's wise old eyes took in the situation with one look, and he removed Ross, who surprisingly said not a word in protest. Margaret scuttled out behind them.

Scarlett fell into a chair. She was shaking all over. From disgust, from humiliation, from anger. Why had she let it happen? I should have spit in his face, clawed him blind. But I didn't, I just took it. She had never been so ashamed.

Eleanor leaned over her. "There's so much you don't know." She drew a chair close to Scarlett's, sat in it, only inches away.

Her voice was gentle but insistent, while her hand stroked Scarlett's bent head—comforting, caring. "What Ross did was unpardonable," she said. "But he is my son, and I know the pain in him that made him do it. He wasn't trying to hurt you, my dear. It was Rhett he was attacking through you; he knows that he'll never be able to match Rhett in anything. Rhett reaches out and takes what he wants, he makes things happen, he gets things done. Ross is a failure at everything.

"Ross always drank, but not the way he's been drinking since Rhett came back to Charleston a year ago. Since the War, Ross was trying to make the plantation go, but he never did get a decent rice crop. Everything was about to be sold up for taxes. So when Rhett offered to buy the plantation from him, Ross had to let it go. It was like a dagger in Ross's heart. The heavy drinking started then.

"I love Rhett best, may God forgive me, I always have. I love Ross, and I love my daughter, Rosemary, but not the way I love Rhett, and I'm afraid they know it. But Ross was first with his father, so he didn't care overmuch. Steven cast Rhett out—disowned him because of his escapades—and made Ross his heir. He loved Ross, he was proud of him. But now Steven is dead, seven years this month. And Rhett is home again, and the joy of it fills my life, and Ross cannot fail to see it."

Mrs. Butler's voice broke, and she wept bitterly.

"Miss Eleanor, don't cry," Scarlett said ineffectively. "Don't feel bad. Please, I need to ask you something."

Mrs. Butler composed her face. "What is it, my dear?"

"I have to know," Scarlett said urgently. "You've got to tell me. Truly, do I—what he said—do I look like that?"

"Precious child," said Eleanor, "it doesn't matter a tinker's dam what you look like. Rhett loves you, and therefore I love you."

God's nightgown! She's saying that I look like a whore, but it doesn't matter. Of course it matters. I want to be a lady. She grabbed Mrs. Butler's hands in a desperate grip. "Oh, Miss Eleanor, help me! Please. I need to know what I'm doing wrong, why I don't look like a lady. I am a lady, Miss Eleanor, I am."

"Of course you are, Scarlett. Appearances are so deceiving. But we can take care of everything with practically no effort at all. You have so much vitality, dear child. You mustn't lose it, it's too valuable. We'll simply find ways to make you somewhat less visible, more like us. Then you'll be more comfortable."

And so will I, Eleanor Butler thought silently, welcoming the opportunity to remake Scarlett in the Charleston mold.

7

*T*HE Charleston that had molded Eleanor Butler and drawn Rhett back after decades of adventuring was an old city, one of the oldest in America. First settled in 1682, it had, from its earliest days, a romantic languor foreign to the brisk pace of the New England colonies. Flowers bloomed year-round; the soil was black, rich. Ships from all over the globe anchored in its harbor for cargoes of the rice grown on vast plantations along the rivers; they delivered the world's luxuries for the pleasure of the small population. It was the wealthiest city in America.

Charleston used its wealth in the pursuit of beauty and knowledge; it used its riches also for the enjoyment of the senses. Each house had its chef and its ballroom, every lady her brocades from France and her pearls from India. There were learned societies and societies for music and dancing. It was civilized and hedonistic, a culture of exquisitely refined grace in which incomparable luxury was tempered by a demanding discipline of intellect and education. Charlestonians painted their houses in all the colors of the rainbow and hung them with shaded porches through which sea breezes carried the scent of roses, like a caress. Inside every house there was a room with globe, telescope and walls of books. In the middle of the day they sat at dinner for six courses; conversation was the sauce of the meal, wit its preferred seasoning.

This was the world that Scarlett O'Hara now intended to conquer, armed only with energy, stubbornness and a dreadful need. Her timing was terrible.

Charleston had been an openhanded, openhearted city. Until the War came. Fittingly, the first shots of the Civil War were fired at Fort Sumter, in Charleston harbor. To most of the world Charleston was the symbol of the mysterious and magical moss-hung, magnolia-scented South. To Charlestonians as well.

And to the North. "Proud and arrogant Charleston" was the refrain in New York and Boston newspapers. Union military officials were determined to destroy the flower-filled, pastel-painted old city. The harbor entrance was blockaded first; later, gun emplacements on nearby islands fired shells into narrow streets and houses in a siege that lasted for almost six hundred days; finally, Sherman's army came with its torches to burn the plantation houses on the rivers. When the Union troops marched in to occupy their prize, they faced a desolate ruin. They also faced a decimated population that had become as proud and arrogant as their northern reputation.

Outsiders were no longer welcome in Charleston.

People repaired their roofs and windows as best they could and locked their doors. Among themselves, they restored the cherished habits of gaiety. They danced in looted drawing rooms, where they toasted the South in water from cracked and mended cups. They called their gatherings starvation parties and laughed.

The military occupation and the outrages of Reconstruction tested their mettle, but they held fast. One by one the other states of the Confederacy were readmitted to the Union, their state governments restored to the people. But not South Carolina. And especially not Charleston. More than nine years after the end of the War, armed soldiers patroled the old streets enforcing curfew. Constantly changing regulations covered everything from the price of paper to the licensing of marriages and funerals. Charleston became more and more derelict outwardly, but ever stronger in its determination to preserve the old ways of life. They weren't defeated. Not so long as they stuck together. After their working hours as clerks or laborers, former plantation owners took the streetcars or walked to the outskirts of the city to rebuild and replant the two-mile oval of the Charleston Race Course.

Little by little, by symbols and by inches, Charlestonians were regaining the essence of their beloved lost world. But there was no room in it for anyone who didn't belong there.

THE Market was the place where Scarlett was to begin the life of a Charleston lady. She would have been happier if it wasn't necessary to go so early, at six o'clock. But needs must.

The Market was like a bazaar, an oasis of color and life in the gray mist of predawn. Torches blazed on brick pillars that supported tall, wide arches open to the surrounding streets, illuminating the bright aprons and head scarves of smiling black women and highlighting their wares, displayed in baskets of every size and shape on long wooden tables. It was crowded with people moving from table to table, talking—to other shoppers or to the vendors in a challenging, laughing ritual of haggling that was obviously enjoyed by all.

"Coffee first, Scarlett?"

"Oh, yes, please."

Eleanor Butler led the way to a nearby group of women. They held steaming tin mugs in their gloved hands, sipping from them while they talked and laughed with one another. "Good morning, Eleanor." "Eleanor, how are you?"

"Ladies, I want you to meet Rhett's wife, Scarlett."

All chattering stopped, and all heads turned to look at Scarlett.

She smiled and bowed to each of the ladies as Eleanor introduced her. "Yes, I just love Charleston. . . . Yes, ma'am, I am Pauline Smith's niece. . . . No, ma'am, I haven't seen the art gallery yet, I've only been here since night before last. . . . Yes'm, I do enjoy a game of whist."

In the next hour Scarlett was introduced to more than twenty ladies and a dozen varieties of fish. Then she and Mrs. Butler ran into Sally Brewton at the onion table.

"We need lots of onions for the artichoke pickles we're putting up," Sally explained. She grabbed one of the brown paper bags from the table and began to drop onions into it.

Scarlett watched with dismay. Impulsively she said, "Excuse me, Mrs. Brewton, but those onions are no good."

"No good? How can they be no good? They're not sprouting."

"These onions were dug up too soon," Scarlett explained.

"They look fine enough, but they won't have any flavor. I know, because when I had to run our place, I grew onions. I'll show you what a good onion should be like." Scarlett sorted through the baskets on the table. "These are the ones you want," she said at last. You can figure me for a country bumpkin, she was thinking, but I'm not ashamed that I got my hands dirty when I had to.

"Thank you," said Sally. Her eyes were thoughtful. "I'm grateful. I did you an injustice, Scarlett. I didn't think anyone as pretty as you could have any sense. What else did you plant?"

Scarlett studied Sally's face. She saw the honest interest and

responded to it. "I had a dozen mouths to feed. I know about all there is to know about yams and carrots and turnips. Cotton, too."

"You must have worked yourself to a shadow." Respect was written clearly in Sally Brewton's eyes.

"We had to eat." Scarlett shrugged. Then she smiled. Sally Brewton made her feel good. "It did make me mighty particular about root crops, though. Rhett said one time that he'd known plenty of people to send wine back, but I was the only one who'd do it with carrots. We were at the fanciest restaurant in New Orleans, and did it ever cause a rumpus!"

Sally laughed explosively. "Oh, Lord!" she hooted. "I'd have given my eyeteeth to have been there."

She bought the basket of onions that Scarlett had designated. Then she turned to Scarlett and looked up into her face. "I hope you'll call me Sally and come see me, Scarlett. I'm at home the first Wednesday of the month, in the afternoon."

Scarlett didn't know it, but she had just advanced to the highest level of Charleston's tight-knit, stratified society. Doors that would have opened a polite crack for Eleanor Butler's daughter-in-law swung wide for a protégée of Sally Brewton's.

THAT afternoon Scarlett had indigestion for the first time in her life. Not from overeating. Eulalie and Pauline had upset her. "We're on our way to see Carreen," Pauline announced when they arrived, "and we figured Scarlett would want to go with us."

Carreen! She didn't want to see Carreen. The traitor had given away a share of Tara. But she couldn't say that. "I'd just love to go," she cried, "but I'm not feeling very well." She dropped her eyes. "You know how it is." There! Let them think I'm having female troubles. They're much too prissy-nice to ask any questions.

She was right. Her aunts made the hastiest possible farewells. "You have yourself a good long rest, now," Eulalie said. "And come to our house in the morning at nine thirty. It's a half-hour walk to Saint Mary's for Mass."

Scarlett stared. Mass had never crossed her mind. Ellen O'Hara had been a devout Catholic, and she had done her best to make religion part of life at Tara. But Scarlett had neglected all religious observance for years. She squirmed with guilt. What was she to do? She couldn't think of any way to get out of going to Mass.

SCARLETT did, of course, go to Mass. To her surprise the ancient ritual was strangely comforting. She went to see Carreen, too. The convent and her sister turned out to be two more surprises. Scarlett had always imagined convents as fortresslike places. But in Charleston the Sisters of Mercy lived in a magnificent brick mansion and taught school in its beautiful ballroom.

Carreen was radiantly happy in her vocation, so changed from the quiet, withdrawn baby sister Scarlett remembered that she didn't seem like the same person at all. How could she be angry

with a stranger? And Carreen—Sister Mary Joseph—was so ex-
travagantly glad to see her that it was a positive pleasure to take
tea with her in the lovely formal garden at the convent.

In what seemed like no time at all, Sunday Mass, followed by
breakfast at her aunt's house, and afternoon tea with Carreen on
Tuesdays were welcome moments in Scarlett's busy schedule.

For she was very busy. A blizzard of calling cards had descended on Eleanor Butler's house in the week after Scarlett
educated Sally Brewton about onions.

Sally Brewton's endorsement of Scarlett had been explicit. "The
girl is most lacking in education, and she has the taste of a Hotten-
tot. But she has vigor and strength, and she's a survivor. We need
her kind in the South, yes, even in Charleston. I'm sponsoring her;
I expect all my friends to make her feel welcome here."

Soon Scarlett's days were a whirlwind of activity. After an hour
or more at the Market and a big breakfast at the house, there was
enough time to pay as many as five calls before dinner. Afternoons were taken up by visits to ladies having their "at home"
days or whist parties or receiving callers with Miss Eleanor or
visiting Anne Hampton at the Confederate Home.

Scarlett loved the constant activity. Even more she loved the
attention paid her. Most of all she loved hearing Rhett's name on
everyone's lips. A few old women were openly critical. They had
disapproved of him when he was young, and they would never
relent. But the younger women regarded Scarlett with poorly
concealed envy. They all had stories about Rhett's exploits during
the War, when his sleek dark ship raced through the Union blockade fleet in Charleston harbor like a death-dealing shadow. They
had a special look on their faces when they talked about him, a
mixture of curiosity and romantic imaginings. Rhett was more
myth than man. And he was Scarlett's husband. How could they
not envy her? But oh, how she wished he'd come home!

Because she was so occupied, Scarlett had been in Charleston
for more than a month before she noticed that she was bored. It
happened at Sally Brewton's, the least boring place in town.

"ALL anybody talked about, Miss Eleanor, was clothes. I thought
I'd go crazy I was so bored!" Scarlett collapsed into the chair opposite Mrs. Butler's. Clothes had lost their fascination for her when

she was reduced to four drab-colored frocks Rhett's mother helped her order from the dressmaker. Even the ball gowns that were being made held small interest. There were only two for the upcoming six-week series of balls almost every night. They were dull, too, with hardly any trim. Still, even the dullest ball meant dancing, and Scarlett dearly loved to dance. Rhett would be back from the plantation, too, Miss Eleanor had promised her. If only she didn't have to wait so long for the Season to start. Three weeks suddenly seemed unendurable with nothing to do but sit around and talk to women. How she wished something exciting would happen!

Her wish was granted very soon. It started as malicious gossip that had people laughing all over town. Mary Elizabeth Pitt, a spinster in her forties, claimed that she had awakened in the middle of the night and seen a man in her room. "With a kerchief that hid the lower part of his face," she said.

"If ever I heard wishful thinking," someone unkindly commented, "that's it."

But the following day the story took an ugly turn. Alicia Savage was also in her forties, but she had been married twice and was a calm-natured, rational woman. She, too, had woken up and seen a man in her bedroom. He was wearing a kerchief over his face and the uniform of a Union soldier.

Mrs. Savage screamed. The soldier went through the curtains onto the piazza before her husband reached her room.

A Yankee! Suddenly everyone was afraid.

The next night and the next, the soldier materialized in a woman's bedroom. A delegation of Charleston men went to army headquarters. They were going to begin their own night patrols. If they surprised the intruder, they'd deal with him themselves.

The commandant agreed to the patrols. But he warned that if any Union soldier was hurt, the responsible man or men would be executed. There'd be no vigilante justice.

Scarlett's fears of the Yankee troops—long years of them—crashed on her like a tidal wave. She felt defenseless, helpless, weak. She begged Eleanor Butler to send a message to Rhett at the plantation.

Eleanor temporized. Yes, yes, she'd send word right away—on the very next trip of the boat that brought duck and other game from the plantation.

"But when will that be, Miss Eleanor? Rhett has to come now!"

Eleanor patted Scarlett's hand. "Soon, dear. Besides, everything will be all right now. There are patrols every night."

For a while it seemed the patrols were effective. There were no reports of intruders, and everyone calmed down. Eleanor Butler even tore up the note she had written Rhett.

SCARLETT came in from her round of morning calls. "Where's Mrs. Butler?" she demanded of Manigo. When he replied that she was in the kitchen, Scarlett ran to the back of the house.

Eleanor Butler looked up at Scarlett's rushed entry. "Good news, Scarlett! I had a letter from Rosemary this morning. She'll be home day after tomorrow."

"Better wire her to stay," Scarlett snapped. "The Yankee got to Harriet Madison last night." She looked at the table near Mrs. Butler. "Ducks? Those are ducks you're plucking! The plantation boat came! I can go back to the plantation on it to get Rhett."

"You can't go alone in that boat with four men, Scarlett."

"I can take Pansy. Here, give me a sack and some of those biscuits. I'm hungry. I'll eat them on the way."

"But Scarlett—"

"But me no buts, Miss Eleanor. I'm going."

I SHOULD never have dashed off this way, Scarlett thought, near panic. Rhett's going to be furious with me. And I must look awful. It's bad enough just to show up where I don't belong; at least I could look pretty instead of being squashed along with Pansy amid boxes and barrels on a scabby boat that smells to high heaven. I had it all planned so different.

It began to rain, and long before the oars started a steady pull toward the left bank of the wide river, she was soaked to the skin and shivering, miserable in body and mind.

The bump of the boat against a dock jarred her from her huddled desolation. She looked up through the blur of rain and saw a figure in streaming black oilskins illuminated by a blazing torch.

"Good trip, boys?" Rhett called.

Scarlett pushed against the crates nearest her to stand. Her legs were too cramped to hold her, and she fell back, toppling the topmost crate with a crash.

"What's making that racket? Are you men drunk?"

"No, sir, Mister Rhett," the boatmen chorused. One of them gestured toward the two women in the stern of the barge.

"My God!" said Rhett.

8

"*D*O YOU feel better now?" Rhett's voice was controlled. Scarlett nodded dumbly. She was in the main house of the plantation, wrapped in a blanket, wearing a work shirt of Rhett's underneath and sitting on a crude stool near an open fire.

"When you dry out, we'll eat," Rhett said.

Scarlett pulled the blanket more closely around her. The room they were in was lit only by the fire. It was a large square, with a packed-earth floor and stained walls that had lost most of their plaster. It smelled of cheap whiskey and tobacco juice. In one corner there was a rough staircase with a sagging railing. Scarlett's and Pansy's clothes were draped over the length of it, the white petticoats like ghosts lurking in deep shadows.

"WHY didn't you stay in Charleston, Scarlett?"

Supper was over, and Pansy had been sent to sleep with the old black woman who cooked for Rhett. Scarlett squared her shoulders.

"Your mother didn't want to disturb you, but I believe you should know what's going on. There's a Yankee soldier creeping into ladies' bedrooms at night."

Rhett smiled derisively. "Am I hearing correctly? Maidenly timidity from the woman who drove a wagon through the entire Yankee army because it was in her way? Come now, Scarlett, the truth. Why did you come all this way? Were you hoping to catch me in the arms of a light-o'-love? Did Henry Hamilton recommend that as a way to get me to start paying your bills again?"

"What on earth are you talking about, Rhett Butler?"

"Such convincing ignorance! I compliment you. But you can't expect me to believe that your crafty old lawyer didn't notify you when I cut off the money I was sending to Atlanta."

"Stopped sending the money? You can't do that!" Scarlett's knees turned to jelly. The house on Peachtree Street— Why, it cost a fortune to run. How would Uncle Henry pay the bills? He'd use her money! No, no that couldn't be. She'd given up all her pride, schemed and cheated, worked day and night for her money. She wouldn't let it go. It was the only thing she had. "You can't take my money!" she said in a cracked whisper.

He laughed. "I haven't *taken* any, my pet. I've only stopped adding to it. As long as you're living in my house in Charleston, there's no reason for me to maintain an empty house in Atlanta. Of course, if you were to return to it, I'd feel obliged to begin paying for it again." Rhett walked over to the fireplace, where he could see her face in the light of the flames. His challenging smile disappeared, and his forehead creased with concern.

"Now tell me, in sober truth, is there really a soldier breaking into bedrooms?"

"Rhett, you didn't mean it, did you? You haven't stopped sending money to Atlanta?"

"I should have known you wouldn't be able to think of anything else once money was mentioned. All right, I'll send some to Henry. Now will you answer me?"

"You swear?"

"Yes, damn it, I swear. Now, what's this about a soldier?"

Scarlett sighed with relief, then told him about the intruder.

"You say Alicia Savage saw his uniform. . . ." Rhett questioned her for almost an hour, then said, "Very well, we'll leave tomorrow as soon as the tide turns." He walked to a door and threw it open. "The sky is clear. It'll be an easy run."

Past his silhouette Scarlett could see the night sky and the moon. She saw the mist from the river that covered the ground outside. A billow of mist enveloped Rhett's feet and ankles, then dissipated into the room. He closed the door and turned. Without the moonlight the room seemed very dark until a match flared. Rhett touched it to a lamp wick, and Scarlett could see his face. She ached with longing. He held the lamp high. "Come with me. There's a bedroom upstairs where you can sleep."

It was not nearly as primitive as the room downstairs. The tall four-post bed had fat pillows and a bright woolen blanket. She let the blanket she was wrapped in fall from her shoulders and climbed the steps beside the bed to burrow under the covers.

He stood over her a moment before he left the room. Scarlett smiled, then slept.

THE NIGHTMARE BEGAN AS IT had always begun—with the mist. She was running, her heart pounding in her ears, running and stumbling through a thick white fog. She was cold, as cold as death, and hungry and terrified. Each time it was the same, it had always been the same. And yet it was not the same. For in the past she had been running and reaching for something unnamed and unknowable; now, ahead of her, she could glimpse through streaks in the mist Rhett's broad back, always moving away. And she knew that he was what she was searching for, that when she reached him, the dream would lose its power and fade away, never to return. She ran and ran, but he was always far ahead. She cried out to him, "Rhett . . . Rhett . . . Rhett . . ."

"Hush, hush now. You're dreaming, it's not real." Strong arms lifted her and held her, and she was warm and safe at last.

Scarlett half woke with a start. There was no mist. Instead, she could see Rhett's face bent close above hers. "Oh, Rhett," she cried. "It was so awful."

"The old dream?"

"Yes, yes—well, almost. I was cold and hungry, and I was so frightened, Rhett, it was terrible."

He held her close. "Of course you were cold and hungry. That supper wasn't fit to eat, and you've kicked off your blankets." He laid her down and pulled the blankets up over her.

"Don't leave me. It'll come back."

"There'll be biscuits for breakfast, and country ham and fresh eggs. Think about that, and you'll sleep like a baby. You've always been a good feeder, Scarlett." His voice was amused. And tired. She closed her heavy eyelids.

"Rhett?" He paused in the doorway. "Thank you for coming to wake me. How did you know?"

"You were yelling loud enough to break the windows." The last sound she heard was his warm, gentle laughter.

TRUE to Rhett's prediction, Scarlett ate an enormous breakfast before she went to look for him. He'd been up before dawn, the cook told her.

Scarlett was so content. Rhett had held her, comforted her, even laughed at her. Just as he used to before things went wrong. She'd been so right to come to the plantation.

She stepped outside and looked around her. A soft moan was her first reaction. The brick terrace under her feet continued to her left for a hundred yards. Broken, fire-blackened and grass-grown, it was a frame for a monumental charred ruin. Jagged remnants of walls were all that remained of the magnificent mansion that had been burned by Sherman's army.

Scarlett was heartsick. The plantation—Dunmore Landing—had been Rhett's home, Rhett's life—lost forever before he could come back to reclaim it.

Nothing in her troubled life had ever been as bad as this. She'd never known the degree of pain he must have felt, must still feel a hundred times a day when he saw the ruins of his home. No wonder he was determined to rebuild it. She could help him! Hadn't she plowed and planted Tara's fields herself? Why, I can work with him, she thought triumphantly. We can do this together.

She turned away from the shell of the house and found herself facing a vista unlike anything she'd ever seen. The brick terrace on which she was standing led onto a series of grass terraces that unfolded in perfectly contoured movement down to a pair of sculpted lakes in the shape of gigantic butterfly wings. Between them a wide, grassy path led to the river and the boat landing. The extravagant scale was so perfectly proportioned that the great distances appeared less, and the whole was like a carpeted outdoor room. The lush grass hid the scars of war. It was a scene of sunlit tranquillity, of nature lovingly shaped into harmony with man.

Dunmore Landing wasn't at all like Tara, Scarlett realized. Life here had been lived on a scale and in a style she knew nothing about. No wonder Charleston people thought they were the be-all and end-all. They had lived like kings.

Movement to the left of the lowest terrace caught Scarlett's eye. It must be Rhett. She began to run. Down the terraces—the undulation increased her speed, and she felt a giddy, intoxicating, joyful freedom; she laughed and threw her arms wide, a bird or a butterfly about to soar into the blue, blue skies.

She was breathless when she reached the place where Rhett was standing. "I've never had such fun!" she said, half gasping. "What a wonderful place this is, Rhett. I can see why you love it. And it can all come back, darling, just like the grass. I understand, I really, truly do understand what you're doing."

Rhett looked at her strangely, cautiously. "What do you 'understand,' Scarlett?"

"Why you're here at Dunmore Landing instead of in town. Why you must bring the plantation back to life. Tell me what you're going to do. It's so exciting!"

Rhett's face lit up, and he gestured toward the long rows of plants behind him. "They burned, but they didn't die. It looks as if they were even strengthened by the burning."

"What kind of tree is it?"

"They're not trees. Scarlett, they're shrubs. Camellias. The first ones ever brought to America were planted here at Dunmore Landing. These are offshoots."

"Do you mean they're flowers?"

"Of course. The most nearly perfect flower in the world. The Chinese worship them."

"But you can't eat flowers. What cash crops are you planting? Why, at Tara we put every foot of land to use." She looked eagerly at him, ready to share her hard-earned knowledge.

"You're a barbarian, Scarlett," he said heavily.

Scarlett's words tumbled out in a burst. "Rhett, why do you have to keep acting as though you hate me?"

Rhett sighed. "Scarlett," he said wearily, "since you came to Charleston, you've been backing me into a corner. Crowding me. I want to be decent. But you won't let me."

"I will, I will let you. I want you to be nice."

"Scarlett, you want love. Unquestioning, unequivocal love. I gave you that once, when you didn't want it. I used it all up."

"I was wrong, Rhett, I'm sorry. I'm trying to make up for it."

"Scarlett, there's no making up for the past. Don't destroy the little that is left. Let me be kind, I'll feel better for it. Now go up to the house and tell Pansy to get ready. I'll meet you at the dock."

What had she done wrong? One minute he was full of excitement; then all of a sudden he was cold, a stranger. She'd never understand him if she lived to be a hundred. She strode rapidly up the green terraces, blind now to their beauty.

THE boat moored to the landing was very different from the scabrous barge that had brought Scarlett and Pansy to the plantation. It was a sleek brown-painted sloop, with bright brass fittings and gilt scroll trim. Scarlett settled herself obediently on a cushioned bench in the small cabin, but as soon as Rhett stepped up on deck, she poked her head out of the hatch to see what was going on. The sloop moved slowly along the riverbank for a short distance and then tied up again.

What was all this? As a series of bulky sacks were thrown to a crewman on the sloop, dozens of black men were leaning on picks and shovels watching. Where on earth could they be? There was a huge clearing in the woods with a big pit dug in it and gigantic piles of pale rock on one side. Chalky dust filled the air.

"Cast off," Rhett shouted.

The sloop moved quickly, caught by the fast river current.

Almost immediately Rhett stepped down the short ladder-stair that led to the cabin. He opened one of the small portholes and closed the hatch. "Good," he said, "we've got a following wind and a strong current. We'll be in the city in record time." He dropped onto the bench opposite Scarlett and lounged back, sleek and sinuous as a cat.

"What was that quarry we stopped at?" Scarlett asked.

"That, my dear, was my passport back into the bosom of my people. It's a phosphate mine. There are dozens of them along the river. Phosphate makes the best fertilizer in the world. There are customers waiting for as much of it as we can produce."

"So you're getting richer than ever."

"Yes, I am. But, more to the point, this is respectable Charleston money. I can spend as much of my ill-gotten, speculator profit as I like now without disapproval. Everyone can tell themselves that it comes from phosphates, even though the mine is puny."

"Why don't you make it bigger?"

"I don't have to. It serves my purpose just as it is. I have respectability, and I can spend my time and money and sweat on what I care about. Right now, that's restoring the gardens."

Rhett extracted a cheroot from his pocket and lit it. "Scarlett, I have a serious question to ask you. What would it take to convince you that you should leave me in peace and go back to Atlanta?"

Scarlett gaped at him, genuinely astonished. "You're joking," she accused.

"No, I am not. I've never been more serious in my life, and I want you to take me seriously, Scarlett. I am working harder than

I've ever had to work. I burned my bridges in Charleston thoroughly and publicly. I was one of their own, and I defied everything they built their lives on. Winning my way back into Charleston's good graces is like climbing an ice-covered mountain. One slip, and I'm dead. So far I've made some headway. I can't take the risk of your destroying all I've done."

Scarlett laughed with relief. "Is that all? You can set your mind at rest if that's what's worrying you. Why, everybody in Charleston just loves me."

Rhett drew on his cigar. "I was afraid I'd be wasting my breath," he said at last. "I was right. I'll admit you've been more restrained than I expected. But you're like a powder keg lashed to my back, Scarlett. You could blow up any minute. I want you gone. What will it take, Scarlett? What do you want?"

He really means it, she thought with despair. She had come to Charleston to get Rhett back, and she had not won.

"I want you," Scarlett said with stark honesty.

Rhett was silent. She could see only his outline and the pale smoke from his cigar. She wanted him so much that she felt physical pain. But she sat tall, waiting for him to speak.

"A half million in gold," said Rhett.

"What did you say?" I must have heard wrong. I told him what was in my heart, and he hasn't answered.

"I said I'll give you half a million dollars in gold if you will go away. It's a handsome bribe, Scarlett. Your greedy little heart can't possibly prefer a futile attempt to save our marriage to a fortune bigger than you ever hoped for."

Scarlett needed to think. Was it really a futile attempt? She refused to believe it.

"What about my offer, Scarlett?" Rhett said calmly.

"I need to think."

"Think, then, while I finish my cigar. Think what it will be like to have a king's ransom, all at one time and all yours."

Scarlett began to think with desperate concentration. She had to find a way to stay. She couldn't go away, not for all the money in the world.

Rhett rose and walked to the porthole. The sunlight was bright on his face. How much he'd changed since he left Atlanta! thought Scarlett. Then he had been drinking as if he was trying to blot out the world. But now he was Rhett again, with his sun-darkened skin and his clear eyes as dark as desire. He was every-thing a man should be. She wanted him back, and she was going to get him, no matter what. Scarlett took a deep breath. She was ready when he turned toward her and raised one eyebrow in interrogation. "What's it to be, Scarlett?"

"You want to make a deal you said, Rhett." Scarlett was busi-nesslike. "But you're not bargaining. You're bluffing about cutting off the money you send to Atlanta. You're almightily concerned about being welcome in Charleston, but folks won't have a very high opinion of a man who doesn't take care of his wife.

"The second thing—the money—you're right. I'd be glad to have it. But not if it means going back to Atlanta now. Right this minute I haven't got a friend in the whole state of Georgia. But as soon as people in Atlanta have enough time to forget a few things, I figure I can make up for my mistakes there.

"So I've got a deal to offer you. You stop acting so hateful to me, you act nice and help me have a good time. We go through the Season like a devoted, happy husband and wife. Then, come spring, I'll go home and start over."

She held her breath. He had to say yes, he just had to. The Season began the day after Christmas and lasted for almost eight weeks. They'd be together every day. There wasn't a man on two feet that she couldn't have eating out of her hand if he was around her that much.

"You'd go after the Season with the money, you mean."

"Well, of course, with the money."

"That's not exactly my idea of a deal, Scarlett. There's nothing in it for me. You take the money I'm willing to pay you to leave, but you don't leave. How do I benefit?"

"I don't stay forever, and I don't tell your mother what a skunk you are." She was almost certain that she saw him smile.

"Do you know the name of the river we're on, Scarlett? It's the Ashley River, and it calls to mind that estimable gentleman, Mr. Wilkes, whose affections you once coveted. I was a witness to your capacity for dogged devotion, Scarlett, and your single-minded determination is a terrifying thing to behold. Now you have decided to put me in the elevated place once occupied by Ashley. The prospect fills me with alarm—"

205

Scarlett interrupted, she had to. He was going to say no, she could tell. "Oh, fiddledeedee, Rhett. I know there's no point in going after you. You're not nice enough to put up with it. Besides, you know me too well. So I'm willing to dicker," she said.

Rhett's abrupt laugh was genuine. "I do believe that the real Miss O'Hara has joined us," he said. "These are my terms: You will confide to my mother that I snore, and therefore we always sleep in separate rooms; after the Saint Cecilia Ball, which concludes the Season, you will express an urgent desire to rush back to Atlanta; and once there, you will appoint a lawyer to meet with my lawyers to negotiate a binding separation agreement. Furthermore, you will never again set foot in Charleston. Nor will you write or otherwise send messages to me or to my mother."

Scarlett's mind was racing. "I might agree to your terms," she said, "but not your timing. If I pack up the day after all the parties are done, everybody will notice. Why don't we say I'll go the middle of April?"

"I'm willing for you to tarry awhile in town after I go back to the plantation. But April first is more appropriate."

Better than she'd hoped for! The Season plus more than a month. "Rhett Butler, if you swear you'll be nice for the whole time before I leave, you've got a bargain. If you turn mean, then it's you that broke it, not me, and I won't leave."

"Mrs. Butler, your husband's devotion will make you the envy of every woman in Charleston."

He was mocking, but Scarlett didn't care. She'd won.

9

THAT afternoon, while Scarlett was resting in her room, Rhett carried a wreath of Christmas greens he had brought from the plantation to Alicia Savage. They had known each other well as children, and they talked companionably about the past. "Scarlett's scared half out of her wits about the Yankee bedroom prowler," said Rhett after he and Alicia finished reminiscing. "Tell me what he looked like. I have a theory about him."

"I only saw him for an instant, Rhett."

"That should be enough. Tall or short?"

"Tall. Yes, really very tall," Alicia remembered, and young. The uniform hung so loosely on his frame that it might not have been his at all. Bit by bit Alicia pieced together her memories. Then her words faltered.

"You know who it is, don't you, Alicia?" said Rhett.

"I must be wrong."

"You must be right. You have a son the right age—about fourteen or fifteen—and you're sure to know his friends. I thought it had to be a Charleston boy. Do you really believe a Yankee soldier would break into a woman's bedroom just to look at the shape of her under a coverlet? This isn't a reign of terror, Alicia, it's a miserable boy who's confused about what his body is doing to him. He wants to know what a woman's body is like without corsets and bustles, wants to know so much that he's driven to stealing looks at sleeping women. Poor devil. I suppose his father was killed in the War, and there's no man for him to talk to."

"He has an older brother—Tommy Cooper is the boy's name. His father died at Bull Run. Tommy never knew him. His brother's ten or eleven years older—Edward Cooper."

"It's no wonder, then. I met Cooper at the house. Tommy'll get no help from him."

"Edward is just too much in love with Anne Hampton to see his brother's needs."

"As you like, Alicia. But I'm going to have a little conference with Tommy."

Alicia put her hands on each side of Rhett's face and kissed him softly on the lips. "It's good to have you back home again, neighbor. Good luck with Tommy."

RHETT was sitting on the Coopers' piazza drinking tea with Tommy's mother when the boy came home from school. Mrs. Cooper introduced her son to Rhett. "Mr. Butler is going to take you to his tailor, Tommy. He has a nephew in Aiken who's growing as fast as you are, and he needs you to try on things so he can pick out a Christmas present that will fit."

As soon as they were well away from the house, Rhett put an arm around the boy's shoulders. "Tom," he said, "I have it in mind to teach you a few valuable lessons. The first is how to lie convincingly to a mother. Because I don't have a nephew in

Aiken, and we're not on our way to the tailor. We're going to a house where I want you to meet some friends of mine."

Tommy Cooper agreed without argument. Before the afternoon was over, the boy was looking at Rhett with such hero worship that Rhett knew he'd be saddled with Tom Cooper for years to come.

He was also confident that Tom would never forget the friends they'd gone to see. One of the specialities of the house, which was "for gentlemen only," was the gentle, discreet introduction of young boys to the pleasures of manhood. It was one of Charleston's cherished traditions.

Rhett's lips curved in a smile. Traditions did have their uses. For one thing, there'd be no more Yankee midnight prowler. Rhett went home to have a self-congratulatory drink before it was time to pick up his sister, Rosemary, at the train station.

SCARLETT was on the couch, settled back against the cushions, wishing that Rhett's sister wasn't coming home. She had no idea what Rosemary would be like, and she'd rather not find out. She knew from bits of gossip that Rosemary was born when Eleanor Butler was over forty and Rhett was off adventuring. Rosemary was also plain as a mud fence, and she was an old maid. Now that Rhett had returned to Charleston with his fabulous wealth, Rosemary would have a substantial dowry. But she seemed to be always away, visiting a cousin or a friend, and there was not even a hint of an attachment, much less a betrothal. Rhett was crazy about Rosemary, and Scarlett didn't know what to expect. She was terrified that Rosemary wouldn't like her or that she'd be another Ross. Her brother-in-law's florid letter of apology had done nothing to make her stop loathing him. Ross had left Charleston after the incident and gone to Wilmington. She was glad.

Scarlett tensed when she heard the outside door open a few minutes before suppertime. Rosemary had arrived.

Rhett entered the library and smiled at his mother. "Your wandering girl is home at last," he said. "She's sound in mind and limb, and as fierce as a lion from hunger."

Scarlett looked at the door with apprehension. Why, she's got the same black eyes and hair as Rhett. But it's more the way she is—she just kind of takes over, like he does. I don't like it, I don't like it at all.

Her green eyes narrowed, and she studied Rosemary. She's not really as plain as people said, it's that she's got her hair all skinned back in that big knot on the nape, and she's picked the worst possible frock in that dull browny-green.

"So this is Scarlett." Rosemary crossed the room in four strides. Scarlett stood up, smiling, and tipped her face upward for a social kiss. But instead of touching cheeks, Rosemary stared frankly at Scarlett's face. "Rhett said you were feline," she said. "I see what he means, with those green eyes. I do hope you'll purr at me and not spit, Scarlett. I'd like for us to be friends."

Scarlett's mouth gaped soundlessly. She was too startled to speak. Her eyes found Rhett, and her temper flared. He was lounging against the door, his mouth twisted in sardonic amusement. Brute! she thought. You put her up to that.

"Supper," said Rhett. "I see Manigo coming to announce it."

ROSEMARY'S bumptiousness gave Scarlett a headache. For Rhett's sister was passionately and loudly opinionated and argumentative. She was also a bluestocking, distressingly forthright and totally lacking in feminine wiles and vanity. She was uncomfortable with all men except Rhett; she rejected the conventions of society about how a woman should look and think and behave.

Rhett loved her. He respected her prickly independence, and he gave her the rarest gift of all—his inner self. He was completely honest with Rosemary, talked to her as an equal and even confided the secrets of his heart to her, as he had never done to any other person. She recognized the immensity of his gift, and she adored him. In the fourteen months that Rhett had been home, the overtall, ill-at-ease, innocent spinster and the oversophisticated, disillusioned adventurer had become the closest of friends.

That night, after bedtime, Rosemary tapped on the door of the library where Rhett was reading, then entered and closed the door behind her. Naturally, they talked about Scarlett.

"I want her to go away and leave all of us alone," Rhett said.

"But she's your wife!"

"I left her, Rosemary. She wouldn't divorce me as I offered, but she knew the marriage was over."

"Then why is she here?"

Rhett shrugged. "It's a long, tiring story," he said. And owly, methodically, rigidly unemotional, Rhett told his sister about Scarlett's two earlier marriages, about his proposal and Scarlett's agreement to marry him for his money. He also told her about Scarlett's near obsessive love for Ashley Wilkes throughout all the years he'd known her.

"But if you knew that, why on earth did you marry her?"

"Why?" Rhett's mouth twisted in a smile. "Because she was so full of fire and so recklessly, stubbornly brave. Because she was such a child beneath all her pretenses. Because she was unlike any woman I had ever known. She fascinated me, infuriated me, drove me mad. I loved her as consumingly as she loved him. From the day I first laid eyes on her. It was a kind of disease." There was a weight of sorrow in his voice.

He bowed his head into his two hands and laughed shakily. "What a grotesque practical joke life is. Now Ashley Wilkes is a free man and would marry Scarlett on a moment's notice, and I want to be rid of her. Naturally that makes her determined to have me. She wants only what she cannot have."

Rhett raised his head. "I'm afraid," he said quietly, "afraid that it will all begin again. I know that she's heartless and completely selfish, that she's like a child who cries for a toy and then breaks it once she has it. But there are moments when she tilts her head at a certain angle, or she smiles that gleeful smile, or she suddenly looks lost—and I come close to forgetting what I know."

"My poor Rhett." Rosemary put her hand on his arm.

He covered it with his own. Then he smiled at her, and he was himself again. "You see before you, my dear, the man who was once the marvel of the Mississippi riverboats. I've gambled all my life, and I've never lost. I'll win this hand, too. Scarlett and I have made a deal. I couldn't risk having her here in this house too long. Either I would fall in love with her again, or I would kill her. So I dangled gold in front of her, and her greed outbalanced the undying love she professes for me. She will be leaving for good when the Season is over. Until then, all I have to do is keep her at a distance and outwit her." Then his eyes sobered. "It would destroy Mama if she knew that I'd walked out on my marriage, no matter how unhappy it was. This way, Scarlett will leave, I will be the injured party, and there'll be no disgrace."

"And no regrets?"

"Only for having been a fool once—years ago. I'll have the very powerful solace of not being a fool the second time."

Rosemary stared, unabashedly curious. "What if Scarlett changed? She might grow up."

Rhett grinned. "To quote the lady herself— 'When pigs fly.' "

It was Sunday, and Scarlett was in the library with Rhett and his mother. Suddenly Eleanor Butler dropped her tatting into her lap and said, "I've decided to give Rosemary the grand tour of Europe for her Christmas gift, Rhett. I gave it considerable thought. No one in Charleston has been able to do that for many years, practically since the time you would have gone if your father hadn't sent you to military school instead.

"However, there's no real risk of ostracism. Charlestonians are pragmatic. We recognize that wealth is desirable and poverty extremely disagreeable. And if one is poor oneself, it's helpful to have rich friends. Right now, no one in Charleston can afford to disapprove of the Butlers, because Rosemary might just decide to accept the courtship of a son or brother of the family, and her marriage settlement could solve any number of awkwardnesses."

"Mama, you're a shameless cynic." Rhett laughed.

Eleanor Butler simply smiled.

"What are you laughing at?" said Rosemary as she opened the door. "Rhett, tell me the joke."

"Mama was being worldly," he said. Long united in a pact to protect their mother from the realities of the world, they smiled at one another like conspirators. Scarlett felt shut out, and she turned her back on them. See if I care, Rhett Butler, that you cater to your old-maid sister like she was Queen of the May. And if you think you can make me jealous, you'll just have to think again!

Suddenly Scarlett's eyes glittered with excitement. Jealous! What a fool I've been! Of course, that's it. Why did it take me so long to see it? The name of the river—Ashley. Rhett was crazy jealous of Ashley. He's always been crazy jealous of Ashley, that's why he wanted me so much. All I have to do is make him jealous again. Not of Ashley—heavens no. I'll find somebody else, somebody right here in Charleston. That won't be hard at all. The Season starts the twenty-sixth. That's only six days away! There'll be parties and balls and dancing. This might be snobby old

Charleston, but men don't change with geography. I'll have a string of beaux hanging after me before the first party's half done. I can hardly wait.

SCARLETT held the white camellias Rhett had sent her to the cluster of curls at the nape of her neck and twisted her head to see herself in the looking glass. "Pansy, you'll have to do my hair different. Pile it on top," she said. She could pin the flowers in between the waves, that wouldn't be too bad. Oh, why did Rhett have to be so mean, telling her that his precious old plantation flowers were the only jewels she could wear? It was bad enough that her ball gown was so dowdy.

"Yes'm." Pansy began to brush the long dark mass of hair, eradicating the curls that had taken so long to arrange.

Scarlett looked at her reflection with growing satisfaction. Yes, it was much better to wear her hair up. And her diamond earbobs would show up better. She was going to wear them, no matter what Rhett said. She had to be dazzling, she had to win the admiration of every man at the ball. That would make Rhett sit up and take notice.

A half hour later Scarlett was ready. She took one final look in the tall pier glass. The deep blue watered silk of her gown shimmered in the lamplight and made her powdered bare shoulders and bosom look as pale as alabaster. Her diamonds sparkled brilliantly, as did her green eyes. A wide black velvet bow sat atop the gown's bustle, emphasizing her tiny waist. Narrow black velvet ribbon was tied around her throat and each wrist, and white camellias filled a silver lace bouquet holder. She had never looked lovelier, and she recognized it.

SCARLETT's first ball in Charleston was a surprise. The candlelit ballroom was alive with music and laughter, the age-old, beloved noise of fortunate, lighthearted people enjoying themselves. It was as if the old world—the beautiful carefree world of her youth—still existed, as if there had never been a war.

Her eyes could see the scabby paint on the walls and the spur gouges in the floor, but she refused to notice. Better to forget the War. There was music, and there was dancing, and Rhett had promised to be nice. Nothing more was needed.

Rhett was more than merely nice; he was charming. Unfortunately, he was just as charming to everyone else as he was to her.

Scarlett told herself that she mustn't care, and after a while she didn't. As each dance ended, she was immediately surrounded by men who begged her for the dance to follow. It was not simply that she was a fresh face in a crowd of people who all knew each other. She was compellingly alluring. Her decision to make Rhett jealous had added a reckless glitter to her eyes and a heated flush of excitement to her cheeks. She was being admired and flirted with, and she was in her element.

ANOTHER Sunday meant attending Mass at Saint Mary's with her aunts. Scarlett daydreamed about the moment when Rhett would abandon his stiff-necked pride and admit that he still loved her. For he did, didn't he? Whenever he held her in his arms to dance, she felt like her knees turned to water. Surely she couldn't feel the lightning in the air when they touched unless he felt it, too. Could she?

When Scarlett got back to the Butler house, she was pleasantly surprised to find Anne Hampton there. Scarlett liked being extra nice to the shy young girl who was so much like Melanie. Anne was so openly admiring that her company was always a pleasure.

But Anne and the widow from the Confederate Home who was with her were almost totally occupied with the bowls full of camellias that had been sent down from the plantation.

"Oh, look!" Anne exclaimed. "There's the Reine des Fleurs."

"And a Rubra Plena!" The thin elderly widow cupped her pale hands to hold the vibrant red blossom. "I used to keep mine in a crystal vase on the pianoforte."

Anne's eyes blinked rapidly. "So did we, Miss Harriet!"

"My Alba Plena isn't as healthy as I'd hoped," Rhett said. "The buds are all kind of stunted."

Anne laughed. "You won't see any flowers until January, Mr. Butler," she explained. "The Alba's a late bloomer."

Rhett's mouth twisted in a rueful smile. "So am I, it seems, where gardening is concerned."

My grief! thought Scarlett. What kind of sissiness is that for a man like Rhett to say! She turned her back on them and sat in a chair close to where Eleanor Butler was doing her tatting.

"This piece is almost long enough to trim the neck of your claret gown when it needs freshening," she said to Scarlett with a smile. "Halfway through the Season it's always nice to have a change. I'll be finished with it by then."

"Oh, Miss Eleanor, you're always so sweet. I feel my bad mood going right away. Honestly, I marvel at you being such good friends with my aunt Eulalie. She's not like you at all. She's forever sniffling and squabbling with Aunt Pauline."

Eleanor dropped her tatting shuttle. "Scarlett, you astonish me. Of course Eulalie's my friend; I think of her as practically a sister. Don't you know that she almost married my younger brother? She came to visit after Pauline married Carey Smith and settled in Charleston. My brother Kemper was smitten at once. Everyone expected them to marry. Then he was thrown from his horse and killed. Eulalie's considered herself a widow ever since."

Aunt Eulalie in love! Scarlett couldn't believe it.

"I was sure you knew," said Mrs. Butler. "She's your family."

But I don't have any family, Scarlett thought, not the way Miss Eleanor means. Not close and caring and knowing all about everybody's heart secrets. All I have is nasty old Suellen, and Carreen with her nun's veil and her convent vows. Suddenly Scarlett felt very lonely, despite the cheerful faces and conversation around her.

DURING the days that followed, at the many receptions and balls of the Season, Scarlett recaptured all the giddy excitement of what she remembered as the best time of her life. She was a belle, with men clustered around her. It was like being sixteen again.

But it was not long before the thrills became flat. She was not sixteen, and she didn't really want a string of beaux. She wanted Rhett. He kept up his end of their bargain: he was attentive to her at parties and pleasant. Yet he seemed to be unaware of the admiration she was provoking. Or worse, uninterested.

She had to make him notice! She decided to choose one man from her dozens of admirers. Someone handsome, rich, younger than Rhett. Someone he'd have to feel jealous of.

MIDDLETON Courtney was tall and fair, with sleepy-lidded pale eyes and a flashing smile. He was the epitome of what Scarlett considered a sophisticated man-about-town. And when he bowed over her hand in greeting, Scarlett closed her fingers over his. He looked up from his bow and smiled. "Dare I hope that you'll honor me with the next dance, Mrs. Butler?"

"If you hadn't asked me, Mr. Courtney, it would have broken my poor heart."

When the polka ended, Scarlett opened her fan and fluttered it near her face. "My goodness," she said breathlessly, "I'm afraid that if I don't get a little air, I'm liable to keel right over into your arms, Mr. Courtney. Will you be so kind?" She took his proffered arm, and he escorted her to a bench beneath a window.

Courtney seated himself beside her. Rather close. His eyes moved slowly down her throat to her white bosom. He was as skillful as Scarlett was at the game they were playing.

Very soon the public romance between Mrs. Butler and Mr. Courtney was the most talked about topic of the Season: the number of times they danced together at each ball . . . the time Courtney took Scarlett's punch cup from her hand and put his lips where hers had been on the edge. . . .

Middleton's wife, Edith, looked increasingly drawn and pale. And no one could understand Rhett's imperturbability.

Why didn't he do something? the little world of Charleston society wondered.

10

*T*HE yearly races were second only to the Saint Cecilia Ball as the crowning event of Charleston's social season. Before the War, the Season had included a full week of racing, and the Saint Cecilia Society hosted three balls. Then came the years of siege; an artillery shell ignited a path of fire through the city that consumed the building where the balls had always been held; and the long, landscaped oval track, its clubhouse, and its stables were used as a Confederate Army encampment and hospitals for the wounded.

In 1865 the city surrendered. In 1866 an enterprising and ambitious Wall Street banker named August Belmont bought the monumental carved-stone entrance pillars of the old racecourse and had them transported north to become the entrance to his Belmont Park racetrack.

The Saint Cecilia Ball found a borrowed home only two years after the end of the War, and Charlestonians rejoiced that the Season could begin again. It took longer to regain and restore the fouled and rutted land of the racecourse. Nothing was quite the same—there was one ball, not three; Race Week was Race Day; the entrance pillars were never recovered; and the club-house was replaced by half-roofed tiers of wooden benches. But on the bright afternoon in late January, 1875, the entire population of old Charleston was *en fête* for the second year of racing.

Rhett presented his three ladies with parasols in green and white—the club colors—and inserted a white camellia into his buttonhole. "The Yankees are taking the bait," he told them. "The esteemed Mr. Belmont himself has sent down two Thoroughbreds, and Guggenheim has one. They don't know about the broodmares Miles Brewton hid in the swamp. Their get grew into a mettlesome family, and now Miles has a wonder of a three-year-old that's going to make every big-money pocket a lot lighter."

"You mean there's betting?" Scarlett asked. Her eyes glittered.

"Why else would anyone race?" Rhett laughed. He tucked folded bank notes into Scarlett's glove. "Put it all on Sweet Sally, and buy yourself a trinket with your winnings."

What a good mood he's in, Scarlett thought. He's noticing me, really noticing me, now that he thinks I'm interested in somebody else. It's going to work!

When they entered the grounds of the racecourse, Rhett seated Scarlett between Rosemary and Eleanor. She was barely settled when an excited stir ran through the crowd. The horses were coming onto the track. Scarlett stared, eyes shining. Nothing had prepared her for the bright colors of the racing silks. Gaudy and shining and festive, the riders paraded past the grandstand while the band played a rollicking tune. Scarlett laughed aloud. It was a child's laughter, free and unconsidered, expressing joyful surprise. "Oh, look!" she said. She was so enraptured that she was unaware of Rhett's eyes watching her instead of the horses.

There was an interval for refreshments after the third race. A green tent sheltered long tables of food, and waiters circulated throughout the crowd bearing trays of Champagne-filled glasses. Scarlett took a glass from a silver tray.

"Scarlett." She turned quickly to the speaker. It was Rosemary. "They'll be sounding the bell any minute. Let's go back before the rush starts."

PEOPLE were starting to return to the stands. Scarlett looked at them through the opera glasses she'd borrowed from Miss Eleanor. There were her aunts; thank heaven she hadn't run into them in the refreshment tent. And Sally Brewton, with her husband, Miles.

Scarlett moved the opera glasses from side to side. It was fun to watch people when they didn't know you were looking. Oh, there's Anne Hampton. Does she see me? She's turning this way.

My stars, she's positively glowing. Has Edward Cooper proposed at last? Must be; she's looking up at him as if he could walk on water. Scarlett moved the glasses upward to see if Edward was being as obvious as Anne . . . a pair of shoes, trousers, jacket—

Her heart leaped into her throat. It was Rhett.

He must be talking to Edward. Her gaze lingered for a moment. Rhett looked so elegant. She shifted the glasses, and Eleanor Butler came into view. Scarlett froze, not even breathing. It couldn't be. She scanned the area near Rhett and his mother. Nobody else was there. Slowly she moved the glasses back to look at Anne again, then again at Rhett, then back to Anne. There was no doubt about it. Scarlett felt sick, then searingly angry. That miserable little sneak! She's been praising me to the skies all this time to my face, and behind my back she's wildly in love with my husband. I could strangle her to death with my bare hands!

Scarlett swung the glasses back to Rhett. Was he looking at Anne? . . . No, he was laughing with Miss Eleanor . . . chatting with the Wentworths. Scarlett kept Rhett in view until her eyes blurred. He hadn't looked in Anne's direction even once. She was staring at him like she could eat him with a spoon, and he didn't even notice it. There's nothing to fret about. It's just a silly girl with a crush on a grown-up man.

Scarlett looked at Rhett with yearning naked on her face, the glasses in her lap. He placed his hand under Miss Eleanor's elbow, and they began to climb the steps to their seats. Scarlett waited eagerly for them to arrive.

Rhett changed places with his mother so that she could be

warmed by what sunlight there was, and Scarlett had him beside her at last. She forgot Anne at once.

When the horses came out on the track for the fourth race, the spectators stood up in a tidal wave of anticipation. Scarlett was almost dancing with excitement.

"Having a good time?" Rhett was smiling.

"Wonderful! Which horse is Miles Brewton's, Rhett?"

"Sweet Sally is number five, the very glossy black. The dark horse, you might say."

The pistol shot sounded, and the race began. Scarlett didn't know that she was shouting, jumping up and down, pounding on Rhett's arm. When Sweet Sally won by a half-length, she let out a yell of victory. "We won! Isn't it marvelous? We won!"

Rhett rubbed his biceps. "I agree. It's truly a marvel—the swamp rat over the best bloodstock in America."

Scarlett frowned. "Rhett! Don't tell me you're surprised? You sounded so confident. Didn't you bet on Sweet Sally, too?"

"I didn't bet at all." His jaw was hard with resolve. "When the gardens at Dunmore Landing are cleared and planted, I'm going to begin bringing the stables back to life. I've already retrieved some of the cups that Butler horses won when our colors were known all over the world. I'll place my first bet when I have a horse of my own to bet on."

SCARLETT received small spiritual benefit from Mass the next day. Her focus was on her own spirits, and they were very low. She'd hardly laid eyes on Rhett at the big party given by the jockey club after the races.

Walking back after Mass, she tried to make an excuse that would get her out of eating with her aunts, but Pauline wouldn't hear of it. "We have something very important to discuss with you," she'd said. Scarlett braced herself for a lecture about dancing too much with Middleton Courtney.

As it turned out, his name wasn't mentioned at all.

"We've learned that you haven't written to your grandfather Robillard for years, Scarlett," Eulalie said.

"Why should I write to him? He's nothing but a crabby old man who's never lifted a finger for me in my whole life."

Eulalie and Pauline were shocked speechless. Good! thought

Scarlett. You don't have an answer to that, do you? He's never done anything for me, and he's never done a thing for you, either. Who gave you the money to keep body and soul together when this house was about to go for taxes? Not your precious father, that's for sure. It was me. It's my money that puts clothes on your backs and food on your table. So you can gape at me like a pair of goggle-eyed frogs, but there's not a thing you can say!

But her aunts found plenty to say. About loyalty to one's family, duty and manners and good breeding.

Scarlett set her coffee cup on its saucer with a crash. "Don't preach over me. I don't care a fig for Grandfather Robillard. He was horrid to Mother, he's been horrid to me, and I hate him."

It felt good to lose her temper. There'd been too many times when she'd had to curb her tongue. Too many tea parties, too many receiving lines, too many hours of listening politely to Charlestonians brag about the glories of their fathers and grandfathers. Now she unleashed on her aunts all the disgust she had felt at her own craven desire to please.

"You know I'm right! Grandfather treats everybody like dirt. I'll bet he never answers all the mealymouthed letters you write him. He likely doesn't even read them. I know I never did. They were always the same thing—whining for more money!"

Scarlett covered her mouth with her hand. She'd gone too far. She'd broken three of the unwritten inviolate rules of the southern code of behavior: she'd said the word money; she'd reminded her dependents of the charity she'd given; she'd kicked a downed foe. When she looked at her weeping aunts, she was stricken with shame. "I'm sorry," she whispered, and she began to cry.

A moment passed before Eulalie wiped her eyes. "I heard that Rosemary has a new suitor," she said in a watery voice. "Have you met him, Scarlett? Is he from a good family?"

Scarlett winced. "Miss Eleanor knows his people," she said, "and says they're very nice. Rosemary won't have anything to do with him. You know how she is." She looked at her aunts' worn faces with real affection and respect. They had kept the code. She knew they would never refer to the way she had behaved.

She straightened her shoulders and lifted her chin. "His name is Elliott Marshall. Did you hear that he's a Yankee?"

Pauline and Eulalie gasped.

Scarlett nodded. "From Boston," she said. "Some big fertilizer outfit opened an office down here, and he's the manager. . . ."

She settled back in her chair, ready for a long stay.

When the morning was spent, Scarlett kissed Pauline and Eulalie good-bye at the front door. "Thank you," she said simply.

"Do try, if you can, to come with us to Savannah for Father's birthday. We're taking the train on the fifteenth, after Mass."

"Thank you, Aunt Pauline, but I couldn't manage it. We've already accepted invitations for every night of the Season."

"But my dear, the Season will be over by then. The Saint Cecilia's on Friday, February the thirteenth. I think that's unlucky myself, but nobody else seems to care."

How could the Season be so short? Scarlett had thought there was lots of time left to get Rhett back.

"We'll see," she said hurriedly. "I've got to go now."

SCARLETT was surprised to find Rhett's mother at home alone. "Emma Anson invited Rosemary to dinner at her house," Eleanor told her. "And Rhett is out with the Cooper boy. He's teaching Tommy how to sail." Eleanor suggested a quiet dinner on the card table before the fire in the library. "Just the two of us."

"I'd like that very much, Miss Eleanor." Suddenly it was what Scarlett wanted above all things. It had been so nice to have quiet meals that way, she thought. Before the Season. Before Rosemary. A voice in her mind added: Before Rhett came back from the Landing. It was true, though she hated to admit it. Life was so much easier when she wasn't constantly listening for his step, watching for his reactions, trying to guess what he was thinking.

The warmth of the fire was so relaxing that Scarlett caught herself saying without thinking, "I love you, Miss Eleanor."

Eleanor took her hand. "Dear Scarlett, I love you, too." She sighed softly. "So much so that I'm not going to make any unwelcome comments. I just hope you know what you're doing."

Scarlett squirmed inwardly. Then she bridled at the implied criticism. "I'm not 'doing' anything!" She pulled her hand away.

Eleanor ignored Scarlett's anger. "How are Eulalie and Pauline?" she asked easily.

"They're fine. Bossy as ever. They're trying to make me go to Savannah with them for Grandfather's birthday."

"Good heavens!" Mrs. Butler's tone was incredulous. "He must be over ninety! I know he was in his late thirties when he married your grandmother, in 1820. He was an incredibly dashing man. So handsome—dozens of women were in love with him." Eleanor smiled reminiscently.

"Tell me about Grandmother," said Scarlett.

Eleanor shook her head. "I don't know how to describe your grandmother. Solange wasn't like anybody else in the world."

"Was she very beautiful?"

"Yes—and no. That's the problem with talking about her, she was always changing. She was so—so French. They have a saying, the French, that no woman can be truly beautiful who is not also sometimes truly ugly."

Scarlett couldn't understand what Miss Eleanor was trying to say. "There's a portrait of her at Tara, and she looks beautiful," she said stubbornly.

"Yes, she would, for her portrait. She could be beautiful or not, as she chose. She chose to be anything she liked. She'd turn her slanted eyes on you, and suddenly you'd find yourself irresistibly drawn to her. Your grandfather was every inch the military man, accustomed to command. But your grandmother had only to smile, and he became her slave. She was all the world to him.

"I remember when she decided that she must be surrounded by pink light because she was getting older. He said that no soldier would live in a pink room. It was too effeminate. She said lots of pink would make her happy. It ended up that not only the walls of the rooms inside were painted but even the house itself. He would do anything to make her happy."

Eleanor sighed. "Poor Pierre. When she died, he died, too, in a way. He kept everything in the house exactly the way she had left it. Often you remind me of her," Eleanor added.

"How so, Miss Eleanor?"

"Your eyes are shaped the same, that little upward tilt at the corner of them. And you have the same intensity, you fairly vibrate with it. Both of you strike me as in some way more fully alive than most people."

Scarlett smiled. She felt very satisfied.

Eleanor Butler looked at her fondly. "Now I believe I'll have my nap," she said. She thought she'd handled that conversation very well. She'd said nothing untrue, but she'd managed to avoid saying too much. She certainly didn't want her son's wife to know that her grandmother had had many lovers and that dozens of duels had been fought over her. No telling what kind of ideas that might put in Scarlett's head.

Mrs. Butler closed her eyes and tried to rest. She was profoundly disturbed by the obvious trouble between her son and his wife. It was not something she could ask Rhett about. If he wanted her to know, he would have told her. And Scarlett's reaction to her hint about the unpleasant situation with the Courtney man made it clear that she didn't want to confide her feelings, either. There was nothing she could do except hope for the best. Rhett was a grown man and Scarlett a grown woman. Even though, in her opinion, they were behaving like children.

SCARLETT was trying to rest, too. For the first time in her life she felt old. And very tired. What was the use of love if all it did was ruin things? Anne Hampton was hopelessly in love with another woman's husband. Hadn't she, Scarlett, done the same thing when she was Anne's age? Fallen in love with Ashley and ruined her life with Rhett by clinging to that hopeless love long after she could see—but wouldn't—that the Ashley she loved was only a dream. Would Anne waste her youth the same way, dreaming of Rhett?

What's wrong with me? she thought. I'm brooding like an old hen. I've got to do something—go for a walk—anything to shake off this awful feeling.

"We're going out," she told Pansy.

Scarlett walked for miles—quickly and silently, uncaring whether Pansy was keeping up. Secrets, she thought. Everyone pretends about everything.

SOON after Scarlett got back and Pansy undressed her, she curled up under the covers, trying to hide from her own desperate unhappiness. If only she could sleep, forget everything, escape.

The latch grated, and light poured into the room as the door swung open. Scarlett turned toward it, startled.

Rhett was standing in the doorway, a lamp in his raised hand. It cast harsh shadows on the strong planes of his windburned face and salt-stiff black hair. He was still wearing the clothes he'd worn sailing; they clung, wet, to his hard chest and muscled arms and legs. His expression was dark, with barely controlled emotion, and he loomed huge and dangerous.

Scarlett's heart leaped with primitive fear, yet her breath quickened from excitement. This was what she had dreamed of—Rhett coming into her bedroom with passion overriding his cool self-control.

He strode to the bed, closing the door with a kick. "Get up," he said. His big hand set the lamp down on the table with such force that it rocked perilously. He threw back the quilts, grabbed her arms and dragged her from the bed.

Her dark, tumbled hair fell across her shoulders and over his hands. The lace that edged the neck of her nightdress quivered from the pounding of her heart. Hot blood stained her cheeks red and deepened the green color of her eyes. Rhett threw her painfully against the bed's thick carved post and backed away.

"Damn you for an interfering fool," he said hoarsely.

Scarlett held on to the bedpost to keep from falling. She felt the surging thrill of danger in her veins.

"Don't play the frightened maiden with me, Scarlett. I know you better than that." Rhett's mouth twisted. "How fetching you look, my dear. Bosom heaving and eyes wide with innocence. The pity of it is that you probably are innocent by your warped definition. Never mind the pain you've caused a harmless woman by casting your net over her witless husband."

Scarlett's lips curved in an uncontrollable smile of victory. He was furious about her conquest of Middleton Courtney! She had done it—made him admit that he was jealous. Now he'd have to admit that he loved her, she'd make him say it.

He clenched his fists, visibly taking command of his fury. "Today an old friend—a cousin—drew me aside and volunteered to serve as my second when I challenge Middleton Courtney to a duel. Regardless of the truth of the matter, your good name had to be defended. For the sake of the family."

Scarlett bit her lower lip. "What did you say to him?"

"Exactly what I am about to say to you. 'A duel will not be necessary. My wife is unaccustomed to society and acted in a way subject to misinterpretation, because she didn't know any better. I'll instruct her in what is expected of her.'"

His hands moved rapidly, closed cruelly around her wrists. "Lesson one," he said. Rhett's face was close above her, his eyes boring into hers. "I do not mind if the entire world thinks I'm a cuckold, my dear, devoted little wife, but I will not be forced to fight Middleton Courtney." Rhett's breath was warm on her lips.

"Lesson two," he said. "If I kill the jackass, I will have to leave town or be hung by the military, and that would be inconvenient for me. It would also be the irony of the age to risk death in order to save your little soul from dishonor. Therefore—lesson three: You will follow my instructions for your behavior at all public appearances until the Season is ended. You will distribute your attentions evenly among the beguiled male population, and I will advise you which gentlemen to favor." He released her wrists and thrust her away from him.

Away from the heat of Rhett's body Scarlett felt like ice. Her mind was icy, too, as the things he had said rang clearly through it. He didn't care. . . . He had been laughing at her. . . . How dare he laugh at her in public and revile her to his kin and throw her around in her own room like a sack of meal?

Scarlett lifted her fists to hit him. Rhett raised his palms to ward off her blows, and laughter rumbled low in his throat.

"You can save your breath, Rhett Butler. I'll need no advice from you. I hate your precious Charleston, and I'm leaving tomorrow." She faced him head-on, her hands on her hips, her head high, her chin out. Her body was visibly trembling in the clinging silk.

Rhett looked away. "No, Scarlett," he said. His tone was leaden. "Flight would only serve to confirm guilt. I'd still have to kill Courtney. You blackmailed me into allowing you to stay for the Season, and stay you will." He walked to the door. He looked back at her and smiled mockingly. "And don't try to do anything clever, my pet. I will be watching you."

"I hate you!" Scarlett shouted. She threw the mantel clock, then the fireplace poker, at the closing door.

Scarlett paced the room until she was exhausted. Then she slumped into a chair. As always, when Scarlett was heartsore, she thought of Tara. There was peace there, and new strength. . . .

And Suellen. If only Tara was hers, all hers. How could Carreen have thrown away her share the way she had?

Scarlett's head snapped up. What good was a share in Tara to the convent in Charleston? Maybe they got a third share of any profit from the cotton crop, but how much could that be? At best, thirty or forty dollars a year. Why, they'd jump at a chance to sell to her.

Rhett wanted her to stay, did he? Fine! She'd stay, but only if he helped her get Carreen's third of Tara. Then, with two thirds in her hand, she'd offer to buy out Will and Suellen. If Will refused to sell, she'd throw them out.

A stab of conscience halted her thoughts, but Scarlett pushed it away. What did it matter how much Will loved Tara? She loved it more. And she needed it. It was the only place she cared about. Will would understand; he'd see that Tara was her only hope.

Scarlett yanked on the bellpull. Pansy came to the door. "Tell Mr. Butler I want to see him, here in my room."

She put on a warm velvet dressing gown, then brushed her hair smooth and tied it back with a velvet ribbon. Her bleak eyes met themselves in the reflection of the looking glass.

She had lost. She wasn't going to get Rhett back.

She pressed her hands to her forehead, as if to contain the maelstrom of confused thoughts. There had to be one thing she could concentrate on. All her life she'd been successful if she put all her attention on one goal.

Tara . . . Tara it would be. When she finished gaining control of Tara, then she would think about all the rest.

RHETT's expression was unreadable except for the wariness in his eyes. "You wanted to see me, Scarlett?"

"Yes, I do. I want to offer you a trade."

He said nothing. Scarlett kept her voice cool and businesslike. "You and I both know that you can force me to stay in Charleston and go to the balls and receptions. And we both know that once you get me to one, there's not a single thing you can do about what I might say or do. I'm offering to stay and to act however you want me to act—if you'll help me get something I want."

Rhett sat down and took out a cheroot. "I'm listening."

She explained her plan.

"I have to admire your nerve, Scarlett," said Rhett when she had finished. "I never questioned whether you could hold your own against General Sherman's army, but trying to outwit the Catholic Church might be biting off more than you can chew."

"I'm not trying to outwit anybody, Rhett, just make an honest deal. Are you going to help me or not?"

"I'm willing to help, but I don't see how. What if the mother superior turns you down? Will you still stay through the Season?"

"I said I would, didn't I? Besides, you know everybody in the world, you can always use your influence."

Rhett smiled. "What touching faith you have in me, Scarlett. I know every rascal within a thousand miles, but I have no influence at all with the good people in this world." His dark eyes were gleeful. "I wish you all the luck in the world, Scarlett. Consider it my benediction." He left her room with his composure intact; then he laughed with genuine delight. Scarlett would keep her promise, she always did. With her help he'd smooth over the scandal; then in only two weeks the Season would end, and Scarlett would be gone. He'd be free of the tension she had brought to his life in Charleston, he'd be free to get back to the Landing. There was so much that he wanted to do on the plantation. Meanwhile, Scarlett's bullheaded assault on Carreen's convent would divert him until his life was his own again.

As RHETT had expected, Scarlett's relations with the mother superior were far from simple. "She won't say yes, and she won't say no!" Scarlett complained after her first, second and third visits to the convent. She was baffled and frustrated. Rhett listened with kind, patient attention while she raged, keeping his laughter inside. He knew that he was the only person she had to talk to.

In addition, Scarlett's efforts provided him with fresh delights almost daily as she escalated her assault on the church. She began by going to Mass every morning, confident that word of her devotion would get back to the convent. The mother superior was still noncommittal.

"I believe I'm wearing my rosary beads down to half their size, Rhett!" she exclaimed. "How can that awful woman be so mean?"

"Maybe she thinks this will save your soul," Rhett suggested.

"Fiddledeedee! My soul is just fine, thank you very much."

Wednesday morning in the second week of Scarlett's siege was dark and cold and wet. She walked all the way to the convent through the rain. "Mother Superior left this morning early to go to Savannah for a meeting at the order's school there," said the nun who opened the convent's door. No one knew exactly how long the meeting would last, maybe a week or more.

I don't have a week or more, Scarlett shouted inwardly. She plodded back to the house through the downpour.

The rain stopped in the afternoon. Miss Eleanor and Rosemary decided to go up to King Street shopping. Scarlett went downstairs to the library. Maybe Rhett would be there to provide some sympathy. She couldn't talk to anyone else about her frustration.

"How goes the reformation of the Catholic Church?" he asked, raising one eyebrow.

She burst into an angry account of the mother superior's flight.

"You might go down to Savannah after the Saint Cecilia for your grandfather's birthday," Rhett said. "If it's an important church meeting, the bishop will be there; perhaps you'll have better luck with him."

Scarlett tried to think about Rhett's suggestion, but she couldn't concentrate with him so near. "I'll see," she said, and she left in a rush, before tears began to stream from her eyes. I'm turning into a spineless crybaby, she thought, just the kind of creature I despise. So what if it takes a little longer to get what I want? I will have Tara . . . and Rhett, too, if it takes a hundred years.

SCARLETT felt miserably frumpy in her tired claret velvet ball gown and camellias. Thank heaven the Saint Cecilia was the last ball and the end of the Season.

I would have called anybody a liar if they'd said I could ever get tired of dancing, but I've had more than my fill. Oh, if only everything was settled about Tara! She had followed Rhett's advice, she'd thought about going to Savannah. But she had decided to wait for the mother superior's return to Charleston. Of course, Rhett was going to the Landing. . . . She wouldn't think about that now. If she did, she'd never be able to get through the evening.

The ball was held in a building called the Hibernian Hall. Scarlett smiled at Rhett as they entered. He had told her all about the Saint Cecilia Society—how it was completely run by men, how only men could be members.

When Scarlett reached the entrance to the ballroom, she was overwhelmed by a beauty that was magical, too lovely to be real. The huge room was lit brilliantly, yet softly, by candlelight. From four cascades of crystal that seemed to float high above. From paired gilt-and-crystal sconces on the long side walls. From tall, gilt-framed mirrors that reflected the flames again and again in opposing images. From tall, multiarmed silver candelabra on long tables at each side of the door.

Scarlett laughed with delight and stepped across the sill.

"ARE you having a good time?" Rhett asked her much later.

"My, yes! It really is the best ball of the Season." She meant it, the evening had been everything a ball should be. The governors of the society, it seemed, had filled in the names on all the ladies' cards in advance. Scarlett was partnered by old men, young men, longtime Charlestonians, visiting guests, so that every dance held the tantalizing potential of surprise. And no embarrassment. Middleton Courtney's name wasn't on her card. She had nothing to think about except the pleasure of dancing.

It was the same for everyone. Scarlett giggled when she saw her aunts dancing every dance. There were no wallflowers here. And no awkwardnesses. She saw Rhett with at least three terribly young debutantes, but never with Anne Hampton. Scarlett wondered briefly how much the wise old governors knew. She didn't care. The sixteenth dance was coming up soon. It was reserved, Miles Brewton told her when they were waltzing, for sweethearts and married couples. At the Saint Cecilia, husbands and wives were always newly in love, he said.

So when Rhett took her in his arms and asked her if she was enjoying herself, she said yes with all her heart.

AT ONE o'clock the orchestra played the last waltz, and the ball was over, the Season was over.

The doors to the Hibernian Hall opened, and people came pouring through, talking, laughing, pausing on the porch, reluctant to see the end of the evening.

Scarlett plucked Rhett's sleeve. "Oh, do let's walk home, Rhett. The air feels so good, and the carriage will be stuffy."

"It's a long walk, Scarlett."

"I don't care. I'd love to walk some."

He took a deep breath of the fresh night air. "I would, too," he said. "I'll go and tell Mama."

BOTH SCARLETT AND RHETT HAD taken quite a bit of punch. They were in the condition known as high flown, where everything was somewhat magnified in effect. The darkness was blacker, the air warmer, the memory of the pleasant evening even more enjoyable than the ball itself. Scarlett yawned happily and tucked a hand into Rhett's elbow. Without a word they began to walk into the darkness toward home.

Rhett's tall form in a black evening cape was a part of the darkness. Scarlett tightened her hold on his arm. She could feel the warmth of his body, sense the bulk and strength of it.

"It was a wonderful party," she said too loudly. Her voice echoed, sounding strange to her ears. She laughed softly, then smiled with warm contentment, and in the light of the next streetlamp, she saw that Rhett was smiling, too. There was no further need to talk. It was enough that they were both smiling, walking together, in no hurry to be anyplace else.

Their route took them past the docks. Rhett adjusted his long stride automatically to match Scarlett's shorter one, and the sound of heels on the brick sidewalk became a single clack, clack, clack—testimony of the comfortable unity of the moment.

The streetlamps were widely spaced, and one had gone out. In the patch of greater darkness Scarlett noticed that the stars seemed close enough to touch. "Rhett, look at the sky," she said softly. "The stars look so close." He stopped walking, put his hand over hers to signal her to stop, too. "It's because of the sea," he said, his voice low and warm. "Listen and you can hear it breathing."

They stood very still, and the rhythmic slap, slap of the moving water against the seawall became audible.

Scarlett tasted salt on her lips. "Do you miss the blockade running, Rhett?"

He laughed once. "Let's just say I'd like to be ten years younger." He laughed again, amused at himself. "Sailing gives me the pleasure of being on the water and feeling the wind blowing free." He moved forward, pulling Scarlett into motion.

Scarlett thought of the winglike sails of the small boats that skimmed the harbor, almost flying. "I want to do that," she said. "I want to go sailing more than anything in the whole world. Oh, Rhett, will you take me? You don't absolutely have to go back to the Landing tomorrow. Say you will, please, Rhett."

He thought for a moment. Very soon she'd be out of his life forever. "Why not? It's a shame to waste the weather," he said.

Scarlett fell into step again, smiling to herself. It was wonderful to have something to look forward to.

11

THE costume Scarlett had assembled the next morning was a wide-brimmed straw hat with yards of bright blue tulle wrapped around the crown and tied under her chin in a bow. She had her favorite parasol with her, a saucy, pale blue, flowered silk pagoda shape, with a dark blue, tasseled fringe.

Rhett himself looked like a field hand, she thought, in those beat-up old breeches and that plain shirt. A battered canvas bag was slung over his shoulders.

She sat quietly on the board seat in the stern while Rhett attached the sails to the mast and tested the lines. "Ready?" he said.

"Oh, yes!"

"Then let's cast off." He freed the lines that hugged the tiny sloop to the dock, and the fast-running ebb tide grabbed the boat and pulled it into the river. He sat on the seat beside Scarlett, hooked his elbow over the tiller between them and began to haul up the mainsail. There was a great noise of creaking and rattling. Scarlett stole a sideways look at Rhett. He was frowning in concentration. But he looked happy, as happy as she had ever seen him.

"ARE you ready to go in?"

"Oh, no, Rhett! Not ever." Scarlett was in a transport of delight with the wind and the sea, unconscious of the spray, the water running across her boots, the total ruin of her hat. She had no thoughts, only sensation. The sloop was a mere sixteen feet long, its hull barely inches above the sea. It rode waves like an eager young animal, climbing to the crests, then swooping into the troughs with a dashing plunge that left Scarlett exultant. She was part of it—she was the wind and the water and the salt and the sun.

Rhett looked at her rapt expression, smiled at the sodden foolish tulle bow under her chin. They'd stay out a bit longer. The sun was warm on his back, the wind sharp and salty on his face. It was a good day to be alive.

He lashed the tiller and moved forward to get the canvas bag. The two sweaters he pulled out were stretched and misshapen with age. "Put this on, Scarlett." He held one of them out to her.

"I don't need it. It's like summertime today."

"The air's warm, but not the water. It's February, whether it seems like summer or not. The spray will chill you without your knowing it."

Scarlett took the sweater. "You'll have to hold my hat."

"I'll hold your hat." Rhett pulled the second, grimier sweater over his head. Then he helped Scarlett. Her head emerged, and the wind assaulted her disheveled hair, pulling it free from dislodged combs and hairpins and tossing it in long, dark, leaping streamers. She shrieked and grabbed wildly at it. "My grief, I'm a mess," she shouted.

She had never in her life looked so beautiful. Her face was alight with joy, rosy from windburn, glowing amid the wild dark cloud of hair. She tied the ridiculous hat firmly on her head, then flung out her arms and arched her back in a luxurious catlike stretch. The sleeves of the sweater were so long that they extended past her hands, flapping in the wind.

"Careful, my pet." Rhett laughed. "You might blow away." He freed the tiller and prepared to come about. "Look, Scarlett," he said urgently. "Out there to starboard—to your right."

Scarlett saw a gleaming gray shape curve above the water. "A shark!" she exclaimed. "No, two—three sharks."

"My dear imbecilic child, those are dolphins, not sharks. Hold tight. Maybe we can travel with them. They love to play."

There were seven dolphins in the pod. Immediately in front of the sloop one of the dolphins leaped from the water, bowed its back and dived with a splash back into the water.

Two dolphins broke water ahead. Their graceful leaps made Scarlett clap her hands. The dolphins swam alongside, across the bow, diving and surfacing, blowing, rolling, leaping. The show was enchanting.

Because of it Rhett was careless. He didn't see the dark patch of cloud that was spreading across the horizon behind them. When he looked—too late—over his shoulder, the squall was racing over the water and the sky.

"Get down into the belly of the boat, Scarlett," he said quietly, "and hold on. We're about to have a storm."

She looked behind, and her eyes widened. Without a word she slid down and found a handhold beneath the seat.

Rhett was making rapid adjustments to the rigging. "We'll have to run before it," he said; then he grinned. "You'll get wet, but it will be a hell of a ride." At that moment the squall hit. Day turned to liquid near-night as the clouds loosed sheets of rain on them.

The boat was pitching and yawing. It raced down, down— almost standing on its nose, then up . . . up . . . up. There was a wall of water that was higher than the tip of the mast. The sloop hung on the top, shuddering, for an endless terrifying moment.

"Rhett," she shouted. Oh, God, where was Rhett? Then, just as the sloop dived down the other side of the wave, she found him.

He was kneeling—his back and shoulders straight, his head and chin high—and he was laughing into the wind and the rain and the waves. His left hand gripped the tiller, and his right hand was outstretched, holding on to the line that was wrapped around his forearm, the sheet that led to the fearful pull of the huge wind-filled mainsail. The fight with the wind, the death danger. He's loving this!

Scarlett looked up at the towering threat of the next wave, and for a wild, despairing instant she waited for it to destroy her. Then she told herself that she had nothing to fear. Rhett could manage anything, even the ocean. She lifted her head, as his was lifted, and gave herself over to the wild, perilous excitement.

Scarlett did not know about the chaotic power of the wind. As the little sloop rode up the side of a thirty-foot wave the wind stopped. It was only for a few seconds, but the mainsail flattened and the boat slewed to broadside. Scarlett had no hint that anything was wrong until Rhett shouted, "Jibe! Jibe," and threw his body painfully over hers.

She sensed the rushing swing of the heavy boom close to her head. Then, suddenly, there was a crack, and the thick mast broke and was carried into the sea by the weight of the sail. The hull of the boat bucked, then lifted to starboard and rolled slowly, until it was upside down. Capsized in the cold, storm-torn sea.

SHE'D NEVER KNOWN SUCH COLD could exist. Cold rain pelting her, colder waters surrounding her, pulling at her. Her whole body must be frozen. Her teeth were chattering uncontrollably, making such a noise in her head that she couldn't think.

I'm dying. Oh, God, don't let me die. I want to live.

"Scarlett!" She knew that voice, it was Rhett's voice. And that was Rhett's arm around her, holding her. But where was he? She couldn't see anything through the water that kept hitting her face, glazing and stinging her eyes.

She opened her mouth, and at once it was filled with water. She blew the water from her mouth. "Rhett," she tried to say.

"Thank God." His voice was very close. Behind her. "Now listen carefully, my darling. We've got one chance, and we're going to take it. The sloop is right here; I'm holding on to the rudder. We've got to get under it and use it for protection. That means we've got to go under the water and come up under the hull of the boat. Do you understand?"

Everything in her cried out, No! If she went under, she'd drown. Panic seized her. She couldn't breathe. She wanted to hold on to Rhett, and she wanted to scream and scream—

Stop it. You've got to live through this, and you'll never do it if you act like a gibbering idiot. The words were clear. And the voice was her own.

"Wh-wh-what sh-should I d-d-do?" Her teeth were chattering.

"Take a deep breath and close your eyes. I'll get you there." Scarlett inhaled in jerky spurts. Then she was pulled down, down. In seconds it was over. She gulped air gratefully.

Rhett was gripping her around her waist. If only her hands weren't so cold.

"Take hold of this cleat, I'm going to cut the laces on your boots, Scarlett. Those heavy skirts and petticoats will have to go, too. Just hold on tight. I won't be long."

It seemed like forever.

Scarlett used the time to assess her surroundings. Things weren't too bad—if she could ignore the cold. The overturned sloop made a roof over her head, so that the rain was not hitting her. For some reason the water was calmer, too. She couldn't see it—the inside of the hull was totally dark—but she knew it was so.

She felt Rhett's touch on her foot; then his hand was at her waist. Suddenly a tremendous weight slid down her legs, and her shoulders bobbed up out of the water. She cried out in surprise.

Then Rhett burst through the water. He was very close to her. "How do you feel?" he asked.

"Frozen nearly to death, if you really want to know."

"Now I'm going to cut the laces on your corset, Scarlett. You can't breathe easily in that cage." There was an embarrassing intimacy in the movement of his hands under the sweater; it had been years since he had last put his hands on her body.

"Now breathe deep," said Rhett when he pulled the cut corset away. "Women today never learn how to breathe. Fill your lungs all the way. I'm rigging a support for us with some line I cut. You'll be able to turn loose that cleat when I'm done and massage your hands and arms. Keep breathing. It'll warm up your blood."

Scarlett tried to do what Rhett said, but her arms felt terribly heavy. It was much easier just to let her body rest in the harness-like rope support under her arms and rise and fall with the waves. She was feeling very sleepy. . . .

"Scarlett!" Rhett's voice was very loud. "Scarlett! You cannot go to sleep. You've got to keep moving. Kick your feet. Kick me if you want to, but move your legs." He began to rub her shoulders vigorously, then her arms.

Scarlett closed her eyes. She felt very tired.

With no warning Rhett slapped her face so hard that her head jerked backward. She came full awake, shocked and angry. "How dare you, Rhett Butler."

"That's better," said Rhett harshly. "If you let yourself give in to the cold, Scarlett, you'll die. I know you want to sleep, but that's the sleep of death. And I will not allow you to die."

Scarlett was aware of the paralyzing cold again as Rhett rubbed life back into her flesh. "Are we going to get out of this?" she asked without emotion. She tried to move her legs.

"Of course we are. The incoming tide is carrying us ashore." Nothing in Rhett's voice revealed his knowledge that gale-force winds would make all normal tidal activity meaningless. The storm might be carrying them out of the harbor into the Atlantic Ocean.

"How long before we get there?" Scarlett's tone was querulous.

"I don't know," Rhett answered. "You'll need all your courage, Scarlett."

"I don't need courage as much as something to eat," she said.

"Scarlett, my pet, your gluttony may be the saving of us. I'd forgotten all about the bag with the rum and hardtack. It's stowed under the bow. Pray it's still there."

THE rum spread life-restoring tentacles of warmth through Scarlett. Rhett put his arms around her and held her close to his body to share its warmth. She was so tired. If only she could rest her head against Rhett and sleep. Her head drooped.

Rhett shook her. "Scarlett, do you hear me? Scarlett! You can't give up now, my darling. We're very near shore. Come on. Let me see some of that gumption of yours. Hold up your head, it's almost over."

"So cold . . ."

"Damn you for a quitter, Scarlett O'Hara! I should have let Sherman get you in Atlanta. You weren't worth saving."

The words registered in her fading consciousness, and her head lifted to meet the dimly sensed challenge.

"Take a deep breath," Rhett commanded. "We're going in." He dived under the water, with her struggling body held close. They surfaced outside the hull, near a line of tall, cresting combers. "Almost there," Rhett gasped. He bent one arm around Scarlett's neck and held her head in his hand while he swam expertly through a breaking wave and used its power to carry them into the shallows.

A thin rain was falling. Rhett rose unsteadily to his feet and stumbled forward onto the beach, clasping Scarlett's limp form to him. He ran clumsily through the sand to a bowllike area sheltered from the gusting winds. There he gently placed Scarlett's body on the soft sand.

His voice broke as he called Scarlett's name over and over again while he tried to bring life into her chilled whiteness by rubbing every part of her with his two hands and slapping her cheeks softly and urgently.

When her eyes opened, their color looked as strong as emeralds. Rhett shouted in primitive triumph.

"Land," she said. And she began to cry in gasping sobs.

Rhett put one arm under her shoulders and lifted her into the protection of his bent, crouching body. With his free hand he touched her hair, her cheeks, mouth, chin. "My darling, my life. I thought I'd lost you. I thought I'd killed you. I thought— Oh, Scarlett, you're alive. Don't cry, my dearest, it's all over. You're safe. It's all right. Everything—" He kissed her forehead, her throat, her cheeks. Scarlett's pale skin warmed with color, and she turned her head to meet his kisses with her own.

And there was no cold, no rain, no weakness—only the burning

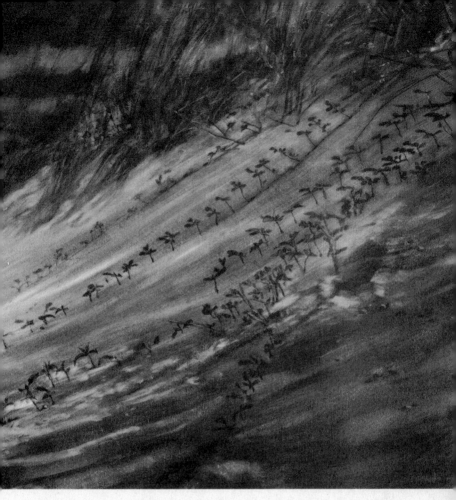

of Rhett's lips on her lips, on her body. And the pounding of her
heart in her throat against his lips, the strong beat of his heart
beneath her palms when she tangled her fingers in the thick,
curling hair on his chest.

Yes! I did remember it, it wasn't a dream. Yes, this is the dark
swirling that draws me in and closes out the world and makes me
alive, so alive. "Yes!" she shouted again and again, meeting
Rhett's passion with her own. Until in the swirling, spiraling
rapture there were no longer words or thoughts, only a union
beyond mind, beyond time, beyond the world.

HE LOVES ME! WHAT A FOOL I was to doubt what I knew.

Scarlett opened her eyes. Rhett was sitting beside her, his arms wrapped around his knees. Why, it's pouring rain. We'll have to find some shelter before we make love again. She reached out and traced Rhett's spine with her fingernails.

He jerked away as if she'd burned him, turning to face her, then springing to his feet. She couldn't read his expression.

"I didn't want to wake you," he said. "I'm going to look for a place to dry out and build a fire. There are shacks on all these islands."

"I'll go with you." Scarlett struggled to get up. Rhett held his hand out to help her rise, and she clasped it eagerly.

THE cottages built by Charlestonians on the nearby islands were retreats from the summer's heat. They were no more than shacks with kitchen fireplaces—perfect shelter for shipwreck survivors.

Rhett broke open the door to the cottage with a single kick. Scarlett followed him inside. Why was he so silent? He'd hardly said a word to her, not even when he was carrying her in his arms through a thicket at the base of the sand dunes. I want him to talk, she thought, I want to hear him saying how much he loves me.

He found a worn patchwork quilt in a cupboard. "Take off those wet things and wrap up in this," he said. He tossed the quilt onto her lap. "I'll start a fire."

Scarlett dropped her pantalets on top of the soaked sweater and wrapped herself in the quilt. She was dry for the first time in hours, but she began to shiver. She moved to the fireplace, where a fire leaped into crackling life. It lit Rhett's brooding face.

"We're only a couple of miles from Fort Moultrie," he said. "I'll go get help." He walked into the small pantry.

"Bother Fort Moultrie!" Scarlett wished he'd stop rooting around in the pantry. How could she talk to him when he was in there?

Rhett emerged holding a bottle of whiskey and two cups. "I'll pour us a drink," he said with a brief smile.

"I don't want a drink. I want—"

He interrupted before she could tell him what she wanted. "I need a drink," he said. He poured the cup half full, drank it in one long swallow, then shook his head. "No wonder they left it here; it's real rotgut. Still . . ." He poured again.

Scarlett watched him with a look of amused indulgence. Poor

darling, how nervous he is. When she spoke, her voice was heavy with loving patience. "You don't have to be so skittery, Rhett. It's not like you compromised me or anything. We're two married people who love each other, that's all."

Rhett stared at her over the rim of the cup, then put it carefully down on the table. "Scarlett, what happened out there had nothing to do with love. It was a celebration of survival, that's all. You see it after every battle in wartime. The men who don't get killed fall on the first woman they see and prove they're still alive by using her body. In this case you used mine, too, because you'd narrowly escaped dying. It had nothing to do with love."

The harshness of his words took Scarlett's breath away.

But then she remembered his hoarse voice in her ear, the words "my darling," "my life," "I love you" repeated a hundred times. No matter what Rhett might say, he loved her. She knew it in the innermost center of her soul. He's still afraid that I don't really love him! That's why he won't admit how much he loves me.

She began to move toward him. "You can say anything you like, Rhett, but it won't change the truth. I love you, and you love me, and we made love to prove it to each other."

Rhett laughed harshly. "A primitive, hasty coupling should never be confused with love."

Scarlett put a hand to her face and wiped away her tears. She was very close to him now. "You do love me," she sobbed. The quilt fell to the floor when she let go of it to reach out to Rhett. "Take me in your arms and tell me you don't love me, and then I'll believe it."

Rhett's hands abruptly caught her head, and he kissed her with bruising, possessive strength. Scarlett's arms closed behind his neck as his hands moved down her throat and her shoulders, and she gave herself up to abandonment.

But Rhett's fingers suddenly closed around her wrists, and he pried her arms apart, away from his neck, away from him.

"Why?" she cried. "You want me."

He cast her away, releasing her wrists and stumbling backward. "Yes, I do want you, and you're a poison in my blood, Scarlett, a sickness of my soul. I know what happens to an addict. He becomes enslaved, then destroyed. It almost happened to me, but I won't risk it again. I won't destroy myself for you." He crashed through the door and out into the storm.

The icy wind howled through the open door. Scarlett grabbed up the quilt, wrapped it around her bare skin. It took all her strength to close the door. She had very little strength left.

She curled up in front of the fire. She was tired, so very tired. She slid into a sleep so profound that it was more nearly coma.

"EXHAUSTION," said the army doctor Rhett had brought back from Fort Moultrie, "and exposure. It's a miracle your wife isn't dead, Mr. Butler. Wrap her in those blankets, and let's get her back to the fort." Rhett swaddled Scarlett's limp body quickly and lifted her in his arms.

Scarlett's eyes opened. Her clouded mind registered the blue uniforms around her; then her eyes rolled back in her head. "Better hurry," the doctor said, "she's slipping away."

At the fort, Scarlett was given sweetened milk with laudanum, and she slept fitfully. She was dreaming disjointed fragments of her memories and fears. There was the never-ending desperate hunger of the bad days at Tara. And Yankee soldiers coming closer to Atlanta. Her mother passed through her dream, and Gerald O'Hara jumped a fence, then another, then fence after fence into infinity.

Scarlett heard voices.

"The bad dreams are over now, Scarlett. You're going to be well in no time." Anne Hampton's eyes were shining with earnestness.

Eleanor Butler's face appeared over Anne's shoulder. "We've come to take you home, my dear," she said.

Scarlett couldn't believe it was still daytime, the same day that she'd left the house on the Battery in a straw hat to go sailing. "Where is Rhett? Why isn't he taking me home?"

Anne spoke quietly. Rhett had waited until the doctor said that Scarlett was out of danger; then he'd taken the ferry to Charleston to set his mother's mind at rest.

"I wouldn't let Rhett go out again," added Mrs. Butler. "I told Manigo to put him straight to bed. He was blue with cold."

SCARLETT was so tired when they arrived at the house that she fell again into a deep sleep. There were no nightmares this time. She knew that Rhett was only a few steps away. She slept for fourteen strength-restoring hours.

She saw the flowers the minute she woke up. Hothouse roses.

There was an envelope propped against the vase. Scarlett reached greedily for it.

His bold handwriting was starkly black on the cream-colored paper. Scarlett touched it lovingly before she began to read:

> There is nothing that I can say about what happened yesterday except that I am profoundly ashamed and sorry to have been the cause of such great pain and danger for you.
>
> Your courage and valiant spirits were truly heroic, and I shall always regard you with admiration and respect.
>
> I regret bitterly all that occurred after we escaped from the long ordeal. I said things to you that no man should say to a woman, and my actions were reprehensible.
>
> I cannot, however, deny the truth of anything I said. I must not and will not ever see you again.
>
> According to our agreement, you have the right to remain at my mother's house until April. I will visit neither Charleston nor Dunmore Landing until I receive information that you have returned to Atlanta. You cannot find me, Scarlett. Don't try.
>
> The cash settlement I promised will be transferred to you immediately in care of your uncle Henry Hamilton.
>
> I ask you to accept my sincere apologies for everything about our lives together. It was not meant to be. I wish you a happier future.
>
> Rhett

Scarlett stared at the letter, at first too shocked to hurt. Then too angry. Finally she tore the heavy paper slowly into shreds, talking as she destroyed the thick dark words. "Not this time you don't, Rhett Butler. You ran away from me that time in Atlanta after you made love to me. And I drooped around, lovesick, waiting for you to come back. Well, now I know a lot more than I did then. I know you can't live without me. No man could make love to a woman the way you made love to me and then never see her again. You'll come back, just like you came back before. But you won't find me waiting. You'll have to come find me. Wherever I am."

She slid out of bed and ran for the bellpull. Pansy'd better come quick. I want to be packed and at the station by ten of twelve, in time for the train to Savannah.

"Morning, Miss Scarlett. It's mighty fine to see you looking so fit after what happen—"

"Stop that babbling and get out my valises." Scarlett paused. "I'm going to Savannah. It's my grandfather's birthday."

She'd meet her aunts at the depot. And tomorrow she'd find the mother superior and make her talk to the bishop. No point in going home to Atlanta without the deed to Tara in her hand.

"I WONDERED what all the fuss was about," said Rosemary. She eyed Scarlett's fashionable clothes with curiosity. "Are you going someplace?"

"Where is Miss Eleanor? I want to tell her good-bye."

"She's already left for church."

Scarlett looked at the clock. She hadn't much time. The hackney was waiting outside. She dashed into the library and grabbed paper and pen. She scrawled a few sentences, saying that she was going to Savannah for her grandfather's birthday and was sorry to miss seeing Eleanor before she left. "Rhett will explain everything," she added. "I love you."

"Please give this to your mother," she said to Rosemary. "I must hurry. Good-bye."

"Good-bye, Scarlett," said Rhett's sister. She watched Scarlett and her maid and her luggage move off down the street. Rhett hadn't been so well organized when he departed late the night before. She had begged him not to go, because he'd looked so unwell. But he had kissed her good-bye and set off. It wasn't hard to figure out that somehow Scarlett was driving him away.

With slow, deliberate movements Rosemary struck a match and burned Scarlett's note. "Good riddance," she said aloud.

12

SCARLETT clapped her hands with delight when the hackney pulled up in front of Grandfather Robillard's house, in Savannah. It was pink, just like Miss Eleanor had said.

Scarlett hurried up the steps and through the opened door. Her aunts and Pansy could see to the luggage, she was dying with curiosity about the inside of the house.

Yes, it was pink everywhere—the hall, the drawing room—pink, with shiny white woodwork and columns, all trimmed with glimmering gilt. Everything looked perfect, too, not peeling and shabby like the houses in Charleston and Atlanta. What a perfect place to be when Rhett came after her. He'd see that her family was every bit as important and impressive as his.

Rich, too. Her eyes moved rapidly, assessing the value of the meticulously maintained furnishings. The old skinflint! Grandfather never sent a penny to help me after the War, and he doesn't do a thing for the aunts, either.

Scarlett prepared for battle. Her aunts were terrified of their father, but she wasn't. Now that she had taken her life back into her own hands, she felt vibrant with strength. She coolly removed her hat and her fur cape and her apple-green kid gloves, and dropped them onto a marble-topped console in the hall.

But when a basso voice bellowed, "Jerome!" from the rear of the house, she felt her palms grow damp.

The imposing black manservant who had admitted her now gestured Scarlett and her aunts toward the open door at the end of the hall. The bedroom had formerly been a spacious parlor, and it was crowded with all the parlor furniture, plus a massive four-posted bed. Pierre Robillard was in the bed, sitting erect against a mass of huge pillows, glaring at his visitors.

"Hello, Grandfather," Scarlett said. "I've come to see you for your birthday. It's Scarlett, Ellen's daughter."

"I haven't lost my memory," said the old man. His strong voice belied his fragile body.

Scarlett bit her tongue to keep silent. No wonder Mother was so happy to have Pa take her away from home!

"Et vous, mes filles. Qu'est-ce que vous voulez cette fois?" Pierre Robillard growled at his daughters. Eulalie and Pauline rushed to the bedside, both speaking at once.

My grief! They're talking French! What on earth am I doing here? Scarlett sank down onto a gold brocade sofa, wishing she was someplace—anyplace—else.

Finally Pauline came over and whispered in Scarlett's ear. "Père wants us to leave now. Say good night, and come with me."

THE next morning after breakfast, Eulalie and Pauline took Scarlett into each of the rooms on the first floor, talking eagerly about the parties and receptions they had seen in their youth. Scarlett had felt isolated in Charleston's web of intermarried generations. It was good to be in the house where her mother had been born and reared, in a city where she was part of the web.

"You must have some cousins in Savannah," she said to the aunts. "Can I meet them?"

Pauline and Eulalie looked confused. Cousins? There were the Prudhommes, their mother's family. But only one very old gentleman was in Savannah, the widower of their mother's sister. The rest of the family had moved to New Orleans many years ago. "Père had lots of cousins in France, brothers, too—two of them," Pauline explained. "But he was the only one to come to America."

Eulalie broke in. "But we have many friends in Savannah, Scarlett. You can meet them. We'll be paying calls today."

THE next day Scarlett sent a telegram to her uncle Henry, giving her address in Savannah. She hesitated, then added a question. Had Rhett transferred any money to her? His letter said he was sending the half million.

The letter—it couldn't be true. Rhett was only bluffing when he wrote all those hurtful things. He'd come after her. It would be harder for him to swallow his pride than it would for any other man, but he'd come. He had to. He couldn't do without her. Especially not after what had happened on the beach. . . .

Scarlett paid for the telegram and listened attentively when the telegraph operator gave her directions to the Convent of the Sisters of Mercy. Then she set off at such a rapid pace that Pansy almost had to run to keep up. While she was waiting for Rhett to come for her, she should have just enough time to track down Carreen's mother superior.

Savannah's Convent of the Sisters of Mercy was a big white building, with a cross over its tall front door. The elderly nun who opened the door for Scarlett said, yes, Charleston's mother superior was there. No, she couldn't see Mrs. Butler right now. There was a meeting in progress. No, she didn't know how long it would last. Perhaps Mrs. Butler would like a tour of the new cathedral. After that, perhaps the mother superior could be sent a message.

Scarlett was about to say that she'd simply come back later, when the nun's words gave her an idea. They were building a new cathedral, were they? That cost money. Maybe her offer to buy back Carreen's share of Tara would be looked on more favorably here than in Charleston. Suppose she offered to buy a stained-glass window in the new cathedral in exchange for Carreen's share of Tara?

She smiled. "I'd be honored to see the cathedral, Sister."

SCARLETT looked up at the soaring twin spires of the handsome Gothic-design cathedral. The workmen on the scaffolding that surrounded the nearly completed towers looked small and nimble. Her pulse was quickened by the organized hubbub on the ground, sounds of hammering, sawing and especially the familiar resiny smell of fresh-cut lumber. She heard barely a word of the descriptive wonders outlined by the young priest who was her escort.

"Begging your pardon, Father." The speaker was a huge man with a red face, wearing a red shirt whitened by mortar dust. "If you could be saying a small blessing on the work, Father? The lintel to the Chapel of the Sacred Heart was set not an hour ago."

Why, he sounds just like Pa at his most Irish. Scarlett bowed her head for the blessing, as did the groups of workmen. Her eyes smarted from the quick tears for her father that she blinked away.

I'll go see Pa's brothers, she decided. No matter that they must be about a hundred years old, Pa would want me to say hello at least.

She walked with the priest back to the convent and to another placid refusal by the elderly nun when she asked to see the mother superior. Scarlett kept her temper, but her eyes were dangerously bright. "Tell her I'll be back this afternoon," she said.

DURING dinner Pauline asked Scarlett where she had been that morning. When Scarlett reported that she'd been to the cathedral, Pauline put her finger to her lips. Père, she said, was, unfortunately, extremely opposed to Roman Catholicism. He got very angry about the church. That was the reason she and Eulalie always left Charleston after Mass to come to Savannah and left Savannah on Saturday to return to Charleston. This year had a particular difficulty; because Easter was so early, they would be in Savannah for Ash Wednesday. Naturally they had to attend Mass, and they could leave the house early and unobserved. But how could they keep their father from seeing the ash on their foreheads when they returned to the house?

"Wash your face," said Scarlett impatiently, thereby revealing her ignorance and the recent date of her return to religion. She dropped her napkin on the table. "I've got to be off," she said briskly. "I . . . I'm going to visit my O'Hara uncles and aunts." She didn't want anyone to know that she was trying to buy the convent's share of Tara. Especially not her aunts, they gossiped too much. Why, they might even write to Suellen. She smiled sweetly. "What time do we leave in the morning for Mass?" She'd be sure to mention it to the mother superior. No need to let on that she'd forgotten all about Ash Wednesday.

What a bother it was that she'd left her rosary in Charleston. Oh, well, she could buy a new one at her O'Hara uncles' store. If she remembered correctly, they had everything in there from bonnets to plows.

SCARLETT was trying to remember where her uncles' store was, and having no luck. Maybe I'll just forget about going to see them. They don't deserve any visits from me after the way they neglected me all these years, she thought, ignoring the letters from Savannah that she'd never answered, until finally they stopped coming.

She was about to consign her father's brothers and their wives to oblivion when she looked at the storefronts on the other side of Broughton Street—Savannah's place to shop—and saw the bold gilt letters that spelled out O'HARA. "Come on," she said to Pansy. And she plunged into the tangled traffic that filled the busy street.

The O'Hara store was more than twice the size of Scarlett's store, in Atlanta, and she looked around enviously. "I'd like to see Mr. O'Hara, if you please," she said to the tall, aproned man behind the counter.

"I'm Mr. O'Hara. How might I be of service to you?" His voice had just a hint of brogue in it.

Scarlett explained hurriedly that she was looking for an elderly Mr. O'Hara, Mister Andrew or Mister James.

"I'm their nephew."

"Oh. Then you must be my cousin. I'm Katie Scarlett, Gerald's daughter. From Atlanta." Scarlett held out both her hands. A cousin! A big, strong, not-an-old-man cousin of her own. She felt as if she'd just been given a surprise present.

"Jamie O'Hara, that's me," he said with a laugh, taking her hands in his. "At your service. And what a gift you are to a weary businessman, to be sure. Pretty as a sunrise. Tell me now, how do you come to be here? Come—let me get you a chair." Scarlett forgot all about the convent and the mother superior. And about Pansy, too, who settled herself on a low stool in the corner.

Jamie O'Hara returned from the back room with a chair for Scarlett. There were four customers waiting to be served. In the next half hour more and more came in, so there was no chance for him to say a word to Scarlett. At last there was a brief moment to talk. "Uncle James will be longing to see you," he said. "He's an old gentleman, but still active enough. His wife died, God rest her soul, and Uncle Andrew and his wife as well. Uncle James lives in the house with me and my wife and children. It's not far from here. Will you come to tea this afternoon and see them all? My son Daniel will be back soon from making deliveries, and I'll walk you to the house. We're celebrating my daughter Patricia's birthday today. All the family will be there."

Scarlett said she'd love to go to tea. Her father had eight brothers, and Scarlett wondered which of them was Jamie's father. No matter, she'd find out at the birthday party.

IN THE daylight of the open street, Scarlett looked up at her cousin Jamie with carefully concealed curiosity. He was a middle-aged man, running to weight and softness. He had the dark, curly hair and blue eyes and round, florid face of the O'Haras. And he wasn't a gentleman. Scarlett couldn't specify how she knew that, but it was as clear as glass. Maybe there was something wrong with his clothes. Whatever it was, he looked so . . . so common. Gerald O'Hara had always looked like a gentleman, no matter how rumpled his coat might be. It didn't occur to Scarlett that her mother's quiet authority might have been at work on her father's transformation to gentleman landowner.

"We'll be walking past your grandfather's house," Jamie said, striking horror to Scarlett's heart. What if her aunts saw them? Suppose she had to introduce them? They always thought Mother married beneath her; Jamie would be all the proof they could ever want. . . . What was he saying? She had to pay attention.

"Leave off your servant girl there. She'd feel out of place with us. We don't have any servants."

No servants? Everybody has servants! What kind of place do they live in, a tenement?

To Scarlett's relief they walked along the street behind her grandfather's house, not by the square in front of it, where her aunts liked to promenade for their constitutionals. Pansy went willingly through the back gate. Then, very soon, James turned onto a handsome avenue called South Broad and announced, "Here we are," in front of a tall, substantial brick house.

"How nice!" Scarlett said with all her heart.

It was almost the last thing she got to say for some time. Instead of climbing the stairs to the big door on the high stoop, Jamie opened a smaller door at street level and ushered her into the kitchen and an overwhelming onslaught of people, all of them redheaded and all noisily welcoming when he shouted out above the hubbub, "This is Scarlett, my uncle Gerald O'Hara's beautiful daughter, come all the way from Atlanta to see Uncle James."

A large, stout woman, with hair redder than any of them, held out a roughened hand to Scarlett. "Welcome to the house," she said placidly. "I'm Jamie's wife, Maureen. Pay no attention to these savages; come sit by the fire and have a cup of tea." She took Scarlett's arm in a firm grip and drew her into the room. She plucked Scarlett's fur cape from her shoulders and handed it to one of the girls. And in an instant Scarlett found herself in a chair, holding the biggest cup she had ever seen in one hand, while with the other she was shaking hands with a shy young girl with dark, curly hair who said, "I'm your cousin Kathleen."

"What's all this now?" The thin, querulous tones cut through the racket. Scarlett looked across the kitchen and saw a tall old man who must be her uncle James.

"You have a visitor, Uncle James," said Maureen. "Come by the fire and see Scarlett."

The old man sat in the chair next to Scarlett's and looked at her. "I always said Gerald had the most style of any of us; didn't I tell you that, Jamie?" he began. "He was a fine small man, was Gerald, God rest his soul. And do you know how he came by that plantation of his? He won it. Playing poker with my money!" James' laughter was warm with life and amusement.

"Tell Scarlett about how he came to leave Ireland, Uncle James," said Maureen. "Perhaps she never heard the tale."

Scarlett stirred restlessly in her chair. "I heard it a hundred times," she said. Gerald O'Hara loved to boast about fleeing Ireland with a price on his head after he killed an English landlord's rent agent with one blow of his fist. Everyone in Clayton County had heard it a hundred times.

Maureen smiled. "A mighty man, for all his small size, so I've always been told. A father to make a woman proud."

"He was that," said James. "When do we have the birthday cake, Maureen? And where is Patricia?"

"Patricia's fixing her own feast, Uncle James," said Maureen. "We're to go next door as soon as Stephen tells us she's ready."

Stephen? Patricia? Next door?

Maureen saw the questions on Scarlett's face. "Did Jamie not tell you? There are three households of O'Haras here. You've only just begun to meet your people."

I'LL never get them all straight, thought Scarlett desperately. If only they'd stay in one place!

But there was no hope of that. Patricia was holding her birthday party in the double parlors of her house. The children—and there were many of them—were playing games, running, hiding, popping out from behind chairs and draperies. Scarlett was grateful for Maureen's red hair. All her children—the ones Scarlett had met next door, plus Patricia, who was pregnant, and Daniel, the son at the store—were at least recognizable. The others were a hopeless muddle, and so were their parents.

"We'll be cutting the cake now," Maureen said. She slipped her arm through Scarlett's. "Then we'll have a bit of music."

Scarlett walked with Maureen to a red plush settee and settled herself on the edge of the seat. A knife clattering against a glass demanded everyone's attention.

"We've come to celebrate Patricia's birthday," Jamie said, "even though it will not arrive until next week. Today is Shrove Tuesday, a better time for feasting than the middle of Lent. We also have a further cause for celebration. A beautiful long-lost O'Hara has been found again. I lift this glass in a toast to cousin Scarlett and bid her welcome to our hearts and our homes." Jamie threw back his head and poured the dark contents of his glass down his throat.

Then from a corner a fiddle began to play, and the O'Hara wives and daughters came in a procession, carrying platters to the

round table in the center of the room. There were meat pies, a roast of beef, a clove-studded ham. Bowls of steaming potatoes were followed by creamed carrots and roast onions. Finally, Maureen entered, carrying a cake trimmed with huge pink roses.

One of the girls began to shoo the children into the other parlor, and in a surprisingly short time there was calm where there had been chaos.

Everyone, it seemed, wanted to talk to Scarlett. And she found herself telling them all about her store and the new houses on the edge of Atlanta. Everyone was loudly approving. They didn't

think that talking about money was taboo. They told her she was wonderful.

"Will you give us some music now, Daniel?" said Maureen, and suddenly everyone was up and moving around. Daniel played a tune on the fiddle while the women cleared the table and the men moved the furniture back against the walls. Scarlett realized then what Daniel had begun to play. It was "Peg in a Low Back'd Car," Pa's favorite. She was close to tears.

But the music wouldn't allow sadness; it was too merry. Billy— Patricia's husband—produced a concertina. Then he reached over and picked up a tin whistle from the mantel. "Let's have some real music. Stephen—" He tossed the thin silver tube to a dark, silent man. "And for you, dear mother-in-law—" His hand dropped something in Maureen's lap.

A young boy clapped wildly. "The bones! Cousin Maureen's going to play the bones." And Maureen lifted her hand with a clacking noise, and Scarlett saw that the "bones" were really thick pieces of smooth wood.

Daniel pulled the bow over the strings, and in an instant the big room rang with the music of an Irish reel. The children clapped, Scarlett clapped, everyone clapped. Except Maureen. She threw up the hand holding the bones, and the sharp staccato clacking made an insistent rhythm that the other players obeyed. A half-dozen children got up and began to leap and hop across the room. Scarlett's hands grew hot from clapping, and her feet were moving as if she wanted to leap about with the children.

When the reel came to an end, she fell back against the settee, exhausted. Still half in a trance from the music, she looked at the windows and was jolted back to reality. It was getting dark. The cup of tea she'd come for had stretched into hours. "Oh, Maureen, I'm going to be late for supper," she gasped. "I've got to go. My grandfather will be furious."

"Let him be, the old loo-la. Stay. The party's only beginning."

"I wish I could," said Scarlett. "But I promised I'd be back."

"Ah, well then. A promise is a promise. You'll come again?"

"I'd love to. Will you invite me?"

Maureen laughed comfortably. "There's no inviting done here. We're all a family, and you're a part of it. Come anytime you like. . . . Jamie! Scarlett's got to go. Put your coat on, man, and give her your arm."

Oh, I wish I didn't have to leave, Scarlett said to herself.

13

THE next day Scarlett went to Ash Wednesday Mass with her aunts. They were visibly shocked when they got home and she announced that she was going to order breakfast. Scarlett's reintroduction to religion was so recent that she thought fasting meant simply having fish on Fridays instead of meat.

Pauline explained that only one meal a day was allowed during the forty days of Lent, and no meat at that meal. Sundays were the exception. Still no meat, but three meals were allowed.

"I don't believe it!" Scarlett exclaimed. "We never did that at home."

"You were children," said Eulalie, "but I'm sure your mother fasted as she should."

Pauline suggested that Scarlett join her and Eulalie for their walk around the square. "Sister and I always find that a constitutional is a great restorative," she said brightly. Then her mouth quivered pathetically. "It keeps one's mind off food, too."

Scarlett agreed at once. She had to get out of the house.

By the time they returned, she was positive she'd walked around every one of the twenty-odd squares that dotted Savannah and gave it its unique charm. But at least it was time for dinner. . . . Scarlett couldn't remember ever tasting fish that was quite so delicious.

By four o'clock Scarlett was starving again. And there'd be nothing at all to eat until dinnertime tomorrow. No, it wasn't possible! She walked to the bellpull and jerked it four times. "Go put your coat on," she told Pansy when the girl came running. "We're going out."

SCARLETT ate two cookies in the bakery, and she carried two sacks of baked goods home and up to her room, hiding them under her cape.

A telegram had been placed neatly in the center of her bureau. Scarlett dropped the sacks and ran to get it.

"Henry Hamilton," it said as signature. Damn! She'd thought it was from Rhett, telling her that he was on his way to fetch her. But as she read Uncle Henry's message, Scarlett began to smile:

YOUR TELEGRAM RECEIVED STOP ALSO LARGE BANK DRAFT FROM YOUR HUS-
BAND STOP WHAT FOOLISHNESS IS THIS QUESTION MARK RHETT ASKED ME
TO NOTIFY HIM YOUR WHEREABOUTS STOP LETTER FOLLOWS STOP

So Rhett was looking for her. Just what she'd expected. Ha! She'd been so right to come to Savannah. She hoped Uncle Henry had had the sense to tell Rhett right away and by telegram, not letter. Why, he might be reading his right this minute.

Scarlett danced around the room, holding the telegram against her heart. Rhett might even be on his way now. The train from Charleston arrived just about this time of day.

An hour later Rhett hadn't come. She was in a very bad mood when she went downstairs. And there was Jerome with her grandfather's supper tray! It was almost enough to make her turn Huguenot or Presbyterian, like the old man.

WHEN Scarlett went downstairs the next morning, she found her aunts in a nervous frenzy of preparation for her grandfather's birthday dinner. "I have to go buy a present for Grandfather," she said. "Is there any shopping you want me to do for you?" And don't dare, she said silently, offer to come with me. I've got to go to the convent to see the mother superior.

They were astonished that Scarlett had not yet selected her gift. Scarlett left before they could describe the depth of their astonishment. "Old loo-las," she said under her breath. She wasn't at all sure what the Irish phrase meant, but the sound of it was enough to make her smile.

THE same elderly nun answered the doorbell. Scarlett readied herself for combat. But, "The mother superior is expecting you," said the nun. "If you'll follow me . . ."

Scarlett was almost dazed when she left the convent ten minutes later. It had been so easy! The mother superior agreed at once to talk to the bishop. She'd send word, she said, very soon. She herself would be returning to Charleston the following week.

Scarlett was euphoric. Her smile and her eyes were so bright that the grocer nearly forgot to charge her for the box of chocolate candies she had selected for her grandfather's birthday present.

Her high spirits began to dim slightly when she got back to the Robillard house and learned that her grandfather would actually come to table for the six courses of his particularly favorite foods. Her spirits plummeted when the aunts informed her that she wasn't allowed to eat many of the delicacies that would be served.

"Flesh is forbidden during Lent," said Pauline sternly. "Be certain that no gravy touches the rice or vegetables you eat."

"But be careful, Scarlett. Don't let Père notice," added Eulalie in a whisper. "He doesn't approve of fasting."

"There'll be soup for us. And fish," Pauline said with sudden cheerfulness. "Cake, too, a beautiful cake. A true feast, Scarlett."

"Remember, sister," warned Eulalie, "gluttony is a sin."

Scarlett could feel herself losing control of her temper. It's only a dinner, she reminded herself, just calm down. It can't be all that bad. After all, what could one old man do?

He could, Scarlett learned at once, refuse to allow anything other than French to be spoken. Her "Happy Birthday, Grandfather" was ignored. Her aunts' greetings were acknowledged by a cold nod, and he sat down in a huge thronelike chair at the head of the table.

Pierre Auguste Robillard was no longer a nightshirted, frail elderly man. Impeccably clothed in an old-fashioned frock coat and starched linen, he looked impressive when he was seated. His white hair was like an old lion's ruff, his eyes were hawklike under his thick white brows, and his big, bony nose looked like a predator's beak. Scarlett braced herself for she knew not what.

Jerome entered, bearing a silver tureen. He placed it in front of his master and lifted the lid with a white-gloved hand. The delicious aroma of shrimp bisque spread throughout the room.

Jerome held the soup plates next to the tureen as Pierre Robillard silently filled each one. Then he tasted his soup. He shrugged eloquent dissatisfaction and dropped his spoon into his bowl.

Eulalie let out a strangled sob.

You old monster! Scarlett thought. She began to eat her soup. It was a velvety richness of flavor. But Eulalie's eyes were downcast, and Pauline's spoon was in the bowl, like her father's. Scarlett began to get angry. He's going to ruin everything, and on purpose, too. She wasn't going to let him keep her from her dinner!

Jerome removed the soup plates and set down dinner plates and fish knives and forks for the planked shad. When it came, Grandfather ate two small bites, and Pauline and Eulalie gave up with most of the fish still on their plates. The old man's displeasure was repeated with the potted doves that were served next.

Scarlett thought she would explode. It was just plain impossible that he didn't like the food. No, there was another reason he wasn't eating. She could see it in his eyes. They gleamed when he looked at her aunts' pitiful disappointment. He'd rather make them suffer than enjoy eating his dinner. His birthday dinner, too.

Scarlett looked at her grandfather and despised him for the way he was tormenting her aunts. But even more she despised them for tolerating his tortures. They don't have a shred of gumption, she thought. And I'm as bad as they are. Why can't I just speak up and tell him how nasty he's acting?

But she continued to sit quietly, just as if she were a child, as if her mother, Ellen Robillard O'Hara, were there at the table. And for love of her, for need of her approval, Scarlett was incapable of defying the tyranny of Pierre Robillard.

She sat for what seemed an eternity, watching as her grandfather tasted and rejected each carefully selected dish that was offered him. By the time Jerome brought in the birthday cake, the tension and misery of Scarlett's aunts were palpable.

"AND did he eat it?" Scarlett asked dramatically. "He did not! I wanted to wring his scrawny neck!"

Maureen O'Hara rocked back and forth, laughing with delight.

"I don't see what's so funny," Scarlett said.

"It's the roguishness of it all, Scarlett. Your poor old aunts plotting their hearts out to please him, and himself sitting in his nightshirt, plotting against them. And don't you know he's got that man of his sneaking in all those wonderful dishes for him to eat behind his closed door? The old rascal." Maureen's laughter was so contagious that Scarlett finally joined in. She'd done the right thing, coming here after the disastrous birthday dinner.

Funny, she'd thought she would never set foot in a kitchen again once the bad days at Tara were over. But this was different. It was a happy place to be. She wished she could stay, but she had to get back to her grandfather's house.

She drained her teacup hurriedly. "You've saved my life, Maureen. I thought I'd go crazy if I had to stay with my aunts. But I've really got to go back now."

"What a pity. I'll hope you'll stay longer for the dancing on Saturday, Scarlett. Maybe Colum will be back by then, too."

Scarlett shook her head. "I can't. I'd love to, but I won't still be in Savannah." Her aunts expected her to go back to Charleston with them on Saturday morning. She didn't think she would, for surely Rhett would come for her long before then. Maybe he was at her grandfather's right now.

She jumped to her feet. "I've got to run. Thank you, Maureen. I'll stop by again before I leave."

HENRY HAMILTON'S PROMISED letter was delivered to the Robillard house just as dark was setting in. Scarlett grabbed it like a line thrown to the drowning and took it up to her room. She wanted to savor every word in private.

The letter began without salutation:

> What mess have you made this time? On Monday, I was visited by a pompous old fool who presented me with an astonishing draft drawn on his bank and payable to you. The amount was one-half million dollars, and it was paid by Rhett. On Tuesday, I was badgered by another old fool, this one a lawyer, asking me where you were. His client—your husband—wanted to know. I did not tell him you were in Savannah. . . .

Scarlett groaned. No wonder Rhett hadn't come for her. She peered again at the old lawyer's spidery handwriting:

> Your telegram arrived after he left, and at the time he called on me, I didn't know where you were. I have not told him yet, because I do not know what you're up to, and I have a pretty good idea that I want no part of it.
>
> This lawyer had two questions from Rhett. The first was your whereabouts. The second was—do you want a divorce?
>
> Now, Scarlett, I don't know what you're holding over Rhett's head to get that kind of money from him, and I don't want to know. Whatever he might have done to give you grounds to divorce him is none of my business, either. I've never dirtied my hands with a divorce action, and I'm not going to start now. Besides, there is no divorce in South Carolina, and that is Rhett's legal residence now.
>
> If you persist in this tomfoolery, I warn you that I won't handle your legal business for you anymore. If you're thinking of divorcing Rhett so you'll be free to marry Ashley Wilkes, you'd do well to think again. Ashley is doing better than anyone expected he would, and if you push yourself into his life, you'll ruin everything. Leave the poor man alone, Scarlett.

Leave Ashley alone, indeed! I'd like to know how prosperous he'd be if I had left him alone. Uncle Henry, of all people, should have better sense than to jump to all kinds of nasty conclusions.

Uncle Henry was the closest thing she had to a father—or a friend—in Atlanta, and his accusations cut deep. Scarlett scrawled a response for Pansy to take to the telegraph office:

SAVANNAH ADDRESS NO SECRET STOP DIVORCE NOT WANTED STOP MONEY IN GOLD QUESTION MARK

Maybe she should go to Atlanta and talk to Uncle Henry and her bankers. No! She had to put first things first. Rhett was trying to find her. She smiled to herself. He doesn't fool me with that divorce talk. Or by transferring the money as if our deal was being carried out. The only thing that counts is that he wants to know where I am. He won't stay away long once Uncle Henry tells him.

"DON'T be ridiculous, Scarlett," said Pauline in a cold tone. "Of course you'll be going home tomorrow. We always go back to Charleston on Saturday."

"That doesn't mean I have to. I told you, I'm staying in Savannah for a while." Rhett was looking for her. She'd receive him right here, in this elegant pink-and-gold room. He'd beg her to come back. She'd agree; then he'd take her in his arms and kiss her. . . .

On Saturday, Scarlett insisted on going to the train depot with her aunts. When she returned to the house, a telegram from Uncle Henry was waiting for her:

I HAVE NOT AND WILL NOT HAVE ANYTHING WHATSOEVER TO DO WITH IN-VESTING THE MONEY THAT WAS TRANSFERRED BY YOUR HUSBAND STOP IT IS IN YOUR ACCOUNT AT YOUR BANK STOP I HAVE EXPRESSED MY REPUGNANCE FOR THE CIRCUMSTANCES SURROUNDING THIS TRANSACTION STOP DO NOT EXPECT ANY HELP FROM ME STOP

Scarlett sank onto a chair when she read it. Her heart was racing. The old fool! A half-million dollars— Banks were still closing all over the country. She'd have to go to Atlanta, change the money to gold, add it to her safe box. But that would take days. Plenty of time for her money to disappear.

A half-million dollars. She had to protect it, but how?

She rang for Pansy. Pale and wild-eyed, Scarlett said, "Get your coat on. We're going out."

She had herself under control when she hurried into the O'Hara store and asked her cousin to recommend a banker. "I've decided to stay in Savannah awhile longer, and I need to have a few dollars transferred from my bank at home. I figured you'd be able to put in a good word for me, being a prosperous businessman and all."

"I'll be proud to escort you to the president of the bank, Scarlett, but you'll do better to tell him you're old Robillard's granddaughter than that you're O'Hara's cousin. The word is, he's a very wealthy old gentleman." Jamie offered her his arm.

When Jamie introduced her to the bank president as Pierre Robillard's granddaughter, the man nearly split his britches bowing and scraping. Obviously her grandfather was much much richer than she'd imagined. Then, after Jamie left, when she told him she wanted to rent a safe box and transfer a half million to it, she thought he'd swoon at her feet. Scarlett smiled to herself. I don't care what anybody says, having lots of money is the best thing in the world.

JEROME brought Scarlett her mail on a silver tray. There was a brief letter from Uncle Henry. He was furious that she'd transferred the money to the Savannah bank. Too bad. Scarlett crumpled up the letter and dropped it on the floor.

The fat envelope was from Aunt Pauline. She tore it open:

> We are profoundly ashamed of your outrageous behavior. If we had known that you were coming with us to Savannah without so much as a word of explanation to Eleanor Butler, we would have insisted that you leave the train and go back.

What the devil was Aunt Pauline saying? Was it possible that Miss Eleanor didn't mention the note I left her? Or that she didn't get it? No, it wasn't possible. Aunt Pauline was just making trouble.

Scarlett's eyes moved quickly over Pauline's complaints about the folly of Scarlett's traveling after her ordeal when the boat capsized and about Scarlett's "unnatural reticence" in not telling her aunts that she'd been in the accident.

Why couldn't Pauline tell her what she wanted to know? There wasn't a word about Rhett. There. At last:

> And dear Eleanor is understandably concerned that Rhett felt it necessary to travel all the way to Boston for the meeting about his fertilizer shipments. He should not have gone north immediately after his long immersion in cold water. . . .

Of course! That's why Rhett hasn't come after me yet. Does Aunt Pauline say when he's coming back?

Scarlett read eagerly to the end of the letter. But there was no mention of what she wanted to know. *Now what am I going to do? Rhett might be gone for weeks. Or he might be on his way back right this very minute.*

THE next day there was a note from the mother superior. The bishop was going to consider Scarlett's request to allow her to buy back Carreen's dowry.

Tara. I'm going to get Tara! She could see it so clearly in her mind. The house, gleaming fresh white on top of the hill. Spring, with clouds of tender dogwood blossoms and the heady scent of wisteria; then summer, the crisp, starched white curtains billowing from the open windows, the thick sweetness of honeysuckle flowing through them into all the rooms, all restored to their polished, quiet perfection. *Yes, summer was the best. The long, lazy Georgia summer, when twilight lasted for hours and lightning bugs signaled in the slow, thickening darkness.*

Oh, if only the bishop would hurry!

SCARLETT felt that she needed to get away from her grandfather's mausoleum of a house and have a little fun. She thought of the O'Haras, and she hurried to the house on South Broad Street. She could hear the music and laughter even before Jamie opened the door.

"It's Scarlett!" he said with pleased surprise. "Come in, Scarlett darling, and meet my brother Colum. He's here at last, the best of all the O'Haras, saving only yourself."

Colum was years younger than Jamie. He was short of stature and stocky. His florid, round face was bright, his eyes flashing blue, and his head a halo of silver curls. He was the very image of Gerald O'Hara.

Colum smiled at Scarlett when Jamie introduced them, and the warmth gleaming from his eyes made her feel that meeting her was the happiest experience of his entire life. "And are we not the luckiest family on the face of the earth, to have such a breathtaking creature one of us?" he said. "It only wants a tiara to complete your gold splendor, Scarlett darling. If the queen of the fairies could see you, wouldn't she tear her spangled wings to ribbons in envy?"

"I believe I'm hearing the famous Irish blarney," Scarlett said, returning Colum's smile. It was impossible not to.

"Not a bit of it. I wish only that I had the gift of poetry to say all I'm thinking."

Jamie hit his brother on the shoulder. "You're not doing too badly, you rogue. Step aside and give Scarlett a seat. I'll fetch her a glass. Colum found us a keg of real Irish ale on his travels, Scarlett darling. You must have a taste." Jamie spoke name and endearment the way Colum did, as if they made one word: Scarlettdarling.

As the evening wore on, she noticed that everyone smiled at Colum a lot, as if reflecting his pleasure. He was clearly enjoying himself so much. He was leaning back in a straight chair, tipped to rest against the wall near the fire, waving his hand to direct and encourage Jamie's fiddling and Maureen's rat-tat-tat with the bones. His boots were off, and his stockinged feet half danced on the rungs of the chair. He was the picture of a man at his ease; even his collar was off, and the neck of his shirt was open.

"Tell us, Colum, about your travels," someone would urge from time to time, but Colum always put them off. He needed music, he said, and a glass, to refresh his heart and his dusty throat. Tomorrow was time enough for talking.

Scarlett's heart, too, was refreshed by the music. But she couldn't stay very long. It was late, and she had to go home.

That evening stirred the emotions that had warred within her all her life. Scarlett's essential self was as much her heritage from her father as was her name. She was impetuous, strong-willed and had the same forthright vitality and courage that had carried him across the Atlantic and to the pinnacle of his dreams—master of a great plantation and husband to a great lady.

Her mother's blood gave her the fine bones and creamy skin that spoke of centuries of breeding. Ellen Robillard also instilled in her daughter the rules and tenets of aristocracy.

The O'Haras drew her like a lodestone. Their earthy vigor and lusty happiness spoke to the deepest and best part of her nature. But she wasn't free to respond. Everything she'd been taught by the mother she revered forbade her ever knowing that freedom.

She roamed restlessly through the silent rooms of her grandfather's house, imagining the music and dancing at the O'Haras', but she'd been taught that such boisterous merriment was vulgar and lower class. Why, then, was it so hard to stop herself from envying her Irish kin?

I won't think about that now, she decided. I'll think about Tara instead. And she retreated into the idyll of her Tara, as it had been and as she'd make it again.

Then a note came from the bishop's secretary, and her idyll exploded in her face. He wouldn't grant her request. Scarlett didn't think at all. She clutched the note to her breast and ran, heedless and alone, to Jamie O'Hara's house. They'd understand how she felt, the O'Haras would. Pa told me so, again and again. "To anyone with a drop of Irish blood in them, the land they live on is like their mother. It's the only thing that lasts, that's worth working for, worth fighting for. . . ."

She burst through the door, and ahead of her she saw the compact, stocky body and silver head of Colum O'Hara. He was dressed in a dark suit. Through the daze of her pain Scarlett stared at the Roman collar at his throat. A priest! No one had told her Colum was a priest. Thank God. You could tell a priest anything, even the deepest secrets of your heart.

"Help me, Father," she cried. "I need someone to help me."

"SO THERE you have it," Colum concluded. "Now, what can be done to remedy it?" He sat at the head of the long table in Jamie's dining room. All the adults from the three O'Hara houses were in chairs around the table. Scarlett looked at their solemn faces. What can they do? They're just Irish immigrants.

But she soon learned that there was quite a lot these Irish immigrants could do. Patricia's husband, Billy Carmody, was foreman of all the bricklayers working on the cathedral. He said a mention from Tom MacMahon, the contractor, that the work might be slowed down would make the bishop promise anything.

Colum would talk to Tom MacMahon. Colum, they all agreed, was the best to do anything that needed doing.

He smiled at Scarlett. "You'll have your Tara, wait and see."

"Tara!" Old James laughed. "That Gerald. For a small bit of a man, he always did have a high opinion of himself!"

Scarlett stiffened. No one was going to make fun of her pa.

Colum spoke very softly to her. "Whist, now, he means no insult. I'll explain it all later."

And so he did, when he was escorting her to her grandfather's house.

"Tara is a magical place to us Irish, Scarlett. It was the center of all Ireland, the home of the High Kings, far far back when the world was young and hopeful. For hundreds and thousands of years the High Kings ruled their sweet green island, and there was music throughout the land. Five roads led to the hill of Tara from every corner of the country, and every third year did all the people come to feast in the banquet hall and hear the poets sing. This is not a story only, but a great truth; the sad words of the end are written in the great books of the monasteries. 'In the Year of Our Lord five hundred fifty and four was held the last feast of Tara.' "

Scarlett was spellbound by Colum's story and his voice. They walked on in silence for a while. Then Colum said, "It was a noble dream your father had to build a new Tara in America. When next I go to Tara, I'll think of him and of his daughter."

"Do you mean it's still there? It's a real place?"

"It's a gentle green hill with magic in it and sheep grazing on it, and from the top you can see for great distances the same beautiful world the High Kings saw. It's not far from the village where I live, where your father and mine were born, in County Meath."

Scarlett was thunderstruck. Pa must have gone there, too; he must have stood where the High Kings stood!

When they reached the Robillard house, she stopped reluctantly. "I don't know how to thank you," she told him. "I feel a million times better now. I'm so sure you'll make the bishop change his mind."

Scarlett went into the house. In all her life she had faced her crises alone. Sometimes she had refused to admit she needed help, more often there had been nowhere she could turn. It was different now. There were people to help her. Her family had willingly lifted her burden from her shoulders. Scarlett wasn't alone anymore.

"SCARLETT, pull that chair up closer to my bed," Pierre Robillard demanded. "I have something to say. Where have you been?"

"I've been at my cousin Jamie's house."

"You've been consorting with those Irish peasants?" The old man quivered with outrage.

Scarlett's anger swelled to meet his. "Yes, I have, and I intend to see them again. I like them very much."

Pierre Robillard was disturbed by Scarlett's defiance. Just so had her mother defied him so many years before, and he had lost her forever. His heart had broken then; Ellen was his favorite child, the daughter most like her mother. He didn't love Scarlett. All the love he had was in the grave with his wife. But he wouldn't let Scarlett go without a fight. He wanted his last days to be comfortable, and she could see to it.

"Scarlett," he said quietly when she was seated, "I am almost ninety-four years old, and it is not likely that I will live much longer. I am asking you, my grandchild, to stay with me for the time I have left."

Scarlett started to speak, but the old man raised one thin hand to stop her. "I am prepared to make you a generous offer. If you will remain in this house as its chatelaine and see to my comforts and conform to my wishes, you will inherit my entire estate when I die. It is not inconsiderable."

Scarlett was dumbfounded. He was offering her a fortune!

Pierre Robillard misunderstood her hesitation; he thought she was overcome with gratitude. "I do not know," he went on, "what circumstances have led you to consider dissolving your marriage. But you will abandon any idea of divorce—"

"You've been reading my mail!"

"Anything that comes under this roof is my business."

Scarlett was so enraged she couldn't find words to express it. She stood up. "How dare you?" she shouted.

"You will not raise your voice in this house, young woman. I am not one of your shanty-Irish relations."

Scarlett backed away from the bed. "No wonder my mother left this house and never came back," she said.

"Stop being melodramatic, girl. Your mother left this house because she was headstrong and too young to listen to reason. She'd been disappointed in love, and she took the first man who asked her. She lived to regret it."

Scarlett turned her back on him. I don't believe him. I won't listen to that kind of talk. "There's not enough money ever been minted to keep me here," she said when she turned to face him again. "Money can't make living in a tomb bearable." She looked at Pierre Robillard with blazing green eyes in a deathly pale face. "I'll leave first thing in the morning."

14

"DON'T be a crybaby, Pansy, nothing's going to happen to you. The train goes straight through to Atlanta; then it stops. Just look out the window, and you'll be home before you know it."

"But Miss Scarlett, what am I to do without you to do for? I'm a lady's maid. When are you going to be home?"

"It all depends. Now climb up in that coach."

It all depends on Rhett, Scarlett thought, and Rhett better come soon. I don't know if I'm going to manage with my cousins or not. She turned and smiled at Jamie's wife. "How am I ever going to thank you for taking me in, Maureen?" It was her bright, girlish, social voice.

Maureen took Scarlett's arm and walked her away from the train and Pansy's forlorn face in the dust-streaked window of the car. "Everything is grand, Scarlett. Kathleen is near floating with joy that she'll be your lady's maid now. It's what she wants to train for anyhow, and she worships the ground under your feet. It's the first time the silly girl's been happy since Colum brought her here. The poor girl's pining for Ireland, and that's the truth of it. Anyway, you belong with us, not at the beck and call of that old loo-la. The brass of him, expecting that you'd stay there to housekeep for him. We want you for the love of you."

Scarlett felt better. It was impossible to resist Maureen's warmth and hospitality. Still, she hoped it wouldn't be long.

IT SEEMED that the dogwood trees came into bloom overnight. Suddenly one morning, when Scarlett and Maureen were walking to the Market, there were clouds of blossoms above the grassy median in the avenue outside the house.

"Ah, isn't this a lovely sight?" Maureen sighed gustily. "Come quickly, there's a grand shopping to do. I'll bake this afternoon, and after Mass tomorrow we'll spend the day at the park."

Was it Saturday already? Scarlett's mind raced, calculating and remembering. Why, she'd been in Savannah almost a full month! A vise squeezed her heart. Why hadn't Rhett come? Where was he? His business in Boston couldn't have taken this long.

"Boston," said Maureen, and Scarlett stopped short. She grabbed Maureen's arm. "What were you saying about Boston?"

"I said 'tis a shame that Stephen is leaving today for Boston. There'll be no trees flowering there, I'm bound."

Scarlett walked quietly at Maureen's side. Questions battered against the walls of her mind, like birds trapped in a cage. Had she made a mistake not going back to Charleston with her aunts? Had she been wrong to leave in the first place? Maybe she should talk to someone about it.

I'll talk to Colum! He'll know what to do. In his own way Colum was like Rhett. He was complete in himself, like Rhett. Colum got things done, too, just like Rhett, and laughed about the doing, just like Rhett.

Maureen said, "And why are you smiling, I'd like to know."

Scarlett turned the smile onto her friend. "Because I'm happy that it's spring," she said.

"Jamie, I'm thinking I should take Kathleen with me when I go," said Colum. "She's been here long enough to get over being homesick, but I can see her heart's still aching."

Scarlett nearly poured boiling water on her hand instead of in the teapot. "Where are you going, Colum?"

"Back to Ireland, darling. I'm only visiting."

"But the bishop hasn't changed his mind about Tara yet. And there's something else I want to talk to you about."

"Well, I'm not leaving this minute, Scarlett darling. There's time for everything. What do you think? Should Kathleen go back?"

"I don't know," said Scarlett. "Ask Maureen." What difference did it make what Kathleen did? It was Colum that mattered. How could he just pick up and leave when she needed him?

Scarlett only picked at the cheese toast and potato soup they had for supper. She felt like crying.

"Oof," Maureen groaned when the kitchen was tidy again. "I'm going to take my old bones to bed early tonight. I'm tired. You, too, Mary Kate and Helen. Tomorrow's a school day."

Scarlett stretched in front of the fire. "Good night," she said.

"Stay a bit," Colum said, "while I finish my pipe. Jamie's yawning so, I can tell he's about to abandon me."

Scarlett took a chair across from Colum's, and Jamie patted her head on his way to the stairs.

Colum drew on his pipe. "A glowing hearth is good for talking by," he said. "What's on your mind and your heart, Scarlett?"

She sighed deeply. "I don't know what to do about Rhett, Colum. I'm afraid I might have ruined everything." She started from the beginning, with the truth about her marriage. "I didn't love him, at least I didn't know it if I did. I was in love with someone else. And then when I knew it was Rhett I loved, he didn't love me anymore. That's what he said, anyhow. But I don't believe that's true, Colum; it just can't be."

"Did he leave you?"

"Yes. But then I left him. And I wonder if it was a mistake."

It was well after midnight when, with infinite patience, Colum unraveled Scarlett's story. "You did just what you should have, my dear," he said. "I can understand your husband, Scarlett. He's fighting himself, and for a strong man that's a mighty battle. He'll come after you, and you must be generous to him when he does, for he will be battle sore."

"But when, Colum?"

"That I cannot tell you. I know this, though. It's he that must do the seeking, you can't do it for him. He has to fight himself alone, until he faces his need for you and admits it is good."

"You're sure he'll come?"

"That I'm sure of. And now I'm to bed. You do the same."

That night Scarlett nestled into her pillow to enjoy the satisfaction that Colum's certainty had given her. Rhett would be here—maybe not as soon as she wanted, but she could wait.

THE next morning, when Scarlett went downstairs for breakfast, Colum was reading the newspaper in the kitchen.

"I came to ask you a favor, Scarlett," he said. He wanted some feminine advice in selecting things for people back in Ireland. "I can manage the lads myself, but the lasses are a mystery."

Scarlett laughed at his perplexed expression. "I'd love to help, Colum, but you have to pay me—with a cup of coffee."

"Come along, then. A cup of coffee would be welcome."

They went to the Pulaski House, a huge and very fashionable hotel. When they were seated on a tufted velvet settee in one of the ornate, marble-columned reception rooms, Scarlett looked around with satisfaction. "This is nice," she said happily.

"You look right at home in your elegant finery amidst all the grand marble and potted palms," Colum said, smiling. People in Ireland, he explained, led lives more simple than Scarlett knew. More simple, perhaps, than she could even imagine. They lived on their farms in the countryside, with no city nearby at all, only a village with a church and a blacksmith and a public house, where the mail coach stopped. And so the gifts for the girls couldn't be city things. They wouldn't know what to do with a length of satin or a painted fan.

Scarlett put her cup in its saucer with a decisive clink. "Calico!" she said. "I'll bet you they'd love calico. It comes in bright patterns and makes up into pretty frocks."

"And boots," Colum said. He took a packet of paper from his pocket and unfolded it. "I have the names and sizes here."

Scarlett laughed at the length of the paper. Every person in County Meath must have put their name on Colum's list.

"Tell me more about Ireland," she said.

"Ah, it's a rare beautiful island," said Colum softly. He talked with love in his lilting voice about green hills crowned with castles; of rushing streams rimmed with flowers; of fragrant hedgerows in misty rain; of a sky wider and higher than any other sky, with a sun as gentle and warming as a mother's kiss. . . .

"You sound almost as homesick as Kathleen."

Colum laughed at himself. "I won't weep when the ship sails. Why don't you come with us, Scarlett, and see the home of your people? It would be a grand adventure. The ship takes only two weeks and a day to Galway."

"That's very fast."

"It is that. The winds blow toward Ireland and carry the homesick travelers home as fast as a cloud flying across the sky. It's a grand sight to see all the sails set and the big ship fairly dancing over the sea. It's a lovely thing, sailing. You feel so free you think you could fly."

"I know," said Scarlett. "That's just what it's like."

"THERE SHE IS," COLUM SAID when Scarlett appeared in the kitchen doorway the next morning.

Everyone was bustling about, getting the children's books and lunch bags sorted out and shooing them off to school. Then Jamie kissed Maureen on the lips, Scarlett on the top of her head and Kathleen on the cheek, and he went off to the store.

"Now you just stay as you are, Scarlett," Maureen ordered. "Kathleen and I will have the kitchen cleared in no time. Colum O'Hara, you stay where you are, too; I don't want your big boots getting in my way. I want you under my eye, too; it's little enough I get to see of you. If it wasn't for old Katie Scarlett's birthday, I'd beg you not to leave so soon for Ireland."

"Katie Scarlett?" said Scarlett.

"And did no one tell you?" Maureen said. "Your grandmother that you were named for is going to be a century old next month."

"And still sharp-tongued." Colum chuckled.

"I'll be home for the feast," Kathleen said happily.

"Oh, I wish I could go," Scarlett said. "Pa used to tell so many stories about her."

"But you can, Scarlett darling. And think what a joy for the old woman."

Kathleen and Maureen rushed to Scarlett's side, urging, encouraging, persuading, until Scarlett was giddy. Why not? she asked herself.

When Rhett came for her, she would have to go back to Charleston. Why not put it off a little longer? She hated Charleston.

Scarlett laughed aloud. "I'm going to go!" she said. Charleston could wait until she got back. Rhett could wait, too. Lord knows she'd waited for him often enough. Why shouldn't she visit that other Tara? She'd be Irish and happy for a while yet, before she settled down to Charleston's rules.

Two days later Stephen O'Hara returned from Boston. And not long after, Scarlett found herself in an open carriage with Colum and Kathleen, on her way to the docks along Savannah's riverfront.

"You're sure we'll not miss our ship, Colum?" Kathleen fretted. "You were late coming for us. Jamie and them left an hour ago."

"Whist, stop your worrying, Kathleen mavourneen. The *Brian Boru* won't sail without us; the captain's a friend of many years."

The carriage jolted down a cobblestoned ramp to the river, careened around a solid phalanx of barrels awaiting loading and clattered to a jouncing halt. Ships of every size and kind were tied up to jutting wooden piers.

Colum jumped from the buggy and held up his hand to Kathleen to help her down. "Go on over, now, and give your cousins a kiss to say good-bye." He pointed toward Maureen.

When Kathleen ran off, he spoke quietly to Scarlett. "You'll not forget what I told you, now, Scarlett darling?"

"I won't forget." She smiled, enjoying the harmless conspiracy.

"You'll be Scarlett O'Hara and no other on this voyage and in Ireland," he said with a wink. "It's nothing to do with you or yours, Scarlett darling, but Butler is a famous name in Ireland, and all of its fame is heinous."

Scarlett didn't mind at all. She was going to enjoy being an O'Hara for as long as she could.

THE *Brian Boru* was a luxury ship, catering to the expensive tastes of rich Americans who traveled to Ireland. There was a disproportionately large hold, compared to the usual passenger ship, because Irish Americans carried with them gifts for all their relatives and returned with multiple souvenirs of their visits.

A broad platform with sturdy railings was built across the top of the paddle wheel on which Scarlett stood with Colum to wave a final good-bye to her cousins.

Slightly to one side of the O'Haras stood Stephen. He raised his hand once in a signal to Colum. It signified that Scarlett's trunks had been opened and repacked en route to the ship. Among the layers of petticoats and frocks were the tightly wrapped, oiled rifles and the boxes of ammunition Stephen had purchased in Boston.

Like their fathers and grandfathers before them, the O'Haras were all militantly opposed to English rule over Ireland. But only in the past ten years had an organization begun to grow. Disciplined and dangerous, financed from America, the Fenians were becoming known throughout Ireland. They were heroes to the Irish peasant; anathema to English landowners; and to English military forces, revolutionaries fit only for death.

Colum O'Hara was the most successful fund-raiser and one of the foremost clandestine leaders of the Fenian brotherhood.

15

$\int$CARLETT and Kathleen stood side by side watching the flat shoreline recede into a soft blur of green, then disappear. What have I done? Scarlett thought in momentary panic. Then she looked ahead at the limitless expanse of the sun-flecked Atlantic, and her heart beat faster with the thrill of adventure.

"Oh!" Kathleen cried out. Then, "Oooh," she moaned.

"What's wrong, Kathleen?"

"Oooh. I'd forgot the seasickness," the girl gasped.

Scarlett put her arm around Kathleen's waist and led her to their cabin. That evening Kathleen's chair at the captain's table was empty, but Scarlett and Colum did full justice to the gargantuan meal that was served. Afterward Scarlett took a bowl of broth to her unfortunate cousin and spoon-fed her. Thank heavens I haven't got a puny stomach, she thought.

SCARLETT woke abruptly at dawn and ran with frantic clumsiness into the small convenience room that adjoined her cabin. There she fell to her knees and vomited into the *chaise privée*.

She couldn't be seasick, not her. Not when she loved sailing so much. Why, in Charleston, when the tiny sailboat was climbing the waves in the storm, she hadn't even felt queasy. She couldn't imagine what was wrong with her. . . .

Slowly, slowly Scarlett's bent head rose from its drooping weakness. Her eyes opened wide with discovery. Excitement raced through her, and she laughed deep in her throat.

I'm pregnant. I'm pregnant! I remember; this is how it feels.

Scarlett leaned back against the wall. Oh, I feel wonderful. I don't care how awful my stomach feels, I feel wonderful. I've got Rhett now. He is mine. I can't wait to tell him.

Sudden tears of happiness poured down her cheeks. Oh, how she wanted this baby. Rhett's baby. Their baby. It would be strong, she knew it—a bold, fearless little thing, like Bonnie.

How Rhett had loved Bonnie. Scarlett's mind flooded with memories. His wide back bent over the cradle, his deep voice making silly baby-talk sounds—never in all the world was there a man so besotted with a baby. He was going to be so happy when she told him. She could see his dark eyes flashing with the joy of it.

And I'm happy, too, Scarlett thought.

Her life would be fine, with Rhett loving her, loving their baby. They'd be the happiest, lovingest family in the whole world.

CROSSING the Atlantic on the *Brian Boru* was like a continuous Saturday night at the O'Haras'—only more so. All day there was something to do: checkers, shuffleboard, games of chance. In the evening the passengers sang along with the professional musicians and danced, and even when the dancing was done, there was a game of whist in the ladies' card saloon. Scarlett was always in demand as a partner. The stakes were higher than any she'd known, and every turn of a card was exciting. So were her winnings. The *Brian Boru*'s passengers were living proof that America was the land of opportunity, and they didn't mind spending their lately gained wealth.

"Ach, Scarlett darling," Colum said at the end of the first week, "you're cleaning out their pockets at the card table."

She laughed. It was true. She was winning a fortune. And what a good thing that there was still a week at sea. She wouldn't have to touch a penny of Rhett's money. As his wife, she spent profligately on the Peachtree Street house and on her wardrobe and luxuries. But the half million he had given her was different. Inviolable. She intended to give it back to him. He had offered it as payment for separation, and she could not accept it, because she would not accept separation.

SCARLETT stood at the ship's rail, between Colum and Kathleen, as the *Brian Boru* entered the sparkling blue waters of Galway Bay.

Colum saw Ireland ahead, and his heart swelled with love for her and pain for her sufferings. And he renewed his vow to destroy the oppressors of his country and to restore her to her own people. He felt no anxiety about the weapons concealed in Scarlett's trunks. Customs officials in Galway concentrated mainly on ships' cargoes, making sure that duty owed to the British government was paid. Even so, it was very good fortune, Colum thought, that he'd convinced Scarlett to come. Her petticoats were much better for hiding guns than the boots and calicoes he'd bought.

Kathleen held tight to the ship's rail, happy to be nearing Ireland. Home, she thought, home. . . .

Scarlett drew in her breath. There was a castle on that little island. A castle! It couldn't be anything else. She could hardly wait to discover what this Ireland was like.

"OUR baggage will be brought to the hotel," Colum said when he returned to the bench where he'd left Scarlett and Kathleen. "It's all arranged. Then tomorrow we'll be on our way to Mullingar and home.

"Come along now, you two," he continued. "We'll have competition getting a hackney, today being Saturday and Market Day."

"Market Day?" Scarlett echoed.

Kathleen clapped her hands. "Market Day in a big city like Galway! Oh, Colum, it should be something grand."

It was grand and exciting and foreign to Scarlett. The entire grass-covered square in front of the Railway Hotel was teeming with life, alive with color. When the hackney set them down on the hotel steps, she begged Colum to join in at once, never mind seeing their rooms or eating dinner. Kathleen echoed her. "I want to take some stockings home to give the girls."

Colum grinned. "All right, then. I'll see to the rooms. Kathleen, you see to Scarlett so she doesn't get lost. Have you any money?"

"I have all my winnings from whist," said Scarlett. She opened her purse and handed Colum a wad of bills. His eyebrows rose.

"You must have almost two hundred dollars here."

"Two forty-seven."

"Here." Colum said. "Here's a few shillings for each of you. You can shop while I do the money exchanging for all of us; then meet me at that pie stall." He pointed toward a fluttering yellow flag in the center of the square.

"Come on, Scarlett," Kathleen said, "take my hand."

In seconds the two cousins were on the grass of the busy square.

Everywhere Scarlett looked she saw ankles and legs in bright stripes. No wonder Kathleen had talked about stockings! The Galway girls wore low-cut black leather shoes—not boots—and their skirts were four to six inches above their ankles. What skirts, too! Full and swinging and bright as the stockings.

"I want some stockings, too, Kathleen! And skirts and a shirtwaist. They're lovely! Come."

Near the square's center were tables piled with finery. Scarlett felt giddy from the lavishness of choice as she began to shop. She didn't understand the English money. It was all too confusing, with pounds and halfpennies and shillings. . . . But it didn't really matter. It was all free, from whist winnings.

By the time Colum found them and they went to the Railway Hotel, they were loaded down with clothes. Scarlett had bought skirts in every color and every weight, and dozens of stockings and shirtwaists, and yards of lace and a long blue cape, plus linen fichus and stacks of shawls.

"I'm worn out," she groaned happily when she dropped down onto the plush settee in the living room of their suite.

I LOVE Irish trains, Scarlett thought when she saw all the individual compartments. How nice to have your own little room instead of sitting in a car with a bunch of strangers. She settled comfortably in the deep seat, eager to pull out of the station so she could look at the countryside.

Ireland didn't disappoint her. "My stars, Colum," she said after they'd been traveling for several hours, "this country's positively peppered with castles! There's one on practically every hill. Why are they all falling down? Why don't people live in them?"

"They're very old, for the most part, Scarlett darling. People found more comfortable ways to live."

She nodded. That made sense. "What's the name of the place the O'Haras live?" she asked.

"Adamstown," Colum replied. "The name's not very Irish— the owner's English."

"Somebody owns the whole town?"

"It's not a town. It's hardly even a village. It was named for the son of the Englishman who first built it—a small gift for Adam, the estate was. It's been inherited since then by his son and grandson and so on. The one that has it now never sees it. He lives mostly in London. It's his agent who manages things."

There was bitterness in Colum's words. Scarlett decided she'd better not ask questions.

When at last Colum announced that they would be getting off the train at the next stop, Scarlett was delighted. The novelty of the train and the castle-peppered views had begun to wear off. She was ready to get where they were going.

But the station sign said MULLINGAR, not ADAMSTOWN. Poor lamb, Colum said, hadn't he told her? They could only go part-way on the train. They'd eat dinner here; then they would make the rest of the journey by road. It was only twenty miles or so; they'd be home before dark.

Twenty miles! Why, that was as far as from Atlanta to Jonesboro. It would take ages, and they'd already been on the train for practically six hours. It took all Scarlett's will to smile pleasantly when Colum introduced his friend Jim Daly. Daly wasn't good-looking, but his wagon was.

Daly owned a bar, and it made Scarlett feel pleasantly wicked to be entering the malty-smelling large room, with its long, polished oak bar. But she had no time to take in the details before Daly ushered her through it into a hallway. The O'Haras were having dinner with him and his family in their private quarters, above the public house.

It was a good dinner, but she might just as well have been in Savannah. All the talk was about the Savannah O'Haras. Jim Daly's mother, it turned out, was another O'Hara cousin.

After dinner they found a small carriage waiting outside the bar, with their trunks already on the top of it. If Scarlett's trunk weighed much less now than at the train depot, no one mentioned it. Scarlett stepped up and took a seat. Kathleen sat beside her, Colum opposite. "May God travel your road with you," called the Dalys.

THE carriage slowed. The road had begun to wind in sharp, short bends. "We'll be reaching Ratharney soon," Colum said, "then a few more miles, and we're in County Meath."

Kathleen sighed happily. Scarlett's eyes sparkled. County Meath. Pa talked like it was paradise, and I can see why. She sniffed the sweet afternoon through the open window, a blend of faint perfume from the pink flowers and a rich country smell of sun-warmed grass from the invisible fields beyond the thick hedgerows and a pungent herbal tang from within the hedgerows themselves.

"Have you told Scarlett about Molly yet, Colum?" Kathleen asked. "She has a right to a warning, I would say."

"Who's Molly?"

"She's the first of the Adamstown O'Haras you'll meet," said Colum, "and a half sister to Kathleen and me."

"And that's a half too much by my thinking," Kathleen said.

"Tell," Scarlett encouraged.

Colum and Kathleen were also half brother and sister, she learned. Their father, Patrick—one of Gerald O'Hara's older brothers—had married three times. The children by his first wife included Jamie, who'd gone to Savannah, and Molly, who was, said Colum, a great beauty.

Patrick married his second wife—Colum's mother—after his first wife died, and after her death he married Kathleen's mother, who was also the mother of Stephen.

Patrick, God rest his soul, was dead these fifteen years, but there was her uncle Daniel, who was still living, and his children and grandchildren.

"I'll never get them all straight," Scarlett said.

Then Colum explained about Molly. She was married to Robert Donahue, who owned a prosperous big farm of a hundred and some acres. Molly was not devoted to her O'Hara kinfolk, Colum said neutrally, and Kathleen snorted. But that was perhaps because her husband was their landlord. Robert Donahue sublet a smaller farm to the O'Haras.

When Colum began to enumerate Robert's children, Scarlett dismissed the onslaught of names. She paid no close attention until he spoke about her own grandmother, old Katie Scarlett. "She still lives in the cottage her husband built for her when they married, in 1789. Nothing will persuade her to move. Sean, Molly's brother, he lives in the cottage with her. And the girls—like Kathleen here—do for them."

Scarlett's brain was reeling. She didn't dare ask about Sean, for fear of having another dozen names thrown at her. In any case, there wasn't time. Molly's house was just ahead.

16

*T*HE lane to Molly's house ran through the center of a small apple orchard; twilight tinted the airy blossoms mauve against the dark blue, low sky. Strict ribbon beds of primroses edged the square house. Everything was very tidy.

Molly herself was impeccable in dress and in manner and expressed "a thousand welcomes" when Scarlett was presented.

She was undeniably beautiful, with velvety clear skin and bright blue eyes.

Scarlett was favorably impressed. "I'm so happy to meet you, Molly, and so grateful that you're going to put me up in your lovely house," she gushed. Not that the house was all that much. The parlor wasn't any bigger than the smallest bedroom in her Peachtree Street house.

"MY GRIEF, Colum! How could you have gone off and left me there all by myself?" Scarlett complained the next day. "That awful Robert is the most boring man in the world, talking about his cows all through *dinner*, as they told me about fifty-eight times, not supper. What on earth difference does it make?"

"In Ireland the English have dinner in the evening, the Irish have supper."

"But they're not English."

"They have aspirations. Robert had a glass of whiskey once in the big house with the earl's agent when he was paying the rents."

"Colum! You're joking."

"I'm laughing, but I'm not joking. Don't worry yourself about it; what matters is, was your bed comfortable?"

"I suppose so. I could have slept on corncobs I was so tired. It feels good to be walking, I must say. That was a long ride yesterday. Is it far to Grandmother's place?"

"A quarter mile, no more, by this boreen."

"Boreen. What a pretty word. We'd say track for a little path like this. But it wouldn't have these hedgerows."

They emerged in an instant into a clearing. Ahead of them was a thatched cottage, its white walls and small blue-framed windows fresh and bright. "It's adorable, Colum!"

The door was open, and there was a strange smell, earthy and sort of sour. It made her nose wrinkle.

"That's the peat fire, Scarlett. You're smelling the true warm heart of Ireland. Molly's coal fire is naught but Englishness."

Scarlett followed Colum into the cottage.

"And is that you at last, Colum O'Hara? Have you brought me the gift of my own Gerald's girl?" The voice was thin and cantankerous, but not weak. A kind of wonder filled Scarlett's being. This was Pa's mother that he had told about so many times.

She pushed past Colum and went to kneel beside the old woman, who was sitting next to the chimney. "I am Gerald's girl, Grandmother. He named me after you, Katie Scarlett."

The original Katie Scarlett was small, her skin darkened by nearly a century of open air and sun and rain. But the faded blue eyes were unclouded and penetrating. "Let me look at you, girl," she said. Her leathery fingers lifted Scarlett's chin.

"By all the saints, Gerald told the truth when he wrote! You've got eyes green as a cat's." She crossed herself rapidly. "Where did they come from? Was your dear mother a witch?"

Scarlett laughed. "She was more like a saint, Grandmother."

"Is that so? And married to my Gerald? The wonder of it all. Colum, you'll light a candle of thanksgiving for me in the church. For the blessing of seeing Katie Scarlett before I go to my grave."

Scarlett's eyes filled with tears. "Thank you, Grandmother."

"Not at all, not at all," said old Katie Scarlett. "Take her away, Colum, I'm ready for my rest now." She closed her eyes.

Colum touched Scarlett's shoulder. "We'll go."

KATHLEEN ran out of her cottage nearby, sending the hens in the yards scattering. "Welcome to the house, Scarlett," she cried. "Tea's in the pot stewing." She'd made a fresh loaf of barm brack for Scarlett, a delicious fruit-filled light bread.

Scarlett was amazed at the change in Kathleen. She looked so happy to be home, so sure of herself.

Scarlett had thought about asking Kathleen to come over to Molly's to stay. Scarlett really needed her. Molly's maid was hopeless at arranging hair. But this happy Kathleen was not someone who'd jump to do her bidding, Scarlett could tell. She'd just have to make do. She sighed and went into the house.

It was so small. Bigger than Grandmother's cottage, but still too small for a family. The outside door led directly to the kitchen. It was only half the size of Scarlett's bedroom in Atlanta. There was a big stone fireplace in the center of one wall. Perilously steep stairs rose up to an opening high in the wall to the left of the chimney; a door to its right led to another room.

My soul, Scarlett thought, my family's really very poor. Why on earth did Kathleen cry her eyes out to come back to this?

In the hours that followed, Scarlett saw for herself why Kathleen had found the relative luxury of life in Savannah an inadequate replacement for life in County Meath. A steady succession of women, girls, boys, men appeared at the door. All were invited to "come in and sit by the fire." The musical Irish voices greeted Scarlett and welcomed her, greeted Kathleen and welcomed her home again, all with a warmth so heartfelt that Scarlett could all but hold it in her hand. It was as different from the formal world of paying and receiving calls as day differs from night.

This is the best vacation a person could possibly have, Scarlett thought. I'll have so much to tell Rhett. Maybe we'll come back together sometime.

In the distance a bell tolled, and Kathleen said, "You'll help me pull out the table, Colum? The men will be coming to dinner. I don't know where Bridie's got to."

One by one the men of the cottage came in from the fields. Scarlett met her father's brother Daniel, a tall, vigorous, angular man of eighty, and his four sons, ages twenty to forty-four.

The missing Bridie ran through the door just as Kathleen was ladling stew into blue-and-white bowls. Bridie was wet. Her shirt clung to her arms, and her hair dripped down her back.

"Did you tumble into a well, then, Bridie?" asked the youngest brother, whose name was Timothy.

"I was washing myself in the river," Bridie said. Then she began to eat, ignoring the uproar caused by her statement. Even Colum, who rarely criticized, raised his voice.

"Brigid O'Hara. Do you not know the Boyne claims a life for every mile of its length every year?"

The Boyne. . . . "Pa told me about the Battle of the Boyne," Scarlett said. "The O'Haras lost all their lands because of it."

"We did," Colum said. "The river marks the boundary of this land. I'll show it to you if you want to see, but it's not for using like a washtub, Brigid. What possessed you?"

"Kathleen told me cousin Scarlett was coming, and a lady's maid must be washed before she touches the lady's clothes or hair. So I went to wash." She looked full at Scarlett for the first time. "It's my intention to please so you'll take me back to America with you." Her blue eyes were solemn, her soft, rounded chin thrust out with determination. Scarlett liked the look of her. There'd be no homesick tears from Bridie, she was sure. But she could only use her until the trip was over. No southerner ever had a white maid. She looked for the right words to tell the girl.

Colum did it for her. "It was already decided you'd go to Savannah with us, Bridie, so you could have avoided risking your life."

"Hurrah!" Bridie shouted. Then she blushed crimson. "I'll not be so rowdy when I'm in service."

Colum was smiling again. "Scarlett will tell you what a lady's needs might be, but not before it's the hour to depart. There's two weeks and a day you'll be sharing quarters on the ship, time enough to learn all you're able to learn."

Daniel had spoken not at all throughout the meal. When it was over, he stood and bowed ceremoniously to Scarlett. "Young Katie Scarlett O'Hara, you honor my house, and I bid you welcome. Your father was greatly loved, and his absence has been a stone in my breast for all these fifty years and more."

She was too surprised to say a word. By the time she thought of something, Daniel, with his sons, was on his way back to his fields.

Colum rose, then moved to the hearth. "Scarlett darling, Daniel's given you the blessing of the head of the house."

"Colum's right," said Kathleen. "When you can't bear another minute of Molly, you'll have a place here if you want it."

"Where do you put everybody?" Scarlett asked with curiosity.

"There's the loft. The boys have their side, Bridie and me the other. And Uncle Daniel has the bed by the fire." Kathleen pulled on the back edge of a wooden settee along the wall by the stairs, and it folded open and down to reveal a thick mattress covered by a woolen blanket. "He felt too lonely in his room after Aunt Theresa died." Kathleen gestured toward the door. "The bed's still in there for you anytime you've the mind."

Scarlett couldn't imagine that she ever would. Seven people in one small house were at least four too many in her opinion. It was time to go back to Molly's house. Molly was having a tea party in Scarlett's honor.

THE food was good, but that's the only good thing I can find to say, Scarlett thought as she smiled brilliantly and shook hands with each of Molly's departing guests. God's nightgown! I've never seen such a tacky bunch of people in all my born days.

The competitive overrefinement of would-be gentry—the elevated little finger of the hand lifting the teacup, the dainty, mouse-size bites of scones that characterized Molly and her acquaintances—seemed as ridiculous to Scarlett as in fact they were. She had eaten with excellent appetite and ignored the hinted invitations to deplore the vulgarity of people who dirtied their hands with farm work. "What does Robert do, Molly—wear kid gloves all the time?" she'd finally asked, delighted to see the lines that showed up in Molly's perfect skin when she frowned.

I reckon she'll have a few words to say to Colum about bringing me here, but I don't care.

"COLUM, I think I'm going to kill dear cousin Molly. Why, this morning she practically swooned when she saw me in these Galway clothes. No chirpy little lady voice then, let me tell you. She lectured me about ruining her position and being an embarrassment to Robert. How dare Molly lecture me?"

Colum patted Scarlett's hand. "She's not the best companion, Scarlett darling, but Molly has her virtues. She did lend us the trap, and it's too fine a day to waste on rancor. You look like a lovely Irish lass in your striped stockings and red petticoat."

Colum was right. Why should she let Molly ruin her day? Scarlett touched the drawstring bag hanging between her breasts. It was hidden by her shirt and Galway blue cloak. No one would ever know she was wearing two hundred dollars in gold instead of a corset. The freedom was almost indecent. She had not been out of the house without stays since she was eleven years old.

They went to Trim, an ancient town with a rich history and a famous castle. The hours sped by, and twilight was setting in when they started the short journey home.

"I'll stop in here at the bar and learn if there's a letter for me," Colum said when they reached Adamstown. He looped the pony's reins around the village pump. "But we can't stay too long, Scarlett. You'll have to get into your finery for Molly's dinner table. You cannot thumb your nose at her under her own roof. She's tried too hard to shed those kinds of petticoats to be able to support seeing them in her dining room."

Scarlett put her hand on Colum's arm. "Do you think I can stay at Daniel's?" she asked. "I truly hate being at Molly's."

Colum laughed. "Don't take this wrong, Scarlett darling, but she'll likely promise anything if I promise to take you elsewhere. She'll never live down what you said about Robert's elegant kid gloves for cow tending. It's already the most cherished story in every kitchen from here to Mullingar."

Colum had a talk with Molly, and by suppertime Scarlett was installed in the room off the kitchen of Daniel's cottage. She adjusted with astonishing ease to the simplicity. With a comfortable bed and Kathleen's tireless, unobtrusive cleaning and cooking, Scarlett had only to enjoy herself on her holiday. And she did—enormously.

DURING the following week Scarlett was busier and in ways happier than she had ever been. Whenever he had time, Colum took Scarlett out adventuring, as he called it. Protected by cloak and hood, she soon learned to pay no attention to the gusting wind from the west or the brief light rains that so often rode on it.

Just such a rain was falling when Colum took her to the "real Tara." Scarlett's cloak billowed around her when she reached the top of the uneven stone steps up the side of the low hill where Ireland's High Kings had ruled and feasted and battled and in the end been defeated.

There's not even a castle. Scarlett looked around her and saw nothing except a scattering of grazing sheep. She shivered, surprising herself. *A goose walked over my grave.* The childhood explanation flickered in her mind, making her smile.

"Come with me." Colum held out his hand to Scarlett, and together they walked slowly across the rich grass to an uneven area of grassy lumps in the earth. Colum stopped. "Saint Patrick himself stood where we are standing now. He was a simple missionary then, facing the power of the High King and his magicians. Patrick had only his faith and his mission of truth and the need to tell it. The wind must have been cold. His need must have been like a consuming flame. He had already broken the High King's law, lighting a great bonfire on a night when it was the law that all fires should be put out. He could have been killed for the trespass, he knew that. He had purposed the great risk to draw the eye of the king and prove to him the magnitude of the message he, Patrick, bore. He did not fear death; he feared only that he would fail God. That he did not do. King Laoghaire, from his ancient jeweled throne, gave the bold missionary the right to preach without hindrance. And Ireland became Christian."

There was in Colum's quiet voice something that compelled Scarlett to listen and to try to understand. She'd never thought about saints as people, as able to be afraid. Now, looking at Colum's short, stocky figure and graying hair tousled by the wind, she could imagine the face and figure of another ordinary-looking man in the same stance of readiness. He wasn't afraid to die. How could anyone not be afraid to die? I don't understand, and I never will, she thought. The realization came slowly: there are things too deep, too complex for everyday understanding. Scarlett felt alone and exposed to the western wind.

Colum walked on, leading her. "There," he said, "that row of mounds. That is all we have left of the banquet hall of the thousand candles. The O'Haras were there, Scarlett darling—all the heroes were there. A thousand guests it held, lit by the thousand candles. What mighty appetites they had—for the venison, boar and roast goose, for the mead and the poteen, for the music. Ach, what revelry! Can you see it, Scarlett? Can you see your pa?"

She laughed with Colum. Yes, Pa would have been calling for his cup to be filled just one more time. "There'd be horses," she said confidently. "Pa always had to have a horse."

Colum put his arms around her and hugged her, then let her go. "I knew you'd feel the glorious fact of it," he said. There was pride in his words, pride in her. Scarlett smiled at him, her eyes like living emeralds.

The wind blew her hood onto her shoulders. The shower was past. She looked up at the clean-washed blue sky.

Then her gaze fell, and she saw Ireland before her, green upon green of fresh-growth fields thick with life. She could see so far, to the mist-edged curve of the earth. Something ancient and pagan stirred deep within her, and the barely tamed wildness that was her hidden being surged hotly through her blood. This was what it was to be a king—this height above the world, this nearness to the sun and the sky. She threw her arms wide to embrace being alive on this hill, with the world at her feet.

"Tara," said Colum. "It's the centuries, Scarlett darling. All the life lived here. You can feel it brushing your skin and speaking without sound. It's time, years beyond our counting. And mystery."

THE NEXT DAY COLUM surprised Scarlett by showing up early, riding a horse and leading a second. "I borrowed us some mounts. Come along now."

There was no saddle, and Scarlett hadn't ridden bareback and astride since she was a child. But it all came back, as if she'd never stopped riding this way.

"Where are we going?" They were on a boreen she'd never walked.

"To the Boyne. I've something to show you."

The river. Scarlett's pulse quickened.

The boreen ended, and suddenly the river was there. The banks were so low that the water all but lapped over them. Brown and gold, like no water Scarlett had ever seen. The sunlight lay on top of the river like molten gold swirling in slow eddies of water as dark as brandy. "It's beautiful," she said, her voice soft. She hadn't expected beauty.

To hear Pa talk, it should be red from all the blood that was spilled, and rushing and wild. But it hardly looks like it's moving at all. So this is the Boyne. She'd heard about it all her life, and now she was here. Scarlett felt an emotion unknown to her, something she couldn't name.

"This is the ford where Bridie does her washing," said Colum. "We're going across. Get your reins steady." His horse stepped into the water. Scarlett gathered up her skirts and followed.

On the opposite bank they dismounted, and Colum tied the horses to a tree. Trees grew close to the river here, and Scarlett found a sunny patch to sit in, her back against a tree trunk.

Colum sat down beside her. "I've a story to tell you," he said. "This land we're on is called Ballyhara. Two hundred years ago, less a few, it was home to our people. This is O'Hara land.

"Two thousand years ago, plus a few, the first O'Haras settled here and made the land their own. One thousand years ago the Vikings discovered the green richness of Ireland and tried to take it for their own. Irish—like the O'Haras—watched the rivers where the dragon-headed longboats might invade, and built strong protections against the enemy.

"The Vikings were driven away," continued Colum, "and the O'Haras tilled their land for two hundred years and more. They built a strong castle, with room for themselves and their servants.

When invasion came again—not Vikings, but English who had once been French—more than half of Ireland was lost to them, but the O'Haras prevailed behind their strong walls and tended their land for another five hundred years.

"Until the Battle of the Boyne, when the land became English. The O'Haras—those that were left—were driven across the ford. One of the children grew up a tenant farmer for the English across the river. His grandson married our grandmother, Katie Scarlett. At his father's side he looked across the waters of the Boyne and saw the castle of the O'Haras torn down, saw an English house rise in its place. But the name remained: Ballyhara.

"The English Ballyhara was built for a young lord. He was as fair and handsome as Apollo, they say. He determined to make Ballyhara the finest estate in all Ireland. His village, though not so grand as Dublin, had a single street wider than the capital's widest street. His stables were like a cathedral; his windows as clear as diamonds; his gardens, a soft carpet to the Boyne.

"His only sorrow was that he had but one son and one grandson, and that grandson became lord of Ballyhara, as did his son after him. I remember him, the young lord of Ballyhara. He rode a tall roan horse, and when the gentry trampled our corn with their horses as they hunted the fox, he always threw coins to us children. I couldn't understand why my father took the coins away from us and cursed the lord for the giving of them."

Colum stood and began to pace the riverbank. When he continued his story, his voice was thin from the strain of controlling it. "The famine came, and with it the starvation and death. 'I cannot stand to see my tenants under such suffering,' said the lord of Ballyhara. 'I will buy two strong ships and give them free and safe passage to America, where there is food in abundance.' The farmers and villagers kissed his hand for his goodness, and many of them prepared for their voyage.

"My father raged at his two brothers Matthew and Brian for accepting the Englishman's gift. But they were firm to go. . . . They drowned, with all the rest, when the rotten ships sank in the first heavy sea. They gained the bitter name 'coffin ships.'

"A man of Ballyhara lay in wait in the stables. And when the young lord came to mount his tall roan horse, he seized him, and he hanged the golden-haired lord of Ballyhara in the tower by the

Boyne, where once the O'Haras had watched for dragon ships."

Scarlett's hand flew to her mouth.

"When the English soldiers came," Colum continued, "the men left at Ballyhara would not point to the man in the stable. The English hanged them all." Colum's face was white in the sun-spattered shade of the trees.

He turned to Scarlett. "We have time to ride across Ballyhara if you want to see it," he said. "It's been deserted for near thirty years. No one will go near it." He held out his hand, and the smile on his ashen face was real. "Come. The horses are just here."

Colum's horse broke a path through brambles and tangled growth, and soon Scarlett could see the mammoth stone walls of a tower ahead of them. It was like the ones she'd seen from the train, made of stone and part crumbled away. Moss stained the base of it, and vines clung to its sides. It looked like it might be as much as thirty feet across and twice that high.

Colum reined in and cupped his hands around his mouth. *"Seachain,"* he shouted, *"seachain."* The strange syllables echoed from the stones.

He turned his head, and his eyes were merry now. There was

color in his cheeks. "That's Gaelic, Scarlett darling, the Old Irish. A *cailleach*—a wise woman—lives in a hut somewhere nearby. She's a witch as old as Tara, some say. I called out to warn her we're passing. She might not like being surprised. I don't say I believe in witches, mind, but it never does any harm to be respectful."

They rode into the clearing around the tower. How old did Colum say it was? No matter. She wasn't afraid of it. The tower was only a building. It's not scary at all. In fact, it kind of invites me over. She rode closer.

"You're very brave, Scarlett darling. There are those who say the tower's haunted by a hanging man."

"Fiddledeedee! There's no such thing as ghosts." Scarlett laid her hand against the stone. It was smooth from eons of weathering. She could feel the warmth of the sun in it and the cold of the rain and the wind. An unaccustomed peacefulness entered her heart. "You can tell it's old," she said, knowing that her words were inadequate, knowing that it didn't matter.

"It survived," Colum said. "Like a mighty tree with roots that go deep to the center of the earth."

"Roots that go deep." Where had she heard that before? Of course, Rhett had said that about Charleston. "I'm going back to a place with roots that go deep," he had said. Now she understood what he had meant. Scarlett smiled, stroking the ancient stones. She could tell him a thing or two about roots going deep. Just wait till the next time he started bragging about how old Charleston was.

The house at Ballyhara was built of stone as well. It was a big house, with flanking wings that were themselves bigger than almost any house Scarlett knew. Built to last, she said to herself. It was a shame nobody lived in it. A waste "Didn't the Ballyhara lord have any children?" she asked Colum.

"No." Colum sounded satisfied. "There was a wife, I believe, who went back to her own people. Some say she went mad."

Scarlett sensed she'd better not admire the house to Colum. "Let's look at the village," she said. It was a town, too large to be a village, and there was not a whole window anywhere or an unbroken door. It was derelict and despised, and it made Scarlett's flesh crawl. Hatred had done this. "What's the best way home?" she asked Colum.

17

O'HARAS from all over County Meath and beyond came to honor Katie Scarlett on her one-hundredth birthday. They brought gifts and stories and food and kegs of ale. Old Katie Scarlett received guests and gifts like a queen, sitting in her high-back chair by the hearth and drinking whiskey in her tea.

There was food and poteen and music. Dancing filled the center of the farmyard, and no one slept at all, save old Katie Scarlett whenever she had a mind to.

I didn't know there could ever be such a party, Scarlett thought to herself. Why not stay in Ireland a little longer and have fun? Charleston would still be there when she arrived. Rhett would still be there, too. Let him wait. The baby in her womb made Rhett hers anytime she wanted to claim him.

The next day she asked Colum if he knew about another sailing. There was indeed, he said. A fine ship that sailed on May 9.

"May ninth. That's a lot later than we planned, Colum."

"It's no time at all, once you're dead, Scarlett."

ON APRIL 26 the *Brian Boru* sailed from Galway with two staterooms unoccupied. She had arrived on the twenty-fourth, a Friday, with passengers and mail. There was a big envelope for Colum from Jamie in Savannah. The envelope finally reached the post station in the pub in Adamstown on Wednesday. Included in the envelope was a letter from Billy Carmody, the foreman for the cathedral. The bishop—with a little persuading—had agreed to allow Scarlett to redeem her sister's dowry.

Tara! Scarlett planned to do such marvelous things. She would make the kitchen warm and friendly, like the Irish ones. As for Will and Suellen, she'd do something very generous for them; for Will anyhow, he deserved it. And Wade and Ella would come live with her and Rhett in Charleston. Rhett really was fond of them. And then the baby would come. And by the summer they'd be at Tara—a Tara reborn and beautiful and home.

THE following Wednesday, Scarlett received another letter. The envelope was covered with writing and rubber-stamped dates. It had gone from the Peachtree Street house to her grandfather's, and he hadn't sent it to Maureen's for weeks. She tore it open impatiently. It was from some government bureau in Atlanta.

The document was dated March 26, 1875. The day she'd sailed from Savannah on the *Brian Boru*. Scarlett's eyes skimmed over the first few lines, then stopped. She read more slowly. All the color drained from her face. "Kathleen, where's Colum?"

"He's with the Old One, Scarlett."

She had to see Colum. Something had gone terribly wrong.

Colum was in the yard in front of the cottage. Scarlett's unnatural calm vanished when she saw him, and she was screaming when she reached his side. "Take me home, Colum. Damn you and all the O'Haras. I should never have left home."

Crumpled in her hand was a statement from the sovereign state of Georgia that it had entered into its permanent records the absolute decree of divorce granted to one Rhett Kinnicutt Butler on the grounds of desertion by his wife, one Scarlett O'Hara Butler, by the military district of South Carolina.

"There is no divorce in South Carolina," said Scarlett. "A lawyer told me so." She said it again and again until her throat was raw and she could no longer force sound through it.

Colum led her to a quiet corner of the vegetable garden. He sat beside her and talked, but he couldn't make her listen, so he took her clenched hands in his for comfort and stayed quiet beside her. Through the twilight. Into the darkness. Bridie came looking for them when supper was ready, and Colum sent her away.

"Tell them in the house not to worry, Bridie. Scarlett only needs a bit of time to get over the shock. The news came from America: her husband's grievously sick. She's afraid he'll die."

Bridie ran back to report. The family prayed.

Another hour went by. Stars glowed in the nearly moonless sky.

"What am I to do, Colum?" Scarlett's rasping voice was loud in the darkness.

"We'll go home as we planned, Scarlett darling." His voice was calm, soothing. "What's done can be undone."

"I should have stayed. I'll never forgive myself."

"Whist, now. Should-haves solve nothing. It's the next thing to happen that needs thinking about."

"He'll never take me back. Not if his heart's so hard that he'd divorce me. I kept waiting for him to come after me, Colum. I was so sure he would. How could I have been such a fool? You don't know the all of it. I'm pregnant, Colum. How can I have a baby when I don't have a husband?"

"Doesn't that take care of it? You've only got to tell him."

Of course. Jagged laughter tore at her throat. There was no piece of paper ever written that would make Rhett Butler give up his baby. He could have the divorce canceled. Rhett could do anything. "Everything's going to be all right. . . . Isn't it, Colum?"

"That it is, Scarlett darling."

LIKE so many people before him, Colum underestimated the strength of Scarlett O'Hara. She insisted that she, Colum, and Bridie leave for Galway the next day, a day early.

Scarlett did very well with her good-byes to the family. The previous day's shock had armored her in a shell of numbness. She broke down only once, when she said good-bye to her grand-mother. Later, in the carriage to Mullingar and in the train to Galway, Scarlett sat silent.

When they reached the Railway Hotel, Colum said, "I'll see you ladies to your room. Then I'm going to go down to the harbor and arrange about loading the trunks."

"I'll go with you," said Scarlett. "I want to see the ship."

Colum humored her. And Bridie asked to come, too.

The early evening breeze off the water was sweet with salt. Scarlett breathed deeply of it, remembering Charleston's salted air. She was unaware of the slow tears rolling down her cheeks.

They found the ship, which was called the *Evening Star*. A uniformed man came off the gangplank with two big canvas sacks on his shoulders. "And isn't that Father Colum O'Hara himself?" he bellowed. He heaved one of the sacks to the ground and took off his hat to Scarlett and Bridie. "I'm just taking the post from America over to the station for sorting tomorrow," said Frank Mahoney. "Will you want a look, Colum?

"That's kind of you, Frank." Colum searched the sack and found the envelope he'd been expecting from his brother. "I thank you, Frank. Would you allow me to buy you a pint?"

"There's no need. I did it for the pleasure of breaking the English rules." Frank hoisted the sack again and was off.

There were a half-dozen smaller letters in the envelope.

"Here's one for you, Scarlett," Colum said, and put a blue envelope in her hand. He had just opened Stephen's letter when he heard a cry and felt a weight sliding against him. Before he could throw out his arms, Scarlett was lying at his feet. The blue envelope and thin pages fluttered in her limp hand.

A hackney sped them back to the hotel.

"SHE fainted, that's all, Father," said the doctor when he left Scarlett's bedroom. "She'll be fine."

Colum thanked him, paid him, saw him out. Then he sat heavily on a chair by the lamplit table, put his head in his hands. He questioned whether Scarlett O'Hara would ever be fine again. The crumpled blue pages from her aunt Pauline were on the table beside him. In their midst was a newspaper clipping. "Yesterday evening," it read, "in a private ceremony at the Confederate Home for Widows and Orphans, Miss Anne Hampton was joined in matrimony to Mr. Rhett Butler."

SCARLETT'S mind spiraled up, up, spinning, swirling, up, up, out of the black toward consciousness, and she opened her eyes. Darkness surrounded her. The lamp had burned out, and Bridie was asleep in her chair, unseen in a corner of the huge room. Scarlett's throat constricted with fear. She was alone and lost in the dark.

Stop it! Her mind forced panic away, demanded that she take hold of herself. Then, like a physical blow, memory attacked her. Rhett was lost to her . . . divorced from her . . . married to Anne Hampton. She couldn't believe it, but she had to, it was true.

I never knew him. I never knew him at all. Who was it that I loved? What's going to become of me?

THAT night, in the frightening darkness of a hotel room in a country thousands of miles from her homeland, Scarlett O'Hara did the most courageous thing she had ever been called on to do. She faced up to failure.

It's all my fault. I should have gone back to Charleston as soon as I knew I was pregnant. I chose to have fun. I just didn't think about what Rhett might believe when I ran away, I didn't think past the next day. I didn't think at all. I never have.

All the impetuous, unconsidered errors of her life crowded around Scarlett in the black silence of the night, and she forced herself to look at them. Charles Hamilton—she had married him to spite Ashley, she hadn't cared for him at all. Frank Kennedy—she'd lied to him so that he'd marry her and give her money to save Tara. Rhett—she'd married him when she didn't love him, and she'd made no effort at all to make him happy, she'd never even cared that he wasn't happy . . . not until it was too late.

Oh, God, forgive me. I hurt and hurt and hurt all of them, because I didn't stop to think what they were feeling.

Melanie, too. I can't bear to remember how nasty I was to her. I never once felt grateful for the way she loved me and stood up for me. I never even told her I loved her.

Despair and shame gripped Scarlett's heart. Now she had to think, and think carefully, before she decided what to do. She had to think about the baby.

Scarlett laid her hands gently on her belly. She'd take care of it better than any baby in the history of the whole world. Her mind filled with images of Rhett and Bonnie. He always loved Bonnie more than he loved me. I'll have a new Bonnie. And when she's old enough—when she loves me, and only me, more than anyone on earth—then I'll let Rhett see her, see what he's missed. . . .

What am I thinking? I must be crazy. Only a minute ago I realized how much I hurt him, and now I'm planning to hurt him worse. I won't be like that, I won't.

Rhett's gone; I've admitted it. I can't give in to regrets or revenge. What I have to do is make a new life from scratch.

Throughout the remainder of the night Scarlett concentrated on the future. Finally the pieces fell into place. She knew what she was going to do. As soon as light filtered through the curtains into the room, Scarlett called out, "Bridie?"

The girl jumped up from the chair, blinking sleep from her eyes. "Thanks be to God you're restored!" she exclaimed.

"I need some breakfast, Bridie. I've got to get my strength back."

AFTER breakfast Scarlett sat down at the writing table. She wrote, folded and sealed two letters, then stared at the blank paper in front of her for a long time. Her very marrow shrank from what she had to do. She had to write to Uncle Henry, eat humble pie and ask him to help her. He was the only one she could trust. Scarlett gritted her teeth and reached for the pen.

Once she had put the words on paper that would turn over control of her Atlanta businesses and her precious horde of gold in the Atlanta bank to Henry Hamilton, she felt physically ill. Not that the old lawyer would cheat her, but she was giving up control of her money, her safety.

But she continued to write. She was going to take a long vacation, she wrote, do some traveling. She would be out of touch, no mail could reach her. The words blurred, but Scarlett blinked the tears away. It was essential to cut all ties, or Rhett would be able to track her down. And he must not know about the baby.

Thirty minutes later Scarlett knocked on the door of Colum's room. She was hollow-eyed from lack of sleep, but perfectly composed. The worst was over; now she had things to do. She smiled at her cousin when he opened his door.

"A thousand welcomes," Colum said. "It's good to see you smiling."

"Soon I'll be able to laugh, I hope. . . . Did the letter from America get lost?"

"No. I have it. I understand what happened."

"Do you?" Scarlett smiled again. "Then you're wiser than I am. I'll likely never understand." She put the three letters she'd written on a table. "I'll tell you about these in a minute. First I have to tell you that I'm not going with you and Bridie. I'm going to stay in Ireland." She held up her hand. "No, don't say anything. I've thought it all through. There's nothing for me in America anymore."

"You're being too hasty, Scarlett darling. Your husband got a divorce once, he'll do it again when you tell him about the baby."

"You're wrong, Colum. Rhett will never divorce Anne. She's his kind, from his people, from Charleston. And besides, she's like Melanie. You never knew Melly, but Rhett did. He respected her and admired her. This girl he's married is worth ten of me, the same as Melly was, and Rhett knows it.

"But the main thing is that I can't go back. People would never believe the baby was made in wedlock. I left Charleston the day after—after the baby was started." Scarlett's face blanched with painful longing.

"Your husband knows the truth. He'll acknowledge the baby."

Scarlett's eyes flamed. "Oh, he'd acknowledge it all right, and he'd take it from me. Colum, you can't imagine how Rhett is about his babies. He's got to own the child."

Suddenly a smile appeared on her lips. "Poor Colum. Don't fret. I know you're trying to help me, and I'm grateful. You've been such a good friend to me. I hope you'll always be my friend."

Colum assured her that he would. He thought to himself that he'd never seen a soul so in need of help.

"I want you to take these letters to America for me, please, Colum. This one's to my aunt Pauline, so she'll have the pleasure of knowing I got her letter. This one's to my Atlanta lawyer, there's business I have to settle. Both should be posted in Boston. I don't want anyone to know where I really am. And this one I want you to hand-deliver. It's to the bank in Savannah. I have a pile of gold and my jewelry in their vault, and I'm counting on you to bring it back safe for me. Now I also need you to find me a lawyer I can trust. I'm going to use Rhett Butler's money to buy Ballyhara, where the O'Haras began. This child's going to have a heritage Rhett could never provide."

"Scarlett darling, I beseech you. Wait a bit. It's too soon for you to be making such big decisions."

"This is my way, Colum, and I mean to take it. I plan to go back to Daniel's tomorrow and ask to stay until Ballyhara's mine."

Colum spread his hands and admitted defeat.

Later he escorted Scarlett to the office of an English lawyer, and the search for the owner of Ballyhara was set into motion.

The following day Colum went to the Market, and he took the purchases Scarlett wanted back to the hotel. "Here you are, then, Mrs. O'Hara," he said. "Black skirts and shirts and shawl and cloak and stockings for the poor new widow, and I've told Bridie that's what the news was that gave you the collapse. Your husband was taken by sickness before there was time for you to reach his side. And here's a wee gift from me. I'm thinking that when widow's weeds pull your spirits down, you'll feel better for having them on." Colum deposited a heap of bright-colored petticoats in Scarlett's lap.

Scarlett's eyes brimmed with emotion. "Now I'll be Scarlett O'Hara, an Irish lass with a secret red petticoat. I'm free, Colum!

I'm going to make a world for myself by my rules, not anybody else's. And I'm going to learn to be happy."

Colum averted his eyes from the grimly determined expression on Scarlett's face.

18

THE ship's sailing was delayed two days, so Colum and Bridie were able to escort Scarlett to the train station the next morning.

Scarlett knew that her carefully thought-out plan was riddled with holes. She had no certainty about anything. The lawyer might not be able to find the owner of Ballyhara. The owner might not be willing to sell. The price might be more, even, than all the money Rhett had given her.

I won't think about it, she thought, there's nothing I can do about any of those things now. . . .

IN MULLINGAR, she bought a pony and trap, and drove it home to Adamstown. It wasn't as stylish a rig as Molly's, but the pony was younger and larger and stronger. And she'd made a start.

The family were shocked when she returned, and sympathetic for her loss. They asked was there anything they could do for her.

"You can teach me," said Scarlett. "I want to learn about an Irish farm." She followed Daniel and his sons through their work routines. After she'd learned all she could about Daniel's farm, Scarlett put herself out to charm Molly's loathsome husband, Robert. His farm was five times the size of Daniel's. After Robert, it was his boss, Mr. Alderson, manager of the earl's entire estate. Not even in the days when she was captivating every man in Clayton County had Scarlett been so charming. Or worked so hard. Or succeeded so well.

After a month she knew almost as much about Adamstown as Alderson did. It was just about that time that she received the letter from her Galway lawyer.

The widow of Ballyhara's deceased owner had remarried only a year after his death and had herself died five years ago. Her heir, the son of her second marriage, said he would consider any offer in excess of fifteen thousand pounds. Scarlett studied the survey map of Ballyhara that was attached to the letter. It was much bigger than she'd thought.

Why, it's both sides of the road to Trim. And there's another river. The boundary is the Boyne on this side and the Knightsbrook on the other. Two rivers. I've got to have it. But—fifteen thousand pounds for a ramshackle ghost town and unworked land?

Ballyhara wasn't just land, it was O'Hara land, the land stolen from her people. Scarlett made a firm offer of fifteen thousand pounds and went to Adamstown to post the letter.

Then she went to the ford over the Boyne and, tucking up her skirts, crossed to the tower. She often went there now when she was worried or sad. She could lay her hands on its great stones and find the solace and comfort she needed in its enduring ancient solidity. Sometimes she talked to it. More rarely she stretched her arms over its stones and wept upon it. She never heard a sound other than her own voice; she never sensed the presence of the eyes that were watching her.

COLUM returned to Ireland on June 18. He sent a telegram from Galway: WILL ARRIVE TWO FIVE JUNE WITH SAVANNAH GOODS. The village was in an uproar. There had never been a telegram in Adamstown. Two hours later another telegram arrived for Scarlett from Galway: OFFER ACCEPTED. LETTER AND CONTRACT FOLLOW.

Scarlett drove her pony trap to Tara with a jubilant heart. It was compellingly necessary on this glorious sunlit day to visit Tara, where the High Kings had once dined, to see from Tara's hill the sweet green land that was now her chosen home. She walked to the Lia Fail, the stone of destiny. Colum had told her about the Lia Fail. It was the coronation test of the ancient kings. If it cried aloud, the man being tested was acceptable as Ireland's High King. Scarlett leaned against the weathered granite pillar and looked dreamily at the blue sky above her. So peaceful. Maybe that's why I needed to come to Tara. I've been so busy I'd forgotten to be happy, and that was the most important part of my plan. Can I be happy in Ireland? Can I make it my real home?

A tiny stir of life moved in her body. "Oh," she whispered. She placed her hands gently over the small swelling under her skirts and stood facing the wind. Green and gold fields and summer-thick green trees filled the world as far as her eyes could see. "All this is yours, little Irish baby," she said. "Your mother will give it to you. Yours, your green high Tara."

Scarlett then made her way to the town of Ballyhara. Now that everything was certain about buying it, she could look closely, see what she had. All told, there were forty-six buildings in the town, plus two churches. Five of the houses were quite grand, two dozen were only cottages. All were deserted.

Scarlett was determined that the baby would be born in the place that would be its home. The Big House at Ballyhara. She was going to be busy all the time from now on. She only had twenty weeks to work in before the birth. It wasn't hard to calculate the date. Nine months from February 14, Saint Valentine's Day. Scarlett's mouth twisted. What a joke that was. . . . She wouldn't think about that now. She'd keep her mind on November 14 and the work to be done before then. She smiled.

She'd said back in Galway that she was going to be happy, and now she was.

COLUM was surprised when Scarlett met his train in Mullingar. Scarlett was surprised when he stepped out of the baggage car and not the coach. And when a companion stepped out after him. "This is Liam Ryan, Scarlett. Jim Ryan's brother." Liam was a big man, dressed in the green uniform of the Royal Irish Constabulary. How could Colum befriend one of them? she thought. They arrested their own people, under orders from the English.

Did Colum have the gold? Scarlett wanted to know. He did, and Liam Ryan with his rifle to guard it.

"I've got men from the bank to take it," said Scarlett. "I'm using Mullingar for safety, it's got the biggest garrison of military."

As soon as she saw the gold stored in the vault and signed the papers for the purchase of Ballyhara, Scarlett took Colum's arm and hurried him out onto the street.

"I've a pony trap, we can get going. There's so much to do, Colum. I've got to find a blacksmith right away. Will you help me? He'll be well paid to move to Ballyhara to work. Oh! I'll need men to clear the fields, and carpenters and roofers and painters to mend the houses!" Her eyes were shining.

Colum extricated himself from her grasp. "All will be done,

Scarlett darling, but first I've things to do in Mullingar. I'll be home in three days, you've my word on it. We'll meet at Daniel's."

"We'll meet at Ballyhara," said Scarlett impatiently. "I've already moved in. It's the yellow house halfway down the street." She turned and strode away to her trap.

LATE that evening, after Jim Ryan's bar was closed for the night, its door was left on the latch for the men who quietly slipped in one by one to meet in a room upstairs. Colum laid out in detail the things they had to do. "It's a God-sent opportunity," he said with incandescent fervor, "an entire town of our own. All Fenian men, all their skills concentrated in one place, where the English would never think to look. The whole world already thinks my cousin's daft for paying such a price for property she might have bought for nothing, just to spare the owner paying taxes on it. The English are too busy laughing at her to be suspicious of what goes on there. We've long needed a secure headquarters. Scarlett's begging us to take it, though she doesn't know it."

"YOU'VE done wonders, Colum, I'm really impressed." Scarlett stood in the center of Ballyhara's wide street and looked at the activity everywhere along the length of it. Hammering could be heard from every direction, and new windows sparkled in a dozen buildings. "But did we really need to finish the bar first?" she asked.

"You'll find more willing workers if there's a place for them to have a pint when their work's done."

"So you've said, but I still can't see why it won't just make them worse. Why, if I didn't keep after them, nothing would ever get done on time. It's practically August already, and not one single field's been cleared yet. How can I plant in the spring if the fields aren't cleared and manured in the fall?"

"You've got months yet, Scarlett darling. Just look what you've already done in only weeks."

Scarlett looked, and she smiled. "That's true," she said.

Scarlett's house was a perfect portrait of her, work first and comfort later. The kitchen had a plain narrow wooden bedstead, a small turf fire in the big stone fireplace, and only one chair, which was placed by a big table under the window. The table held a large account book. The surveyor's map of Ballyhara was nailed to the wall nearby. So was a mirror, above a shelf that held jars of powder, rouge and creams.

She had already mentally designated the houses she was going to give the family. They'd all have grand, spacious homes. Colums was the smallest, but he had chosen his himself. She had chosen a much bigger house for Daniel and Kathleen, and one for each of the sons. She'd also give them farmland, as much as they wanted. The O'Haras would be so surprised when the houses were done and she told them! The gifts were her cherished secret; she hadn't even told Colum yet. It added to her pleasure every time she looked at Ballyhara's street that she knew just which houses would be O'Hara houses.

COLUM appeared at Scarlett's door late in August, when the sky was still rosy with dawn. Ten burly men stood behind him. "Here are the men to clear your fields," he said.

Scarlett screeched with delight. "Let me get my boots, and I'll be right out. Take them to the first field beyond the gate."

She tried to hurry, but excitement made her clumsy. And it was getting more difficult every day to get her boots on. *My grief, I'm as big as a house already. I must be going to have triplets.*

The devil take it! Scarlett grabbed her shawl and ran along the street with her feet bare.

The men were grouped glumly around Colum on the weed-choked drive inside the open gate. "Never seen such a sight." "Those be more like trees than weeds." "Looks like all nettles to me." "A man could spend a lifetime clearing an acre."

"A fine lot you are," Scarlett said clearly. "Are you afraid to get your hands dirty?"

They looked at her with disdain. They'd all heard about the little woman with the driving ways.

"We were discussing the best way to get started," Colum said soothingly.

Scarlett was in no mood to be placated. "I'll show you how you get started." She put her left hand on the lower curve of her belly to support it, then she leaned over, and her right hand grasped a big handful of nettles. With a grunt and a heave she ripped them from the earth. "There," she said contemptuously, "now you're started." She threw the spiny plants at the men's feet. Blood was oozing from wounds all over her hand. Scarlett spit in her palm, then wiped it on her skirt and walked heavily away.

The men stared at her back. First one, then another, then all of them took their hats off.

Later, when Colum entered her kitchen, Scarlett was fixing breakfast. "Want some?" she asked.

Colum sniffed the air. "Porridge again? I'd rather have boiled nettles. You need a woman to help you." He expected her to protest; she automatically denied every suggestion that she couldn't do everything herself. But she agreed. Colum smiled; he had just the woman for the job, he said. She was housekeeper at a big house of an estate on the other side of Trim, and she was willing to take care of Scarlett and this house until the Big House was repaired. Then she'd hire the women needed to run it, and she'd run them.

"You'll admit, Scarlett darling, that you've nothing in America quite like a big house in Ireland. It needs a practiced hand. You'll need a steward, a butler, footmen—"

"Stop!" Scarlett was shaking her head furiously. "I'll only be using a few rooms of that pile of stone up there to start with. So this paragon of yours will have to give up her high-and-mighty position."

"I'll ask her, then." Colum was sure she would agree, even if she had to scrub floors. Rosaleen Mary Fitzpatrick was the sister of a Fenian who'd been executed by the English, and the granddaughter of men who'd gone down in the Ballyhara coffin ships. She was the most passionate member of Colum's inner circle of insurgents.

Scarlett spooned porridge onto a plate and ate hungrily, talking rapidly between mouthfuls. She told Colum her plan for the family, to have all the O'Haras living in moderate luxury at Ballyhara.

Colum waited until she had finished eating before he said, "They won't do it. They've been farming the land they're on for nearly two hundred years."

"Of course they will. Everybody always wants better than they've got."

He shook his head in reply.

"I'll prove you wrong. If you'll hitch my pony to the trap, I'll ask them right now!"

Colum opened his mouth, then closed it. There was no point in arguing. And he was certain that Daniel would never move.

SCARLETT burst in on Colum just before summer's late darkness fell. The family had—very kindly—turned down her invitation to come to Ballyhara.

She had not cried when she received the notice of the divorce, nor even with the announcement that Rhett had married again. But on this warm rainy night in August she sobbed for hours, until she fell asleep on Colum's comfortable couch. He covered her with a lightweight coverlet and went to his bedroom.

In the morning he found Scarlett sitting at his kitchen table, eating the only eggs he had. "You know, Colum, you might start thinking about good tenants for my houses. They'll have to be prosperous, though, because I'll expect good rents."

SCARLETT was profoundly hurt, even though she didn't show it again and never referred to it. She continued to ride over to Daniel's in the trap several times a week, and she worked just as hard as ever on Ballyhara, although her pregnancy was increasingly burdensome. By the end of September the town was done, and the population was growing by leaps and bounds.

There were two more bars, a cobbler's shop, a grocery store, an elderly priest—Father Flynn—for the small Catholic church, and two teachers for the school, which would begin classes soon. The post rider from Trim came every day to leave the mail with the scholarly gentleman who had opened a bookshop. And a doctor had leased the largest of the houses, to begin occupancy the first week of November.

This last was the best news of all for Scarlett. She'd have her own doctor right at hand. Now all she had to do was get the house ready.

"Where is this perfect Fitzpatrick woman of yours, Colum?"

"She'll be here on October first, that's Thursday next."

Scarlett smiled, but with difficulty. "The truth is Colum, I'm worn out. I'll be glad to rest some."

Her back hurt all the time now; her legs, too. And her feet and

ankles were so swollen that walking was agony. And she had six—
no, six and a half—more weeks of this.

There was a knock on the door. "I'll go," Colum said.

He came back to the kitchen with a package in his hand. "That
was Mrs. Flanagan, from the store, with the tobacco you ordered
for Grandmother. I'll take it to her for you."

"No." Scarlett heaved herself to her feet. "She asked me to get
it. I want to take it to her."

"GERALD's girl!" said her grandmother. "It's glad I am to see you."

"I've brought your tobacco," Scarlett said cheerfully.

"What a grand thing to do. Will you have a pipe with me?"

"No, thank you, Grandmother. I'm not quite that Irish yet."

The tiny cottage was quiet except for the sound of her grandmother's soft sucking pulls on her pipe. Scarlett put her feet up on
a stool and closed her eyes. The peacefulness was balm.

When she heard shouting outside, she hurried as best she could
into the farmyard. What she saw was terrifying. There were soldiers in Daniel's farmyard, and Irish constables, and an officer on
a horse, with a saber in his hand. She hobbled across to Kathleen,
who was weeping in the doorway.

"Here's another one of them," said one of the soldiers. "Look at
her. These miserable Irish breed like rabbits."

"You!" Scarlett called loudly. "You on the horse. What are you
and those common creatures doing at this farm?"

"Are you addressing me, girl?" The officer looked down his
long nose.

She stared at him with cold green eyes. "I am not a girl, sir, and
you are not a gentleman, even if you pretend to be an officer."

His mouth dropped open. The hot joy of combat filled Scarlett
with energy.

"What are you doing here?" she said again. "Explain yourself."

The officer remembered who he was. His mouth closed and his
back stiffened. "I am executing an order of Her Majesty's government to evict the people resident on this farm for nonpayment of
rent." He waved a scrolled paper.

Scarlett's heart was in her throat. Beyond the soldiers she could
see Daniel and his sons running from the fields with pitchforks
and cudgels, ready to fight.

"There's obviously been a mistake," she said. "What amount is supposed to be unpaid?" Hurry, she thought, you long-nosed fool. If any O'Hara man—or men—hit a soldier, he'd be sent to prison, or worse.

The officer took forever to open the scroll. "Thirty-one pounds eight shillings and nine pence," he said. Scarlett heard shouting from the field, saw the big O'Hara men running, waving fists and weapons. She clawed frantically at the string around her neck, at the pouch where she kept her money, and breathed a prayer of thanks. She was carrying the wages of all the workers at Ballyhara. More than fifty pounds.

She lifted the cord from her neck, over her head, and she jingled the pouch in her hand. "There's extra for your trouble, you ill-bred cad," she said. Her arm was strong and her aim true. The pouch struck the officer in the mouth. Shillings and pence scattered down the front of his tunic and onto the ground. "Clean up the mess you've made," said Scarlett, "and take away that trash you brought with you!"

She turned her back on the soldiers. "For the love of God, Kathleen," she whispered, "get over in the field and stop the men before there's real trouble."

LATER Scarlett confronted old Daniel. She was livid. "Why didn't you tell me you needed money? I'd have given it to you."

"The O'Haras don't take charity," said Daniel.

"Charity? It's not charity when it's your own family."

Daniel looked at her with old, old eyes. "What isn't earned by your own hands is charity. We've heard your history, Scarlett O'Hara. When my brother Gerald lost his wits, why did you not call upon his brothers in Savannah? They're your own family."

Scarlett's lips trembled. He was right. She had carried her burden alone. She looked at her uncle, the proud tilt of his head, and she understood. She understood, too, why she'd been wrong to offer Ballyhara as a substitute for land he'd farmed all his life. "Robert raised the rent, didn't he? Because I made that smart remark about his gloves."

"Robert's a greedy man. There's no saying that it's anything to do with you."

"Will you allow me to help? It would be an honor."

Scarlett saw approval in old Daniel's eyes. And he agreed.

"I thank you," said Scarlett formally. I'm happy, she thought. I hurt from head to toe, but I'm happy. If this baby isn't proud to be an O'Hara, I'll wring its neck.

19

"*Y*ou need a cook," said Mrs. Fitzpatrick. "I do not myself cook well."

Scarlett didn't think she was going to like this woman, no matter what Colum said. Right off the bat, when I asked her what her name was, she answered, "Mrs. Fitzpatrick." She knew I meant her first name. I've never called a servant Mrs.

Mrs. Fitzpatrick was a tall woman, solid as a tree. Her skin was flawless; her lips were a thin wide slash; and her dark, surprisingly delicate eyebrows formed a perfect thin arch above her blue eyes, strange contrast to her snow-white hair. She was wearing a severe gray gown with white linen collar and cuffs. Her strong capable hands were folded in her lap. There was an English seasoning in her Irish voice. Still soft, but it had lost some music to clipped consonants.

I know what she is, Scarlett realized, she's businesslike. The thought made her feel better. She could deal with a businesswoman whether she liked her or not.

"I am confident that you will find my services useful," said Mrs. Fitzpatrick, "and I shall be honored to be housekeeper for The O'Hara."

What did she mean?

"Do you not know? Everyone is talking of nothing else." Mrs. Fitzpatrick's mouth parted in a gleaming smile. "They're calling you The O'Hara, head of the family O'Hara. In the days of the High Kings each family had its leader, its champion. Some distant ancestor of yours was The O'Hara. Today that title has been reborn for you."

"I don't understand. What do I have to do?"

"You've already done it. You're respected, admired and honored. You have only to be what you are. You are The O'Hara."

The O'Hara. Scarlett tried it silently on her tongue. The O'Hara. It was like a drumbeat. Deep, hidden, buried, primitive, something within her kindled. The O'Hara. "You have only to be what you are," she'd said. What does that mean?

Scarlett looked into Mrs. Fitzpatrick's eyes. "Please have some tea with me," she said. "We need to talk about a cook and other things. We have only six weeks, and a lot to do."

SCARLETT had never been in the Big House. Mrs. Fitzpatrick hid her astonishment and her own curiosity about it. She helped Scarlett turn the huge brass key in the great rusted lock. "Mildew," she said when the smell hit them. "We'll need an army of women with pails and scrubbing brushes. Let's have a look at the kitchen first. No cook worth having is going to come to a house without a first-class kitchen."

Curved colonnades connected two large wings to the main block of the house. They followed the one to the east first and found themselves in a large corner room. Doors opened onto interior corridors that led to more rooms. "You'll put your steward, the manager of the estate, to work here," said Mrs. Fitzpatrick. "This is obviously the estate office."

"I'll be the steward at Ballyhara, Mrs. Fitzpatrick." Scarlett's firm jaw told the housekeeper that there was no point in arguing. "Now let's find this kitchen you're so worried about."

They walked to the other wing. Scarlett was appalled by the condition of the house. How would it ever be done in six weeks? It has to be, that's all. The baby must be born in the Big House.

"Magnificent," said Mrs. Fitzpatrick. The kitchen was cavernous, two stories high, with skylights in the roof. A tremendous stone chimney nearly covered the wall at the far end of the room, with doors on each side of it. One led to a scullery, the other to an empty room. "The cook can sleep here, that's good. And that"— Mrs. Fitzpatrick pointed upward—"is the most intelligent arrangement I've ever seen." A balustraded gallery ran the length of the kitchen at the second-story level. "The rooms above the cook's and the scullery will be mine. The maids and cook will never know when I might be watching them. That should keep them alert. Now I'd like to see the storerooms. Do you want to come?"

"Not really. I'll sit outside." One door led out into an overgrown walled garden. A second door opened onto the colonnade. Scarlett lowered herself to the paved floor and leaned against a column. A heavy fatigue pressed on her. She'd no idea the house would need so much work.

Mrs. Fitzpatrick came out. "It will do," she said succinctly.

"ARE you finding Mrs. Fitzpatrick helpful, Scarlett?" Colum asked.

She had to admit she was. "I've told her to clean out a room for me and order in a bed. But Colum, she's spending money like there's no end to it. Three maids I've got already, just to get things nice enough so that a cook will be willing to come. Oh, I'll be so happy when this baby arrives."

"How much longer?"

"About three weeks. . . . Colum?" He'd been away, and Scarlett didn't feel as easy with him as she used to, but she needed to ask him anyhow. "Have you heard about this 'The O'Hara' business?"

He had, and he was proud of her. "You're a remarkable woman, Scarlett O'Hara. And spitting in the eyes of the English officer— well, they say you put out the sight in one of them from a hundred paces."

"That's not true!"

"And why should a grand tale be tarnished by the truth?"

Scarlett laughed, then said, "I haven't laughed since you went away. Stay home for a while, will you?"

"That I will. I want to be one of the first to see the child. I'm hoping you'll name me a godfather."

"But I was counting on you to baptize the baby."

"I cannot do that, Scarlett darling. That's the job of a parish priest. I'm a missionary priest, working to ease the sufferings of the poor. I perform no sacraments. But the grandest of godfathers I'll be, if you'll ask me, Scarlett darling."

"Of course I'll ask you."

"Then I've got what I came for. Now I can go. But one more promise, Scarlett. Stay in your house Saturday evening, with your door shut tight. It's Allhallows Eve, and the Irish believe all the fairies and goblins and ghosts are out, from all the time since the world began. Pay heed to the customs, and close yourself in safe from seeing them. And if you're really feeling Irish, have a supper of whiskey washed down with ale."

"No wonder they see spooks! But I'll do as you say, Colum."

THE WEATHER HAD TURNED RAINY, with torrents of rain that lasted sometimes for hours. The three maids stood in the doorway of the Big House bedroom Scarlett had chosen for her own. They dropped clumsy curtsies. They were leaving early.

Mrs. Fitzpatrick sighed. "The rain wouldn't have bothered them if today wasn't Halloween. I suppose they think if clouds darken the sky, it's the same as nightfall." She looked at the gold watch pinned on her bosom. "It's only two. . . . Let's get back where we were. I'm afraid that all this wet will keep us from finishing, Mrs. O'Hara. I wish it weren't so, but I'm not going to lie to you. You need new plaster in some spots, and that means dry walls. Then time for the plaster to dry afterward before the wall is painted or papered. Two weeks just isn't enough."

Scarlett's jaw hardened. "I am going to have my baby in this house, Mrs. Fitzpatrick. I told you that from the beginning."

Her anger flowed right off Mrs. Fitzpatrick's sleekness. "I've got a surprise for you," said the housekeeper. "We found it in the attic. Come look." She opened the door to an adjoining room.

Scarlett burst out laughing. "God's nightgown! What is it?"

"A state bed. Probably made for a visit from the viceroy. Isn't it remarkable?" It was immense—at least ten feet long and eight wide. Four thick oak posts carved to look like Greek goddesses supported a tester frame on their laurel-wreathed heads.

"What's a viceroy?"

"The head of the government in Ireland."

"Well, I'll say this for it, with a tester and curtains it will be like a room in itself. You're a marvel, Mrs. Fitzpatrick."

Their laughter was companionable as they walked down the granite staircase to the ground floor. "This is a downpour, not a rain," the housekeeper said. "It can't last at this rate. Would you like a cup of tea? The kitchen's warm and dry; I've had the stove going all day to test it."

"Might as well." She followed Mrs. Fitzpatrick to the kitchen. "This is all new," said Scarlett suspiciously. She didn't like any spending without her approval. "And what did this cost?" She tapped the big, heavy wood table.

"A few bars of soap. It was in the tack room, filthy dirty."

Scarlett felt guilty, and cross, too. Her back was hurting worse than usual. She put her hands over the pain. Then a new pain ripped through her side and down her leg. She grabbed the table for support and stared dumbly at the liquid streaming down her legs to pool on the stone floor.

"The water broke," she said at last, "and it's red. Mrs. Fitzpatrick, please get me up on this table and give me something to soak up the water . . . or the blood. Then hightail it to the bar and tell somebody to ride for a doctor. I'm about to have a baby."

THE ripping pain was not repeated. With cushions under her head and the small of her back Scarlett was quite comfortable. I'd really feel fine, she thought, if there wasn't so much blood. Something's wrong.

Where is the doctor? It wasn't supposed to be like this, I was going to be in a viceroy's bed, not on a table from the tack room.

Why doesn't it stop raining? Pouring, more like it. Wind's rising, too. Oh, where is Mrs. Fitzpatrick? Oh, God. . . .

I'm not going to lose hold of myself, I'm not. The O'Hara doesn't do that kind of thing. . . . What was that? The doctor?

Mrs. Fitzpatrick came in. "I've brought sheets and blankets and soft pillows. Colum's getting the doctor. He tried to cross the river to Adamstown, but he couldn't make it. He's gone to Trim."

"I figured. I'd like a fresh sopper. This one's soaked through."

Mrs. Fitzpatrick tried to hide the horror on her face when she saw the blood-soaked towel. She wadded it up and hurried to one of the stone sinks with it.

"What time does your watch say, Mrs. Fitzpatrick?"

"Five sixteen. I reckon the storm's making travel slow."

THE kitchen door opened. "Scarlett darling, is it very bad?"

"Oh, Colum!" Scarlett pushed herself to half sitting. "Is the doctor with you? There's something bad wrong."

"There's no getting to Trim, the river's over the road. I found a midwife in Dunshauglin, she's on the way. She'll know what to do, lamb. Try not to fret."

The midwife bustled in just after eight, her manner crisp and competent. She took off her cape and walked briskly to the stone sink to wash her hands. At the sight of the blood-soaked towels she wilted, gestured frantically to summon Mrs. Fitzpatrick. They had a whispered conference.

Scarlett lowered her eyelids over sudden tears.

"Let's just see what we have here," said the midwife with false cheer. She felt Scarlett's abdomen. "A fine strong baby. He just greeted me with a kick." She turned to Colum, then pulled him toward the sink. "You should stay, Father—for the last rites."

Scarlett heard her. "Oh, dear God," she cried.

"Hold her legs," the midwife ordered Mrs. Fitzpatrick.

Scarlett screamed when the woman's hand thrust into her womb. "Stop! The pain, make it stop." When the examination was over, she was moaning from the hurt. Blood was splattered everywhere.

"I'll have to try it with both hands," the midwife said.

Scarlett groaned. Mrs. Fitzpatrick stepped in front of the woman. "I have six children," she said. "Get out of here. Colum, get this butcher out of this house before she kills Mrs. O'Hara."

The room was lit suddenly by a flash of brilliance through skylights and windows, and rain slashed against the glass. When lightning scored the sky again, the midwife screamed. Colum took her by the upper arm. "Quiet yourself, woman."

"Get her out of here, Colum," said Mrs. Fitzpatrick. "Then bring the smith. He doctors animals; a woman can't be that different."

Colum looked at Mrs. Fitzpatrick with dull, hopeless eyes. "He'll not come, Rosaleen, no one will come now it's dark. Have you forgot what night this is?"

Mrs. Fitzpatrick wiped Scarlett's temples with a cool, damp cloth. "If you don't bring him, Colum, I'll do it. I've a knife and a pistol. It only needs showing him there's more certain things to fear than ghosts."

Colum nodded. "I'll go."

JOSEPH O'Neill, the blacksmith, crossed himself. His face glistened with sweat. "I've doctored a horse, once, same as this, but a woman I cannot do such violence to." He looked down at Scarlett and shook his head. "I cannot."

There were lamps along the edges of all the sinks, and lightning flashing one jagged bolt after another. The huge kitchen was brighter than day, save for the shadowed corners.

"You've got to do it, man, else she'll die," said Colum.

Scarlett stirred on the table, moaning piteously.

"Joseph! I order you."

The smith shuddered. He raised his arm over Scarlett's mounded belly. Lightning glittered on the blade of the knife in his hand.

"Who is that?" said Scarlett distinctly. "Who's that lovely lady, Colum, in the beautiful white gown?"

"Saint Patrick preserve me!" cried the smith. He dropped the knife and backed away in terror, his hands stretched before him, palms outward.

The wind swirled, caught a branch, hurled it crashing through the window above the sink. Shards of glass fell to the floor. Shrieking noise was everywhere.

The flames in the lamps wavered, and some went out. Quietly, in the midst of the storm's intrusion, the kitchen door was opened and closed again. A shawled figure walked across the kitchen, among the terrorized people, to the window. It was a woman with a creased round face. She reached into the sink and twisted one of the towels, wringing out the blood.

"What are you doing?" Rosaleen Fitzpatrick stepped toward the woman. Colum halted her. He recognized the *cailleach*, the wise woman who lived near the tower.

One by one the wise woman piled bloodstained towels atop one another until the hole in the window was filled. Then she walked to the smith and kicked him sharply. "You're in the way, smith, go back to your forge." She turned to Colum. "Light the lamps again," she said.

Colum lit all the lamps.

"Thank you, Father," she said politely. "Come hold two lamps high by the table. You," she turned to Mrs. Fitzpatrick, "do the same. I'll ready The O'Hara."

A cord around her waist held a dozen or more pouches made of different-colored rags. She reached into one and withdrew a vial of dark liquid. Lifting Scarlett's head, she poured the liquid into her mouth.

The *cailleach* chuckled, then took a tin snuffbox from one of her pouches. Colum and Mrs. Fitzpatrick stood like statues with the lamps, but their eyes followed every move.

The snuffbox contained a paste. The woman rubbed it into the skin of Scarlett's belly. Then she looked at Colum and Mrs. Fitzpatrick. "She will scream, but she will not feel pain."

Before they could reply, she took a thin knife, wiped it with something from one of her pouches and stroked it the length of Scarlett's belly. Scarlett's scream was like the cry of a lost soul.

Before the sound was gone, the *cailleach* was holding a baby in her two hands. She blew into the baby's mouth, once, twice, thrice. The baby's arms jerked, then its legs.

Colum whispered the Hail Mary.

A whisk of the knife cut the cord, the baby was laid on folded sheets and the woman was back beside Scarlett. "Hold the lamps closer," she said.

Her hands moved quickly. She poured more dark fluid between Scarlett's lips, then a colorless one into the wound in her belly. A cracked humming accompanied the small precise movements as she sewed the wound together.

"Wrap her in linen while I wash the babe," she said.

When Colum and Mrs. Fitzpatrick were finished, the woman was back. Scarlett's baby was swaddled in a soft white blanket. "The midwife forgot this," the *cailleach* said. Her chuckle brought an answering throaty sound from the baby, and the infant girl opened her eyes. She had long black lashes and two tiny lines for eyebrows. Her olive skin was very dark against the white blanket.

SCARLETT tried to hold on to the darkness, to stay asleep, to push the world away. But the pain tore at her, made her move to flee it, and the moving gave it such strength that she whimpered helplessly. The cool glass vial tipped, and she was freed. Later, when she floated again to the edges of consciousness, she opened her mouth in readiness, eager for the dreamless darkness. Instead there was a cold, wet cloth wiping her lips, and a voice she knew. "Scarlett darling . . . open your eyes. . . ."

Colum. It was Colum. She opened her eyes halfway.

"I've something for you, Scarlett darling. Here. Look."

Scarlett turned her head on the pillow. A pale bundle in someone's hands was there. "Your daughter." Colum parted the folds of the blanket, and she saw the tiny sleeping face.

"Oh," Scarlett breathed. So small and so perfect. She looks sunbrowned, like—like a baby pirate. She looks like Rhett!

Scarlett felt a strange warmth wash through her. The baby

opened her eyes. They stared into Scarlett's. And Scarlett felt love. Without conditions, without bounds, without self. Perhaps it was because the baby looked like Rhett; perhaps it was because Scarlett always valued most what she fought hardest for. Whatever the origin, pure, consuming love had come to Scarlett O'Hara after a lifetime of emptiness, not knowing what she lacked.

SCARLETT refused to take any more painkiller. The long red scar on her body was like a streak of white-hot steel, but it was forgotten in the overwhelming joy she felt whenever she touched her baby or even looked at her.

The child was baptized in Scarlett's bedroom because Scarlett was too weak to walk. Father Flynn stood near the viceregal bed, where she was propped up against pillows. Colum was godfather; Kathleen and Mrs. Fitzpatrick were godmothers. The baby was named Katie Colum O'Hara. She waved her arms and kicked her legs when the water touched her, but she didn't cry.

Kathleen wore her best blue frock, although she should have been in mourning. Old Katie Scarlett had died. But everyone agreed that Scarlett should not be told until she was stronger.

When the ceremony was over, Colum poured a tot of whiskey for Father Flynn and the godparents, then escorted the priest to Kennedy's bar, where he bought a few rounds for all there in honor of the occasion. He hoped against hope that it would stop the rumors that were already flying all over County Meath.

Joe O'Neill, the blacksmith, had cowered in a corner of Ballyhara's kitchen until daylight, then scuttled to his smithy to drink himself brave. "Ready was I to save the life of The O'Hara when the witch come through the stone wall and throws me with terrible force onto the floor," he told anyone who would listen, and there were many.

"She cast a spell on The O'Hara then and ripped the babe from the womb. I saw the babe, and I'm telling you it was a man-child. But the demon turns her back and then presents to Father O'Hara a spindly frail female. Now tell me, if I didn't see a changeling, what was it I saw that terrible night? It was the devil's work, and the babe is naught but a ghoul."

The story got to Ballyhara after a week. "I feel that I should warn Scarlett," Colum said to Rosaleen Fitzpatrick, "but what can

313

I tell her? That people are superstitious? That Allhallows Eve is a dangerous birth date for a baby? I cannot find any advice to give her. There's no way to protect the baby from talk."

"I'll see to Katie's safety in this house," Mrs. Fitzpatrick said. "Talk will be forgotten in time. You know that, Colum."

A WEEK later Mrs. Fitzpatrick took a tray of tea and sandwiches to Scarlett's room and stood patiently while Scarlett bombarded her with the same plaint she'd been making for days.

"I don't see why I have to stay stuck up here in this room forever. I feel plenty well enough to be up and about— Oh, look! Come look! Look at Katie's eyes. They're changing from blue. I can see the first little specks of green. She's going to have my eyes!"

Scarlett nuzzled the baby's neck. "You're Momma's girl, aren't you, Katie O'Hara? No, not Katie. Anybody can be a Katie. I'm going to call you Kitty Cat, with your green eyes." She lifted the solemn baby up to face the housekeeper.

"Mrs. Fitzpatrick, I'd like to introduce you to Cat O'Hara."

Rosaleen Fitzpatrick felt more frightened than at any time in her life.

20

THE enforced idleness of her convalescence gave Scarlett many hours to think. What she thought about first and foremost was her love for Cat. It's loving that's making me so happy, Scarlett realized. It has nothing to do with being loved.

I didn't dream anybody could ever feel as happy as I do now, every time I look at Cat. I was happy even before Cat came. I was happy because the O'Haras took me just the way I was. They never made me feel I had to change.

Oh, I'm never going to try to change Cat. I'm never going to make her different from what she is. I'm always going to love her like I do now—with my whole heart—no matter what.

Mother never loved me like I love Cat, Scarlett realized. She wanted me to be different from me, she wanted me to be just like her. But Mother was wrong. Being a lady like her isn't the only way to be. It isn't even the best way to be. Not if it doesn't make you happy. Happy is the best way to be because then you can let other people be happy, too. Their own way.

What was it Mrs. Fitzpatrick said? "You only have to be what you are." What I am is Scarlett O'Hara, who makes mistakes sometimes and does things right sometimes, but who never pretends to be what she's not. I'm The O'Hara, and I'm proud of it. It makes me happy and whole.

MRS. Fitzpatrick was Scarlett's constant companion during the long convalescent weeks after Cat was born. The two women had become close. Scarlett invited the housekeeper to call her Scarlett and asked, "What's your first name?"

Mrs. Fitzpatrick never told her. It wouldn't do for any informality to develop, she said firmly. She suggested that Scarlett could call her Mrs. Fitz, and she would call Scarlett Mrs. O. But only when they were alone together.

Mrs. Fitz had told her about old Katie Scarlett dying. And about the old woman who had appeared, as if by magic, to deliver Cat in the middle of the Halloween tempest. Colum had told her who the woman was—the *cailleach* from the tower. Scarlett owed the wise woman her life, and Cat's. She had to thank her.

THE cold took Scarlett by surprise. October had been warm enough, how could one month make so much difference? She wrapped the folds of her cloak around the well-blanketed baby and walked through the stable yard to the route she'd used so often in the trap.

"I KNOW you're there someplace," Scarlett shouted at the thicket that bordered the tower's clearing. Then she waited confidently.

A few minutes later Scarlett heard a rustling in the holly bushes and the wise woman stepped out. "This way," she said.

There was a path, which Scarlett followed to a grove of trees. The wise woman bent low under the branches. Scarlett did the same. After a few steps she was in a clearing that held a small hut. "Come in," said the woman. She opened the door.

"Let me have the babe," said the wise woman, hands outstretched. Scarlett passed Cat over at once.

"She's a fine child. What have you named her?"

"Katie Colum O'Hara," said Scarlett.

"Katie Colum," the wise woman repeated. " 'Tis a weak, soft sound for this strong child. My name is Grainne, a strong name." Scarlett didn't know how she should reply. Then the woman lifted Cat and whispered in her little ear. "I spoke in the Old Irish. It was a charm," she explained.

Scarlett began thanking the woman for what she'd done, but Grainne stopped her.

"There are few who feel thankful when I enter their lives," she said. "I wonder you don't feel anger at what I did to your body."

"You saved my life and my baby's, too."

"But I took life away from all other babes."

"What do you mean?" said Scarlett.

"I lifted the womb with the baby, and I had not the skills to restore it. You will never have another child."

There was a terrible finality in the woman's words. No more babies? Now, when she'd finally discovered the encompassing joy of being a mother? It couldn't be. It was too cruel.

Cat made a soft mewing sound. Scarlett knew that she was getting hungry. *What am I taking on so for? Don't I already have the most wonderful baby in the whole world? I'm not going to fret about imaginary babies when my Cat is real and wants her mother.* "I've got to go," said Scarlett. "It's time to feed the baby." She held out her hands for Cat.

"One more word," said Grainne. "A warning. Keep your babe close. There are those who say she was brought by a witch and must be bewitched therefrom." Scarlett shivered.

Grainne kissed Cat's soft head. "Go well, Dara," she said; then she gave the baby to Scarlett. "I will call her Dara. It means oak tree. I am grateful for seeing her. But do not bring her again. It is not wise for her to have aught to do with me. Go now."

Scarlett was glad to obey.

Colum had been away. When he came home, Scarlett walked down to his house for tea. And advice. She wanted to buy a small closed buggy. It was too cold to go around in the trap. "Will you pick one out for me, Colum?"

He'd be willing, he said, but she could do her own choosing. The buggy makers would bring their wares to her. As would the makers of anything else. She was the lady of the Big House.

Within a week Scarlett was driving a neat black buggy behind a neat gray horse. She also had a "parlor suite" of green-upholstered oak furniture with ten extra chairs, and a table large enough to seat six for a meal. All these sat on a Wilton carpet in the room adjoining her bedroom. No matter what Mrs. Fitz said, she saw no reason at all to use the downstairs rooms for entertaining when there were plenty of empty rooms upstairs and handy.

Cat's padded basket was beside her on the seat of the buggy everywhere Scarlett went, and she showed Cat off at every shop and house in Ballyhara. People crossed themselves when they saw the dark-skinned baby with the green eyes, and Scarlett was pleased. She thought they were blessing the baby.

SCARLETT and Cat spent Christmas Day at Daniel's house. There were nearly enough people coming through the open door to keep Scarlett's mind off the Christmases at Tara in the old days, when the family and house servants went out onto the wide porch after breakfast in response to the cry "Christmas gift." When Gerald O'Hara gave a drink of whiskey and a plug of tobacco to every field hand as he handed him his new coat and new boots. When Ellen O'Hara said a brief prayer for each woman and child as she gave them lengths of calico and flannel, together with oranges and stick candy. Sometimes Scarlett missed the flashing smiles on black faces almost more than she could bear.

On New Year's Day, Scarlett got her first hint of what it really meant to be The O'Hara. After breakfast Colum accompanied her through the town. It was good luck for the whole year, he explained, if a dark-haired person visited a house on New Year's Day. The head of a clan was ten-times-over good luck. But the tradition required that the person enter, then be escorted out, then be escorted back in again.

"Thank goodness there are still so many empty buildings," Scarlett gasped when it was over. "I'm awash with tea and foundering from all the cake in my stomach. Did we have to eat in every place?"

"Scarlett darling, how can you call it a visit if there's no hospitality offered and received?"

A month later, on February 1, was the feast day of Saint Brigid.

It was considered the beginning of the farm year in Ireland. Accompanied by everyone who worked and lived in Ballyhara, Scarlett stood in the center of a big field and, after saying a prayer for the success of the crops, sank a spade into the earth, lifted and turned the first sod. Now the year could begin.

"You need some clothes," Mrs. Fitz said one day. "I've heard there's a dressmaker who wants to rent a house."

"What's wrong with the way I look?"

"You wear earth-stained peasant clothes, and you're the lady of the Big House."

"Oh, fiddledeedee, Mrs. Fitz. How could I ride out to see if the timothy grass is growing if I had on lady-of-the-house clothes?"

"Then you aren't interested in renting to the dressmaker?" said Mrs. Fitzgerald.

"I'm always interested in another rent. And one of these days I'll order some frocks. After the planting."

"There's still another rent possible," Mrs. Fitz said carefully. "Brendan Kennedy thinks he could do well if he added an inn to his bar. There's the building next to him could be used."

"Who on earth would come to an inn in Ballyhara? That's crazy."

Mrs. Fitzgerald abandoned talk of the inn for the moment. Colum would have to work on it; he was much more persuasive than she was. The Fenians had been steadily growing in strength and numbers throughout Ireland. With Ballyhara they now had what they most needed: a secure location where leaders from every county could meet to plan strategy, and where a man fleeing the militia could safely go. Except that strangers were too noticeable in a town that was hardly larger than a village.

"We really need the inn," Rosaleen said to Colum that night.

"You're right, Rosaleen," he soothed, "and I'll talk to Scarlett. But not right away. She'll wonder why we're both pressing. I'll do it when I believe the moment's right."

Mrs. Fitzpatrick had to settle for that. She consoled herself by remembering that at least she'd gotten the dressmaker in.

Scarlett decided to buy some pretty frocks. She was going to America. If she left soon after Easter, she could be back in plenty of time for the harvest.

I'll feel the baking heat of Georgia sun one more time, she thought. I'm entitled to that. I miss it sometimes so terribly. But somehow Tara's more like a dream than a memory. It belongs in the past, like the Scarlett I used to be. I'll keep my shares of Tara for Wade and Ella's inheritance, but I'll sell everything in Atlanta and cut those ties. Ballyhara's my home now.

Her mind concentrated on the best way to tell Wade and Ella about their wonderful new home. They wouldn't believe she wanted them. Why should they? In truth she never had. Until she discovered what it felt like to love a child, to be a real mother.

It's going to be hard, Scarlett told herself many times, but I *can* make up for the past. I've got so much love in me that it just spills over. I want to give some to my son and my daughter. They might not like Ireland at first, it's so different; but once we go to Market Day a couple of times, and I buy them their own ponies . . .

Scarlett reserved the best stateroom on the *Brian Boru* for departure from Galway on the Friday following Easter.

But she did not make the sailing. On Easter Sunday night old Daniel O'Hara died, and Scarlett had to stay in Ireland for his wake and burial.

She finally booked a cabin on a ship sailing April 26, a year exactly after the date she was originally supposed to have ended her "vacation" in Ireland.

ON THE day before she was to leave for America, Scarlett ran, half dancing, to Ballyhara town to pick up the last of the dresses she'd ordered from the dressmaker. While the frocks were being wrapped in tissue paper Scarlett looked out at the town and saw Colum going into the abandoned Protestant church on the other side of the wide street. Oh, good, she thought, he's going to use it after all. It makes no sense for the whole town to be squashed into that little chapel for Mass every Sunday, when there's that great big church standing empty. Just because it was built by Protestants is no reason for Catholics not to take it over. I'll just go tell him how happy it makes me that he's changed his mind.

"I'll be right back," she told the dressmaker. She hurried over to the church and opened the door. A loud noise sounded, then another, and Scarlett felt something sharp hit her sleeve.

A shaft of light from the open door fell directly onto a strange man, who had spun to face her. His stubbled face was twisted into a snarl. He was half crouching, pointing a pistol at her.

He shot at me. White-hot anger filled Scarlett, and she lunged forward. The second shot echoed deafeningly from the vaulted stone ceilings. Scarlett threw herself to the floor screaming.

"I'll ask you to be quiet, Scarlett darling," said Colum. There was steel in his voice, and ice.

Scarlett looked up. She saw Colum's right arm around the neck of the man, Colum's left hand around the man's wrist, the pistol pointing at the ceiling. "Drop it, Davey boy," he said. The pistol fell with a metallic crash onto the stone floor. Colum released the man, made two fists with his hands and clubbed him. The unconscious form fell at Colum's feet.

Scarlett got slowly to her feet. "What is going on here?" she enunciated carefully.

Colum walked briskly past Scarlett and quietly closed the door, slid the bolt across. "Now, Scarlett darling, we have to talk." The warmth and lilt were back in his voice. "It's an unfortunate happening to be sure, Scarlett darling—"

"Don't 'Scarlett darling' me. That man tried to kill me. Who is he? What's going on here?"

Colum walked to a place where thin slats of sunlight slanted down from the boarded-over windows. Scarlett couldn't believe her eyes. He was smiling at her. "Ach, the pity of it is, if we'd had the inn, this would never have happened. I wanted to keep you out of it, Scarlett darling. It's a worrisome thing once you know."

Colum told her about the Fenian brotherhood. Not until he'd finished did she find her voice.

"Judas! You filthy, lying traitor. I trusted you. I thought you my friend." She felt heartsick. Everything was a betrayal, all of it. He'd been using her. They all had—all her O'Hara cousins in Savannah and in Ireland, all the people in Ballyhara town. Her happiness was a delusion. Everything was a delusion.

"Will you listen now, Scarlett? Remember your South with the boots of the conqueror upon her, and think of Ireland, her beauty and her life's blood in the murdering hands of the enemy. The English stole our language. Teaching a child Irish is a crime. They took our land, which is our mother. They left us nothing.

"When your Tara was being taken from you, Scarlett, you battled for it. Were lies needed, you could lie; deceptions, you could deceive. So it is with us who battle for Ireland.

"You are loved by me, Scarlett, by us all. You thought I was your friend, you say. So I am, Scarlett, and will be until time ends. And yet Ireland is my soul. But she does not take away the love I have for you; she makes it more."

Scarlett understood no more than half of what Colum was saying. Yet he enthralled her, as he always did when he spoke that way.

The unconscious man on the floor groaned. Scarlett looked at Colum with fear. "Is that man a Fenian?"

"Yes. He's on the run from the English."

"You gave him that gun." It was not a question.

"Yes, Scarlett. I have concealed weapons throughout this English church. I am the armorer for the brotherhood. When the day arrives, many thousands of Irishmen will be armed for the uprising, and those arms will come from this English place."

"When?" Scarlett dreaded his reply.

"There's no date set. We need more shipments."

"That's what you do in America."

"It is. I raise the money, others buy weapons with it, and I bring them into Ireland."

Scarlett was shaken. She groped for understanding. Suppose she hadn't been there when the English came to Daniel's house? Suppose all her money was gone and Cat was hungry? Suppose the English soldiers really were like Yankees? She knew what it was to be helpless before an army. She knew the feeling of hunger. They were memories no amount of gold could ever erase.

"How can I help you?" she asked Colum. He was fighting for Ireland, and Ireland was the home of her people and her child.

21

THE long, slow miles the ship took to travel up the Savannah River seemed to go on forever. Scarlett was on deck with Cat in her arms. There was the city. And the docks. "Oh, Cat, this is the South, feel the sun? Oh, my darling, my Cat, Momma's home."

Savannah hadn't changed, Maureen's kitchen hadn't changed. The affection. The swarms of O'Hara children. Cat was embraced at once into the daily rhythms of the three-house home. She regarded the other children with curiosity, pulled their hair, submitted to hers being pulled, became one of them.

Scarlett was jealous. *She won't miss me at all, and I cannot bear to leave her, but I have to. Too many people in Atlanta know Rhett, and they might tell him about her. I'd kill him before I'd let him take her from me.*

She sent telegrams to Uncle Henry Hamilton at his office and to Pansy at the house on Peachtree Street, and took the train for Atlanta on the twelfth of May. She was both excited and nervous, but she was radiant in emerald-green Irish linen.

THE hubbub at the Atlanta depot made Scarlett's heart race with excitement. How alive were the noise and hurry and push.

She looked eagerly out the window of her carriage at the houses on Peachtree Street. The Merriwethers' had a new roof, the Meades' a new color paint. And there was her house! Oh. *Was it always so close to the street? For pity's sake, what difference does it make? I've decided to sell it anyhow.*

But this was no time to sell, said Uncle Henry Hamilton when she got to his office. The depression was no better, and the hardest-hit market of all was real estate, especially big places like hers. People were moving down, not up. The little houses, now, like the ones on the edge of town, they were selling fast. She was making a fortune there. Why did she want to sell anyhow? It wasn't as if the house cost her anything. Rhett paid all the bills.

Uncle Henry probably blames me for the divorce, Scarlett thought. *And it doesn't matter a bit. He's wrong in judging me, just like everybody else in Atlanta was wrong in judging me.*

"If you don't want to bother with selling my property, I won't take it against you, Henry," she said. "Just tell me so." There was a simple dignity in her manner.

"I'm an old man, Scarlett. It would probably be better for you to hook up with a younger lawyer."

Scarlett rose from her chair, held out her hand, smiled with real fondness for him.

It was only after she was gone that he could put words to the difference in her. *Scarlett's grown up. She didn't call me Uncle Henry.*

"Is Mrs. Butler at home?"

Scarlett recognized Ashley's voice immediately. She hurried from the sitting room into the hall. "Ashley, dear, I'm so happy to see you." She held out both her hands to him.

He clasped them tightly in his, looking down at her. "Scarlett, you've never looked lovelier. Foreign climates agree with you. Tell me what you've been doing."

"Come in and sit down." She led the way into the sitting room, took one corner of a settee, patted the seat beside her. "Sit here beside me, Ashley, do. I want to look at you."

Ashley Wilkes was doing fine. He'd lost that hangdog look he'd had. And he was still a handsome man. His thin aristocratic features had become more distinguished with age. She smiled at him. It was good to see him. Especially looking so fit.

"How's Aunt Pitty? And India? And Beau?"

Pitty and India were just the same, said Ashley with a quirk of his lips. Pitty got the vapors at every passing shadow, and India was very busy working to improve the moral tone of Atlanta. Beau was a real little man; he already knew more about the lumber business than his father, said Ashley, his gray eyes lighting up with pride. And, he added, the boy had the makings of a scholar.

Maybe the boy would be all right, Scarlett decided. If he knew lumber already, there was hope for him. Now she had one more promise to Melly that she wanted to settle. Scarlett put her hand on Ashley's sleeve. "I've got a big favor to beg," she said.

"Anything, Scarlett." Ashley covered her hand with his.

"I'd like for you to promise that you'll let me send Beau to university and then on a grand tour. It would mean a lot to me. And I've come into a lot of money lately, so that's no problem—"

"Scarlett. . . ." Ashley's smile was gone. He looked very serious. "Scarlett, dear. I know how you came into that money. Uncle Henry let it slip. I understand how you must feel. But there's no need. Rhett was never worthy of you, you're well rid of him. You can put it all behind you now, as if it never happened."

Great balls of fire, Ashley's going to propose!

"You're free from Rhett. Say you'll marry me, Scarlett, and I'll pledge my life to making you happy, as you deserve to be."

There was a time when I would have traded my soul for those words, Scarlett thought. It's not fair that now I hear them and don't feel anything at all. Oh, why was Ashley doing this? Before the question was formed in her mind, she knew the answer. It was because of the old gossip. Ashley was determined to redeem her in the eyes of Atlanta society. If that wasn't just like him! He'll do the gentlemanly thing even if it means tearing up his whole life.

Poor Ashley. Rhett had said it once: Ashley belonged to that time before the War. He's got no place in the world today. I can't be angry or mean. I don't want to lose anyone who was part of the glory days. All that's left of that world is the memories and the people who share them.

"Dearest Ashley," Scarlett said, "I don't want to marry you. That's the all of it. I'm not going to play belle games with you. I care for you too much for that. You've been a big piece of my life all along, and you always will be. Say you'll let me keep that."

"Of course, my dear. I'm honored you feel that way. I won't distress you by referring again to marriage." He smiled, and he looked so young, so much like the Ashley of Twelve Oaks that Scarlett's heart turned over. Dearest Ashley. Everything was all right. No. Better than all right. Now they could truly be friends. The past was neatly finished.

"What are your plans, Scarlett? Are you home for good?"

"I'm selling up, Ashley, I don't want to be tied down at all for a while. After I visited in Savannah, I paid a visit to Pa's family in Ireland, then I went traveling. Somehow I never got around to seeing London. Do you think London's a good idea?" Scarlett knew, from Melanie, that he considered London the perfect city. He'd talk his head off and forget to ask any more questions.

When Scarlett walked him to the door later, she said, "I enjoyed the afternoon so much, Ashley."

"It was a rare pleasure." Ashley accepted his hat and gloves from the maid. "Good-bye, Scarlett."

"Good-bye. Oh— Ashley, you will grant the favor I asked, won't you? If you don't let me set up a fund for Beau, I'll cry. And you know that no gentleman ever deliberately makes a lady cry."

Ashley bowed over her hand. "I was thinking how much you'd changed, Scarlett, but I was wrong. You can still wrap men around your little finger and make them like it. I'd be a bad father to deny Beau a gift from you."

"Oh, Ashley, I do love you, and I always will. Thank you."

And run to the kitchen and tell that, Scarlett thought as she watched the maid close the door behind Ashley. Might as well give all the old cats something good to gossip about. Besides, I do love Ashley, in a way they'd never understand.

IT TOOK much longer than she'd expected for Scarlett to accomplish her business in Atlanta. She didn't leave for Tara until June 10. But once on the train to Jonesboro she was able to relax. In spite of the delays, she had done everything she'd set out to do. The saloon had been sold, and the store. She'd realized enough from those two sales to put up another hundred houses on the edge of the city. That would keep Ashley prosperous for years. And she would make a fortune.

Her little houses had made a profit. A lot of profit. She was downright shocked when she saw her bank account. It made it much easier to instruct the builder to send all the future profits to Stephen O'Hara in Savannah. Now he'd have all the money he needed to carry out Colum's instructions.

It was funny about the Peachtree Street house, Scarlett thought. You'd think it would hurt to part with it. But when that girls' school made an offer, the only thing I felt was relief. I'm free now. And most wonderful of all, I'm going home to Tara.

WILL Benteen was waiting for her at the Jonesboro depot. Scarlett hugged him ferociously.

"Landsake, Scarlett, it's good to see you."

"It's good to see you, too, Will." It was so true. Will was so dear to her. Maybe because he loved Tara as much as she did.

Scarlett climbed up onto the seat of the wagon. "Tell me the news, Will," she said when they were on the road.

"Well, let me see. Ella and our Susie are thick as thieves, and that's done Ella a world of good. You ain't hardly going to know Wade when you see him. He started shooting up when he hit fourteen, last January, and it don't look like he's ever going to stop. For all the weedy look, though, he's strong as a mule. Works like one, too."

Scarlett smiled. A born farmer. How he'll love Ballyhara.

"Suellen lost a baby last year, but we've got three healthy girls.

Course I'd have liked a boy, but I'm not complaining. Wade's been all the son any man could hope for. He's a fine boy, Scarlett. I'm that fond of Wade, I agreed to talk to you for him. He's always been kind of scared of you, Scarlett, you know that. What he wants me to tell you is he don't want no more schooling."

Scarlett shook her head. "His daddy went to university and so will Wade. No offense, Will, but a man can't go very far without an education."

"No offense taken, but I figure you're wrong. Wade can read and write and do all the calculations a farmer's ever going to need. And that's what he wants. Farming. Farming Tara. He says his grandpa built Tara with no more schooling than he's got."

Will looked directly ahead at the dusty red road and continued in his slow cracker drawl. "They showed me the new papers about Tara over to the county courthouse. Seems like you got hold of Carreen's share. I don't know what your thinking is, Scarlett, but my figuring is that Tara should be Wade's. The land should stay in the family. I'm hoping you'll leave him where he is."

"I'll think about it," Scarlett promised. The wagon creaked along the familiar road, and she saw that the land she'd known as cultivated fields was now all gone back to scrub. Scarlett felt like crying, but she forced herself to smile.

SCARLETT was glad she hadn't told anyone in Savannah about her plan to take Wade and Ella back to Ireland with her. Now she didn't have to explain why she'd left them at Tara, that her own children didn't want her, that they were strangers to her and she to them. It hurt, and she blamed herself.

Everything had hurt at Tara. She'd hardly recognized anything in the house. Suellen had used the money every month to buy new furnishings. Scarlett hated it all. It made her feel like a stranger.

She had been glad to leave Tara, and that hurt, too. At least her son was taking her place. She saw her new lawyer in Atlanta after the Tara visit, and she made a will, leaving her two-thirds share of Tara to Wade. She signed the document with a flourish, and then she was free.

To go back to Savannah and her Cat. Who healed all Scarlett's hurts in a second. The baby's face lit up when she saw her, and the little arms reached out to her.

STEPHEN GAVE SCARLETT HER instructions for the trip back to Galway. She didn't like them. But Colum had told her Stephen was in charge of all arrangements; so she donned her mourning clothes and kept her complaints to herself.

The ship was named the *Golden Fleece*, and it was the latest thing in luxury. It did not make a direct crossing, but it was not until Scarlett was actually on the gangplank that she saw the big NOTICE OF DEPARTURE with the ship's itinerary. The *Fleece* loaded passengers in Savannah, Charleston and Boston, disembarked them in Liverpool and Galway.

Scarlett turned in panic, ready to run back to the dock. She couldn't go to Charleston! Rhett would know she was on the ship—Rhett always knew everything, somehow—and he'd learn about Cat and take her away.

Then anger drove away Scarlett's panic, and she turned again to walk up onto the ship's deck. Rhett Butler wasn't going to make her turn tail and run. She was sure that Stephen was smuggling guns to Colum in her trunks, and they were depending on her. Also, she was eager to get back to Ballyhara.

Scarlett went to her suite. More than a year had passed since Rhett had divorced her, then immediately married Anne Hampton. During that year Scarlett had been able to block out the pain he had caused her. Now it tore at her heart.

THE ship sailed up the coast during the night, entering Charleston harbor at first light. Scarlett hadn't slept at all. She went out on deck for the sunrise. There was a rose-tinted mist on the wide waters of the harbor. Beyond it the city was blurred and insubstantial, like a city in a dream.

As the sun cleared the horizon the mist lifted, and she saw that they were entering the waters where she'd sailed with Rhett and laughed at the dolphins with him and been struck by the storm with him.

Slowly the city grew more distinct, glowing pink and green, pastel in the shimmering morning air. Then the ship was passing the promenade along East Battery. Scarlett could see the tall columns of the Butler house, the piazzas, the front door, the windows to her bedroom. . . . She picked up her skirts and ran.

She ordered breakfast served in her suite.

THE *GOLDEN FLEECE* WAS sailing at five o'clock. The sooner Scarlett got away from Charleston, the happier she would be. This must be the hottest place on earth. No rain, no wind. Just heat. She went up on deck. Poor baby Cat must be practically cooked. As soon as they got out of the harbor, she'd bring Cat up for whatever breeze the ship's movement might cause.

Clattering hoofbeats and feminine laughter caught Scarlett's attention. She glanced down at an open victoria on the dock. With three fabulous hats on the women in it. Wide-brimmed, decorated with plumes held by sparkling jewels, and swirled with airy tulle netting, from Scarlett's perspective the hats were like wonderful parasols. I'd look fantastic in a hat like that, she thought. She leaned slightly over the rail to look at the women. They were elegant, even in the heat, and not hurrying to get on the ship they were holding up.

The Panama-hatted man with them stepped down into the street. He took off his hat and reached up to hand the first woman down. Scarlett clutched the railing. Dear God, it's Rhett.

Slowly her brain registered what she was seeing: Rhett was bowing, kissing one gracefully extended hand after another. "Good-bye and thank you," said the women.

How well Rhett looked. His skin was brown, his smile as white as his linen suit. What was he saying? Something outrageously charming, she was sure, in that low, intimate voice he saved for women. Curse him. She wanted that voice murmuring to her.

The ship's whistle shrieked. Scarlett could hear rapid footsteps, the rumble of the gangplank, but she kept her eyes fixed on Rhett. He was smiling. She could see his strong, masculine, unforgettable pirate's face. "My beloved," she whispered.

The ship was moving away from the dock. Rhett put his hat on and turned away. Don't go, cried Scarlett's heart.

Rhett glanced over his shoulder as if there had been a sound. His eyes met hers, and surprise stiffened his body. For a long, immeasurable moment the two of them looked at each other while the space between them widened. Then Rhett touched two fingers to his hat brim in salute. Scarlett lifted her hand.

He was still standing there on the dock when the ship turned into the channel. When Scarlett could see him no longer, she sank numbly into a deck chair.

SHE HAD TO FIND OUT WHO THOSE women were and why they were with Rhett, or she'd go mad.

They were English, she learned in the dining saloon that night. The distinctive accent was dominating the captain's table. Scarlett asked the steward to change her seating to the small table near the wall. The table near the wall was near the captain's table.

The English passengers were talking about Charleston. "My dears," the older of the women trumpeted, "I've never seen anyplace as dreary in my life. Beastly climate."

There was a chorus of agreement.

"On the other hand," said a youthful female voice, "that terribly attractive Butler man said the winters are quite delightful. He invited us back."

"I'm sure he invited you back, Felicity," said the older woman. "You behaved disgracefully."

"Frances, I did no such thing. I was only having some fun for the first time on this wretched trip." Felicity and the other young woman, Marjorie, both thought Rhett the most intriguing man they'd ever met.

"A shame he's so devoted to his wife," Marjorie said.

"Such a colorless little thing, too," Felicity said.

"Out and out rebound, I heard. Didn't anyone tell you? He was married before, to an absolute tearing beauty. She ran off with another man, and Butler's never gotten over it."

Scarlett smiled. She was enormously gratified to know that gossip had her leaving Rhett and not the other way around.

Scarlett thought about the meeting with Rhett in Charleston, which was really no meeting at all. Had he felt the same shock of recognition she had when their eyes met? It wasn't possible that she could feel so bound to him by a look and that he would not feel the same way. Was it?

22

COLUM was waiting at the end of the gangplank when the *Golden Fleece* docked in Galway. At the sight of his stocky figure in worn black clericals, and smiling Irish face, Scarlett felt that she'd come home. Her luggage went past customs without any questions other than "And how old is that beautiful baby, then?" To which Scarlett replied proudly, "Three months shy of a year, and already trying to walk."

Traffic was snarled, and it took nearly an hour to drive the short distance from the port to the train station. It was because of the Galway Races, said Colum. There was steeplechase and flat racing, he explained, five days' worth every July.

But Scarlett wanted to hear about Ballyhara. "How are the fields, Colum? Is the wheat nearly ripe? Is the hay cut yet?"

"Wait and see, Scarlett darling. You'll be pleased."

Scarlett was more than pleased. She was overcome. The townspeople had erected arches covered with fresh greenery over her route through Ballyhara town. They stood outside the arches waving and cheering her return. "Oh, thank you, thank you," she cried over and over, with tears brimming from her eyes.

At the Big House, Mrs. Fitzpatrick and the servants were lined up to greet her. Then, less than an hour later, Scarlett was dressed in her Galway peasant clothes, striding quickly over her fields.

Fragrant mounds of golden hay stood in field cocks seven feet tall on the meadows, and the wheat fields were richly yellow. There would be a bounteous harvest, and Scarlett was content, for the land of the O'Haras was fruitful again.

"It's so good to be back," Scarlett said to Kathleen next morning. "I have about a million messages from everybody in Savannah." She settled herself happily beside the hearth and put Cat down to explore the floor.

Things had changed while she was away. Kathleen was going to be leaving Adamstown soon. She was going to marry a boy from Dunsany. Kevin O'Connor had asked her only the Saturday before.

Scarlett hugged Kathleen. "How exciting! You'll let me give the wedding, won't you? We'll have a wonderful party."

To her disappointment Scarlett learned that she couldn't hold the wedding party at the Big House. Tradition demanded that the wedding take place in the house the couple would live in.

In August the potatoes were harvested. It was the best crop they'd ever had, the farmers said. Then they began to reap the wheat. Scarlett loved to watch them. The shiny sickles flashed in the sun, and the golden stalks fell like rippling silk.

Scarlett gave Kathleen a gift of a hundred pounds and contributed several geese and barrels of porter to the wedding feast. Even that was going over the edge a bit, Colum warned her. The groom's family were the hosts.

"Well, if I'm going to go over the edge, I might as well go way over," Scarlett told him. "I'm coming out of mourning."

Scarlett danced every reel at the wedding party, wearing striped stockings and blue and red petticoats under a dark green skirt. Then she cried all the way home to Ballyhara. "I'm going to miss her so much, Colum."

"Twelve miles isn't the end of the earth, Scarlett darling. Get yourself a good riding horse instead of driving your buggy, and you'll be in Dunsany in no time at all."

Scarlett could see the sense to that. What she refused to consider was Colum's quiet suggestion that she think about marrying again. She woke up in the night sometimes and saw Rhett's eyes meeting hers when her ship was leaving Charleston. What had he been feeling? Alone in the vastness of the ornate bed Scarlett wondered, and dreamed of impossible things, and sometimes wept from the ache of wanting him.

SCARLETT looked at the long, laden tables set up the length of Ballyhara's wide street. Each was decorated with a ribbon-tied sheaf of wheat and surrounded by smiling people. This was the best part of being The O'Hara. They had all worked, and now they were all together to celebrate the results of that work.

There was food and drink, a carousel for the children, a wooden platform for dancing later in front of the unfinished inn. The air was golden with afternoon light, the wheat was golden on the table, a golden feeling of happiness bathed everyone in shared repletion. It was exactly what harvest home was meant to be.

The sound of horses coming made mothers look for their younger children. Scarlett's heart stopped for a moment when she couldn't find Cat. Then she saw her sitting on Colum's knee at the end of the table.

A group of militia rode into the end of the street. Three men, three officers, their polished brass buttons more golden than wheat. They reined in before the deserted church, and the noise around the tables died away.

"Which way to the Big House?" said one of the officers. "I'm here to talk to the owner."

Scarlett stood up. "I am the owner," she said.

The officer looked at her bright peasant clothes. "Very amusing, girl, but we're not here to play games."

Scarlett felt a wild, elated anger. She stepped up onto the bench she'd been sitting on and put her hands on her hips. She looked insolent and she knew it. "No one invited you here—soldier—to play games or anything else. Now what do you want? I am Mrs. O'Hara."

A second officer walked his horse forward a few steps. He dismounted and came on foot to stand in front of and below Scarlett's position on the bench. "We're to deliver this, Mrs. O'Hara." He removed his hat and one of his white gauntlets and handed a scrolled paper up to Scarlett. "The garrison is going to second a detachment to Ballyhara for its protection."

Scarlett could feel tension, like a storm, in the warm end-of-summer atmosphere. She unrolled the paper and read it slowly. When the full meaning of the document was clear to her, she lifted her head and smiled so everyone could see her. Then she turned the full force of her smile on the officer looking up at her. "That's mighty sweet of the colonel," she said, "but I'm really not interested, and he can't send soldiers to my town without my agreement. Will you tell him for me? I don't have any unrest here in Ballyhara. We get along real fine." She held the vellum sheet down to the officer. "You-all look a mite parched. Would you like a glass of ale?" The admiring expression on her face had enchanted men just like this officer from the day she turned fifteen. He blushed and stammered exactly like dozens of young men she'd beguiled in Clayton County, Georgia.

"Thank you, Mrs. O'Hara, but—uh—regulations— That is, personally I'd like nothing better—but the colonel wouldn't—um—"

"I understand," said Scarlett kindly. "Maybe some other time?"

THE first toast of harvest home was to The O'Hara. It would have been the first toast anyway, but now the salute was a loud roar.

WINTER made Scarlett restless; except for riding, there was nothing active to do. She was overjoyed when Saint Brigid's Day arrived, on February 1, and the growing year began again. She turned the first sod with such enthusiasm that soil flew.

But new fields had been cleared, and they put an impossible burden on the farmers. Scarlett nagged at Colum to move some more laborers into the town. He wouldn't let strangers in, but he found a compromise. Scarlett could hire men just for the summer. He'd take her to the hiring fair at Drogheda. The horse fair would be on, too, and she could buy the horses she needed.

On the day of the fair Scarlett was dressed like a village lass, not landed gentry. "No one will believe you can pay for a carousel ride, let alone a horse," Colum told her.

"I know what I'm doing. If I look rich, the dealer will think he can stick me with any old broken-down thing he has."

Drogheda was a very big fair. "Will you choose the lads first or the horses?" Colum asked. "They're at different ends."

"Oh, bother! The best ones will get snapped up in the beginning. I'll tell you what— You pick out the boys, and I'll go for the horses. Find me when you finish. Now, which way do I go?"

"Back in that corner, where the banners are. You'll see some of the best horses in Ireland there."

There were big canvas tents that served as temporary stables for the horses. Ha! thought Scarlett. Nobody's going to sell me an animal in bad light. She pushed into the noisy crowd milling around inside the tent and looked over one horse after another.

She didn't like the system in Ireland at all. You couldn't just walk up to the owner and ask him what he wanted for his animal. The minute there was any interest one of the traders would jump in to name a price that was way out of line one end or another, and then badger buyer and seller into an agreement. Then they'd grab your hand and slap down on it, and that meant you had bought yourself a horse.

She liked the looks of a pair of roans that the dealer shouted were perfectly matched three-year-olds. Scarlett put her hands behind her back. "Walk them out in the light, where I can see them," she said. Owner and dealer protested furiously.

Scarlett insisted, but very sweetly. Then she caught hold of one horse's head and examined his teeth. She burst out laughing. Three-year-old, my maiden aunt! "Take 'em in," she said with a wink at the dealer. "I've got a grandfather younger than them." She was enjoying herself very much.

After an hour, though, she'd only found three horses. She looked enviously at the people buying hunters. There were jumps set up outside in the open, and they could get a good look at what they were buying. Hunters were such beautiful horses, too. She turned away from the view of the jumping. She needed three more plow horses.

"Where is this Pegasus of yours, Bart? I don't see anything flying over the jumps."

I'm losing my mind, Scarlett thought. That sounded like Rhett's voice. She turned quickly, looking out into the sunlight, blinking. That's his back, isn't it? It is, I'm sure it is. He's got no reason to be in Ireland, but I couldn't be wrong about that voice.

He turned to speak to the slightly built, fair-haired man beside him. It was Rhett. She was trembling.

The fair-haired man said something, pointed with his crop and walked away. Rhett was there alone. Don't move, Scarlett ordered herself when Rhett started to walk away. But she couldn't obey. She burst from the shadows of the tent and ran after him. "Rhett!"

He stopped awkwardly and spun around. Then he smiled the mocking smile she knew so well. "You do turn up in the most unexpected places, Scarlett," he said.

He's laughing at me, and I don't care. I don't care about anything as long as he'll say my name and stand near me. "Hello, Rhett," she said, "how are you?"

"What brings you to Ireland? I thought you were in England."

Scarlett's heart leaped to the meaning of what he'd said. He'd taken the trouble to find out where she was going, he cared about her, he wanted to keep her from disappearing. Happiness flooded her heart.

Without planning or thought of consequences Scarlett looked at the man who had been her husband for so many years of lies. "I love you, Rhett," she said with simple dignity.

"How unfortunate for you, Scarlett. You always seem to be in love with another woman's husband." He lifted his cap politely. "I have another commitment. Please excuse me now." He turned his back and walked away. Scarlett looked after him. She felt as if he'd slapped her face.

For no reason. She'd made no demands on him; she'd made a gift of the greatest thing she'd learned to give. And he'd trampled it into the muck.

Scarlett stood there, a brightly colored, small isolated figure amid the noise and movement of the horse fair. Then the world came back into focus, and she saw Rhett and his friend near another tent, in a circle of intent spectators. A man was holding a restless bay by the bridle.

Her feet moved by themselves, marching across the space separating her from them. The dealer's voice was like some ritual chant: "A hundred and twenty, sir, you know that's a handsome price. . . . And you, sir, one forty? The gentleman's come up to one twenty-five. Say one forty's your price, and we'll be making a deal. . . . Say one thirty?"

Scarlett stepped into the triangle of seller, buyer and dealer. "One forty," she said clearly. The dealer stared, confused. Scarlett spit into her right hand and slapped it loudly against his. Then she spit again, looking at the seller. He lifted his hand, slapped once, twice against hers in the age-old seal of a deal made. The dealer could only spit and seal in acquiescence.

Scarlett looked at Rhett's friend. "I hope you're not too disappointed," she said in a honeyed tone.

"Why, of course not. That is to say—"

Rhett broke in. "Bart, I'd like you to meet . . ." He paused.

Scarlett did not look at him. "Mrs. O'Hara," she said to Rhett's bewildered companion. She held out her spit-wet right hand. "I'm a widow."

"John Morland," he said, and took her grimy hand. He bowed, kissed it, then smiled ruefully into her blazing eyes. "You must be something to see taking a fence, Mrs. O'Hara. Talk about leaving the field behind! Do you hunt around here?"

"I . . . um . . ." What could she say? "I confess, Mr. Morland, I just gave in to a woman's impulse. I had to have this horse."

"I felt the same way. But not quickly enough, it seems," said the cultivated English voice. "I'd be honored if you'd join the hunt from my place sometime. It's near Dunsany."

Scarlett smiled. No wonder the name John Morland was familiar. She'd heard all about Sir John Morland at Kathleen's wedding. "He's a grand man, for all that he's a landlord," said the bridegroom, Kevin O'Connor, a dozen times.

"I'm familiar with Dunsany," Scarlett said. "And I'd dearly love to hunt with you sometime."

"Saturday next?"

Scarlett smiled wickedly. She spit in her palm and lifted her hand. "Done!"

Morland laughed. He spit in his, slapped hers once, twice. "Done! Stirrup cup at seven and breakfast after."

For the first time since she'd pushed in on them, Scarlett looked at Rhett. He was looking at her as if he'd been looking a long time. There was amusement in his eyes, and something else that she couldn't define. Great balls of fire, you'd think he'd never met me before. "Mr. Butler, a pleasure to see you," she said graciously. She dangled her dirty hand elegantly in front of him.

Rhett removed his glove to take it. "Mrs. O'Hara," he said with a bow.

Scarlett turned to the dealer. "Guineas, is that right?" She hiked up her skirts to take a bundle of bank notes from the garter above her knee. She counted the money into the seller's hand. Her skirts swirled when she turned and walked away.

"What a remarkable woman," said John Morland

Rhett smiled. "Astonishing," he said in agreement.

23

*E*VERYTHING had to be done faster than fast. The dressmaker worked on Scarlett's riding habit, the cobbler worked on her boots, the stableman labored with rags and oil over a sidesaddle that had been left in the tack room thirty years before Scarlett arrived. When Saturday dawned, she was as ready as she'd ever be.

Her horse was a bay gelding named Half Moon. He was very big, nearly seventeen hands, with a deep chest and long back and powerfully muscled thighs. He was a horse for a big man; Scarlett looked tiny and fragile and very feminine on him. She was afraid she looked ridiculous.

And she was quite certain that she'd make a fool of herself. She didn't know Half Moon's temperament. She was also riding side-saddle, as all ladies did.

The sidesaddle was a serious handicap. She couldn't communicate with the horse through pressure of her knees, because one knee was hooked around the sidesaddle's pommel, the other one rigid because only by pressing on the one stirrup could a lady counterbalance her unbalanced position. I'll probably fall off before I even get to Dunsany, she thought with despair.

COLUM had described a fox hunt to Scarlett, but she wasn't prepared for the first impact of it. Morland Hall was an amalgamation of building over two centuries, with wings and chimneys and walls attached higgledy-piggledy around a stone-walled courtyard that had been the keep of the fortified castle erected by the first Morland baronet in 1615. The square courtyard was filled with mounted riders and excited hounds. Scarlett forgot her apprehensions at the sight. The men wore pinks—misnamed bright red jackets.

"Mrs. O'Hara!" Sir John Morland rode over to her, his top hat in his hand. "Welcome. I didn't believe you'd come."

Scarlett's eyes narrowed. "Did Rhett say that?"

"On the contrary. He said wild horses wouldn't keep you away." There was no guile in Morland.

Scarlett's eyes moved quickly, searching for Rhett. What a lot of people! Damn this veil anyhow, everything looks blurred. She was wearing the most conservative riding clothes fashion allowed. Unrelieved black wool with a high neck, and low black top hat with a veil pulled tight over her face.

Rhett was looking at her. She looked away quickly when she finally saw him. He's counting on me to make a spectacle of myself. I'll show Mr. Rhett Butler.

"Ride along easy, well back, and watch what the others do," Colum had said. Scarlett began as he advised. She felt her palms sweating as she looked ahead at the panorama of red and black backs streaming down the slope in front of her, at the horses jumping effortlessly over the low stone wall at the base of the hill.

This is it, she thought. She shifted her weight and felt Half Moon moving faster, faster, surefooted veteran of a hundred hunts. Then the wall was behind her, and she had hardly noticed the jump. Scarlett laughed aloud. Her fear was gone. There was only excitement, and the new determination to overtake and pass and leave Rhett Butler far behind.

SCARLETT stood with the muddy train of her habit looped over her left arm and a glass of Champagne in her right hand. The paw of the fox that she'd been awarded would be mounted on a silver base if she'd allow it, said John Morland.

"I'd love it, Sir John."

"Please call me Bart. All my friends do."

"Please call me Scarlett." She was giddy from the exhilaration of the hunt and her success. Everywhere she looked, there were servants, wealth, people having a good time, a good life. It was like a story in a book, like life before the War. She could almost forget that Rhett was there. Almost.

"Congratulations, Scarlett." Rhett was at her side, and she hadn't seen him approaching. Scarlett's arm jerked, and Champagne spilled on her skirts.

"Damn it, Rhett, did you have to sneak up like that?"

"I'm sorry." He offered her a handkerchief. "And I'm sorry for my boorish behavior at the horse fair. My only excuse is that I was shocked to see you there."

Scarlett bent to wipe at the dampness on her skirts. It gave her a chance to collect her thoughts. I will not show how much I care, she vowed. I will not show how much he hurt me.

When she looked up, her eyes were sparkling. "You were shocked," she said. "Imagine what I was. What on earth are you doing in Ireland?"

"Buying horses. I'm determined to win at the races next year. Morland's stables have a reputation for producing likely yearlings. I go to Paris Tuesday to look at some more. What brought you to Drogheda in local costume?"

Scarlett laughed. "Oh, you know how I love to dress up. I borrowed those clothes from one of the maids at the house I'm visiting." She looked from side to side, searching for John Morland. "I've got to make my manners and get going," she said. "My friends will be furious if I'm not back pretty soon." She looked at Rhett for an instant, then hurried off. She didn't dare stay. Not close to him like that. Not even in the same room. . . .

The rain began when she was a little more than five miles from Ballyhara. Scarlett blamed it for the wetness on her cheeks.

"A GENTLEMAN to see ye," said the maid, holding out a card.

Scarlett ran down the stairs. "Bart! What a surprise. Come in, we can sit on the steps. I don't have any furniture." She was genuinely pleased to see him, but she couldn't take him up to her sitting room. Cat was having her nap there.

Bart Morland sat down on the steps as if it were the most natural thing in the world to have no furniture. He'd had the devil of a time finding her, he said, until he ran into the postman in the bar. That was his only excuse for being so late delivering her trophy from the hunt.

Scarlett looked at the silver plaque with her name and the fox paw on it. It was not a thing of beauty.

"Disgusting, isn't it?" said Bart cheerfully.

Scarlett laughed. She liked John Morland. "Would you like to say hello to Half Moon?"

"Thought you'd never suggest it."

They walked through the colonnade and out to the stable. Scarlett was going to pass it by on the way to the pasture and Half Moon, but Bart stopped her. Could he go inside? Her stables were famous, and he'd never seen them.

The stalls were separated by granite columns with Doric capitals. Tall vaulting sprang up from the columns to meet and cross and create a ceiling of stone that looked as light and weightless as air and sky. "Don't you find it extraordinary to have a stable that looks like a cathedral? I'd put an organ in it and play Bach to the horses all day."

"Probably give them strangles."

Morland had a whooping laugh that made Scarlett laugh, too.

Walking beside him, Scarlett searched for some way to start him talking about Rhett.

There was no need. "I say, what luck for me that you're friends with Rhett Butler," Bart exclaimed. "If he hadn't introduced us, I'd never have gotten a look at those stables of yours."

"How do you happen to know him?" Scarlett asked quickly.

He didn't really know Rhett at all, Bart replied. Some old friends had written to him a month ago saying that they were sending Rhett to look at his horses. "He's a remarkable fellow, really serious about horses. I wish he could have stayed longer. Are you old friends? He never got around to telling me."

Thank goodness, thought Scarlett. "I have some family in Charleston," she said. "I met him when I was visiting there."

"Then you must have met my friends the Brewtons. I'm mad for Sally just like everybody else."

Bart chuckled as he recounted the gossip Sally Brewton had included in her letter. Rhett had fallen into the oldest snare in history, it seemed. Some orphanage was having an outing at his country place, and one of the orphans turned up missing when it was time to leave. So what did he do but go off with the school-teacher to search for it. The child was found, but not until after dark. Which meant, of course, that the spinster teacher was compromised, and Rhett had to marry her. The best part was that he'd been run out of town years before when he refused to make an honest woman out of another girl he'd been indiscreet with. "You'd think he would have learned to be careful after the first time."

Scarlett was elated, and yet she felt like crying. What a sly boots

Anne Hampton is. Or maybe it was just that it took so long to find the orphan. And that Anne looks so much like Melly.

They'd reached the pasture fence, and Half Moon approached warily. Morland reached into a pocket of his jacket and pulled out an apple. The horse nickered in anticipation. "Look here, Scarlett," Bart said as he broke the apple. "I've got something a bit ticklish to talk to you about." Alice Harrington, he explained— she was the stoutish one at the hunt who'd ended up in the ditch—was having a house party at Midsummer Night, and she wanted to invite Scarlett, but didn't have the nerve. He'd been appointed diplomat to sound her out about it.

Scarlett had a hundred questions. Essentially they boiled down to when, where, and what to wear. Colum would be furious, she was sure. The English landowners, known as the Anglo-Irish, were the enemy. But she didn't care. She wanted to get dressed up and drink Champagne.

HARRINGTON House was a huge block of a house made of Portland stone. It wasn't far from Ballyhara. A footman came out of the front door, and he handed Scarlett down from the buggy.

"Mrs. O'Hara!" shouted Alice Harrington. She moved toward Scarlett and bellowed that she was happy to see her. "Let me introduce everyone."

The guests were outside having tea. The table was set up on the lawn, under a tremendous beech tree. Scarlett was introduced to an elderly man in tweeds named General Smyth-Burns; to Charlotte Montague, a tall, thin woman with beautifully dressed gray hair; and to Alice's cousin Desmond Grantley, who was as rotund as she. John Morland was there, too, and he waggled his fingers at Scarlett in greeting.

Desmond Grantley held a chair for Scarlett and asked if she would permit him to bring her an assortment of sandwiches and cakes. Scarlett generously said she would. She looked at the circle of what Colum scornfully called gentry and thought that he shouldn't be so pigheaded. These people were really very nice. She was sure she was going to have a good time.

The worst thing was there'd be no hunt. Hunting was for autumn and winter. The only reason Sir John Morland had arranged one was to show off his horses to his rich American guest. But there were many things Scarlett enjoyed. There was croquet, boating on the lake, plus a game called tennis, quite the latest rage, she was told.

After dinner Saturday everyone rummaged through big boxes of costumes that had been brought to the drawing room. Alice's husband, Henry, draped Scarlett in a long, glittering silk cloak and put a crown of fake jewels on her head. "That makes you tonight's Titania," he said.

There was buffoonery and uninhibited laughter and a lack of self-consciousness that Scarlett envied. "I know it's all very silly," John Morland said apologetically through a huge papier-mâché lion's head. "But it is Midsummer Night, we're all allowed to go a bit mad."

When the long, long Irish twilight was done and darkness fell, the house party went out onto the lawn to look at the bonfires. Scarlett felt a wave of guilt. Colum had told her she shouldn't go to an Anglo house party. She knew she should be at Ballyhara. Midsummer Night was almost as important as Saint Brigid's Day in farming tradition. Bonfire ceremonies marked the turning point in the year, its shortest night, and gave mystical protection for the cattle and the crops.

"Why aren't you at the Ballyhara fire?" asked Bart.

"Why aren't you at yours?" Scarlett snapped.

"Because I'm not wanted there." His voice in the darkness sounded very sad. "I did go once. All the joy went out of the celebration when I arrived, so I left."

"I should have left here," Scarlett blurted.

"What an absurd thing to say. You're the only real person here. You're the exotic bloom in the patch of weeds, Scarlett."

She hadn't thought of it that way. It made sense, too. People always made much over guests from far away. Still, Scarlett realized that she should never have left her own place and her own people.

WEEKS later, when the wheat was almost ready to harvest, a rider brought a note to Scarlett and invited himself into the kitchen for a cup of tea while he waited for her reply.

Charlotte Montague would like to call on her.

Who on earth was Charlotte Montague? Scarlett had to rack her brain before she recalled the pleasant, unobtrusive older woman at the Harringtons'.

But what could she want? Scarlett's curiosity was piqued. She hastily wrote a note inviting Mrs. Montague to tea that afternoon.

SCARLETT was wearing her Galway skirts when Mrs. Montague called. She wouldn't pretend to be what she was not. Charlotte Montague was wearing a gray linen jacket and skirt, with a lace jabot that Scarlett's fingers itched to touch.

The older woman took off her gray kid gloves and gray feathered hat before she sat down next to the tea table. "Thank you for receiving me, Mrs. O'Hara. I doubt that you want to waste time talking about the weather; you'd prefer to know why I'm here, is that correct?" Mrs. Montague had an interesting wryness in her voice.

"I've been dying of curiosity," said Scarlett.

"I have learned that you're a successful businesswoman, both here and in America. . . . Don't be alarmed. What I know, I keep to myself; it's one of my most valuable assets. I'm a businesswoman, too. I would like to tell you about my business, if I may."

Scarlett could only nod.

To put it at its most basic level, she arranged things, said Mrs. Montague. She was born into a good family, but she had married a younger son. Even before he died, she had grown tired of being always in need of money while trying to keep up appearances. After she was widowed, she found herself in the position of poor relation, a position that was intolerable.

What she had was intelligence, education, taste, and entrée to all the best houses in Ireland. "I am—in a manner of speaking—a professional houseguest. I give advice—in clothing, in entertaining, in decorating houses, in arranging marriages or assignations. And I am paid generous commissions by merchants—dressmakers, jewelers, furniture dealers. I am skillful and tactful, and it is doubtful that anyone suspects that I am being paid."

Scarlett was fascinated.

"I'm telling you this because I have a business proposal for you. You have beauty and brains and money. You can be an original. If you put yourself in my hands, I will make you the most admired, the most-sought-after woman in Ireland. In two to three years the whole world will be open to you. You will be famous. And I will have enough money to retire in luxury."

"I'm Irish," Scarlett said. "I don't want to be sought after by the English."

Mrs. Montague smiled. "Your Irishness is one of the intriguing things about you. Striped stockings and boiled potatoes one day, partridge and silks the next. It will only add to your legend. Write to me when you decide."

HARVEST, harvest-home celebration, golden autumn days. Scarlett rejoiced in the rich crops, mourned the end of the growing year. September was the time for the half-yearly rents, and she knew her tenants would have profit left over. It was a grand thing, being The O'Hara. She gave a big party for Cat's second birthday. All the Ballyhara children played in the big empty rooms on the ground floor and tasted ice cream for probably the first time. Every one of them went home with a shiny coin. Scarlett made sure they went home early because of all the superstitions about Halloween.

But people were afraid of fairy changelings, and later mothers scrubbed their children with water in which angelica root had steeped all day. It was a known protection against witches.

THE horn did it. Scarlett was exercising Half Moon when both of them heard the horn and then the hounds. Somewhere close by in the countryside people were hunting. For all she knew, Rhett might even be with them. She wrote to Charlotte Montague the next day.

Two weeks later Mrs. Montague was installed at the Big House, in a suite of rooms near Scarlett's. "Now we begin," she said.

24

SCARLETT understood that accepting invitations placed an obligation on her to return them, and she couldn't invite people to a place that had furniture in only two rooms. She was lucky, she supposed, that Charlotte Montague wanted to transform the Big House for her.

The costs made Scarlett wince, but she had agreed to give

Charlotte a free hand, and it was too late to back out. Besides, money just didn't matter to her now the way it used to.

So Scarlett took refuge in the estate office and Cat made the kitchen her own, while workmen did unknown, expensive, noisy things to her house for months on end. At least Scarlett had the farm to run. Also, she was buying horses.

"I know little or nothing about horses," said Charlotte Montague. It was a statement that made Scarlett's eyebrows skid upward. She'd come to believe that there was nothing on earth Charlotte didn't claim to be an expert on. "You'll need at least four saddle horses and six hunters, eight would be better; and you must ask Sir John Morland to assist you in selecting them."

Scarlett had been hoping to have a reason to see Bart. He might have some news of Rhett. She rode over to Dunsany the next day. Morland was delighted by her request. Of course he'd help her find the best hunters in all Ireland. . . .

"Do you ever hear from your American friend, Bart?" Scarlett hoped the question sounded casual.

"Rhett? Yes. He's determined to enter the filly he bought from me in the Charleston races. Her dam was out of . . ."

Scarlett stopped listening. Morland's life was built around horses. He would talk bloodlines all the way back to the Flood! Why couldn't he tell her what she wanted to know? Was Rhett happy? Had he mentioned her? Then she looked at the young baronet's animated face and forgave him. In his own eccentric way he was one of the most charming men in the world.

From Charlotte she knew that John was relatively immune to husband-hunting women because he had little money. His title and his property were impressively old, but he had no income except his rents, and he spent almost every shilling of that on his horses.

"Did Rhett say anything about me?" Scarlett finally asked.

"Yes, he asked me if you might possibly sell Half Moon. He's thinking about starting up the Dunmore Hunt again."

"He'll have to come back to buy horses, I guess," she said.

"No, he'll have to trust me. His wife's expecting, you see, and he won't leave her side. But now that I'll be aiming you at the cream of the crop, I couldn't help Rhett anyhow."

Scarlett was so preoccupied with Bart's news that he had to

shake her arm to get her attention. When did she want to start the search for her hunters? he asked.

Today, she answered.

Throughout the winter Scarlett went every Saturday with John Morland to one hunt or another in County Meath, trying out hunters that were for sale. It wasn't easy to find mounts that suited her, for she demanded that the horse be as fearless as she was. She rode as if demons were chasing her, and the riding eventually made it possible for her to stop imagining Rhett as father to any child but Cat.

By spring she had succeeded in relegating Rhett to the past and seldom thought of him at all.

THAT fall Scarlett spent a long, exhausting day being measured by Mrs. Sims, the dressmaker Charlotte Montague had brought over from Dublin. If what Charlotte had promised was true, Scarlett was soon going to have both worlds, Irish and English.

Scarlett thought of her good fortune again when she presided at the harvest-home banquet. Ballyhara had another good crop—not as good as the two previous years, but still enough to make every man's pocket jingle. Everyone in Ballyhara celebrated. Everyone except Colum, Scarlett noticed. He looked as if he hadn't slept in ages. Well, she wasn't going to let his gloom ruin her good mood. Harvest home was a party. Besides, the hunting season would be starting any day now.

"IF YOU'RE ready, we will take a tour," said Charlotte Montague. Scarlett put down her teacup. She was more eager than she wanted to admit.

Charlotte led the way upstairs first, to long corridors lined with bedrooms for guests, then back down again to what Scarlett still called, in American usage, the second floor. "Your bedroom, your bath, your boudoir, and Cat's playroom, bedroom." The doors flew open as Charlotte unveiled her labors. Scarlett was enchanted with the pale-green-and-gilt furniture in her rooms, and the child-size chairs and tables in Cat's rooms.

"Your private rooms are French," said Charlotte. "They represent your Robillard self. Your O'Hara self dominates the reception rooms on the ground floor." She led Scarlett downstairs and through the hall. She opened tall double doors on one side of it and ushered Scarlett into the dining room.

"My stars," Scarlett exclaimed, "I don't know enough people to fill up all those chairs."

"You will," said Charlotte. She led Scarlett on to a breakfast room and morning room. Then she walked across to more doors. "The great salon and ballroom," she announced. "I admit to being very pleased with this."

One long wall was made up of widely spaced French doors with tall gilt mirrors between them. The ceiling was painted with scenes from the heroic legends of Irish history. The High Kings' buildings on the hill of Tara looked rather like Roman temples. Scarlett loved it.

"The furniture throughout this floor is Irish made. So are the fabrics—wools and linens—and the silver, china, glass. This is where The O'Hara is hostess. Come, there's only the library still to see."

Scarlett liked the leather-covered chairs and chesterfield. "You've done a wonderful job, Charlotte," she said sincerely.

SCARLETT rode to Sir John Morland's hunt in style. She was riding a saddle horse and was accompanied by two grooms leading Half Moon and Comet, one of her new hunters. Mrs. Sims, the dressmaker, had made a tremendously becoming riding habit for her. The skirts flowed elegantly over her new sidesaddle, and she was very pleased with herself.

"How glad I am to see you, Scarlett," said Bart Morland. "Half Moon is looking ready for a good run. Come along over here and have a stirrup cup with my special guest."

Scarlett smiled graciously at the young member of Parliament for County Meath. He was very handsome, she thought, this Mr. Parnell. She'd heard the name before— Oh, yes, she remembered now. Colum really detested this Parnell. She'd have to pay attention so she could tell Colum all about him. After the hunt. For now Half Moon was eager to go, and so was she.

"I CAN'T for the life of me understand how you can be so stubborn, Colum." Scarlett had passed from enthusiasm to explanation to rage. "You've never even bothered to go hear the man speak, for pity's sake. Well, I heard him, and he wants exactly what you always talked about—Ireland for the Irish, and no evictions, and even no landlords. What more can you ask?"

Colum's patience cracked. "I can ask that you not be such a trusting fool! Do you not know that your Mr. Parnell is a landlord himself? And a Protestant. He's looking for votes, with his home-rule policy, not justice. The man's a politician."

"There's simply no talking to you! But I know this much—there's no reason to smuggle in guns and start a war if you can get what you want without it. I lived through a war. All it did was kill most of my friends and ruin everything. I'm telling you right now, Colum O'Hara, there's a way to get Ireland back for the Irish without killing and burning, and that's what I'm for. No more money for Stephen, do you hear? And no more guns hidden away in my town. I want to be rid of them. Right away."

"And rid of me as well, are you saying?"

"If you insist, then—" Scarlett's eyes filled with tears. "What am I saying? What are you saying? Oh, Colum, don't let this happen. You're my best friend." The tears spilled over.

Colum took her hand in his. "Ach, Scarlett darling, forgive me. It's the Irish temper in the two of us talking."

"Colum, promise me you'll get rid of those guns. Promise me you won't start a war."

"I promise you, Scarlett darling."

Scarlett had gotten what she wanted. Before she went home, she detoured to the little chapel and made her confession to Father Flynn. Losing her temper with Colum was part of it, but not the main part. She was there to be absolved of the sin that made her own blood run cold. She had thanked God when John Morland told her that six months earlier Rhett's wife had lost her baby.

Not long after Scarlett left, Colum O'Hara entered the confessional. He had lied to her, a heavy sin. After doing his penance, he went to the Anglican church to make sure the arms were sufficiently well concealed in the event she decided to investigate.

CHARLOTTE Montague and Scarlett left for the house party that was Scarlett's debut into society after Mass on Sunday. The party was to last a week. Scarlett didn't like being away from Cat for so long, but her birthday party was only just over—Mrs. Fitz was still in a tight-lipped fury about the damage all the running children had done to the parquet in the ballroom—and she was certain that Cat wouldn't miss her. With all the new furnishings to inspect, Cat was a very busy little girl.

Scarlett was more excited than nervous. Charlotte was nervous enough for both of them, although it didn't show; Scarlett's future in the fashionable world would be decided now. Charlotte's future, also. Yes, Scarlett looked lovely in her green merino traveling costume. And her slim, uncorseted body was sure to set tongues wagging. She looked precisely like what Charlotte had insinuated to chosen friends: a beautiful, not-too-young American widow, with fresh colonial looks and charm; somewhat gauche, but refreshing as a result; wealthy, well bred, with an aristocratic French bloodline, but vigorous and exuberant; all in all an intriguing addition to the circles of people who knew too much about one another and were avid for someone new to talk about.

Scarlett's confidence ebbed when she saw the house, an immense Gothic-style structure with stained-glass windows as tall as a cathedral's. You're The O'Hara, she reminded herself, and she marched up the entrance steps with her chin high.

By the end of dinner that night she was smiling at everyone. The food was excellent, but Scarlett barely tasted it. She was feasting on admiration. There were forty-six guests in the house party, and they all wanted to know her.

"And on New Year's Day, I have to knock on every single door in the town, go in, go out, go in again and drink a cup of tea. I declare, I don't know why I don't turn yellow as a Chinaman, drinking half the tea in China the way I do," she said gaily to the man on her left. He was fascinated by the duties of The O'Hara.

When the hostess turned the table, Scarlett enchanted the retired general on her right with a day-by-day account of the siege of Atlanta. Her southern accent was not at all what one expected from an American, they reported later to anyone who'd listen. She was also a "damn'd intelligent woman" and a "damn'd attractive woman."

The following morning, and for five mornings after, there was a hunt. Scarlett was adept and fearless. Her success was assured.

The Anglo-Irish gentry admired nothing quite as much as they did a fine rider.

Charlotte Montague had to be vigilant, or she'd be caught looking like a cat who'd just finished a bowl of thick cream.

"DID you enjoy yourself?" she asked Scarlett on the way back to Ballyhara.

"Every minute, Charlotte! Bless you for getting me invited. Everything was perfect. It's so thoughtful having those sandwiches in the bedroom. I always get hungry late at night."

Charlotte laughed until her eyes were streaming with tears. When she could speak, she explained. At the more sophisticated houses the ladies' bedrooms were supplied with a plate of sandwiches that could be used as a signal to admirers. Set on the floor of the corridor outside a lady's room, the sandwiches were an invitation for a man to come in.

Scarlet blushed. "My grief, Charlotte, I ate every crumb."

Charlotte Montague smiled complacently. If any one thing had been needed to create a legend for Scarlett O'Hara, the mistake about the sandwiches had accomplished it. Now she'd be known as refreshingly colonial but satisfactorily sophisticated. Charlotte began to make preliminary plans for her retirement. Only a few more months to go.

"I shall arrange for delivery of the *Irish Times* every day," she said to Scarlett, "and you must study it. Everyone you meet in Dublin will expect you to be familiar with the news it reports."

"Dublin? You didn't tell me we were going to Dublin."

"Didn't I? I do apologize, Scarlett. Dublin is the center of everything, you will love it. And the castle is so thrilling."

"A castle? Does the Queen live there?"

"No, the castle in Dublin is ruled by Her Majesty's representative, the viceroy. You will be presented to him and to the vicereine in the Throne Room. . . ." Mrs. Montague painted a word picture for Scarlett of pomp and splendor that made Charleston's Saint Cecilia sound like nothing at all.

BY MID-DECEMBER Scarlett was pacing the long hallways of the Big House like a caged animal. She had forgotten how much she hated winter. She bought Cat a Shetland pony, after promising herself not to hobble Cat just because she'd lost Bonnie in a riding accident; and when there were a few hours of sun, she watched while Cat rode her pony in great joyful loops across the frozen meadow. Cat was as restless as she was. It was all Scarlett could do to persuade her to stay indoors, even in the stables.

On Christmas Eve, after Cat fell asleep, Colum helped Scarlett bring out Cat's present. It was a stuffed toy pony on rockers.

The next morning Cat looked at it with scorn. "It's not real."

"It's a toy, darling—for indoors in this nasty weather."

Cat climbed on it and rocked. She conceded that for a pony that wasn't real it was not a bad toy.

Scarlett breathed a sigh of relief. She wouldn't feel quite so guilty now when she went to Dublin. She was to meet Charlotte Montague at the Gresham Hotel there the day after New Year's.

SCARLETT had no idea Dublin was so near. It seemed she was barely settled in the train at Trim before Dublin was announced. Charlotte's maid met her at the station.

They took a hackney to the hotel. When they arrived, Charlotte was waiting in the sitting room of their suite of rooms. "Come and have tea," she said. "We have a great deal to do."

That evening Mrs. Sims arrived, with three assistants carrying muslin-wrapped gowns and dresses. Each evening gown was more elegant than the one that preceded it. "Do not gain so much as a millimeter around the middle, Scarlett, or you'll have to be fitted all over again," Charlotte warned.

"I'll run it all off shopping," Scarlett said. "I saw wonderful shops on the drive from the station."

Charlotte smiled indulgently. She'd receive a commission from every shop Scarlett patronized. "You'll have all the shopping your heart desires, but only in the afternoons. In the mornings you'll be sitting for your portrait."

"What do I want with a portrait of myself?"

"The portrait is important. Take my word."

"I'll do it because you say so, but I won't like it."

The next morning they had breakfast in the sitting room. Afterward a woman came in whom Scarlett had never seen before. "This is Serafina," said Charlotte. "She's going to do your hair."

It took nearly an hour. Finally Mrs. Sims and an assistant arrived. The assistant lifted the muslin wrap from the gown she was holding, and Scarlett drew in her breath. The white satin glistened in the light, and the light made the silver embroidery shine as if it were a living thing. It was a fantasy of a gown. Scarlett stood and reached out to touch it.

"Gloves first," Mrs. Sims commanded. "Every finger would leave a mark." Scarlett took the long white kid gloves Charlotte held out to her. When she had smoothed them all the way up, Serafina dropped a silk handkerchief over Scarlett's head and removed the wrapper she wore. Then Mrs. Sims lowered the dress onto Scarlett's upraised arms and fastened the back.

There was a knock at the door. "Well timed," said Mrs. Montague. "That will be Monsieur Hervé. We'll want Mrs. O'Hara over here, Mrs. Sims." Charlotte led Scarlett to the center of the room, where Mrs. Sims' assistant put slippers on Scarlett's feet.

Scarlett could hear Charlotte opening the door and speaking in a low voice.

"Mrs. O'Hara," said Charlotte Montague, "please allow me to present Monsieur François Hervé."

A rotund bald man walked in front of Scarlett and bowed.

"Fantastique," he said, and snapped his fingers. Two men carried the enormous pier glass to a spot between the windows. When they stepped away, Scarlett saw herself.

The white satin gown was more décolleté than she'd realized. She stared at the daring expanse of bosom and shoulder. Then at the reflection of a woman she hardly recognized. Her hair was piled high on her head in a mass of curls so artful that they looked almost happenstance. The white satin glimmered the narrow length of her body, and a silver-encrusted white satin train spread in a sinuous semicircle around the white satin slippers.

The years of habitual girlishness fell away. She was looking at a woman, not the flirtatious belle of Clayton County. And she was mystified and excited by this stranger. Her chin lifted in supreme self-confidence, and she looked directly into her own eyes with challenge and approval.

That's it, whispered Charlotte Montague to herself. That's the woman to take all Ireland by storm.

"Easel," murmured the artist. "Quickly. I shall do a portrait that will make me famous."

AFTER TEN DAYS OF SITTINGS and fittings and shopping, Scarlett went home to Ballyhara. She was in love with Dublin and could hardly wait to return. How very very lucky she was. She had both—country and city, The O'Hara and that still unknown woman in the pier glass.

SCARLETT left Cat engrossed in a picture book of animals, her other presents still unwrapped. She ran down the drive to Colum's gatehouse with the cashmere muffler she'd brought him and her impressions of Dublin to share.

"Oh, I'm sorry," she said when she saw that he had a guest. The well-dressed man was a stranger to her.

"Come meet John Devoy," said Colum. "He's just in from America."

Devoy was polite, but clearly not pleased to be interrupted. Scarlett made her excuses and left. *Now what kind of American comes to Ballyhara and isn't pleased to meet another American? He must be one of Colum's Fenians, that's it! And he's annoyed because Colum isn't part of that crazy revolution thing anymore.*

The reverse was the truth. Devoy was seriously leaning toward support for Parnell, and he was one of the most influential American Fenians. If he abandoned support for the revolution, the blow would be nearly mortal. Colum argued passionately against home rule long into the night. "The man wants power and will use any treachery to get it," he said about Parnell.

"What about you, Colum?" Devoy retorted. "Sounds to me like you can't stand a better man getting your job done—and done better."

After Devoy went to Kennedy's Inn for the night, Colum sat in the darkness brooding on Devoy's angry outburst. *Could the man be right? Was power the motive, and not love for Ireland? How could a man know the truth of his own soul?*

THIN, watery sunlight shone briefly as Scarlett drove a spade into the earth on Saint Brigid's Day. It was a good omen for the year to come. To celebrate, she treated everyone in Ballyhara town to porter and meat pies at Kennedy's. It was going to be the best year of all. Scarlett was sure of it. The next day she went to Dublin for the six weeks known as the Castle Season.

25

HE and Charlotte had a suite of rooms at the Shelbourne Hotel this time, not the Gresham. The Shelbourne was *the* place to stay in Dublin for the Season. Everything was imposingly grand—the space, the staff, the guests.

In addition to a suite, a private drawing room was reserved for Scarlett's use. The finished portrait stood on an easel in a corner of the green-brocaded room. Scarlett looked at it with wonder. Did she really look like that? That woman wasn't afraid of anything, and she felt as nervous as a cat.

"After you're presented," Charlotte said, "you'll serve tea and coffee in your drawing room every afternoon. People will bring others to meet you."

Who? Scarlett wanted to ask. But she didn't bother. Charlotte always knew what she was doing.

SCARLETT waited in a group of white-gowned girls and women outside the closed double doors to the Throne Room of Dublin Castle. Why on earth had she agreed to do this? she asked herself. In part she was The O'Hara, determined to conquer the English. In part she was an American girl dazzled by the grandeur of the British Empire's royal panoply. At bottom, Scarlett had never in her life backed away from a challenge and never would.

"Madam The O'Hara of Ballyhara."

God's nightgown, that's me. She repeated Charlotte Montague's coaching litany to herself: Walk forward, stop outside the door. The gentleman usher will open the doors. Wait for him to announce you.

"Madam The O'Hara of Ballyhara."

Scarlett looked at the Throne Room. Well, Pa, what do you think of your Katie Scarlett now? she thought. I'm going to stroll along that fifty miles or so of red carpet runner and kiss the Viceroy of Ireland, cousin of the Queen. Scarlett glanced at the majestically dressed gentleman usher, and her right eyelid quivered in what might almost be a conspiratorial wink.

The O'Hara walked like an empress to face the viceroy's red-bearded magnificence and present her cheek for the ceremonial kiss of welcome.

CHARLOTTE MADE NO ATTEMPT to hide her satisfaction. She entered Scarlett's bedroom with the stiff squares of white cardboard fanned in her hand. "My dear Scarlett, you were a dazzling success. These invitations arrived before even I was up and dressed. The State Ball. Saint Patrick's Ball. A small dance in the Throne Room. Most of the peers in Ireland have never been invited to one of the small dances."

In fact, Scarlett was the Season's hit. Her goings and comings were reported faithfully in the gossip column of the daily *Irish Times*. Gentlemen flocked to meet the rich widow who was also fantastically beautiful. Mothers swarmed her reception room with daughters in tow to meet the gentlemen.

Scarlett looked at her portrait every afternoon before the first visitors arrived. She was learning herself. Charlotte Montague observed the metamorphosis with interest. The practiced flirt vanished, replaced by a serene, somewhat amused woman, who had only to turn her smoky green eyes on man, woman or child to draw them, mesmerized, to her side.

THERE were still two weeks left in the Season when Scarlett went again to Dublin Castle. The First Drawing Room shimmered gold. Gilded columns supported the ceiling. Gilt covered the intricately carved chandeliers and the massive canopy above the gold-and-red thrones. Gold lace trimmed men's court dress of brocaded silk skirted coats and white satin knee breeches. Gold buckles decorated their satin dancing pumps. Gold buttons, gold epaulets, gold braid gleamed on the dress uniforms of regimental officers. The men were almost more splendid than the women.

Almost, but not quite, for the women were jeweled at neck, ears and wrists, and wore gowns of rich materials—satin, velvet, brocade, silk—embroidered often in glowing silks or gold and silver threads.

Scarlett made her way across the room to curtsy to the viceregal host and hostess. The music started as she finished.

"May I?" A gold-braided red arm crooked to offer support for her hand. Scarlett smiled. It was Charles Ragland. She'd met him at a house party, and he had called on her every day since her arrival in Dublin. He made no secret of his admiration. Charles' handsome face blushed every time she spoke to him. He was awfully sweet and attractive, even though he was an English soldier. She rested her hand on Ragland's arm, and he escorted her into the pattern of the quadrille.

"You are very beautiful tonight, Scarlett."

"Thank you, Charles."

The pattern of the dance shifted, and he was gone. She looked up at her new partner. "My God!" she said aloud. It was Rhett.

"How flattering," he said with his twisty half smile. No one else smiled like that. Scarlett felt as if she were floating above the polished floor, buoyant with happiness.

And then, before she could speak again, the quadrille took him away. Her mind was racing: Why is Rhett here? Could it be because he wanted to see me? Because he couldn't keep away?

The quadrille moved at its stately tempo, and when it ended, she was facing Charles Ragland. It took all her self-control to murmur a hasty excuse before she turned to search for Rhett.

Her eyes met his almost immediately. He was only an arm's length away. Scarlett's pride kept her from reaching out to him. "What a pleasant surprise," she said, and the cool tone of her voice pleased her.

Rhett held out his hand. "May I have this dance, Mrs. O'Hara?" He smiled and took her into his arms as the music began. She could feel his warm breath on her skin, and it made her weak.

"What are you doing here?" she asked. She had to know.

Rhett chuckled. "I couldn't resist my curiosity," he said. "I was in London on business, and everyone was talking about an American who was taking Dublin Castle by storm. Could that be Scarlett of the striped stockings? I asked myself. Bart Morland confirmed my suspicions. Then I couldn't get him to stop talking about you. He even made me ride with him through that town of yours."

His eyes raked over her from head to toe. "You've changed, Scarlett," he said quietly. "The charming girl has become an elegant, grown-up woman. I salute you, I really do."

"Thank you, Rhett," she said.

"Are you happy in Ireland, Scarlett?"

"Yes, I am."

"I'm glad." His words were rich with deeper meaning. And for the first time in all the years she'd known him, Scarlett understood Rhett, at least in part. He did come to see me, she under-

stood, he's been thinking about me all this time, worrying about how I was. He never stopped caring, no matter what he said. He loves me and always will, just as I'll always love him.

The realization filled her with happiness, and she tasted it like Champagne, sipped it to make it last. Rhett was here with her, and they were, in this moment, closer than they had ever been.

An aide-de-camp approached them when the music ended. "His Excellency requests the honor of the next dance, Mrs. O'Hara."

Rhett raised his eyebrows in the quizzical mockery Scarlett remembered so well. Her lips curved in a smile for him alone.

"Tell His Excellency that I will be delighted," she said. She looked at Rhett before she took the aide's arm. "In Clayton County," she murmured to Rhett, "we'd say that I was in high cotton." His laughter followed her as she walked away.

Scarlett felt no real surprise that Rhett was no longer there when she looked for him later. For as long as she had known him, Rhett had appeared and disappeared without explanation.

When she returned to her rooms at the Shelbourne, she stood before a long pier glass to look at herself and see what Rhett had seen. She looked beautiful and sure of herself, like her portrait.

Her heart began to ache. For in Rhett's caring words, she knew, there had also been sadness and farewell.

In the middle of the night Scarlett O'Hara woke in her luxurious room in the best hotel in Dublin and wept with racking convulsive sobs. *If only . . .* repeated again and again in her head.

But sometime during those dark hours she found the courage to let Rhett go. *If I love him,* she understood, *I must not try to hold on to him. I have to give him his freedom, just the way I try to give Cat hers because I love her.*

I wish I could have told Rhett about her, he'd be so proud of her. I wish the Castle Season was over. I miss Cat dreadfully.

CAT was running with the strength of desperation through the woods at Ballyhara. The boys chasing her shouted and jeered. "There she is!" one shouted, and the others threw the stones.

But the figure stepping from behind a tree was not Cat. It was the *cailleach*, with a gnarled finger pointing. The boys howled with fear and ran.

"Come with me," said Grainne. "I will give you some tea."

"Will there be cakes?" Cat asked.

"There will," said the *cailleach*.

WHEN the Saint Patrick's Ball ended, at four in the morning, the Castle Season was over. The next event was the Punchestown races. Everyone would be there, Charlotte told her.

Scarlett declined. "I love racing, Charlotte, but I'm ready to go home now. I'll pay for the hotel reservations you made."

No need, said Charlotte. She could sell them for four times their cost. And she herself had no interest in racing and horses.

She thanked Scarlett for making her an independent woman. "You are independent as well, Scarlett. You are in the world now. Do with it what you will."

26

*T*HE spring was sunnier than anyone could remember one ever being, and the wheat had already hazed the fields with tender fresh green. Scarlett was delighted to be home.

"How is Ree doing?" she asked Cat. It was like the child to

name her Shetland pony King, and nice she used the Gaelic word.

"Ree doesn't like it when I ride him with a saddle. I don't like it either. Bareback is better."

"No, my precious. You've got to learn to ride with a saddle, and so does Ree. Let's ride to the town. Would you like that?"

"Cat doesn't like town. Can we ride to the tower?"

"That's a good idea."

"Will we go see Grainne?"

Scarlett's hands tightened on her reins. "How do you know Grainne?" Who had taken Cat there? And why?

"She gave Cat some tea."

Scarlett didn't care for the sound of it. Cat only referred to herself in the third person when something made her nervous or angry. "What didn't you like about Grainne?"

"She thinks Cat is another little girl, named Dara."

"Oh, honey, she knows it's you. That's a very special name she gave you when you were just a little baby. It's Gaelic, like the name you gave Ree. Dara means oak tree, the best and strongest tree of all."

"That's silly. A girl can't be a tree. She doesn't have leaves."

"Look, Cat, there's the tower." There were no stairs outside, Scarlett explained to Cat, just as old Daniel had explained to her. A ladder gave people access to the door, set twelve feet above the ground. When danger came, people could run to the tower, pull the ladder up behind them and fire arrows or throw stones down on the attackers from the narrow slit windows.

"I like the tower," said Cat.

"I do too, sweetheart," said Scarlett.

THE blackthorn was already blooming in the hedges and it was still April. What a season they were having! Scarlett was driving the buggy into Trim for a package of summer clothes Mrs. Sims had sent. But what on earth was going on? Why was the bridge all jammed up with people?

Scarlett leaned down from the buggy and touched a hurrying woman on the shoulder. "What's happening?"

The woman looked up, her face excited. "It's a flogging. Better hurry, or you'll miss it."

A flogging. Scarlett didn't want to see some poor devil being whipped. But the mass of people avid to see the spectacle caught her up in their press. Her horse was buffeted, her buggy rocked. The only thing she could do was get down and hold the bridle and soothe the horse, walking at the pace of the people around her.

When forward motion stopped, Scarlett could hear the whistling of the lash and the dreadful sound it made when it landed.

"One hundred. That's it," she heard.

Scarlett didn't shut her eyes until too late. She saw the mutilated body. He was tied onto an upright spoked wheel, and his broad back was a giant red wound with flesh and skin hanging from it. Scarlett turned her head away.

"All right, then, lad, help me cut him down. It's over." Scarlett raised her head. A British sergeant was talking to an ashen-faced private. They cut the leather thong from behind the wheel, and the body fell into the blood-soaked mud beneath it. "The cart will come later to take him away."

A woman in a black cloak ran to the men. She caught the sergeant's gold-striped sleeve. "Your officer promised I could bury him," she cried. "He gave me his word."

The sergeant shoved her away. "I only had orders for the flogging, the rest is none of my business. Leave me be, woman."

The black-cloaked figure stood watching the soldiers walk into the bar. Then she made one sound, a shuddering sob. Her hood fell away, revealing a pale fine-boned face, golden hair, blue eyes in shadowed circles of grief.

Scarlett had to do what little could be done. "I know a doctor in Trim," she said. "I'll go get him."

"A doctor?" Her voice was English-accented.

"He'll prepare your husband for burial," said Scarlett quietly.

THE woman's name was Harriet Kelly; her husband's, Daniel Kelly. Their son, Billy Kelly, a sturdy blond boy, was eight. That was all Scarlett knew until Daniel Kelly was in the closed coffin inside the Catholic chapel.

Scarlett brought Harriet Kelly and her son from Trim to Ballyhara, and it was more than a week before she learned the bare bones of Harriet's story. Daughter of an English clergyman, Harriet had taken a post as a governess on an estate. Well educated but completely ignorant of the world, she'd fallen in love with one of the grooms. When he asked her to run away with him, she thought it the most romantic adventure in the world.

The adventure ended on the small farm of Daniel Kelly's father. There were no references and so no jobs for a runaway groom or governess. Danny worked the stony fields with his father and brothers, blamed Harriet for his fall from grace, consoled himself with whiskey. He was arrested when he attacked an English officer in a bar. His family gave him up for dead. Harriet pleaded for her husband's life. She was granted his body for burial.

"I'll take my son to England, Mrs. O'Hara, if you will lend me the fare. My parents are dead, but I have cousins who will give us a home. I'll find work and repay you from my wages."

"What nonsense," said Scarlett. "I have a little girl running wild as a woods colt. Cat needs a governess. Besides, she's already attached herself to Billy like a shadow. You'd be doing me a favor if you'd stay, Mrs. Kelly."

NEVER in memory had there been such a growing season. The grain was already half again as tall as normal, and the potato fields were thick with strong green growth. One glorious sunny day followed another.

By the end of May, however, the waters of the Boyne were so low that one could see the stones laid centuries before as footing for the ford. The farmers were looking anxiously at the sky. The fields needed rain.

Cat reported that Grainne had more butter than she could eat. "People are buying spells for rain," she said.

"You've decided to be friends with Grainne?"

"Yes. Billy likes her."

Scarlett smiled. Whatever the good-natured Billy said was law to Cat. They'd invented a new game that they called sink the Vikings. They put a rope ladder on the tower. Billy hauled rocks up, and then they'd throw them through the slits, into the river.

SCARLETT went to a house party in Roscommon in early June.

"Isn't the weather splendid?" said everyone at the party. They played tennis on the lawn after dinner in the soft clear light that lasted until after ten o'clock.

Scarlett was pleased to be with so many of the people she'd

liked most in Dublin. The only one she didn't greet with enthusiasm was Charles Ragland. "It was your regiment that flogged that man to death, Charles. I'll never forget, and I'll never forgive."

Charles was surprisingly unapologetic. "I'm truly sorry that you saw it, Scarlett. Flogging's a filthy business. But we're seeing things that are even worse, and they must be stopped."

He declined to give examples, but Scarlett heard from general conversation that violence against landlords was cropping up all over Ireland. Fields were torched, cows had their throats cut, an agent for a big estate near Galway was killed. There was hushed, anxious talk about a resurgence of the Whiteboys, organized bands of marauders that had terrified landowners years before.

Scarlett forgave Charles. But, she said, he mustn't expect her to forget. "I'll even take the blame for the flogging if it will make you remember me," he said ardently. Then he blushed. "You know, don't you, that I'm most abominably in love with you?"

"Yes, I know, and I like you very much—"

"Do you, my angel? Might I hope that—"

"I don't think so, Charles. Don't look so desperate. It's not you. I don't think so with anybody." The sandwiches in Scarlett's room slowly curled up their edges during the night.

"THE O'Hara was under a spell, and the witch and her changeling were talking in a tongue known to no man." Nell Garrity had seen it with her own eyes, she said. "Casting spells on the clouds to make them pass us by, they were."

"The changeling rides a wolf disguised as a pony by day."

"And did you never hear the tale of her birthing? It was on Allhallows Eve. . . ."

The stories were being carried from hearth to hearth.

Rosaleen Fitzpatrick hurried to Colum's house and burst in without knocking. He looked up at her, but he remained seated in his chair. The smell of whiskey clung to his clothes.

"Just what I thought I'd be finding!" she exclaimed. "You can't do your drinking in the bar like an honest man, you've got to hide your weakness here."

"Leave me be, Rosaleen," Colum said wearily. "I'm mourning the death of Ireland's hopes."

"And what about the hopes of your cousin? Will you drown

yourself in another bottle when Scarlett is mourning the death of her darling babe? Because I tell you, Colum, the child is in mortal danger."

"Katie Colum O'Hara," mumbled Colum.

"Her blood will be on your hands," said Rosaleen with cold clarity. "You've got to do something, Colum."

COLUM made a leisurely round of visits to every house, cottage and bar in Ballyhara and Adamstown the following day and night. He listened keenly for indications that Rosaleen's warning about danger to Cat had a basis, but he heard nothing, to his great relief. Then he visited Scarlett in her office, where he found her studying the estate ledgers.

He had just received a letter from the Savannah O'Haras, he said. He had a delicious piece of news for her. Grandfather Robillard had died and left his estate to Pauline and Eulalie. They were in the pink house together and were reputed to be richer than anyone in Savannah.

ON MIDSUMMER Day the clouds borne on the west wind began to pile together, black and heavy, instead of scudding past. The men and women who were building the bonfire for the night's celebration could smell rain. It would be a celebration indeed if the rains returned and the crops were saved.

The storm broke at first dark, with a deluge of rain. People fell to the ground and covered their heads. Hail peppered them with stones of ice as big as walnuts. Cries of pain and fear filled the moments of silence between lightning cracks.

It lasted a half hour, then the sky cleared. The bonfire was sodden; it would not be lighted this night. And the fields of grass and wheat were flattened by the hail. A keening rose from the throats of the Irish of Ballyhara. Its piercing sound cut through the stone walls of the Big House, and Scarlett shuddered.

"WE'VE lost our harvest," Scarlett said. She was standing on a table in the middle of Ballyhara's wide street, facing the people of the town. "But I'm going now to Trim and Drogheda to buy supplies for the winter. There'll be no hunger in Ballyhara. That I promise you, my word as The O'Hara."

365

Scarlett

They cheered her then. But by their hearths at night they talked
about the changeling and the tower where the changeling had
stirred the ghost of the hanged lord to vengeance.

THE clear skies and relentless heat returned, and lasted. The
Irish Times was made up entirely of speculations on the weather
and items about outrages against landlords' property and agents.
At least Scarlett didn't have to worry about her tenants. They
knew she'd take care of them.

But it wasn't easy. Supplies of flour and meal became scarce,
and she was so happy to find anything at all that she paid whatever was asked, often for inferior goods.

She continued to go to parties, but now she was looking for
information from other landowners, not for entertainment.

SCARLETT arrived a day late at Kilbawney Abbey for Lady Gif-
ford's house party. She'd been going from pillar to post looking
for flour and meal, and had lost track of what day it was.

"I've been waiting for the opportunity to shake your hand,
young woman." A knickerbockered old gentleman, the Marquess
of Trevanne, pumped Scarlett's hand vigorously.

"Thank you, sir," said Scarlett. What for? she wondered.

She deserved congratulations, the marquess roared, for rescu-
ing Ballyhara. He'd told Arthur not to be such a fool, not to waste
his money buying ships from those thieves who claimed the timbers were sound. Eighty thousand pounds he'd paid, more than
half his patrimony, enough to buy all of County Meath. They had
been boys together. No man ever had a truer friend than Arthur
was to him. He had wept—yes, ma'am, actually wept—when
Arthur hanged himself. He'd always known Arthur was a fool, but
who could have dreamed he'd be such a fool as that? Arthur loved
that place, he gave his heart to it and, in the end, his life.

It was criminal that Constance abandoned it the way she did.
The marquess was grateful to Scarlett for doing what Arthur's
own widow didn't have the decency to do.

What was the old man telling her? The young lord of Ballyhara
hadn't hanged himself; a man from the town had dragged him
to the tower and hanged him. Colum said so. The marquess must
be wrong. . . . Or Colum was wrong. He'd only been a child,

366

he only knew what people said, he wasn't even in Ballyhara then. . . . The marquess wasn't in Ballyhara either, he only knew what people said. It's all too complicated.

All the talk at the house party was of the weather. Ireland had never before in its history had a drought, but now there was almost no corner of the country that didn't need rain. There'd be trouble for sure when rents were due in September.

Scarlett's heart felt like lead. It was horribly difficult to keep up the appearance of cheerfulness, but she had to.

The final night of the party was July 14, Bastille Day. Charles Ragland came in for the dancing after dinner. Scarlett let him kiss her in the shadow of the great oak tree. It had been so terribly long since she'd been kissed or felt a man's strong arms around her. She felt herself melting in his embrace.

"Beloved," Charles said hoarsely.

"Shhh. Just kiss me till I'm dizzy, Charles."

Dizzy she became. She held on to his broad muscular shoulders to keep from falling. Her cheeks were pale, her eyes very bright.

"May I offer you a sandwich tonight?" she asked quietly.

CHARLES was an experienced, skillful lover. His hands were gentle, his lips firm and warm. Scarlett closed her eyes and received his caresses. Then he spoke her name, and she felt the ecstatic sensations slipping away. No, she thought, no, I don't want to lose it, I mustn't. She closed her eyes tighter, thought of Rhett, pretended that the hands were Rhett's hands, the lips Rhett's lips.

It was no good. It was not Rhett. The sorrow of it made her want to die. She turned her face away from Charles' questing mouth and wept until he was at rest.

"My darling," he said, "I love you so."

"Please," Scarlett sobbed, "oh, please go away."

"What is it, darling, what's wrong?"

"Me. Me. I was wrong. Please leave me alone." Her voice was so small, so poignant with despair that Charles reached out to comfort her, then drew back in full knowledge that there was only one comfort he could give. He moved quietly as he gathered his clothes, and he shut the door behind him with only the slightest sound.

ROSALEEN FITZPATRICK LOOKED at the anguish in Colum's eyes and hardened her expression. Too long had she poured sympathy on his wounded spirit; it had not helped. He was tortured by his sense of failure and betrayal. After more than twenty years of working for Ireland's freedom, he had been discarded by the Fenian leaders. After success at his assigned task, after filling the arsenal in the church at Ballyhara, Colum had been told it was all valueless. Parnell's political actions had more meaning. Colum had always been willing to die for his country; he could not bear to live without believing that he was helping her.

Rosaleen put aside her allegiance to Fenianism. Colum's suffering meant more to her than Ireland's, for she loved him in a way that no woman should permit herself to love a priest, and she could not let him destroy himself through doubt and anger.

"What kind of Irishman are you, then, Colum O'Hara? You hear what's happening. The people are fighting on their own and lack a leader. They do not want Parnell, no more than you. You created the means for an army. Why don't you go now and build the army, to use the means, instead of drinking yourself to blindness?"

Colum looked at her, and his eyes slowly filled with hope.

SCARLETT was working on the accounts, and they were terribly depressing. The only money she had coming in was the profit from the little houses she was building on the edge of Atlanta. Well, at least that money was no longer going to the Fenians. If only Joe Colleton, the builder, would shave a little in building those houses.

Scarlett shook her head impatiently. He'd never do that. He was just like Ashley, bone honest and full of ideals.

Scarlett's eyes grew thoughtful.

She ought to send Harriet Kelly to Atlanta. Scarlett had been pleased to have Cat's governess in the house. Harriet was good company. The only drawback was Mrs. Fitz's hostility to an Englishwoman at Ballyhara.

Harriet would be a perfect wife for Ashley. They were another two of a kind, hopeless in the real world. Harriet was a ninny in lots of ways, but she stuck by her obligations—had her own kind of gumption. Ashley needed that kind of steel behind him. He needed somebody to take care of, too. It couldn't be doing him any good having India and Aunt Pitty fussing over him all the time.

No, it wouldn't do at all. Cat would be heartbroken without Billy. Scarlett bent her head and worked doggedly on the accounts. With no grain to sell and no rents to collect, she was going to lose money this year. The knowledge bothered her because she had always made money in business, and losing it was a highly disagreeable change.

But Scarlett had grown up in a world where it was accepted that sometimes a crop failed or a storm wreaked havoc. She knew that next year would be different and certainly better. She was not a failure because of the disaster of the drought and the hail. Besides, the losses would barely make a dent in her fortune. She could be extravagant for the rest of her life and the crops at Ballyhara could fail every year, and she would still have plenty of money.

Scarlett sighed. For so many years she had worked and scrimped and saved, thinking that if only she could have enough money, she would be happy. Now she had it, thanks to Rhett, and somehow it didn't mean anything at all. Except that there was no longer anything to work for, to scheme and strive for.

She wasn't foolish enough to want to be poor and desperate again, but she needed to be challenged, to use her quick intelligence, to conquer obstacles. And so she thought with longing about the coming fall and the start of the hunting season, about jumping fences and ditches and taking chances on a powerful horse that she controlled by force of will.

27

"*S*UCH good news, Scarlett!" She'd never seen Harriet Kelly looking so excited. Why, she's much prettier than I thought. With the right clothes . . .

"A letter has come from one of my cousins in England. This cousin, Reginald Parsons, has arranged for Billy to be admitted to the school his son attends—"

"Wait a minute, Harriet. What are you talking about? Billy's going to the school in Ballyhara, I thought."

"Naturally he'd have had to if there was no alternative."

Scarlett's jaw set. "What's wrong with the school here?"

"Nothing is wrong with it, Scarlett. It's a good Irish village school. I want something better for Billy. Surely you understand that."

Scarlett was prepared to defend Ballyhara's school, Irish schools, Ireland itself if need be. Then she took a good look at Harriet. The gray eyes, normally hazy with dreams, now looked like steel. She was ready to fight anyone, anything for her son. Scarlett had seen that same thing before, the lamb turned lion, when Melanie took a stand about something she believed in.

Scarlett sighed. "I'd like to suggest a different alternative, Harriet. You and I both know that in England, Billy will always be branded the Irish son of an Irish stable groom. In America he can become anything you want him to be. . . ."

EARLY in September, Scarlett and Cat waved good-bye to Billy and his mother as their ship sailed for America. Harriet's face had the radiance of resolve and hope. Scarlett had written to Ashley and Uncle Henry Hamilton, asked them to help Harriet find a place to stay and work as a teacher. The rest was up to Harriet.

Back at Ballyhara, Scarlett helped Cat turn the tower into Cat's private place, to be visited only by invitation. They swept the dried cobwebs of centuries out of the high doorway, then with buckets of water from the river they scrubbed the walls and floor of the room. It took them over a week to get the place clean. Then Cat went patiently back and forth, house to tower, with her favorite picture books, her paint box, and patchwork quilts. The quilts went into a deep, wide niche in the thick wall of the tower. For her nap, Cat said.

They finished just in time for what would have been harvest home in a normal year. Colum had advised Scarlett not to try and make a celebration when there was nothing to celebrate. He helped her distribute the sacks of food that she had bought.

"They didn't even say thank you," she said bitterly when the ordeal was over. "You'd think it might just dawn on a few people that I'm hurting from the drought, too. My wheat and grass were ruined, the same as theirs, and I'm losing all my rents."

She couldn't verbalize the deepest hurt of all. The people of Ballyhara, her people, had turned against her.

LIKE EVERYONE ELSE IN Ireland, Scarlett read the newspapers that autumn with alarm that grew into outrage. For her the alarm was caused by the number of evictions reported. The farmers' efforts to fight back were perfectly understandable as far as she was concerned. Attacking a bailiff or constable with fists or pitchfork was only a normal human reaction, and she was sorry that it stopped none of the evictions. It wasn't the fault of the farmer that crops had failed and there was no money for rents.

But Scarlett's reactions became the same as her neighboring estate owners' when the Whiteboys entered in. There had been scattered incidents during the summer. But the Whiteboys were more organized now and more brutal. Night after night barns and hayricks were torched, cattle and sheep killed, shopwindows smashed. And more and more, as autumn turned to winter, there were attacks against English soldiers and Irish constables, and against gentry in carriages or on horseback. Scarlett took two grooms along on the roads to the meets.

And she worried constantly about Cat. The child was four now, and she wandered through woods and fields like a wild creature at home there. Scarlett was determined not to cage her daughter, but she began to wish she were less independent, less fearless.

SCARLETT set off for the long-awaited hunt in Galway on a Tuesday in December. She met the hawk-faced man on the black horse on the third day of the hunt. She had noticed him before; it was impossible not to. He rode with arrogant recklessness. People surrounded him at the hunt breakfast, all of them talking, the man saying little. He was tall enough for her to see his aquiline face and dark eyes and hair almost blue, it was so black.

"Who is that tall man?" she asked a woman she knew.

"My dear! That's the Earl of Fenton. Everyone says Luke is the most wicked man in Britain."

Scarlett made no comment. Privately she thought he looked like he needed taking down a peg or two. And when Fenton walked his horse alongside hers later, Scarlett was glad she was on Half Moon; it put her almost at his eye level.

"Good morning," said Fenton, touching the brim of his top hat. "I understand we're neighbors, Mistress O'Hara. I'd like to call and pay my respects, if I may."

"That would be very pleasant. Where is your place?"

Fenton raised his thick black eyebrows. "Don't you know? I'm on the opposite side of the Boyne—Adamstown."

Scarlett was glad she hadn't known. Obviously he'd expected her to. What conceit. "I have some O'Hara cousins who are tenants of yours," she said.

"Indeed? I've never known my tenants' names." He smiled. "It is quite charming, that American candor about your humble origins. It was mentioned in London, even, so you see it's serving your purposes very well." He moved off.

The nerve of the man! And the bad manners—he didn't even tell me his name.

When she got home, she told Mrs. Fitz to give instructions to the butler: she was not at home to the Earl of Fenton the first two times he called.

Then she concentrated on decorating the house for Christmas.

SCARLETT opened the parcel from Atlanta as soon as it was delivered to her office. Harriet Kelly had sent a present for Cat from Billy and a nice fat letter. Harriet's letters were always full of surprises. Scarlett settled herself with a pot of coffee to read it.

Among eight tightly written pages was the unbelievable story that India Wilkes had a serious beau. A Yankee, no less. Scarlett relished the idea. India Wilkes—Miss Confederacy Noble Cause herself. Let a Yankee in breeches come along and give her the time of day, and she'll forget there ever was a war.

Scarlett skimmed the pages quickly. Then she found what she was looking for. Ashley had asked Harriet to marry him.

It's what I wanted, isn't it? It's silly for me to feel a twinge of jealousy. I'll send a magnificent present.

"Have you another cup in that pot, Mistress O'Hara? It was a chilly ride over here."

Scarlett stared up at the Earl of Fenton. Oh, I must look a sight, I hardly even brushed my hair this morning. "I told my butler to say I'm not at home," she blurted.

Lord Fenton smiled. "But I came the back way. May I sit down?"

"I'm amazed you wait to be asked. Please do. Ring the bell first, though. I've only got one cup, seeing I wasn't at home to visitors."

Fenton tugged the bellpull, took a chair close to hers. "I'll use your cup if you don't mind."

"I do mind. So there!" Scarlett blurted. Then she burst out laughing. "I haven't said 'so there' in twenty years. You're a very irritating man, milord."

"Luke."

"Scarlett."

"May I have some coffee?"

"The pot's empty. . . . So there."

Lord Fenton looked a little less overbearing when he laughed, as he did then.

SCARLETT visited her cousin Molly that afternoon with questions about the Earl of Fenton. Molly didn't know anything save that this was the first time in nearly five years that he had come to his Adamstown estate.

Scarlett returned to Ballyhara no wiser than she'd left it. After dinner she wrote to friends she'd made during the Season. "Such a fuss in these parts," she scribbled, "about Lord Fenton popping up here. He's been absentee for so many years that even the shopkeepers don't have any good gossip about him."

She smiled. If that doesn't bring out all the skeletons in his closet, I don't know what will.

The next morning she dressed in one of the gowns she'd worn at her drawing rooms in Dublin. I don't give a fig about looking attractive for that irritating man, she told herself, but I will not let him sneak up on me again when I'm not ready for guests.

The coffee grew cold in the pot.

Fenton found her in the fields exercising Comet, one of her hunters, that afternoon. She was wearing her Irish clothes and riding astride. "How sensible you are, Scarlett," he said. "And that looks like a fine horse. Would you care to match him against mine in a race?"

"I'd be delighted," Scarlett said with honeyed sweetness. "But the drought left everything so parched that the dust behind me will probably choke you half to death."

Fenton raised his eyebrows. "Loser provides Champagne to lay the dust in the throat of both," he challenged.

"Done. To Trim?"

"To Trim." Fenton wheeled his horse and began the race before Scarlett knew what was happening. She was coated with dust when they thundered across the bridge into town in a tie.

"You owe me a drink," said Fenton when they reined in.

"The devil you say! It was a tie."

"Then I owe you one as well. Or would you prefer to break the tie by racing back?"

Scarlett kicked Comet sharply and took a head start. She could hear Lord Fenton laughing behind her.

The race ended in the forecourt of Ballyhara. Scarlett won, but barely. She grinned happily, pleased with herself, pleased with Lord Fenton for the fun she'd had.

He touched the brim of his dusty hat with his crop. "I'll bring the Champagne for dinner," he said. "Expect me at eight." Then he galloped off.

Scarlett stared after him. The nerve of the man! I think I've just been tricked good and proper. She began to laugh.

THE Earl of Fenton was an entertaining and polished dinner companion. At the end of the meal the Champagne was served.

Luke held up his glass to examine the color, tasted the wine and nodded approval to the butler. Then he lifted his glass again, in a toast to Scarlett. "Shall we drink to amusing ourselves?" he said.

Scarlett could feel herself blushing. She was certain she had just been propositioned. She raised her glass. "Let's drink to you being a good loser of very good Champagne," she said with a smile.

Later, Scarlett turned Luke's words over and over in her mind. Had he come to Adamstown just to see her? And did he intend to seduce her? If he did, he was in for a surprise. But it would be fun to make such an arrogant, self-satisfied man fall hopelessly in love with her. She was looking forward to riding with Fenton in the morning, as she'd promised.

THEY raced again, this time to Pike Corner, and Fenton won. Then back to Adamstown, and Fenton won again. Scarlett wanted to get fresh horses and try again, but Luke declined with a laugh. "You might break your neck in your determination, and I'd never collect my winnings."

"What winnings? We had no bet on this race."

He smiled and said nothing, but his glance roved over her body.

"You're insufferable, Lord Fenton!"

"So I've been told. But never with quite so much vehemence. Do all American women have such passionate natures?"

You'll never find out from me, Scarlett thought. She was annoyed with herself. I should know better than to let him goad me into losing my temper. Rhett always used to make me fly off the handle, and it gave him the upper hand every time.

Rhett. . . . Scarlett looked at Lord Fenton's black hair and dark mocking eyes and superbly tailored clothes. He did have a look of Rhett about him. But only at first. There was something very different, she didn't know exactly what. "I thank you for the race, Luke," she said. "Now I've got to be going."

A momentary look of surprise showed on his face, then he smiled. "I expected you to have breakfast with me."

Scarlett returned his smile. "I expect you did." She could feel his eyes on her as she rode away. When a groom rode over to Ballyhara in the afternoon with a bouquet of hothouse flowers and Luke's invitation to dinner at Adamstown, she wasn't surprised. She wrote a note of refusal for the groom to take back.

Then she ran upstairs, giggling, to put on her riding habit again. She was arranging his flowers in a vase when Luke strode into the drawing room. "You wanted another race, if I'm not mistaken."

"You're not mistaken about that," Scarlett said.

SCARLETT and Lord Fenton raced their horses on the roads around Ballyhara and Adamstown. Also over fences, ditches, hedges and the Boyne. Almost every morning for a week Luke made her laugh, made her angry, made her feel alive. But the excitement she felt when she forced her courage to its reckless limits was threatening as well as thrilling. Scarlett sensed something powerful and unknown, hidden deep within her, that was in danger of breaking free of her control.

Mrs. Fitz warned her that the townspeople were disturbed by her behavior. "The O'Hara is losing their respect," she said sternly. "Your social life with the English is different, it's distant. This racketing around with the earl rubs their noses in your preference for the enemy."

"I don't care if their damn noses are rubbed bloody. My life is my own business."

Scarlett's vehemence startled Mrs. Fitzpatrick. "Is it like that, then?" she said. "Are you in love with him?"

"No, I'm not."

Rosaleen Fitzpatrick kept her thoughts to herself after that. But she saw trouble in the feverish brightness of Scarlett's eyes.

AM I in love with Lord Fenton? Mrs. Fitzpatrick's question forced Scarlett to question herself. No, she answered at once.

She thought about what she'd learned from friends responding to her letters. Fenton was notorious, they all said. He possessed one of the greatest fortunes in Britain, was an intimate of the Prince of Wales, maintained a huge town house in London, where rumored bacchanals were held. There were stories about broken hearts and shattered reputations. He was immoral, cruel, dangerous. Therefore, of course, the most fascinating man in the world.

Scarlett's eyes narrowed. I'm not about to let Lord Fenton add my name to his long list of conquests.

But she couldn't help wondering what it would be like to be kissed by him.

LORD Fenton whipped his horse into a burst of speed and passed Scarlett, laughing aloud. She bent forward, crying to Half Moon to go faster. Almost immediately she had to pull back on the reins when Luke stopped and turned his horse to block the way.

"I could have crashed right into you," she said.

"Exactly what I had in mind," said Fenton. Before Scarlett understood what was happening, he had caught hold of Half Moon's mane and drawn the two horses close. His other hand closed over the back of Scarlett's neck and held her head immobile while his mouth fastened over hers. Scarlett's heart pounded with surprise, fear and—as the kiss lasted on and on—a thrill of surrender. When he released her, she was shaken.

"Now you'll stop refusing my invitations to dinner," said Luke.

Scarlett gathered her wits. "You presume too much," she said.

"Do I? I doubt it." Luke held her against his chest while he kissed her again. Scarlett felt a surging response, a longing for his hands on her body and his brutal lips against her skin.

Then the nervous horses moved, breaking the embrace. She mustn't do this, she thought, she mustn't give herself to him. If she did, he'd lose interest as soon as he conquered her. And she didn't want to lose him. She wanted him. This was no lovesick boy, like Charles Ragland, this was a man. She could even fall in love with a man like this.

Scarlett stroked Half Moon, calming him, thanking him in her heart for saving her from folly. When she faced Lord Fenton, she was smiling. "I won't come to dinner, Luke, but you may follow me to Ballyhara for coffee."

Scarlett couldn't read the meaning of the scowl on Fenton's face, and she felt something very like fear. She turned Half Moon back the way they had come and urged him into a walk, then a trot.

SHE had already dismounted when Luke rode into the stable yard. He swung from his horse, throwing the reins to the only groom there. Scarlett had to lead Half Moon inside the stable to find another boy.

She stopped in her tracks, afraid to move. Cat was in the stall directly in front of her, standing barefoot atop Comet, with her small arms outstretched for balance. She had on a heavy sweater, bunched over her tucked-up skirts, and her black hair was a mass of tangles. She looked like an urchin.

"What are you doing, Cat?" said Scarlett quietly. She knew that a loud noise could spook the horse.

"I'm practicing circus," said Cat. "Like the lady in my book."

Scarlett kept her voice even. This was more frightening than Bonnie. "Your feet must feel very cold on Comet's back."

"Oh." Cat slid onto the floor at once, next to the metal-shod hoofs. "I didn't think of that." Scarlett held her breath. Then Cat climbed over the gate, with her boots and wool stockings in her hand. "I knew the boots would hurt."

Scarlett saw Lord Fenton standing quietly and staring at Cat.

"This is my daughter, Katie Colum O'Hara," she said. And make of it what you will, Lord Fenton, she thought.

Cat looked up, studied Fenton's face before she spoke. "My name is Cat. What is your name?"

"Luke," said the Earl of Fenton.

"Good morning, Luke. Would you like the yellow of my egg? I'm going to eat my breakfast now."

"I would like that very much," he said.

Cat led the way to the house, with Lord Fenton walking beside her, adjusting his stride to hers. "I had my breakfast before," she told him, "but I'm hungry again, so I will have breakfast again."

"That strikes me as eminently sensible," he said.

Scarlett followed the two of them. She felt confused. Fenton was the last man on earth she would have expected to love children, and yet he seemed to be fascinated by Cat.

Tears filled her eyes. Oh, yes, she could love this man. What a father he could be to her beloved child. She looked at his sleek dark head, inclined toward Cat. He looked very tall and broad and powerful. Invincible. She wanted him for herself and for Cat.

SCARLETT nearly laughed at the scene Luke and Cat presented. Cat was absorbed in the delicate business of cutting off the top of her boiled egg without shattering it; Fenton was watching Cat with equal concentration. Suddenly, without warning, desperate grief drove Scarlett's amusement away. Those dark eyes watching Cat should be Rhett's, not Lord Fenton's! Painful longing—so long held at bay—flooded Scarlett's heart. She ached for Rhett's presence, for his voice, for his love.

If only I'd told him about Cat before it was too late. . . .

Don't be a fool, she said to herself. What was past was past, and she had to think about the future.

After breakfast Cat said good-bye and ran outdoors, but Lord Fenton stayed. "Tell me about your daughter," he said to Scarlett.

"She only likes the white of the egg," Scarlett answered, smiling to mask her worry. Suppose Luke asked about Cat's father?

But Fenton asked only about Cat, if she was always so self-possessed, if she had always been precocious. Scarlett warmed to his genuine interest and talked about the marvels of Cat O'Hara. Finally she looked at the clock and laughed. "My grief, I've been bragging for an age. You should have shut me up."

"Not at all. I'm interested."

"Watch out or you'll make me jealous. You act like you're falling in love with my daughter."

Fenton raised his eyebrows. "Love is for shopkeepers and

penny romances. I'm interested in her." He stood and bowed, lifted Scarlett's hand and brushed it with a light kiss. "I leave for London in the morning, so I'll take leave of you now."

Scarlett stood up, close to him. "I'll miss our races."

"I'll call on you and Cat when I return."

Well! thought Scarlett after he was gone. He sure is scared of the word love.

She concluded that Lord Fenton showed all the symptoms of a man falling in love against his will. It made her very happy.

28

*L*ORD Fenton was very much on Scarlett's mind during the following weeks. And when she pulled the wishbone of the Christmas goose with Cat, she wished that he would return from London soon.

On New Year's Day of 1880 an icy wind tore at Scarlett's shawl when she made the rounds of visits in her town. Colum took a drink in every house and talked politics with the men until Scarlett thought she would scream.

"Will you not come to the bar, then, Scarlett darling, and raise a glass to a brave new year and new hope for the Irish?" said Colum after the last cottage had been visited.

"No, I'm tired and cold, and I'm going home, Colum. Come with me, and we'll have a quiet time by the fire."

"A quiet time is what I dread most. Quiet lets the darkness creep into a man's soul." Colum walked unsteadily through the door of Kennedy's bar, and Scarlett trudged slowly up her drive.

She pushed open the heavy front door of the Big House and dropped her shawl on a chair, then looked around.

"Happy New Year, The O'Hara," said the Earl of Fenton. He was on the landing of the staircase.

Scarlett stared up at him. Oh, why had he caught her looking this way? But it didn't matter. He was back. "Happy New Year," she said. And it was.

Fenton stepped to one side, and Scarlett saw Cat on the stairs behind him, a gleaming jeweled tiara on her tousled head. She walked down the steps to Scarlett, her mouth twitching to keep from grinning. Behind her trailed a long crimson velvet robe bordered with ermine. "Cat's wearing your regalia, Your Lady-ship," Luke said. "I've come to arrange our marriage."

Scarlett's knees gave way and she sat on the marble floor. This couldn't be true. It was too easy.

"It seems our surprise was a success, Cat," said Luke. He took the heavy robe and the tiara from her. "You may go now. I have to talk to your mother."

Cat ran giggling up the stairs. Luke walked to Scarlett. With his right hand he reached down to her. She gave him her hand, and he lifted her to her feet. His eyes were very dark. "We'll go into the library," he said. "There's a fire and a bottle of Champagne for a toast to seal the bargain."

Scarlett allowed him to lead the way. He wanted to marry her. She couldn't believe it. She was numb, speechless with shock.

Luke held a glass out to her. Scarlett took it. Her mind was beginning to register what was happening, and she found her voice. "Why did you say bargain, Luke?" Why hadn't he said he loved her and wanted her to be his wife?

Fenton touched the rim of his glass to hers. "What else is marriage but a bargain, Scarlett? Our respective solicitors will draw up the contracts. You know, surely, what to expect."

Scarlett set her glass on a table. Then she lowered herself into a chair. Something was horribly wrong. "I would like you to tell me, please," she said slowly, "what to expect."

Fenton shrugged. He was, he said, one of the wealthiest men in England, and she'd find him quite generous. He would naturally provide her with all her clothing, carriages, jewels, et cetera. She could keep Ballyhara for her lifetime. After her death Ballyhara would go to their son, even as Adamstown would be his upon Luke's death. "For of course, the essential feature of the bargain is that you provide me with an heir. Once I get a son on you, your life is your own, with the usual attention to discretion."

He drained his glass. Scarlett could thank Cat for making her a countess, said Luke. "You're the kind of woman I enjoy playing with, breaking to my will. It would have been interesting. But not as interesting as that child of yours. I want my son to be like her—fearless. The Fenton blood has been thinned by inbreeding. Your peasant vitality will remedy that. You are a valuable possession, Scarlett. You will give me an heir to be proud of."

Scarlett had been staring at him like an animal mesmerized by a serpent. Now she took her glass from the table. "I will when hell freezes over!" she cried. Then she threw the glass into the fire. The alcohol flared in an explosion of flame. "There's your toast to seal your bargain, Lord Fenton. Get out of my house."

Fenton laughed. "Forget your injured vanity, Scarlett," he said with a sneer, "and consider your daughter. She will become the Lady Catherine. 'Katie' is, of course, out of the question, it's a kitchen maid's name. As my daughter, she will have an impregnable position in the world, access to the best of everything. Can you deny all that to her because your lower-class yearning for romance is unfulfilled? I don't think so.

"But enough of this. It bores me. Send word when you've come to your senses, Scarlett. You'll agree to my bargain. I always get what I want." Fenton began to walk to the door.

Scarlett called to him to stop. There was one thing she had to know. "Did it ever cross your mind, Lord Fenton, that your wife might be barren? Or that you couldn't father a child?"

Fenton smiled. "My manhood is proven by the bastards I've scattered all through Europe. As for you, there's Cat. I am going to Dublin to open my house there for the Season. Send word when you capitulate. A letter will find me on Merrion Square." He bowed to her with full courtly flourishes and left, laughing.

Scarlett held her head proudly high until she heard the front door close behind him. Then she began to sob. How could she have been so wrong about everything? The man had no love in him. And what was she going to do now? Her mind was filled with the picture of Cat on the stairs, crowned and laughing with delight. What should she do?

"Rhett," Scarlett cried, "Rhett, we need you so much."

SCARLETT had fantasies of revenge: she would laugh in Fenton's face before the altar and tell him that she could never bear another child.

Hatred burned in her heart. Scarlett extended it to all the English, and she decided to renew her support of Colum's Fenian brotherhood.

"But I have no use for your money, Scarlett darling," he told her. "The work now is in planning the moves of the Land League."

"There must be something I can do to help."

There was nothing. Land League membership was open only to tenant farmers, and there would be no action until rents came due in the spring. One farmer on each estate would pay, all the others would refuse, and if the landlord evicted, all would go to live at the cottage where the rent was paid up. Scarlett couldn't see the reason for that. The landlord would just rent to someone else.

Ah, no, said Colum, that's where the league came in. They'd force everyone else to stay away, and without farmers the landlord would lose his rents. It was the idea of a genius, he said.

ON SAINT Brigid's Day there was a light rain. Scarlett said the ritual prayers for a good farm year with a fervor no other prayer had ever held, and she had tears on her cheeks when she turned the first sod. Only God could save them. No one could stand another year like the last one.

Scarlett returned to the house and got her things organized to be packed for Dublin. She would be leaving in less than a week. She didn't want to go—Lord Fenton would be there, and how could she face him? With her head held high. It was the only way.

SCARLETT'S second Season in Dublin was an even greater triumph than her first. She was The O'Hara of Ballyhara, Irish and proud of it. She was an original!

Lord Fenton seemed to turn up everyplace she went. Scarlett greeted him with cool good manners and ignored the expression of contemptuous confidence in his eyes. He had no power to hurt her anymore. Not as himself. But she was pierced by pain again and again when she glimpsed the back of a tall dark-haired man clad in velvet or brocade and it turned out to be Fenton. For Scarlett looked for Rhett in every crowd. He'd been at the castle the year before, why not this year . . . this night . . . this room?

But it was always Fenton.

SCARLETT returned to Ballyhara thankful to get away from Dublin. The final weeks of the Season had seemed endless. It was good to be home, and it was pure heaven to have Cat's strong little arms nearly strangle her with a fierce hug of welcome.

"Where shall we go for our walk?" Scarlett asked her. Cat said she'd like to go visit Grainne.

"She likes you, Momma. She likes me more, but she likes you a lot."

"That would be nice," said Scarlett. She'd be glad to go to the tower. It gave her a feeling of serenity, and there was little serenity in her heart.

SCARLETT closed her eyes and rested her cheek on the ancient smooth stones for a moment. Cat fidgeted, anxious to see Grainne.

Then Scarlett pulled on the rope ladder to the high door to test it. It was weathered, and she thought she'd better see about having a new one made. If it broke, and Cat fell . . .

"Grainne will be expecting us, Momma."

"All right, honey, I'm coming."

The wise woman looked no older, no different from the first time Scarlett had seen her. Cat busied herself in the small dark cottage, getting cups from their shelf. She was very much at home. "I'll fill the kettle at the spring," she said as she carried it outside. Grainne watched her lovingly.

"Dara visits me often," said the wise woman. "It's her kindness to a lonely soul, and I haven't the heart to send her away. Lonely knows lonely. The other children try to stone her, but Dara is too quick for them."

"They do what?"

The children from the town, Grainne said placidly, hunted the woods for Dara. She knew how to escape them, though. They wouldn't dare chase her into her tower, they were afraid of it, haunted as it was by the ghost of the young hanged lord.

Scarlett was aghast. Her precious Cat tormented by the children of Ballyhara! She would evict their parents! She started up out of her chair.

"You will burden the child with the ruin of Ballyhara?" said Grainne. "Sit you down, woman. Others would be the same. They fear anyone different to themselves. What they fear, they try to drive away."

Scarlett sank back onto the chair. She knew the wise woman was right. She'd paid the price for being different herself. Her stones had been coldness, criticism, ostracism. But she had brought it on herself. Cat was only a little girl. She was innocent. "It's intolerable!" Scarlett cried. "I've got to make them stop."

"Ach, there's no stopping ignorance. Dara is safe in her tower, and it is enough for her. Listen to an old woman, The O'Hara. Listen. Where there is no sorrow, there is no joy. Leave Dara be."

As if the old woman had called her, Cat came back in. She set the heavy water-filled kettle on the iron hook over the coals. Scarlett had to turn her head to keep from grabbing Cat in her arms.

"Watch me, Momma," said Cat in a while. She was carefully pouring steaming water into an old brown china teapot. "I put in all the right leaves, Grainne." She looked proud and happy.

Scarlett caught hold of the wise woman's shawl. "Tell me what to do," she begged.

"You must do what's given you to do. God will guard Dara."

I don't understand anything she says, thought Scarlett. But somehow her terror was relieved. She drank Cat's brew in the companionable silence of the shadowy room, glad that Cat had this place to come to. And the tower. When she got home, Scarlett gave orders for a new, stronger rope ladder.

SCARLETT went to Punchestown for the races this year. She'd been invited to Bishopscourt, the seat of the Earl of Clonmel, who was known as Earlie. To her delight Sir John Morland was also a guest. To her dismay the Earl of Fenton was there.

Scarlett rushed over to Morland. "Bart! How are you? You're the biggest stay-at-home. You're never anywhere."

Morland was gleaming with happiness. "I've been busy, Scarlett. I've got a winner, I'm sure of it, after all these years."

He'd talked like this before. Bart was always sure each foal was the next Grand National champion. "I named her Diana, fleet of foot and all that, you know, plus John for me. It came out Dijon when I put it together. Mustard, I thought. Hot and peppery. That's not a bad profile. So Dijon it is. She's going to make my fortune. Better lay a fiver on her, Scarlett, she's a sure thing."

"I'll make it ten pounds, Bart."

"I'll be really sunk if I'm wrong about Dijon, Scarlett. My tenants are doing that rent-strike thing the Land League dreamed up. Leaves me without money for oats."

Scarlett was horrified. She'd never dreamed the Land League

would be used against anyone like Bart. "I can't believe it, Bart. What are you going to do?"

Morland's face lost some of its glow. "I don't know," he said. "All I've got are my rents. I've never evicted. But now I'm up against it, I might have to. . . . I say, Scarlett, I forgot to mention it. I received some very good news from our friend Rhett Butler."

Scarlett's heart leaped. "Is he coming over?"

"No. I wrote to him about Dijon, you see. But he wrote back that he couldn't come. He's to be a father in June. They took extra care this time—kept the wife in bed for months—and everything's splendid now. They're both happy as larks. Never saw a man in my life cared as much about being a father as Rhett."

Scarlett caught hold of a chair for support. Whatever unrealistic daydreams and hidden hopes she might have had were over.

EARLIE had reserved a section of the stands for his party. Scarlett stood with the others, scanning the racecourse through mother-of-pearl opera glasses. The turf track was brilliant green.

"Do you fancy anything, Scarlett?" said a smooth voice in her ear. It was Fenton.

"I haven't decided yet, Luke."

When the riders came onto the track, Scarlett cheered with the rest and agreed with Morland that Dijon was the handsomest horse there. All the time she was talking and smiling, her mind was methodically making its way through the options of her life. It would be highly dishonorable to marry Lord Fenton. He wanted a child, and she could not give him one. Except Cat, who would be safe and secure.

What kind of honor do I owe Lord Fenton? He has none himself, why should I feel he's entitled to it from me?

Dijon won. Everyone crowded around John Morland, shouting and pounding on his back. Under cover of the happy rowdiness, Scarlett turned to Lord Fenton. "Tell your solicitor to see mine about the contracts," she said. "I choose late September for the wedding date. After harvest home."

"COLUM, I'm going to marry the Earl of Fenton."

Colum stared at Scarlett's pale, determined face. "I'll not allow it," he shouted. "The man's a devil and an Anglo."

Scarlett's shoulders hunched in a brief, dejected shrug. "It doesn't matter. I've made up my mind. I'm going to marry Lord Fenton and move to London in September."

"You're a disgrace to your people, Scarlett O'Hara."

"That's a lie," she said wearily. "Say that to your precious Fenians, who've been using me all this time. Don't worry, Colum, Ballyhara will stay just as it is, with the inn for the men on the run and the bars for you-all to talk against the English in. That's really what you care about, not me."

"No!" The cry burst from Colum's lips. "Ach, Scarlett, you're grievous wrong. You're my pride and my delight. 'Tis only that Ireland is my soul and must be first." He held out his hands to her in supplication. "Say you believe me, Scarlett."

Scarlett tried to smile. "I do believe you. And you have to believe me. The wise woman said, 'You'll do what's given you to do.' That's what you're doing with your life, Colum, and it's what I'm doing with mine."

Scarlett's steps dragged as she walked to the Big House. She had gone to Colum before anyone else, expecting understanding and compassion. He had failed her, and she felt very alone.

A FEW days later a messenger from Fenton came with a letter and a package. In the letter he said that he would be in England until the week of the wedding. The announcement would not appear until after the London Season. And Scarlett should have her gown designed to complement the jewels sent with the letter.

Inside the package she found a square, shallow box of oxblood leather, finely tooled in gold. The hinged top lifted and Scarlett gasped. The case was lined in padded gray velvet to display a necklace, two bracelets and a pair of earrings.

The settings were fashioned of heavy old gold, and the jewels were pigeon-blood rubies—matched stones, each as large as her thumbnail. For the first time Scarlett understood the difference between jewelry and jewels. Her fingers were trembling when she clasped the bracelets on her wrists. She couldn't do the necklace by herself, she had to ring for a maid. When she saw herself in the looking glass, Scarlett drew in a long breath. Her skin looked like alabaster, with the dark richness of the rubies against it. She remembered that the tiara, too, was set with rubies. She would look like a queen when she was presented to the Queen. London was going to be a much more challenging game than Dublin. She might even learn to like London very much.

The maid lost no time telling the news to the other servants and her family in Ballyhara town. The magnificent jewels plus the weeks of morning coffee could only mean one thing. The O'Hara was going to wed that rack-renting villain the Earl of Fenton.

And what will become of us? The question and apprehension spread from hearth to hearth like a brushfire.

SCARLETT went to see Mrs. Sims in April. "You'll have to swear on a stack of Bibles not to tell a soul," Scarlett warned her.

Dublin's most exclusive dressmaker gave Scarlett her most freezing stare. "No one has ever had cause to question my discretion, Mrs. O'Hara."

"I'm to be married, Mrs. Sims, and I want you to create my gown." She held out the jewel case in front of her and opened it. "These will be worn with it."

Mrs. Sims' eyes and mouth made O's.

"There's only one wedding gown to have, Mrs. O'Hara. White silk velvet with overlaid Galway lace. The lace must be made, then sewn onto the velvet. How long do I have?"

"Will five months do?"

Mrs. Sims' well-kept hands disheveled her well-groomed hair. "So short. . . . If I can get two extra needlewomen . . ."

Scarlett stood and held out her hand. "I leave the gown in your care, Mrs. Sims. I have every confidence in you. Let me know when you need me to come to Dublin for the first fitting."

Mrs. Sims took her hand and squeezed it. "Oh, I'll come to you, Mrs. O'Hara."

COLUM went with Scarlett to the hiring fair in Drogheda in May. Both of them were unusually quiet, each of them preoccupied with private concerns. For Colum the worry came from the increase in militia all over County Meath. An entire regiment was coming to nearby Navan, said his informants. The Land League's rent strikes had stirred up the landlords. Now evictions were done without warning and houses burned before the people could drag their furnishings out.

Scarlett remembered the hiring fair for only one thing. Rhett had been with Bart Morland there. She avoided even looking in the direction of the horse sales; when Colum suggested they walk around and enjoy the fair, she all but shouted when she told him no, she wanted to get home. There'd been a distance between them ever since she told Colum she was going to marry Lord Fenton.

Scarlett began to think she saw disapproval everywhere, even on the faces of Ballyhara's shopkeepers when she made the special effort to buy things from them in these lean months before the harvest. She worked in the hayfields day after day, glad to be busy, grateful for the ache in her arms and legs after the labor. Grateful, most of all, for the rich crop. Her fears about another bad harvest gradually went away.

Midsummer Night, June 24, completed the cure. The bonfire was the biggest ever, and the music and dancing restored her spirits. When the toast to The O'Hara was shouted over the fields, Scarlett felt that all was right with the world.

Still, she was a little sorry she'd refused all the house party invitations for the summer. She had to, she was afraid to leave Cat. But she was lonely, and she had too much time on her hands, too much time to think and worry. She was almost happy when she received the semihysterical telegram from Mrs. Sims, saying that the lace had not arrived from Galway.

Scarlett was smiling when she drove her buggy to the depot in Trim to catch the train for Dublin.

29

THERE was just time enough in the morning to dash to Mrs. Sims' workshop, calm her down, gather the specifics of the lace she had ordered, and race to the station for the train to Galway. Scarlett settled herself comfortably and opened the newspaper.

My grief, there it is. The *Irish Times* had printed the announcement of the wedding plans on the front page. Scarlett smiled at the part about "The O'Hara of Ballyhara, a beautiful ornament to the innermost circles of viceregal society" and "exquisite and dashing equestrienne."

At Galway, a porter carried her small case from the station to the nearby Railway Hotel. The reception area was jammed with people in town for the races.

Scarlett weaved her way to the reception desk and asked to speak to the manager. He was a balding man in a black frock coat and striped pants. She smiled winningly. "I'll need a room tonight. I am Mrs. O'Hara of Ballyhara."

The manager glanced at a *Times* on the desk and bowed. "I trust you'll accept our finest suite."

Scarlett smiled. There was really a lot to be said for marrying an earl. "Send my bag to my rooms. I'll be back later."

Scarlett started toward the door and bumped headlong into Sir John Morland. She hardly recognized him. There was no color in his normally ruddy face and no light in his usually warm, interested eyes. "Bart, my dear, are you all right?"

He seemed to have trouble bringing her face into focus. "Oh, sorry, Scarlett. Not quite myself, I'm afraid."

She took hold of his arm. "Come along, Bart. Have coffee with me." Scarlett walked him to the dining room wondering what on earth had happened to him.

After a great deal of coffee she found out. John Morland broke down and cried when he told her. "They burned my stables, Scarlett. I'd taken Dijon to race at Balbriggan, and when we came home, the stables were just black ruins. My God, the smell! I hear the horses screaming in my dreams. . . . It was my tenants. Because of the rents, you see. How could they hate me so much? I tried to be a good landlord, I tried. What had my poor burned horses ever done to them?"

There was nothing she could say. All Bart's heart was in his stables. . . . Wait, he'd been away with Dijon, his special pride and joy. "You've got Dijon, Bart. You can start over, breed her. You can have the stables at Ballyhara. You can't let things beat you, Bart. You can't give up, you just can't."

John Morland's eyes were like cold embers. "I'm going to England tonight on the eight-o'clock boat. I've sold up. Dijon's entered in the claiming race this afternoon, and when it's over, so is Ireland for me." He looked as if he would never be able to feel anything ever again.

Then as Scarlett watched, a transformation took place. Sir John

Morland, baronet, came back to life by effort of will. His shoulders firmed, and he smiled. "Poor Scarlett, I fear I've put you through the wringer. Do forgive me. I'll soldier on. One does. Come along to the track with me. I'll put a fiver on Dijon for you, and you can buy the Champagne with your winnings."

Scarlett had never in her life respected anyone as much as she did Bart Morland at that moment. She found a smile to meet his.

"I'll match your fiver with one of my own. Done?" She spit in her palm, held it out. Morland spit, slapped, smiled.

IN CLAIMING races, Scarlett recalled, all the horses running were for sale, their prices set by their owners. At the end of the race the owner was obliged to sell for the price he'd set. But Scarlett didn't believe for a minute that horses couldn't be bought before the race began, no matter what the rules were. When they reached the racecourse, she asked Bart for the number of his box. She wanted, she said, to tidy up. Instead, she found the office where the claiming would take place. She intended to buy Dijon and send her to Bart later, when he was settled in England.

"What do you mean Dijon's already been claimed?" she said.

The top-hatted official was careful not to smile. "You're not the only one with foresight, madam. It must be an American trait. The gentleman who put in the claim was American, too."

Scarlett felt desperate. She had to have Dijon for Bart. "Oh, please. What can I do? It's really awfully important."

"You might ask the new owner if he would be willing to sell."

"Yes. I'll do that. Will you point him out to me?"

The top-hatted man consulted a sheet of paper. "His name is Butler, Rhett Butler.

Rhett! Here! Bart must have written him about selling up, about Dijon. He must be doing what I was going to do. He came all the way from America to help a friend.

Or to get a winner for the next Charleston races. It doesn't matter. I'm going to see Rhett. Scarlett realized that she was running, pushing people aside without apology.

"Box eight," she gasped at a steward. He gestured. Scarlett climbed the steps into the box. Out on the great turfed oval twelve brightly shirted riders were whipping their horses toward the finish. People were shouting, urging on the horses. Scarlett didn't hear a thing. Rhett was watching the race through field glasses. Even ten feet away she could smell the whiskey on him. He was rocking on his feet. Drunk? Not Rhett. He could always hold his liquor. Had Bart's disaster upset him that much?

Look at me, her heart begged. Let me see something for me in your eyes. You loved me once.

Cheering and groans hailed the end of the race. Rhett lowered the glasses. "Damn, Bart, that's my fourth loser in a row."

"Hello, Rhett," she said.

His head snapped, and she saw his dark eyes. They held nothing for her, nothing but anger. "Why, hello, Countess." His eyes raked her from her kidskin boots to her egret-plumed hat. "You are certainly looking—expensive." He turned abruptly. "You should have warned me, Bart, so I could stay in the bar. Let me by." And he pushed out of the box on the side away from Scarlett.

Her eyes followed him as he plunged into the crowds. Then they filled with tears. John Morland patted her shoulder. "I say, Scarlett, I apologize for Rhett. He's had too much to drink. That's two of us you've had to deal with today. Not much fun."

Not much fun. Is that what Bart called it? What gives Rhett the right to be angry and insulting? Why is it fine and dandy for him to divorce me so he can marry a proper Charleston girl and have proper Charleston babies, but it's oh so disgraceful for me to marry again and give his child all the things that he should be the one to give her. "I hope he falls over his own drunken feet and breaks his neck," she said to Bart Morland.

"Don't be too hard on him, Scarlett. He had a real tragedy last spring. I told you about the baby, didn't I? Beastly awful thing happened. His wife died having it, then the baby died."

"What! Where did he go?" Scarlett cried.

"I don't know, Scarlett. The bar—his hotel—anywhere."

"Is he going with you tonight to England?"

"No. He said he had some friends he wanted to look up. I must say I'm surprised he got so drunk. He took me to my hotel last night, put me to bed. Was in fine fettle. But when I came downstairs this morning, Rhett ordered coffee and a newspaper, then suddenly bolted— Scarlett, what is it? What are you crying for? Did I say something wrong?"

"Oh, no, no, no, dearest Bart. You didn't say anything wrong at all. He loves me. He loves me. That's the rightest, most perfect thing I could ever hear."

Rhett came after me. That's why he came to Ireland. Not for Bart's horse, he could have bought her by mail. He came for me as soon as he was free again. I've got to go home. I don't know where to find him, but he can find me. The wedding announcement shocked him, but it won't stop him. Nothing stops Rhett from going after what he wants. He wants me, and he'll come to get me. I know he'll come to Ballyhara. I've got to be there.

"Good-bye, Bart, I've got to go now," said Scarlett.

"Don't you want to see Dijon win? What about our fivers?" John Morland shook his head. She was gone. Americans! Fascinating types, but he'd never understand them.

SHE'D missed the train to Dublin by ten minutes. The next train east went to Moate. It would take her more than halfway to Trim. She'd walk the rest of the way if she had to.

Every stop was torture. She had to be home, waiting, when Rhett arrived.

It was after four when Scarlett got out of the train. "Where can I buy a good horse?" she asked the stationmaster. "I don't care what it costs." She had almost fifty miles still to go.

The owner of the horse wanted to bargain. But Scarlett threw gold sovereigns at him and galloped off.

Just before seven Scarlett led the limping horse across the bridge into Mullingar. At the livery stable she handed the reins to a groom. "I'll give him to you if you'll sell me one of the hunters you keep for the officers at the fort." By ten after seven she was on her way, with twenty-six miles still ahead of her.

She rode past Trim Castle and onto the road to Ballyhara at nine o'clock. Every muscle in her body ached, but the misty twilight was gentle and soft on eyes and skin. There was the wooden bridge over the Knightsbrook. Once over the bridge, it was only a mile to Ballyhara town. She urged the horse on with her heels.

SOMETHING'S wrong. Ballyhara town's up ahead, and there are no lights in the windows. Usually the bars are glowing like moons by now. Scarlett had passed the first five dark houses before she saw the group of men at the crossroads in front of the Big House

drive. Redcoats. Militia. Of course—that's why the windows are
dark, they don't want to have to pull any pints for the English. I'll
get rid of them, and then things can get back to normal.

She reined in and swung her leg over the back of the horse.
She could see a soldier—no, an officer—walking toward her from
the group at the crossroad. She'd give him a piece of her mind.
She walked stiffly down the center of her town's wide street.

He stopped in front of the post office. "You there, with the
horse. Halt, or I'll fire." Scarlett stopped short. Not because of the
officer's command; it was his voice. The one voice in all the world
she'd hoped never to hear again as long as she lived.

"The rest of you, in your houses, there'll be no trouble if you
send out the priest Colum O'Hara. I have a warrant for his arrest.
No one will be hurt if he gives himself up."

Scarlett had a mad impulse to laugh. This couldn't be happening. She did know the voice; she'd last heard it next to her ear,
speaking words of love. It was Charles Ragland. Once, only once
in her entire life, she had gone to bed with a man who wasn't her
husband, and now he had come from the far end of Ireland to her
town to arrest her cousin. Well, at least she could be sure of one
thing—if she didn't die of shame when she looked at him,
Charles Ragland was the one officer in the entire British army
who would do what she wanted him to do. Go away and leave her
and her cousin and her town alone.

She dropped the horse's reins and strode forward. "Charles!"

Just as she called his name Charles Ragland shouted, "Halt!"
He fired his revolver into the air.

Scarlett winced. There was the crack of a second shot, and
Ragland seemed to jump into the air, then fell sprawling. Scarlett
started to run. "Charles, Charles!" She heard more shots, heard
shouting, ignored it all. "Charles!"

"Scarlett!" she heard, from another direction, and "Scarlett,"
weakly, from Charles when she knelt by him. He was bleeding
horribly from his neck, red blood spurting onto his red tunic.

"Scarlett darling, get down." Colum was somewhere nearby,
but she couldn't look at him now.

"Charles, oh, Charles, I'll get a doctor." Charles raised his
hand, and she took it between hers. She felt the tears on her face.
He mustn't die, not Charles, he was a good, gentle man. There

was noise all around. Something whined past her head. Dear God, people were shooting, the British were trying to kill her people. There were boots running, and Colum was shouting, and oh, God, please help, what can I do to stop this? Charles' hand is getting cold. "Charles! Charles, don't die!"

"There's the priest!" someone shouted. Shots fusilladed from the dark windows of the houses of Ballyhara. A soldier fell.

An arm closed around Scarlett from behind, she threw up her arms to defend herself. "Later, my dear, no fighting now," said Rhett. "This is the best chance we'll ever have. I'll carry you, just go limp." He threw her across his shoulder, his arm behind her knees, and ran crouching into the shadows. "What's the back way out of here?" he said.

"Put me down and I'll show you," said Scarlett. Rhett lowered her to her feet. His big hands closed on her shoulders, and he pulled her to him impatiently, then kissed her, briefly, firmly, and let her go.

"I'd hate to be shot without getting what I came for," he said. She could hear the laughter in his voice. "Now, Scarlett, get us out of here."

She took his hand and ducked into a dark passageway between two houses. The firing was loud and close. "Follow me; this goes to a boreen. We can't be seen once we're in it."

The hedgerows were high and thick. As soon as Scarlett and Rhett ran four paces into the boreen, the sound of battle became muffled. Scarlett stopped to catch her breath, to look at Rhett, to comprehend that at last they were together. Her heart was swelling with happiness.

But the seemingly distant sound of shooting demanded her attention, and she remembered. Charles Ragland was dead. The militia was after Colum, was shooting at the people of her town. "We've got to get to the house," she said. "I've got to warn the servants to stay away from town until this is over. Hurry."

Rhett caught her by the arm as she started to move. "Wait, Scarlett. I've just come from the house. It's dark and empty, with all the doors left open. The servants are gone."

Scarlett wrenched her arm from his clasp. She moaned with terror as she grabbed up her skirts and ran, faster than she had ever run in her life. Cat. Where was Cat? She had to get to Cat.

BEHIND THE BOREEN, IN THE wide street of Ballyhara, there were five red-coated bodies and three wearing the rough clothing of farmers. The bookseller lay across the sill of his shattered window, blood-streaked bubbles falling from his lips with the whispered words of prayer. Colum O'Hara prayed with him as he died.

Colum crossed the small room. He seized the twig broom on the hearth and thrust it into the bed of coals. It burst into flame.

A shower of sparks flew from the torch when Colum ran into the moonlit street. "Follow me, you English butchers," he shouted as he plunged toward the deserted Anglo church, "and we'll die together for the freedom of Ireland."

Two bullets tore into his chest. He staggered for seven uneven steps more until another three shots spun him right, then left, then right again and to the ground.

SCARLETT raced up the wide front steps and into the dark great hall, Rhett one stride behind her. "Cat!" she screamed. "Cat!" The word echoed from the stone stairs and marble floor. "Cat!"

Rhett grabbed her upper arms. "Scarlett!" he said loudly, "Scarlett, get hold of yourself. We've got to get away. The servants must have known something. The house isn't safe."

"Cat!"

Rhett shook her. "Stop that. The cat's not important. Where are the stables, Scarlett? We need horses."

"Oh, you fool," said Scarlett. "I've got to find Cat—Katie O'Hara, called Cat. She's your daughter."

Rhett's hands closed painfully on Scarlett's arms. "What the devil are you talking about?" He looked down into her face. "Answer me, Scarlett," he demanded, and he shook her.

"There's no time for explanations. All that isn't important now." Scarlett tried to break free, but he was too strong.

"It's important to me." His voice was rough with urgency.

"All right, all right. It happened when we went sailing and the storm came. You remember. I found out I was pregnant in Savannah, but you hadn't come for me, and I was angry, so I didn't tell you right away. How was I to know you would be married to Anne before you could hear about the baby?"

"Oh, dear God," Rhett groaned, and he released Scarlett.

"Where is she?" he said. "We've got to find her. We've got to!"

"We will, Rhett. There's a lamp on the table by the door. Strike a match so we can find it."

The yellow flame of the match lasted long enough to locate a lamp and light it. Rhett held it up. "Where do we look?"

"She could be anywhere." She led him through the dining room and morning room. "Cat," she called, "where are you?"

"COLUM!" Rosaleen Fitzpatrick ran from Kennedy's bar into the middle of the British troops, pushing, shoving to get through, then down the wide street toward Colum's sprawled body.

"Don't shoot," shouted an officer. "It's a woman."

Rosaleen threw herself on her knees and put her hands over Colum's wounds, rocking from side to side, keening.

She closed the lids over his dead eyes with gentle fingers and whispered good-bye. Then she caught up the smoldering torch and leaped to her feet, waving it to bring the flame back to life. So quick was she that not a shot was fired until she reached the passageway that led to the church. "For Ireland and her martyr Colum O'Hara!" she cried triumphantly, and she ran into the arsenal, brandishing the torch. For a moment there was a silence. Then the stone wall of the church exploded in a tower of flame and a deafening blast of sound.

THE sky was lit brighter than day. Scarlett ran, calling to Cat, as one explosion followed another and the town of Ballyhara burst into flame.

She ran upstairs, with Rhett at her side. "Cat," she called, again and again. "Kitchen," said Scarlett, "she loves the kitchen. We can call down." She raced through the sitting room, through the door onto the gallery. Scarlett stopped and leaned across the balustrade. "Kitty Cat," she called, "please answer Momma." She kept her voice calm.

Orange light flickered in the copper pans on the wall beside the stove. Red coals glowed on the hearth. Scarlett strained her ears and her eyes. She was about to turn away when the very small voice spoke. "Cat's ears hurt."

Oh, thank God! Scarlett rejoiced. "I know, baby, that was an awfully loud noise. I'll come around and down to you."

Scarlett gestured. Rhett followed her along the gallery and through the door.

"Scarlett, look," said Rhett. "We must hurry." The open windows above the drive framed a distant cluster of lights, torches, moving toward the house. Scarlett saw Rhett's face in the orange light of the fire-filled sky, capable and strong. Now she could lean on him. Cat was safe. He put his hand beneath her arm, supporting her even as he hurried her.

Down the stairs they ran and through the ballroom. The colonnade to the kitchen wing was glaringly bright, and they could hear a blurred roaring of far-off angry shouts. Scarlett slammed the kitchen door behind them, and Rhett bolted it.

"We've got to get to the stables," said Scarlett. "There's a door to the kitchen garden, it's got high walls, though. I don't know if there's another door out of it. Do you know, Cat?"

"Are we running away?"

"Yes, Kitty Cat, the people who made the awful noise want to hurt us. That's why we have to hurry now."

"The tunnel to the servants' wing would be faster," said Cat.

"Cat, take your mother and me to the tunnel, please," Rhett said. "Would you mind if I carried you?"

"If we have to hurry, you'd better carry me."

Rhett knelt, held out his arms, and his daughter walked trustingly into them. He clasped her in the brief embrace he could not withhold. "Onto my back, then, Cat, and tell me where to go."

The tunnel had high, grated windows. There was barely enough light to see, but Rhett moved at a steady speed, jouncing Cat in a gallop. She was shrieking with delight.

My Lord, our lives are in terrible danger, and the man's playing horsie! Scarlett didn't know whether to laugh or cry.

From the servants' wing Cat directed them through a door into the stable yard. The horses were maddened with fright. Rearing, neighing, kicking at the gates to the stalls. "Hold Cat while I let them out," Scarlett said urgently, Bart's story vivid in her mind.

"You take her. I'll do it." Rhett put Cat in Scarlett's arms.

When all the horses were released except Comet and Half Moon, Scarlett and Cat ran to Rhett's side. "Bareback will do," Scarlett said. They could see torches moving inside the house now. Suddenly a ladder of flame raced up a curtain. Rhett was on

Comet's back now, holding Half Moon by the mane to keep him steady. Scarlett handed his daughter up to him and climbed the mounting block, then onto Half Moon.

"Cat, you show Rhett the way to the ford. We'll take the Adamstown road to Trim. You show the way. I'll keep up. Now go."

They stopped at the tower. "Cat says she'll invite us to her room," said Rhett evenly. Over his broad shoulder Scarlett could see flames licking into the sky beyond. Adamstown was on fire, too. Their escape was cut off. She jumped from her horse.

"They're not far behind," she said. "Hop down, Cat, and run up that ladder like a monkey." She and Rhett sent the horses running along the riverbank, then followed Cat.

"Pull up the ladder. They can't get to us then," Scarlett told Rhett.

"But they'll know we're here," he said. "I can keep anyone from getting in; only one can come up at a time. Quiet now, I hear them."

Scarlett crawled into Cat's cubbyhole and drew her little girl into her embrace.

"Cat's not afraid."

"Shhh, precious. Momma's scared silly."

Cat covered her giggling with her hand.

THE voices and the torches came nearer. Scarlett recognized the boasting of Joe O'Neill, the blacksmith. "And didn't I say we'd kill the English to a man if they ever dared to march into Ballyhara?" Scarlett held her hands over Cat's ears. How frightened she must be, my fearless little Cat. The child nestled close, and Scarlett rocked her from side to side in her lap.

Other voices overlapped O'Neill's. "The O'Hara'd gone over to the English, did I not say it long ago?" "Did you see her, now, down on her knees by the redcoat?" "Shooting's too good for her, I say. Burning's better." "The changeling's what we've to burn, the dark one that brought the afflictions." Scarlett held her breath. The voices were so close, so inhuman. She looked at the outline of Rhett's shadow beside the opening to the ladder. She sensed his alertness. He could kill any man who climbed the ladder, but what could stop a bullet if he showed himself? Rhett. Oh, Rhett, be careful.

The mob reached the tower and stopped. "The tower . . . they're in the tower." Scarlett's heart hammered in her ears. Then O'Neill's voice cut through the others.

"Not there. See the rope still hanging down?" "The O'Hara's clever, she'd be tricking us that way," another argued. "You go up and see." "The changeling talks with the ghost up there, they do be saying. I'm leaving this haunted place." "If they're up there, The O'Hara and the changeling, isn't slow starving a death as good as burning?" "Put your torches to the ropes, then, lads. They'll not get down without breaking their necks!"

Scarlett smelled the rope burning, and she wanted to shout in jubilation. They were safe! No one could come up now. Tomorrow she could make a rope from strips of the quilts on the floor beneath her. It was over. They were safe! She bit her lips to stop herself from laughing, from crying, from calling Rhett's name so she could feel it in her throat, hear it in the air, hear his deep, sure, laughing response, hear his voice speak her name.

It was a long time before the voices and the sound of trampling boots faded away. Even then Rhett did not speak. He came to her and to Cat, and held them both in his embrace. It was enough. Scarlett rested her head against him, and it was all she wanted.

Much later, when Cat was asleep, Scarlett laid her down and covered her with a quilt. Then she turned to Rhett. Her arms circled his neck, and his lips found hers.

"Why, Mr. Butler," she whispered shakily when the kiss ended, "you fairly take my breath away."

Muted laughter rumbled in his chest. He unlocked her embrace gently. "Come away from the baby. We have to talk." Rhett backed out of the niche and walked to a window. His profile was like a hawk's against the firelit sky. Scarlett followed him. She felt as if she could follow him to the ends of the earth. He had only to call her name. No one had ever said her name quite the way Rhett did.

"We'll get away," she said confidently when she was beside him. "There's a hidden path. Cat will know it."

"Is there anything Cat doesn't know?"

"She doesn't know you're her father." Scarlett saw the muscles tighten in his jaw. "You fixed it so I couldn't tell!" Scarlett said hotly. "You divorced me when it was supposed to be impossible, and then before I could turn around, you got married. What was I supposed to do? Hang around your front door with my baby wrapped in my shawl like some kind of fallen woman? How could you do such a thing? That was rotten of you, Rhett."

"Rotten of me? After you went charging off without a word to anybody? My mother was worried sick until your aunt Eulalie told her you were in Savannah."

"But I left her a note. I wouldn't upset your mother for the world. I love Miss Eleanor."

Rhett caught her chin in his hand, turned and held her face in the uneven garish light from the window. Suddenly he kissed her, then he put his arms around her and held her to him. "It happened again," he said. "My darling, hot-tempered, pigheaded, wonderful, infuriating Scarlett, do you realize we've been through this before? Missed signals, missed chances, misunderstandings that need never have happened. We've got to stop it. I'm too old for all this drama."

He buried his lips and his laughter in her tangled hair. Scarlett closed her eyes and rested against his broad chest. After a long time his arms tightened with demand, and Scarlett felt new, thrilling energy race through her veins. She lifted her face to his, and there was neither rest nor safety in the blinding ecstasy she felt when their lips met. Her fingers combed his thick hair, grabbed, held his head down and his mouth on hers until she felt faint and at the same time strong and fully alive.

When their kisses grew too urgent, Rhett broke away. He gripped the stone sill of the window. "There are limits to a man's control, my pet," he said, "and the one thing I can think of that's more uncomfortable than a wet beach is a stone floor."

"Tell me you love me," Scarlett demanded.

Rhett grinned. "What makes you think that? I come to Ireland on those damned clanking, chugging steamships so often because I like the climate here so much."

She laughed. Then she hit him on the shoulder with both fists. "Tell me you love me."

Rhett trapped her wrists in a circle of his fingers. "I love you, you abusive wench." Rhett's expression hardened. "And I'll kill Fenton if he tries to take you from me."

"Oh, Rhett, I don't even like Luke. I was only going to marry him because I couldn't have you." Rhett's skeptical raised eyebrows forced Scarlett to continue. "Well, I did sort of like the idea of being a countess . . . and getting all his money for Cat."

Rhett's black eyes glinted with amusement. He kissed Scarlett's imprisoned hands. "I've missed you," he said.

THEY talked through the night, sitting close together on the cold floor with their hands clasped. Rhett could not get enough of learning about Cat, and Scarlett delighted in telling him. "I'll do my best to make her love me more than you," he warned.

"You don't stand a chance," Scarlett said confidently.

"We'll see. I have a way with women, I've been told."

"And she has a way with men. She'll have you jumping through hoops before a week's out. There was a little boy named Billy Kelly— Oh, Rhett, guess what. Ashley's married. I did the matchmaking. . . ." The story of Harriet Kelly led to the news that India Wilkes had finally found a husband, which led to the news that Rosemary was still a spinster.

"And likely to stay one," Rhett said. "She is at Dunmore Landing restoring the rice fields."

"Is she happy?"

"She glows with it. She would have packed my things herself if it would have hurried my departure."

Scarlett's eyes questioned him. Yes, Rhett said, he had left Charleston. It had been a mistake to think that he could ever be content there. "I'll go back to Charleston, but I'll go to visit, not to stay." He'd told himself that he wanted the stability of family and tradition. But in the end he began to feel the nagging pain where his wings had been clipped. He loved Charleston—he loved its beauty and its grace and its soft-scented salt breezes and its courage in the face of loss and ruin. But it wasn't enough. He needed challenge, risk, some kind of blockade to be run.

Scarlett breathed a quiet sigh. She hated Charleston. Thank heaven Rhett wasn't going to take them back there.

In a quiet voice she asked about Anne. Rhett was silent for a long time. Then he spoke, and his voice was heavy with sorrow. "She deserved better than me. I was more than half crazy about that time. You'd gone, and no one knew where you were. I believed you were punishing me, so to punish you and to prove that

I didn't care about your leaving, I got the divorce. An amputation."

Rhett prayed he hadn't hurt Anne, he said. He'd searched his soul, and he could find no willful hurt. She loved him too much to suspect that tenderness and affection were only the shadows of a man's loving. He would never know what blame he should take for marrying her. She'd been happy. One of the injustices of the world was that it was so easy to make the innocent and caring ones happy with so little.

Scarlett put her head on his shoulder. "It's a lot, making somebody happy," she said. "I didn't understand that until Cat was born. Somehow I learned from her."

"You've changed, Scarlett. You've grown up. I have to get to know you all over again."

"I have to get to know you, period. I never did, even when we were together. I'll do better this time, I promise."

"Don't try too hard, you'll wear me out." Rhett chuckled, then kissed her forehead.

"Stop laughing at me, Rhett Butler— No, don't. I like it, even when it makes me mad." She sniffed the air. "It's raining. That should finish off the fires. When the sun comes up, we'll be able to see if anything's left. We should try and get some sleep. We're going to be very busy in a few hours." She nestled her head into the hollow of his neck and yawned.

While she slept Rhett lifted her into his arms and sat down again, holding her as she had held Cat. The gentle Irish rain made a curtain of soft silence around the old stone tower.

AT SUNRISE, when Scarlett woke, the first thing she saw was Rhett's hollow-eyed face, and she smiled contentedly. Then she stretched.

They could hear Cat's soft snoring, and Scarlett took Rhett's hand and drew him with her to a window. The sight that met their eyes was sobering. Dozens of dark fingers of smoke reached up from every direction, making dirty stains on the tender rose color of the sky. Scarlett's eyes filled with tears. Rhett put his arm around her shoulders. "We can build it all back, darling."

Scarlett blinked away the tears. "No, Rhett, I don't want to. Cat's not safe in Ballyhara, and I guess I'm not either. I won't sell, this is O'Hara land, and I won't let it go. But I don't want another big house, or another town. My cousins can find some farmers to work the land. No matter how much shooting and burning, the Irish will always love the land.

"But I don't belong here, not anymore. Maybe I never did, really. . . . I don't know where I belong, Rhett. I don't even feel at home anymore when I go to Tara."

To Scarlett's surprise Rhett laughed, and the laughter was rich with joy. "You belong with me, Scarlett. And the world is where we belong, all of it. We're not home-and-hearth people. We're the adventurers, the buccaneers, the blockade runners. Without challenge, we're only half alive. We can go anywhere, and as long as we're together, it will belong to us. But my pet, we'll never belong to it. That's for other people, not for us."

He looked down at her, the corners of his mouth quivering with amusement. "Tell me the truth on this first morning of our new life together, Scarlett. Do you love me with your whole heart, or did you simply want me because you couldn't have me?"

"Why, Rhett, what a nasty thing to say! I love you with all my heart, and I always will."

The pause before Scarlett answered his question was so infinitesimal that only Rhett could have heard it. He threw his head back and roared with laughter. "My beloved," he said, "our lives are never going to be dull. I can hardly wait to get started."

A small grimy hand tugged on his trousers. Rhett looked down.

"Cat will go with you," said his daughter.

He lifted her to his shoulder, his eyes glistening with emotion. "Are you ready, Mrs. Butler?" he asked Scarlett. "The blockades are waiting for us."

Cat laughed gleefully. She looked at Scarlett with eyes that were bright with shared secrets. "The old ladder is under my quilts, Momma. Grainne told me to save it."

Alexandra Ripley thought it was a practical joke. In April 1986, as she was furiously working to finish her novel *New Orleans Legacy,* her agent, Robert Gottlieb, called her with a question. Would she be

interested in writing the sequel to *Gone With the Wind?* Annoyed at the interruption, she snapped, "Oh, sure, Robert. That's not funny," and hung up. But when she called back later, she learned it was no joke— though it was very much top se- cret. A sequel to Margaret Mitch- ell's classic novel of the South *was* being planned, and when Gottlieb asked again if Ripley would be in- terested in writing it, her answer was summed up in one word— "Wow!"

Wow indeed. It would take Ripley four years from that tele- phone call, and stamina she never knew she had, to complete the se-

Alexandra Ripley

quel. But it was a job worth doing. When *Scarlett* was finally published—brought out simultaneously in forty countries—it be- came an international, and record-breaking, best seller. It went in- stantly to the top of best-seller lists and has been bought by CBS television for a miniseries.

Among the reasons Alexandra Ripley was a natural choice for the job of writing the book was that she already had a reputation as a fine historical novelist. *New Orleans Legacy,* a Condensed Books selec- tion in 1987, went on to become a national best seller; and her first novel, *Charleston,* was even compared to *Gone With the Wind.* (Charleston is also the city where Ripley was born and in which she spent her early years.) This author is proud to call herself a southern writer, and she admits that she would have been upset if anyone but a dyed-in-the-wool southerner had been chosen to write the sequel.

"What I tried to do in *Scarlett* was an echo of *Gone With the Wind,*" Ripley says. To prepare herself for the formidable task ahead, she read the original book at least six times, and even wrote out several scenes, underlining certain passages with colored pencils and bracketing others, in order to develop a feeling for Margaret Mitchell's style. "She broke every conceivable rule of grammar," Ripley says, "and yet it worked like gangbusters." Ripley also watched the motion picture over and over again, and she admits that she kept the performances of its two stars, Vivien Leigh and Clark Gable, very much in mind as she wrote.

Choosing the locales for *Scarlett* proved difficult. There was still Atlanta to represent the Old South, a landscape that Ripley enlarged to include Charleston and Savannah. But now the Civil War was over and Scarlett—and the author—needed a change of scenery. "I was poking around in the history of that period," Ripley says, "and came upon a reference to uprisings in Ireland. And I thought, Tara, O'Hara, and the Irish people fighting one another, just like our Civil War . . . How could I have missed it?" Because she is particular about the historical details of her novels, she journeyed with her husband to Ireland to seek out the roads and byways Scarlett might have traveled and the places where she might have lived. Although most of the great Georgian mansions were "too grand" for Scarlett, they finally found a house in County Roscommon that came to serve as the model for the Big House in Ballyhara.

Alexandra Ripley's own home is a charming eighteenth-century farmhouse in the Virginia countryside, where she lives with her husband, John, a professor of rhetoric at the University of Virginia. It is here that she creates her books, curled up in a chintz-covered easy chair and writing in longhand on a pad of paper. Lately, though, Ripley hasn't seen much of that big easy chair. The incredible success that greeted the publication of *Scarlett* has kept her on the road with demands for personal appearances and interviews around the country. She longs to settle down again and begin writing the book on the tobacco barons that she put on hold when she said yes to *Scarlett*. Until then, Alexandra Ripley, like her heroine, can say, "This will be over soon, and then I can go home. . . ."

The Deceiver

Frederick Forsyth

Sam McCready is no ordinary spy. He's the Deceiver, an expert in deception and disinformation. And he's been a thorn in the side of the KGB for years.

But now the cold war is over, and so is Sam's career. The British secret service no longer wants a man with the Deceiver's unorthodox talents.

The British secret service has just made a big mistake.

"A master of Cold War suspense. . . . Flawless espionage fiction."
—*Publishers Weekly*

PROLOGUE

IN THE summer of 1983 the then chief of the British Secret Intelligence Service sanctioned the formation of a new desk designed to have a wide-ranging jurisdiction that would span traditional frontiers. The main impetus was the recent arrival of Yuri V. Andropov as General Secretary of the Communist Party of the Soviet Union. For fifteen years Andropov had been chairman of the KGB. Favoring his old agency, he instituted an upsurge of aggressive espionage and active measures by the KGB against the West. Andropov highly favored the use of disinformation—the spreading of demoralization by the use of lies, character assassination, and the sowing of discord among the allies with planted untruths.

Mrs. Thatcher, then earning her Soviet-awarded title of the Iron Lady, took the view that two could play at that game and that Britain's own intelligence agency might offer the Soviets a return match.

The new desk was given a ponderous title: Deception, Disinformation, and Psychological Operations. Of course, the title was at once reduced to Dee-Dee and Psy Ops, and thence simply to Dee-Dee. The new head of Dee-Dee was tagged the Deceiver.

The man chosen was not a head office careerist with the prudence of a true civil servant but a former field agent plucked from East Germany. He was Sam McCready, and he ran the desk for seven years. But all good things come to an end. In the late spring of 1990 a conversation took place in the heart of Whitehall. . . .

THE YOUNG AIDE ROSE FROM behind his desk in the outer office with a practiced smile. "Good morning, Sir Mark. The permanent under secretary asked that you be shown straight in."

He opened the door to the private office of the permanent under secretary of the Foreign and Commonwealth Office—the FCO—and ushered the visitor through it. The permanent under secretary, Sir Robert Inglis, rose with a welcoming smile.

"Mark, my dear chap, how good of you to come."

You do not become, however recently, chief of the Secret Intelligence Service—the SIS—without developing a certain wariness when confronted by such warmth from a relative stranger. Sir Mark steeled himself for a difficult meeting.

When he was seated, Sir Robert, the country's senior Foreign Office civil servant, opened the scarred red dispatch box lying on his desk and withdrew a red book with a black spiral binding.

"I have," he began, "read your proposals—'SIS in the Nineties.' You seem to have met the requirements most thoroughly."

"Thank you, Robert," said the chief. "Then may I count upon the Foreign Office's support?"

The diplomat's smile could have won prizes on a TV game show. "My dear Mark, we have no difficulties with your proposals. But there are just a few points I would like to take up with you."

Here it comes, thought the chief of the SIS.

"I don't know what your staffing position is, but we are facing some difficulties over staffing the expanded Service that will result from the end of the cold war and the liberation of Central and Eastern Europe. You know what I mean?"

Sir Mark knew exactly what he meant. With the virtual collapse of communism over the previous two years, the diplomatic corps was looking to expanded opportunities right across Central Europe and the Balkans. By inference Sir Robert was suggesting that with the cold war now laid out in the morgue, the position for his colleague in secret intelligence would be just the reverse.

The diplomat dropped his smile and leaned forward earnestly. "What I wish to discuss with you is the allocation of space in our embassies, and to whom."

Sir Mark groaned inwardly. The FCO has one ace card always ready to play. The great majority of intelligence officers who are serving abroad do so under the cover of the embassy. That makes the embassy their host. No allocation of a cover job—no posting.

"In future, I fear, we will simply not be able to offer positions to some of your more . . . colorful staffers. Officers whose cover is clearly blown. Brass-plate operators. In the new Europe they would stick out like sore thumbs."

Both men knew that agents abroad fell into three categories. "Illegal" agents were not within the cover of the embassy and were not the concern of Sir Robert Inglis. Officers serving inside the embassy were either "declared" or "undeclared."

A declared officer, or brass-plate operator, was one whose real function was widely known. In the past, dissidents and malcontents in the communist world knew just whom to come to and pour out their woes, as to a father confessor. It had led to rich harvests of information and some spectacular defectors. Sir Robert was saying that he wanted no more such officers.

Sir Mark was having none of it. "I hear what you are saying, Robert, but I will not start my term as chief of the SIS with a purge of officers who have served long, loyally, and well."

"Find other postings for them," suggested Sir Robert. "Desk jobs here at home."

"You mean what is called unattractive employments," said the chief. "Most will not take them."

"Then they must go for early retirement." The senior diplomat leaned forward again. "Mark, my dear chap, this is not negotiable. I will have the Five Wise Men with me on this, be assured of it, seeing that I am one myself. We will agree to handsome compensation, but . . ."

The Five Wise Men are the permanent under secretaries of the Cabinet Office, the Foreign Office, the Home Office, the Ministry of Defense, and the Treasury. Among them, these five wield enormous power in the corridors of government.

Sir Mark was deeply unhappy, but he knew he would have to concede. "Very well, but I will need guidance on procedures."

What he meant was that for his own position among his own staff he wanted to be visibly overruled.

"Guidance will be forthcoming at once," Sir Robert Inglis said. "What I propose is a single precedent for the whole group."

"A scapegoat?"

"An unpleasant word. Early retirement with generous pension

411

rights can hardly be called victimization. You take one officer whose early departure could be envisaged without demur, hold a hearing, and thus set your precedent."

"One officer? Had you anyone in mind?"

Sir Robert steepled his fingers and gazed at the ceiling. "Well, there is always Sam McCready."

Of course. The Deceiver. Sir Mark was aware that the Foreign Office regarded him as a sort of unleashed Genghis Khan. Odd, really. Such a . . . crumpled fellow.

SIR Mark was driven back across the Thames to his headquarters, Century House, in a deeply introspective mood. He knew the senior civil servant in the Foreign Office had not merely proposed the departure of Sam McCready—he was insisting on it. From the chief's point of view Sir Robert could not have chosen a more difficult demand.

In 1983, when Sam McCready had been chosen to head up the new desk, Sir Mark, like others, had speculated that he would not last long. The Deceiver, or so ran the received wisdom, was too rough a diamond to cope easily with the in-house politics of Century House.

To Sir Mark's surprise Sam McCready had flourished like the proverbial green bay tree. He seemed to command total loyalty from his staff.

He could talk the lingo with the other field agents when they came home for furlough or a briefing, and from them amass an encyclopedia of information that would never have been divulged otherwise. He could share a beer with the technical cadres—the nuts-and-bolts men and women—and from them obtain a phone tap, mail intercept, or false passport while other desk heads were still filling out forms.

All this—and other irritating foibles, like bending the rules and disappearing at will—hardly endeared him to the Establishment. But what kept him in place was simple—he delivered the goods, he provided the product. So he had stayed . . . until now.

Sir Mark sighed. For the moment he need do nothing. Sir Robert Inglis would confer with his colleagues and produce the "guidance" that would enable the troubled chief to say truthfully but with a heavy heart, "I have no alternative."

IT WAS EARLY JUNE WHEN THE guidance came down from the Foreign Office and enabled Sir Mark to summon his two deputies, Basil Gray and Timothy Edwards, to his office.

"That's a bit bloody stiff," said Basil Gray. "Can't you fight it?"

"Not this time," said the chief. "Inglis has got the bit between his teeth, and he has the other four Wise Men with him."

"Well," sighed Timothy Edwards. "One has to concede we won't have the operations we used to have in Eastern Europe, or need the manpower there. They have a point."

"How kind of you to say so." The chief smiled.

Basil Gray he had promoted himself, his first act on being appointed chief. Timothy Edwards he had inherited. He knew Edwards was hungry to succeed him in three years' time; knew also that he had not the slightest intention of recommending him.

"So what happens now?" asked Edwards.

"We will have to set a precedent," said Sir Mark, "to clear the way for the smooth passage into early retirement for the rest."

"Anyone in mind?" asked Gray.

"Sir Robert Inglis does. Sam McCready."

Basil Gray stared across with his mouth open. "Chief, you can't fire Sam."

"No one's firing Sam," said Sir Mark. He echoed Robert Inglis' words. "Early retirement with generous compensation is hardly victimization."

"It's sad, of course, because we all like Sam," said Edwards predictably. "But the chief does have a Service to run."

"Precisely. Thank you," said Sir Mark.

"We'll have to offer him three alternative employments," Gray pointed out. "Perhaps he'll take one."

"Possibly." Sir Mark grunted. He opened a folder. "Those available are the commandant of the training school, the head of Administration/Accounts, and the head of Central Registry."

Edwards smiled thinly. That should do the trick, he thought.

Two weeks later the subject of these conferences prowled around his office while his deputy, Denis Gaunt, stared gloomily at the sheet in front of him.

"It's not all that bad, Sam," he said. "They want you to stay on. It's just the question of the job."

"Someone wants me out," said McCready flatly.

London flagged under a heat wave that summer. The window was open, and both men had removed their jackets. Gaunt noticed that the buttons of McCready's shirt had not been inserted into the right holes, so that it rode up on one side. By lunch, he suspected, some secretary would have put it right. The women around Century House always seemed to want to do something for Sam McCready.

It baffled Gaunt, the matter of McCready and the ladies. He was of medium build, with thinning brown hair, and clothes that always looked as if he had slept in them. He had been widowed for some years, but he had never remarried, preferring apparently to live alone in his little flat in Kensington.

There must be somebody, Gaunt mused. But no one ever asked, and no one was ever told.

"Surely you could take one of the jobs," said Gaunt. "It would cut the ground right out from under their feet."

"Denis," replied McCready gently, "I am not a schoolteacher, I am not an accountant, and I am not a bloody librarian. I'm going to make them give me a hearing."

THE hearing at Century House began on a Monday morning in the conference room one floor down from the chief's office. In the chair was the deputy chief Timothy Edwards, the man the chief had picked to ensure the required verdict. He was flanked by the controller of Domestic Operations and the controller for Western Hemisphere. To one side of the room sat a young man from records, who had a large pile of folders in front of him.

Sam McCready sat in the chair facing the table. At fifty-one he was still lean and looked fit. Otherwise, he was the sort of man who could pass unnoticed. That was what had made him in his day so good, so damned good. That, and what he had in his head.

They all knew the rules. Turn down three unattractive employments, and they had the right to retire you. But he had the right to a hearing, to argue for a variation. Denis Gaunt would speak on his behalf. Denis, with his brilliant smile and public school tie, would be able to handle them better than he could.

Edwards coughed for silence. "All right. We are here to study Sam's application for a variation of a head office order. Denis, I believe you are going to speak for Sam?"

Denis Gaunt rose. "Look, we all know the rules. And we all know the realities. Sam has asked not to be assigned to the training school, or the accounts, or the files, because he is a field man. And one of the best, if not the best."

"No dispute," murmured the controller for Western Hemisphere. Edwards shot him a warning look.

"The point is," suggested Gaunt, "that if it really wanted to, the Service could probably find a place for Sam. I am suggesting the Service ought to make that effort because of years of service—loyal, often very uncomfortable, and sometimes extremely dangerous. I would like us to consider a few cases handled by Sam over the previous six years. Starting with this one . . ."

The man of whom they were speaking stared impassively from his chair, at the rear of the room. None present could guess at the anger, even despair, beneath that weathered face.

"I think we all recall it," said Gaunt. "The matter concerning the late Soviet general Yevgeni Pankratin. . . ."

PRIDE AND EXTREME PREJUDICE

CHAPTER ONE

THE Russian colonel stepped out of the shadows slowly and carefully. All meetings with his British controller were dangerous and to be avoided if possible. But this one he had asked for himself. He had things to say—to demand—that could not be put in a message in a dead-letter box. A loose sheet of metal on the roof of a shed down the railway line flapped and creaked in a puff of predawn May wind of that year, 1983.

"Sam?" he called softly.

Sam McCready had also been watching. He had been there for an hour, in the darkness of the abandoned railway yard in the outer suburbs of East Berlin. He had seen, or rather heard, the Russian arrive, and still he had waited to ensure that no other feet were moving amidst the dust and the rubble. Satisfied they were alone, he had flicked the match with his thumbnail, so that it had flared briefly and died away. The Russian had seen it and emerged from behind an old maintenance hut. Both men had reason to prefer the gloom, for one was a traitor and the other a spy.

McCready moved out of the darkness to let the Russian see

him, paused to establish that he too was alone, and went forward. "Yevgeni. It's been a long time, my friend."

McCready did not embrace or even shake hands. Yevgeni Pankratin, colonel of the Red Army, was a cold one—aloof, self-contained. He had first been spotted in Moscow in 1980 by a sharp-eyed attaché at the British embassy. A diplomatic function, banal conversation, then the sudden tart remark by the Russian about his own society. Two months later there had been a first tentative approach, which Colonel Pankratin had not rebuffed. Then he had been posted to Potsdam, to the Group of Soviet Forces Germany, the 330,000-man army that kept the East Germans in thrall, the West Berliners in fear, and NATO on the alert for a crushing breakout across the central German plain.

McCready had taken over; it was his patch. In 1981 he had made his own approach, and Pankratin was recruited. People betray their countries for many reasons, but Pankratin was the true mercenary—he just wanted money. One day he would come out, he had said, but when he did, he intended to be rich. He had called the dawn meeting in East Berlin to raise the stakes.

Pankratin reached inside his trench coat and produced a bulky brown envelope. Without emotion he described what was inside it as McCready secreted it inside his duffle coat. Names, places, movements, divisional readiness, weaponry upgrades. The key, of course, was what Pankratin had to say about the SS-20, the terrible Soviet mobile-launched medium-range missile with independently guided triple nuke warheads. According to Pankratin, they were moving closer to the border.

"There is more," said the Russian. "I understand I am slated for promotion. To major general. And a transfer back to Moscow."

"Congratulations. As what, Yevgeni?"

Pankratin paused to let it sink in. "Deputy director, joint planning staff, Defense Ministry."

McCready was impressed. To have a man in the heart of 19 Frunze Street, Moscow, would be incomparable.

"And when I come out, I want an apartment block. In California. Deeds in my name. Santa Barbara, perhaps. I have heard it is beautiful there."

"It is," agreed McCready. "An apartment can be arranged."

"Not an apartment. A block of apartments. To live off the rents."

"Yevgeni, you are asking for between five and eight million American dollars. I don't think my people have that kind of money, even for your product."

The Russian's teeth gleamed beneath his military mustache. "When I am in Moscow, the product I will bring you will be beyond your wildest expectations. You will find the money."

BRUNO Morenz knocked on the door and entered in response to the jovial *"Herein."* His superior was alone in the office, delicately stirring his first cup of coffee of the day.

Like Morenz, the Herr Direktor was nudging fifty, but there the similarity ended. Dieter Aust was short, plump, beautifully barbered and tailored. Morenz was taller, burly, gray-haired. But he stooped and appeared to shamble as he walked, untidy in his tweed suit. Moreover, he was a low-to-medium-rank civil servant, who would never aspire to be director of the Cologne outstation of the West German Secret Intelligence Service, the BND.

Morenz accepted Aust's invitation to sit, and wondered what, if anything, he had done wrong. The answer was, nothing.

"My dear Morenz, I won't beat about the bush. Next week our colleague Dorn retires. His duties will be taken over by his successor, a much younger man. There is, however, one duty that requires a man of more mature years. I would like you to take it over."

Morenz nodded, as if he understood. He did not.

"Now and again this country has visitors—foreign dignitaries— who at the end of a day of official meetings feel in need of distraction . . . entertainment. Some visitors prefer female company. Paid-for female company."

"Call girls," said Morenz.

"In a word, yes. Well, rather than have important foreign visitors accosting hotel porters or haunting the red-light district, the government prefers to suggest a certain telephone number." Aust took three slim folders from his desk and handed them to Morenz. "There are three girls. Different physical types. I am asking you to take this over because you are a mature married man. Just keep an avuncular, supervisory eye on them. Make sure they have regular medicals, keep themselves presentable. Not a burdensome task, really. It should not interfere with your other duties."

Morenz lumbered to his feet with the files. Great, he thought as he left the office. Thirty years' loyal work for the Service, and I get to baby-sit hookers for foreigners who want a night on the town.

THAT autumn Sam McCready sat in a darkened room deep in the subbasement of Century House, in London, headquarters of the British Secret Intelligence Service, or SIS, referred to by insiders as the Firm. He was watching a flickering screen upon which the massed might of the U.S.S.R. rolled endlessly over Red Square. The parade to celebrate the great October socialist revolution had been held the day before, on November 7.

The camera left the vista of rumbling tanks and panned across the row of faces atop Lenin's mausoleum. The General Secretary himself was not there. Yuri V. Andropov, who had taken power in late 1982, was dying by inches out at the Politburo clinic at Kuntsevo. Chernenko, who would succeed him in a few months, was up there with the other aged leaders, including Ustinov, the minister of defense.

"Hold it," said McCready. The technician at his side moved a hand over the controls, and the picture froze. "That one, third from the left. Can you enhance? Bring it closer?"

The technician fine-tuned carefully. The officer McCready had indicated was half hidden by a full general, but it was the mustache, unusual among Soviet officers, that clinched it. The shoulder boards on the greatcoat said major general.

"Bloody hell," whispered McCready. "He's done it." He turned to the impassive technician. "Jimmy, how the hell do we get hold of an apartment block in California?"

"WELL, the short answer, my dear Sam," said Timothy Edwards two days later, "is that we don't. He's too rich for us."

"But his product is priceless," protested McCready.

"No dispute," Edwards said smoothly. He was younger than McCready by a decade and already an assistant chief, a highflier with a good degree and private wealth. "Look," he said, "the chief's been in Washington. He mentioned your man, just in case he got his promotion. Our cousins have always had his product since you brought him in. They've been delighted with it. Now it seems they'll be happy to take him over, money and all."

"He knows me. He might not work for anyone else."

"Come now, Sam. You're the first to agree he's a mercenary. He'll go where the money is. And we'll get the product. Please ensure there's a smooth handover." He paused and flashed his most winning smile. "By the way, the chief wants to see you. Tomorrow morning, ten a.m. I don't think I'm out of order in telling you he has in mind a new assignment. A step up, Sam. A desk, perhaps."

"I'm a field man," said McCready.

"Why don't you listen to what the chief has to say?"

Twenty-four hours later Sam McCready was made head of Dee-Dee and Psy Ops. The CIA took over the handling, running, and paying of General Yevgeni Pankratin.

IT WAS hot in Cologne the August of 1985. Those who could, had sent the wives and children away to the lakes, the mountains, the forests and would join them later. Bruno Morenz had no holiday home. He soldiered on at his job. His salary was not large and was not likely to increase with three years to retirement.

He sat at an open-air café, sipping a tall glass of keg beer and staring gloomily at the passersby.

Behind his amiable façade Bruno Morenz was a deeply unhappy man. He was locked into a loveless marriage to his wife, Irmtraut, a woman of quite bovine stupidity and potatolike contours who had, as the years ebbed away, even stopped complaining of his lowly salary and lack of promotion. Of his job she knew only that he worked for one of the government agencies. She kept their small apartment in the suburb of Porz more or less tidy, and his evening meal would be on the table ten minutes after he arrived home, semicongealed if he was late.

Bruno had worked hard, paid his taxes, and had little enough fun in life. In three years they would pension him off. There would be a small party in the office, Aust would make a speech, and Bruno would be gone. To what? He would have his pension and the savings from his "other work," which he had carefully hoarded in a variety of accounts around Germany under a variety of pseudonyms. There would be enough there to buy a retirement home and do what he *really* wanted.

Behind his amiable façade Bruno Morenz was also a very secretive man. He had never told Aust or anyone else in the Service about his other work—in any case, it was strictly forbidden. He had never told Irmtraut about *any* of his work or his secret savings.

What Bruno really wanted was to be free, to start again. For Bruno Morenz, well into middle age, had fallen head over heels in love. And the good part was that Renate, the stunning, lovely, youthful Renate, was as much in love with him as he was with her.

There, in that café, on that summer afternoon, Bruno finally made up his mind. He would do it; he would tell her. He would tell her he intended to leave Irmtraut well provided for, quit the job, and take her away to a new life with him in the dream home they would have up in his native north, by the coast.

RENATE Heimendorf was twenty-six, a tall and handsomely proportioned brunette. At the age of eighteen she had become the mistress and plaything of a wealthy businessman three times her age. When the man dropped dead of a heart attack five years later, she managed to pillage their expensively furnished love nest of its contents, which, together with the jewelry he had given her over the years, fetched at sale a tidy sum.

She decided to go into business. Skilled at coaxing a form of arousal from overweight, out-of-condition, middle-aged men, there was really only one business into which she could go.

She leased a second-floor apartment in Hahnwald, a quiet and respectable suburb of Cologne. It had a sitting room, kitchen, bathroom, two bedrooms, and an entry hall and passageway. The larger bedroom was at the end of the passage, so that the bathroom was between the two sleeping rooms. Just before the door of the larger bedroom, built into the wall on the left, was a two-yard-wide coat closet that borrowed space off the bathroom.

She slept in the smaller bedroom, using the larger one as her working room. After moving in, she had carried out some structural refurbishment, including the soundproofing of the master bedroom. Few sounds from inside it could penetrate outside to disturb or alarm the neighbors. The room, with its unusual decor and exotic accoutrements, was always kept locked.

She was good; successful, anyway. Many of her clients returned regularly. She had been in the game for three years and in two more intended to retire, clean up just once in a rather major way, and live on her investments in luxury somewhere far away.

That afternoon there was a ring at her doorbell. A glance through the peephole revealed the rumpled gray hair of Bruno Morenz, her minder from the Foreign Ministry. She sighed, put on a smile of ecstatic welcome, and opened the door.

"Bruno, daaaaarling . . ."

Two days later Timothy Edwards took Sam McCready out to lunch at Brooks' Club in London. Over coffee in the library Edwards broached what was on his mind.

"Sam, there is a new era coming. An era whose leitmotiv may well have to be the phrase 'by the book.' A question of some of the old ways, the rule-bending, having to become—how shall I put it?—restrained."

"Restrained is a very good word," agreed Sam.

"Excellent. Now, a riffle through the records shows that you still retain certain assets who really have passed their usefulness. Old friends, perhaps, whose discovery by their own employers might cause the Firm real problems."

"Such as?" asked McCready.

"Poltergeist. Sam, he's a full-time staffer of the BND. There'd be all hell let loose if they ever discovered he moonlighted for you. It's against all the rules. We do not run employees of friendly agencies. Get rid of him, Sam. Stop the retainer. Forthwith."

"He's a mate," said McCready. "We go back a long way. To the Berlin Wall going up. He did well then, ran dangerous jobs for us."

Edwards rose. "Get rid of him, Sam. I'm afraid that's an order."

MAJOR Ludmilla Vanavskaya sighed, stretched and leaned back in her chair. She was tired. It had been a long haul. She reached for her packet of Soviet-made Marlboros, noticed the full ashtray, and pressed a bell on her desk. When a young corporal entered, she just pointed to the ashtray with her fingertip. He quickly removed it, returning with it cleaned a few seconds later. She nodded. He left again and closed the door.

There had been no talk, no banter. Major Vanavskaya had that effect on people. In earlier years some of the young bucks had noticed the shining short-cropped blond hair above the crisp service shirt and slim green skirt and had tried their luck. No dice. At thirty-five she wore no more uniforms, just the severe, tailored charcoal-gray suit over the white blouse with the floppy bow at the neck.

Some still thought she was beddable, until they caught a salvo from those freezing blue eyes. In the KGB, not an organization of liberals, she had a reputation as a fanatic. Fanatics intimidate.

The major's fanaticism was her pursuit of traitors. An utterly dedicated Communist, she hated them with a cold passion. At the independent Third Directorate, also called the Armed Forces Directorate, the traitors were high ranking and dangerous. Two years of work had gone into the file that now lay open in front of her. Two years of checking and cross-checking, of correlating tiny fragments of information until a picture began to emerge. She was convinced that somewhere in the army there was a deliberate leak. And he was high, damned high.

There was a list of eight names on the top sheet of the file before her. Five were crossed out. Two had question marks. But her eye always came back to the eighth. She lifted a phone and was put through to the male secretary of General Shaliapin, head of the Third Directorate.

"Yes, Major. A personal interview? I see. The problem is, the comrade general is in the Far East. . . . Not until next Tuesday. . . . Very well, then. Next Tuesday."

Major Vanavskaya put down the phone. Four days. Well, she had already waited two years—she could wait four more days.

"I THINK I've clinched it," Bruno told Renate with childlike delight the following Sunday morning. "I've just got enough for the freehold purchase and some more left over for decorating and equipping it. It's a wonderful little bar."

They were in bed in her own bedroom—it was a favor she sometimes allowed him because he hated the working bedroom as much as he hated her job.

"Tell me again," she cooed. "I love to hear about it."

He grinned. "Okay. It's called the Lantern Bar, and the sign is an old ship's lantern. It stands on the open quay right on the Bremerhaven dockfront. There's an old-fashioned brass-topped bar—we'll be behind that serving the drinks—and a nice snug apartment upstairs. I've paid the deposit. Completion is at the end of September. Then I can take you away from all this."

Renate could hardly keep herself from laughing. She had no intention of being taken away from "all this," least of all to a bleak quay in Bremerhaven. But it amused her to prolong Bruno's delusion so that his eventual misery would be all the greater.

An hour after Bruno and Renate's conversation in Cologne, a black Jaguar sedan swept off the M3 motorway and sought the quieter lanes of Hampshire. It was Timothy Edwards' personal car, and his Service driver was at the wheel. In the back was Sam McCready, who had been summoned by a telephoned appeal from the assistant chief.

The sedan swept into the graveled forecourt of a substantial Georgian country house and came to a halt. Timothy Edwards ten years earlier had married the daughter of a duke, who had been considerate enough to drop off his perch in early middle age and leave about three million pounds to Lady Margaret.

"I was told to say they will be round the back, sir, on the terrace," said the driver.

There were four cane chairs in a group. Three were occupied. The two men in the rattan chairs rose.

"Ah, Sam," said Edwards. "Glad you could make it. I don't think you know Chris Appleyard," he added, as the tall American held out his hand.

"Guess not," said Appleyard. He had the leathery look of a Texan cowhand. "Nice to meet you, Sam. Know your reputation."

McCready knew who he was from the name and from photographs: deputy head, European division, CIA. The woman, in the third chair, leaned forward and held out a hand. "Hi, Sam, how're you doing these days?"

Claudia Stuart, at forty still a great-looking woman. She held his gaze and his hand a mite longer than necessary.

"Fine, thanks, Claudia. Just fine." They had met years earlier in Berlin when Claudia was with the CIA's West Berlin station and Sam was recruiting the then Colonel Pankratin. It was she who had taken over the colonel.

"Sorry to hear about May," said Claudia.

"Thank you," said McCready. May. Sweet, loving, and much loved May, his wife. Three years since she died. Multiple sclerosis can act fast or slow. With May it had been fast. In one year she was in a wheelchair and two years later, gone. He had lived alone in the Kensington apartment since then.

A butler appeared with an extra flute of Champagne on a salver. McCready raised an eyebrow. Edwards whispered in the butler's ear, and he came back with a tankard of beer. McCready sipped.

"We have a problem, Sam," said Appleyard. "Claudia, tell him."

"Pankratin," said Claudia. "Remember him?"

McCready studied his beer and nodded.

"In Moscow we've run him mainly through drops. Arm's length. Very little contact. Fantastic product, and very pricey payments. Now he says he's got hold of an unregistered copy of the Soviet army war book. The entire order of battle. For the whole of the Western front. We want it, Sam. We want it very badly."

"So go get it," said Sam.

"This time he won't use a dead-letter box. He will only hand it over to someone he knows and trusts. He wants you."

"In *Moscow?*"

"No, in East Germany. He begins a tour of inspection soon. Lasts a week. He wants to make the pass Tuesday or Wednesday morning, in the deep south of Thuringia, up near the Bavarian border. He wants to use lay-bys—road pull-offs."

Sam glanced up at Edwards. "Have you explained, Timothy?"

"Touched on it," said Edwards, then turned to his guests. "Look, I have to make it clear that Sam actually can't go. He's been black-flagged by the SSD. It means that if they catch him again over there, they'll shoot him." Edwards was referring to the formidable East German secret police, or *Stasi*.

Appleyard whistled. "You must have really shaken them up."

"One does one's best," said Sam sadly. "By the way, if I can't go, there is one man who could. Timothy and I were discussing him last week at the club."

Edwards nearly choked on his flute of Krug. "Poltergeist? Pankratin says he'll only make the pass to someone he knows."

"He knows Poltergeist. Back in '81, when I brought him in, Poltergeist had to baby-sit him till I could get there. Actually, he liked Poltergeist. He'd recognize him again and make the pass."

Edwards straightened the silk at his neck. "Very well, Sam. One last time."

"It's dangerous, and the stakes are high. I want a reward for him. Ten thousand pounds."

"Agreed," said Appleyard without hesitation. He took a sheet of paper from his pocket. "Here are the details Pankratin has provided for the method of the pass. Two alternate venues are needed. A first and a backup. Can you let us know in twenty-four hours the lay-bys you've picked? We'll get it to him."

Sam rose. "By the way, this 'Tuesday'— Which one is it?"

"A week from the day after tomorrow," said Appleyard. "Eight days away."

CHAPTER TWO

Sam McCready spent most of the next day, Monday, poring over large-scale maps and photographs. By midafternoon he had two locations that would suit. One was a sheltered lay-by just off East Germany's Highway 7, between the industrial city of Jena and the more pastoral town of Weimar. The second was on the same road, but halfway between Weimar and Erfurt, not three miles from the Soviet base at Nohra.

At five McCready proposed his choices to Claudia Stuart at the American embassy, in Grosvenor Square. A coded message went to CIA headquarters, Langley, Virginia; they approved and passed the message to Pankratin's controller in Moscow.

Before sundown on Monday, McCready sent a coded message to the head of the SIS station in Bonn, who read it, destroyed it, picked up the telephone, and made a local call.

Bruno Morenz was halfway through his supper that evening when his wife remembered something. "Your dentist called. Says he should look at that filling again. Tomorrow. Could you come to his office at six."

Bruno hoped she had the message right. There were two bars where McCready might want to meet him. One was called office, the other clinic. And six meant during the lunch hour.

On Tuesday morning McCready took the breakfast-hour flight to Cologne. At five to twelve he entered the old-style, half-timbered bar in the Krebsgasse. The small tinted windows made the interior dim. He sat in a booth in the far corner, ordered two steins of

Rhine beer, and waited. Bruno Morenz slid into the chair opposite him five minutes later.

"It's been a long time, old friend," said McCready.

Morenz sipped his beer. "What do you want, Sam?"

Sam told him. Morenz shook his head.

"Sam, I'm fifty-two. Soon I retire. In the old days it was different, exciting. Now, frankly, it frightens me."

"They're offering ten thousand pounds cash."

Morenz stared at him. "Why me?"

"He knows you. He likes you. I hate to ask you this way, but
this is really for me. For old times' sake."

Bruno finished his beer and rose. "All right, Sam. For you. For
old times' sake. But then, I swear, I'm out. For good."

They agreed to rendezvous the following Monday at dawn.

ACROSS two time zones, in Moscow, Major Ludmilla Vanavskaya had her interview with General Shaliapin. He sat behind
his desk, read her file carefully, then pushed it back toward her.

"Circumstantial," he said.

"So far, Comrade General," Vanavskaya conceded. "But a *lot* of
circumstances. Those SS-twenty rockets in East Germany two
years ago—the Yanks knew too quickly. And the movements of the
red banner fleet. Those bastards in NATO always seem to know."

Shaliapin smiled at the young woman's passion. "There may be
a leak," he admitted, "or several. Negligence, loose talk, an array
of small agents. But you think it's one man. . . ."

"This man." She tapped the photo on top of the file.

General Shaliapin leaned over the desk and jabbed a stubby
forefinger at the flushed major.

"I cannot order the arrest of a senior staff officer on the basis of
this. Not yet. I need something hard. Just one tiny thing."

"Let me put him under surveillance," urged Vanavskaya.

"Discreet surveillance."

"All right, Comrade General. Discreet surveillance."

"Then I agree, Major. I'll make the staff available."

"JUST a few days, Herr Direktor. I would like to take my wife
away for the weekend, plus Monday, Tuesday, and Wednesday."

It was Wednesday morning, and Dieter Aust was in an expansive mood. "My dear Morenz, five days is not a problem. I will rearrange the rosters."

That evening at home Bruno Morenz told his wife he would have to leave on business for five days. "Herr Direktor Aust wants me to accompany him on a trip."

"That's nice," she said, engrossed in the TV.

Morenz in fact planned to spend a long, romantic weekend with Renate, give Monday to Sam McCready's briefing, and make his run across the East German border on Tuesday. Even if he had to spend the night in East Germany for the second rendezvous, he would be back in the West by Wednesday evening and could be home in time for work on Thursday. Then he would hand in his notice, work it out through the month of September, make his break with his wife, and leave with Renate for Bremerhaven.

ON THURSDAY, Major Vanavskaya suffered her first serious setback. She had her surveillance team in place, ready to begin shadowing her military target. But first she had needed to know what his daily movements were. To find this out, she had contacted one of the several KGB Third Directorate spies inside the military intelligence organization, the GRU.

"I'm sorry, Major," the young KGB man told her on the phone. "Your man leaves tomorrow for a tour of our principal garrisons in Germany. Yes, I have his schedule here."

He had dictated it to her before she put the phone down. She remained for a while deep in thought, then put in her own application for permission to visit KGB headquarters in East Berlin.

BRUNO made a point of getting through his chores as fast as he could on Friday and escaping from the office early. As he knew he would be handing in his notice as soon as he returned, he even cleared out some of his drawers. His last chore was to sort out the few papers in his small office safe. At the bottom, beneath them all, was his service issue automatic. The Walther PPK was so dusty from disuse that he thought he ought to clean it before handing it back. His cleaning kit was at home in Porz. At ten to five he put it in the side pocket of his seersucker suit and left.

He shopped in the center of town before driving out to Hahnwald—some good veal, fresh vegetables, a bottle of real

French claret. He would make them a cozy supper. His final purchase was a large bunch of flowers.

He parked his Opel Kadett round the corner from her street. He had not told her he was coming. He would surprise her. With the flowers. She would like that. He had his own key to her apartment, so he let himself in quietly to make the surprise even nicer.

The hall was quiet. He opened his mouth to call her when he heard a peal of her laughter from down the passage. He realized with a start that she might have a client. But then she would be in the soundproofed working bedroom, with the door closed. He was about to call again when someone else laughed. It was a man. Morenz stepped from the hall into the passageway.

The master bedroom door was open a few inches, the gap partly obscured by the fact that the big closet doors were also open. "What a jerk," said the man's voice. "He really thinks you're going to marry him?"

"Stupid bastard! Just look at him." Her voice.

Morenz put down the flowers and the groceries and nudged the bedroom door open with the tip of his shoe. Renate was sitting on the edge of the king-size bed, smoking a joint. Lounging on the bed was a man Morenz had never seen before—lean, young, tough, in jeans and a leather motorcycle jacket. They both saw the movement of the door and jumped off the bed. The man had a mean face and dirty blond hair. In her private life this was Renate's regular boyfriend, as rough as they came.

Morenz's eyes were fixed on the video flickering on the TV set beyond the end of the bed. No middle-aged man looks very dignified when making love, and Morenz watched his own image with a growing sense of shame and despair. Renate was with him in the film, occasionally making gestures of disdain at the camera.

Renate recovered from her surprise quickly. Her face flushed with anger. "What the hell are you doing here?"

"I wanted to surprise you," he mumbled.

"Yeah, well, you've bloody surprised me. Now bug off. Go home to your potato sack in Porz, you fat old fool."

That was when he hit her. Not a punch—an openhanded slap to the side of the face. Something snapped in him, and he hit her. He was a big man, and the blow knocked her to the floor.

The pimp reached inside his jacket. It seemed he was armed.

Morenz pulled out his PPK. He wanted to scare the pimp into letting him go. But the pimp went on pulling his pistol. Morenz squeezed the trigger. Dusty it may have been, but the Walther went off.

The single bullet hit the pimp right in the heart. The man jerked, an expression of disbelief on his face, but his right arm kept coming up, clutching his Beretta. Morenz fired again. Renate chose that moment to rise from the floor. The second slug caught her in the back of the head.

Morenz felt numb. Eventually he left the room and pulled the door closed behind him. He was about to leave the apartment when it occurred to him to wonder why the coat closet should be open. He looked inside and noticed that the rear panel appeared to be loose. He pulled the loose panel toward him. . . .

When Morenz left the apartment, he took with him the video-tape of himself, the groceries, the flowers, and a black canvas grip that did not belong to him. Two miles from Hahnwald he dropped the groceries and flowers into separate garbage cans by the road-side. Then he drove for almost an hour, threw the videotape and his gun into the Rhine, turned out of Cologne, deposited the canvas grip, and finally made his way home to Porz.

"My trip with the Herr Direktor has been postponed," he told his wife. "I'll be leaving very early on Monday morning instead."

He went out and got drunk that night. He noticed that his hands were shaking and that he kept breaking out in sweat. He thought he had a summer cold coming on. Or the flu. He was not a psychiatrist, and there was none available to him. So no one told him he was heading for a complete nervous breakdown.

THAT Saturday, Major Vanavskaya arrived in East Berlin and was driven to KGB headquarters. She checked at once on the whereabouts of the man she was stalking. He was in Cottbus, heading for Dresden, moving in a military convoy, and out of her reach. Her surveillance mandate did not cover East Germany. It could be extended, but that would require paperwork. Always the damned paperwork, she thought angrily.

THE following day Sam McCready spent the morning conferring with the head of Bonn station. In the evening he took delivery of a BMW car and drove to Cologne. He lodged at the Holiday

Inn out at the airport, where he took a room for two nights.

Bruno Morenz arrived at the Holiday Inn about seven on that Monday morning and joined McCready in his room. The Englishman ordered breakfast for both from room service, and when the waiter had gone, he spread out a huge road map of Germany.

"We'll do the route first," he said. "Tomorrow you leave here at four a.m. Take the E thirty-five here past Frankfurt. Then head east past Bayreuth and up to the border. That's your crossing point, near Hof. The Saale Bridge border station. It's no more than a six-hour drive. You want to be there about eleven. I'll be there ahead of you, watching from cover. Are you feeling all right?"

Morenz was sweating, even with his jacket off. "It's hot in here," he said. McCready turned up the air-conditioning.

"After the border turn left onto the E forty and head into Weimar. Four miles west of the town, on the right of the road, is a lay-by."

Carefully and meticulously McCready ran him through the procedure he should follow and, if the first pass aborted, how and where he should spend the night and where and when to attend the second, backup rendezvous with Pankratin.

AT NINE that morning the cleaning lady, Frau Popovic, arrived for work at the apartment in Hahnwald. She knew Fräulein Heimendorf liked to sleep late, so she always let herself in and started with the other rooms; then she would tidy the lady's bedroom. The locked room at the end of the passage she never entered. She had been told it was used for storing furniture.

She was vacuum-cleaning the passage when she noticed a large brown stain at the base of the locked door. She went to get a bucket of water and a brush to scrub it off. She was working on her hands and knees when she kicked the door. To her surprise it opened. Seconds later she was running, screaming, down the stairs to hammer at the door of the ground-floor apartment and arouse the retired bookseller who lived there. He called the 110 emergency number and asked for the police.

The first to arrive was a *Streifenwagen*, or stripe car, with two uniformed policemen. According to procedure, they first called the emergency doctor, whose job was simply to establish the fact of death. Then they called the police *Präsidium* and described what they had found. The message went up to the *Mordkommission*, or murder squad, always known as First K, on the tenth and eleventh floors of the building on Waidmarkt Square. The director of First K assigned a commissar and two assistants. They arrived at the apartment as the doctor was leaving.

The commissar, whose name was Peter Schiller, met him on the steps. "What have we got?" he asked.

"One male, one female. Died of gunshot wounds, I'd say."

"Time?" asked Schiller.

"One to three days. Rigor mortis is well established."

Schiller gave a low whistle when he saw the contents of the master bedroom. Renate Heimendorf and her pimp were still where they had fallen, the woman's head lying close to the door where the blood had leaked outside. The pimp was across the room, slumped with his back to the TV set.

Treading carefully, Schiller flipped open the closets and drawers. "A hooker," he said to his assistant. "Call girl, whatever."

The assistant, Wiechert, said, "I've seen the man somewhere before. . . . Hoppe. Bernhard Hoppe. Bank robbery, I think."

"Oh, good," said Schiller ironically, "that's all we need. A gangland killing."

SAM McCready put down his second cup of coffee and folded up the map. He had shown Morenz the latest photograph of Pankratin and explained that the man would be in the baggy fatigues of a Russian army corporal and driving a GAZ jeep.

"Unfortunately, he thinks he will be meeting me. We must just hope he recognizes you from Berlin and makes the pass anyway. Now, to the car. It's a BMW sedan, black, with Würzburg registration plates. Under the battery shelf there is a flat compartment, big enough to take the book you will be given.

"You are Hans Grauber, age fifty-one, married with three children. You work for BKI Optical Glassware in Würzburg—they exist—and the car is a duplicate of one of theirs. You have an appointment at three p.m. tomorrow with the director of foreign sales at the Zeiss works in Jena. If all goes well, you can agree to place an order for Zeiss precision lenses, and return to the West the same evening. If you need further discussions, you may have to overnight. That's just if the border guards ask you for details.

"So here are your passport, pictures of your wife and children, credit cards, driving license, keys, the baggy raincoat—the lot. You'll only need the attaché case and the overnight bag. Study the contents of the attaché case. The papers all concern your desire to purchase Zeiss products for your firm. The clothes and wash kit are genuine Würzburg purchases. Now, old friend, let's have lunch."

During the meal, from room service, Morenz drank wine greedily, and his hands shook.

"Are you sure you're all right?" asked McCready.

"Sure. This damned summer cold, you know? And a bit nervous. That's natural."

McCready nodded. Nerves were normal before an illegal run into the Sovbloc. Still, he did not like the shape Morenz was in. He had seldom seen a case of nerves like this. But he had no choice.

In the Hahnwald apartment, the bodies were bagged and then removed to the city morgue. The entire apartment had yielded nineteen sets or partial sets of fingerprints. Three were eliminated; they belonged to the two deceased and to Frau Popovic. That left sixteen.

"Probably clients," muttered Schiller.

"But one set the killer's?" suggested Wiechert.

"I doubt it. He probably wore gloves."

The major problem, mused Schiller, was not lack of motive, but too many. Was the call girl the intended victim? Was the murderer an outraged client, a former husband, a vengeful wife, a business rival? Or was her pimp the real target? He had been confirmed as Bernhard Hoppe, ex-con, bank robber, gangster—a real lowlife. Schiller suspected it was going to be a tough one.

There was something odd about the flat. But Schiller could not figure out what it was. He spent an hour puttering about while Wiechert complained that he wanted his dinner. At ten past eight Schiller shrugged and called it a day. He sealed the flat, left one uniformed man in the hallway in case someone returned to the scene of the crime, and went home.

At four the next morning he awoke beside his sleeping wife and realized what it was that bothered him about that flat. He telephoned and awoke an outraged Wiechert and told him to meet him at the Hahnwald house at seven.

AT FIVE TO ELEVEN THAT Tuesday morning Sam McCready was concealed amid pine trees on a hill south of the Saale River. He had been brought there in a Range Rover by Kit Johnson, a communications man from the SIS Bonn station. Now the Range Rover was parked out of sight in the forest. From the tree line the two men could see the West German border post half a mile below them. Beyond it was a gap in the hills and the East German border post, half a mile farther on.

Because the East Germans had built their controls well inside their own territory, a driver would be inside East Germany as soon as he left the West German post. Then came a two-lane highway between high chain link fencing. Behind the fencing were the watchtowers. The reason for the half-mile corridor was so that anyone bursting through the eastern border post could be cut to pieces by the machine guns before reaching the West.

At two minutes to eleven McCready picked out the BMW moving sedately through the cursory West German controls. Then it purred forward into the corridor, heading for the land controlled by the East's most dreaded secret police, the *Stasi*.

CHAPTER THREE

"IT HAS to be the bathroom," said Commissar Schiller just after seven a.m. as he led a sleepy Wiechert back into the flat.

"It looks all right to me," grumbled Wiechert.

"Look at this closet in the passage. It's two yards wide, right? So when you enter the bathroom and turn to your right, there should be two yards to the bathroom wall, the width of the cupboard outside. Try it."

Wiechert entered the bathroom. "One yard," he said.

"Exactly. That's what puzzled me. There's a yard missing."

Poking around in the hall closet, it took Schiller thirty minutes to find the door catch, cunningly concealed in a knothole. When the rear of the closet swung open, Schiller reached in, flicked a switch, and the inner light came on.

The secret compartment was ten feet long, the same length as the bathroom, but it was only three feet wide. To the right was the rear side of a one-way mirror that exposed the whole bedroom. On a tripod at the center of the mirror, facing into the bedroom, was a video camera. The entire far end of the narrow passageway was ceiling-to-floor shelving, containing numbered videocassettes.

Schiller phoned Rainer Hartwig, director of First K.

"Well done," said Hartwig when he had the details. "Stay there. I'll get two fingerprint men down to you."

IT WAS eight fifteen. Dieter Aust was shaving while listening to the morning television news. He thought little of the item about a double murder in Hahnwald until the newscaster said, "One of the victims, call girl Renate Heimendorf . . ."

That was when the director of the Cologne BND cut himself quite badly on his pink cheek. In ten minutes he was in his car and driving fast to his office, where he arrived almost an hour early.

"The vacation contact number Morenz gave us," Aust said to his secretary. "Let me have it, would you?"

When he tried it, he got the disconnected tone. He tried Morenz's home number, and to his amazement he found himself speaking to Frau Morenz. They must have come home early.

"Could I speak to your husband, please? This is Director Aust."

"But he's with you, Herr Direktor," she explained patiently. "Out of town. On a trip. Back late tomorrow night."

"Ah, yes, I see. Thank you, Frau Morenz."

He put the phone down, worried. Morenz had lied. What was he up to? He put through a secure-line call to BND headquarters in Pullach, near Munich, and spoke to the deputy director of the Operations Directorate, Dr. Lothar Herrmann.

"The murdered call girl. And her pimp. How were they killed?" Herrmann asked.

"They were shot."

"Does Morenz have a personal sidearm?"

"I—er . . . believe so."

"Then it must have been issued here. I will call you back."

Dr. Herrmann was back on the phone in ten minutes.

"He has a Walther PPK, service issue. It was tested on the range and in the lab before we gave it to him. Where is it now?"

"It should be in his personal safe," said the badly flustered Aust. "I will find out and call you back."

Aust had the master key for all the safes in the department. Five minutes later he was talking to Herrmann again.

"It's gone," he said. "He might have taken it home, of course."

"That is strictly forbidden. So is lying to a superior officer, whatever the cause. I think I had better come to Cologne."

BRUNO Morenz cruised the BMW into the East German border control and was waved into an inspection bay. A green-uniformed guard appeared at the driver's-side window.

"*Aussteigen, bitte. Ihre Papiere.*"

He climbed out and offered his passport. Other guards began to surround the car, all quite normal.

"Hood open, please, and trunk."

He opened both; they began the search. Morenz forced himself not to look as a guard studied the battery.

"The purpose of your journey?"

Morenz explained he was going to Jena to discuss purchases of optical lenses from Zeiss. They waved him into the customs hall. It's all just normal, he told himself.

They went through his attaché case, studied the letters exchanged between Zeiss and BKI in Würzburg. Morenz prayed the stamps and postmarks were perfect. They were. His bags were closed. He took them back to the car. A guard with a huge Alsatian stood nearby.

At that moment there was a scream and several shouts from the column of cars across the dividing reservation, the column trying to get out. Everyone spun around to look. Morenz was back behind the wheel. He stared in horror.

There was a blue minivan at the head of the column. West German plates. Two guards were dragging a young girl out of the back, where they had discovered her hiding in a recess in the floor. She was screaming. The young driver of the van was hauled out in a circle of submachine gun barrels.

"Go," snapped the guard beside Morenz. He let the clutch out, and the BMW surged forward. He looked in the rearview mirror and saw the driver and the girl being hauled into a concrete building, still screaming. He drove north, sweating profusely, his nerve now completely gone, a burned-out case.

McCready had watched him enter the corridor between the two border posts, then lost sight of him behind a curve of the hill.

"He's through," McCready remarked to Johnson.

"Want to tell Bonn or London?" asked Johnson.

McCready shook his head. "There's nothing they can do," he said. "Nothing anyone can do now. It's up to Poltergeist."

AT THE flat in Hahnwald, the two fingerprint men had finished with the secret compartment. They had lifted three sets of prints.

Schiller entered the closet and surveyed the racks of cassettes at the back. He took one at random, went into the master bedroom, and slotted it into the video. Two minutes later he switched it off, a rather shaken young man.

The senator from Baden-Württemberg had been photographed by his constituents in many poses—kissing babies, opening church fetes, addressing the conservative ladies.

But they probably had not seen him like this.

MORENZ checked his watch. It was two o'clock. He was ahead of time. He wanted to be at the lay-by for the rendezvous at ten to four—no earlier or it would look suspicious. He decided to go past Jena and Weimar to the Erfurt pull-off, go right around the roundabout, and come back toward Weimar. That would kill time.

A green-and-white car from the Wartburg people's police, or VOPO, came past him in the overtaking lane. The two uniformed highway patrolmen stared at him with expressionless faces.

He held the wheel steady, fighting down the rising panic. They know, a small treacherous voice inside him kept saying. It's all a trap. The Russian has been blown.

Don't be silly, his cogent mind urged. Then he thought of Renate, and the black despair joined hands with the fear.

Listen, you fool, said his mind, the bodies won't be discovered for weeks. By then you'll be out of the country with your savings. And they'll leave you alone because of the tapes.

The VOPO car slowed and studied him. He began to sweat. The fear was rising and winning. He could not know that the young policemen were car buffs and had not seen the new BMW sedan before.

COMMISSAR Schiller spent thirty minutes with the director of First K, the murder squad, explaining what he had found.

"It's going to be a bastard," Hartwig said. "Had she started blackmailing already, or was this to be her retirement fund? We don't know." He rose from his desk. "Come on. We're going back. I want to see this place for myself."

It was actually Director Hartwig who found the notebook. It was taped under the lowest shelf where the videos were stored. He ran through the names in the notebook, which corresponded with the numbers on the videocassettes. Some he recognized, some not. The ones he recognized included two senators, a parliamentarian (government party), a banker (local), three industrialists, a judge, a famous surgeon, and a television personality.

"Eighty-one names," he said. "Eighty-one tapes. There must be enough here to bring down several state governments."

"That's odd," said Schiller. "There are only sixty-one tapes."

They both counted them. Sixty-one.

"You say there were three sets of prints lifted here?"

"Yes, sir."

"Assuming two were from Heimendorf and Hoppe, the third is probably the killer. And I have a horrible feeling he's taken twenty tapes with him. Come on. I'm going to the president with this. It's got beyond a murder—way beyond."

DR. HERRMANN was finishing lunch with his subordinate, Aust.

"My dear Aust, we know nothing as yet. We simply have reason for concern. The police may quickly arrest and charge a gangster, and Morenz may return on schedule after a sinful weekend with a girlfriend. For the moment I want you to try and trace him. I will attempt to find out just what is the state of the police investigation."

THE police president of Cologne, Arnim von Starnberg, listened gravely to Schiller's report. He was flanked by Hartwig of the murder squad and Horst Fraenkel, director of the whole *Kriminalamt*, or crime office, known as the K.A. Both senior officers had felt it right to come straight to him. When he heard the details, he agreed.

"You will remain completely silent about this, Herr Schiller," said von Starnberg. "You and your colleague Wiechert. Your careers depend on it. You understand?"

He dismissed Schiller and turned to the others.

"How far exactly have you got?"

Hartwig produced a number of large high-definition photographs. "Well, Herr President, we now have the bullets." He tapped two photographs. "We need to find the gun that fired them. Second, the fingerprints. There were three sets in the camera room. We believe one set must belong to the killer. We also believe it was he who stole the twenty missing cassettes."

"Where are the other sixty-one tapes?" asked von Starnberg.

"In my personal safe," said Fraenkel.

"Have them brought straight up here. No one must view them."

When he was alone, President von Starnberg began telephoning. The responsibility for the affair went up the official hierarchy faster than a monkey up a tree, all the way to the justice minister, in Bonn. In the late afternoon the country's internal security service, the BfV, was routinely informed of the investigation and its progress. Ironically, the BfV is headquartered in Cologne, back where it all started. The interdepartmental memorandum on the case landed on the desk of a senior officer in counterintelligence called Johann Prinz.

BRUNO Morenz rolled slowly west along Highway 7. He came to a curve, and there was the lay-by. He checked his watch—eight minutes to four. The road was empty. He slowed and pulled into the lay-by.

According to instructions, he released the trunk and removed the tool kit. Then he flicked the catch and raised the hood. His stomach began to churn. In his mind's eye he saw SSD agents crouching in the bushes, waiting to make a double arrest.

He took a wrench, the right size for the job, and bent to loosen the nut connecting the water pipe to the radiator. A trickle of water escaped. He changed the wrench for one the wrong size and tried vainly to tighten the nut again.

He glanced at his watch. Six minutes past four. Where the hell are you? he asked. Almost at once there was a slight crunch of gravel as a vehicle came to a halt. He kept his head down. The Russian would come up to him and say, "If you are having trouble, perhaps I have a better set of tools," and offer him the flat wooden toolbox from the jeep. The Soviet army war book would be under the wrenches, in a red plastic cover.

Boots crunched on gravel. Morenz straightened. An East German police car was parked five yards away. One green-uniformed policeman stood by the open driver's door. The other was beside Morenz, gazing down into the BMW's open engine bay.

Morenz wanted to vomit. He felt his knees becoming weak.

"*Was ist los?*" the policeman asked.

Of course it was a ploy. The inquiry if anything was wrong was to precede the screams and shouts and the arrest.

"I thought I was losing water," Morenz said.

The policeman studied the radiator. He removed the wrench from Morenz's hand, stooped, and came up with another one. "This one will fit," he said.

Morenz used it and retightened the nut. The trickle stopped.

The cop gazed at the BMW engine. "Nice car," he said. "What are you doing out here?"

"I wished to see Weimar . . . the Goethe memorial."

"You are heading in the wrong direction. Weimar is that way."

He pointed down the road behind Morenz. A gray-green Soviet GAZ jeep rolled past. The driver, eyes shaded by a forage cap, gazed at Morenz, met his eyes for a second, took in the parked VOPO car, and rolled on. An abort. The Russian would not approach now.

"Yes. I took a wrong turn out of town. I was looking for a place to turn when I saw the water gauge misbehaving."

The VOPOs supervised his U-turn and followed him back to Weimar. They peeled off at the entry to the town. Morenz drove on to Jena and checked into the Black Bear Hotel.

AT EIGHT, on his hill above the Saale River, Sam McCready put down his binoculars. The gathering dusk made it impossible to see the East German border post and the road behind it. Something had gone wrong up there behind the minefields and the razor wire. Bruno was two hours overdue.

Waiting was always the worst, the waiting and the not knowing what had gone wrong.

DR. HERRMANN of the BND had a contact in the BfV, the internal security service. That evening at six he rang the BfV in Cologne and asked to be put through.

"Johann? This is Lothar Herrmann. . . . No, I'm not. I'm here in

Cologne. . . . I was hoping I could offer you dinner. . . . Excellent. Well, look, I'm at the Dom Hotel. Why don't you join me in the bar? About eight? . . . I look forward to it."

Johann Prinz put the phone down and wondered what had brought Herrmann to Cologne. Visiting the troops? Possibly. . . .

Two hours later they sat at the corner dining table and ordered. For a while they fenced gently. How are things? Fine. . . . Over the crab cocktail Herrmann moved a little closer.

"I suppose they've told you about the call girl affair?"

"Yes," Prinz said. "Got the file this afternoon."

"Nasty affair," Herrmann murmured as the steak arrived.

"And getting worse," agreed Prinz. "Bonn won't like those sex tapes floating around."

Herrmann kept his face impassive, but his stomach turned over. Sex tapes? *What* sex tapes? He affected mild surprise and poured more wine. "Got that far, has it? I must have been out of the office when the latest details arrived. Mind filling me in?"

Prinz did so. "First K have been told to put every man onto this case. The search, of course, is for the gun and the owner of the fingerprints."

Herrmann lost all his appetite, sensing a scandal of cataclysmic proportions. "I wonder if the culprit could be a foreigner?"

Prinz grinned. "Ah, now I see. Our external intelligence service has an interest?"

Herrmann shrugged. "We do, of course, have some records of our own. Fingerprints of foreigners. . . . Alas, we haven't got copies of the prints our friends in the K.A. are seeking."

"You could ask officially," Prinz pointed out.

"Yes, but then why start a hare that will probably lead nowhere? Now—unofficially—for old times' sake you have my word, if I turn anything up, it comes straight back to you. A joint effort by the two services."

"All right," Prinz said, "for old times' sake. Just this once."

Later that night a sealed brown envelope arrived at the Dom Hotel for Dr. Herrmann. The envelope contained three large photographs—two of various 9-mm slugs, one of a set of fingerprints. If the prints matched up with his expectations, he was going to face a very major quandary. Whom to tell, and how much. If only Morenz would show up.

At ten a.m. Wednesday, Major Vanavskaya, in Berlin, checked again on the whereabouts of the man she was tracking. He was with the garrison outside Erfurt, she was told. He leaves at six tonight for Potsdam. Tomorrow he flies back to Moscow.

And I'll be with you, you bastard, she thought.

At half past eleven Morenz drove carefully out of Jena, heading west, toward Weimar. The lay-by was bigger than yesterday's. He pulled into it, got out his tool kit, and opened the hood. At two minutes after twelve the GAZ jeep rolled onto the gravel and stopped. The man who got out wore baggy cotton fatigues and knee boots. He had corporal's insignia and a cap pulled over his eyes.

"If you are having trouble, perhaps I have a better toolbox," he said. He laid his wooden toolbox on the cylinder block and flicked open the catch. There was a clutter of wrenches inside. "So, Poltergeist, how are you these days?" he murmured.

Morenz's mouth was dry. "Fine," he whispered, pulling the wrenches to one side. The red plastic–covered manual lay underneath. The Russian took a wrench and tightened the loose nut. Morenz stuffed the book inside his raincoat, jamming it under his left arm. The Russian replaced his wrenches and closed the box.

"Give me ten minutes to get clear," he muttered. He straightened up, waved his right arm, and walked back to his jeep.

Morenz stood up and waved after him. "*Danke*," he called as the jeep drove away. Morenz felt weak. He would pull over later and stash the manual in the compartment beneath the battery. Right now he needed a drink. Keeping the manual pinned beneath his armpit, he dropped the engine cover, tossed his tools into the trunk, and climbed into the car. He had a hip flask in the glove compartment. He took a deep, satisfying pull. Five minutes later, his confidence restored, he turned the car back to Jena.

The crash was not even his fault. South of Jena, in the suburb of Stadtroda, a Trabant came bucketing out of a side road. He nearly stopped in time, but his reflexes were poor. The much stronger BMW crunched the rear of the East German mini.

Morenz began to panic almost at once. Was it a trap? The Trabant driver climbed out of his car, stared at his crushed rear, and stormed up to the BMW. He had a pinched, mean face and angry eyes. "What the hell do you think you're doing?"

Jamming his left arm tight to his body to hold the manual in place, Morenz climbed out and reached for a wad of ostmarks. People began to stroll toward the scene.

"Look, I'm sorry," he said. "I'll pay for the damage."

The angry East German looked at the money. "That's not the point," he said. "I had to wait four years for this car."

That was when the police car arrived. Routine patrol, but Morenz began to shake. The policemen got out. One looked at the damage. The other approached Morenz.

"*Ausweis, bitte,*" he said. Morenz used his right hand to bring out his passport. The hand was trembling. The cop looked at the hand, the bleary eyes, the unshaven chin. "You've been drinking," he said. He sniffed and confirmed it. "Right. Down to the station. Come on. Into the car."

That was when Bruno Morenz finally disintegrated. He swung his free arm violently back, hit the policeman under his nose, breaking it, and knocked the man down. Then he leaped into the police car, whose engine was still running, slammed it into gear, and drove off, swerving wildly. He was facing the wrong way, north toward Jena. The other policeman, stunned, managed to fire off four shots from his sidearm. Three missed. The fourth bullet drilled a hole in the VOPO car's gas tank.

CHAPTER FOUR

Aᴛ ᴏɴᴇ p.m. Dr. Lothar Herrmann, back at his desk in Pullach, took the awaited phone call from the BND ballistics laboratory. The technician had compared the scratches on the two sample slugs he still retained from a Walther PPK issued ten years ago with those on the photographs he had been given.

"A perfect match? I see. Thank you," said Dr. Herrmann. He called the fingerprint section and received the same reply. He exhaled deeply and reached for the phone again. There was nothing for it; this had to go to the director general himself.

What followed was one of the most difficult interviews of Dr. Herrmann's career. The D.G. was obsessive about the efficiency of his agency and its image, and the news Herrmann brought was like a body blow.

"Find him," the D.G. ordered Herrmann. "Find him quickly,

and get those tapes back." As Herrmann turned to leave, the D.G. added another remark. "Dr. Herrmann, the English have a saying that I commend to you. 'Thou shalt not kill; yet need not strive/ Officiously to keep alive.' "

In a lifetime's career in the BND, it was the broadest hint Dr. Herrmann had ever been given.

AT TWO o'clock Sam McCready was still on the hillside, where he and Johnson had been since seven, waiting for Morenz to appear. Johnson was reading a local newspaper he had bought at a service station when his car phone trilled discreetly. He picked it up, listened, and offered the handset to McCready.

"GCHQ," he said, referring to the British government communication headquarters, near Cheltenham, England. "They want to speak to you."

McCready talked for several minutes, and when he put the phone down, he was pale. "According to our radio listening post," he told Johnson, "there's been a crash outside Jena. A West German car, make unknown, hit a Trabant. The West German slugged one of the VOPOs who attended the crash, and drove off—in the VOPO car. Of course, it might not be our man."

Johnson looked sympathetic, but he no more believed it than McCready. "What do we do?" he asked.

McCready sat on the tailgate of the Range Rover, his head in his hands. "We wait," he said. "There's nothing else we can do."

AT FOUR p.m. Dr. Herrmann called Dieter Aust, in Cologne. "I want you to interview Frau Morenz personally," he said. "Try and get from her any clue as to where he might go, any vacation home, any relative's house—anything at all. Use your entire staff to follow up any lead she gives you. Report back to me."

Herrmann put down the phone. Based on something he had seen in Morenz's file, he then sent a blitz category–coded signal to Wolfgang Fietzau, the BND agent on the staff of the German embassy, Belgrave Square, London.

AT FIVE o'clock the phone set on the tailgate of the Range Rover trilled. McCready picked it up. He thought it would be London. The voice was thin, tinny, as if the speaker were choking.

"Sam? Is that you, Sam?"

McCready stiffened. "Yes," he snapped, "it's me."

"I'm sorry, Sam. I'm so sorry. I messed it up."

"Are you okay?" said McCready urgently. Morenz was wasting vital seconds.

"I'm finished, Sam. I didn't mean to kill her. I loved her, Sam."

McCready slammed down the phone, severing the connection. No one could make a phone call to the West from an East German phone booth. But the SIS maintained an East German safe house in the Leipzig area. A call to that number from inside East Germany would run through pass-on equipment that would throw the call up to a satellite and back into the West. But calls had to be four seconds long—no more—to prevent the East Germans locating the safe house. Morenz had babbled on for nine.

"He's cracked up," said Johnson. "Gone to pieces."

"Tell me something I don't know," snapped McCready. "What the hell did he mean—'I didn't mean to kill her.' "

Johnson was pensive. "He comes from Cologne?"

"That's right."

Johnson took the local newspaper and pointed out the second lead story on the front page. McCready read it, put it down, and stared across toward the north.

"Oh, Bruno, my poor friend. What the hell have you done?"

AT TEN p.m. GCHQ phoned McCready for the last time. "I'm afraid it's over," said the duty officer. "No, they haven't got him yet, but they will. They must have discovered something in the BMW. Heavy radio traffic, coded, between local SSD and East Berlin. Oh, and all border points are on full alert—guards doubled, the lot. Sorry."

At ten thirty Timothy Edwards came on the line. "We're all very sorry, but it's over," he said. "Come back to London at once, Sam."

"They haven't got him yet. I should stay here. I may be able to help. It's not over yet."

"Bar the shouting, it is," insisted Edwards. "There are things here we have to discuss—the loss of the package being not the least of them. Our American cousins are not a happy group. Please be on the first plane out of Munich or Frankfurt, whichever is the first of the day."

Major Ludmilla Vanavskaya rose early that Thursday, as was her wont, and did her sit-ups in her room at the KGB barracks. Her flight was not till midday, but she intended to pass by the KGB headquarters for a last check on the itinerary of the man she hunted.

She knew he had returned from Erfurt to Potsdam in convoy the previous evening and spent the night there. They were both due to take the same flight back to Moscow at noon. They would not meet—she was posing as a humble stenographer—but as soon as they entered Soviet airspace, he would be under surveillance.

At eight she walked into the KGB headquarters building and made her way to the communications office. They would be able to call Potsdam and confirm that the flight schedule was unchanged. While waiting for her information, she took coffee and shared a table with a young lieutenant, who was plainly very tired.

"Up all night?" she asked.

"Yep. Night shift. The krauts have been in a flap."

"Why?" she asked.

"Oh, they intercepted a West German car down at Jena and found a secret cavity in it. Reckon it was being used by one of their agents."

There was a wall map at the end of the canteen. She rose and went over to it. Jena, Weimar, Erfurt—all in a line, a line followed by the convoy of the man she hunted. Yesterday . . . Erfurt. And Jena fourteen miles away. Close, too damned close.

At nine London time McCready took his seat in the conference room at Century House. Claudia Stuart was opposite, looking at him reproachfully. Chris Appleyard, who had flown to London to escort the Soviet war book personally back to Langley, smoked and stared at the ceiling. His attitude seemed to be, You screwed it up; you sort it out. Timothy Edwards took the chair at the head.

"All right," he said, "it appears your man Poltergeist has come apart at the seams and blown the mission away. Let's see if there is anything we can salvage from the mess."

"The damned thing is," said Claudia in exasperation, "he's seen Pankratin. When the *Stasi* get him and go to work, he'll talk. We've lost Pankratin as well."

"Where is Pankratin now?" asked Edwards.

"According to his schedule, he's boarding a military flight from Potsdam to Moscow right about now."

"Can't you get to him and warn him?"

"No, dammit. When he lands, he's taking a week's furlough in the country. We can't get our emergency warning code to him till he gets back to Moscow—if he ever does."

"What about the war book?" asked Edwards.

"I think Poltergeist's got it on him," said McCready. He got their undivided attention.

Appleyard stopped smoking. "Why?"

"Timing," said McCready. "The rendezvous was at twelve. Assume he quit the lay-by at about twelve twenty. The crash was at twelve thirty, ten minutes and five miles away, on the other side of Jena. I think he had it on him—under his jacket, maybe. So he ran for it."

"Where would he go?" asked Edwards. "Has he friends near there? A safe house? Anything?"

McCready shook his head. "There's a safe house in East Berlin. He knows it from the old days. I've tried it—no contact. In the south he knows nobody. Never even been there."

"Could he hide out in the forests?" asked Claudia.

"It's not that kind of area. Not like the Harz, with its dense forests. Open rolling farmland, towns, villages, hamlets, farms."

"Then we've lost him," said Claudia. "Him, the war book, and Pankratin. The whole deal."

The meeting ended on that gloomy note. When the Americans had gone, Edwards detained McCready at the door. "Sam, I know it's hopeless, but stay with it, will you? When they get Poltergeist—and they must—I want to know at once. We're going to have to placate our cousins somehow."

Major Ludmilla Vanavskaya took a seat in the private office of Colonel Otto Voss of the SSD, at his headquarters building, at 22 Normannenstrasse, in Lichtenberg, East Berlin.

"What can I do for you, Comrade Major?" he asked politely. He was well aware who really ruled the roost in the German Democratic Republic.

"You are handling a case in the Jena area," said Vanavskaya. "A

West German agent who ran off after a crash and left his car behind. Could you let me have the details so far?"

Voss filled in the details not included in the situation report that the Russian had already seen.

"Let us assume," said Vanavskaya when he was finished, "that this agent had come to collect or deliver something. Was anything found in the car or in the secret cavity that could be what he either brought in or was trying to take out?"

"No, nothing. All his private papers were merely his cover story. If he brought something in, he had already delivered. If he sought to take something out, he had not collected."

"Or it was still on his person."

"Possibly, yes. We will know when we interrogate him."

"Have you any reason to know whether he was to make a personal contact or just administer a dead-letter box?"

"We believe he was here to make a personal meet," said Voss. "Although the crash was at twelve thirty yesterday, he actually came through the border at eleven on Tuesday. If he simply had to drop off a package or pick one up from a dead-letter box, he could have done it by nightfall on Tuesday. As it was, he spent Tuesday night at the Black Bear, in Jena."

Vanavskaya's heart sang. A personal meet somewhere in the Jena-Weimar area, along a road probably, a road traveled by the man she hunted at almost exactly the same time. "Have you identified this West German agent?" she asked.

Concealing his triumph, Voss opened a file and passed her an artist's impression. It had been drawn with help from the staff of the Black Bear. It was very good. Without a word Voss then passed her a large photograph. The two were identical.

"His name is Morenz," said Voss. "Bruno Morenz. A full-time career officer of the BND, based in Cologne."

Vanavskaya was surprised. So it was a West German operation. She had always suspected that her man was working for the CIA or the British. "You haven't got him yet?"

"No, Major. I confess I am surprised at the delay. But we will. The police car was found abandoned near Apolda, just north of Jena. Its petrol tank had a bullet hole through it. So our man is on foot, has no papers, a Rhineland accent, physically not in good shape. He will stick out like a sore thumb."

"I want to be present at the interrogation," said Vanavskaya. She was not squeamish. She had seen them before.

"Then don't be far away, Major. We will have him probably by midday."

Vanavskaya returned to the KGB building, canceled her flight from Potsdam, and contacted General Shaliapin. He agreed.

CHAPTER FIVE

MAJOR Vanavskaya could not sleep Thursday night. She lay awake in the darkness, wondering how on earth the East Germans, reputedly so efficient, could lose a man like Morenz in an area twenty miles by twenty miles. There was something missing, some part of the puzzle of how Bruno Morenz had disappeared.

At four in the morning she rose, and returned to the KGB offices, perturbing the night staff with her demand for a secure line to SSD headquarters. When she had it, she spoke to Colonel Voss. He had not left his office at all.

"That picture of Morenz," she said. "Where did you get it?"

"The HVA," said Voss.

Of course, the HVA, East Germany's foreign intelligence arm, which specialized in running networks inside West Germany. Its head was the legendary Colonel General Marcus Wolf. He had perpetrated some brilliant coups against the West Germans, notably the running of Chancellor Brandt's private secretary.

Vanavskaya called and awoke the local head of the Third Directorate and made her request, citing General Shaliapin's name. The man said he would see what he could do. He called back in half an hour. It seemed that General Wolf was an early bird, he said; she would have a meeting with him in his office at six.

MAJOR Vanavskaya was shown into Marcus Wolf's office, two floors above that of Colonel Voss. The East German spymaster disliked uniforms and was in a well-cut dark suit. He also preferred tea to coffee and had a particularly fine blend sent to him from Fortnum and Mason, in London. He offered the Soviet major a cup.

"Comrade General, that photograph of Bruno Morenz. It came from you?"

Marcus Wolf regarded her steadily over the rim of his cup. If he had sources inside the West German Establishment, which he did, he was not going to confirm it to this stranger.

"Could you possibly get Morenz's curriculum vitae?" she asked.

Marcus Wolf considered the request. "Why?" he asked softly.

She explained in detail. "It's only a suspicion," she said. "A feeling there is a piece missing. Maybe something in his past."

Wolf approved. He liked lateral thinking. He rose, went to a filing cabinet, and withdrew a sheaf of eight sheets without saying a word. It was Bruno Morenz's life story. Vanavskaya exhaled in admiration. Wolf smiled.

Major Vanavskaya read the pages. "He has a sister," she said.

"Yes," said Wolf. "You think she may know something?"

"It's a long shot," she said. "If I could go and see her . . . But I would need a cover. Not Russian, not East German."

Wolf shrugged self-deprecatingly. "I have certain 'legends' ready for use, of course. It is part of our strange trade."

There was a Polish Airlines flight to London—LOT 104— staged through Berlin-Schönefeld airport at ten a.m. It was held for ten minutes to enable Ludmilla Vanavskaya to board. She had papers of a Polish schoolteacher visiting a relative.

THE phone on Sam McCready's desk trilled at midday. The caller was a man from the NATO desk at Century House. "There's a chit came through in the morning bag," he said. "It may be nothing; if so, throw it away. I'm sending it up by messenger."

The chit arrived five minutes later. When he saw it and the timing on it, McCready swore loudly.

The East German listening station at Cheltenham had been told to pass to McCready without delay anything they got. But no one had thought to alert those who listen to *allied* traffic.

The message he held was from Pullach, timed at four twenty-two p.m. on Wednesday. It was to the staffer at the West German embassy in London, and it said:

Ex: Herrmann
Pro: Fietzau

Top urgent. Contact Mrs. A. Farquarson, née Morenz, believed living London. Ask if she has seen or heard of or from her brother in last four days.

He never told me he had a sister in London, thought McCready. He dragged a telephone directory from a shelf. There were fourteen Farquarsons, but no Mrs. A. He began to ring them in sequence. He was lucky at the eighth; the listing was for Robert Farquarson. A woman answered.

"Yes, this is Mrs. Farquarson."

A hint of German accent? "Mrs. Farquarson, I am from the immigration department at Heathrow. Would you by chance have a brother named Bruno Morenz?"

A long pause. "Is he there? At Heathrow?"

"I'm not at liberty to say, madam. Unless you are his sister."

"Yes, I am Adelheid Farquarson. Could I speak to him?"

"Not at the moment, I'm afraid. Will you be at that address in, say, fifteen minutes? It's rather important."

"Yes, I will be here."

It was a large studio apartment at the top of an Edwardian villa in Primrose Hill. Mrs. Farquarson greeted McCready in a painter's smock and showed him into a cluttered studio with paintings on easels and sketches strewn on the floor.

She was a handsome woman, gray-haired like her brother. McCready put her in her late fifties, older than Bruno. She offered him a seat and met his gaze levelly. McCready noticed two empty coffee mugs on a nearby table. He contrived to touch one while Mrs. Farquarson sat down. The mug was warm.

"What can I do for you, Mr. . . . ?"

"Jones. I would like to ask you about your brother, Bruno."

"Why?"

"It's an immigration matter."

"You are lying to me, Mr. Jones. My brother is not coming here. You are a policeman?"

"No, Mrs. Farquarson. But I am a friend of Bruno. Over many years. Please believe that, because that *is* true."

"He is in trouble, isn't he?"

"Yes, I'm afraid so. I'm trying to help him. It looks as if he has killed his mistress. And he has run away. Disappeared."

She rose and walked to the window, staring out at the late summer foliage of Primrose Hill Park. "Oh, Bruno. You fool. Poor, frightened Bruno." She turned and faced him. "There was a man from the German embassy here yesterday morning. He did not

450

tell me what you have—just asked if Bruno had been in touch. He hasn't. I can't help you, either, Mr. Jones. Do you know where he has gone?"

"That's the problem. I think he has gone into East Germany. Somewhere in the Weimar area. Perhaps to stay with friends. But so far as I know, he's never been near Weimar in his life."

"What do you mean? He lived there for two years."

McCready was stunned. "I didn't know. He never told me."

"No, he wouldn't. He hated it there. They were the unhappiest two years of his life. He never talked about it."

"I thought your family was Hamburg born and raised."

"We were until 1943, when Hamburg was destroyed by the RAF. The great fire-storm bombing. Bruno and I were orphaned that night." She paused and stared past McCready, seeing again the flames raging through the city where she was born.

"When it was over, the authorities took charge of us, and we were evacuated. I was fifteen; Bruno was ten. We were split up. I was billeted with a family outside Göttingen. Bruno was sent to stay with a farmer near Weimar. After the war we were reunited and returned to Hamburg. Times were very hard, you know."

McCready nodded. "Yes. I'm sorry."

She shrugged. "It was the war. Anyway, in 1947 I met a British sergeant. Robert Farquarson. We married and came to live here. He died eight years ago. I have only seen Bruno three or four times since I married, and not in the past ten years."

"You told that to the man from the embassy?"

"Herr Fietzau? No. He did not ask about Bruno's childhood. But I told the lady from the pensions department. She left only an hour ago."

"Pensions?"

"Yes. She said Bruno still worked in optical glassware, for a firm called BKI, in Würzburg. But it seems BKI is owned by Pilkington Glass, of Britain, and with Bruno's retirement approaching, she needed details of his life to assess his full entitlement. She was not from Bruno's employers?"

"I doubt it."

"I'm sorry. I seem to have been very foolish."

"You weren't to know. She spoke good English?"

"Yes, perfect. Slight accent—Polish, perhaps."

McCready had little doubt where the lady had come from. He rose. "Try hard to think what he said in those years after the war. Is there anyone, anyone at all, to whom he might go in his hour of need for sanctuary?"

She thought long and hard. "There was one name he mentioned, someone who had been nice to him. His primary school teacher. Fräulein . . . Neuberg. . . . No, Neumann. That was it. Of course, she's probably dead by now."

"One last thing, Mrs. Farquarson. Did you tell this to the lady from the glass company?"

"No. I just told her Bruno had once spent two years as an evacuee on a farm not ten miles from Weimar."

Back at Century House, McCready borrowed a Weimar telephone directory from the East German desk. There were several Neumanns listed, but just one with Frl., short for Fräulein, in front of it. A spinster. It was a long shot, very long.

He next visited the section inside Century House whose specialty is the preparation of untrue identity cards. He then rang Lufthansa. They had a flight at five fifteen to Hanover. He asked Denis Gaunt to drive him to Heathrow.

THE Polish Airlines flight from Heathrow to Warsaw via East Berlin was due to take off at three thirty. But an engine fault delayed takeoff until six. In the departures lounge Major Ludmilla Vanavskaya glanced at the televised departure information, noted the delay, cursed silently, and returned to her book.

MCCREADY was leaving the office when the phone rang. It was Edwards. "Sam, someone in Funny Paper has been on to me. Now look, Sam, you are not—absolutely not—getting my permission to go into East Germany. Is that clear?"

"Absolutely, Timothy. Couldn't be clearer."

"Good," said the assistant chief, and put the phone down.

Denis Gaunt had heard the voice at the other end of the phone and what it had said. "Sam, I know you've been in more tight places than a shepherd's right arm, but you've been black-flagged in East Germany, and the boss has forbidden you to go back."

"Forbidding is one thing," said McCready. "Preventing is another."

When he strode through the departure lounge of terminal 2 to catch the Lufthansa flight to Hanover, he cast not a glance at the trim young woman with the shiny blond hair and piercing blue eyes who sat reading two yards from him. And she did not look up at the medium-built, rather rumpled man with thinning brown hair in a gray raincoat as he walked past.

McCready landed at Hanover at eight local time. Major Vanavskaya landed at Berlin-Schönefeld at nine. McCready rented a car and drove to his destination in the forests outside Goslar. Vanavskaya was met by a KGB car and driven to Normannenstrasse 22, where she had to wait an hour to see Colonel Otto Voss.

McCready had telephoned his host from London; he was expected. The man met him at the front door of his substantial home, a beautifully converted hunting lodge set on a sweep of hillside, with a view, in daylight, far across a long valley clothed in conifers. Only five miles away the lights of Goslar twinkled in the gloom. The man McCready had come to visit had chosen to spend his comfortable retirement within sight of the very border that had once made his fortune.

McCready was shown into a paneled sitting room hung with the heads of boars and the antlers of stags. A bright fire crackled in a stone hearth; even in early September it was chilly at night in the high hills.

His host had changed over the years. The once lean physique was now fleshed out, and the round pink face, topped by white candy-floss hair, looked more harmless than ever. Until you looked into his eyes. Cunning eyes, wily eyes. He had once been the uncrowned underworld king of Berlin.

For twenty years, from the building of the Berlin Wall, in 1961, until his retirement, in 1981, Andre Kurzlinger had been a *Grenzgänger*, a border crosser. He brought people out—for money. Although Berlin was his bailiwick, he also ran lines through the East German–West German border, which ran from the Baltic to Czechoslovakia.

"So, Sam, my friend, it has been a long time." He stood with his back to the fire, a retired gentleman in a velvet smoking jacket. "You are retired also now?" he asked.

"No, Andre, I still have to work for my crust. Not as clever as you, you see."

Kurzlinger liked that. He pressed a bell, and a manservant brought crisp Moselle wine in crystal glasses.

"Then," asked Kurzlinger as he surveyed the flames through the wine, "what can an old man do for the mighty *Spionage* service of Her Majesty?"

McCready told him. The older man continued staring at the fire, but he shook his head. "I am out of it, Sam. Retired. Now they leave me alone. But you know, they have warned me, as I think they have warned you. If I start again, they will come for me. In my time I did them a lot of damage, you know."

"I know," said McCready.

"Also, things change. My rabbit runs were all discovered eventually. Closed down. My contacts have all gone cold."

"I have to go over," said McCready slowly, "because we have a man over there. He is sick, very sick. But if I can bring him out, it will probably break the career of Otto Voss."

Kurzlinger did not move, but his eyes went very cold. Years ago, as McCready knew, he had had a friend. A very close friend. The man had been caught crossing the Wall. Talk was, later, that he had raised his hands. But Voss had shot him all the same.

"Come," said Kurzlinger, "we will eat. I will introduce you to my son."

The handsome young blond man of about thirty who joined them at table was not actually Kurzlinger's son, of course. But he had formally adopted him. "I brought Siegfried out of the East," he said. "He had nowhere to go, so now he lives here with me."

McCready continued eating. He suspected there was more.

"Have you ever heard," said Kurzlinger over the grapes, "of the Arbeitsgruppe Grenzen?"

McCready had. The Borders Working Group. Sometimes when the East Germans wanted to spirit an agent into the West, they would actually cut a rabbit run through their own defenses, using the experts of the Arbeitsgruppe Grenzen for the job. These engineers, working at dead of night, would burrow under the razor wire, cut a thin line through the minefield, and leave no trace of where they had been.

That still left the two-hundred-yard-wide plowed strip—the shooting ground, where a real refugee would probably be caught in the searchlights and machine-gunned. Finally, on the western side, there was the fence. The Arbeitsgruppe Grenzen would cut a hole for the agent as he went through, and lace it up after him.

"Siegfried used to work for the AGG," said Kurzlinger. "Siegfried, our friend here needs to go across. Can you help?"

"There used to be one rabbit run," Siegfried said. "I cut it myself. I left a fishing line on the ground where I cut the path through the minefield. I was going to use it myself, but I came out a different way."

"Where is it?" asked McCready.

"Not far from here," said Siegfried. "Between Bad Sachsa, in West Germany, and Ellrich, in the East."

"What is the best time to go?" asked McCready.

"Four o'clock. Before dawn. The light is darkest, and the guards are tired. We will need camouflage smocks in case we are caught by the lights."

They discussed details for another hour. Siegfried and McCready left at one o'clock for the slow, two-hour drive through the mountains.

"If you get through," said Siegfried, "walk the six miles into Nordhausen. Avoid the village of Ellrich—the dogs will bark. Take the train from Nordhausen south to Erfurt, and the bus to Weimar. There will be workers on both."

They drove quietly through the sleeping town of Bad Sachsa and parked at the outskirts. Siegfried stood in the darkness with a compass and a penlight. When he had his bearing, he plunged into the pine forest, heading east. McCready followed him.

Four hours earlier Major Vanavskaya had confronted Colonel Voss in his office. She explained about Bruno Morenz's evacuation during the war.

"A farm?" said Voss. "Which farm? There are hundreds in that area."

"His sister didn't know the name. Just that it was not ten miles from Weimar itself. Draw your ring, Colonel. Bring in troops. Within the day you will have him."

Colonel Voss called Abteilung XIII, the intelligence and security service of the National People's Army, the NVA. Phones rang in the NVA headquarters out at Karlshorst, and trucks began to roll south toward Weimar.

CHAPTER SIX

SIEGFRIED lay on his belly at the edge of the tree line and studied the dark contours of the forest that marked East Germany. McCready lay beside him. It was three a.m. on Saturday.

Five years earlier Siegfried had cut his rabbit run from the base of a tall pine tree on the eastern side in the direction of a gleaming white rock high up on the western side. His problem now was that he was heading the other way and the rock was behind him, screened by the trees. It would become visible only from far out in no-man's-land. He judged the line as best he could, crawled forward, and began to snip at the chain link fence.

When Siegfried had his hole, McCready saw his arm rise in a beckoning motion. He crawled out of cover toward the wire. Siegfried had chosen his spot well—halfway between two of the watchtowers. Although the right-hand searchlight had a clear view of their intended path, the man behind it must have been tired or bored, for it went off for minutes on end. The sweep of the left-hand searchlight was partially blocked by trees.

Siegfried jerked his head and crawled through the hole. McCready followed, dragging his gunnysack. It was tempting to run across the hundred yards of plowed strip, but there could be trip wires linked to sound alarms. It was safer to crawl. At the halfway point the searchlight to their right came on. Both men froze in their green smocks and lay face down.

The pale light splashed over them, hesitated, moved back, and went off again. Ten yards farther on, Siegfried found a trip wire and gestured McCready to crawl around it. Another forty yards, and they reached the minefield. Here the thistles and grasses were chest-high. No one tried to plow up the minefield.

The German looked back. High above the trees McCready could see the white rock, pale against the dark forest. Siegfried swiveled his head and checked the giant tree against the rock. He was ten yards to the right of his line. He crawled again, down the edge of the minefield. After two minutes McCready heard his breath hiss out in triumph. He held a strand of fishing line between finger and thumb.

"Follow the fishing line," Siegfried whispered. "It will take

you through the minefield to the tunnel under the wire. The path is only two feet wide. When do you come back?"

"Twenty-four hours," said McCready. "Or forty-eight. After that, forget it. I will not be coming."

He disappeared on his belly into the minefield.

He went forward through the mines, following the nylon line. Occasionally he tested it to make sure it was still straight. He knew he would not see any mines. These were not big plate mines that could throw a truck into the air. They were small antipersonnel mines—buried, pressure operated, and vicious enough to blow away a leg or to tear out the chest cavity.

McCready saw the rolling waves of razor wire looming ahead of him—the end of the minefield. The fishing line led him to a shallow scrape under the wire. He rolled on his back, pushed the wire upward with his tote bag, and kicked with his heels. Inch by inch he slid beneath the entanglement. Above him he could see the glittering razors that made this kind of wire so much more painful than barbed wire.

When he came out on the eastern side, he found the nylon strand attached to a small peg that was almost out of the ground. Another tug, and it would have come loose, aborting the whole crossing.

He held his compass in front of him and crawled away on a heading of ninety degrees until he came to a track. There he stripped off his smock, bundled it around his compass, and hid them beneath pine needles ten yards inside the forest. He walked away toward the east, noting every marker—fallen trees, piles of logs, twists and turns—to guide him on his return. After a mile he came out on a road and saw the spire of the Lutheran church of Ellrich village ahead of him. He skirted it, as briefed, walking through fields of cut wheat until he intercepted the road to Nordhausen, five miles farther on.

Outside Nordhausen he had a lucky break. Over the picket fence of a darkened house, a bicycle was propped against a tree. It was rusty but usable. He took it, walked for a hundred yards, then mounted it and rode to the railway station. It was five to six. The first train to Erfurt was due in fifteen minutes.

There were several dozen workingmen waiting on the platform. Sam hoped his scuffed reefer jacket, corduroy trousers, and forage cap would escape scrutiny. He presented some money, was issued a ticket, and the train steamed in—an old-fashioned steam locomotive, but on time. He consigned his bicycle to the luggage van and took his place on the wooden seats. The train rolled into Erfurt at six forty-one. He retrieved his bicycle and pedaled away toward Weimar.

Just after half past seven a tractor came up behind him and stopped. It had a flat trailer behind it, and an old man was at the wheel.

"*Steig mal rauf,*" he called above the snarl of the dilapidated engine. McCready waved his gratitude, hurled the bicycle onto the flatbed, and climbed on. The noise of the engine prevented conversation, which was just as well, for McCready's German, though fluent, was not that of lower Thuringia.

Ten miles out of Weimar, McCready saw the wall of soldiers. They were spread out across the fields to left and right. The tractor slowed for the roadblock and stopped. A sergeant shouted up to the driver, asking for the old man's papers. He looked at them, gave them back, and came down to where McCready sat.

"*Papiere,*" he said. McCready handed over his I.D. card. It said he was Martin Hahn, farm worker, and had been issued by the Weimar administrative district. McCready did not volunteer that he was a hitchhiker, and no one asked.

The sergeant gave back the papers and waved the tractor on. Three miles from the town the tractor turned off onto a farm track. McCready jumped down, pulled his bicycle to the ground, waved his thanks, and pedaled off, staying close to the curb to avoid the trucks disgorging troops in their green uniforms.

Coming into Weimar on the Erfurterstrasse, McCready rode straight on toward the ancient town center. On Karl Marx Platz he dismounted and began to push the bicycle, his head down, as the VOPO cars rushed by him in both directions.

Number 14 Bockstrasse was an old building, long in need of repair. The paint and plaster were peeling, and the names on the bell pushes were faded. But he could make out against flat number 3 the single name Neumann. He left his bicycle in the stone-flagged hall and walked up. Number 3 was on the second floor. He took off his cap, straightened his jacket, and rang the bell. It was ten to nine.

After a while there was a shuffling sound, and the door opened slowly. Fräulein Neumann was very old, in a black dress, white-haired, and she supported herself on two canes. She looked up at McCready and said, *"Ja?"*

He smiled broadly, as if in recognition.

"Yes, it is you, Fräulein. You won't remember me. Martin Kroll. You taught me at primary school forty years ago. May I come in?"

She stood aside, and he entered. A dark hall, musty with age. She led the way, hobbling on arthritic knees and ankles, into her sitting room. He waited for her to sit, then took a chair.

She stared at him levelly. "So I taught you once, in the old primary school on Heinrich Heinestrasse. When was that?"

"Well, it must have been '43 and '44. I was in a class with . . . Well, I recall Bruno Morenz. He was my buddy."

She pulled herself to her feet, hobbled to the window, and looked down. A truck full of VOPOs rumbled past.

"Always the uniforms and the guns," she said softly. She hobbled back to her seat. "You are British, aren't you?"

"Why do you say such an extraordinary thing?" he asked.

"Two reasons. I remember every boy I ever taught at that school, and there was no Martin Kroll among them. And secondly, the school was not on Heinrich Heinestrasse. Heine was Jewish, and the Nazis had erased his name from all streets."

McCready could have kicked himself. "If you scream or raise the alarm," he said quietly, "I will not harm you. But they will come for me and take me away and shoot me. And they may not believe that you have never seen me before."

She smiled for the first time. "Young man, when you are eighty-eight, there is nothing they can do to you that the good Lord is not going to do quite soon now. Why did you come?"

"Bruno Morenz. You do remember him?"

"Oh, yes, I remember him. Is he in trouble?"

"Yes, Fräulein, bad trouble. He came on a mission—for me. He is here, not far away. He fell ill, sick, in the head. A complete breakdown. He is hiding out there somewhere. He needs help."

"The police, all those soldiers—they are for Bruno?"

"Yes. If I can get to him first, I may be able to help. His sister, in London, said he had been very unhappy here in the war and his only friend had been his schoolteacher, Fräulein Neumann."

She rocked backward and forward for some time. "Poor Bruno," she said at length. "Poor frightened Bruno. Always so frightened. Of the shouting and the pain."

"Why was he frightened, Fräulein Neumann?"

"Bruno was billeted with a farmer outside the town, a brutal man who drank much. Also, an ardent Nazi. One evening Bruno must have made some uncomplimentary remark about Hitler, something he learned from his father, a Social Democrat. The farmer took his belt to him and whipped him. Hard. After that he did it many times. Bruno used to run away."

"Where did he hide, Fräulein?"

"In the barn. He showed me once. He made a hole in the hay bales up in the loft. He used to crawl in there and wait until the farmer had fallen into his usual drunken sleep."

"Where exactly was the farm?"

"The hamlet is called Marionhain. Just four farms in a group. It lies between the villages of Ober and Nieder Grünstedt. Take the road out toward Erfurt. Four miles out turn left down a track. Look for a barn set two hundred yards away from the group, at the end of the meadow. Do you think you can help him?"

McCready rose. "If he is there, Fräulein, I will try. Thank you for your help."

The track off the main road was where she had said it would be. A small sign said OBER GRÜNSTEDT. He cycled down to a junction a mile farther on. The road split. To his left lay Nieder Grünstedt. He could see a wall of green uniforms surrounding it. On either side of him lay fields of uncut maize, five feet high. He crouched low and pedaled away to his right. He skirted Ober Grünstedt and saw an even narrower track. Half a mile down it, he could make out a group of farmhouses and barns. Marionhain.

He hid his bicycle in the maize. To his right he saw a single tall barn, of brick and black-tarred timbers, set away from the main group. On the horizon the tide of green uniforms began to move out of Nieder Grünstedt.

Dr. Lothar Herrmann of the BND was also working that Saturday morning. The trail of the missing Bruno Morenz had gone cold. Now he was in a difficult predicament. No arrest had been made in the case of the Heimendorf slayings.

Dr. Herrmann opened a thick file dealing with cross-border radio traffic. He noted that there seemed to be an awful lot of it. Some kind of flap among the VOPOs in the Jena area. Then his eye caught a phrase used in a conversation between a VOPO patrol car and Jena Central: "Big, gray-haired, Rhineland accent." He became pensive. That rang a bell. . . .

An aide entered and placed a message in front of his boss. It was a complimentary pass-on from the internal security service, the BfV. It simply said that a sharp-eyed operative at Hanover airport had noted the face of a man entering Germany on a London flight under the name of Maitland. The BfV man had checked his files and passed his identification on to the head office in Cologne. The man Maitland was Mr. Samuel McCready.

Dr. Herrmann looked at the intercepts from Jena and the message from Hanover. He wouldn't dare, he thought. Then another part of his mind said, Yes, he damned well would.

McCREADY left the cover of the maize and crossed the few yards of grass to the barn. The door creaked on rusty hinges as he let himself in. Light streaked into the gloom from a dozen splits in the woodwork, making motes of dust dance in the air and revealing old carts, horse tackle, and rusting troughs. He glanced up. The upper floor, reached by a vertical ladder, was piled with hay. He went up the ladder and called softly, "Bruno."

There was no reply. He walked past the piled hay and saw a fragment of raincoat fabric between two bales. He gently lifted one of the bales away.

Bruno Morenz lay in his sanctuary on his side. His eyes were open, but he made no movement.

"Bruno, it's me. Sam. Your friend. Look at me, Bruno."

Morenz swiveled his gaze toward McCready. He was gray-faced and unshaven. His eyes appeared unfocused. They tried to register as he looked at McCready. "Sam?"

"Yes. Sam. Sam McCready."

"Don't tell them I'm here, Sam. They won't find me if you don't tell them."

"I won't tell them, Bruno. Never." He helped Morenz into a sitting position, his back against the hay bales. "We must hurry, Bruno. I'm going to try to get you out of here."

Morenz shook his head dully. "Stay here, Sam. It's safe here. No one could ever find me here."

No, thought McCready, a drunken farmer never could. But five hundred soldiers could and would. He tried to get Morenz to his feet, but it was hopeless. The weight of the man was too much. His legs would not work. He clutched his hands across his chest. There was something bulging under his left arm. McCready let him slump back into the hay. Morenz curled up again. McCready knew he would never get him back to the border near Ellrich, under the wire, and across the minefield. It was over.

Through a crack in the planking he saw the green uniforms swarming over the farms of Ober Grünstedt. Marionhain would be next.

"I've been to see Fräulein Neumann. She's nice."

"Yes, nice. She won't tell them I'm here."

"Never, Bruno. Never. She said you have your homework for her. She needs to mark it."

Morenz unbuttoned his raincoat and eased out a fat red manual. Its cover bore a gold hammer and sickle. Morenz's tie was off and his shirt open. A key hung on a piece of twine around his neck. McCready took the manual.

"I'm thirsty, Sam."

McCready held out a small silver hip flask that he had taken from his back pocket. Morenz drank the whiskey greedily. McCready looked through the crack. Soldiers were coming down the track while others fanned out through the fields.

"I'm going to stay here, Sam," said Morenz.

"Yes," said McCready, "so you are. Good-bye, old friend. Sleep well. No one will ever hurt you again."

"Never again," murmured the man, and slept.

McCready was about to rise when he saw the glint of the key against Morenz's chest. He eased the twine from around his neck, stowed the manual in his tote bag, slithered down the ladder, and slipped away into the maize.

It took him twelve hours to get back to the border. Siegfried was waiting for him at the fence.

On the drive back to Goslar he flicked over the key he had taken from Bruno Morenz. It was made of steel, and engraved on the back were the words FLUGHAFEN KÖLN. Cologne airport.

AT ONE O'CLOCK ON THAT Saturday afternoon the soldiers made contact with Colonel Voss, who arrived in a staff car with a woman in a civilian suit. They went up the ladder and examined the body in the hay. A thorough search was made. The barn was almost torn apart, but no sign was found of any written material, least of all a thick manual.

A soldier pried a small silver flask from the dead man's hand and passed it to Colonel Voss. He sniffed it and muttered, "Cyanide." Major Vanavskaya took it and turned it over. On the back was written HARRODS, LONDON. She used a very unladylike expression.

AT NOON on Sunday, McCready entered Cologne airport. He changed his Hanover-to-London ticket for a Cologne-London one, checked in, and wandered toward the luggage lockers to one side of the concourse. He took the steel key and inserted it into locker 47. Inside was a black canvas grip.

"I think I will take the bag, thank you, Herr McCready."

He turned. The deputy head of the Operations Directorate of the BND was standing with two large gentlemen ten feet away.

"Why, Dr. Herrmann. How nice to see you again. And what brings you to Cologne?"

"The bag . . . if you please, Mr. McCready."

It was handed over. Herrmann passed it to one of his team.

"Come, Mr. McCready, let me escort you to your plane. You would not wish to miss it."

They walked toward passport control.

"A certain colleague of mine . . ." suggested Herrmann.

"He will not be coming back, Dr. Herrmann."

"Ah, poor man. But just as well, perhaps."

They arrived at passport control. Herrmann smiled at last. "We also know how to listen to cross-border radio chitchat. Good journey, Mr. McCready. My regards to London."

THE news came to Langley a week later. General Pankratin had been transferred. In future he would command a military detention complex of prison camps in Kazakhstan.

Claudia Stuart learned the news from her man in the Moscow embassy. At the time she was still basking in the plaudits that rained down from on high as the military analysts studied the complete Soviet order of battle. She was prepared to be philosophical about her Soviet general. As she remarked to Chris Appleyard, "He keeps his skin and his rank. Better than the lead mines of Yakutia. As for us— Well, it's cheaper than an apartment block in Santa Barbara."

INTERLUDE

THE hearing resumed on the following morning. Timothy Edwards remained formal courtesy itself while privately hoping the entire affair could be wound up with minimum delay.

"Thank you for reminding us of the events of 1985," he said, "though I feel one might point out that in intelligence terms, that year now constitutes a vanished age."

Denis Gaunt was having none of it. He knew he was entitled to recall any episode he wished from the career of his desk chief to persuade the board to recommend a variation of decision. He crossed to the clerk from records to ask him for another file.

"I think, gentlemen, we might consider a series of events in 1986 that alone might justify a reconsideration of the early retirement of Sam McCready. Events that started on Salisbury Plain. . . ."

THE PRICE OF THE BRIDE

CHAPTER ONE

THERE was still a hint of fog hanging away to their right, over the stretch of woodland known as Fox Covert, presaging a warm, clear day to come. On the knoll that dominated the rolling stretch of ground known as Frog Hill, the group of army officers took their station to observe the forthcoming maneuvers. Both sets of opponents would be British soldiers, divided into the Blues and the Greens. The usual designation of one group as the Reds had been changed, in deference to the composition of the officers on the knoll. Umpires who would eventually decide the outcome of the battle were scattered across the open country.

At the center of the officer group was the senior British general, the commanding officer of Southern Command. Beside him stood his personal guest, the senior ranking general of the visitors. Between and slightly behind them stood a bright young subaltern, fresh out of language school, who murmured a running translation into the ears of both men.

The British group of officers—just over thirty men—wore an air of gravity, as if well aware of the importance of the occasion. For this was the first year of perestroika and the first time Soviet officers had been invited to England as guests of the British army.

The Russians were as grave as the British, or more so. There were seventeen of them, and each had been carefully picked and screened, an expert in his field.

They had arrived at Tidworth Army Base the previous evening. The first dinner at the officers mess had been fairly formal. The Russians were aware that among the seventeen of them there had to be five at least who were watching the rest.

No one mentioned this to the British group, among whom there were four who were actually from counterintelligence—the watchers. At least the British watchers were only there to watch the Russians and not their fellow countrymen.

The British also had twenty operatives from the Security Service posted around the officers mess. These watchers were now tending the lawns and flower beds, waiting table, or polishing bits of brass, keeping the building under observation. As the chief of general staff had mentioned at a briefing several days earlier, "One really would prefer not to lose one of the buggers."

The war game began on schedule at nine o'clock and proceeded throughout the day. During the paratroop drop by 2nd Battalion, Parachute Regiment, a major of Two Para found himself standing next to a Soviet airborne colonel.

"I see," observed the Russian, "that you still favor the two-inch company mortar."

"A useful tool," agreed the Britisher. "Effective and reliable."

"I agree," said the Russian in slow, accented English. "I used them in Afghanistan."

"Indeed. I used them in the Falklands," said the major.

That evening the dinner at Tidworth barracks was more relaxed. The wine flowed; vodka was in evidence. The major from Two Para found himself next to a major from Soviet military intelligence, the GRU. He thought he would practice his smattering of Russian. *"Govoritya-vi pa-Angleeski?"* he asked.

"Ochen malo," the Russian replied with delight, then dropped

into halting English. "Very little, I am afraid. I try with books at home, but it is not so good."

"Better than my Russian, I'm sure," said the paratrooper. "By the way, I'm Paul Sinclair."

The Russian held out his hand. "Pavel Kuchenko."

It was a good dinner and ended at eleven o'clock with songs in the bar. A number of the officers would appreciate that the following morning would permit a lie-in until seven o'clock.

In fact, Major Kuchenko was up at five and spent two hours seated quietly behind the lace curtains covering his bedroom windows. He thought he spotted three men in the half gloom, who might be watchers. He also spotted, precisely at six o'clock, Colonel Arbuthnot depart on what was apparently his regular morning jogging run. He had seen him do the same the previous morning.

Colonel Arbuthnot was not a difficult man to spot, for his left arm was missing. He had lost it years earlier during a campaign to prevent a communist revolution in Oman. He was now the catering officer at Tidworth officers mess. Every morning he took a five-mile jog down the road and back, an accepted figure in white tracksuit with cowl hood, the loose left sleeve neatly pinned to his side. Major Kuchenko watched him thoughtfully.

The second day of war games passed without incident, and finally all the officers agreed the umpires had done a good job in awarding victory to the Greens. The third dinner was very jolly, with copious toasts and later a rendering of "Malinka" from a young Russian ops staff captain. No one noticed that Colonel Arbuthnot's room, which was not locked, was entered by someone who left sixty seconds later as quietly as he had come and who later rejoined the group at the bar.

At TEN minutes to six the next morning a figure in a white cowled tracksuit, the empty left sleeve pinned to the side, trotted from the mess toward the main gate. A watcher at a window of another building made a note, but took no action.

At the gate the corporal of the guard came out of the guardroom and threw up a salute to the runner, who raised a hand in salutation, then turned and jogged toward Tidworth.

At ten past six the corporal glanced up, stared, then turned to his sergeant. "I've just seen Colonel Arbuthnot go past," he said.

"So?" asked the sergeant.

"Twice," said the corporal.

The sergeant shrugged. "Must have forgotten something," he said. He would regret that remark later.

Major Kuchenko ducked into some trees beside the road after half a mile and slipped out of the stolen white tracksuit. When he went back to the road, he was in gray flannel slacks and tweed jacket over a shirt and tie. A mile behind him jogged an annoyed Colonel Arbuthnot, who had wasted ten minutes searching for his tracksuit before concluding that his orderly must have taken it for laundering. He was wearing his spare, and he had not yet noticed he was also missing a shirt, tie, jacket, and slacks.

A car that came from behind Kuchenko stopped at his wave. "I'm awfully sorry," Kuchenko said, "but my car seems to have broken down. Back there. I was wondering whether I could get some help from a garage in North Tidworth?"

"I can run you up there," said the driver. "Jump in."

The paratroops major would have been amazed at Kuchenko's sudden mastery of English. But the foreign accent was still there.

"Not from these parts, are you?" asked the driver.

"No. I am from Norway. Touring your British cathedrals."

Kuchenko was dropped by the kindly driver in the center of the sleepy town of North Tidworth at ten minutes to seven. He found a phone booth and dialed a London number. It was answered at the fifth ring.

"I'd like to speak to Mr. Joe Roth," said Kuchenko.

"Yeah, this is Joe Roth," said the voice at the other end.

"Pity," said Kuchenko. "You see, I really hoped I might talk to Chris Hayes."

In his small but elegant Mayfair apartment, all Joe Roth's professional antennae went onto red alert. He had only been awake for twenty minutes when the phone rang. His job as assistant public affairs officer at the American embassy did not require him to check in until ten.

Joe Roth was CIA, but he was not the Company's head of London station. That honor went to William Carver. As such, Carver was "declared," which meant that just about everyone who mattered knew what his job was. Carver was the official representative of the Company in London.

Roth came from the Office of Special Projects, a bureau formed only six years ago to handle projects and active measures that Langley regarded as sufficiently sensitive to merit the station heads' later being able to claim innocence, even to America's allies.

All CIA officers have a real name and an operational or professional name. The real name in friendly embassies actually is real; Joe Roth, who was undeclared, really was Joe Roth. To have his professional name thrown at him down a phone line at seven a.m., and in a voice with a non-British accent, was like a warning buzzer.

"I'm sorry," he said carefully. "You've got Joe Roth here. Who is that speaking?"

"Listen carefully, Mr. Roth, or Mr. Hayes. My name is Pyotr Alexandrovich Orlov. I am a full colonel of the KGB."

"Look, if this is a joke—"

"Mr. Roth, my calling you by your operational name is no joke to you. My defection to the U.S.A. is no joke to me. And that is what I am offering to do. I have an enormous amount of information of great value to your Agency. You must make your decision quickly, or I go back while there is time."

"Where exactly are you now, Colonel?"

"In a phone booth in a small town near Salisbury Plain. I have been with a group of Soviet officers attending British military maneuvers. Staying at Tidworth barracks. My cover there was as Major Pavel Kuchenko of the GRU. I walked out one hour ago. If I am not back within one hour, I cannot go back at all. It will take me half an hour to get back. You have thirty minutes, Mr. Roth."

"Okay, Colonel. I'll go with it—so far. I want you to call me back in fifteen minutes. You will have your answer."

"Fifteen minutes. Then I walk back," said the voice.

Roth's mind was racing. He was thirty-nine, and he had spent twelve years in the Agency. Nothing like this had ever happened to him before. Most Soviet defectors, he knew, came after initial, tentative approaches to the known Agency men in the area. Usually the potential defector was asked to stay in place and provide a stream of information before finally coming over. The amount he could send out, or at least bring with him, would affect his standing, his rewards, his life-style. In the trade it was called the bride price.

And here was a man claiming to be a full colonel of the KGB who wanted just to walk in, right in the heart of England. And to the Americans, not the Brits. Or had he already approached the Brits? Been turned down? Roth's mind raced across the possibilities, and the minutes ticked away.

Five past seven—five past two in Washington. Everyone asleep. He ought to call Calvin Bailey, head of Special Projects, his boss. But the time—there wasn't time. He flipped open a wall cabinet to reveal his private computer. Swiftly he tapped himself into the mainframe deep beneath the American embassy in Grosvenor Square. He put the computer into encrypted mode and asked the mainframe to consider senior KGB officers known to the West. Then he asked, Who is Pyotr Alexandrovich Orlov?

The CIA mainframe computer in London is linked straight through to Langley, Virginia. In response to Roth's question, letters in green began to flash up on Roth's small screen.

PYOTR ALEXANDROVICH ORLOV. KGB. FULL COLONEL. PAST FOUR YEARS BELIEVED IN THIRD DIRECTORATE. BELIEVED MASQUERADING AS GRU MAJOR INSIDE RED ARMY JOINT PLANNING STAFF MOSCOW. PREVIOUS POSTINGS KNOWN AS OPS PLANNING MOSCOW CENTER AND FIRST CHIEF DIRECTORATE (ILLEGALS DIRECTORATE) YAZENEVO.

Roth whistled as the message ended. If Orlov had really been for four years posing as a GRU major on the joint planning staff of the Soviet Defense Ministry, he would be a walking encyclopedia.

He checked his watch. Seven fourteen. No time to call Langley. He had sixty seconds to decide. . . . The phone rang.

"Mr. Roth, I can just get back in time if I have to."

Roth took a deep breath. Career on the line, boy, right on the line. "Okay, Colonel Orlov, we'll take you. I'll contact my British colleagues—they'll have you safe within thirty minutes."

"No." The voice was harsh, brooking no opposition. "I come to the Americans only. No other deal. I want you to pick me up yourself. In two hours. The railway station at Andover. Then to Upper Heyford U.S.A.F. base. You get me on a transport to America. It's the only deal I will take."

"All right, Colonel. You got it. I'll be there."

It took Roth ten minutes to throw on street clothes; grab a passport, CIA identification, money, and car keys; and head downstairs for his car, in the basement garage.

HE ENTERED THE FORECOURT OF the Andover railway station at ten past nine. There was a stream of cars sweeping in and leaving, travelers hurrying into the station concourse. Only one man was not moving. He leaned against a wall, in a tweed jacket and gray trousers, and scanned a morning paper. Roth approached him.

"I think you must be the man I have come to meet," he said softly. The reader looked up, calm gray eyes, a hard face in its mid-forties.

"That depends if you have identification," said the man. It was the same voice as the one on the phone. Roth tendered his CIA pass. Orlov nodded. Roth gestured to his car, engine still running. Orlov looked around, as if saying good-bye for the last time to a world he had known, then stepped into the car.

Two hours later, at the Oxfordshire base of the U.S.A.F., Roth drove straight to the base commander's office. There were two calls to Washington; then Langley cleared it with the Pentagon, which instructed the base commander. A communications flight out of Upper Heyford to Andrews Air Force Base, in Maryland, that afternoon at three p.m. had two extra passengers.

That was five hours after everything had hit the fan from Tidworth to London and back. About ten minutes before nine the absence of Major Kuchenko was noted, and a steward was dispatched to his room. The steward returned to say the major's room was empty, but his gear was still there. A complete search of the mess building was made, but to no avail.

A British intelligence captain slipped out to talk to the invisible watchers from the Security Service. Their log showed that two officers in tracksuits had gone jogging that morning but only one had returned. The corporal of the guard, summoned from his bed, related the double departure of Colonel Arbuthnot, who was confronted and hotly denied he had ever returned to the main gate, and left again. The intelligence captain had a hurried conversation with the senior British general, who became extremely grave and asked the senior Russian to accompany him to his office.

When the Russian general emerged, he was white with anger and demanded a staff car to take him to his embassy in London. It was ten o'clock. The telephoning began.

By noon the Soviet ambassador, Leonid Zamyatin, had lodged a vigorous protest with the British Foreign Office, alleging kidnapping, and demanded immediate access to Major Kuchenko. The protest bounced straight back down from the Foreign Office to all the covert agencies, who in unison held up their lily-white hands and replied, "But we haven't got him."

Now the rage of the Russians was being matched by the puzzlement of the British. The manner in which Kuchenko (they were still calling him that) had made his escape was bizarre, to put it mildly. Defectors headed for sanctuary usually prepared in advance. With all the British agencies protesting their innocence, that left the possibility of other agencies based on British soil.

Bill Carver, the CIA station head in London, was in an impossible position. Langley had informed him about Roth. Carver knew it would be taken as deeply offensive for the Americans to spirit a Russian out of England under the nose of the Brits without telling them. But Carver was warned to delay until Roth's flight cleared British airspace. So he made himself unavailable all morning, then asked for an urgent meeting with Timothy Edwards at three p.m.

When Edwards confronted him, Carver explained that Roth had been given no choice but to take Kuchenko/Orlov at zero notice or let him go back and that Orlov would absolutely come only to the Americans. Privately, Edwards knew that he too would have acted exactly as Roth had, given the opportunity of such a prize, but he remained cool and offended. Having formally received Carver's report, he at once informed his own Defense Ministry, Foreign Office, and sister service, Security.

An hour later Ambassador Zamyatin arrived at the Foreign Office and was seen by the Foreign Secretary himself. Though he received the explanation with skepticism, he was privately prepared to believe Sir Geoffrey Howe, whom he knew to be a very honorable man. With a show of continuing outrage the Russian went back to the embassy and told Moscow.

In Washington, the director of Central Intelligence looked across his desk at the head of Special Projects, Calvin Bailey.

"Your young Mr. Roth. He certainly upset the Brits pretty badly. Would you have taken the same risk?"

"I don't know," said Bailey. "We won't know until we talk to Orlov." Bailey had few personal friends in the Agency. People found him aloof, chilly. But he was good at his job.

The D.C.I. nodded. In the covert world, as in all others, the rule was simple. If you took a gamble and it paid rich dividends, you were a smart fellow, destined for the highest office. If the gamble failed, there was always early retirement.

When the military flight landed at Andrews, just after six p.m. Washington time, there were five Agency cars waiting on the tarmac. The two men were escorted off the plane and enveloped by the dark-windowed sedans waiting below. Bailey met Orlov, nodded coolly, and saw the Russian ensconced in the second car.

Bailey turned to Roth. "I'm giving him to you, Joe. You brought him out; you debrief him."

"I'm not an interrogator," said Roth. "It's not my specialty."

Bailey shrugged. "You'll have all the backup—translators, analysts, specialists in every area he touches on. And the polygraph, of course. Take him to the Ranch—they're expecting you. And Joe—I want it all. As it comes, at once, my eyes only, by hand."

The Ranch is a CIA safe house, a genuine farm in the horse-raising country of southern Virginia. Not too far from Washington, it is buried in deep woodland, approached by a long driveway, and guarded by teams of very fit young men, who have all passed the unarmed combat and weapons training courses at Quantico.

Orlov was shown to a comfortable two-room suite with the usual appurtenances of a good hotel—television, video, tape player, easy chairs, small dining table. Food was served—his first meal in America—and Joe Roth ate with him. On the flight over, the two men had agreed to call each other Peter and Joe.

"It won't always be easy, Peter," said Roth as he watched the Russian dealing with a large hamburger. "Tomorrow you have to take a polygraph test. If you pass that, you have to tell me . . . many things. Everything, in fact. Everything you know or suspect."

Orlov smiled. "Joe, you do not have to"—he searched for the phrase—"mince the words. I have to justify the risk you have taken to get me out. What you call the price of the bride, yes?"

Roth laughed. "Yes, Peter, that's what we need to have now. The price of the bride."

IN LONDON, Timothy Edwards summoned Sam McCready.

"I've screwed our American cousins as hard as I can. Deep offense taken, outrage at all levels—that sort of thing. Bill Carver is deeply mortified. He sees his own position here as damaged. He will press Langley to give us the Orlov product, as and when it comes. I want to form a small group to have a look at it. I'd like you to be in charge—under me."

"Thank you," said the Deceiver. "But I'd go for more. I'd ask for personal access. It could be that Orlov knows things that are specific to us. Those things won't be high on Langley's list."

"That might be hard," mused Edwards. "But I can ask."

"Another thing. I'd like to check on Orlov with Keepsake."

Edwards stared hard at McCready. Keepsake was a British "asset," a Russian working for the SIS. He was so highly placed and so sensitive that only four men in Century House were aware who he was. McCready was his case officer, the man who ran him.

"Is that wise?" asked Edwards.

"I think it is justified."

"Be careful."

THE black car the following morning was clearly parked on a double yellow line, and the traffic warden had no hesitation in writing out a ticket. He had just slipped it under the windshield wiper when a slim, well-dressed man in a gray suit emerged from a shop and began to protest. It was such an everyday scene that no one noticed, even on a London street.

From afar, an onlooker would have seen the driver tugging at the warden's sleeve, urging him to look at the plates. The warden saw the CD plate of the diplomatic corps next to the registration plate, but was unimpressed. Foreign diplomatic staff might be immune from the fine, but not from the ticket. To prove he really was a diplomat, the driver produced an identity card, which he forced the warden to look at. The warden glanced, shrugged, and moved away. In a rage the driver screwed up the parking ticket and hurled it into the car, before climbing in and driving off.

What the onlooker would not have seen was the paper stuck inside the I.D. card saying, "Reading Room, British Museum, tomorrow, two p.m." Nor would he have noticed the driver smooth out the crumpled ticket and read on the reverse side, "Colonel Pyotr Alexandrovich Orlov has defected to the Americans. Do you know anything about him?"

The Deceiver had just contacted Keepsake.

THE treatment, or handling, of a defector is always a sensitive and complicated business.

The defector must first be housed in an environment that does not appear menacing, but that precludes both his escape and the possibility of reprisals. The U.S.S.R.—and notably the KGB—are notoriously unforgiving toward those they regard as traitors and have been wont to hunt them down and liquidate them. The higher the defector's rank, the worse the treason.

One thing that debriefers are always keenly interested in is motivation. Why did you decide to come over? (The word defect is never used.) By far the most common reason given is disillusionment with the system. For many this is the genuine reason, but not always. It may be that the defector had his hand in the cashbox, or he may have been about to face discipline for a tangled love life. Everything will be checked out; sooner or later the hosts will know the real reason, the real status. For the moment everything is listened to very sympathetically.

When the area of secret intelligence is finally broached, pitfalls are set. Questions are asked to which the debriefing officers already know the answers. If the defector lies about things that he ought to know the truth of, he immediately becomes suspect. In among the questions to which the answers are already known come others to which true answers are *really* valuable. This is the pay dirt. Can this new defector tell the host agency anything it doesn't already know, and if so, how important?

In the case of Colonel Pyotr Alexandrovich Orlov, now codenamed Minstrel, the CIA came to the view within four weeks that it had fortuitously tapped into a mother lode of pure gold. The man's product was fantastic.

He narrated to Joe Roth the story of his life, from his birth near Minsk to the day he decided, six months ago, that he could tolerate no more of a regime he had come to despise. He never denied a deep love for his motherland of Russia, and he showed the normal emotion at the knowledge he had left it behind forever.

He passed three separate lie detector tests concerning his background, career, and political change of heart. And he began to reveal information of the first order. From his four years inside the joint planning staff at army headquarters, he had a wide knowledge of the dispositions of the Soviet army and air force, and of the navy's ships. And he provided fascinating insights into the defeats suffered by the Red Army in Afghanistan.

Prior to working in the Third Directorate, Orlov had been with the Illegals Directorate, that department inside the First Chief Directorate responsible for the running of illegal agents world-wide. The illegals are the most secret of all agents who spy against their own countries (if they are nationals of them) or who live in foreign countries under deep cover.

Although his knowledge was four years out of date, Orlov seemed to have an encyclopedic memory and began to blow away the very networks he had once helped establish and run, mainly in Central and South America, which had been his previous area.

THE day after Joe Roth began to share his life with Colonel Orlov in Virginia, Sam McCready quietly entered the portals of the British Museum and headed for the great circular reading room under its domed cupola.

McCready made for a reading table and courteously asked the man already seated there if he minded the intrusion. The man, his head bowed over a volume from which he took occasional notes, silently gestured to the chair opposite, and went on reading.

"How are you, Nikolai?"

"Well," murmured the man, making a note on his pad.

"There is news?"

"We are to receive a visit next week. At the *Rezidentsia*. General Drozdov himself."

McCready made no sign, but he was amazed by the name. Drozdov was the head of the Illegals Directorate and rarely ventured outside the U.S.S.R. To come into the lion's den of London was most unusual and could be very important.

"Is that good or bad?" he asked.

"I don't know. It may be something to do with Orlov. There has been the most almighty stink over that. Or maybe . . ."

"Is there another reason for his coming?"

Keepsake sighed and raised his eyes for the first time. McCready stared back. He had become a friend of the Russian over the years, trusted him, believed in him.

"It's just a feeling," said Keepsake. "Nothing concrete, just an odor on the wind. Maybe they suspect something."

"Nikolai, it cannot go on forever. We know that. Sooner or later the pieces will add together. Do you want to come out now? I can arrange it. Say the word."

"Not yet. Soon, perhaps, but not yet. There is more I can send. By the way, please do not intercept Drozdov. If there *are* suspicions, he would see it as another straw in the wind. He is coming as a Swiss businessman from Zurich. British Airways, Tuesday."

"I'll ensure he is left completely alone," said McCready. "Anything on Orlov?"

"Not yet," said Keepsake. "I know of him, never met him. But I'm surprised at him defecting. He had the highest clearance."

"So do you," said McCready.

The Russian smiled. "Why does he interest you?"

"Nothing concrete," said McCready. "As you said, an odor on the wind. The manner of his coming, giving Joe Roth no time to check. For a sailor jumping ship, it's normal. For a colonel of the KGB, it's odd. He could have done a better deal."

"I agree," said the Russian. "I'll find out what I can."

Face-to-face meetings were hazardous, therefore infrequent. The next one was set up at a small and seedy café in Shoreditch, in London's East End. Early in the following month, May.

AT THE end of April, during a meeting in the White House with the director of Central Intelligence, the President was unusually flattering about the CIA. The gratitude expressed by a number of agencies and departments as a result of Orlov's product had reached as high as the Oval Office. When he returned to Langley, the D.C.I. summoned the head of Special Projects, Calvin Bailey.

"Congratulations are in order, Cal," the D.C.I. said. "The Navy Department loves it, says keep it coming. The Mexicans are delighted; they just wrapped up a network of seventeen agents."

"Thank you," said Calvin Bailey carefully. He was a cautious man, not given to overt displays of human warmth.

"Fact is," said the D.C.I., "we all know Frank Wright is retiring at the end of the year. I'm going to need a new D.D.O. Maybe, Calvin, just maybe I think I know who it ought to be."

Bailey's morose shrouded gaze flashed into a rare smile. In the

CIA the director himself is always a political appointment. Under him come the two main divisions of the Agency: Operations, headed by the deputy director Ops (D.D.O.), and Intelligence (analysis), headed by the deputy director Intel (D.D.I.). These two posts are the highest to which a professional can aspire.

Having delivered his bouquet, the D.C.I. turned to more mundane matters. "Look, it's about the Brits. They say they're very grateful for all the Minstrel product we've been sending over, but as regards Soviet agents being run in England, so far it's all code names. Can Minstrel recall any actual names, or offices held— something to identify a hostile agent in their own pond?"

Bailey thought it over. "We've sent the Brits everything that remotely concerns them," he said. "I'll ask Minstrel again, have Joe Roth see if he can remember a real name. Okay?"

"Fine, fine," said the D.C.I. "One last thing. They keep asking for access. Over there. We owe them, Cal. This time around I'm prepared to indulge them. I think we can go that far."

"I'd prefer to keep him over here. He's safe here."

"We can keep him safe over there. Look, we can put him on an American air base. They can talk to him under supervision."

"I don't like it," said Bailey.

"Cal"—there was a hint of steel in the D.C.I.'s voice—"I've agreed to it. Just see to it."

Calvin Bailey drove down to the Ranch for a personal talk with Joe Roth. He found his subordinate tired and drawn. Debriefing a defector is a tiring business.

"Washington is delighted," Bailey told him. "Everything he says checks out. Soviet army, navy, and air force deployments, weapons levels, readiness states, the Afghan mess—Pentagon loves it all. You've done well, Joe. Very well."

He went on to tell Roth of the D.C.I.'s hint about the forthcoming vacancy for deputy director Operations. "If it goes through, Joe, there'll be a second vacancy—for head of Special Projects. My recommendation will count for a lot. It'll be for you, Joe."

Roth was grateful, but not ecstatic. He seemed more than tired. There was something else on his mind.

"Is he causing problems?" asked Bailey. "Does he need female company? These things can be arranged."

"No, I've offered him that. He just shook his head. We work out together. It helps. Run through the woods until we can hardly stand. I've never been in such good shape. He's older, but he's fitter. That's one of the things that worries me, Calvin. He's got no flaws, no weaknesses. He's a total pro."

"That's why he's the best we've ever had, Joe. Don't knock it. Be grateful."

"Calvin, that's not the main reason he bugs me. There's something else. He's holding something back."

Calvin Bailey went very quiet and very still. "The polygraph tests don't say so."

"No, they don't. That's why I can't be sure I'm right. I just feel it. There's something he's not saying."

Bailey leaned across and stared hard into Roth's face. "Could there be any chance that, despite all the tests, he might still be a phony, a KGB plant?"

Roth sighed. "I don't think so, but I don't *know*. For me there's a ten percent area of doubt. And I can't work out why."

"Then find out, Joe. Find out," said Calvin Bailey. He did not need to point out that if there was anything phony about Colonel Orlov, two CIA careers were likely to go straight into the trash can.

Roth found Orlov in his living room, lying on a settee, listening to his favorite music—the ballad singers of the '6os and early '7os. Whenever he visited the Russian, Roth was accustomed to hearing Simon and Garfunkel, the Seekers, or the slow honeyed tones of Elvis Presley coming from the tape deck.

"You want we should talk some more?" Orlov asked.

"No," said Roth. "I just stopped by to see if you were okay. I'm going to turn in. It's been a long day. By the way, we are going back to England soon. Let the limeys talk to you for a while."

Orlov frowned. "My deal was to come here. Only here."

"It's okay, Peter. We'll be staying on an American air force base. I'll be there to protect you from the big bad Brits."

Orlov did not smile at the joke.

Roth became serious. "Peter, is there a reason you don't want to go back to England? Something I should know?"

Orlov shrugged. "Nothing specific, Joe. Just gut feeling."

"Nothing will happen to you in England. I give you my word. You going to turn in now?"

"I stay up for a while. Read, play music," said the Russian.

IN FACT, THE LIGHT BURNED IN Orlov's room until half past one in the morning. When the KGB assassination team struck, it was a few minutes before three.

Orlov was told later that they had silenced two guards on the perimeter with powerful crossbows, traversed the lawn at the rear of the house undetected, and entered the house via the kitchens.

On the upper floor, the first Roth or Orlov heard was a burst of submachine gun fire from the lower hall, followed by the rapid pounding of feet up the stairs. Orlov awoke like a cat, came out of his bed, and was across the living room in no more than three seconds. He opened the door to the landing and caught a brief glimpse of the night duty guard from Quantico swerving off the landing and down the main stairs. A figure in a black cat suit and ski mask halfway up the stairs loosed a brief burst. The American took the blast in the chest.

Orlov slammed his door and turned back toward the bedroom. He entered it as the man in black ran through the door from the corridor, followed by an American. The last thing Orlov saw before he slammed his bedroom door shut was the KGB assassin turn and blast the American behind him. The killing gave Orlov time to throw the lock.

But it was only a respite. Seconds later the lock was blasted away and the door kicked open. The KGB man threw down his empty machine pistol and pulled a Makarov 9-mm automatic from his belt. He pointed it straight at Orlov's face and hissed contemptuously, "*Predatel* [traitor]!"

There was a cut-glass ashtray on the bedside table. In a last gesture of defiance Orlov swept it up and sent it spinning toward the Russian's face. As he did so he yelled back, "*Padla* [scum]!"

The man in black sidestepped the heavy glassware, but it cost him a fraction of a second. In that time the Quantico team leader stepped into the doorway and fired twice with his heavy Colt .44 Magnum. The Russian was thrown forward as his chest exploded in a welter of blood.

Kroll, the man who had fired, was white with rage, and panting. "You okay?" he snapped.

Orlov nodded. He was pale but calm.

"Someone screwed up," said the American. "There were two of them. Two of my men are down, maybe more outside."

480

A shaken Joe Roth came in, still in pajamas. "Peter, I'm sorry. We have to get out of here. Now. Fast."

There was an army base only twenty miles from the Ranch. Within two hours Roth, Orlov, and the remainder of the Quantico team were temporarily housed there. Before nightfall they moved to another CIA safe house, in Kentucky, and much better protected.

WHILE the Roth-Orlov group was at the army base Calvin Bailey returned to the Ranch. He wanted a full report from the Russian in the black ski mask who had confronted Orlov at point-blank range.

The young officer of the Green Berets was nursing a bruised wrist from when he had fallen. The special-effects blood had long been wiped off him, and he had changed out of the black jumpsuit with the two holes in the front and removed the harness containing the tiny charges and sacs of realistic blood.

"Verdict?" asked Bailey.

"He's for real," said the Russian-speaking officer. "He thought he was being liquidated by his own side."

"He didn't suspect you?" asked Bailey.

"No, sir. I saw it right in his eyes. He believed he was going to die. He just went right on fighting. Quite a guy."

"I think," Bailey said to Roth by telephone later, "that we have our answer. He's okay, and that's official. Try and get him to recall a name—for the Brits. You're flying over next Tuesday."

ROTH spent two days with Orlov while the Russian racked his memory for the names of Soviet agents planted in Britain. As he had specialized in Central and South America, Britain had not been his primary concern. But at the end of the second day something came back to him.

A civil servant in the Ministry of Defense, in Whitehall. But the money was always paid into the man's account at the Midland Bank in Croydon High Street.

"It's not a lot," said the man from the Security Service, MI5, when he was given the news. He was sitting in the office of Timothy Edwards, at Century House. "He might have moved long since. Might have banked under a false name. But we'll try."

He went back to Curzon Street, in Mayfair, and set the wheels in motion. Surprisingly, the chase was very quick. Only one M.O.D. civil servant banked at the Midland in Croydon High Street. The records of the accounts were sent for. The man still lived locally. He had a checking account and a savings account. Over the years a total of twenty thousand pounds had been paid into his deposit account, always in cash and fairly regularly. His name was Anthony Milton-Rice.

The Whitehall conference that evening involved the director general and deputy director general of MI5 and the assistant commissioner of the Metropolitan Police in charge of Special Branch. The meeting was chaired by the chairman of the Joint Intelligence Committee. He started the questioning.

"Who exactly is Mr. Milton-Rice?"

The deputy director of MI5 consulted his notes. "Grade two civil servant on the staff of the Procurement Office."

"Pretty low grade?"

"Sensitive work, though. Weapons systems, access to evaluations of new armaments."

"The point is," said the director general, "we have very little to go on. Not enough to get a conviction. He could plead that he backs the horses, always on track, gets his cash that way."

The policeman nodded his agreement. Without a confession the Crown Prosecution Office wouldn't even bring a case.

"We'd like to shadow him first," said the director general. "Around the clock. If he makes one contact with the Russians, he's in the bag, with or without a confession."

It was agreed. The watchers—that elite team of MI5 agents—were put on alert to envelop Anthony Milton-Rice twenty-four hours a day, starting the following morning as he approached the Defense Ministry.

ANTHONY Milton-Rice was a man of routine. On workdays he left his house in Addiscombe precisely at ten to eight and walked the half mile to East Croydon Station. He boarded the same commuter train every day and rode into London, descending at Victoria Station. From there it was a short bus ride to Parliament Square and the Defense Ministry building.

The morning after the conference about him, he did exactly the same. He did not notice the group of youths who boarded the train at Norwood Junction until they entered his compartment. There were screams and shouts of alarm as the teenagers, engaged in an orgy of casual robbery and assault called steaming, swept through the carriage, snatching women's handbags and jewelry and demanding men's wallets at knife point, threatening anyone who seemed to resist them.

At the next station up the line, the young thugs quit the train, scattered, and disappeared, leaving behind them hysterical women, badly shaken men, and frustrated transport police.

The train was delayed while the police took statements. It was only when they tapped the commuter in the pale gray raincoat dozing in the corner on his shoulder that the man toppled slowly forward onto the floor. There were further screams as the first blood from the thin stiletto wound to his heart began to seep from beneath the crumpled figure. Mr. Anthony Milton-Rice was very dead.

IVAN'S Café, appropriately named for a meeting with a Russian, was situated in Crondall Street, in Shoreditch. When McCready entered, he took a cup of tea from the counter and wandered over to the wall where two tables were side by side. Keepsake occupied the one in the corner and was engrossed in *Sporting Life*. McCready unfolded his *Evening Standard* and proceeded to study it.

"How was the good General Drozdov?" he asked quietly, his voice lost in the babble of the café.

"Amiable and enigmatic," said the Russian. "I fear he may have been checking us out. I will know more if K-Line decide to visit." K-Line is the branch of the KGB charged with internal security.

"Have you ever run a man called Anthony Milton-Rice?" asked McCready. "A civil servant in the Ministry of Defense?"

"Never heard of him. Never handled his product."

"Well, he's dead now. Could he have been run directly from Moscow through the Illegals Directorate?"

"If he was working for us, that's the only explanation," muttered the Russian. "Why did he die?"

McCready sighed. "He was denounced. To us. And then he was dead."

"Who denounced him?" asked Keepsake, stirring his tea.

"Colonel Pyotr Orlov," said McCready quietly.

"Ah," said Keepsake in a low murmur. "I have something for you there. Orlov is a loyal and dedicated KGB officer. His defection is as phony as a three-dollar bill. He is a plant, a disinformation agent. And he is well prepared and very good."

CHAPTER THREE

TIMOTHY Edwards listened carefully to McCready's evaluation and then asked calmly, "And you are quite certain you believe Keepsake?"

McCready had expected this question. Keepsake had worked for the British for four years. There was always the possibility that he might be a double, his true loyalties still with Moscow.

"Keepsake's product has been tested against every known criterion," said McCready. "It's pure."

"Yes, of course," said Edwards smoothly. "Unfortunately, our cousins would say exactly the opposite—that *our* man was lying and theirs was for real."

"I don't think they should be told about Keepsake," retorted McCready. "Keepsake has an instinct that suspicions are growing in Moscow that they have a leak somewhere. For the moment it could be very dangerous to widen the circle who know about him."

Edwards made his decision. "Sam, I agree. But I'm going to see the chief on this one. Stay in touch."

During the lunch hour, which Edwards spent eating a sparse meal with the chief in the top-floor suite of offices, a military version of the Grumman Gulfstream III landed at the U.S.A.F. base at Alconbury.

When Roth, Orlov, Kroll, and the rest descended from the Grumman, they were taken to a single-story building set aside and equipped with living quarters and kitchen, conference rooms, and one electronically bugged room for the debriefing of Colonel Orlov. The British team was cleared to enter the base the following morning.

McCready's phone rang at three p.m., and Edwards asked to see him again.

"Proposals accepted and agreed," said Edwards. "We back our judgment that Keepsake is telling the truth and that the Americans have themselves a disinformation agent. The problem is that whatever Orlov is here for, it seems that for the moment he is producing good product, which makes it unlikely our cousins would believe us. So how do you suggest we handle it?"

"Let me have him," said McCready. "Joe Roth is in charge, and I know Joe. He's no fool. Maybe I can push Orlov hard enough to sow some seeds of doubt. Get the cousins to contemplate the notion that he may not be all he seems."

"All right," said Edwards. "You take it."

He made it sound like his own decision, his own act of magnanimity. In reality the chief had insisted that the Deceiver be in charge of handling Orlov.

McCready set off for Alconbury by car early the following morning. Denis Gaunt, on whom McCready was putting an increasing degree of trust and reliance, drove. For much of the journey McCready sat silently, his mind running back over what Keepsake had told him. In London years earlier the Russian had been marginally associated with the first preparatory stages of a deception operation of which Orlov could only be the final fruition. It had been code-named Project Potemkin.

"The target is the CIA," Keepsake had said. He did not know who the exact victim would be or how the sting would be accomplished, but this had to be Potemkin coming into operation at last. "The proof will be in two parts," he had said. "No information provided by Orlov will ever actually produce massive and irreversible damage to Soviet interests. Second, you will see an enormous loss of morale taking place inside the CIA."

At the moment the latter was certainly not the case, mused McCready. His American friends were riding high on their newfound asset. He determined to concentrate on the other area.

At the main gate of the air base McCready asked for Joe Roth. Minutes later Roth appeared in an air force jeep.

"Sam, good to see you again."

"Nice to see you back, Joe. That was quite a vacation you took."

"Hey, I'm sorry. I was given no choice, no chance to explain."

"That's okay," said McCready easily. "All has been explained. All is smoothed over."

They drove in line across the base to the isolated block where the CIA team was housed. A single corridor divided its entire length, from which doors led off to the various rooms. Roth led

McCready and Gaunt to a room in the center of the block. Its windows were closed and shuttered; the only illumination was electric. Easy chairs formed a comfortable group around a coffee table in the center; straight chairs and tables ringed the walls.

Roth ordered some coffee. "I'll go get Minstrel," he said.

When Roth was out, McCready nodded to Gaunt to take a chair by the wall. The message was, watch and listen; miss nothing. From down the corridor McCready heard the haunting melody of "Bridge over Troubled Waters." The sound stopped, and Roth ushered into the room a chunky, tough-looking man in running shoes, slacks, and a polo sweater.

"Sam, let me present Colonel Pyotr Orlov. Peter, this is Sam McCready."

The Russian stared at McCready with expressionless eyes. He had heard of him. Most high-ranking officers of the KGB had by then heard of Sam McCready. But he gave no sign.

McCready crossed the room, his hand outstretched. "My dear Colonel Orlov. I am delighted to meet you," he said warmly.

Coffee was served, and they seated themselves, McCready facing Orlov, Roth to one side. McCready began gently, and Orlov's answers came fluently and easily. But after the first hour McCready became more and more perplexed, or so it seemed.

"It's all very fine, wonderful stuff," he said. "But everything you have given us is code names. We have Agent Wildfowl somewhere in the Foreign Office; Agent Kestrel in the navy. Nothing could actually lead to a detection or an arrest."

"Mr. McCready, as I have explained many times, during my period in the Illegals Directorate I specialized in Central and South America. I did not have access to the files of agents in Britain."

"Yes, of course," said McCready. "But I was thinking more of your time in planning. As we understand it, that entails preparing cover stories for people about to be infiltrated or just recruited. Also, systems for making contact, passing information, paying off agents. It involves the banks they use, the sums paid. All this you seem to have . . . forgotten."

"My time in planning was eight years ago. Bank accounts are in eight-figure numbers. It is impossible to recall them all." There was an edge to his voice. He was getting annoyed.

"Or even one number," mused McCready, as if thinking aloud. "Or even one bank."

"Sam." Roth leaned forward. "What are you driving at?"

"I am simply trying to establish whether anything Colonel Orlov has given you or us over the past six weeks will really do massive and irreversible damage to Soviet interests."

"What are you talking about?" It was Orlov, on his feet, plainly angry. Roth was on his feet too.

"Sam, could I have a word with you? Privately. Outside."

He made for the door. McCready rose and followed him. Roth did not stop walking until he was outside the building.

"Sam, what the hell do you think you're doing?"

McCready shrugged. "I'm trying to establish Orlov's bona fides," he said. "That's what I'm here for."

"Let's get this absolutely straight," said Roth tightly. "You are not—as in *not*—here to establish Minstrel's bona fides. That has already been done. By us. You are here as a concession from the D.C.I. to share in Minstrel's product. That's all."

"And what do you think that product is really worth, Joe?"

"A lot. Soviet military deployments, weapons levels, plans—"

"Which can all be changed," observed Sam, "quite quickly and easily." He could not repeat what Keepsake had told him in the café, but he could still hear the murmuring voice beside him.

Sam, this new man in Moscow, Gorbachev. You know little about him as yet. But I know him. This perestroika he talks about, this glasnost. You know what these will mean, my friend? In two years—by 1988, maybe 1989—all these military details won't matter anymore. All that this Orlov is telling the Americans will be for the archives. But the big lie when it comes—that will be important. Wait for the big lie.

"And the networks in South America," said Roth. "Dammit—they've rolled up scores of Soviet agents."

"All locally recruited help," said McCready. "Not an ethnic Russian among them. Tired, clapped-out networks, greedy agents, low-level informants. Disposable."

Roth was staring at him hard. "You think he's phony, don't you? You think he's a double. Where did you get that, Sam? Do you have an asset in Moscow that we don't know about?"

"Nope," said McCready flatly. Strictly speaking, he was not

even lying. "I just want to push him hard. I think he's holding something back. You're no fool, Joe. I believe that in your deepest heart you have the same impression."

That shaft went home. Roth nodded. "All right. We'll ride him hard. He hasn't come here for a vacation, after all. And he's tough. Let's go back."

They resumed at a quarter to twelve. McCready returned to the question of Soviet agents in Britain.

"One I have already given you," said Orlov, "if you can detect him. The man who banked in Croydon, at the Midland."

"We have traced him," said McCready evenly. "His name is, or rather was, Anthony Milton-Rice."

"What do you mean, *was?*" queried Roth.

"He died yesterday morning," said McCready. "Liquidated. Just an hour before we could get the surveillance team around him."

There was a stunned silence. Then Roth was on his feet again, absolutely outraged. They were back outside in two minutes.

"What the hell do you think you're playing at, Sam?" he shouted. "You could have told me."

"I wanted to see Orlov's reaction. I thought if I told you, you might break the news yourself. Did you see his reaction?"

"No. I was watching you."

"There wasn't one," said McCready. "I would have thought he'd be pretty stunned. Worried, even. Tell me, when did Orlov produce the product about the spy in our Defense Ministry?"

Roth told him.

"Five days," mused McCready. "Before it reached us. Time enough . . ."

"Now just a minute," protested Roth.

"Which gives us three choices," McCready continued. "Either it was a remarkable coincidence. Or someone on your side leaked. Or it was set up in advance. I mean, the killing was prepared for a specific hour on a specific day. A certain number of hours before that time, Orlov had a rush of memory. Before we could get our act together, the denounced agent was dead."

"I don't believe we have a leak in the Agency," said Roth tightly. "And I don't believe Orlov is a phony."

"Then why isn't he coming clean? Let's go back to him."

When they returned, McCready changed his tone. "Colonel

Orlov," he said gently, "you are a stranger in a strange land. You have anxieties about your future. So you wish to keep certain things back—for insurance. We understand that. But your standing with the Agency is now so high you need no more insurance. Now, are there any other real names you can offer us?"

There was utter silence in the room. Slowly Orlov nodded. There was a general exhalation of breath.

"Remyants," he said, "Gennadi Remyants."

Roth's exasperation was almost visible. "We know about Remyants," he said. He looked up at McCready. "Washington-based representative of Aeroflot. That's his cover. The FBI turned him two years ago. Been working for us ever since."

"No," said Orlov. "You are wrong. Remyants is *not* a double. His exposure was arranged by Moscow. Remyants is a KGB major of the Illegals Directorate. He runs four separate Soviet networks in mainland U.S.A. and knows all the identities."

Roth whistled. "If that is true, then it is real pay dirt. *If* it is true. Guys, I have to go down to London to talk with Langley."

Joe Roth got his link to Calvin Bailey at eight p.m. London time, three o'clock in Washington. They spoke in clear voices, their tones slightly tinny because of the encrypting technology through which both voices had to pass for security.

"Sam McCready believes Minstrel is a phony, a plant," said Roth.

"That's crazy. Minstrel's product has been great. What's McCready's beef?"

"We covered two areas. On Minstrel's military product he said Moscow could change it all, as long as they knew what Minstrel was telling us."

"What else didn't satisfy Mr. McCready?"

"He thought the Soviet networks in Central and South America were tired—clapped-out was the word he used."

"Look, Joe, Minstrel has blown away a dozen networks run by Moscow in four countries down there. He's smashed up years of KGB work. McCready's talking crap."

"He did have one point. All Minstrel has given the Brits are code names. Nothing to identify a single Russian asset here. Except one, and he's dead. You heard about that?"

"Sure. Rotten luck. A miserable coincidence."

"Sam thinks it's no coincidence. He thinks Minstrel works for Moscow Center."

"Did he offer you any hard evidence for this?"

"No. I asked him if he had an asset inside Moscow who had denounced Minstrel. He denied it, but I think he was lying."

"If they have a man, it's their man who is lying," Bailey told him. "Of course Moscow would leak to the Brits that our triumph was hollow. And the Brits would be susceptible to that scam because of their annoyance at not getting Minstrel to themselves. So far as I am concerned, the British tip-off is disinformation."

"Sam had one success," said Joe Roth. "He got Minstrel to come up with a new name. Gennadi Remyants." Roth went on to reveal what Orlov had said about Remyants' true loyalties to Moscow. The simple way to find out would be to pick up Remyants and break him.

Bailey was silent. Finally he said, "Maybe. We'll think it over. I'll talk to the D.D.O. and the Bureau. In the meantime, keep McCready away from Minstrel. Give them both a break."

JOE Roth invited McCready to join him for breakfast the following morning at his apartment. "I make a pretty mean breakfast. Juice, eggs over easy, waffles, coffee suit you?"

McCready laughed down the phone. "Juice and coffee will do fine."

When he arrived, Roth was in the kitchen, proudly demonstrating his talent with ham and eggs. McCready weakened and took some.

"Sam, I wish you'd revise your opinion about Minstrel," said Roth over the coffee. "I spoke with Calvin last night. He wasn't pleased. Figures we gave you a generous break on Minstrel. Our view is that your man—the one who doesn't exist—is lying. Orlov has passed three polygraph tests. That's proof enough."

For answer, McCready produced a slip of paper from his pocket and laid it in front of Roth. It read:

We discovered that there were some East Europeans who could defeat the polygraph at any time. There is an occasional individual who lives in that part of the world who has spent his life lying about one thing or another and therefore becomes so good at it that he can pass the polygraph test.

Roth snorted and tossed the paper back. "Some academic with no experience of Langley."

"Actually," said McCready mildly, "it was said by Richard Helms two years ago."

Richard Helms is a legendary director of Central Intelligence. Roth looked shaken.

"Joe, one thing Moscow has always longed for is to have the Brits and the Yanks fighting like Kilkenny cats. That's exactly what we're heading for, and Orlov's only been in the country forty-eight hours. Think about it."

IN WASHINGTON, the D.C.I. and the FBI had agreed that the only way to test Orlov's statement about Remyants was to pick him up. The arrest was fixed for that evening, when Remyants left the Aeroflot office in downtown Washington, about five o'clock.

The Russian emerged from the building and walked down the street, unaware of the six armed FBI agents who moved in behind him as he crossed a small park to where he had left his car. The agents intended to make the arrest as the Russian got into his car.

The park contained a series of paths with various benches between ragged and litter-strewn lawns. It had become a meeting place for drug pushers and their customers. On one of the benches, as Remyants crossed toward the parking lot, a black man and a Cuban were negotiating a deal. Each dealer had backup men close by.

The fight was triggered by a scream of rage from the Cuban, who rose and pulled a knife. One of the black man's bodyguards drew a handgun and shot him down. At least eight others from the two gangs pulled weapons and started firing. The FBI agents dropped, rolled, and drew their guns.

Remyants took a single soft-nosed bullet in the back of the head and toppled forward. His killer was shot at once by an FBI agent. The two gangs—the blacks and the Cubans—scattered in different directions. The whole firefight took seven seconds and left two men dead—one Cuban and the Russian, killed in the cross fire.

The Cuban was later identified as Gonzalo Appio; his fingerprints were already on file with the FBI. He was known as a drug dealer and contract hit man and was suspected by the FBI of being a gunman for the DGI, Cuba's KGB-dominated secret police.

The FBI passed the file to Langley, where it caused deep concern. It was the D.D.O., Frank Wright, who went around Bailey and spoke to Joe Roth in London. "We need to know, Joe—now, fast—if there is any substance to the British reservations about Minstrel. Gloves off, Joe. Lie detector, the works. Get up there and find out why things keep going wrong."

Colonel Pyotr Orlov noticed the change in the people around him as soon as Roth arrived back at Alconbury. Within minutes the jocular familiarity had vanished. The CIA staff became withdrawn and formal. Orlov waited patiently.

When Roth took his place opposite him in the debriefing room, two aides wheeled in a machine on a trolley. Orlov had seen it before. The polygraph. "Something wrong, Joe?" he asked.

"Yes, Peter, something very wrong."

In a few brief sentences Roth informed the Russian of the fiasco in Washington. Something flickered in Orlov's eyes. Fear? Guilt? The machine would find out.

Orlov made no protest as the technicians prepared him for the lie detector test. Roth began as always with simple questions about Orlov's background. These were designed to establish a response norm. The fine pen drifted over the rolling paper in gentle rises and falls. Then Roth went for the hard ones.

"Are you a double agent working for the KGB?"

"No."

The pen kept drifting slowly up and down.

"Is the information you have given so far truthful?"

"Yes."

"Is there any vital information you have not given us?"

Orlov was silent. Then he gripped the arms of his chair. "No."

The fine pen swerved violently up and down several times.

"I'm sorry, Peter, but that was a lie."

There was silence in the room. Finally the Russian, who was looking at the floor, raised his eyes.

"Joe, my friend, can I speak to you? Alone?"

Roth nodded abruptly. When they were alone, all the technology disconnected, he said, "Well?"

The Russian gave a long sigh. "Joe, did you ever wonder at the

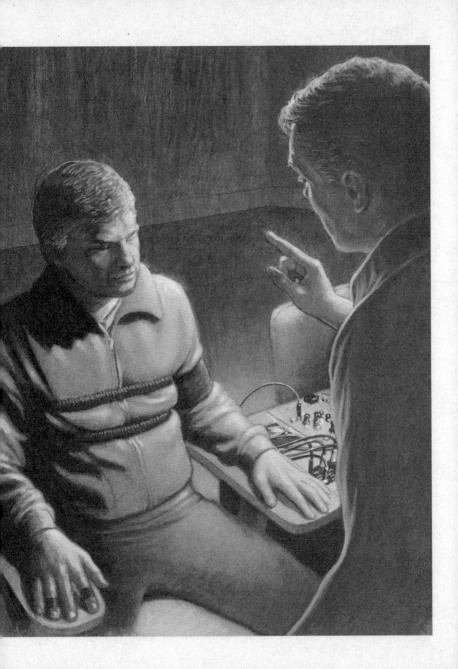

manner of my defection? The speed? Not giving you a chance to check with Washington?"

"Yes, I did. Frankly, I was never completely satisfied with your explanations. Why did you defect that way?"

"Because I didn't want to end like Volkov."

Roth sat as if he had been punched in the belly. Everyone in the business knew of the disastrous Volkov case. In early September, 1945, Konstantin Volkov, Soviet vice-consul in Istanbul, Turkey, turned up at the British consulate general and told an astonished official that he was really the deputy head of the KGB in Turkey and wanted to defect. He offered to blow away 314 Soviet agents in Turkey and 250 in Britain. Most vital of all, he said there were two British diplomats in the Foreign Office working for Russia and another man high in the SIS.

The news was sent to London while Volkov returned to his consulate. In London, the matter was given to the head of the Russian section, who flew out to Istanbul. The last that was seen of Volkov was a heavily bandaged figure being hustled aboard a Soviet plane bound for Moscow, where he died after hideous torture in the Lubyanka. The British head of the Russian section had arrived too late—not surprisingly, since he had informed Moscow from his London base. His name was Kim Philby, the very Soviet spy whom Volkov's evidence would have exposed.

"What exactly are you saying to me, Peter?"

"I had to come over the way I came because I knew I could trust you. You were not high enough."

"Not high enough for what?"

"Not high enough to be him." The Russian spoke slowly and clearly, as if liberating himself from a long-held burden. "For seventeen years the KGB has had a man inside the CIA. I believe that by now he has risen very high."

CHAPTER FOUR

JOE Roth lay on his cot in his bedroom in the isolated building on Alconbury field and wondered what to do.

If Orlov's claim was true, the manhunt alone could tear the Agency apart. If it was true, the damage assessment would take years—the realignment of thousands of agents, codes, foreign networks, and alliances. The question that raged through Roth's mind as he tossed the night away was, Who the hell can I go to?

Just before dawn he made up his mind, rose, dressed, and packed a suitcase. Before leaving, he looked in on Orlov, who was sound asleep, and said to Kroll, "Look after him for me. No one enters; no one leaves. That man has just become incredibly valuable."

Roth drove to London, went to his apartment, and took a passport in another name. He secured a seat on a private British carrier to Boston and connected at Logan Airport into Washington National. It was dusk when he drove a rented car into Georgetown, parked, and walked down K Street to the far end, close to the campus of Georgetown University.

The house he sought was a fine building of red brick, distinguished from others near it only by extensive security systems. At the door he flashed his CIA pass and asked that a message be passed to the man he had come to see. Minutes later he was shown into a paneled library redolent of leather-bound books and a hint of cigar. He sat and waited. Then the door opened, and the director of Central Intelligence entered.

The D.C.I. was over seventy, an unusual age for the post, but he was an unusual man. He had served with the OSS in World War II, running agents into Nazi-occupied France and the Low Countries. He was known in the corridors of Langley as a tough old bastard. He rewarded talent and intelligence, but his passion was loyalty. For traitors he had only a visceral loathing.

He listened to Roth's narration, giving no sign of what he felt, save a tightening of the muscles around the dewlapped jaw.

"You came straight here?" he asked when Roth finished. "You spoke to no one else?"

Roth explained how he had come like a thief in the night into his own country. The old man nodded. He rose and went to fill a tumbler from the brandy decanter on the antique side table, pausing to tap Roth reassuringly on the shoulder.

"You did well, my boy," he said. "Seventeen years, you say?"

"According to Orlov. All my own superior officers, right up to Frank Wright, have been with the Agency that long. I didn't know who else to come to."

"No, of course not." The D.C.I. returned to his chair and sat lost in thought. Finally he said, "It has to be the Office of Security.

495

But not the chief. No doubt he's totally loyal, but he's a twenty-five-year man. There's a very bright young man who works as his deputy. Ex-lawyer. I doubt if he's been with us more than fifteen."

The D.C.I. summoned an aide and caused several phone calls to be made. It was confirmed that Max Kellogg, the deputy head of the Office of Security, was forty-one and had joined the Agency from law school fifteen years earlier. Kellogg, flustered and apprehensive, arrived just after midnight from his home in Alexandria.

"Tell him," said the D.C.I.

Roth repeated his story. The lawyer took it all in without blinking, missed nothing, asked two questions, and shut up.

"I have decided to keep Minstrel at Alconbury," said the D.C.I. "He's probably as safe there, even safer, than back over here. You'll fly in the morning"—he checked his watch—"this morning, by designated flight straight to Alconbury. No holds barred now. I want to know two things fast. Is it true, and if so, who? Report direct. As of now, you two work for me—only for me."

ROTH and Kellogg tried to get some sleep on the Grumman from Andrews to Alconbury. They were ragged and tired when they arrived. They hardly paused to wash and brush up before going to Colonel Orlov's room. As they entered, Roth heard the familiar tones of Art Garfunkel coming from the tape deck.

Orlov was cooperation itself. He seemed resigned to the fact that he had now divulged the last piece of his precious insurance. The price of the bride had been offered in full. The only question was whether it would be acceptable to the suitors.

"I never knew his name," he said in the debriefing room. "He was known only as Agent Sparrowhawk, and he was run personally by General Drozdov."

"Where and when was he recruited?"

"In Vietnam, in '68 or '69. I was with planning, and we had a big operation down there, mainly in and around Saigon. Locally recruited help was Vietnamese, of course—Vietcong. But we had our own people. One of them reported that the Vietcong had brought him an American who was dissatisfied. Our local *Rezident* cultivated the man and turned him. In late 1969 General Drozdov personally went to Tokyo to talk with him."

"How do you know this?"

"There were arrangements to be made, communication links set up, funds to be transferred. I was in charge."

They talked for a full week. Orlov recalled banks into which sums had been paid over the years, and the months on which these transfers were made. The sums increased as the years passed, probably to account for promotion and better product.

Max Kellogg noted everything and reran his tapes through the night. Finally he said to Roth, "There is only one career that fits all these allegations. I don't know whose it is, but the records will prove it. It's a question of cross-checking now. I can only do that in Washington, in the Central Registry. I have to go back."

He flew the following day, met with the D.C.I., and then closeted himself with the records. Despite the secrecy, word began to spread through Langley. Something was up. There was a flap going on, and it had to do with internal security. Morale began to flag.

AT GOLDERS Hill, in North London, there is a small park that contains a menagerie of deer, goats, ducks and other wildfowl. McCready met Keepsake there on the day Max Kellogg flew back to Washington.

"Things are not so good at the embassy," said Keepsake. "The K-Line man has started asking for files that go back years. I think a security investigation has been started."

"Is there anything we can do?"

"It would help if I could give them something really useful—some good news about Orlov, for example."

With a defector-in-place like Keepsake it is customary for his new masters to give him some genuine intelligence to send home to allay suspicion. It was agreed that two days later Keepsake would be passed a copy of a draft memorandum in Denis Gaunt's hand to the effect that Orlov was now ensconced at Alconbury, where the Americans had fallen for him hook, line, and sinker—and so had the British.

"How are things with Orlov?" inquired Keepsake.

"Everything has gone quiet," said McCready. "I had one half day with him, got nowhere. I think I sowed some seeds of doubt in Joe Roth's mind. He went back to Alconbury, talked again with Orlov, then shot off back to the States on a different passport. He thought we hadn't spotted him. Seemed in a hell of a hurry.

Hasn't reappeared—at least not through a regular airport. May have flown direct into Alconbury on a military flight."

Keepsake stopped tossing crumbs to the ducks and turned to McCready. "They have invited you back to resume?"

"No. It's been a week. Total silence."

"Then he has produced the big lie, the one he came to produce. That is why the CIA is involved within themselves."

"Any idea what it could be?"

Keepsake sighed. "There are two things the KGB has always lusted after. One is to start a major war between the CIA and the SIS. Have they started fighting you?"

"No, they are being very polite. Just noncommunicative."

"Then it is the other. The other dream is to tear the CIA apart from the inside. Destroy its morale. Project Potemkin. Orlov will denounce someone as a KGB agent inside the CIA. Look for the man to whom the CIA suddenly grows cold. That will be the man, and he will be innocent."

EDWARDS was aghast. "Let Moscow know that Orlov is now based at Alconbury? If Langley ever finds out, there'll be a war. Why in heaven's name do that?"

"A test. If Moscow does not react, makes no attempt to harm Orlov, that will be the proof. Even the Americans will believe that. They'll be angry, of course, but they'll see the logic."

"And if the KGB attack and kill Orlov? You're going to be the one to tell Calvin Bailey?"

"They won't," said McCready.

"By the way, Calvin's coming here. On vacation, with wife and daughter. There's a file on your desk. I'd like the Firm to offer him some hospitality. He's been a good friend of Britain over the years."

Glumly McCready stumped downstairs and looked at the file. Denis Gaunt sat opposite him.

"He's an opera buff," said McCready, reading from the file. "You like opera?"

"Sure."

"Fine. You can mother-hen Calvin and Mrs. Bailey while they're here. Get tickets for Covent Garden and Glyndebourne. Use Timothy's name. This miserable job must have some perks, though I'm damned if I ever get any."

MAX KELLOGG SHUT HIMSELF inside the archives and lived there for ten days. Halfway through his investigation two agents were dispatched to Europe. One visited banks in Vienna and Frankfurt; the other, Stockholm and Helsinki. When they had what they came for, they returned to Washington and put their trophies on the desk of Max Kellogg.

From an original group of more than twenty CIA officers who had served in Vietnam in the relevant period—and Kellogg had expanded the time frame to include two years on either side of the dates quoted by Orlov—a dozen were quickly eliminated. One by one, the others went out of the frame. Either they were not in the right city at the right time or they could not have divulged a certain piece of information because they never knew it. Except one.

Kellogg knew he had his man. When he was ready, when he had it all, he went back to the house of the D.C.I., in Georgetown.

THREE days before he went, Calvin and Mrs. Bailey with their daughter, Clara, flew to London and installed themselves in a Mayfair apartment retained by the CIA for visiting V.I.P.s. Bailey loved London; he loved to visit the old castles and stately mansions built in a bygone era, to wander the cool cloisters of ancient abbeys and seats of learning.

On his second evening Joe Roth stopped by for a drink. He wanted to tell Bailey of the strain caused by Orlov's bombshell, but the D.C.I. had been adamant. No one, not even the head of Special Projects, was to be allowed to know—yet. So Joe Roth lied. He told Bailey the debriefing of Orlov was progressing well but at a slower pace. Naturally, the product Orlov remembered most clearly had already been divulged. Now it was a question of dragging smaller and smaller details from his memory.

As Roth sipped his drink Sam McCready turned up at the door. He had Denis Gaunt with him, and introductions were made again. Bailey was delighted with the tickets to the operas at Covent Garden and Glyndebourne. They would form the high point of the family's twelve-day visit to London.

"And then back to the States?" asked McCready.

"No. A quick visit to Paris, Salzburg, and Vienna, then home," said Bailey. McCready nodded. Salzburg and Vienna both had operas that were among the best in the world.

M<small>AX</small> K<small>ELLOGG</small> <small>SAT WITH THE</small> D.C.I. in the latter's library two nights later, with his files and his notes, copies of bank drafts, and photographs; and he talked.

The D.C.I. sat on the other side of the old oak refectory table placed between them to carry the paperwork. The old man seemed hunched into his velvet smoking jacket. The lights shone on his bald and wrinkled head. When Kellogg had finally finished, he asked, "There can be no doubt?"

Kellogg shook his head.

The D.C.I. sighed. "Go home, Max. Stay silent. I'll send for you when I need you again. Take a break. Rest."

Max Kellogg rose and left. The old man sat alone and thought of the old days, of friends and colleagues—bright young men and women—whom he had sent beyond the Atlantic wall and who had died under interrogation because of an informer, a traitor. He stared at the photo before him.

"You bastard," he said softly.

T<small>HE</small> following day a chit from the cipher room was brought to Sam McCready's office, at Century House. Denis Gaunt read it, whistled, and passed it over. It was a request from the CIA in Langley: during his vacation in Europe, Calvin Bailey was to have access to no classified information.

"Orlov?" asked Gaunt.

"Gets my vote," said McCready. "What the hell can I do to convince them?"

He made his own decision on that. He got a message to Keepsake, asking for a meeting without delay.

T<small>HAT</small> same evening Joe Roth sat at the refectory table at the D.C.I.'s mansion. The director sat opposite him, Max Kellogg to his right. The old man looked grim.

"Begin again, Max. At the beginning. Just the way you told it to me."

Kellogg glanced at Roth, adjusted his eyeglasses, and took a sheet from the top of the pile.

"In May 1967 Calvin Bailey was sent as a provincial officer, a G-twelve, to Vietnam. Here is the posting. He was assigned, as you see, to the Phoenix program. You've heard of that, Joe."

Roth nodded. At the height of the Vietnam War the Americans had mounted an operation to counter the drastic effects the Vietcong were having on the local population through selective, public, and sadistic assassinations. The notion was to use counterterror to identify and eliminate Vietcong activists.

It soon became the practice for Vietnamese to denounce any person against whom they had a grudge. Usually such people were handed over to the Vietnamese secret police or the army, the ARVN, who interrogated, tortured, and killed them.

"There were young Americans, fresh out of the States, who saw things down there that no man should be asked to watch. Some quit, some needed professional help. Calvin Bailey turned to the very philosophy of the men he had been sent to fight. This experience turned him into a communist sympathizer.

"In 1968 Bailey reported he had recruited two Vietnamese cousins, Nguyen Van Troc and Vo Nguyen Can, and infiltrated them into the Vietcong's own intelligence setup. According to Bailey, he ran these men for two years. According to Orlov, it was the other way around. They ran him. Look at this."

He passed Roth two photographs. One photograph showed two young Vietnamese males, taken against a background of the jungle. One man had a cross over his face, indicating he was now dead. The other photograph, taken much later, showed a group of Vietnamese officers on a veranda, being served tea.

"Look at the man on the left."

Roth looked. It was Nguyen Van Troc, ten years older but the same man. He wore a senior officer's shoulder boards.

"He's now deputy head of Vietnamese counterintelligence," said Kellogg. "Point made.

"Next we have Minstrel's assertion that Bailey was passed on to the KGB right there in Saigon. Minstrel named a now dead Swedish businessman as the KGB *Rezident* for Saigon in 1970. Swedish counterintelligence broke his cover story in 1980. Bailey could have seen him whenever he wanted.

"Next, Tokyo. Minstrel says Drozdov himself went there in the same year, 1970, and took over Bailey, giving him the name Sparrowhawk. And Bailey was there on those dates. Here is his movement order by Air America, our own airline. It all fits. He returned to America in 1971, a dedicated KGB agent."

"Fix yourself a drink, Joe," growled the D.C.I. "It gets worse."

"Minstrel named four European banks into which Moscow had made transfers of cash to the traitor. Here are the accounts—one each in Frankfurt, Helsinki, Stockholm, and Vienna. Here are the deposit slips—large sums and in cash. Payments all made within a month of the accounts being opened. Four tellers were shown a photograph; three identified it as the man who opened the accounts. This photograph."

Kellogg slipped a photograph of Calvin Bailey across to Roth. He stared at the face of Calvin Bailey in the photo, as if at the face of a stranger. He could not believe it. He had eaten with the man, drunk with him, met his family.

"In all, twenty-four precise items were extracted from Orlov, and twenty-one check out. That leaves three, much more recent. Joe, when Orlov called you that day in London, what name did he use?"

"Hayes," said Roth.

"Your professional name. How did he know it?"

Roth shrugged.

"Finally, we come to the two recent killings of the agents named by Orlov. Bailey told you to get the Orlov product to him first, by hand. Right?"

"Yes. But that is normal. He wanted to check it over first."

"When Orlov fingered Milton-Rice, Bailey got that first?"

Roth nodded.

"The Brits three days later?"

"Yes."

"And Milton-Rice was dead before the Brits could get to him. Same with Remyants. I'm sorry, Joe. It's watertight. There's just too much evidence."

Kellogg closed his last file and left Roth staring at the material in front of him—photos, bank statements, airline tickets. It was like a jigsaw puzzle assembled, not a piece missing. Even the motive—those awful experiences in Vietnam—was logical.

Kellogg was thanked and dismissed. The D.C.I. stared across the table. "What do you think, Joe?"

"You know the British think Minstrel's a phony," said Roth.

The D.C.I. made an irritable gesture of dismissal. "They have no proof, just the loser's resentment at not having gotten Minstrel to themselves. This is proof, Joe. Pages and pages of it."

Roth stared dumbly at the papers. He felt sick. Quietly he said, "What do you want me to do, sir?"

The D.C.I. rose and paced his elegant library. "I am the director of the Central Intelligence Agency. Appointed by the President himself. I am asked to protect this country as best I can from all her enemies. Some within, some without. We cannot have a massive scandal. There can be no arrest and trial, Joe. The trial has been here, the verdict has been reached, and the sentence must be from me, God help me."

"What do you want me to do?" repeated Roth.

"For a traitor there can be only one sentence, Joe. You will return to England, and before he can skip to Vienna and thence across the border into Hungary—which is assuredly what he has been preparing since Minstrel came over—you will do what has to be done."

"I'm not certain I can do that, sir."

The D.C.I. leaned over the table, and stared into the younger man's eyes. His own were as hard as obsidian. "You will do it, Joe. Because it is my order and because you will do it for your country. Go back to London and do what has to be done."

"Yes, sir," said Joe Roth.

CHAPTER FIVE

THE steamer pulled away from Westminster Pier precisely at three and began its leisurely journey downriver toward Greenwich. As it neared mid-river a man in a light gray suit quietly rose and walked to the stern, where he stood gazing down into the churning wake. Minutes later another man, in a light summer raincoat, went to join him.

"How are things at the embassy?" asked McCready.

"Not so good," said Keepsake. "The fact of a major counterintelligence operation is confirmed. So far, only the behavior of my junior staff is being gone over. But when they have been cleared, the focus of search will move higher—toward me."

"How long do you think you've got?"

"A few weeks at most."

"Be careful, my friend. Err on the side of caution."

"Don't worry." Keepsake smiled. "How are things with you?"

"Not good. We believe Orlov has denounced Calvin Bailey."

Keepsake whistled. "Sam, you must persuade them they are wrong, that Orlov is lying. There is a life at stake here."

"You don't really think—"

"Oh, yes, I do," said the Russian. "The D.C.I. is a passionate man. He will take the option of ensuring silence. Forever. But of course it will get out. The rumors will start quite soon because the KGB will ensure that they start. Orlov will have won."

"They still think Orlov's product is immensely valuable and pure. They believe him."

The Russian stared at the foaming water beneath the stern. "Did I ever tell you of my ashtray theory?"

"No," said McCready, "I don't think you did."

"When I taught at the KGB training school, I told my pupils that you take a cut-glass ashtray and smash it into three pieces. If you recover one piece, you have only a piece of glass. If you recover two, you have two thirds of an ashtray, but you cannot stub out your cigarette. To have the whole and usable article, you need all three pieces of the ashtray."

"So?"

"Orlov has never given the Americans a whole ashtray. Something really secret that the U.S.S.R. does not want to give away. Ask them to give Orlov an acid test. He will fail it. But when I come out, I will bring the whole ashtray. Then they will believe."

McCready pondered. Finally he asked, "Would Orlov know the name of the Fifth Man?"

Keepsake thought it over. "Almost certainly," he said. "Orlov spent years in the Illegals Directorate. We have both been in the Memory Room, but only he would have seen the black book."

Deep in the heart of KGB headquarters lies the Memory Room, commemorating the precursors of the present generation of KGB officers. Among the portraits hanging there are those of the most damaging spy ring ever recruited by the KGB among the British.

The recruitings took place mainly among a group of students at Cambridge University in the mid- and late '30s. One was Donald Maclean, who left Cambridge to join the Foreign Office. In the late '40s he was instrumental in passing hundreds of atomic secrets to Moscow. Another in the Foreign Office was Guy Burgess, a chain-smoking drunk and homosexual, who acted as go-between for Maclean and their Moscow masters. Both were finally blown in 1951 and fled to Moscow.

A third was Sir Anthony Blunt, also gay, a superb intellect and talent spotter for Moscow. A distinguished art historian, he was finally exposed and disgraced only in the 1980s.

The most successful of all was Kim Philby, who joined the SIS and rose to control the Soviet desk. The flight of Burgess and Maclean, in 1951, pointed the finger at him too, and he was ousted from the Service.

The portraits of all four hang in the Memory Room. But there was a fifth, and his portrait is a black square. The British had known that there was a Fifth Man, but they could never prove who it was. His identity was to be found only in the black book.

Over the years the enigma racked British intelligence. Was the Fifth Man still alive—perhaps highly placed in the government, the civil service, or the intelligence community? The matter could rest only when that man was finally identified. The KGB, of course, had jealously guarded that secret all those years.

"Tell the Americans to ask Orlov for the name," said Keepsake. "He will not give it to you. But I will find it out and bring it with me when I come over."

"They may not wait if you are right about the D.C.I.'s reaction."

"Is there no other way you can persuade them to stay their hand?" asked the Russian.

"There is. But I must have your permission."

Keepsake listened for several minutes. Then he nodded. "If this Roth will give his solemn, sworn word. And if you trust him to keep it. Then, yes."

WHEN Joe Roth stepped out of the airport terminal the next morning, having flown through the night from Washington, he found Sam McCready at his elbow. The bastard had evidently known about his false passport all along and had checked passenger lists from Washington.

"Jump in," said McCready when they reached the pavement. "I'll give you a lift to Mayfair."

Roth shrugged. Why not? He wondered what else McCready knew or had guessed. The British agent kept the conversation to small talk until they entered London's outskirts.

"What was the D.C.I.'s reaction?" he asked.

"Don't know what you're talking about."

"Come on, Joe. We've had a note at Century. 'Keep Bailey away from all classified material.' So we know he's under suspicion. You're saying it's not because Orlov has accused him of being a Soviet agent?"

"Don't push me, Sam. This is Company business now."

"Joe, for God's sake. It's gone too far. Orlov's lying to you, and I fear you are going to do something terrible."

Joe Roth lost his temper. "Stop the car," he shouted.

McCready swerved the Jaguar into the curb. Roth reached into the back for his suitcase and unlatched his door. McCready grabbed his arm.

"Joe, tomorrow, two thirty. I have something to show you. Pick you up outside your apartment block at two thirty."

"Get lost," said the American.

"A few minutes of your time. Is that too much to ask?"

Roth stepped out of the car and swung away down the pavement, looking for a cab.

But he was there, outside his apartment block, at half past two the next day. McCready waited in the Jaguar until Roth climbed in, and drove without saying a word. The journey to Mount Street was less than half a mile, and it was there that McCready stopped.

Halfway down Mount Street is one of London's finest fish restaurants, Scott's. At three precisely a trim man in a pale gray suit stepped out the doors and paused. A black limousine from the Soviet embassy eased down the street to pick him up.

"You asked me if we had an asset in the KGB in Moscow," said McCready quietly. "I denied it. I was not entirely lying. He's not in Moscow; he's here in London. You're looking at him."

"I don't believe it," whispered Roth. "That's Nikolai Gorodov. He's the head of the whole KGB *Rezidentura* in Britain."

"In the flesh. And he works for us, has done for four years."

"Prove it," said Roth.

"If Gorodov scratches his left ear with his right hand before he gets into the car, he's our man," said McCready.

The black limousine was abreast of the restaurant. Gorodov never glanced toward the Jaguar. He just raised his right hand, reached across his chest, tugged at his left earlobe, and climbed in. The embassy car purred away.

Roth breathed deeply several times. "I have to tell the D.C.I.," he said. "Personally. I can fly back."

"No deal," said McCready. "I have given Gorodov my word. I want to tell you about the ashtray theory." He told Roth what Keepsake had told him on the river steamer. "Ask Orlov for the name of the Fifth Man. He knows, but he will not tell you. But Keepsake will bring it with him when he comes over."

"When is that to be?"

"Soon now. A few weeks at most. Moscow is suspicious."

"One week," said Roth. "Bailey leaves for Salzburg and Vienna in one week. The D.C.I. thinks he's going to slip into Hungary."

"Have him recalled to Washington as a matter of urgency. If he obeys, that merits a further delay. If he refuses, I'll throw in the towel."

Roth considered the proposition. "I'll try it," he said. "First I'm going to Alconbury. Tomorrow, when I get back, if Orlov has refused to name the Fifth Man, I'll send a cable to the D.C.I., asking for Bailey's instant recall to Langley. As a test. I think the D.C.I. will grant that, at least. It will cause a delay of several weeks."

"More than enough, old friend. Keepsake will have come across by then, and we can all level with the D.C.I. Trust me."

Roth was at Alconbury just after sundown. He dined with Orlov that night and put to him the notion of the Memory Room, in Moscow.

Orlov nodded. "Sure, I have seen it. All inducted officers are taken there. To see the heroes and admire them."

Roth steered the conversation to the portraits of the five Englishmen.

Chewing on a mouthful of steak, Orlov shook his head. "Only four pictures. Burgess, Philby, Maclean, and Blunt."

"But there's a fifth frame, with just black paper in it?" suggested Roth.

Orlov was chewing much more slowly. "Yes," he admitted. "A frame, but no picture."

"So there *was* a Fifth Man?"

"Apparently." Something flickered in Orlov's eyes.

"Peter, who *was* the Fifth Man? His name, please."

"I do not know, my friend. I swear that to you." He smiled. "You want me to take the lie detector on it?"

Roth smiled back, but he thought, No, Peter, I rather think you can beat the lie detector—when you want to. He resolved to return to London in the morning and send his cable asking for Bailey's recall. If there was one tiny element of doubt, he would not carry out D.C.I.'s order. Some prices were just too high.

THE following morning the cleaning ladies came in to the Alconbury quarters. Roth was eating breakfast opposite Orlov in the mess hall, trying to talk above the noise of a rotary floor buffer in the corridor outside, when Orlov mentioned that he needed to go to the men's room. Seconds after he had left, Roth noticed a change in the tone of the buffing machine. He walked out into the corridor to look at it. The buffer stood alone, its brushes turning, its motor emitting a single high whine.

He had seen the cleaner when he went in for breakfast—a thin lady in print overalls, curlers in her hair, and a scarf wrapped over them. Now she was gone. At the end of the corridor the men's room door was still swinging gently.

Roth yelled, "Kroll!" and raced down the corridor. She was on her knees in the middle of the men's room floor, her plastic bucket of cleaning fluids and dusters spilled around her. In her hand she had the silenced Sig Sauer that the dusters had hidden. From the far end of the room a cubicle door opened, and Orlov stepped out. The kneeling assassin raised the gun.

Roth did not speak Russian, but he knew a few words. He yelled, *"Stoi!"* at the top of his voice.

She turned on her knees, Roth threw himself to the floor, there was a low phut, and Roth felt the shock waves near his head. He was still on the tiles when there was a boom from behind him.

Kroll stood in the doorway, his Colt gripped two-handed. There was no need for a second shot. The woman lay on her back on the tiles, a blooming red stain on her overalls.

Orlov still stood by the door of the cubicle, white-faced. "Games," he shouted. "It is enough of CIA games!"

"No game," said Roth as he got up. "This was the KGB."

It took Roth two hours to secure Orlov and the rest of the team a fast passage back to America and to arrange their immediate transfer to the Ranch. When the air force transport lifted off for the States, Roth headed back to London, bitterly angry.

He drove to the American embassy. There was only one thing to do to back the claim that Gorodov was a real defector and Orlov a phony. McCready would have to pull Gorodov out *now* so that Langley could talk to the man directly and sort it out once and for all. As he went to his desk to make the call to McCready in Century House, his head of station passed him in the corridor.

"Oh, by the way," said Bill Carver. "Something just came in, courtesy of Century. Seems our Soviet friends are moving things around. Their *Rezident*, Gorodov, flew back to Moscow this morning. It's on your desk."

Roth did not make the call to McCready. He sat at his desk. He was stunned. He was also vindicated—he and his Agency. He had no more doubts now, not a shred. The D.C.I. was right. What had to be done had to be done.

"I'm sorry, Sam," Timothy Edwards said, "but it's an utter bloody fiasco. I've just had a word with the chief. We are seriously contemplating that Keepsake was a Soviet plant all along."

"He wasn't," said McCready flatly.

"So you say. Did he give you any indication that he intended to return to Moscow?"

"No."

"When was he due to quit and come across to us?"

"Two, three weeks," said McCready. "He was going to tell me when his situation had become hopeless, then jump the fence."

"Well, he hasn't. He's gone home. We have to assume now that Moscow *is* his real home. And then there's this damned Alconbury business. You said it was a test. Well, Orlov has passed it with flying colors."

"I still don't believe Keepsake was bent. He promised years ago to bring back one last big consignment before he came over. I have a gut feeling he's gone back for it."

"Gut feeling!" expostulated Edwards. "We can't achieve anything on gut feeling."

"Columbus did. Mind if I see the chief?"

"You're welcome. I don't think you'll get any change."

But McCready did. The chief listened to his proposal, then asked, "And supposing he's loyal to Moscow, after all?"

"Then I'll know within seconds."

"But, Sam, this is a job for a field team."

"Keepsake won't trust anyone else. You know that."

The chief sighed. "True. If anyone goes, you go. Is that it?"

" 'Fraid so."

The chief thought it over. To lose Keepsake would be a devastating blow. If there was a tenth of a chance that McCready was right and Gorodov was not a plant after all, the Service should try to pull him out of there. But the political fallout of a major scandal—the Deceiver caught red-handed in Moscow—would ruin him. He sighed. "All right, Sam. You can go. But you are on your own. As of now I have never heard of you."

McCready prepared to go on those terms. It took him three days to make his plans.

On the second day Joe Roth rang Calvin Bailey.

"Calvin, I've just come back from Alconbury. I think we should talk. Why don't you let me offer you dinner tomorrow night? I know this marvelous old inn up the Thames, at Eton. They say Henry the Eighth used to have Anne Boleyn rowed up the river for secret meetings with her there."

"Really? That old? Okay. Look, Joe, tomorrow night we're at Covent Garden. Thursday is clear."

"Right, Calvin. Thursday it is."

ON THURSDAY three men entered Moscow on different flights. The first in was Rabbi Birnbaum from Zurich.

The passport control officer gazed at the rabbi at length, then turned his attention to the passport. It was American, denoting the holder to be one Norman Birnbaum, age fifty-six.

The rabbi was a stout man in a black suit and wore a full beard and mustache. On his face, topped by a black homburg, his eyes were masked by lenses so thick, the pupils blurred as the man peered to see. Twisted gray ringlets hung from beneath his hatband down each side of his face.

The visa was in order, issued by the Soviet consulate general in New York.

"The purpose of your visit to Moscow?" the officer asked.

"I want to visit my son for a short stay. He works at the American embassy here."

"Moment, please," said the officer. He rose and retired behind a glass door. Orthodox rabbis were rare in the Soviet Union.

Phone calls were made. Someone in Moscow consulted a diplomatic list. Apparently there was a Roger Birnbaum listed at the economic section of the U.S. embassy. The list did not record, however, that Roger Birnbaum's real father had retired to Florida. The rabbi was waved through.

They still checked his suitcase at customs. It contained the usual changes of clothing, wash kit, and a copy of the Talmud in Hebrew. The customs officer let the rabbi go.

Rabbi Birnbaum took the Aeroflot coach into central Moscow, drawing several curious or amused glances all the way. From the terminus building he walked to the National Hotel, on Manezh Square, entered the men's room, and slipped into a cubicle.

When he emerged, he was still in a dark jacket, but the reversible trousers were now medium gray. The hat was inside the suitcase, along with the bushy eyebrows, the beard, and mustache. His hair, instead of gray, was chestnut brown, and his torso was covered by a canary-yellow polo-neck sweater. He took a cab to the British embassy, on the embankment opposite the Kremlin. In fact, his real name was David Thornton, and he was one of the best makeup artists in British films.

The second man to arrive in Moscow came direct from London by British Airways. He was Denis Gaunt, looking like himself, save that his hair was grayed to make him look older. He had a slim attaché case chained to his left wrist, and he wore the blue tie bearing the motif of the Corps of Queen's Messengers.

All countries have diplomatic couriers who spend their lives ferrying documents from embassy to embassy. They are diplomatic personnel, and their luggage is not searched. Gaunt was met by a car and taken at once to the embassy building, arriving there an hour after Thornton. He was then able to give Thornton all the tools of the makeup artist's trade that he had brought in his own suitcase.

The third to arrive was Sam McCready, from Helsinki. Like Gaunt, he had a valid British passport in a false name, and he too was disguised. But in the heat of the aircraft something had gone wrong. His ginger wig had come slightly askew, and a wisp of darker hair showed from beneath it. A fragment of his equally ginger mustache had detached itself from his upper lip.

The passport officer stared at the picture in the passport. The face was the same—hair, mustache, and all. There is nothing illegal about wearing a wig, even in Russia, but a mustache that comes unstuck? The passport officer consulted his senior, who peered through a one-way mirror. A camera clicked several times.

When McCready emerged from the concourse, two unmarked Moskvitch cars were waiting. He too was collected by a car and was driven to the embassy, but he was followed all the way by the two KGB vehicles.

In the late afternoon the photos of the strange visitor arrived at Yazenevo, the headquarters of the KGB's foreign intelligence arm, the First Chief Directorate. They ended up on the desk of the deputy head, General Vadim V. Kirpichenko, after the photographic lab had airbrushed out the wig and mustache.

General Kirpichenko almost laughed out loud. "Well, I'll be damned," he murmured. "It's Sam McCready."

He ordered a twenty-four-hour tail. "If he makes a contact, pick them both up. If he makes a collection from a drop, pick him up."

In the embassy on the embankment, McCready, Gaunt, and Thornton dined alone.

"I hope it works," said Gaunt over the coffee. "The Russians are extremely good at playing chess."

"True," said McCready soberly. "Tomorrow we'll find out how good they are at the three-card trick."

CHAPTER SIX

AT PRECISELY five minutes to eight on a warm July morning an unmarked Austin Montego sedan drove out the gates of Britain's Moscow embassy toward the center of the city.

According to the KGB report, Sam McCready was at the wheel, driving alone. Although his ginger wig and mustache were now impeccably in place, they were clearly visible to the watchers in their several cars. Telephoto-lens pictures were taken at the time, and several more were secured during the course of the day.

The British agent drove carefully through Moscow and out to the Park of Technological Achievement, to the north of the city.

Once there, he left his car and proceeded on foot, enveloped by an invisible screen of KGB.

He bought an ice cream and sat for much of the morning on a bench, pretending to read a newspaper, frequently glancing at his watch as if waiting for someone to show up. No one did except an old lady, who asked him for the time. He showed her his watch without a word. She thanked him and walked on.

She was promptly taken into custody, searched, and questioned. The ice-cream seller was also detained.

Shortly after twelve the Englishman took out a packet of sandwiches and slowly ate them. When he had finished, he dropped the wrapping paper into a wastebasket. The trash basket was kept under observation, and the wrappers were later taken by the KGB and subjected to intensive forensic analysis. Nothing was found except traces of bread, butter, cucumber, and egg.

Just after one p.m. the London agent left the park in his car and drove back to the British embassy. Ten minutes later he left again, in a Jaguar driven by an embassy chauffeur. As the Jaguar left the city, heading for the airport, the leader of the watcher team was patched through to General Kirpichenko.

"He is approaching the concourse now, Comrade General."

"He has made no contact of any kind?"

"No, Comrade General. Apart from the old lady and the ice-cream seller—now both in custody—he has spoken to no one."

It's a mission abort, thought Kirpichenko.

"Let him go," he said. "Watch for a brush-pass inside the airport concourse. If there is none, see him through the departure lounge and into the aircraft."

Later the general would examine his team's telephoto pictures of McCready, in the Montego and at the park, and shout, "You idiots, that's not McCready."

AT TEN past eight on the morning of the same day a Jaguar driven by Barry Martins, the SIS station head, left the embassy and drove sedately toward the elegant old district of the Arbat. A single Moskvitch took up the tail, but this was purely routine. The Jaguar drove aimlessly around the Arbat, the driver occasionally pulling into the curb to consult a map.

At twenty past eight a Mercedes left the embassy. At the wheel, in a blue jacket and peaked cap, was an embassy chauffeur. No one looked in the rear, so no one saw another figure crouched low and covered with a blanket. Another Moskvitch fell in behind.

Entering the Arbat district, the Mercedes passed the parked Jaguar. At this point Martins put down his map and swerved out from the curb, taking space between the Mercedes and the following Moskvitch. The convoy now constituted a Mercedes, a Jaguar, and two Moskvitches, all in line astern.

The Mercedes entered a narrow one-way street, followed by the Jaguar, which then developed engine trouble and came to a halt. The two Moskvitches piled up behind it.

The Mercedes disappeared down the street and turned the corner. Clearing the Arbat, David Thornton, at the wheel, took his guidance from Sam McCready, who without any disguise at all emerged from his blanket and gave directions.

Twenty minutes later, on a lonely road screened by trees in Gorki Park, the Mercedes halted. At the rear, McCready took off the CD plate and stuck a new license plate over the British one. Thornton did the same at the front. McCready retrieved Thornton's makeup box from the trunk and climbed into the rear seat. Thornton swapped his hard, blue peaked cap for a more Russian black leather cap and got back behind the wheel.

At eighteen minutes past nine Colonel Nikolai Gorodov left his apartment in Shabolovsky Street and began to walk toward the headquarters of the KGB. He looked haggard and pale; the reason soon appeared behind him. Two men emerged from a doorway and without a pretense of subtlety took station behind him.

He had gone two hundred yards when a black Mercedes drew to the curb beside him and kept pace. He heard a voice say in English, "Good morning, Colonel. Going my way?"

Gorodov stopped and stared. Framed in the window, shielded by the rear curtains from the two KGB men up the street, was Sam McCready. Gorodov was stunned, but not triumphant.

That, thought McCready, is the look I wanted to see.

Gorodov recovered and said loudly enough for the KGB ferrets to hear, "Thank you, Comrade. How kind."

Then he entered the car, which sped away. The two KGB men paused. They had seen that the license plates of the Mercedes bore the letters MOC, which are exclusive to members of the

Central Committee, and it is a bold KGB foot soldier who dares stop a Central Committee man.

Gorodov leaned back in the seat, his bridges now completely burned behind him.

"If you are a long-term Soviet mole, I am dead," remarked McCready. "Why did you return?"

"As it turned out, a mistake," said Gorodov. "I had promised you something, and I found I could not discover it in London. Then Moscow summoned me back for urgent consultations. I thought I could come for one week, find out what I needed, and return to London. Only when I got here did I learn that it was too late. By the way, I have something for you."

He opened his attaché case and passed McCready a slim file. There were five sheets in the file, each with a photograph and a name. The first four pictures were of Maclean, Burgess, Philby, and Blunt. McCready turned to the fifth page.

The photo was very old. It showed a thin young man, with wild wavy hair and large, owlish glasses. Beneath the photo were two words: John Cairncross. McCready leaned back and sighed.

"Bloody hell. Him all along."

Cairncross had been a senior civil servant during and after the war, serving in a variety of capacities in signals intelligence at Bletchly Park, in the Treasury, and the War Office. He had had access to nuclear secrets in the late '40s. In the early '50s he had come under suspicion, conceded nothing, and been eased out. By 1986 he was in retirement in France.

The Fifth Man. Keepsake had made good on his promise.

Thornton parked again in the trees of Gorki Park, changed places with one of the men in the rear, and went to work. On went the inflatable undervest to give the slimmer man the sturdy bulk of Rabbi Birnbaum. Then the white shirt, black trousers, tie, and jacket. Thornton affixed the beard and mustache and appended the curling gray ringlets of the Orthodox rabbi. With the addition of the black homburg, Rabbi Birnbaum had been re-created exactly— except that he was a different man. Finally the car was changed back to a British embassy vehicle.

The rabbi was dropped off at the National Hotel. After a sustaining lunch he took a cab to the airport. He was booked on the afternoon flight to London, connecting to New York.

Thornton drove the car back into the British embassy compound with his other client crouched under the rug in the back. He went to work again almost at once with an identical ginger wig and mustache. Ten minutes after Denis Gaunt, hot and itchy under the ginger wig he had worn all day for the benefit of the KGB, drove back in his Montego, the other man left for the airport in the Jaguar, driven by a real chauffeur. Within an hour Thornton, transformed into the Queen's messenger, was himself driven there by Barry Martins.

The rabbi drew the usual curious glances, but his papers were in order, and he was passed through the formalities.

The man in the ginger wig and mustache was almost escorted to the door of the departure lounge, so anxious were the KGB to ensure that he neither passed nor received a message.

Last to arrive was the Queen's messenger, his attaché case chained to his left wrist. This time Thornton's precious workbox was in his own suitcase, which could not be searched.

Denis Gaunt remained inside the embassy, to be exfiltrated three days later, posing as a messenger.

The British Airways flight cleared Soviet airspace at five fifteen. Shortly after that, the rabbi walked down to the smoking section and said to the man in the ginger wig and mustache, "Nikolai, my friend, you are now in the West."

Then Sam McCready bought Champagne for them both, and for the Queen's messenger. The scam had worked, and they landed at Heathrow just after seven.

As a concession, Timothy Edwards allowed McCready to take Nikolai Gorodov to his own apartment for the evening.

It was just after ten that evening when Joe Roth arrived, summoned by a phone call from McCready. He found two SIS heavies in the hallway and two more in the corridor outside McCready's modest flat. McCready appeared in slacks and sweater, a glass of whiskey in his hand. "Come on in, Joe. There's someone I have wanted you to meet for a long time."

He led the way into the sitting room. The man at the window turned and smiled. "Good evening, Mr. Roth," said Gorodov. "Good to meet you at last."

Roth stood as if paralyzed. Then he slumped into a chair and took McCready's proffered whiskey. Gorodov sat opposite Roth.

"You'd better tell it," said McCready to the Russian. "You know it better than I."

The Russian sipped his drink as he pondered where to begin. "Project Potemkin started eight years ago," he said. "General Drozdov's aim was to denounce a senior CIA officer as a Soviet plant, destroy morale among the staff, and wreck the relationship with the SIS in Britain. The choice fell on Calvin Bailey for two reasons. We knew he was not much liked inside the Agency. And he had served in Vietnam, a suitable place for a recruitment.

"Drozdov's breakthrough came when he was examining your papers that came to us from the Vietnamese after the fall of Saigon, in 1975. One mentioned a certain Nguyen Van Troc, who had worked for the Americans.

"That paper was the end for Van Troc. He and his cousin were picked up—they had not managed to escape. The cousin was executed, but Van Troc, although brutally interrogated, was finally sent to a North Vietnamese slave labor camp. That was where Drozdov found him, still alive, in 1980. Under torture he confessed he had worked for Calvin Bailey inside the Vietcong.

"Van Troc was taken from the camp, fattened on good food, and dressed in the uniform of a colonel of Hanoi's intelligence arm. Photos were taken of him enjoying tea with other officers. One copy found its way to Langley.

"Drozdov already knew Bailey had been involved in the Phoenix program. He had been spotted by our *Rezident* in Saigon, a man posing as a Swedish businessman. His purely routine visit to Tokyo in 1970 had been noted. So Drozdov only had to brief Orlov to say that he, Drozdov, had been in Tokyo on the same dates.

"Pyotr Orlov was chosen as the disinformation agent about 1981; he has been in training and rehearsal ever since, preparing himself to avoid the traps, beat the polygraph, and always tell you what you wanted to hear.

"After Drozdov had picked Bailey as the victim, Bailey went under intensive scrutiny. When he began to travel to Europe and elsewhere to visit the outstations, the bank accounts began. Drozdov prepared an actor—a dead ringer for Bailey—to fly at a moment's notice to open these accounts so that the bank teller would later recognize Bailey as the client.

"Triumphs secured by the KGB against the CIA were attributed to Bailey. CIA operations that went sour were attributed to Bailey. What Drozdov did was change the dates. Pieces of secret intelligence that we did not learn until the early '80s were, according to Orlov, acquired in the mid-'70s. It looked as if we had found out earlier than we possibly could have—without a CIA traitor, that is.

"But two years ago Drozdov still lacked something. He needed inside-Langley gossip, nicknames known only in the building—your own professional name of Hayes, Mr. Roth. Then a CIA defector named Edward Howard came over, and Drozdov had it all.

"Finally Orlov was allowed to come over, in a manner so bizarre that he could later claim he feared he would be stopped and betrayed by Sparrowhawk if he did it any other way. He denounced the two KGB agents just before they were liquidated. It was all pretimed, but it looked as if there were a leak in Washington. When the customer was ready for the bait, he finally came clean with news of a Soviet mole high in the CIA. No?"

Roth nodded. He looked haggard. "That assassination attempt against Orlov at Alconbury. Why?" he asked.

"That was Drozdov overinsuring. He just wanted to pile on a bit more evidence. The lady was one of the best. She was briefed to wound, not kill, then make her escape."

There was silence in the room. Joe Roth stared at his drink. Then he rose. "I must go," he said shortly.

McCready accompanied him down the stairs. In the hall he clapped the American on the back. "Cheer up, Joe. Hell, everyone in this game makes mistakes. Look on the bright side. You can go back to the embassy and cable the D.C.I. that everything's worked out. Bailey's in the clear."

"I'll think I'll fly back and tell him myself," muttered Roth.

Puzzled by his friend's silence, McCready returned to the apartment. In the sitting room he found Gorodov sitting staring at a copy of the *Evening Standard*. Without a word he flicked it across the table and pointed to an item on page 5:

Police divers today recovered the body of an American tourist from the Thames, at Teddington Lock. According to an official spokesman, the body is believed to have entered the water somewhere near Eton yesterday evening. The dead man has been identified as one Calvin Bailey, an American civil servant on holiday in London.

McCready put down the paper and stared toward the door. "Oh, you bastard," he whispered, "you poor bloody bastard."

Joe Roth took the first morning flight to Washington and went to the Georgetown mansion. He handed in his resignation, effective twenty-four hours later. Before he left, he had made one request. The D.C.I. granted it.

Roth reached the Ranch very late that night.

Colonel Orlov was still awake, listening to a Seekers album from 1965. Kroll came in first and took up position by the wall. There was a bulge under his left armpit. Roth followed and closed the door behind him. Orlov looked up, puzzled.

Roth just stared at him with very cold eyes. Orlov's puzzlement ebbed, and a resigned awareness took its place. No one spoke.

Kroll's hand moved sideways toward the tape deck, and silence returned. Orlov spoke one word, almost his first in Russian since he arrived in America. He said, *"Kto?"* It means, "Who?"

Roth said, "Gorodov."

It was like a punch in the stomach. Orlov closed his eyes and shook his head as if in disbelief. The price of the bride had been paid and accepted, but there would be no wedding.

Kroll pulled out his gun. "Let's go," he said.

Then Colonel Pyotr Alexandrovich Orlov, a very brave man and a patriot, rose and went into the darkness to meet the mighty God who made him.

INTERLUDE

"WELL now, that's all very fine, Denis, and most impressive," said Timothy Edwards when the board reconvened on Wednesday morning. "But we have to ask ourselves, Will these remarkable talents ever be needed in the future?"

"I don't follow you, Timothy," said Denis Gaunt.

Sam McCready looked out at the bright blue sky beyond the windows. There was another world out there, one that he would soon have to join. If his wife, May, were still alive, he would want to retire with her, find a small cottage by the sea in Devon or Cornwall. He had sometimes dreamed of his own small fishing boat, bobbing in a stone-walled harbor.

"I mean simply," Timothy Edwards was saying, "that relations with the U.S.S.R. have changed out of all recognition; there will be no more defectors, just honored guests."

"Sam realizes as well as any of us that we cannot dwell in the past," Gaunt said. "The point is, there are other menaces to our country, and they are on the increase." He took a buff folder from the records clerk. "Let me remind you of the affair that began in April 1986 and ended in the late spring of 1987. Such affairs will happen again, and it will be the Firm's task to head them off— again. Get rid of Sam McCready? Frankly, gentlemen, that could be very foolish."

The controllers for Western Hemisphere and Domestic Operations nodded, while Edwards glowered at them.

" 'On April 16, 1986,' " Gaunt read out, " 'fighters from American carriers in the Gulf of Sidra and fighter-bombers flying from British bases blasted the private living quarters of Colonel Qaddafi, outside Tripoli. Qaddafi vowed vengeance, just as much on Britain as upon America. In the early spring of 1987 we learned how Qaddafi intended to extract that revenge upon Britain, and the case was given to Sam McCready. . . .' "

A CASUALTY OF WAR

CHAPTER ONE

FATHER Dermot O'Brien received the message from Libya by the normal route for such first communications—by mail.

It was a perfectly ordinary letter. The postmark said that it came from Geneva, as indeed it had, and the return address indicated the writer worked for the World Council of Churches, which he did not. Father O'Brien found it in his pigeonhole outside the refectory after breakfast one morning in the early spring of 1987. He took it with him to his bedroom, on the first floor of the old manor house that was the headquarters of his order.

The letter began, "My dear Dermot," and was written in the tone of one old friend involved in pastoral work to another. The meat was in the third paragraph. The writer said that his bishop recalled with pleasure a previous meeting with Father O'Brien and would be delighted to meet him again. The sign-off was simply, "Your good friend Harry."

Father O'Brien gazed from his window across the green fields that he loved so dearly, as dearly indeed as he hated the great enemy that lay beyond the Irish Sea.

The letter intrigued him. It had been almost two years since he had visited Tripoli for a personal audience with Colonel Muammar Qaddafi—leader of the Libyan People's Jamahariya, the socialist republic—the man referred to as the bishop in the letter. It had been a rare and privileged occasion, but despite the extravagant promises, nothing had been forthcoming. No money, no arms for the Irish cause. Finally it had been a disappointment, and the man who had arranged the meeting, Hakim al-Mansour, head of the foreign arm of the Libyan secret service—the Mukhabarat—who now signed himself Harry, had been apologetic.

And now this—a summons, for that was what it was. The snag would be to find a good excuse to travel again so soon. Father O'Brien had but three days earlier returned from Amsterdam, ostensibly from a seminar of the War on Want.

Traveling was, for Dermot O'Brien, a constant part of his life. His order busied itself with missionary and ecumenical work, and he was its international secretary. It was the perfect cover for the war against the English, which had been his calling and his life since he had held the broken head of a dying young man in Derry all those years ago and seen the British paratroopers running down the street, and spoken the last rites, and made his other, personal vow, of which his order knew nothing.

For ten years he had been the principal international fixer for the Provisional IRA. He had raised the funds, secured false passports, and arranged for the safe arrival and storage of the Semtex explosives. With his help, the bombs in Regent's Park and Hyde Park and outside Harrods had ripped out entrails and severed limbs. He regretted that it was necessary, but he knew it was just.

His problem that spring morning was fortuitously solved by a small announcement in the Dublin *Press,* still lying on his bed. He made two calls, and during the second he received a warm welcome to join the group whose forthcoming pilgrimage had been announced in the paper. Then he went to see his superior.

"I need the experience, Frank," he said. "I need the peace and the time to pray. If you can spare me, I would like to go."

The superior glanced at the itinerary and nodded. "Go with my blessing, Dermot. Pray for us all while you are there."

The pilgrimage was one week away. Father O'Brien sent a letter to London, paying the extra to guarantee twenty-four-hour delivery, knowing it would reach the Libyan People's Bureau— the Libyan government's term for its embassies—within three days. That would give Tripoli time to make their arrangements.

THE pilgrimage was by chartered jet from Shannon Airport to Lourdes, in the foothills of the French Pyrenees. There Father O'Brien slipped away from the crowd of pilgrims and boarded the small charter plane waiting for him at the Lourdes airport. It deposited him four hours later at Valletta, Malta, where the Libyans took him over. Their unmarked executive jet landed at a small military base outside Sirte, in Libya. Hakim al-Mansour, urbane and gracious as ever, was there to meet him.

The two men talked in a room at the base, set aside for them and ringed by Mansour's personal guards. When they had finished, the Irishman left again for Malta and Lourdes. He was excited. What he had learned, if it came to fruition, would constitute a huge breakthrough for his cause.

Hakim al-Mansour secured his personal interview with Qaddafi three days later. The great leader was in what Mansour privately called the Bedouin mood that day, lounging on a pile of cushions in a large and ornate tent at his desert encampment, dressed in a white caftan. He appeared as languid as ever as he took a sip of water and asked for Mansour's report.

The younger officer gave his report without frills or exaggerations. Like all those around the Libyan leader, he was somewhat in awe of Muammar Qaddafi. The man was an enigma, and men are always in awe of an enigma, especially one who, with a wave of his hand, could require your immediate execution.

Mansour knew that many foreigners believed Qaddafi to be mad. He, Mansour, knew there was nothing mad about Muammar Qaddafi. The man would not have survived eighteen years of supreme and unquestioned mastery of this turbulent, fragmented, and violent land if he were deranged.

He was in fact a subtle and skilled political operator. He had made his mistakes, and he entertained his illusions—notably about the world outside his own country. On this, Hakim al-Mansour, raised in a British public school, was the expert. Mansour knew Qaddafi had a soft spot for him. It was justified—the head of the foreign arm of the Mukhabarat had, in younger days, proved his loyalty by personally executing three of Qaddafi's political opponents in their European bolt-holes.

That day in April, 1987, Hakim al-Mansour told Qaddafi of the visit of the Irish priest. As he talked, one of Qaddafi's personal doctors, who had been mixing a potion in the corner, approached the Libyan leader, who still suffered nightmares as a result of the American bombing. The doctor gave him a mild sedative.

"The fifty-fifty split of the material—it is accepted?" he asked after swallowing the draft.

"The priest will report that condition," said Mansour. "I am confident the IRA Army Council will agree."

"And the matter of the American ambassador?"

"That too."

Qaddafi sighed in the manner of one on whose shoulders too many of the world's burdens are placed. "Not enough," he said dreamily. "There must be more. On mainland America."

"The search goes on, Excellency. The tools of your vengeance will be found."

Qaddafi nodded several times, then gestured that the interview was over. "See to it," he murmured softly.

THE gathering of intelligence is a strange business. Rarely does one single coup provide all the answers. Mostly the picture appears piece by piece, as in a jigsaw puzzle. Before the end of April two pieces of a new puzzle had arrived at Century House.

One came from the Libyan doctor who had given Qaddafi his medicine. The man had once had a son studying in England. The Mukhabarat had approached him and suggested that if he loved his father, he should carry out a task for the great leader. The bomb they had given him to plant had gone off prematurely. The father had hidden his grief well, but his heart had turned to hatred, and he passed what information he could glean from his position with Qaddafi to the British.

His report of what he had heard in the tent was considered important enough to go straight to the top.

"He's going to do *what?*" asked the chief when he was told.

"It seems he has offered a gift of explosives and weaponry to the IRA," said Timothy Edwards.

"How was the offer made?"

"Apparently via an unknown Irish priest flown into Libya."

"Right. Well, we must find out who this mysterious cleric is. I'll tell the Box and see if they have anything."

Box Five Hundred is the in-house term for MI5, the British Security Service, which has the task of counterterrorism in Northern Ireland, as British territory. The SIS has the mandate for operations outside Britain, including the Republic of Ireland. Two days later an MI5 operation came up with the second piece of the jigsaw puzzle.

A young IRA man, driving a car with an Armalite rifle in the trunk, tried to crash a roadblock manned by the Royal Ulster Constabulary. As the stolen car suddenly surged ahead, an officer, standing well back, brought up his rifle and fired four shots into the accelerating car. One of them took off the top of the teenager's head.

He was only a messenger boy, but to the IRA he merited a funeral with full military honors. It took place in Ballycrane, the dead youth's native village, in south Armagh. The grieving family, hard-line Republicans all, agreed that the service be conducted by Father Dermot O'Brien.

The funerals of IRA men buried in Northern Ireland provide a useful venue for IRA leaders to get together and confer. The IRA chiefs can hold muttered conferences, plan, decide, relay information, or set up future operations. Thus the IRA uses the supposed sanctity of death to plan further slaughter.

When the British learned of this, they were not slow to catch up. It was once said that the most important thing an English gentleman ever learns is precisely when to stop being one.

So the British bug the coffins.

On the night before the funeral at Ballycrane, two Special Air Service soldiers in civilian clothes broke into the funeral parlor where the empty coffin stood waiting. The body, in Irish tradition, was still laid out in the family's front parlor. Within an hour they implanted the bug in the woodwork of the coffin.

From deep cover on a hillside the next day, the SAS soldiers kept watch on the funeral, photographing every face with a camera whose lens resembled a bazooka tube. Another man monitored the sounds emanating from the device in the coffin.

At the open grave, the priest, his cassock billowing in the breeze, intoned the last words and scattered a little earth on the coffin as it went down. Beside Father O'Brien stood a man known to be the deputy chief of staff of the IRA Army Council. Heads down, lips hidden, they began to mutter. What they said went onto the tape on the hillside. It was only a routine operation, but it came up with pure gold. Father O'Brien had reported to the Army Council the full details of Colonel Qaddafi's offer.

"*How* much?" asked Sir Anthony, the chairman of the Joint Intelligence Committee, two days later in London.

"Twenty tons, Tony. That's the offer."

The director general of MI5 closed the file that his colleagues had just finished reading and returned it to his briefcase.

"And the conditions?" asked Sir Anthony. "No doubt about them?"

"None," said the D.G. "Within the twenty tons will be the usual machine guns, rifles, grenades, launchers, mortars, pistols, and bazookas—probably the Czech RPG-7. Plus two metric tons of Semtex-H. Of this, half must be used for a bombing campaign on mainland Britain, to include the assassination of the American ambassador. Apparently the Libyans were very insistent on that."

"I want you to take it all to the SIS," said Sir Anthony at last. "It looks as if this will be an overseas operation. I want you to give them your absolute cooperation, from you downward."

"No question," said the D.G. "They'll have it."

Before nightfall the chief of the SIS and his deputy Timothy Edwards attended a lengthy briefing at the Curzon Street headquarters of their sister service. MI5 would increase surveillance on the IRA Army Council man. So long as Father O'Brien remained in the north, the same would apply to him. When he returned to the Irish republic, the SIS would take over. Surveillance would also be doubled on the one other man mentioned in the graveside conversation, a man well known to British security forces, but who had never yet been charged or imprisoned.

When he returned to Century House, the chief summoned Sam McCready.

"Stop it, Sam," he said finally. "Stop it at its source in Libya or in transit. Those twenty tons must not get through."

Sam McCready sat for hours in a darkened viewing room watching the film of the funeral. Nothing remotely suspicious was said until the priest stood, his head bowed, by the grave, with the IRA Army Council man beside him. The priest raised his head once to offer words of comfort to the teenager's weeping mother.

"Freeze-frame. Close-up. Enhance."

When the face of Father O'Brien filled the screen, McCready stared at it for twenty minutes, memorizing every feature.

Later he sat alone and stared at photographs in his office. One was of Hakim al-Mansour, stepping out of a car in Paris, exquisitely tailored by Savile Row—smooth, urbane, charming, and utterly lethal. Another was of the chief of staff, IRA Army Council, addressing a public meeting in Belfast. There was a third picture: that of the man mentioned by the graveside as the one who would probably be chosen to run the operation. A former commander of the IRA's South Armagh Brigade, he was now head of Special Projects, a very intelligent, highly experienced, and ruthless killer. His name was Kevin Mahoney.

McCready tried to glean some knowledge of the brains behind the faces. To win, he would have to match his mind with theirs. He had two advantages. One, he knew what they had in mind, but they did not know he knew. And two, he could recognize them, but they did not know him. Or did Mansour know his face? The Libyan had worked with the KGB; the Russians knew McCready.

The chief was not prepared to take the risk. "I'm sorry, Sam. You are absolutely not going in yourself. I don't care if there's only a one percent chance they have your face on file, the answer is no. You'll have to find someone else."

So McCready went through the files day after day, sifting and sorting, considering and rejecting. Eventually he came up with a name, a possible. And he took it to Timothy Edwards.

"You're crazy, Sam," said Edwards. "You know he's absolutely unacceptable. MI Five hate his guts. We're trying to cooperate with them, and you produce this—turncoat. We'd never employ him."

"That's the point," said Sam quietly.

Edwards shifted his ground. "Anyway, he'd never work for us."

"He might."

"Give me one good reason why."

McCready gave it.

"Well," said Edwards, "as far as the record goes, the man's an outsider. Use of him is absolutely forbidden. Is that clear?"

"Completely," said McCready.

"On the other hand," added Edwards, "you'll probably follow your own instincts anyway."

McCready steered his car out of the small town of Cricklade and across the unmarked county line into Gloucestershire.

The converted barn was tucked down a side road—an old Cotswold stone affair that had once housed cattle and hay. The conversion to a quiet country house had been done well. It was surrounded by a stone wall set with wagon wheels, and the garden was bright with spring flowers. McCready drove through the gate and drew up outside the timber door. A pretty young woman, weeding a flowered border, put down her trowel and stood up.

"Hello," she said. "Have you come about a rug?"

So, he thought, he's selling rugs as a sideline. Perhaps the information about his book not selling too well was true.

"No, 'fraid not," he said. "Actually, I've come to see Tom."

Her smile faded, and an element of suspicion entered her eyes. "He's writing. In his shed at the bottom of the garden. He finishes in about an hour. Can you wait?"

"Certainly."

She gave him coffee in the bright, chintz-curtained sitting room, and they waited. Conversation wilted. At last they heard the tramp of feet coming through the kitchen. She jumped up.

"Nikki—"

Tom Rowse appeared in the door and stopped. His smile did not flicker, but his eyes took in McCready and became very watchful.

"Darling, this gentleman has come to see you. We've been waiting. Would you like a coffee?"

"Sure, love a coffee."

She left. McCready introduced himself. Rowse sat down. The records had said he was thirty-three. They did not say that he looked extremely fit. They did not need to.

Tom Rowse had been a captain in the Special Air Service regiment. Three years earlier he had left the army, married Nikki, and bought the barn. He had done the conversion himself, working out his rage through the long days. By night he wrote.

It had to be a novel, of course; a nonfiction work would have been banned under the Official Secrets Act. Even so, it had caused outrage in the Curzon Street headquarters of MI5. The book was about Northern Ireland, seen from the point of view of an undercover soldier, and it mocked the counterintelligence efforts of MI5.

For a first novel, it was a modest success. The publishers had since commissioned a second book, on which he was now working. But the word had gone out from Curzon Street that Tom Rowse was an outsider, beyond the pale, not to be helped in any way. He knew it, and he did not give a damn. He had built himself a new world, with his new house and his new wife.

Nikki served coffee, absorbed the atmosphere, and left. McCready spoke for ten minutes. When he had finished, the ex-soldier said, "I'm out, McCready. Right out. Didn't Curzon Street tell you that? I've made myself untouchable. A new life, a home that isn't a soaking scrape in an Irish bog, even a modest living from the books. Why the hell should I go back?"

"I need a man, Tom. Inside. Able to move through the Middle East with a good cover."

"Find another."

"They're putting a man in charge from their side. Someone I think you know. Kevin Mahoney."

Rowse stiffened as if he had been hit. "He will be there?"

"We believe he will be in charge. If he fails, it will destroy him."

Rowse stared out at the landscape for a long time, then rose and went outside. McCready heard low voices and the sound of Nikki crying. Rowse came back and went to pack a suitcase.

CHAPTER TWO

Rowse's briefing took a week, and McCready handled it personally. He borrowed one of the three quiet country houses not an hour's drive from London that the SIS keeps for such purposes.

Rowse saw the film and heard the tape from the graveyard scene. He studied the face of the Irish priest and that of the Army Council man beside him. But his gaze always came back to the cold, handsome features of Kevin Mahoney.

Four years earlier Rowse had almost killed the IRA gunman when he ventured into Northern Ireland from his hideout in the south. He was being driven by another IRA man, and they stopped for petrol at a filling station near Moira. Rowse had been driving behind him, well back, receiving radio briefings from the watchers along the route. He decided to close in.

By the time Rowse reached the filling station, the IRA driver had filled his tank and was back in the car. No one was with him yet. Rowse told his partner to cover the IRA driver and got out. It was while he was busying himself with the petrol pump that the door of the men's room opened and Mahoney came out.

A scruffy woolen cap covered most of Rowse's head, and several days of stubble obscured his face. As Mahoney emerged, Rowse dropped into a crouch, pulled his gun, took up the double-handed aim position, and yelled, "Mahoney—freeze!"

At that moment two old ladies in a Volkswagen pulled into the filling station, straight between Rowse, by the petrol pump, and Mahoney, by the wall. That was enough for the IRA man. He dodged around the back of a parked lorry and ran out into the middle of the highway.

The elderly driver of a Morris Minor jammed on his brakes to avoid hitting the running man. Mahoney kept the Morris between himself and Rowse, hauled the old man out by the jacket, jumped into the driving seat, and was off.

There was a passenger in the car. The old man had been taking his granddaughter to the circus in the Morris. Rowse watched as the passenger door flew open and the child was thrown out. He heard her thin scream from down the road, saw her small body hit the road, then saw her body struck by an oncoming van.

"She was thrown," said Rowse. "I saw his arm. He's really going to be in charge of this?"

"We think so. We don't know where he'll show up. But we think he'll command the operation. You heard the tape."

McCready briefed Rowse on his cover stories. He would have two. The first would be reasonably transparent. With luck, those investigating it would penetrate the lie and discover the second story. With luck (again), they would be satisfied with that.

"Where would you like to start?" asked McCready as the week neared its end.

"Anyone researching international arms traffic for his next novel would soon find out that the two European bases for that traffic are Antwerp and Hamburg," said Rowse.

"True. Do you have any contacts in either city?"

"There's a man I know in Hamburg—Ulrich Kleist. He's dangerous, crazy, but he may have contacts in the international underworld. I saved his butt once. At Mogadishu. He wasn't crazy then. That came later, when someone turned his son into a druggie. The boy died."

"Ah, yes," said McCready. "That can have an effect. Right. Hamburg it is. I'll be with you all the time. You won't see me, but I'll be there, with two of your former colleagues from the SAS regiment. We'll come for you if things get rough."

Rowse nodded. He knew it was a lie, but it was a nice one. For Rowse possessed that quality so beloved of spymasters: he was quite dispensable.

Rowse arrived in Hamburg in May and booked into an unpretentious hotel near the railway station. He had hired a small car and stuck to his modest budget, in keeping with the limitations of a moderately successful novelist trying to research his next book. After two days he found Ulrich Kleist, who was working as a forklift driver on the docks.

The big German had switched off his machine and was climbing down from the cab when Rowse called to him. He spun around, prepared to defend himself, then recognized Rowse. His craggy face broke into a grin. "Tom. Tom, my old friend."

Rowse was embraced in a crushing bear hug. When he was released, he stood back and looked at the former special forces soldier, whom he had first met in a baking Somalian airport in 1977. Kleist was forty now, but he looked much older.

On October 13, 1977, four Palestinian terrorists had hijacked a Lufthansa flight from Majorca to Frankfurt, with eighty-six passengers and a crew of five. The captive jet had landed in succession at Rome, Larnaca, Bahrain, Dubai, and Aden before coming to rest, out of fuel, at Mogadishu, the bleak capital of Somalia.

Here, a few minutes after midnight on October 18, the jet had been stormed by the West German special force, the GSG 9, which modeled itself on, and had been largely trained by, the British SAS. It had been the first foreign "outing" for Colonel Ulrich Wegener's crack troops. They were good, very good, but two SAS sergeants had come along anyway. One was Tom Rowse—that was before he was commissioned.

In all, it took eight seconds. As Uli Kleist entered the center aisle a woman terrorist was climbing to her feet with a grenade in one hand, her other hand reaching for the pin. Kleist had never done it at point-blank range before, so Rowse stepped into the aisle and did it for him.

Ten years later Uli Kleist now stood on a Hamburg quayside and grinned at the slim young man who had fired those two shots over his head in the cramped airliner cabin so long ago.

"What brings you to Hamburg, Tom?"

"Let me buy you dinner, and I'll tell you."

They ate spicy Hungarian food at a *csárda* in one of the back streets of Sankt Pauli. Rowse talked; Kleist listened.

"*Ja*, sounds like a good plot," he said eventually. "About terrorists and arms dealers, and the White House. So there is a living to be made from this thriller fiction?"

Rowse shrugged. "It pays the rent."

The German considered. "I will try and get you some information—research purposes only, yes?" He laughed and tapped his nose, as if to say, Of course, there's more to it than that. "So you have done well since leaving the army. I, not so well."

"I heard about your troubles," said Rowse.

"*Ach*, two years in Hamburg jail. It was worth it."

Kleist's son had been only sixteen when someone turned him on to cocaine, then crack. The boy overdosed and died. Rage had made Uli Kleist rather unsubtle. He had found out the names of the Colombian wholesaler and the German distributor of the drugs, walked into a restaurant where they were dining, and blown both their heads off. A sympathetic judge gave him four years. He served two, and had come out six months before. Word was, there was a contract on him.

They parted at midnight, and Rowse took a cab back to his hotel. A single man on a motorcycle followed all the way. The motorcyclist spoke twice into a hand-held communicator. When Rowse paid off the taxi, McCready emerged from the shadows.

"You haven't got a tail," he said. "Feel like a nightcap?"

They drank beer in an all-night bar, and Rowse filled him in.

"He believes your tale of researching a novel is poppycock?" McCready asked.

"He suspects it."

"Good. Let's hope he puts it about."

Rowse made a remark about feeling like the cheese in a mousetrap.

"In a successful mousetrap," remarked McCready, "the cheese does not get touched."

"I know it, and you know it, but tell that to the cheese."

ROWSE met Kleist the following evening. "I have asked around," the German said, "but what you mentioned is too sophisticated for Hamburg. That kind of material is made in government factories. But there is a man, or so is the whisper."

"Here in Hamburg?"

"No, Vienna. The Russian military attaché there is a certain major, Vitali Kariagin, of the GRU. As you know, Vienna is the main outlet for the Czech manufacturer Omnipol. Some of their exports and some buyers have to be cleared with Moscow. The channeling agent for these permissions is Kariagin."

"Why should he help?"

"Private tastes. It appears he likes girls, the sort to whom you have to give expensive presents. So he himself takes presents— cash presents, in envelopes. By the way, in this . . . novel of yours. Would there be any IRA in it?"

"Why do you ask?" said Rowse.

Kleist shrugged. "They have a unit here. Based in a bar run by Palestinians. They do liaison with other terror groups in the international community, and arms buying. You want to see them?"

"These Palestinians—they know you once blew away four of their number?" asked Rowse.

"Probably. But I still go to drink in their bar."

"Why?"

"Fun. Pulling the tiger's tail."

You really *are* crazy, thought Rowse.

"I THINK you should go," said McCready later that night. "They might see you and wonder why you are here. They won't believe the novel-researching story, and they'll deduce you really *are* out buying weapons for use in America."

The following evening Uli Kleist paid off their cab on the Reeperbahn. He led Rowse into Bernhard Nochtstrasse and stopped at a studded timber door.

He rang the discreet bell, and a small grille slid back. An eye looked at him, there was a whispered conference inside, and the door opened. The doorman and the dinner-jacketed man beside him were both Arabs.

"Evening, Mr. Abdallah," Kleist said cheerfully in German.

Abdallah glanced at Rowse.

"Oh, he's all right, he's a friend," said Kleist. The Arab nodded at the doorman, who let them in. Kleist was big, but the doorman was massive, shaven-headed, and not to be trifled with.

Abdallah led them both to a table and summoned a waiter. Two busty bar girls, both German, left the bar and sat at their table. Kleist grinned. "I told you. No problem."

They sat and drank. Now and then Kleist danced with one of the girls. Rowse toyed with his drink and surveyed the room. Despite the sleazy street in which it was situated, it was lushly decorated, the music was live, and the drink was unwatered. Even the girls were pretty and well dressed.

Apart from the redoubtable doorman, Rowse could see no sign that this was a hangout for anything other than businessmen who were prepared to be parted from a lot of money in the hope of taking one of the bar girls home.

Above the bar was a large one-way mirror; behind it was the manager's office. Two men stood and looked down.

"Who's your man?" one asked in the harsh burr of Belfast.

"German called Kleist. Comes in occasionally. Once GSG Nine; not anymore. Did two years for murder."

"Not him," said the first man. "The one with him. The Brit."

"No idea, Seamus. Just came in."

"Find out. I think I've seen him somewhere before."

They came in when Rowse was visiting the men's room. He was washing his hands when the two men entered. The bigger one stood in front of the urinal. The slimmer, good-looking Irishman stayed by the door. He slipped a small wooden wedge out of his pocket, dropped it, and with one foot eased it under the rest room's entrance door. There would be no distractions.

Rowse caught the gesture in the mirror. When the big man turned away from the urinal, he was ready. He turned, ducked the first hammer blow from the big fist, and lashed a toe kick into the sensitive tendon beneath the man's left kneecap.

The big man's leg buckled, bringing his head down to waist level. Rowse's knee came up hard, finding the point of the jaw. The fight was stopped by his third blow—four rigid knuckles into the base of the throat. Then he turned to the man by the door.

"Easy now, friend," said the man called Seamus. "He only wanted to talk to you." His eyes were cold and watchful.

"*Qu'est-ce qui se passe?*" asked Rowse. On entering the club, he had passed himself as a visiting Swiss.

"Drop it, Mr. Rowse," said Seamus O'Keefe. "For one thing, your picture was on the back of your book, which I read with great interest. For another, you were an SAS man in Belfast years ago. Now I remember where I've seen you before."

"So what?" said Rowse. "I'm out—well out. We had a parting of the ways. I write novels for a living now. That's all."

"So I heard, to be sure. Well then, SAS man, come and have a drink. For old times' sake."

He kicked the wedge away from the door and held it open. On the tiles, the big man hauled himself up. Rowse passed through the door. O'Keefe paused to whisper in the big man's ear.

In the bar Uli Kleist was still at his table. The girls had gone. As Rowse passed, he raised an eyebrow. Rowse shook his head.

"It's all right, Uli," he said. "Stay cool. Go home. I'll see you."

O'KEEFE took Rowse to his own apartment. They drank Jameson's with water. "Tell me about this research, SAS man."

Rowse outlined the plot of his intended next novel.

"Not about the lads in Belfast, then?" said O'Keefe.

"Can't use the same plot twice. This one's about America."

They talked through the night. And drank. Rowse had a rock-hard head for whiskey, which was just as well. At dawn he walked back to his hotel to blow away the whiskey fumes.

The others worked on Kleist in the abandoned warehouse to which they had taken him after Rowse left the club. The big doorman held him down, and another Palestinian used the instruments. Kleist took all he could, but he talked before dawn. They let him die as the sun rose.

The big Irishman from the men's room watched and listened. His orders from O'Keefe were to find out what the German knew about Rowse's presence in Hamburg. When it was over, he reported what he had learned.

"I thought there was more to it than a novel," the IRA station head said. Later he sent a cable to a man in Vienna.

THE Vienna flight was via Frankfurt and took off on time. Rowse was in business class. After takeoff the stewardess distributed newspapers. Rowse could speak only halting German, but the headlines in the *Morgenpost* did not need deciphering.

The face in the picture had its eyes closed and was surrounded by garbage. The headline read SLAYER OF DRUG BARONS FOUND DEAD. The text below said two garbage collectors had found the body near a rubbish bin close to the docks. The police were treating the case as a gangland revenge killing.

SOMEWHAT to Rowse's surprise, Major Kariagin took his call at the Soviet embassy at his first attempt.

For a stranger to telephone Major Kariagin at the embassy was not so odd, bearing in mind the major's secondary task of keeping an eye on the applications made to the Czech arms outlet, Omnipol. He agreed to meet Rowse that evening at Sacher's.

Kariagin did not look like a caricature Russian. He was smooth, groomed, and well tailored. He was known at the famous restaurant. The headwaiter showed him to a corner table away from the orchestra and the babble of the other diners. The two men sat and ordered schnitzel with a dry, light Austrian red wine.

Rowse explained his need for information for his next novel.

Kariagin listened politely. "These American terrorists . . ." he said when Rowse had finished.

"Fictional terrorists," said Rowse.

"Of course. These fictional American terrorists— What would they be looking for?"

Rowse passed over a typed sheet that he took from his breast pocket. The Russian read it and passed it back.

"Impossible," he said. "That list contains items that simply do not come under the heading of conventional weaponry. Booby-trapped briefcases, claymore mines— My country would never dream of supplying such matériel or sanctioning its supply by a friendly state."

"And yet these weapons do appear in the hands of certain terrorist groups," said Rowse. "The Palestinians, for example."

"Possibly, but I have not the faintest idea how."

"I know it's a lot to ask," said Rowse, "but in the pursuit of authenticity, I do have a modest research fund."

He lifted the corner of his folded newspaper, which lay on the third chair at the table. A slim white envelope rested between the pages. Kariagin extracted the envelope and glanced at the deutsche mark bills inside. He looked thoughtful, then slipped the envelope into his breast pocket.

"If I were you, and wished to acquire certain kinds of matériel to sell on to a group of American terrorists—all fictional, of course—I think I might go to Tripoli and try to seek an interview with a certain colonel, Hakim al-Mansour."

"So FAR, so good," McCready said as they stood in the men's room of a bar near the river. "I think you should go there."

"What about a visa?"

"The Libyan People's Bureau at Valletta would be your best chance. If they grant a visa without delay, it will mean you have been preannounced."

"You think Kariagin will tip off Tripoli?" asked Rowse.

"Oh, I think so. You have crossed the first hurdle. The bad guys really are beginning to think you're a renegade trying to make a fast buck by working for some shadowy group of American madmen. Mansour will want a lot more than that, of course."

Rowse flew from Vienna to Rome and thence to the capital of Malta. He made his application to the People's Bureau for a visa to visit Tripoli. The visa came through in twenty-four hours.

The following morning Rowse took the Libyan Airways flight from Valletta to Tripoli. As the ocher-brown coast of Tripolitania came into view across the glittering blue Mediterranean, he thought of McCready's words in the Valletta airport.

"I'm afraid Tripoli is one place I cannot follow you. When you go in there, you will be alone."

CHAPTER THREE

ROWSE followed the other passengers down the steps from the airliner into the blazing sun of a Libyan morning. He entered the air-conditioned cool of the terminal and took his place at the end of the queue waiting for passport clearance.

It took twenty minutes for him to reach the desk. The green-uniformed officer opened his passport and glanced down at a note beneath the grille. Without expression, he raised his gaze and nodded to someone behind Rowse. There was a tug at Rowse's elbow. He turned. Another green uniform—younger, courteous but firm. Two armed soldiers stood farther back.

"Would you please come with me?" the young officer said. He reached under the grille and retrieved Rowse's passport.

The two soldiers closed up from behind, one at each elbow. The officer leading, they turned out of the main concourse and down a long passage. At the far end the officer opened a door for Rowse to enter. The soldiers took up position on the outside.

The officer followed Rowse in and closed the door. It was a bare white room, with barred windows. A table and two chairs stood in the center—nothing else. Rowse took one of the chairs; the officer sat down facing him and began to study the passport.

"I don't understand what is wrong," said Rowse. "My visa was issued yesterday by your People's Bureau in Valletta."

The officer made a gesture with one languid hand to suggest that Rowse should be quiet. He was. A fly buzzed. Five minutes elapsed, and then the door opened. The officer shot to his feet and saluted. Then, without a word, he left the room.

"So, Mr. Rowse, here you are at last."

Rowse turned. He allowed no trace of recognition to cross his face, but he had studied pictures of this man for hours in McCready's briefing sessions. The Libyan head of external intelligence was barely older than Rowse himself. Thirty-three, the dossier had said.

"He's slick and highly educated—by us," McCready had said. "He's also utterly ruthless and quite deadly. Be careful of Hakim al-Mansour."

"My visa is in perfect order," Rowse said indignantly. "So may I ask what is going on?"

"Certainly, Mr. Rowse. The answer is simple. You are being denied entry into Libya."

"But why?" asked Rowse. "All I want to do is try to research some passages for my next novel."

"Please, Mr. Rowse, spare me the bewildered innocence. You are a former soldier of the British special forces, apparently turned novelist. Come, I will escort you back to the plane."

He called an order in Arabic, and the two soldiers entered. One took Rowse's grip. Mansour picked up the passport from the table and led the way out into the sunlight. The Libyan airliner stood ready for takeoff.

"May I know who I have been speaking to?" asked Rowse.

"Not for the moment, my dear fellow. Just call me . . . Mr. Aziz. Now, where will you go from here for your research?"

"I don't know," said Rowse. "I seem to have reached the end of the line."

"Then take a break," said Mansour. "Why not fly on to Cyprus? A lovely island. Personally I always favor the cool air of the Troodos Mountains at this time of year. Just outside Pedhoulas is a charming old hostelry called the Apollonia. I recommend it. Such interesting people stay there. Safe journey, Mr. Rowse."

McCREADY had two SAS sergeants backing him up in Malta, and it was a lucky coincidence that one of them spotted Rowse coming through the Valletta airport. They had not expected him back so soon. Both men were sharing a room at the airport hotel, spelling each other in the arrivals hall. The duty man was reading a sports magazine when he spotted Rowse emerging from customs. Without raising his head, he let Rowse pass and watched him approach the Cyprus Airways desk. Then he used a wall phone to rouse his colleague in the hotel. The colleague raised McCready in central Valletta.

"Damn," swore McCready. "What's he doing back so fast?"

"Dunno, boss," said the sergeant. "But according to Danny, he's inquiring at the Cyprus Airways desk."

McCready thought furiously. Why Cyprus? McCready needed to get to Rowse and find out what had happened in Tripoli. . . .

"Bill," he said down the line, "tell Danny to stay with him. When the coast is clear, get to the Cyprus Airways desk and try to find where they went. Then book us two on the same flight and two more on the next flight, in case I can't get there on time. I'll be out there as soon as I can."

By the time McCready reached the airport, the evening flight for Nicosia had gone—with Rowse and Danny on board. The next flight was not till the following day. McCready checked into the airport hotel. At midnight a call came in from Danny.

"Hallo, Uncle. I'm at the Nicosia airport hotel. Auntie's gone to bed. She's got a super room. Six ten."

"I'm so glad," said McCready. "I'll probably stay there myself when I arrive. How's the holiday so far?"

"Great. Auntie's rented a car for tomorrow. I think we're going up into the mountains."

"That'll be lovely," McCready said jovially to his "nephew." "I'll join you and Auntie as soon as I can."

He put the phone down. "Bugger's going up into the mountains tomorrow," he said gloomily. "What the hell did he learn in that stopover in Tripoli?"

"We'll know tomorrow, boss," said Bill. "Danny'll leave a message in the usual place."

MCCREADY'S plane touched down at the Cypriot capital just after eleven. He was well separated from Bill, although they emerged from the same plane and took the same courtesy shuttle to the airport hotel. McCready settled into the lobby bar while Bill went up to room 610. Danny had left his situation report taped to the underside of the lavatory cistern lid. Bill pocketed it and went back downstairs.

They made the exchange in the men's toilet off the lobby. McCready retired to a cubicle and read the sitrep. According to Danny, shortly after Rowse appeared from the customs hall at Valletta, his tail had followed—a sallow young man in a fawn suit.

The Libyan agent had shadowed Rowse until the Cyprus Airways plane took off, but he had not joined the flight. Another tail had been waiting at the Nicosia airport and had shadowed Rowse to the hotel, where he had spent the night in the lobby.

Rowse had asked reception to order him a hired car for seven the following morning. Much later Danny had done the same. Rowse had also asked for a map and had consulted the reception manager on the best route to the Troodos Mountains.

In the last passage of the sitrep Danny had said he would stay as close as he could and would call the hotel lobby when he had run Rowse to earth. He would ask for Mr. Meldrum.

McCready returned to the lobby and made a brief call to the British embassy. Minutes later he was speaking to the SIS head of station. He soon got what he wanted—an unmarked car with a driver who spoke Greek. It would arrive within the hour.

The call for Mr. Meldrum came at ten past two.

"Hallo, Uncle. Auntie and I have stopped for lunch at a lovely hotel high in the mountains outside the village of Pedhoulas. It's called the Apollonia. I think she may stay here, it's so lovely. The car gave a bit of problem at the end, so I've brought it to a garage in Pedhoulas run by a Mr. Demetriou."

"Never mind. How are the olives?"

"There are no olives up here, Uncle. Just apple and cherry orchards. Olives only grow down in the plain."

McCready put the phone down and headed for the men's room. Bill followed him. They checked the cubicles and talked.

"Is Danny all right, boss?"

"Sure. He tailed Rowse to a hotel high in the Troodos Mountains. The Libyan tail, the olive-skinned one, remained down here. Danny's in the village at a garage called Demetriou's. He'll wait for us there. The car will be here shortly. I want you to take your grip and leave. Wait for us half a mile down the road."

Thirty minutes later Mr. Meldrum's car, a Ford Orion, indeed appeared. The driver was Bertie Marks, an alert young staffer from the Nicosia station who spoke fluent Greek. They picked up Bill by the wayside and headed for the mountains. It was dusk before they entered the picturesque village of Pedhoulas, heart of the Troodos Mountains cherry industry.

Danny was waiting for them in a café opposite the garage.

He pointed out the Hotel Apollonia, and he and Bill surveyed the surrounding countryside. They fixed on the mountain slope across the valley from the hotel's splendid dining terrace, hefted their grips, and disappeared silently into the cherry orchards. McCready and Bertie Marks found a small taverna in the village and checked in.

Rowse had arrived at lunchtime, after a leisurely drive from the airport hotel. There was a room available at the Apollonia, so he took it. Perhaps Mansour had arranged for it to be available—perhaps not. It was a pleasant room, with stunning views over the valley to a hillside covered with cherry trees.

He lunched off a local lamb casserole, washed down by a light Omhodos red wine, followed by fresh fruit. The hotel dining terrace was built on piles out over the valley. Whoever else was staying there, few had turned up for lunch. There was an elderly man with jet-black hair at a corner table, who addressed the waiter in mumbled English, and several Cypriot couples, who might have simply come for lunch. When Rowse entered the terrace, a very pretty younger woman had been leaving. She was quite a head turner, and with her mane of corn-gold hair, she was almost certainly not Cypriot.

After lunch he went to his room and took a nap. He had done what Mansour had advised him to do. The next move, if any, was in the Libyan's court. He only hoped, if the going got rough, that he still had some backup out there somewhere.

The backup was indeed in place by the time Rowse awoke from his nap. The two sergeants had found a small abandoned stone hut among the cherry trees on the mountainside, opposite the hotel terrace. Their high-powered field glasses brought the dining terrace, seven hundred yards away, to a range that appeared to be twenty feet.

Dusk was deepening when they called up McCready and gave him directions to approach their hideout from the other side of the mountain. Bertie Marks drove according to the instructions until they saw Danny standing in their way. McCready left the car and followed Danny to the hut. There Bill handed McCready his image-intensifying night glasses.

On the dining terrace the lights were coming on—a ring of colored bulbs strung around the perimeter of the dining area, with candles in sconces on each table.

"We'll need Cypriot peasant clothes tomorrow, boss," murmured Danny. "Can't move around dressed as we are."

McCready made a mental note to have Marks buy the sort of canvas smocks and trousers worn by the farmworkers.

"Hallo," muttered Bill, who had taken back the night glasses. "Tasty." He passed the glasses to McCready.

A young woman had entered the terrace. She wore a simple but elegant white dress over a golden suntan. Blond hair hung about her shoulders.

"Keep your minds on your work," grumbled McCready. "Where's Rowse?"

The sergeants grinned. "Oh yeah, him. One line of windows above the terrace. Third window to the right."

McCready swiveled his glasses. He saw a figure with a towel around his waist emerge from the shower room. It was Rowse. So far, so good. He checked his watch. Seven fifteen.

Rowse dressed and went downstairs for a drink before dinner. The sun had dropped below the mountains, bathing the far side of the valley in thick gloom while the silhouette of the hills was brilliantly backlit. There were three people on the terrace: a fat man of Mediterranean look, the old fellow with unlikely black hair, and the woman. She had her back to him, staring at the view across the valley. A waiter approached. Rowse nodded to the table next to the woman's, up against the balustrade. The waiter grinned and hastened to show him to it. Rowse ordered ouzo and a carafe of local springwater.

As he took his seat, she glanced sideways. He nodded and murmured, "Evening." She nodded back and continued to gaze at the darkening valley. His ouzo arrived. After a while he said, "May I propose a toast?"

She was startled. "A toast?"

He gestured with his glass to the shadow-shrouded mountains all around them. "To tranquillity. And spectacular beauty."

She gave a half smile. "To tranquillity," she said, and drank a sip of her dry white wine. The waiter brought them two menus. She ordered mountain trout.

"I can't better that. The same for me, please," Rowse told the waiter, who left.

"Are you dining alone?" asked Rowse quietly.

"Yes, I am," she said carefully.

"So am I. And it worries me, for I'm a God-fearing man."

"What's God got to do with it?"

The accent was not British. American? He gestured beyond the terrace. "The view, the peace, the hills, the dying sun. He created all of this, but surely not for dining alone."

She laughed—a flash of clear white teeth in a sun-golden face.

"May I join you? Just for dinner?"

"Why not? Just for dinner."

He crossed to sit opposite her. "Tom Rowse," he said.

"Monica Browne," she replied.

They talked, the usual small talk. He explained that he was a novelist who had been doing some research in the Middle East. He had decided to end his tour with a brief break at this hotel.

"And you?" he asked.

"Nothing so exciting. I breed horses. I've been in Syria buying three Thoroughbred stallions. It takes time for the shipment papers to come through. So I thought it would be nicer here than stewing on the dockside."

He learned that she was married to the much older Major Eric Browne and that together they owned and ran a breeding stud at Ashford. Originally she was from Kentucky, which was where she had gained her enthusiastic knowledge of horses. He knew Ashford vaguely—it was a small town in Kent.

The trout arrived, deliciously grilled over a charcoal brazier. It was served with a local dry white wine. In the bar, its doors open to the terrace, three men were finishing their drinks.

"How long will you have to wait?" asked Rowse. "For the stallions?"

"Any day now, I hope. My shipping agent will call me when they arrive, and I'll ship them out personally."

The men in the bar were shown out onto the terrace to a table. Rowse caught a hint of their accents. He raised a steady hand to his mouth with a forkful of trout.

"Ask yer man to bring another round of the same," said one of the men.

ACROSS THE VALLEY, DANNY said quietly, "Boss."

McCready jackknifed to his feet and came to the small aperture they had made in the stone wall. Danny handed him the glasses, and McCready let out a long sigh.

"Bingo," he said. He handed the glasses back. "Keep it up. I'm going back with Marks to watch the front of the hotel. Bill, come with me."

ON THE terrace, one glance had told Rowse all he needed to know. Two of the Irishmen he had never seen before. The third—clearly the leader—was Kevin Mahoney.

Rowse and Monica Browne took coffee but declined desserts. "No good for the figure," she said.

"And yours should in no way be harmed, for it is quite stunning," said Rowse. She laughed away the compliment, but not with displeasure. She leaned forward.

"Do you know those men?" she asked earnestly.

"No, never seen 'em before," said Rowse.

"One of them seems to be staring at you a lot."

Rowse did not want to turn and look at them, but after that remark it would have been suspicious not to. As he turned, Mahoney's eyes met his. Rowse knew the glance. The puzzlement. Unease. As of someone who thinks he has seen a person somewhere before but cannot place him.

Rowse turned back. "Nope. Total strangers."

"Then they are very rude strangers."

"Can you recognize their accent?" asked Rowse.

"Irish," she said. "Northern Irish."

"Where did you learn to detect Irish accents?" he asked.

"Horse racing. The sport is full of them. And now, it's been lovely, Tom, but if you'll excuse me, I'm going to turn in."

She rose. Rowse followed, his fleeting suspicion allayed.

"I agree," he said. "It was a wonderful dinner. I hope we can eat together again."

She gave him a radiant smile and swept off the terrace. Rowse took another coffee and turned away from the Irish trio to look out across the dark mountains.

"I told you it was a charming place," said a deep, cultured voice behind him.

Hakim al-Mansour, as beautifully tailored as ever, slipped into the vacant chair and gestured for coffee. Across the valley, Danny muttered urgently into his communicator.

"You did indeed, Mr. Aziz," said Rowse. "But if you wanted to talk to me, why did you expel me from Libya?"

"Oh, please—not expel," drawled Mansour. "Just decline to admit. And, well, I wished to talk to you in complete privacy. Even in my homeland there are formalities. Here, nothing but peace and quiet."

"So," Rowse said, "I must thank you for your courtesy in agreeing to help me with my research."

Hakim al-Mansour laughed softly. "I think the time for that particular foolishness is over, Mr. Rowse. You see, before certain . . . animals put him out of his misery, your late friend Herr Kleist was quite communicative."

Rowse spun around on him, bitterly angry. "The papers said he was killed by the drug people, in revenge for what he did."

"Alas, no. The people who did that were interested in finding out what you were really up to in Hamburg, and they thought your friend might know. Or suspect. And he did. His information, coupled with further messages received from Vienna, brought me to the view that you might be an interesting man to talk to. I sincerely hope you are, Mr. Rowse, for your sake. And the time has come to talk. But not here."

Two men had appeared behind Rowse. They were big and olive-skinned.

"I think we should go for a little ride," said Mansour.

"Is this the sort of ride from which one returns?" asked Rowse.

Hakim al-Mansour rose. "That depends very much on whether you are able to answer a few simple questions," he said.

McCready was waiting, having been tipped off by Danny, across the valley. He saw the Libyans' car—with Rowse in the back seat between the two heavies—turn away from the hotel.

"Do we follow, boss?" asked Bill.

"No," said McCready. To try and follow without lights would be suicide on those hairpin curves. To put on headlights would give the game away. "If he comes back, he'll tell us what went on. If not . . . By the way, Bill, can you enter that hotel unseen?"

Bill looked as if he had been insulted.

"Slip that under Rowse's door," said McCready, and he passed the sergeant a tourist brochure.

THE drive took an hour. Twice the Libyan driver pulled to the side of the road, doused his lights, and waited for five minutes. No one came past them. Just before midnight they arrived at a substantial villa. Rowse was decanted and pushed through the door, which was opened by another heavyweight Libyan. With Mansour himself, that made five. Too heavy odds.

And there was another man waiting for them in the large drawing room—a heavyset, big-bellied man in his late forties, with a brutal, coarsened face and big red hands. He was clearly not a Libyan. In fact, Rowse recognized him, though he gave no sign.

Frank Terpil was a CIA renegade, fired by the Agency in 1971. Soon after, he had gravitated to his true and very lucrative vocation—supplying a vast range of terrorist equipment and technology to the most extreme groups around the Middle East, always taking his orders from Muammar Qaddafi. He was regarded in Libya as the American expert.

Rowse was told to take a chair in the middle of the room. A single bulb hung over him. Mansour fastidiously seated himself in a brocade high-backed chair.

Terpil took a nod from Mansour and lumbered over. "Okay, boy, let's talk. You've been going around Europe looking for arms. Very special weapons. What the hell are you really up to?"

"Researching a new novel. I've tried to explain that a dozen times. About soldiers, spies, terrorists—fictional terrorists."

Terpil hit him once on the side of the face—not hard, but enough to indicate there was more where that came from. "Who are you really working for?"

Rowse let the story come out slowly, as he had been briefed, sometimes recalling things exactly, sometimes having to search his memory.

"Which magazine?"

"*Soldier of Fortune*. April . . . May, last year."

"What did the ad say?"

" 'Weapons expert needed, European area, for interesting assignment'—something like that. A box number."

There had been such an ad in the columns of *Soldier of Fortune*. McCready had found it, and a few calls to his friends in the CIA and the FBI had ensured—or so Rowse fervently hoped—that the placer of the ad would not deny he had ever received a reply from Mr. Thomas Rowse of England.

"So you wrote back."

"Yep."

The interrogation went on. They had set up a meet. When? Last November. Where? The George Cinq, in Paris. What was he like?

"Youngish, well dressed, well spoken. Called himself Galvin Pollard. Certainly phony. He said he represented a group of ultra-radicals who were sick and tired of the Reagan administration, of its hostility to the Soviet and Third Worlds, and particularly of the use of American planes to bomb women and children in Tripoli the previous April."

"And he produced a list of what he wanted?"

"Yes."

"This list?"

Rowse glanced at it. It was a copy of the list he had shown Kariagin in Vienna. "Yes."

"Claymore mines. Semtex-H. Booby-trapped briefcases. This is high-tech stuff. What the hell did they want all that for?"

"He said his people wanted to strike a blow. A real blow. He mentioned the White House. And the Senate."

"So what did you get involved for?"

"There was a twenty percent commission. A hundred thousand dollars."

At four in the morning Terpil and Mansour went into a huddle in an adjacent room. Although Rowse did not know it, the gods were smiling on him that night. Mansour needed to bring something to his leader to satisfy the insistent pressure for revenge against America; Terpil needed to prove to his hosts that he was still the man they needed to advise them about America and the West. Finally, both men believed Rowse for the reason that most men believe: because they wanted to.

At half past four the two men returned to the sitting room.

"You may go, Mr. Rowse," said Mansour mildly. "We will check, of course. Stay at the Apollonia until we get in touch."

The two heavies who had brought him drove him back to the

hotel. When he entered his room, he noticed something lying on the carpet. It was a brochure inviting visitors to visit the historic Kykko Monastery and admire the Golden Icon of the Virgin. A single script in pencil beside the paragraph said, "Ten a.m."

CHAPTER FOUR

KYKKO, the largest monastery in Cyprus, was founded in the twelfth century by the Byzantine emperors. The vast edifice stands high on a remote peak west of the Marathassa Valley. A single lane leads up to the monastery gate.

Danny had stayed behind in the stone hut, while Bill, on a motorcycle acquired for him by the Greek-speaking Marks, had ridden ahead to Kykko. At dawn the SAS sergeant was well hidden in the pines above the single track to the monastery. He saw McCready himself arrive, driven by Marks. He watched to see who else came, but it was only the usual stream of tourists.

At twenty past nine Danny reported that Rowse had left the hotel. At ten to ten Bill reported that Rowse had come into sight, driving up the steep track to the monastery. McCready rose from his seat in the courtyard and went inside, wondering at the labor that had brought these massive stones so high into the mountains, and at the skill of the masters who had painted the frescoes in the gold leaf, scarlet, and blue that decorated the interior.

Rowse found McCready in front of the famous Golden Icon of the Virgin. Outside, Bill ensured that Rowse had not grown a tail, and he gave McCready two double blips on the communicator.

"It seems you're clean," murmured McCready as Rowse appeared beside him. There was no strangeness in talking in a low voice; all around them the other tourists conversed in whispers too, as if afraid to disturb the calm of the shrine. "I remember seeing you off at the Valletta airport on your very brief visit to Tripoli. Since then, if you please, every detail."

Rowse started at the beginning. Part of his narrative McCready could confirm from his own and the sergeants' observations. Rowse arrived at the moment he first saw Mahoney and his two cronies.

"Wait a minute. The girl— Who is she?"

"An American racehorse breeder waiting for the arrival of three

Arab stallions she bought last week in Syria. Monica Browne. With an *e*. No problem—just a dining companion."

"Are you sure?"

"Yes, Sam. Quite sure. Just a civilian. And a very pretty one, as it happens."

"So we noticed," muttered McCready. "Go on."

Rowse narrated the arrival of Mahoney and the suspicious glances Monica had intercepted across the terrace.

"You think he recognized you? From that filling station?"

"No. He'd stare like that at any Englishman as soon as he heard the accent. You know how much he hates us all."

"Maybe. Go on."

It was the sudden appearance of Hakim al-Mansour and the interrogation by Frank Terpil that really interested McCready. He made Rowse stop a dozen times to clarify tiny points.

"So far, so good," mused McCready. "Their arms shipment operation seems to be on hold, ready for some go order. What we have to know is when, where, and how. Did they ask where you would want the shipment for the American terror group if they agree to sell?"

"Yes. I told them anywhere in Western Europe."

"Plans for getting it to the States?"

"Told them what you said. I'd load the consignment into a camper van with hidden compartments behind the walls. Drive the van north through Denmark, on the ferry to Sweden, up to Norway, and take it on one of the many freighters crossing to Canada. Just another tourist on a wildlife-watching vacation."

"They like that?"

"Terpil did. Said it was neat and clean."

"All right. We've made our pitch. Now we have to wait and see if you've convinced them. Or if their greed for revenge against the White House will outweigh natural caution. It has been known."

"What happens next?" asked Rowse.

"You go back to the hotel. If they swallow the American scheme, Mansour will contact you. I'll only close in on you for a situation report when the coast is clear."

"And if they don't swallow it?"

"Then they'll try to silence you. But my sergeants will be close by. They'll move in to pull you out alive."

The hell they will, thought Rowse. That would give away London's awareness of the plot. The Irish would scatter, and the whole shipment would reach them by another route at another time. If Mansour came for him, he would be on his own.

McCready then drifted away into the throng. He too knew he could not intervene if the Libyans or the Irish came for Rowse. What he had decided to do, in case the Libyan fox had not believed Rowse, was to bring in a far larger team of watchers and to keep an eye on Mahoney. When he moved, the Irish arms consignment would be moving. Now that he had found Mahoney, the IRA man was the better bet as a trace to the shipment.

Rowse completed his tour of the monastery and emerged into the brilliant sunshine to find his car. Bill, from his cover under the pines, watched him go and alerted Danny that he was on his way back. Ten minutes later McCready left, driven by Marks. On the way down the hill they gave a lift to a Cypriot peasant standing by the roadside and thus brought Bill back to Pedhoulas.

Fifteen minutes into the forty-minute drive, McCready's communicator crackled into life. It was Danny. "Mahoney and his men are ransacking our man's room."

"If I speed up, we might overtake him," suggested Marks.

"Too late," McCready said. "We'd never catch him."

"Poor old Tom," said Bill, from the back.

There was silence all the way to Pedhoulas.

Rowse's key was hanging on its hook in the lobby. He took it himself—there was no one behind the desk—and walked upstairs. As he entered his room a powerful shove from the man behind the door sent him staggering forward. The door slammed shut, access to it barred by the stocky one, identified by McCready as Tim O'Herlihy, a killer from the Derry Brigade; the beefy ginger-haired one by the fireplace was Eamonn Kane, an enforcer from West Belfast. Mahoney sat in the only armchair, his back to the window, whose curtains had now been drawn.

Without a word Kane grabbed the staggering Englishman and flattened him against the wall. Skilled hands ran quickly over Rowse's short-sleeved shirt and down each leg of his trousers.

The room was a mess—every drawer opened and emptied, the contents of the wardrobe scattered. Rowse's only consolation was that he carried nothing that an author on a research trip would not have with him. His passport was in his back trouser pocket. Kane fished it out and tossed it to Mahoney. Mahoney flicked through it, but it told him nothing he did not already know.

"So, Sass-man, perhaps you'll tell me what you're doing here."

"I don't know what you're talking about," said Rowse indignantly.

Kane swung a fist, which caught Rowse in the solar plexus. Rowse grunted and doubled, breathing heavily.

"Don't you, now?" said Mahoney, without rising. "Well, a friend of mine in Hamburg identified you there a couple of weeks back. Tom Rowse, former captain in the SAS, asking some very funny questions. Two tours in the Emerald Isle behind him, and now he turns up in the middle of Cyprus just when my friends and I are trying to have a nice quiet holiday."

"Look," said Rowse. "Okay, I was in the regiment. But I quit. Denounced them all, the bastards. Now I write novels for a living."

Mahoney nodded to O'Herlihy. The punch from behind caught Rowse in the kidneys. He cried out and dropped to his knees.

"You're lying to me, Sass-man, and I don't like it. I've heard this just-doing-my-research story before. And a certain gentleman from across the water that you were talking with last night—he one of your co-writers?"

"That's between us. You'd better ask him."

"Oh, I did, Sass-man. And he asked me to keep an eye on you. Which I will do, day and night, until you leave. But just between us, here's a little something for the old times."

Kane and O'Herlihy waded in. When Rowse's legs gave way, he went down to the floor, doubling up, protecting the lower stomach and genitals. He felt the toecaps thud into his back, shoulders, and ribs, choking on the wave of pain until the merciful blackness came after a kick on the back of the head.

He came to, lying on his face, and for a while he studied the pattern of the carpet. Then he rolled over—a mistake. He ran a hand to his face. There was one lump on the cheek below the left eye; otherwise it was more or less the same face he had been shaving for years. He tried to sit up, and winced. An arm went behind his shoulders and eased him into a sitting position.

"What the hell happened here?" Monica Browne was on her knees beside him, one arm around his shoulders. "I was passing, saw the door ajar . . ."

Quite a coincidence, he thought, then dismissed the idea.

"I must have fainted and thumped myself as I went down," he said.

"Was that before or after you wrecked the room?"

She helped him up and led him to the bed. He sat on it. She lifted his legs and rolled him onto the mattress.

"Don't go away," she said unnecessarily. "I have some liniment in my room."

She was back in minutes, closing the door behind her and giving the key a swift turn. She unbuttoned his shirt and slipped it from his shoulders, tut-tutting at the sight of the bruises that adorned his torso and ribs. A small bottle was uncorked, and gentle fingers rubbed liniment into the bruised areas. It stung. He said, "Ow."

"It'll do you good, take the swelling down, help the discoloration. Roll over."

She eased more liniment into the bruises on his back.

"They hit you in the legs as well?"

"All over."

She unbuttoned the waistband of his trousers, unzipped them, and eased them off without a fuss. There were a half-dozen bluish areas on the thighs. She massaged the liniment into them. After the sting the sensation was of pure pleasure. She paused and set the bottle down.

"Where did you learn about bruises?" he asked.

"Back in Kentucky my kid brother was an amateur jockey," she said. "I patched him up a few times."

She turned away and reached for the zipper at the back of her cream shantung dress. It slid to the floor in a pool. She turned around. Rowse swallowed.

"But this I did not learn from any brother."

He reached up for her, but she took his wrists and pressed them back on the pillow.

"Lie still," she whispered. "You're far too ill to participate."

But for the next hour or so she seemed quite content to be proved wrong.

Just before four she rose and crossed the room to open the curtains. Across the valley, Danny the sergeant adjusted his focus and said, "Tom, you dirty bastard."

THE AFFAIR LASTED FOR THREE days. The horses did not arrive from Syria, nor any message for Rowse from Hakim al-Mansour.

McCready and Marks stayed at their pension, in Pedhoulas village, while McCready organized more men from Nicosia station. As long as Hakim al-Mansour made no contact with Rowse, the key was the Irishman Mahoney and his two colleagues. While they stayed, the operation would not move into the shipment phase.

On the second day after Rowse and Monica first made love, McCready's team was in place, covering every road in and out of the area. The telephone line to the hotel had been tapped. The monitoring listeners were ensconced in another, nearby hotel.

On the third day Rowse was up as usual just after dawn broke. Monica slept on, and it was Rowse who took the coffee tray from the waiter at the door. When he lifted the coffeepot to pour his first cup, he saw a folded wafer of paper beneath it. The message said simply, "Club Rosalina, Paphos, 11 p.m. Aziz."

The problem of easing Monica out of the way for the few hours it would take to get to Paphos, on the western coast, was solved at midday by her shipping agent, who called to say that the three stallions would be arriving in the port of Limassol that evening. Could she please be present to see them signed for and settled in their stables? She left at four o'clock.

The Rosalina Club turned out to be a casino in the heart of the Old Town. Rowse entered it just before eleven and soon saw the slim, elegant figure of Hakim al-Mansour seated at one of the roulette tables. Rowse slid into a chair next to him.

"Good evening, Mr. Aziz. What a pleasant surprise."

Mansour inclined his head gravely. *"Faites vos jeux,"* called the croupier.

The Libyan placed several high-denomination chips on a combination of the higher numbers. The wheel spun, and the dancing white ball fell into slot number four. The Libyan showed no annoyance as his chips were swept away. That single throw would have kept a Libyan farmer and his family for a month.

"Nice of you to come," said Mansour as he placed more chips. "I have news for you. Good news, you will be pleased to hear. Our glorious leader has acceded to your request. The equipment you seek will be provided—in full."

"I'm delighted," said Rowse. "I'm sure my principals will put it to . . . good use."

"We must all fervently hope so. That is, as you British soldiers say, the object of the exercise."

"How would you like payment?" asked Rowse.

The Libyan waved a deprecatory hand. "Accept it as a gift from the People's Jamahariya, Mr. Rowse."

"I am very grateful. I am sure my principals will be too."

"I doubt it, for you would be a fool ever to tell them. And you are not a fool. So as you will now be making a commission of not one hundred thousand dollars but half a million, perhaps you will split that with me? Shall we say fifty-fifty?"

"Mr. Aziz, sir, you have a deal. When I can pry the money out of the clients, half will come to you."

"I do hope so," murmured Mansour. This time he won, and a pile of chips was pushed toward him. Despite his urbanity, he was delighted. "My arm is very long."

"I need to know about shipment. Where to collect, when."

"And so you shall. Soon. You asked for a port in Europe. I think that can be arranged." He rose and handed Rowse his remaining pile of chips. "Do not leave the casino for another fifteen minutes," he said. "Here—enjoy yourself."

Rowse waited for fifteen minutes, then cashed in the chips. He left the casino and strolled the narrow streets of the Old Town toward his car. As he approached it an old man in blue denim and a forage cap was sweeping the gutters.

"*Kali spera,*" croaked the old road sweeper.

"*Kali spera,*" replied Rowse. He remembered the wad of money from Mansour's winnings, pulled out a large-denomination note, and tucked it into the old man's top pocket.

"My dear Tom," said the road sweeper, "I always knew you had a good heart."

"What the hell are you doing here, McCready?"

"Just keep jiggling your car keys and tell me what happened," said McCready as he pushed his broom. Rowse told him.

"Good," said McCready. "It looks like a ship. That probably means they're tacking your small cargo onto the much larger one for the IRA. Any idea which port?"

"No. Just Europe."

"Go back to the hotel and do what the man says," ordered McCready.

The message to Rowse came twenty-four hours later by telephone. It was not Mansour's voice but another. "Go home, Mr. Rowse. Your olives will arrive by ship at a European port. You will be contacted personally with arrival and collection details."

McCready studied the intercept in his hotel room. Did Mansour suspect something? If he suspected Rowse's real employers, he would know that Mahoney and his group were also under surveillance. So was he ordering Rowse to England in order to take the watchers off Mahoney? Possibly. McCready decided to play both ends. He would leave with Rowse for London, but the watchers would stay with Mahoney.

Rowse decided to tell Monica the next morning. He had got back to the hotel from Paphos before her. She arrived from Limassol at three a.m., flushed and excited. Her stallions were in beautiful condition, now stabled outside Limassol. She only needed the transit formalities to be completed to bring them to England.

Rowse awoke early, but she was ahead of him. They gave him a message at reception, a brief note in one of the hotel's envelopes:

Dear Tom,
  It was beautiful but it's over. I'm gone, back to my husband and my life and my horses. Think kindly of me, as I will of you.
                                                        Monica

He sighed. He also had his life—with his country home and his writing career and his Nikki. Suddenly he wanted to see Nikki very badly.

CHAPTER FIVE

ROWSE's flight touched down just after lunch.

His car was in the long-term car park. Before retrieving it, he rang Nikki. She was ecstatic, her voice shrill with a mixture of relief and delight. "Are you all right, darling?"

"Yes, I'm fine."

"And is it over?"

"Yes, the research is finished, all bar a couple of extra details that I can sort out here in England. How have you been?"

"Oh, great. Guess what happened? Two days after you left, a man came. Said he was furnishing a large company flat in London, looking for carpets and rugs. He bought the lot, all our stock. Paid cash. Sixteen thousand pounds. Darling, we're flush!"

"This buyer, where was he from?"

"Mr. Da Costa? Portugal. Why?"

"Dark-haired, olive-skinned?"

"Yes, I suppose so."

Libyan, Rowse thought. That meant that while Nikki was out in the barn, where they kept the stock of carpets and rugs, someone had been in the house and probably bugged the phone. Mansour certainly liked to cover all the angles. Had he made a single ill-judged phone call to Nikki, as he had been tempted to do, he would have blown away himself and the mission.

"Well," he said cheerfully, "I don't care where he was from. If he paid cash, he's wonderful."

"When are you coming home?" she asked excitedly.

"I'm on my way."

Rowse drove back to Gloucestershire to await the promised contact from Hakim al-Mansour. As he saw it, when he received the information concerning the docking of the arms ship, he would pass the tip to McCready. The SIS would trace the ship backward from that, identify it in the Mediterranean, and pick it up in the Atlantic or in the English Channel, with Mahoney and his team on board. It was as simple as that.

The contact came seven days later. A black Porsche crept into the courtyard of Rowse's home, and a young man climbed out. He was dark-haired, saturnine, and came from a drier, harsher land.

Rowse's face showed only polite inquiry. "Yes?" he said.

"Mr. Rowse? I have a message from Mr. Aziz." His English was reasonable but careful. "Your cargo will arrive at Bremerhaven. Three crates, all marked as office machinery. Bay zero nine, Warehouse Neuberg. Rossmannstrasse. You must remove them within twenty-four hours of their arrival date. Is that clear?"

Rowse repeated the exact address, fixing it in his mind. "One thing. When? Which day?"

"Ah, yes. They arrive at noon of the twenty-fourth."

The young man drove away. Minutes later Rowse was racing to the village to use the public phone.

"WHAT THE HELL CAN THEY mean, the twenty-fourth?" raged McCready for the tenth time. "That's in three days!"

"Mahoney's still in place?" asked Rowse. He had just driven up to London at McCready's insistence, and they were meeting at one of the Firm's safe houses, an apartment in Chelsea.

"Yes. Still propping up the bar at the Apollonia, still surrounded by his team, still waiting for a word from Mansour."

No ship could get from Cyprus to Bremerhaven via Tripoli or Sirte in three days. McCready had consulted a friend at Lloyd's Shipping Intelligence. The man was adamant. Seven days minimum; more likely eight.

So either it was a test for Rowse, to see if the police would raid the Neuberg warehouse—in which case Mansour would have time to divert his ship somewhere else. Or the ship was already at sea. To dock at Bremerhaven on the twenty-fourth, it would now be somewhere west of Lisbon.

Checks were being made by Lloyd's as to the names of ships expected in Bremerhaven on the twenty-fourth with a Mediterranean port of departure. The phone rang. It was the Lloyd's expert, on a patch-through to the Chelsea safe house.

"Nothing from the Mediterranean is expected on the twenty-fourth," he said. "You must have been misinformed."

With a vengeance, thought McCready. In Hakim al-Mansour he had come up against another master of the game. He turned to Rowse. "Apart from Mahoney and his crew, was there *anyone* in that hotel who even smelled of IRA?"

Rowse shook his head.

"I'm afraid it's time for the photograph albums," said McCready. "Go through them. If there's any face that you spotted in your time in Tripoli, Malta, or Cyprus, let me know."

MCCREADY went to see the CIA station head in Grosvenor Square, Bill Carver.

"Well, Sam, I don't know. Diverting a satellite isn't that easy."

McCready considered long and hard. For weeks his concern had been just to stop the arms shipment from getting into the hands of the IRA. Now, needing CIA help, he produced his bombshell: the threat to the American ambassador in London, as reported by the Libyan doctor in Qaddafi's tent.

Bill Carver came out of his chair as if jet propelled. "You'll get your bloody satellite," he exploded, "but next time you damned well better tell me earlier than this."

IT WAS almost midnight before Rowse went wearily back to album 1—the old days. A projector had been installed so that photographs could be thrown onto a screen and alterations made to the faces. Just before one o'clock Rowse paused.

"This one," he told the technician. "Put it on the screen."

"Don't be daft," said McCready. "He's been out of it for years."

The face stared back—tired eyes behind thick-rimmed glasses, iron-gray hair over the creased brow.

"Lose the glasses," Rowse said to the photo expert. "Give him brown contact lenses."

The technician made adjustments. The glasses vanished, and the eyes went from blue to brown. "Thin the hair, more lines, dewlaps under the chin." The technician did as he was told.

"Turn the hair jet black. Hair dye."

The thin gray hair turned deep black. Rowse whistled. "Sitting alone in the corner of the terrace," he said, "at the Apollonia. Talking to no one, keeping himself to himself."

"Stephen Johnson was chief of staff of the IRA—the *old* IRA— twenty years ago," said McCready. "Quit the whole organization ten years ago after a blazing row with the new generation."

Rowse grinned. "Used to be an ace, had a row, quit in disgust, known to be out in the cold, untouchable by those inside the Establishment—remind you of anyone you know?"

"The old bugger," breathed McCready. "He's gone active again."

IN THE middle of the morning McCready took a call from Bill Carver, and they went over to the American embassy. Carver took them to his office in the basement, where he too had a room for viewing photographs all set up.

The satellite had done its job well, rolling gently high in space over the eastern Atlantic, its Long Tom cameras covering a strip of water from the Portuguese, Spanish, and French coasts to more than one hundred miles out into the ocean in a single pass.

The continuous welter of photographs had been broken down into individual snaps of every ship afloat in that rectangle of water.

"The bird photographed everything bigger than a floating Coke can," remarked Carver proudly.

Nearly half the ships were fishing vessels, and McCready discounted them. He concentrated on the freighters and a few large private yachts. His reduced list numbered fifty-three.

One by one, he asked that the small slivers of metal on the great expanse of water be blown up until each filled the screen. Detail by detail the men in the room examined them.

At half past two McCready called a halt. "That man," he said to Bill Carver's technician, "the one standing on the wing of the bridge. Can you come in closer?"

"You got it," said the American.

The freighter grew bigger and bigger, and still the definition held. The forepeak and stern of the vessel disappeared offscreen, and the figure of the man standing alone grew larger. His face was raised.

"Freeze," called Rowse. "Closer."

The technician magnified the face until finally it began to blur.

"Bingo," McCready whispered. "That's him. Johnson."

The tired old eyes beneath the thin jet-black hair stared out at them from the screen. The old man from the corner of the Apollonia dining terrace. The has-been.

"We need the name of the ship," said McCready.

A single low-angle shot had caught the words beside the anchor: REGINA IV. McCready reached for the phone and called his man at Lloyd's Shipping Intelligence.

"Can't be," said the man when he called back thirty minutes later. "*Regina IV* is over ten thousand tons, and she's off the coast of Venezuela. You must have got it wrong."

"No mistake," said McCready. "She's about two thousand tons, and she's steaming north, by now off Bordeaux."

"*Regina* is a very common name. That's why they have numerals after the name, to distinguish one from another. It happens there's a *Regina VI* registered at Limassol, now believed to be berthed at Paphos. About two thousand tons. German skipper, Greek Cypriot crew. New owners—a shell company registered in Luxembourg."

The Libyan government, thought McCready. It would be a simple ruse. Leave the Mediterranean as the *Regina VI*; out in the Atlantic, paint out the single numeral after the V and paint another in before it. Skilled hands could alter the ship's papers, and who would know that the real *Regina IV* was off Venezuela?

AT DAWN of the third day Captain Holst stared out the forward windows of his bridge at the slowly lightening sea. There was no mistaking the maroon flare that had burst into the sky ahead of him. A distress flare. Peering through the half-light, he could make out something else: the yellow fluttering of a flame. He ordered his engine room to make half speed, lifted a handset, and called one of his passengers, in his bunk below. The man joined him less than a minute later.

Captain Holst pointed through the windshield. On the calm water ahead a forty-foot motor fishing vessel rolled drunkenly. She had clearly suffered an explosion in her engine area; black smoke drifted up from below her deck, mingling with a flicker of orange flame. Her topsides were scorched and blackened.

Stephen Johnson took the captain's binoculars and focused on the small fishing boat ahead. FAIR MAID, WHITBY, could be made out on her bow.

"We have to stop and give them help," Holst said in English. "It is the law of the sea."

He did not know what his own vessel was carrying, and he did not want to know. His employers had given him their orders and an extravagant bonus. He knew there must be illicit cargo in there somewhere; the proof lay in the six passengers—two were from Cyprus, and four more were from Sirte—and the changing of the numerals as soon as he had passed the Pillars of Hercules. In twelve hours he expected to be rid of them all. He would sail back through the North Sea, convert again to the *Regina VI*, and return to his home port of Limassol a much richer man.

Johnson looked dubious. "We can't stop," he said.

"We have to."

The light was getting better. They saw a figure, scorched and blackened, emerge from the wheelhouse of the fishing vessel, stagger to the forward deck, make a pain-racked attempt to wave, then fall forward onto his face.

Another IRA officer came up behind Holst. He felt the muzzle of a gun in his ribs. "Sail on by," said a flat voice.

Holst did not ignore the gun, but he looked at Johnson. "If they are rescued by another ship, they will report us. We can give first aid and call the Dutch coast guard. No one comes aboard. When the Dutch cutter appears, we continue. It will cost us thirty minutes."

Johnson was persuaded. "Put up your gun," he said.

Holst moved his speed control to FULL ASTERN, and the *Regina* slowed rapidly. Giving an order in Greek to his helmsman, he left the bridge and made his way to the foredeck.

"Ahoy, *Fair Maid!*" he called, peering down as the fishing boat came under the bow. They saw the fallen man on the deck try to stir, then faint again. Holst shouted an order for a line to be thrown aboard the *Fair Maid*.

There was no need. As the fisherman slid past the *Regina* the man on the deck came to, jumped up with remarkable agility, seized a grappling hook, and hurled it over the *Regina*'s rail. A second man ran out of the fishing boat's cabin and did the same at the stern. The *Fair Maid* stopped drifting.

Four more men ran from the cabin, vaulted to the roof, and jumped straight over the rail of the *Regina*. They were all dressed alike: black one-piece overalls, cleated rubber boots, and black woolen caps. They were members of the SBS—the Special Boat Squadron—the seaborne equivalent of the Special Air Service. A very hard hand took Captain Holst in the solar plexus, and he went down on his knees.

By now there were four Cypriot crewmen on the main deck. One of the men in black shouted a single order to them in Greek, and they obeyed. They went face down onto the deck and stayed there. Not so the four IRA members who came pouring out of the side door of the superstructure. They all had handguns.

Two had the sense to see that a handgun is a poor bargain when faced with a Heckler and Koch MP5 submachine carbine and tossed their pistols to the deck. Two tried to use their guns. One was lucky. He took the brief burst in the legs and survived to spend his life in a wheelchair. The other collected four bullets in the chest.

There were now six black-clad men swarming over the *Regina*'s deck. The third to come aboard had been Tom Rowse. He ran for the companionway that led to the bridge. As he reached the top Stephen Johnson emerged from inside. Seeing Rowse, he threw his hands in the air. "Don't shoot, Sass-man. It's over!" he shouted.

Rowse stood aside and jerked the barrel of his machine pistol toward the staircase. "Down," he said.

The old IRA man began to descend to the main deck. There was a movement behind Rowse—someone in the door of the wheelhouse. He sensed the movement, half turned, and caught the crash of the handgun. The bullet plucked at the shoulder of his cloth overall. There was no time to pause or shout. He fired as they had taught him, a quick double burst, then another.

He had an image of the figure in the doorway taking all four bullets in the chest, being thrown back into the doorjamb, cannoning forward again—the wild swing of the corn-blond hair. Then she was on the steel deck, quite dead, a thin trickle of blood seeping from the mouth he had kissed.

"Well, well," said a voice at his elbow. "Monica Browne. With an *e*."

Rowse turned. "You bastard," he said. "You knew, didn't you?"

"Not knew. Suspected," McCready said gently. In civilian clothes, he had come at a more sedate pace out of the fishing vessel when the shooting was over. "We had to check her out, Tom. She is—was—indeed Monica Browne, but Dublin born and bred. Her first marriage, at twenty, took her to Kentucky for eight years. After the divorce she married Major Eric Browne, much older, but rich. He probably had no suspicion of his wife's fanatical devotion to the IRA. And yes, she did run a stud farm, but not at Ashford, Kent, England. It was at Ashford, County Wicklow, Ireland."

THE covers were taken from the holds, and the cargo searched. After two hours the lieutenant who commanded the SBS team reported to McCready. "Nothing, sir."

"What do you mean, nothing?"

"A lot of olives. Some crates marked Office Machinery."

"Containing?"

"Office machinery, sir. And the three stallions. They're pretty upset, sir."

"So am I," said McCready grimly. "Show me."

He and Rowse followed the officer below. The lieutenant gave them a tour of the ship's four holds. No crate or carton had been

left untouched. There was a feeling in McCready's stomach—that awful feeling that comes with knowing you have been duped and that there will be the devil to pay.

A young SBS man was standing with the horses. He seemed to know about animals; he was talking to them quietly, calming them down. "Sir?" he asked. "Why are they being shipped?"

"Oh. They're Arabs. Thoroughbreds destined for a stud farm," said Rowse.

"No, they're not," said the young commando. "They're riding school hacks. Stallions, but hacks."

Between the inner and outer walls of the specially constructed transport boxes there was a good foot of space. With crowbars they hacked at the planks of the first horse box. As the shattered timber fell away, the search was over. The watching men saw piled blocks of Semtex-H, serried ranks of RPG-7 rocket launchers, and rows of shoulder-borne surface-to-air missiles. The other horse boxes yielded heavy machine guns, ammunition, grenades, mines, and mortars.

"I think," said McCready, "we can call in the navy now."

THE *Fair Maid* had been pumped out to correct her wallowing list. The special-effects smoke grenades that had given her the appearance of being on fire had long been thrown into the sea. Her engine started. Two of the commandos cast her loose, and the fishing boat chugged away.

On the other side of the *Regina's* deck a navy frigate eased alongside, threw graplines, and sent the first of the boarding party across.

Tom Rowse sat down on the coaming of one of the holds, next to the body of Monica Browne. A puff of wind had lifted one corner of the sheet that covered her, and he stared at the beautiful face, so calm in death. The breeze blew a frond of corn-blond hair across the forehead. He reached down to push it back. Someone sat down beside him, and an arm came around his shoulders.

"It's over, Tom. You weren't to blame."

"If I'd known she was here, I wouldn't have killed her," said Rowse dully.

"Then she'd have killed you. She was that kind of person."

"What happens now?" asked Rowse.

McCready stared at the sea and the sky and sighed. "Oh, I will go back to Century House and start again. And go back each night to my small flat and listen to my music and eat my baked beans. And you will go back to Nikki, my friend, and hold her very tight, and write your books and forget all this. It's all over."

"Why did she do it, Sam? Why the hell did she do it?"

McCready leaned forward and drew the sheet back over the face of Monica Browne. "Because she believed, Tom. In the wrong thing, of course. But she believed."

He rose, pulling Rowse up with him.

"Come on, lad, we're going home. Let it be, Tom. Let it be. She's gone the way she wanted, by her own wish. Now she's just another casualty of war. Like you, Tom. Like all of us."

INTERLUDE

T HURSDAY, when the hearing began its fourth day, was the day that Timothy Edwards had determined would be its last. Before Denis Gaunt could begin, Edwards preempted him.

After the close of the Wednesday hearing, his two colleagues behind the table had made their feelings more than plain, proposing that somehow the old Deceiver be retained within the Service. That was emphatically not in Edwards' scenario. Unlike the others, he knew that the move to retire McCready stemmed from the permanent under secretary of the Foreign Office, a man who one day would help decide the identity of the next chief of the SIS. It would be foolish to antagonize such a man.

"Denis, we have all listened with the greatest interest to your recall of Sam's many services, and we are all mightily impressed. The fact is, however, that we now have to face the challenge of the '90s, a period when certain—how shall I put it?—active measures will have no place. Must I remind you of the brouhaha occasioned by Sam's chosen course of action in the Caribbean last winter?"

"Not in the slightest, Timothy," said Gaunt. "I had in mind to recall the episode myself."

"Then please do so," invited Edwards, convinced that his two colleagues would view McCready's actions more as those of a cowboy than of a local representative of Her Gracious Majesty.

Denis Gaunt reluctantly crossed the room to the desk of the

records clerk and took the proffered folder. Despite what he had said, the Caribbean affair was the one he would most have liked to avoid.

"It all really began," said Gaunt, opening the file, "in early December, on a small island in the northern Caribbean."

A LITTLE BIT OF SUNSHINE

CHAPTER ONE

THE *Gulf Lady* came home across a bright and glittering sea an hour before the sun went down. Julio Gomez sat forward, his ample rear end supported by the cabin roof, his moccasined feet on the foredeck. He drew contentedly on one of his foul Puerto Rican cheroots.

He was, in that moment, a truly happy man. In the scarred old box astern of the open fishing deck lay two fine dorados, one for him and one for the skipper, who now held the tiller and steered his game fisherman home to Port Plaisance.

Not that two fish had been his entire day's take; two big amber-jacks he had returned to the sea, taking only the dorados because they are among the finest eating fish in the Caribbean.

Julio Gomez did not like to kill. What brought him on his annual pilgrimage to these waters was the thrill of the hissing reel and the running line, the sheer excitement of the contest between air-breathing man and monstrously strong fighting fish. It had been a wonderful day.

Three miles ahead of the *Gulf Lady* the island straddled the water. Gomez flicked the stub of his cheroot to a sputtering grave in the water and dropped from the cabin roof into the stern. "I'll take over, Jimmy. Give you a chance to swab down."

Jimmy Dobbs gave his ear-to-ear grin, handed over the tiller, took bucket and broom, and began to swab the fish scales and fragments of gut out through the scuppers.

There were, of course, more modern charter fishing boats plying the Caribbean. But the sheer lack of sophistication of the islands pleased Julio Gomez, who spent much of his professional life handling America's modern technology, tapping queries into a computer, steering a car through the tangled traffic of central Miami. For his vacation he wanted the sea, the sun, and the wind.

They berthed just after five at the rickety old wooden fishing quay that ought to have fallen down years ago. The previous governor had said he would ask London for a grant to build a new one, but then he had been replaced by Sir Marston Moberley, who had no interest in fishing. Nor in the islanders, if the bar talk in Shantytown was to be believed—and it always was.

"You free tomorrow, Jimmy?" asked Gomez.

"Sure am. You wanna go again?"

"That's what I'm here for. See you at eight."

Julio Gomez paid a small boy a dollar to carry his fish for him, and together the pair walked into Port Plaisance. It was the sort of town found in most of the smaller Caribbean islands—a jumble of brightly colored wooden houses, with lanes of crushed shells between them. Around the small harbor, where the weekly trading steamer berthed, stood the more resplendent structures—the customhouse, the courthouse, and the war memorial.

Farther into the town were the town hall and, on Parliament Square, the Anglican church, the police station, and the principal hotel, the Quarter Deck. Along the shore, just out of town, stood the governor's residence, Government House, all white and walled in white, with two old Napoleonic cannons by the front gate.

Gomez could have stayed at the Quarter Deck, but he preferred the homey atmosphere of Mrs. Macdonald's boardinghouse. She was a widow, with a cap of snow-white frizzy hair, and as amply proportioned as he was himself. He turned into the street where she lived, ignoring the garish election posters clipped to most of the walls, and saw that she was sweeping down her front steps. She greeted him and his fish with her usual beaming smile.

"Why, Mistah Gomez, that is one very fine fish."

"For our supper, Mrs. Macdonald, and enough for all of us."

Gomez went up to his room. He washed, shaved, and changed into cream slacks and a bright short-sleeved beach shirt. He decided he could use a very large, very cold beer and walked back through the town to the bar of the Quarter Deck.

It was only seven o'clock, but night had come, and the town was quite dark. He passed the police station, where Chief Inspector Brian Jones and an impeccably turned-out force of two sergeants and eight constables represented law and order in the community with the lowest crime rate in the Western Hemisphere. Coming from Miami, Gomez could not but wonder at a society that seemed to have no drugs, no gangs, no muggings, no prostitution, no rapes, and only half a dozen reportable thefts a year. He sighed and entered the bar of the Quarter Deck.

He took a corner stool and ordered his large cold beer. It would be an hour before his fish was ready—time for a second beer to keep company with the first. At five to eight he was reaching into his pocket to settle his bill. When he looked up, he stopped, fixed rigid, and stared at the man who had entered the bar and was ordering a drink at the far end. After two seconds he eased back on his stool so that the next drinker blocked him from view. He could hardly believe his eyes, but he knew he was not wrong. You do not spend four days and four nights sitting across a table from a man, staring into his eyes, seeing hatred and contempt, and later forget that face, even eight years on. Not a single word had he got out of the man—not even a name.

Gomez retired to a corner in the shadows. If the man was here, he was here for a reason. If he had checked into a hotel, he would have a name. Gomez wanted that name. He waited and watched. At nine the man rose and left. Gomez went after him.

In Parliament Square the man climbed into an open jeep and drove away. Gomez looked desperately around. Parked near the hotel entrance was a small motor scooter, its key in the ignition. Wobbling precariously, Gomez set off after the jeep.

The jeep left the town and drove out along the coast road. It passed the island's other residential community, known as Shanty-town, then kept going until it reached the other side of the island. Here it pulled off the coast road and up a short track to a pair of wrought-iron gates that protected a large, walled estate.

The driver must have seen the single head lamp that had been behind him all the way. For as Gomez rode past the entrance the beam of a powerful spot lamp swept over him, holding him in its glare until he passed out of sight down the road.

Gomez returned the scooter to its place outside the hotel thirty minutes later and walked home. He was deeply worried. He had seen where the man was living. But he himself had been seen. He could only pray that he had not been recognized.

Mrs. Macdonald was perturbed at his failure to arrive for sup-per until almost two hours late, and said so. She served the dorado anyway and watched her guest eat it with no pleasure. He was lost in thought and only made one remark.

"Nonsense, man," she chided. "We don't even have them things in these islands."

Julio Gomez spent the night lying awake and considering his choices. The man's presence here was something the British ought to hear about, but the man probably had given no cause to be arrested. He was not on U.S. territory now. This would need an extradition request from Uncle Sam. Gomez had no choice; he would have to return to Florida in the morning.

That same evening a Delta Air Lines flight from Washington touched down at Miami Airport. Among its passengers was a tired British civil servant whose passport said he was Mr. Frank Dillon. That his real name was Sam McCready was known only to the group of senior members of the CIA with whom he had been attending a seminar on intelligence in the '90s.

McCready took a cab to the Sonesta Beach Hotel on Key Biscayne. Here he treated himself to a lobster supper before retiring for a deep and untroubled sleep. He faced, or so he thought, the prospect of seven days of toasting himself by the pool and occasionally raising his gaze from a lighthearted spy novel to watch a Florida girl sway by. It was time, he thought as he fell asleep, for the Deceiver to get a suntan.

ON FRIDAY morning Julio Gomez checked out of Mrs. Macdonald's boardinghouse. His ticket was for the Sunday morning scheduled flight by BWIA to Nassau, with a connection to Miami. There was no travel agent in town—bookings were always made right at the airstrip—so he could only hope that there was a Friday morning BWIA flight. He did not notice that he was being watched as he took a taxi out of the town.

At the airstrip, he was disappointed. The airport building was almost deserted. A single passport officer sat in the sun reading a week-old Miami *Herald*.

"Not today, man," he replied. "Never on a Friday."

Gomez surveyed the field. Outside the single hangar stood a Piper Navajo Chief. A man in ducks and shirt was checking it over. Gomez moved across. "You flying today?" he asked.

"Yep," said the pilot, a fellow American.

"Available for charter?"

"No way," said the pilot. "This is a private plane. Belongs to my employer."

"Where you heading? Nassau?" asked Gomez.

"Nope. Key West."

Gomez's heart rose. "Any chance I can talk to your employer?"

"Mr. Klinger. He'll be here in about an hour."

Gomez found a shady spot near the hangar wall and settled down to wait. Someone in the bushes withdrew, took a motorcycle from the undergrowth, and motored away down the coast road.

SIR Marston Moberley checked his watch, rose from his breakfast table, and sauntered toward his office. That tiresome delegation was due anytime.

Britain retains very few of her colonies in the Caribbean. Only five remain, classed today as dependent territories. They include the Cayman Islands, the British Virgin Islands, the Turks and Caicos, and the island of Anguilla, whose inhabitants conducted the only known revolution in colonial history in order to stay British.

In the winter of 1989 the fifth and last group was the Barclays, eight small islands situated at the western edge of the Great Bahama Bank, due south of the Florida Keys. The tiny group had no more than twenty thousand inhabitants, and only two of the eight islands were inhabited at all. The chief island, and home of the government, rejoiced in the name of Sunshine.

They were not rich islands. Industry was nil, and income not much more. The generous ocean provided most of the food, along with fruit from the forests and gardens tended along the slopes of Sunshine's two hills, Spyglass and Sawbones.

In early 1989 someone in the Foreign Office decided that the Barclays were ripe for independence. The British Cabinet that year was wrestling with a huge trade deficit and slumping popularity polls. The bagatelle of an obscure island group in the Caribbean going independent passed without debate.

The then governor objected, however, and was duly recalled and replaced by Sir Marston Moberley. A tall, vain man, who prided himself on his resemblance to the late actor George Sanders, he had been sent to Sunshine with a single brief: the Barclays were to accept their independence. Candidates for

Prime Minister would be invited, and a general-election day was set. After the democratic election of the Barclays' first Prime Minister, full independence would be granted—nay, insisted upon. Sir Marston was to ensure that the program went through. He and Lady Moberley had arrived on Sunshine in late July.

Two candidates had soon presented themselves for the office of Prime Minister–to-be. Mr. Marcus Johnson, a wealthy businessman and philanthropist, had returned to the islands of his birth after making a fortune in Central America. He now resided on a fine estate the other side of Sawbones Hill and had formed the Barclays Prosperity Alliance, pledged to develop the islands and bring wealth to the people. The more rough-hewn but populist Mr. Horatio Livingstone, who lived in Shantytown, of which he owned a substantial part, had formed the Barclays Independence Front. Livingstone had promised a miraculous rise in living standards, based on the nationalization of property and assets. The elections were but three weeks away, scheduled for January 5.

There was but one fly in Sir Marston's ointment: the CCC, or Committee for Concerned Citizens, which was opposed to independence. It was led by that tiresome man the Reverend Walter Drake, the local Baptist minister. Sir Marston had agreed to receive a delegation from the CCC at nine that morning.

There were eight of them. The Anglican vicar, an ineffectual Englishman, he knew he could deal with. Six were local worthies—the doctor, two shopkeepers, a farmer, a bar owner, and a boarding-house keeper. They were all elderly and of rudimentary education.

The problem was the CCC delegation leader, Walter Drake, a big black bull of a man in a black suit, who now wiped perspiration from his face. He was a compulsive preacher who had secured an education on the American mainland. Drake thumped a pile of paper on the governor's desk.

"That, Governor," he boomed, "is a petition. Yes, sir, a petition. Signed by more than one thousand of our citizens. We want this petition conveyed to London and put before Mrs. Thatcher herself. We believe she will listen to us, even if you will not."

Sir Marston sighed. "And what does your petition require?"

"We want a referendum. We *demand* a referendum. We do not want to be forced into independence. We want to go on as we are, as we have always been. We appeal to London."

DOWN AT THE AIRSTRIP, A TAXI arrived, and Mr. Barney Klinger stepped out. He was a short, rotund man who lived in a substantial property in Coral Gables, next to Miami. The stunning chorus girl who accompanied him was young enough to be his daughter. Mr. Klinger kept a cottage on the slopes of Spyglass Hill, which he used occasionally for discreet vacations away from Mrs. Klinger.

He intended to fly to Key West, put his girlfriend on a scheduled flight to Miami, then proceed home in his own plane, clearly alone, a tired businessman returning from a boring old meeting.

Julio Gomez heaved himself to his feet and approached. "Mr. Klinger, sir?"

Klinger's heart jumped. A private detective? "Who wants to know?"

"Look, I have a problem, sir. I was vacationing down here, and I just got a call from my wife. Our kid's had an accident back home, and I have to get back. There are no flights today. None. I was wondering, could you give me a lift to Key West?"

Klinger hesitated. The man could still be a private eye hired by Mrs. Klinger. He handed his grip to a baggage porter, who began to load the Navajo. "Well," he said, "I don't know."

There were six people grouped around: the passport officer, the baggage porter, Gomez, Klinger, his girlfriend, and another man, who was helping with the luggage. The porter assumed this man was from the Klinger party, and the Klinger party assumed he belonged to the airstrip.

"Gee, honey, we've got to help him," said the chorus girl.

"Okay," said Klinger. "So long as we take off on time."

The passport officer quickly stamped the three passports, the three passengers boarded, the pilot revved up both engines, and three minutes later the Navajo lifted off Sunshine.

Fifty miles short of Key West it disintegrated in midair.

"MY DEAR Mr. Drake," said Sir Marston Moberley, "if you feel this way, why not stand for the post of Prime Minister yourself? According to your view, you would have to win."

Drake stabbed a sausagelike finger in his direction. "You know why, Governor. These candidates are using printing presses, public-address systems, even campaign managers brought in from outside. And they're offering a lot of cash around among the people. And intimidation of those who oppose them."

"I have no evidence of that," snapped the governor.

"Because you won't go outside and see what's going on!" roared the Baptist minister. "But *we* know."

"Surely we need not quarrel," pleaded the Anglican vicar. "The point is, will you send our petition to London, Sir Marston?"

"Certainly I will," said the governor. "It is the least I can do for you. But it is also, I fear, the *only* thing I can do."

As they left the building the doctor, who happened to be the uncle of the police chief, asked, "Do you think he really will?"

"Yes, by surface mail," growled the Reverend Mr. Drake. "It should arrive in London around mid-January. We have to get rid of that governor and get ourselves a new one."

ON MONDAY, Julio Gomez, a detective on the force of the Metro-Dade Police Department, did not show up for work. His partner, Detective Eddie Favaro, was extremely annoyed. They were due in court together that morning, and now Favaro had to go alone. In the late morning he got back to MDPD headquarters and checked with his superior officer, Lieutenant Broderick.

"What's with Julio?" asked Favaro. "He never showed up."

"You're asking me? He's your partner," replied Broderick.

"He didn't check in?"

"Not to me," said Broderick.

Mirroring its own local population, the Metro-Dade Police Department, which covers most of Greater Miami, employs a wide racial mix. Julio Gomez had been of Puerto Rican parentage. His partner of nine years, Eddie Favaro, was an Italian American. Lieutenant Clay Broderick was black. Now he shrugged. "Find him," he said. "You know the rules."

Favaro did indeed. In Metro-Dade if you are three days late back from a vacation without adequate good reason and without checking in, you are deemed to have dismissed yourself.

Favaro checked his partner's apartment, but there was no sign of him. He knew where Gomez had gone—he always went to Sunshine—so he checked with the airline. Its computer revealed the flight reservation and prepaid ticket home, but it also showed the ticket had not been taken up. Favaro went back to Broderick.

"He could have had an accident," he urged.

Broderick sighed. Missing detectives he could do without. "Okay," he said. "I'll call the local police chief."

It took thirty minutes for Lieutenant Broderick to get his connection. Chief Inspector Jones took this call seriously. His was a tiny force, and Metro-Dade's was enormous. But he would show the Americans that Chief Inspector Jones was not half asleep. He decided to handle the case himself.

He started with the Quarter Deck Hotel, but there he drew a blank. He went on to the fishing quay and found Jimmy Dobbs. Dobbs related that Gomez had not shown up for their Friday charter, which was odd, and that he had been staying with Mrs. Macdonald.

The landlady reported that Julio Gomez had left in a hurry on Friday morning for the airport. Jones went there and spoke to the passport officer, who confirmed that Mr. Gomez had taken a lift with Mr. Klinger to Key West on Friday morning. Jones telephoned Broderick back at four p.m.

Broderick summoned Eddie Favaro just after six. His face was grave. "Eddie, I'm sorry. Julio made a sudden decision to come home Friday morning. There was no scheduled flight back, so he hitched a lift on a private plane for Key West. The plane went down into the sea, fifty miles short of Key West. The coast guard says there were no survivors."

Favaro sat down. He shook his head. "Nine years," he whispered. "Nine years he watched my back. What happens now?"

"You know the procedure," said Broderick. "If we can't have a funeral service, we'll have a memorial. Full departmental honors. I promise."

THE suspicions came later that night and the next morning.

On Sunday a charter skipper had taken two boys fishing off Islamorada, a resort well north of Key West. Six miles out, one of the boys took a big bite on his line. It turned out to be the remnants of a life jacket, still bearing the stenciled number of the airplane to which it had belonged and some scorch marks.

The local police sent it up to Miami, where it was established that it had come from Barney Klinger's Navajo and that the scorch marks bore traces not of gasoline, but of plastic explosive.

ON TUESDAY MORNING SAM McCready eased himself onto his poolside lounger on Key Biscayne and opened the Miami *Herald*. The second lead concerned fresh revelations in the disappearance of a light airplane the previous Friday morning.

The news sleuths of the *Herald* had discovered not only that the plane might well have been destroyed by a bomb inside it but that Mr. Barney Klinger was known as the uncrowned king of the illicit trade in spare aviation parts in south Florida.

After narcotics, this abstruse area of illegal behavior is probably the most lucrative. Florida bristles with airplanes in constant need of new or reconditioned spare parts. Since some of these parts sell for a quarter of a million dollars each, the profits for a ruthless operator can be huge.

LIEUTENANT Broderick summoned Eddie Favaro on that same Tuesday morning. "Eddie, what the hell was Julio doing sharing a plane with a sleazeball like Klinger?"

"He was trying to get back home," said Favaro. "He saw a plane, he asked for a ride, is all."

"Why was he trying to get home two days ahead of schedule?"

"That's what puzzles me," admitted Favaro. "He would never have cut short his fishing without a reason. I've got some leave time due me. I want to go over there and find out why."

"If you go there, you're on your own, Eddie. That's British territory—we have no authority there. And I want your gun."

Favaro handed over his police automatic, left, and headed for the bank. That afternoon he landed on Sunshine's airstrip, paid off his chartered four-seater, hitched a lift into Port Plaisance, and checked into the Quarter Deck.

SIR Marston Moberley sat in a comfortable chair in his walled garden and sipped a whiskey and soda. It was his favorite ritual of the day. The garden behind Government House was not large, but it was very private. A well-tended lawn covered most of the space, and bougainvilleas and jacarandas festooned the walls with their brilliant colors. The walls surrounding the garden were eight feet high and topped with shards of glass. In one wall was an old steel door, seven feet tall but long out of use. On its outer side two semicircular steel hasps were secured by a padlock the size of a small dinner plate. All were long fused by rust.

Sir Marston enjoyed the cool of the evening. He sipped his whiskey with appreciation, then almost choked when his ears were assailed by the scream of rending steel. He rose. He had time to say, "I say, what on earth— Now look here—"

The roar of the first bullet shocked and stunned him. The slug went through a fold of loose fabric in the sleeve of his cotton shirt. It hammered into the coral-block wall of the house behind him and fell back onto the path, misshapen and twisted. The second hit him full in the heart.

CHAPTER TWO

DESPITE the twin booms of the handgun from the garden, there was no immediate reaction from inside the house. Only two people were there at that hour. Lady Moberley was out visiting the local hospital.

Jefferson, the chef-butler, was belowstairs preparing a fruit punch for the evening meal. He would say later that when the blender was switched on, the noise filled the kitchen.

The governor's adjutant was Lieutenant Jeremy Haverstock, a downy-cheeked young subaltern seconded from the Queen's Dragoon Guards. He was in his room at the far end of Government House, with the window closed and the air-conditioning at full blast. He too heard nothing.

By the time Jefferson came out into the garden, the assassin had clearly withdrawn through the steel gate. Jefferson saw his employer lying flat on his back, arms wide, a dark blotch still spreading across the front of his dark blue cotton shirt.

At first Jefferson thought his master had fainted, and he ran down to help him up. When he saw the hole in the chest more clearly, he ran, panic-stricken, to fetch Lieutenant Haverstock. The young officer arrived seconds later, still in his boxer shorts.

Haverstock examined the body without touching it, established that Sir Marston was extremely dead, and sat down in the ex-governor's chair to ponder what to do. The subaltern decided that (a) he had a dead governor on his hands, (b) someone had shot him and escaped, and (c) he should inform a higher authority. At this point Lady Moberley came home.

Jefferson heard the crunch of the wheels of the official Jaguar limousine on the gravel of the front drive and rushed out to intercept her. His breaking of the news was lucid, if not very tactful.

"Oh, Lady, de governor been shot. He dead."

Lady Moberley hurried to the veranda and was met by Haverstock, coming up the steps. He assisted her to her bedroom and comforted her as she lay down, more bewildered, it seemed, than grief-stricken. He then dispatched Jefferson to summon the island's only doctor—who also happened to be the only coroner—and Chief Inspector Jones, who was the doctor-coroner's nephew. The lieutenant instructed the distraught butler to explain nothing to them, simply to ask each man to come urgently.

It was a fruitless request. Poor Jefferson told Chief Inspector Jones the news in the hearing of three wide-eyed constables, and Dr. Caractacus Jones in front of his housekeeper. The news spread like wildfire.

While Jefferson was away, Lieutenant Haverstock pondered how to tell London. Apart from the open phone line, the governor's messages had always gone to London via the British High Commission in Nassau, the Bahamas. For this an elderly C2 system was used. It sat on a table in the governor's private office. To look at, it was an ordinary Telex machine, and was switched to encrypted mode through a second box, which sat beside it. The trouble was, to operate the encoder, one had to insert corrugated disks, which were kept in the governor's safe. The dead man's secretary, Myrtle, had the combination of the safe, but she was away visiting her parents on Tortola, in the Virgin Islands. Haverstock did not know the combination.

Eventually he simply rang the High Commission in Nassau. An incandescent first secretary told him crisply to seal Government House and hold the fort until backup could arrive from Nassau or London. The first secretary then radioed the Foreign Office, in London, and the wheels began to roll.

On Sunshine, the news spread through Port Plaisance, and on his regular evening call a radio ham told a fellow enthusiast in Chevy Chase, near Washington. The latter, being a public-spirited fellow, called The Associated Press, which emitted a dispatch. In London, Reuters took the story off its rival's tape and tried to get confirmation from the Foreign Office. Just before dawn the Foreign Office admitted that the appropriate steps were being taken.

The appropriate steps had involved the waking of a considerable number of people scattered in and around London. The Foreign Office alerted the Home Office, and they in turn raised the commissioner of the Metropolitan Police. The commissioner woke Simon Crawshaw of the Specialist Operations Division, who got on to the commander controlling his Serious Crimes Branch. Commander Braithwaite rang through to the twenty-four-hour Reserve Office and asked, "Who's in the frame?"

The Reserve Office at New Scotland Yard maintains a list of senior detectives available at short notice to assist a police authority outside the metropolitan area.

The duty sergeant consulted his roster. "Mr. Hannah, sir."

"Ask him to call me at home. Now," said the commander.

Thus it was that just after four a.m., on a black December morning, the phone woke Detective Chief Superintendent Desmond Hannah, in bed in Croydon. He listened to the instruction from the Reserve Office and then called a number in West Drayton.

"Bill? Des Hannah. What's up?"

He listened for five minutes, then asked, "Bill, where the hell is Sunshine?"

BACK on the island, Dr. Caractacus Jones had examined the body and pronounced it very dead. Darkness had descended over the garden, and he worked by flashlight. Not that there was much he could do. He was a general practitioner, not a forensic pathologist. He could issue a death certificate, but he had never cut up a dead governor, and he did not intend to start now.

Lieutenant Haverstock returned from the private office. "A senior officer will be sent from Scotland Yard," he announced. "Till then we must keep everything just as it was."

Chief Inspector Jones had posted a constable on the front door to keep away sightseers. He had prowled the garden and discovered the steel door through which the assassin had apparently entered and left. Jones at once posted a second constable outside the door and ordered him to keep everyone away from it. It might contain fingerprints the man from Scotland Yard would need.

Inside the garden Chief Inspector Jones pronounced, "The body must not be moved until morning."

"Don't be a damned fool, boy," said his uncle, Dr. Jones. "It will go rotten." In the heat of the Caribbean, bodies are normally interred within twenty-four hours. The alternative is unspeakable.

The three men considered their problem.

"It will have to be the icehouse," said Dr. Jones at length. "There's nowhere else."

The icehouse was down on the docks. Haverstock took the dead man's shoulders, and Chief Inspector Jones took his feet. With some difficulty they maneuvered the body up the steps, across the sitting room, and out into the hall. Lady Moberley put her head around her bedroom door, glanced over the banisters, uttered a series of oh-oh-oh-ohs, and retired again.

Sir Marston was placed in a police Land-Rover and driven down to the docks, followed by most of the population of Port Plaisance. There he was laid out with great ceremony in the icehouse, where the temperature was well below zero.

Her Majesty's late governor of the Barclay Islands spent his first night in the afterworld sandwiched between a large marlin and a very fine blackfin tuna. In the morning the expression on all three faces was much the same.

IN LONDON, Detective Chief Superintendent Hannah was closeted with Commander Braithwaite in New Scotland Yard.

"You take off just before twelve on the BA flight from Heathrow for Nassau," said the commander. "Tickets are being arranged."

"And the team?" asked Hannah.

"Ah, the team, yes. Fact is, Des, they're being provided in Nassau. The Foreign Office is arranging it."

Desmond Hannah smelled a large rat. He was fifty-one, an old-fashioned thieftaker who had worked his way up the ladder from bobby on the beat to chief superintendent. He liked things to be done right. On any assignment a Murder Squad detective could expect a backup team of at least four: a scene-of-crime officer—or SOCO—a lab liaison sergeant, a photographer, and a fingerprint man. The forensic aspect could be crucial.

"I want them from here, Bill."

"Can't be done, Des. The High Commission in Nassau has arranged for the Bahamian police to provide the forensic backup. I'm sure they're very good."

"Postmortem? They doing that too?"

"No," said Commander Braithwaite reassuringly. "We're sending Ian West out to Nassau for that. The body's still on the island. As soon as you've had a look, get it shipped back to Nassau."

Hannah was slightly mollified. At least in Dr. Ian West he would have one of the best forensic pathologists in the world.

"Now why don't you get a decent breakfast? The car will be here for you at nine. Your detective inspector will have the murder bag. He'll meet you at the car."

Just before nine Desmond Hannah appeared with his suitcase in the inner courtyard, where the car was waiting for him. He looked around for Harry Wetherall, the detective inspector with whom he had worked for three years. He was nowhere to be seen. A pink-faced young man of about thirty came hurrying up. He carried the murder bag, a small suitcase that contained a variety of tools for discovering, removing, and retaining clues.

"Who are you?"

"D.I. Parker, sir," said the young man.

"Where's Wetherall?"

"He's ill, I'm afraid. Asian flu or something. The Reserve Office asked me to step in. It's awfully good to be working with you."

Blast Wetherall! thought Hannah. Damn his eyes!

They rode out to Heathrow largely in silence. At least Hannah was silent. Parker ("It's Peter, really") expatiated on his knowledge of the Caribbean. He had been there twice with Club Med.

At Heathrow, the press was already in evidence. Two organizations with money to spend had persuaded booked passengers to vacate their seats and take a later flight. Others were trying to get on the two Miami flights of the morning, while their head offices arranged charter planes from Miami into Sunshine.

After takeoff Hannah asked Parker gently, "And how many murder investigations have you been on?"

"Well, this is my first, actually. But in my spare time I study criminology. I think it's so important to understand the criminal mind."

Hannah turned his face to the porthole in pure misery.

Sam McCready was sitting on his balcony sipping his first coffee of the day and gazing out over the azure sea when he heard the rustle of the Miami *Herald* coming under his door.

The AP story was at the bottom of the front page. The headline said simply BRITISH GOVERNOR SLAIN? He read it several times.

At nine a.m. he was making himself known at the British consulate in Miami as Mr. Frank Dillon of the Foreign Office. By ten he had what he had come for: a secure line to the embassy in Washington. He spoke for twenty minutes to the head of the SIS station, a colleague he knew well from London days.

An hour later McCready left the consulate with a wad of dollars, duly signed for, and an attaché case containing a portable telephone and an encrypter with a range that would enable him to make secure calls to the consulate in Miami and have them passed on to Washington.

He returned to the hotel, packed, checked out, and called an air taxi company at the airport. They agreed on a two p.m. takeoff for the ninety-minute run to Sunshine.

EDDIE Favaro had decided there was only one place he could start—the game-fishing community down at the quay. Having no transport, he walked. Almost every wall and tree he passed bore a printed poster urging the islanders to vote for one candidate or the other. On a warehouse wall near the docks was another message, crudely painted. It said WE WANT REFERENDUM.

At the fishing quay groups of men were discussing the news of the murder. Favaro made his inquiry. He showed some fishermen a picture of Julio Gomez.

"Sure, he was here last week. But he go out with Jimmy Dobbs. That's Jimmy's boat over there, the *Gulf Lady*."

There was nobody on the *Gulf Lady*. He leaned on a mooring post to wait. Like all cops, he knew the meaning of patience. Jimmy Dobbs showed up at ten.

"Mr. Dobbs? My name's Eddie. This your boat?"

"Sure is. You here for the fishing?"

"Friend of mine recommended you," said Favaro. "Julio Gomez."

The black man's honest face clouded. He led Favaro to the end of the jetty, out of earshot of anyone else. "Julio Gomez dead," he said gravely.

"I know," said Favaro. "I'd like to find out why. He fished with you a lot, I think."

"Every year. He good man, nice guy."

"He tell you what his job was in Miami?"

"Yep. Once. You a friend or a colleague?"

"Both, Jimmy. Tell me, when did you last see Julio?"

"Right here, Thursday evening. We'd been out all day. He booked me for Friday morning. Never showed up."

"No," said Favaro. "He was at the airstrip, trying to get a flight to Miami. Why did we have to walk down here to talk?"

"They some bad people on these islands," Dobbs said simply.

Favaro realized he could now identify an odor he had smelled in the town. It was fear. Somehow fear had now come to paradise.

"When he left you, where did he go?"

"To Mrs. Macdonald's. He always stayed with her."

Mrs. Macdonald was not at home. Favaro decided to come back later. First he would try the airport.

THE jumbo carrying Superintendent Hannah and D.I. Parker touched down at Nassau at three p.m. local time. A senior officer of the Bahamian police boarded first and escorted them out of the cabin down to a waiting Land-Rover. They were driven straight to the V.I.P. lounge, where they met the British deputy high commissioner and a more junior staffer, called Bannister.

"I'll be coming to Sunshine with you," said Bannister. "Some problem over there with communications. I'll fix a new set so you can talk to the High Commission here on a secure link."

He sounded brisk and efficient. Hannah liked that. He met the four men from the forensic team provided by the Bahamian police. When the final details had been settled, the group headed downstairs. Thirty yards away a chartered ten-seater was waiting to take Hannah and his party to Sunshine. Between the building and the airplane two camera teams had been set up. Microphones were thrust at him, notepads held ready.

"Mr. Hannah, are you confident of an early arrest?"

"Is Sir Marston's death linked to the election campaign?"

He nodded and smiled, but said nothing.

AT THREE thirty a small Cessna dropped its wings over Sunshine and turned for the final run-in to the grass airstrip. Sam McCready looked through the Perspex at the dusty strip coming toward them. Outside the reception shed a figure in a short-sleeved beach shirt was talking to a man in boxer shorts and singlet. A car stood nearby. The palm trees rose on either side of the Cessna, and the small plane thumped onto the grit.

"SURE, I remember that plane. It was dreadful when I heard later that those poor people were dead." The baggage porter who had loaded the Navajo Chief the previous Friday was named Ben, and he was prepared to talk.

Favaro produced a photograph. "Did you notice this man?"

"Sure. He was asking the owner for a lift to Key West."

"Did he seem worried, anxious, in a hurry?"

"So would you be, man! He done told the owner his wife called him and their kid was sick. The girl say they should help him."

"Was there anyone else nearby?"

"Only the other man helping load the luggage," Ben said. "Employed by the owner, I think."

"What did he look like, this other loader?"

"Never seen him before. Black man, not from Sunshine. Bright-colored shirt, dark glasses. Didn't say nothing."

The Cessna rumbled up to the customs shed. Favaro saw a rumpled-looking man of medium build get out, take a suitcase and attaché case from the locker, and go into the shed.

Favaro was pensive as he studied the scene. Julio Gomez had no wife and child. He must have been desperate to get home to Miami. But why? Favaro was convinced that he had been under threat. The bomb was not for Klinger. It was for Gomez.

He thanked Ben and wandered back to the taxi that waited for him. As he climbed in, a British voice at his elbow said, "I know it's a lot to ask, but could I hitch a ride into town?"

It was the man who had just got off the Cessna. "Sure," said Favaro. "Be my guest."

"Awfully kind," said the Englishman. On the five-minute ride into town he introduced himself. "Frank Dillon," he said.

"Eddie Favaro," said the American. "You here for the fishing?"

"Alas, no. Just for a bit of peace and quiet."

"No chance," said Favaro. "There's chaos here. There's a whole crowd of London detectives due in soon, and a whole bunch of journalists. Last night someone shot the governor."

"Good Lord!" The Englishman seemed genuinely shocked.

Favaro dropped him on the steps of the Quarter Deck, dismissed the cab, and walked the few hundred yards to Mrs. Macdonald's boardinghouse. Across Parliament Square a big man was addressing a subdued crowd of citizens from the back of a flatbed truck. It was Mr. Livingstone himself.

"And I say, brothers and sisters, you should share in the wealth of these islands! You should share in the fish caught from the sea. You should share the fine houses of the few rich who live up on the hill. . . ."

The crowd did not look very enthusiastic. The truck was flanked by two large men, and there were similar men throughout the crowd, seeking to start a cheering response. They cheered alone. Favaro walked on. This time Mrs. Macdonald was in.

DESMOND Hannah touched down at twenty to six. It was almost dark. Four other, lighter aircraft had just made it in time and were able to depart back to Nassau before the light faded. Their cargoes were the BBC, ITV, the *Sunday Times* man sharing with the *Sunday Telegraph*, and Sabrina Tennant and her team from BSB, the British Satellite Broadcasting company.

Hannah, Parker, Bannister, and the four Bahamian officers were met by Lieutenant Haverstock and Chief Inspector Jones. By the time formalities were completed and the cavalcade had descended on the Quarter Deck Hotel, darkness had fallen. Hannah was tired. He dined with Parker and Lieutenant Haverstock, which enabled him to get a firsthand account of what had actually happened the previous evening. Then he turned in.

The press found the bar with practiced speed. Rounds were ordered and consumed. No one noticed a man in a rumpled tropical suit drinking alone at the end of the bar, listening to their chatter.

"WHERE did he go after he left here?" Eddie Favaro asked Mrs. Macdonald. He was seated at her kitchen table.

"He went over to the Quarter Deck for a beer," she said. "I told him not to be late, or the dorado spoil and go dry."

"And was he on time?"

"No, man. He was an hour and more late. The fish done spoil. And him talking nonsense."

"What did he say? This . . . nonsense."

"He seemed worried bad. Then he said he seen a scorpion."

Favaro stiffened. "Did he say *a* scorpion, or *the* scorpion?"

She frowned at the effort of recollection. "I thought he said 'a.' But he mighta said 'the,' " she admitted.

Favaro thanked her and went back to the hotel. He knew how his friend and partner had died, and he thought he knew why. In some mysterious manner, here in these paradise islands, Julio Gomez had seen—or thought he had seen—the coldest killer either of them had ever met.

CHAPTER THREE

DESMOND Hannah began work the following morning just after seven. His starting place was Government House.

He had a long interview with the butler, Jefferson, who described how he had found the body, but averred that he had not heard the shot. Later this use of the word shot would convince Hannah that the butler was telling the truth. But Hannah did not yet know how many shots there had been.

The forensic team from Nassau was working on the grass, looking for spent cartridges from the killer's gun. Hannah examined the steel gate in the garden wall as the Bahamian fingerprint man dusted for prints. There were none. Hannah estimated that if the killer had entered by the gate and fired immediately, the governor would have been standing between the gate and the coral wall below the steps to his veranda. If any bullet had passed through him, it should have hit that wall. Hannah switched the forensic team from the lawn to the path that ran along the base of the wall. Then he went back to the house to talk to Lady Moberley.

The governor's widow awaited him in the drawing room. She was a thin, pale woman with mousy hair, and skin that had been yellowed by years in the tropics.

Jefferson appeared with a chilled lager beer on a tray. Hannah hesitated, then took it. Lady Moberley took a grapefruit juice. She looked at the beer with raw hunger. Oh dear, thought Hannah.

There was really nothing she could contribute. So far as she knew, her husband had had no enemies. Political crime was unheard of in the islands. She herself had been away at the time, visiting the small mission hospital on the slopes of Spyglass Hill.

Hannah thanked her and rose. Parker was outside, tapping at the window. Hannah went out to the terrace. Parker was in a state of great excitement. "You were right, sir! Here it is."

He held out the flattened remnant of a lead bullet.

"Thanks for handling it," Hannah said bleakly. "Next time shall we try tweezers and a plastic bag?"

Parker went pale.

"Put it in the murder bag until we can send it to ballistics," said Hannah. He sighed. This was going to be a hard slog.

Dr. Caractacus Jones arrived, as requested. Hannah asked him, in his capacity as the island's coroner, to sign a release for the body to be removed to Nassau for a postmortem.

Bannister, the junior staffer from the Nassau High Commission who had accompanied them to the Barclays, typed the release on Government House notepaper. He had just installed the new communications system and was prepared to transmit.

Hannah then asked Dr. Jones to show him the body. Down at the icehouse, two of Chief Inspector Jones' police constables slid the cadaver of their former governor, now like a frozen log, out from between the fish and carried him to the shade of the nearby warehouse, where they laid him on a table.

Hannah made as thorough an examination of the rigid body as he could. Dr. Jones stood by his side. After peering at the frozen hole in the governor's chest, Hannah noticed two neat, circular holes in the left shirtsleeve.

"Two bullets, minimum," he said quietly. "We are missing a second bullet."

"Probably still in the body," said Dr. Jones.

"No doubt," said Hannah. "But damned if I can see any sign of entry or exit holes."

He ordered the dead governor replaced in the icehouse.

"Tell me, Doctor. Is there anyone on this island who really knows everything that goes on and everyone who lives here?"

Dr. Jones grinned. "For the real history of these islands, you should visit Missy Coltrane. She's like . . . the grandmother of the Barclays. If you want someone to guess who done this, she might."

Back at Government House, the governor's Jaguar was in the forecourt, and Oscar Stone, the chauffeur, was polishing it.

"Oscar?" Hannah asked. "Do you know Missy Coltrane?"

"Oh yes, sah. She fine lady."

"Do you know where she lives?"

"Yes, sah. Flamingo House, top of Spyglass Hill."

"Take me to see her, will you?"

The Jaguar wound its way out of town, then began to climb the lower slopes of Spyglass Hill, six miles west of Port Plaisance. Wooden shacks stood back from the road, fronted by dusty yards where chickens scratched. Small brown children heard the car coming and scampered to the roadside to wave frantically. Hannah waved back.

They rounded two final curves and emerged on the top of the hill. There stood a pink villa, Flamingo House.

A teenage girl answered the door, bare black legs emerging from a simple cotton frock.

"I'd like to see Missy Coltrane," said Hannah.

She nodded and admitted him, showing him into a large and airy sitting room. Open double doors led to a balcony with spectacular views over the island and the glittering blue sea.

The room was cool despite having no air-conditioning. Hannah noticed it had no electricity at all. Three brass oil lamps stood on low tables. The array of memorabilia indicated it was the home of an elderly person. Hannah sauntered around as he waited.

On one wall was a portrait of a man in the uniform of a British colonial governor. He stood staring out at the room, gray-haired and gray-mustached, with a tanned, lined, and kindly face. The small label beneath the painting said SIR ROBERT COLTRANE, K.B.E., GOVERNOR OF THE BARCLAY ISLANDS, 1945–1953.

So Missy Coltrane must be Lady Coltrane, the former governor's widow. Hannah moved to a display cabinet of the former governor's military trophies. There was the deep purple ribbon of the Victoria Cross, Britain's highest award for gallantry in the field, and the date of its award, 1917. Other items the warrior had carried on his campaigns were grouped around his medals.

"He was a very brave man," said a clear voice behind him.

Hannah spun around, embarrassed.

She had entered silently, the rubber tires of her wheelchair making no sound on the tiles. She was small and frail, with a cap of shining white curls and bright blue eyes. Behind her stood a manservant, a giant of awe-inspiring size. She turned to him.

"Thank you, Firestone. I'll be all right now."

He nodded and withdrew. She gestured for Hannah to be seated, and smiled. "Now, you must be Detective Chief Superintendent Hannah from Scotland Yard. What can I do for you?"

"I must apologize for calling you Missy Coltrane to your housemaid," he said. "No one told me you were Lady Coltrane."

"No more," she said. "Here I am just Missy. I prefer it that way. As you may detect, I was not born British, but in South Carolina."

"Your late husband"—Hannah nodded toward the portrait—"was governor here once."

"Yes. We met in the war. Robert had been through the First War. He didn't have to come back for a second dose, but he did. He got wounded again. I was a nurse. We fell in love, married in 1943. There were twenty-five years between our ages, but it didn't matter a damn. After the war he was made governor here. He was only fifty-six when he died. Delayed war wounds."

Hannah calculated. She would be sixty-eight, too young for a wheelchair. She seemed to read his mind.

"I slipped and fell," she said. "Ten years ago. Broke my back. But you didn't come four thousand miles to discuss an old woman in a wheelchair. How can I help you?"

Hannah explained. "Whoever shot Sir Marston must have hated him enough to do it. But I cannot perceive a motive. You know these people. Who would want to do it, and why?"

Lady Coltrane wheeled herself to the open doors and stared out for a while. "Mr. Hannah, I do know these people. I love them, and I hope I may think that they love me." She turned and gazed at him. "In the world scheme of things these islands matter for nothing. Yet these people seem to have discovered something that has eluded the world outside. They have found out how to be happy. Not rich, not powerful, but happy.

"Now London wants us to have independence. And two candidates have appeared to compete for the power. I know them both. Knew them when they were boys. Knew them when they left in their teens to pursue careers elsewhere. And now they are back."

"You suspect either of them?" asked Hannah.

"It is the men they have brought with them. These are violent men, Mr. Hannah. There have been threats, beatings. Perhaps you should look at the entourages of these two men."

At Government House, a plump Englishman with several chins above his clerical collar jumped up from a chair in the sitting room as Hannah walked in. Parker was with him.

"Ah, Chief, this is the Reverend Simon Quince, the Anglican vicar. He has some interesting information for us."

Hannah wondered where Parker had got the word chief from. He hated it. "Any luck with that second bullet?"

"Er, no—not yet."

"Better get on with it," said Hannah. Parker disappeared through the French windows. Hannah closed them. "Well now, Mr. Quince. What would you like to tell me?"

"This is all very distressing," said the vicar, "coming to you about a fellow of the cloth. I don't know whether I should."

"Why don't you let me be the judge of that?" suggested Hannah mildly.

The reverend calmed down and sat. "It happened last Friday," he said. He told the story of the delegation from the Committee for Concerned Citizens and their rebuff by the governor. When he had finished, Hannah frowned.

"What exactly did Reverend Drake say?" he asked.

"He said," repeated Quince, " 'We have to get rid of that governor and get ourselves a new one.' "

Hannah rose. "Thank you, Mr. Quince. May I suggest you say no more about this, but leave it with me?"

The grateful vicar scuttled out. Hannah would now have to check out the fire-breathing Baptist, Walter Drake, as well.

Jefferson brought him lunch on a tray. While he was eating it he learned from Chief Inspector Jones that no one had left the island in the last forty hours.

"Not legally, at any rate," said Hannah. "Mr. Jones, do you keep a firearms register?"

"Of course."

"Fine. Would you check it through and visit everyone who has a listed firearm? We are looking for a large-caliber handgun. Particularly a handgun that cannot be produced, or one that has been recently cleaned and gleams with fresh oil."

When he had gone, Hannah asked to see Lieutenant Haverstock. "Do you by any chance own a service revolver or automatic?"

The young subaltern shook his head.

"Any guns in Government House at all?"

"No, not to my knowledge. Anyway, the killer came from out-side, surely? Through the garden wall?"

Hannah had examined the wrenched-off lock on the steel gate. There was little question that someone had used a very strong crowbar to force the old steel to snap. But it also occurred to Hannah that the snapping of the lock might have been a ruse on the part of someone coming through the house. What Hannah needed was that second bullet and the gun that had fired it.

SAM McCready also sat at lunch. When he'd entered the open-sided veranda dining room of the Quarter Deck, every table was full. Out on the square, men in bright beach shirts and wrap-around dark glasses were positioning a flatbed truck with posters from Marcus Johnson. The great man was due to speak at three.

Sam had looked around the terrace and seen a single vacant chair. It was at a table that was occupied by one other luncher. "Mind if I join you?" he'd asked.

Eddie Favaro waved at the chair. "No problem."

"You here for the fishing?" asked McCready as he studied the menu.

"Yep."

"You know," said McCready after ordering seviche, a dish of raw fish marinated in fresh lime juice. "If I didn't know better, I'd have said you were a cop."

Favaro put down his beer and stared at him. "Why?"

"Instinct. You carry yourself like a cop. Would you mind telling me why you're really here?"

"Why the hell should I?"

"Because," McCready suggested mildly, "you arrived just be-fore the governor was shot. And because of this."

He handed Favaro a sheet of Foreign Office notepaper. It an-nounced that Mr. Frank Dillon was an official of that office and begged "to whom it may concern" to be as helpful as possible.

Favaro handed it back. "Officially I'm on vacation," he began. "No, I don't fish. Unofficially I'm trying to find out why my part-ner was killed last week, and by whom."

"Tell me about it. I might be able to help."

Favaro told him how Julio Gomez had died. "I think he may

have seen a man on Sunshine and been seen himself. A man we used to know as Francisco Mendes, alias the Scorpion."

In the summer of 1984 a motorcyclist in red-and-white leather, astride a Kawasaki, had drawn up outside a liquor store in the Dadeland Mall and emptied the entire magazine of an Uzi submachine carbine into the busy store. Three people had died; fourteen were injured.

When the killer sped off, he was seen by a young motorcycle cop, who gave chase, broadcasting the description as he went. Halfway down North Kendall Drive the man pulled over and shot the oncoming policeman dead. He was twenty-three, and he left a widow and baby daughter.

His radio calls had alerted two prowl cars, and the motorcyclist was caught and placed under arrest. The case was given to Gomez and Favaro. For four days and nights they sat opposite the killer, unable to get a single word out of him.

Gomez believed the killer was Colombian. It was at the height of the cocaine turf wars between the Colombians and the Cubans, and the liquor store had been a Cuban cocaine drop. After four days he and Favaro nicknamed the suspect the Scorpion.

On the fourth day a very high-priced lawyer had turned up. He produced a Mexican passport in the name of Francisco Mendes. It was new and valid, but it bore no U.S. entry stamps. The lawyer conceded that his client might be an illegal immigrant and asked for bail. The judge granted it. Within twenty-four hours the Scorpion was gone.

"And you believe . . . ?" asked McCready.

"I think Julio saw him here and was trying to get back so Uncle Sam would file an appeal for extradition from the British."

"Which we would have granted," said McCready. "I think we ought to inform the man from Scotland Yard. After all, the governor was shot four days later. Even if the two cases turn out not to be linked, there's enough suspicion to hold him."

"I like it. Let's go see your man from Scotland Yard."

HANNAH stepped through the open doors of the plank-built Baptist chapel. Leading the singing was the deep bass voice of the Reverend Walter Drake.

"*Rock of ages, cleft for me . . .*"

591

The Baptist minister caught sight of Hannah in the doorway, ceased singing, and waved his arms for quiet.

"Brothers and sisters!" he roared. "We are indeed privileged today. We are joined by Mr. Hannah from Scotland Yard!"

The congregation turned in their pews and stared. Most were elderly men and women, with a scattering of young matrons and small children.

"Join us, brother! Sing with us!"

A vast matron in a flowered-print frock gave Hannah a wide smile and moved up, offering him her hymnbook. Hannah needed it. Together they finished the rousing anthem.

When the service was over, the congregation filed out, and Drake beckoned Hannah into his vestry, a small room attached to the side of the church. "And what can I do for the man from Scotland Yard?" inquired the pastor.

"Tell me where you were at five p.m. on Tuesday."

"Holding carol service practice here, in front of fifty good people," said the Reverend Mr. Drake. "Why?"

Hannah put to him his remark of the previous Friday morning on the steps of Government House. Drake smiled.

"Ah, you have been talking with Mr. Quince." He pronounced the name as if he had sucked on a raw lime. "You think I killed Governor Moberley? No, sir. I am a man of peace. I meant that we should ask London for a new governor, one who would understand us and propose what we ask."

"Which is?"

"A referendum, Mr. Hannah. Something bad is happening here. Strangers have come among us, ambitious men who want to rule our affairs. If we had a referendum, the great majority would vote to stay British. Is that so wrong?"

"Not in my book," admitted Hannah. "But I don't make policy."

"Neither did the governor. But he would carry a policy out, for his career, even if he knew it was wrong."

"You didn't like Sir Marston, did you?"

"No, God forgive me. He was a hypocrite and a fornicator."

"Fornicator? What does that mean?"

The reverend glanced at him sharply. "Myrtle, the missing secretary. You have not seen her?"

"No. She is away with her parents in Tortola," said Hannah.

"No," said Drake gently. "She is in Antigua General Hospital, terminating a baby."

Oh dear, thought Hannah. And Lady Moberley knew. Poor washed-out Lady Moberley, driven to drink by all those years in the tropics. She was resigned, no doubt. Or perhaps she was not. Perhaps she had been driven a bit too far, just this once?

WHEN Hannah got back to Government House, there was a spate of news waiting for him.

Chief Inspector Jones had checked his firearms register. There were only six workable guns on the island. Three were owned by expatriates—retired gentlemen, two British and one Canadian. They were twelve-bore shotguns used for clay-pigeon shooting. The fourth was a rifle owned by the fishing skipper Jimmy Dobbs for use on sharks. The fifth gun was a presentation pistol owned by another expatriate, an American, and still in its glass-topped case. And the sixth gun was Jones' own.

"Damn," snorted Hannah. Whatever gun had been used, it was not kept legally.

Detective Inspector Parker, for his part, had a report on the garden. It had been searched from end to end and top to bottom. No second bullet. Most likely it was still in the body.

Bannister had received news from Nassau. A plane would be landing at four, in one hour's time, to take the body to the Bahamas for postmortem.

And there were two men waiting to see Hannah in the drawing room. The man called Frank Dillon produced his letter of introduction. Hannah studied it with little pleasure. A London-based official who happened to be taking a holiday in the middle of a murder hunt was as likely as a vegetarian tiger. Then he met the American, who admitted that he was another detective.

Hannah's attitude changed, however, as Dillon narrated Favaro's story. "You have a picture of this man Mendes?" he asked.

"No, not with me. But I could have one wired from Miami to your people in Nassau."

"You do that." Hannah glanced at his watch. "Now you must excuse me—I have to see the body onto the plane for Nassau."

"Are you by any chance thinking of talking to the candidates?" asked McCready as they left.

"Yes," said Hannah. "First thing in the morning."

"Would you mind if I came along?" asked McCready. "After all, they are both . . . political, are they not?"

"All right," said Hannah reluctantly. He wondered whom this Frank Dillon really worked for.

AT THE airstrip, Hannah saw to the loading of the body, accompanied by Bannister, who would return to Nassau along with it. Bannister would see that all their scrapings and samples went on the evening flight to London, to be taken to the Home Office's forensic laboratory, in Lambeth. Hannah had few hopes they would turn up much; it was the second bullet he wanted.

Because he was at the airstrip, Hannah missed the Johnson rally in Parliament Square that afternoon. So did the press corps, who had followed the police convoy out to the airstrip.

McCready did not miss the rally. He was on the veranda of the Quarter Deck Hotel. He noticed half a dozen men in brightly colored beach shirts and dark glasses handing out small pieces of paper and flags on sticks. The flags were in the candidate's blue and white colors. The pieces of paper were dollar bills.

At precisely ten past three a white Ford Fairlane swept up to the speaking platform. Mr. Marcus Johnson leaped out and ascended the steps. He held up his hands in a boxer's victory salute. Led by the bright-shirted ones, there was a round of applause. In minutes Marcus Johnson was into his speech.

"And I promise you, my friends—and you are *all* my friends—when we are finally free, a wave of prosperity will come to these islands. There will be work—in the hotels, in the new marina, in the bars and cafés, in the new industries. From all these things prosperity will flow. And it will flow into *your* pockets—"

He was using a bullhorn to reach everyone in the square. The interruption came from a man who did not need a bullhorn.

"Johnson!" roared Walter Drake's deep bass voice. "We do not want you here! Why don't you go back where you came from and take your Yardies with you?"

There was silence. The stunned crowd waited for the sky to fall. No one had ever interrupted Marcus Johnson before. Without a word Johnson jumped into his car. It sped off, pursued by a second car containing his helpers.

THE REVEREND WALTER DRAKE took his beating in silence. There were four of them, and they came for him that night as he left his church and walked home. They used baseball bats and their feet. When they were finished, they left him on the ground.

Half an hour later he recovered consciousness and crawled to the nearest house. The frightened family called Dr. Caractacus Jones, who spent the rest of the night patching him up.

CHAPTER FOUR

DETECTIVE Chief Superintendent Hannah elected to interview Mr. Horatio Livingstone first. He rang him at his house, in Shantytown, just after sunrise, and the politician said yes, he would be delighted to receive him within the hour.

Oscar drove the Jaguar, with Detective Inspector Parker beside him. Hannah was in the back with Dillon of the Foreign Office.

Shantytown lay three miles down the coast. It was a village of clustered homes made of wooden planks and galvanized sheet roofing, with some five thousand inhabitants. Livingstone posters were everywhere. In its center stood a walled compound. A single gate, wide enough for a car, admitted entry. Beyond the walls could be seen the roof of the house, the only two-story edifice in Shantytown.

The Jaguar halted at the gate, and Oscar sounded the horn. All down the street Barclayans were standing to stare at the gleaming limousine. The governor's car had never been into Shantytown before.

A small window in the gate opened, an eye surveyed the car, and the gate swung open. The Jaguar rolled forward into a dusty yard and stopped by the house. Two men were in the yard. Both wore identical pale gray safari suits. A third man in similar dress stood at an upstairs window. As the car halted, he withdrew.

Hannah, Parker, and Dillon were shown into the sitting room, and a few seconds later Horatio Livingstone appeared. He was a large, fat man, and his jowly face was wreathed in smiles.

"Gentlemen, gentlemen, what an honor. Please be seated."

He seated himself in a large chair. Two other men entered and seated themselves behind him. Livingstone gestured to them. "Two of my associates—Mr. Smith and Mr. Brown."

The two inclined their heads, but said nothing.

"Now, Mr. Hannah, what can I do for you?"

"You will know, sir, that I am here to investigate the murder of Sir Marston Moberley. I'm afraid I have to ask you what you were doing at five p.m. on Tuesday evening."

"I was here, Mr. Hannah, here among my friends, who will vouch for me. I was working on a speech."

"And your associates, they were here? *All* here?"

"Every one of them. Here, inside the compound."

"Your associates— Are they Barclayans?" asked Dillon. Hannah shot him an irritated glance; the man had promised to say nothing.

Livingstone beamed. "Ah, no, I fear not. We Barclayans have so little experience of organizing an election campaign. My associates are from the Bahamas. You wish to see their passports?"

Hannah waved the necessity away. Behind Mr. Livingstone, Mr. Brown had lit a large cigar.

"Would you have any idea, Mr. Livingstone, who might have killed the governor?" asked Hannah.

The fat man adopted a mien of great seriousness. "Mr. Hannah, the governor was helping us all on the road to our final freedom from the British Empire. There was not the slightest motive for me or any of my associates to wish to harm him."

Behind him Mr. Brown held his cigar to one side, and with the much elongated nail of his little finger, he flicked an inch of ash from the tip.

McCready knew he had seen that gesture somewhere before. "Will you be holding any public meetings today?" he asked.

"Yes," Livingstone said. "At twelve I am addressing my brothers and sisters of the fishing community on the docks."

Hannah rose. "I won't take up any more of your time, Mr. Livingstone," he said.

The politician escorted them to the door. Two more gray safari suits saw them off the premises. That made seven. All were pure Negroid except Mr. Brown, who was much paler—the only one who dared smoke without asking, the man in charge of the other six.

"Strange man, didn't you think?" said Dillon in the car. "I wonder where he spent the years between leaving here as a teen-ager and returning six months ago."

"No idea," said Hannah. It was only later, in London, that he would wonder at Dillon's remark about Livingstone's leaving Sunshine as a teenager. It was Missy Coltrane who had told him, Desmond Hannah, that. Dillon had not been there.

At half past nine they arrived at Marcus Johnson's estate, on Sawbones Hill. An assistant in psychedelic beach shirt and black glasses opened the wrought-iron gates and let the Jaguar proceed up the raked gravel drive to a pillared colonial portico. The three Englishmen were led inside the spacious two-story building. They followed their guide, a second brightly shirted "assistant," onto a veranda, where Marcus Johnson received them.

Where Horatio Livingstone had been fat and creased, Marcus Johnson was slim and elegant. He wore an impeccable cream silk suit. The cast of his features indicated he was at least half white. Four heavy gold rings adorned his hands.

Desmond Hannah asked the same questions about the previous Tuesday evening. The reply was the same.

"Addressing an enthusiastic crowd of well over a hundred people in Parliament Square, Mr. Hannah."

"And your . . . entourage?" asked Hannah, borrowing Missy Coltrane's word to describe the election campaign team, in their bright shirts.

"All with me, to a man," said Johnson. Despite the subdued light inside the veranda, the bright shirts never removed their wraparound dark glasses.

"Do you have another public address scheduled for today?" asked Dillon.

"Yes, indeed. At two, on Parliament Square."

"You were there yesterday. There was a disturbance, I believe."

Marcus Johnson shrugged. "The Reverend Drake shouted some rude words. No matter. I had finished my speech. Poor Drake. He wishes the Barclays to remain in the last century. But progress must come, Mr. Dillon. I have the most substantial development plans in mind for our dear Barclays."

McCready nodded. Tourism, he thought. Gambling, industry, pollution, a little prostitution—and what else?

They drove back to Government House.

"Thank you," said Dillon as he climbed out. "Meeting the candidates was most instructive. I wonder where Johnson made all that money in the years he was away."

"No idea," said Hannah. "He's listed as a businessman. Do you want Oscar to run you back to the Quarter Deck?"

"No, thank you. I'll stroll."

In the bar, the press corps were working their way through the beer supply. It was eleven o'clock. They were getting bored with waiting for a good, hard piece of news.

McCready mingled with them. "Horatio Livingstone is speaking on the dock at twelve," he said. "Could be interesting."

They were suddenly alert. "Why?" asked someone.

McCready shrugged. "There was some savage heckling here on the square yesterday," he said. "You were at the airstrip."

They brightened up. A nice little riot would be the thing— Election Violence Sweeps Sunshine Isle. They picked up their gear and sauntered toward the docks.

McCready took time to make a call to the British consulate in Miami. He asked for a seven-seat charter plane to land on Sunshine at four p.m. It was a long shot, but he hoped it would work.

Livingstone's cavalcade arrived from Shantytown at a quarter to twelve. A makeshift platform was erected, and at noon the people's candidate hoisted his bulk up the steps. He spoke into a megaphone held up by one of the safari suits. Four TV cameras had secured elevated positions, from which they could cover the candidate or, hopefully, the hecklers and the fighting.

The BSB cameraman had borrowed the cabin roof of the *Gulf Lady*. To back up his TV camera, he had a Nikon camera with a telephoto lens. The reporter, Sabrina Tennant, stood beside him.

McCready climbed up to join them. "Hello," he said.

"Hi," said Sabrina Tennant. She took no notice of him.

"Tell me," he asked quietly. "Would you like a story that would blow your colleagues out of the water?"

Now she took notice. The cameraman looked up inquisitively.

"Can you use that Nikon to get in close, really close, on any face in that crowd?" asked McCready.

"Sure. I can get their tonsils if they open wide."

"Why not get pictures of all the men in gray safari suits?" suggested McCready. The cameraman looked at Sabrina. She nodded.

"What have you got in mind?" she asked.

"Step into the cabin, and I'll tell you."

She did, and McCready talked for several minutes.

"You're joking," she said at length.

"No, I'm not, and I think I can prove it. But not here. The answers lie in Miami."

Sabrina's only problem was time. Her main feature spot was on *Countdown,* the BSB current affairs program that went out at noon on Sunday in England. She would need to send her material by satellite from Miami by no later than four p.m. on Saturday, the next day. So she had to be in Miami that night.

"Actually, I'm due to leave myself at four this afternoon," said McCready. "I've ordered my own plane from Miami. Happy to offer you a lift."

"Who the hell are you?" she asked.

"Just a holidaymaker. But I do know the islands. And their people. Trust me."

She had no bloody choice, thought Sabrina. If his story was true, this one was too good to miss.

AT TWO an even more disgruntled press corps assembled in Parliament Square. From the point of view of sensations, the morning rally had been a flop. If Hannah did not make an arrest soon, they thought, they might as well pack up and go home.

At ten past two Marcus Johnson arrived in his long white convertible. More sophisticated than Livingstone, he had a microphone with two amplifiers strung from nearby palm trees.

As Johnson began speaking, McCready sidled up to Sean Whittaker, the free-lance reporter-photographer who covered the Caribbean from his Kingston, Jamaica, base for London's *Sunday Express.* A long-lens Yashica hung around his neck. "Would you like a story that would blow your rivals out of the water?"

Whittaker turned and cocked an eyebrow. "What do you know that nobody else does?"

"Why not come with me and find out?"

The two men proceeded across the square, into the hotel, and up to McCready's second-floor room. From the balcony they could see the whole square. "The men in multicolored beach shirts and dark glasses," said McCready. "Can you get full-face close-ups of them from here?"

"Sure," said Whittaker. He adjusted his zoom lens and ran off two rolls of color prints and two of black-and-white.

McCready took him down to the bar, stood him a beer, and talked for thirty minutes.

Whittaker whistled. "Can you prove it?"

"Not here," said McCready. "The proof lies in Kingston. You could get back tonight, finalize it tomorrow morning, and file by four p.m. Nine o'clock in London—just in time."

Whittaker shook his head. "Too late. The last Miami-Kingston flight is at seven thirty. I'd never make it."

"As a matter of fact, I have a plane leaving for Miami at four—in seventy minutes. I'd be happy to offer you a lift."

AT FOUR o'clock Sabrina Tennant arrived at the airstrip with her cameraman. McCready and Whittaker were already there. The air taxi from Miami drifted down at ten past the hour.

When it was about to take off, McCready explained, "I'm afraid I can't make it after all. But the air taxi is paid for, so please be my guests. Good-bye and good luck."

He returned to the Quarter Deck, programmed his portable phone to a secure mode, and made a series of calls. By the time he had finished, he had reason to hope his newfound friends of the press would be accorded every facility.

AT SIX p.m. the doctor called from Nassau. Desmond Hannah took the call in the governor's private office.

"You've got the bullet?" asked Hannah eagerly.

"No bullet," said the forensic pathologist. "It went clean through him. It entered between the second and third ribs, perforated the upper left ventricle of the heart, causing immediate death. It exited through the ribs at the back. It touched no bone on the way through. If you can find it, the slug should be intact—no distortion at all."

"But that's impossible," protested Hannah. "The man had a wall behind him. We've searched the wall inch by inch."

"Well, it came out all right," said the doctor.

"Could it have been slowed up to the point that it fell to the lawn between the governor and the wall?"

"How far behind the man was the wall situated?"

"No more than fifteen feet," said Hannah.

"Then, not in my view," said the pathologist. "The slug would have been traveling fast. It must have hit the wall."

"But it didn't," Hannah protested. Unless, of course, someone had stolen it. "Anything else?"

"One last thing," said the doctor. "The bullet was traveling in an upward trajectory. The assassin must have been crouching or kneeling. The gun was fired about thirty inches off the ground."

Damn, thought Hannah. It must have gone clean over the wall. Or possibly it hit the house, but much higher, near the gutters. In the morning Parker would have to start all over again, with ladders.

Hannah thanked the doctor and put the phone down.

JEFFERSON, the butler, held the ladder while the hapless Parker went up the house wall. He went as high as the gutters, but he found no imprint of the second bullet.

Hannah took his breakfast in the sitting room. Lady Moberley drifted in now and again, arranged the flowers, smiled vaguely, and drifted back out again. She seemed blithely unconcerned whether her late husband's body was brought to Sunshine for burial or taken back to England. Then Hannah realized why. The vodka bottle was missing from the silver drinks tray.

Desmond Hannah finished his breakfast, went outside, and glanced at Parker, up near the gutter.

"Any luck?" he asked.

"Not a sign," Parker called down.

Hannah walked back to the steel gate. The previous evening he had stood on a trestle and stared over the gate at the alley behind it. Between five and six the alley was constantly busy. The killer could not have come in that way without being spotted. Someone must have seen something. Yet no one would come forward.

Hannah stood with his back to the gate, walked forward two paces, and dropped to his knees. He was still too high. He went on his stomach and propped his torso on his elbows, his eyes thirty inches above the grass. He stared at the point where Sir Marston would have been standing. Then he was up and running.

"Parker!" he yelled. "Come down here!"

Parker almost fell off the ladder, so loud was the shout. He scampered down to the garden.

"Stand there," said Hannah, pointing to a spot on the grass. "Jefferson, get me a broom."

Jefferson shrugged. If the white policeman wanted to sweep the patio, that was his business. He went for a broom.

Hannah made Parker stand on the spot where Sir Marston had stood. Crouching on the grass, he aimed the broom handle like a rifle at Parker's chest. The broom sloped upward at twenty degrees.

"Step to one side."

Parker did so. Hannah stood up and walked to the steps that ran up to the terrace. It was still hanging on its wrought-iron bracket, as it had for three days, and before that. The wire basket, packed with loam, cascaded brilliant geraniums. As the forensic team worked on the wall they had brushed the streaming flowers out of their faces.

"Bring that basket down," Hannah told Parker. "Jefferson, get a bed sheet."

Emptying the basket over the bed sheet, Hannah extricated the flowers. When only the loam was left, he separated it into hand-size clods. He broke the clods into grains. And there it was.

Not only had the bullet passed through the governor intact, it had gone between two strands of wire and stopped dead in the middle of the loam. It was in perfect condition.

"Tonight, lad," he told Parker, "you are going back to London. With this. I've got the bullet. Soon I'll have the gun. Then I'll have the killer."

CHAPTER FIVE

IN THE city of Kingston, Sean Whittaker was having a remarkable reception. Just after seven the next morning, the first call had come in. It was an American voice. "My name is Milton. I believe you have some photographs you might care to show me."

They arranged a rendezvous in a public place and met an hour later. The American did not look like the head of the U.S. Drug Enforcement Administration field station in Kingston, as Whittaker had expected. His casual air was more that of a young academic from the university.

"Forgive my saying so," said Whittaker, "but could you establish any bona fides at all?"

"Let's use my car," said Milton.

They drove to the American embassy. Milton flashed his identity card to the marine guard, then led the way to an office.

"All right," said Whittaker, "you're an American diplomat."

Milton did not correct him. He smiled and asked to see Whittaker's pictures. He surveyed them all, but one held his attention.

"Well, well," he said. "So that's where he is."

He opened his attaché case and produced a series of files, selecting one. The photograph on the first page of the dossier had been taken a few years earlier, with a long lens, apparently through an aperture in a curtain. But the man was the same.

"Want to know who he is?" asked Milton.

The British reporter nodded.

"Okay," said Milton, and he read out the contents of the file. There were details of operations run, aliases used, cargoes delivered, profits laundered. Whittaker took notes furiously.

"Phew," he said. "Can I source this on you?"

" 'Highly placed sources within the DEA'—that would do."

The American escorted Whittaker back to the entrance. "Why don't you go down to police headquarters with the rest of the pictures?" he suggested. "You may find you are expected."

At the police building, the bemused Whittaker was shown up to the office of Commissioner Foster. With him was Commander Gray, the head of the Criminal Investigation Division. The two Jamaicans studied Whittaker's pictures of the eight bodyguards in bright beach shirts. Opening a series of files, Commander Gray identified the men one after the other.

"May I cite you gentlemen as the source?" Whittaker asked.

"Certainly," said the commissioner. "All have long criminal records. Three are wanted here as of now. You may quote me."

By midday Whittaker had his story. He transmitted his pictures and text to London, took a long phone call from the news editor, and was assured of a good spread the following day.

IN MIAMI, Sabrina Tennant had checked into the Sonesta Beach Hotel. She took a call just before eight on Saturday morning. The appointment was set for an office building in central Miami. It was a CIA safe building.

She was shown to an office, and met a man who suggested she

call him Bill. He asked her for the still photographs that had been taken of Horatio Livingstone's bodyguards. Bill opened a series of files and showed her other pictures of the same men.

"This one," he said. "What was he calling himself?"

"Mr. Brown," she said.

Bill laughed. "Do you know the Spanish word for brown?"

"No."

"It's *moreno*—in this case, Hernan Moreno."

"Can I have these photos?" she asked.

"I'll have copies made for you," said Bill. "And we'll keep copies of yours."

Later that morning she did a stand-up piece with her cameraman. By midday she had beamed all her material via satellite link to the BSB, in London. She had a long talk with her news editor as the cutting-room staff began to put the feature together.

"It's a bloody cracker," he said. "Well done, love."

McCready had been busy too. He spent part of the morning on his portable telephone to London and part talking to Washington. In London he got through to the director of the Special Air Service regiment. The leathery young general listened to his request.

"As a matter of fact, I do," he said. "I've got two of them lecturing at Fort Bragg at the moment. I'll have to get clearance."

"No time," said McCready. "Look, are they owed leave?"

"I suppose they are," said the director.

"Fine. Then I'm offering them both three days of rest and recreation here in the sun. As my personal guests."

"Sam," said the director, "you are devious. I'll see what I can do. But they're on leave, okay? Just sunbathing, nothing else."

"Perish the thought," said McCready.

At three o'clock that afternoon a battered van drove into Parliament Square. From the driver's seat emerged the enormous figure of Firestone. He went around to the rear, opened the door, and lifted Missy Coltrane out, invalid chair and all. Slowly he wheeled her down Main Street to do her shopping. Her progress was slow, being marked by innumerable greetings.

"G'day, Missy Coltrane." "Good day, Jasper." "Good day, Emmanuel." She asked after wives and children, congratulated a beaming father-to-be on his good fortune, sympathized with a case of a broken arm. She made her usual purchases, paying for them from a small purse she kept in her lap, while from a larger handbag she dispensed candies to a crowd of children. From the shopping area she moved to the quay, where she greeted the fishermen and bought two snappers and a wriggling lobster that had been preordered by the Quarter Deck Hotel. If Missy Coltrane wanted it, she got it. No argument. The Quarter Deck would get the prawns and the conch.

As she returned to Parliament Square she met Detective Chief Superintendent Hannah, descending the hotel steps. He was accompanied by Detective Inspector Parker and an American called Favaro. They were off to meet the four-o'clock plane from Nassau. She greeted them; then Firestone lifted her up into the van.

"Who's that?" asked Favaro.

"An old lady who lives on a hill," said Parker. "She's supposed to know everything about this place."

Hannah frowned. It had occurred to him that Missy Coltrane might know more than she had let on about who had fired those shots on Tuesday evening.

The short-haul island hopper from Nassau landed just after four. The pilot had a package from the Metro-Dade Police Department for Favaro. Parker, with a sample bottle containing the vital bullet in his jacket pocket, boarded.

"There'll be a car for you at Heathrow," said Hannah. "I want that bullet in the hands of Alan Mitchell as fast as possible."

Alan Mitchell, the brilliant scientist who headed the Home Office ballistics lab, would start to work on the bullet first thing on Monday. With his findings Hannah would know exactly what weapon he was looking for. That would narrow the odds.

On the ground, after the plane took off, Favaro showed the photos of Francisco Mendes, alias the Scorpion, to Hannah. They showed a lean, saturnine man with slicked-back black hair and a thin, expressionless mouth. The eyes were blank.

"Nasty-looking bastard," agreed Hannah. "Let's get them up to Chief Inspector Jones."

The head of the Barclayan police was in his office, on Parliament Square. "No, never seen him, man. Not in these islands."

"Would you circulate these, Mr. Jones? Show them around. He

was supposed to have been seen in the bar of the Quarter Deck last Thursday week. Maybe somebody else saw him. The barman, any other customers—you know the score."

Chief Inspector Jones nodded. He knew his patch. He would show the picture around.

AT CHEQUERS, the Buckinghamshire residence of the Prime Ministers of Great Britain, Mrs. Thatcher had been up early as usual and had plowed through four red dispatch boxes of state papers. As she finished, there was a tap on the door, and her press secretary, Bernard Ingham, entered. He held the *Sunday Express* in his hand.

"Something I thought you might like to see, Prime Minister."

She read the centerfold spread, and her brow furrowed. The pictures were there: of Marcus Johnson on the hustings in Port Plaisance, and again, a few years earlier. There were photos of his bodyguards, all taken around Parliament Square on Friday, and matching pictures taken from Kingston police files.

"But this is dreadful!" said the Prime Minister. "I must speak to Douglas."

Her Majesty's Secretary of State for Foreign Affairs, Mr. Douglas Hurd, was with his family at Chevening, his official country residence in the county of Kent.

"Yes, I agree," said the Foreign Secretary. "It's disgraceful if it's true. . . . Yes, yes, Margaret, I'll get on to it in the morning and have the Caribbean desk check it out."

It was her political adviser, Charles Powell, who taped the BSB program *Countdown* at twelve o'clock. Mrs. Thatcher watched the tape in silence. Then she rang Mr. Hurd again.

"I have a tape," said the Prime Minister. "It is quite appalling. I'll send it straight to you. Please screen it when it arrives."

A dispatch rider roared through the gloom of a dismal December afternoon and was at Chevening by half past four.

The Foreign Secretary called Chequers at five fifteen. "I agree, Margaret, quite appalling," said Douglas Hurd.

"I suggest we need a new governor out there now," said the P.M. "We must show we are active, Douglas. You know who else will have seen these stories?"

The Foreign Secretary was well aware that Her Majesty was an avid newspaper reader and watched current affairs issues on television. "I'll get on to it immediately," he said.

He did. At eight that evening the choice had fallen on Sir Crispian Rattray, a retired diplomat and former high commissioner in Barbados. He would report to the Foreign Office in the morning for a thorough briefing, then take the late morning plane to Nassau. He would consult further with the High Commission there, spend the night, and arrive on Sunshine on Tuesday morning to take the reins in hand.

"It shouldn't take long, my dear," he told Lady Rattray as he packed. "Seems I'll have to withdraw the candidacy of these two rascals and see the elections through with two new candidates. Then they'll grant independence, I'll haul the old flag down, the islanders will run their own affairs, and I can come home."

AT NINE o'clock on Sunday morning on Sunshine, McCready found Hannah having breakfast on the terrace at the hotel.

"Would you mind awfully if I used the phone at Government House to call London?" he asked. "I ought to talk to my people about going back home."

"Be my guest," said Hannah.

At half past nine island time McCready put his call through to Denis Gaunt. What his deputy told him about the *Sunday Express* and the *Countdown* program confirmed to McCready that what he had hoped would happen had indeed happened.

Since the small hours of the morning a variety of news editors in London had been trying to call their correspondents in Port Plaisance. None of the calls had come through.

McCready had briefed the switchboard operator at the Quarter Deck that all the gentlemen of the press were extremely tired and were not to be disturbed under any circumstances. A hundred-dollar bill had sealed the compact. The switchboard operator duly told every London caller that his party was out but that the message would reach him immediately. The messages were duly passed to McCready, who duly ignored them. The moment for further press coverage had not yet come.

At eleven a.m. he was at the airport to greet two young SAS sergeants flying in from Fort Bragg, North Carolina, via Miami. Their baggage was meager, but it included one holdall containing their "toys," wrapped in beach towels. The Deceiver brought them back to the hotel and installed them in a room next to his own. They stashed their bags under their beds, locked the door, and went for a long swim. McCready had told them he would need them at ten the next morning at Government House.

Having lunched on the terrace, McCready strolled down through the town to the harbor. Jimmy Dobbs was working on the *Gulf Lady*. McCready spent thirty minutes with him, and they agreed on a charter voyage for the following day.

He was hot and sticky when he arrived at Government House, just before five. Jefferson served him an iced tea while he waited for Lieutenant Haverstock to return. The young officer had been playing tennis at a villa in the hills. McCready's question was simple. "Will you be here at ten o'clock tomorrow morning?"

"Yes, I suppose so," Haverstock said.

"Good," said McCready. "Do you have your full tropical dress uniform with you?"

"Yes," said the cavalryman. "Only got to wear it once. A state ball in Nassau six months ago."

"Excellent," said McCready. "Ask Jefferson to press it and polish up the leather and brasses."

He had dinner with Eddie Favaro at the hotel. Over coffee he asked, "What are you doing tomorrow?"

"Going home," said Favaro. "I have to be back Tuesday."

"Ah, yes. What time's your plane?"

"Booked an air taxi for midday."

"Couldn't delay it until four o'clock, could you?"

"I suppose so. Why?"

"Because I could do with your help. Say, Government House, ten o'clock? Don't be late. Monday is going to be a very busy day."

McCREADY rose at six. A pink dawn, herald of another balmy day, was touching the tips of the palm trees. It was delightfully cool. He went out into Parliament Square, where a taxi awaited him. His first duty was to say good-bye to an old lady.

He spent an hour with her, between seven and eight, took coffee and hot rolls, and made his farewells.

"Now don't forget, Lady Coltrane," he said as he rose to leave.

"Don't worry, I won't. And it's Missy."

At half past eight he dropped in on Chief Inspector Jones. He showed the chief of police his Foreign Office letter. "Please be at Government House at ten o'clock," he said. "Bring with you your two sergeants, four constables, your personal Land-Rover, and two plain vans. Do you have a service revolver?"

"Yes, sir."

"Please bring that too."

IN LONDON, in the ballistics department of the Home Office forensic laboratory in Lambeth, Mr. Alan Mitchell was staring into a microscope. For the fifth time he gently turned the bullet under the lens, staring at the striation marks left by the rifling in the gun barrel, picking out the other scratches that were as individual to a gun barrel as a fingerprint to a human hand. Finally he was satisfied. He whistled in surprise and went for one of his manuals. He had a whole library of them.

There were still other tests to be carried out. He knew that a detective waited impatiently for his findings, but he would not be hurried. He had to be sure, absolutely sure.

McCREADY dismissed his taxi at the gate of Government House and rang the bell. Jefferson recognized him and let him in. McCready explained that he had Mr. Hannah's permission to make another phone call on the international line. Jefferson showed him into the private study and left him.

McCready ignored the telephone and addressed himself to the desk. He had picked the locks the previous day and found what he wanted. They were in the bottom-left-hand drawer—two of them—but he needed only one.

It was an imposing sheet of paper, crisp to the touch and creamy, like parchment. In the center at the top, raised and embossed in gold, was the royal coat of arms. Beneath, in bold black lettering, were the words:

WE, ELIZABETH THE SECOND, OF THE UNITED KINGDOM OF GREAT BRITAIN AND NORTHERN IRELAND, AND OF ALL HER TERRITORIES AND DEPENDENCIES BEYOND THE SEAS, BY THE GRACE OF GOD QUEEN, DO HEREBY APPOINT . . . [here there was a gap] TO BE OUR . . . [another gap] IN THE TERRITORY OF . . . [a third gap].

The facsimile signature read, "Elizabeth R."

It was a royal warrant. *En blanc.* McCready took a pen from the inkstand and filled it in, using his best copperplate script. When he had finished, he blew gently on the ink to dry it and used the gubernatorial seal to stamp it. He had just appointed himself governor of the Barclays. For a day.

CHAPTER SIX

MCCREADY's five guests were assembled in the sitting room. The two SAS sergeants, Newson and Sinclair, stood by the wall in cream tracksuits and cleated training shoes. Lieutenant Haverstock had not changed into his dress uniform. He sat on one of the brocade chairs. Eddie Favaro was on the settee. Chief Inspector Jones stood by the door.

McCready took the warrant and offered it to Haverstock. "This arrived from London at dawn," he said. "Read, mark, learn, and inwardly digest."

Haverstock read the warrant. "Well, that's all right, then," he said, and passed it on.

"My first act," said McCready when they had each read it, "is to empower you all—excepting Chief Inspector Jones, of course—with the authority of special constables. You are hereby deputized. Secondly, I'd better explain what we are going to do."

He talked for thirty minutes. No one disagreed. Then he summoned Haverstock, and they left to change. Haverstock showed McCready the late governor's dressing room, where he found what he wanted right at the back of the wardrobe—the full-dress uniform of a British colonial governor, albeit two sizes too large.

When he reentered the sitting room, the rumpled tourist in the creased jacket was gone. On his feet the George boots, with their boxed spurs, gleamed. The tight trousers were white, as was the tunic jacket, buttoned to the throat. The gold buttons and gilt aiguillettes glittered in the sunlight, as did the spike on his Wolsey helmet. The sash around his waist was blue.

Haverstock was also in white, but his flat officer's cap was in dark blue, with a black peak. His aiguillettes were also gilt, as were the patches of chain mail covering each shoulder. A gleaming black leather strap lay slantwise across his chest and back, at the rear supporting a slim ammunition pouch.

"Right, Mr. Jones. Let us go," said McCready. "We must be about the Queen's business."

Chief Inspector Jones swelled. No one had ever asked him to be about the Queen's business before.

The cavalcade was led by the official Jaguar. Oscar drove, with a policeman beside him. McCready and Haverstock sat in the back, helmets on. Behind them came the Land-Rover, driven by a second constable, with Jones and Favaro beside him. Before leaving, Sergeant Sinclair had slipped Favaro a loaded Colt Cobra, which now nestled in the American detective's waistband.

The two vans were driven by the remaining two constables. Newson and Sinclair crouched by their open side doors. The police sergeants were in the last van.

The Jaguar rolled into Shantytown and stopped at the gate to the walled compound of Mr. Horatio Livingstone. McCready descended. So did Haverstock. A crowd of Barclayans emerged from the surrounding alleys and watched them, mouths agape. McCready did not ask for admission; he just stood in front of the gate while Sergeant Sinclair went over the wall and unlocked it from the inside. Sinclair stood back as McCready entered, with Haverstock at his side. The vehicles rolled after them at a walking pace.

Three men in gray safari suits were halfway across the compound, running for the gate, when McCready appeared. They stopped and stared at the two white-uniformed figures walking purposefully toward the front door. Sinclair disappeared.

McCready walked up the steps and into the house, Haverstock behind him. Favaro and Jones, the two police sergeants, and three constables left their vehicles and came after them.

In the big reception room the policemen took positions by the doors and windows. A door opened, and Horatio Livingstone emerged. "What is the meaning of this?" he shouted.

McCready held out his warrant. "Would you please read this?"

Livingstone read it and handed it back contemptuously.

"I would like you to summon all your Bahamian staff here—with their passports, if you please, Mr. Livingstone."

"By whose authority?" snapped Livingstone.

"I *am* the supreme authority," said McCready.

"Imperialist!" shouted Livingstone. "In fifteen days I will be the authority here, and then—"

"If you decline," said McCready calmly, "I will ask Chief Inspector Jones here to arrest you."

Livingstone glowered at them all. He called one of his aides and gave the order. One by one, the men in safari suits appeared. Favaro circulated, collecting their Bahamian passports. He handed them to McCready.

McCready went through them. "These passports are all false," he said. "These men are not Bahamians. Nor are you a democratic socialist. You are in fact a dedicated Communist who has worked for years for Fidel Castro, and these men around you are Cuban officers. Mr. Brown over there is Captain Hernan Moreno of the Dirección General de Información, the Cuban equivalent of the KGB. The others are also Cubans from the DGI."

It was Moreno who went for his gun first. It was tucked in his waistband at the back, hidden by the safari jacket. He was very fast, reaching for the Makarov before anyone could move.

The Cuban was stopped by a sharp shout from the top of the stairs. *"Fuera la mano, o serás fiambre."*

Hernan Moreno got the message just in time. His hand stopped moving. He froze. So did the six others, who were in the act of following his example.

Sinclair's Spanish was fluent and colloquial. *Fiambre* is a collation of cold meats, and in Spanish slang, a stiff, or corpse.

The two sergeants were at the top of the stairs, having entered through upper windows. Each held a small machine pistol.

"Now please ask your men to put their hands above their heads," said McCready.

Livingstone remained silent.

Favaro slipped up behind him, slid his arm around the man's chest, and eased the barrel of his Colt Cobra into his right nostril. "Three seconds. Then I have an awful accident."

"Do it," rasped Livingstone.

Fourteen hands went up. The three police constables went around collecting the seven handguns and frisking each Cuban. Two knives in calf sheaths were discovered.

"Search the house," said McCready.

The seven Cubans were lined up facing the sitting-room wall,

613

hands on top of heads. Livingstone sat in his club chair, covered by Favaro. The five local police officers searched the house. They discovered a variety of extra weapons, a large sum of American dollars and Barclayan pounds, and a shortwave radio with encrypter.

"Mr. Livingstone," said McCready, "I could ask Mr. Jones to charge your associates with a variety of offenses. Instead I am going to expel them all as undesirable aliens. Now. Within the hour. You may stay if you wish. You are, after all, a Barclayan by birth. But you might feel safer back where you belong, on Cuba."

Livingstone nodded.

The Cubans and Livingstone were marched out to the second of the two vans, waiting in the courtyard. They sat on the floor of the van, hands on heads, while Sergeant Newson, in the front seat, covered them with his machine pistol. The cavalcade formed up again and trundled slowly out of Shantytown to the fishing quay in Port Plaisance.

There the *Gulf Lady* waited, her engine idling. Behind her she towed a garbage scow newly fitted with two pairs of oars.

"Mr. Dobbs," said McCready, "please tow these gentlemen as far as Cuban territorial waters. Then cast them loose. They can row home with the onshore breeze. Lieutenant Haverstock here will accompany you. He will, of course, be armed." McCready looked down at the eight men in the scow. "One last thing. When you reach Cuba, you may tell Senor Castro that taking over the Barclays through a stooge candidate in the elections was a wonderful idea. But it ain't going to work. He'll have to salvage his political career some other way."

More than a thousand Barclayans thronged the quay as the *Gulf Lady* turned and headed for the open sea.

"One more chore, I believe, gentlemen," said McCready, and strode back down the jetty toward the Jaguar, his gleaming white uniform cutting a swath through the crowd of onlookers.

The wrought-iron gates to the estate of Marcus Johnson were locked. Newson and Sinclair went straight over the wall. Minutes later, from inside, there came a soft thunk, as of the edge of a hard hand coming into contact with the human frame. An electric motor hummed, and the gates swung open.

Inside, and to the right, was a small hut with a control panel and telephone. Slumped on the floor was a man in a bright beach shirt. He was thrown into the last van with the two police sergeants.

Marcus Johnson was descending the staircase, pulling a silk bathrobe around himself, when McCready strode in. "May I ask what the hell this means?" he demanded.

"Certainly," said McCready. "Please read this."

Johnson handed the warrant back. "So? I have committed no offense. You will regret this. I have lawyers."

"Good," said McCready. "You may well need them. Now, I want to interview your staff, Mr. Johnson. One has been kind enough to escort us to the door. Please bring him in."

The two police sergeants picked up the gatekeeper, whom they had been supporting between them, and dropped him on a sofa.

"The other seven, please, Mr. Johnson, with their passports."

Johnson thought it over, then called upstairs. A head appeared at the upper banister. Johnson gave the order.

Two men in bright shirts emerged from the veranda and stood beside their master. Five more came down from the upper rooms. Several muffled female squeals were heard. There had apparently been a party going on.

Chief Inspector Jones went around collecting their passports. McCready examined them all, shaking his head as he did so.

"They are not forgeries," Johnson said. "And as you see, all my associates entered Sunshine legally."

"Not quite," said McCready, "since all of them failed to declare that they have criminal records. In fact," he said evenly, "all are members of a criminal conspiracy known as the Yardbirds."

The Yardbirds, or Yardies, had started as street gangs in the slums of Kingston, taking their name from the backyard where they held sway. They began in protection racketeering and developed into purveyors of hemp and the cocaine derivative crack.

Four of the Yardies went for their waistbands, beneath their beach shirts.

"Freeze! Hold it!"

Newson and Sinclair had waited until the upper floor was vacated, except for the girls, before coming in through the windows. Now they were on the upper landing, machine pistols covering the open area below. Hands froze in mid-movement.

"They daren't fire," snarled Johnson. "They'd hit you all."

Favaro came behind Marcus Johnson, slid his left hand under the man's throat, and dug the Colt into his kidneys. "Maybe," he said, "but you go first."

"Hands above your heads, if you please," said McCready.

Johnson swallowed and nodded. The Yardies were ordered to lean against the wall, hands high. The police sergeants relieved them of their guns.

"I am a citizen of these islands," snapped Johnson, "a respectable businessman."

"No," said McCready, "you're not. You're a cocaine dealer. That's how you made your fortune. Running dope for the Medellín cartel and setting up dummy companies to launder cocaine money. And now, if you please, I would like to meet your Colombian chief executive, Senor Mendes."

"Never heard of him. No such man," said Johnson.

McCready thrust a photograph under his nose. "This Senor Mendes, or whatever he is calling himself now."

Johnson remained silent. McCready looked up and nodded to Newson and Sinclair. They had already seen the photograph. The soldiers disappeared. Minutes later there were two short, rapid bursts of fire. Sinclair and Newson appeared, pushing a man in front of them. He was thin and sallow, with straight black hair.

"I could charge your Jamaicans with a variety of offenses under the law here," McCready said to Johnson, "but in fact I have reserved nine seats on the afternoon plane to Nassau. The Bahamian police will be more than happy to escort you all to the Kingston flight. In Kingston you are expected."

The police searched the house. They found further weapons and a large amount of American dollars in an attaché case. In Johnson's bedroom were a few ounces of white powder.

McCready handed the attaché case to Chief Inspector Jones. "Distribute it among the island's charities," he said. "Burn the cocaine."

At four that afternoon the short-haul carrier from Nassau stood on the grass strip, its propellers whirling. The eight Yardbirds, all cuffed, were escorted aboard by two Bahamian police sergeants. Johnson, his hands cuffed behind him, stood waiting to board.

"Perhaps you can get a message to Senor Ochoa, or Senor Escobar, or whoever it is you work for," said McCready. "Tell him that the taking over of the Barclays through a proxy was a brilliant idea. To own the coast guards, customs, and police of the new state, to set up laundering banks—all extremely ingenious. And profitable, with the casinos, the bordellos. But tell him from me, it ain't going to work. Not in these islands."

Five minutes later the short-haul lifted off and headed away.

McCready walked over to a six-seat Cessna parked behind the hangar. Sergeants Newson and Sinclair were aboard, in the back row, on their way back to Fort Bragg. In front of them sat Francisco Mendes, his wrists tied to the frame of his seat.

"You cannot extradite me," he said in very good English, leaning out the open door. "You can arrest me and wait for the Americans to ask for extradition. That is all."

"My dear chap," said McCready, "you're not being arrested, just expelled." He turned to Eddie Favaro. "I hope you don't mind giving him a lift to Miami," he said. "Of course, it could be that as you touch down, you will suddenly recognize him as wanted by the Metro-Dade force. After that it's up to Uncle Sam."

They shook hands, and the Cessna ran up the grass strip, turned, paused, and put on full power. Seconds later it was out over the sea, turning northwest toward Florida.

McCready walked slowly back to the Jaguar, where Oscar waited. Time to go back to Government House, change, and hang the white uniform of governor back in the wardrobe.

WHEN he arrived, Detective Chief Superintendent Hannah was in Sir Marston's office taking a call from London. He had spent the whole afternoon waiting for it. McCready slipped upstairs and came down in his rumpled tropical suit. Hannah was hurrying out of the office, calling for Oscar and the Jaguar.

"It's remarkable," the ballistics expert, Alan Mitchell, had told Hannah. "One of the most extraordinary bullets I've ever examined. Certainly never seen one like it used in a murder before."

"What's odd about it?" asked Hannah.

"Well, the lead, to start with. It's extremely old. Seventy years at least. They haven't made lead of that molecular consistency since the early 1920s. The same applies to the powder."

"But what about the gun?" insisted Hannah.

"That's the point. The gun matches the ammunition. The bullet

617

has exactly seven grooves, with a right-hand twist, left by the barrel of the revolver. Only one handgun ever left those seven right-hand grooves, the Webley 4.55. Remarkable, what?"

Hannah was not an expert in handguns. "Fine, Alan. Now tell me, what is so special about the Webley 4.55?"

"Its age. It's a bloody antique. It was first issued in 1912, discontinued about 1920. It's a revolver with an extremely long barrel—accurate but unwieldy. They were issued as service revolvers to British officers in the First World War. Have you ever seen one?"

Hannah had thanked him. "Oh yes," he'd breathed, "I've seen one."

Now he was rushing across the hall when he saw that strange man Dillon, from the Foreign Office. "Use the phone if you like. It's free," he called, and climbed into the Jaguar.

WHEN he was shown in, Missy Coltrane was in her wheelchair in the sitting room. She greeted him with a welcoming smile. "Why, Mr. Hannah, how nice to see you again," she said. "Won't you sit down and take some tea?"

"Thank you, Lady Coltrane. I think I prefer to stand. I'm afraid I have some questions to ask you. Have you ever seen a handgun known as a Webley 4.55?"

"Why now, I don't think I have," she said meekly.

"I take leave to doubt that, ma'am. You have in fact got one. Your late husband's old service revolver. In that trophy case over there. And I'm afraid I must take possession of it."

He turned and walked to the glass-fronted case. They were all there—the medals, the insignia, the citations. But they had been rearranged. Behind some of them could be dimly discerned some oil smudges where another trophy had once hung.

Hannah turned back. "Where has it gone?" he asked tightly.

"Dear Mr. Hannah, I'm sure I don't know what you are talking about."

Beyond the windows the blue sea was darkling in the fading light. Somewhere out there, deep in its unquestioning embrace, he knew, lay a Webley 4.55.

"It was there, Lady Coltrane. On Thursday, when I came to see you. It was there in the cabinet."

"Mr. Hannah, what exactly is it you suspect of me?" she asked.

"I don't suspect, ma'am. I know. I know what happened. Last Tuesday, at about this hour, Firestone picked you and your chair up with those huge arms of his and placed you in the back of your van, as he did on Saturday for your shopping expedition. He drove you down to the alley behind the governor's residence, set you down, and with his own hands tore the lock off the steel gate. He pushed you through the gate and left you. I believe you had the Webley in your lap. Antique it may have been, but it had been kept oiled, and the ammunition was still inside it. With a short barrel you'd never have hit Sir Marston, but this Webley had a very long barrel—very accurate. The first shot missed and hit the wall. The second did the job and lodged in a flower basket full of loam. That's where I found it. London identified it today."

"Oh dear. Poor Mr. Hannah. It's a wonderful story, but can you prove it?"

"No, Lady Coltrane, I can't. I needed the gun or a witness. I'll bet a dozen people saw you and Firestone in that alley, but none of them will ever testify. Not against Missy Coltrane. But there are two things that puzzle me. Why? Why kill that unlovable governor? Did you *want* the police here?"

She smiled and shook her head. "The press, Mr. Hannah. Always snooping about, always asking questions, always investigating backgrounds. Always so suspicious of everyone in politics."

"Yes, of course. The ferrets of the press."

"And the other puzzle, Mr. Hannah?"

"Who warned you, Lady Coltrane? The gun was there on Thursday. Now it is gone. Who warned you?"

"Mr. Hannah, give my love to London when you get back. I haven't seen it since the blitz, you know. And now I never shall."

Desmond Hannah had Oscar drive him back to Parliament Square. Two youths in front of the hotel were dancing in the dust. One had a cassette player around his neck. The tape was playing a calypso number. Hannah did not recognize it. It was "Freedom Come, Freedom Go." He recognized "Yellow Bird," however—it was coming from the Quarter Deck bar. He recalled that in five days he had not heard a steel band or a calypso.

By the time Hannah strode up the steps of the hotel, he realized there was an air of levity about the streets. It did not match his own mood. He hated to lose a case, but he knew this one would remain on the file. He would return to Nassau on the plane that brought in the new governor and fly on to London. He crossed the terrace bar toward the staircase. There was that man Dillon again, sitting on a stool, nursing a beer. Strange fellow, he thought. Always sitting around waiting for something. Never actually seemed to *do* anything.

ON TUESDAY morning a de Havilland Devon droned in from Nassau and deposited the new governor, Sir Crispian Rattray. From the shade of the hangar McCready watched the elderly diplomat, crisp in cream linen and white Panama hat, descend from the aircraft to meet the welcoming committee.

Lieutenant Haverstock, back from his marine odyssey, introduced him to various notables, including Dr. Caractacus Jones and his nephew, Chief Inspector Jones. After the introductions the small cavalcade drove off toward Port Plaisance.

Sir Crispian would discover that he had little to do. The two candidates appeared to have withdrawn their candidacies and gone on vacation. He would appeal for other candidates. None would come forward. The British government might well concede that a referendum would be appropriate.

Desmond Hannah boarded the empty Devon for the journey to Nassau. Ten minutes after it left, McCready's air taxi from Miami arrived. He had to return his portable telephone to the Miami CIA office and say a few thank-yous to friends in Florida.

The Piper took off, and McCready had a last look down at the interior of the island. On a dusty track a small brown child looked up and waved. McCready waved back. With luck, and for the moment, he thought, the boy could grow up without ever having to live under the red flag or to sniff cocaine.

EPILOGUE

"I AM sure we are all deeply grateful," said Timothy Edwards, "to Denis for his excellent presentation. I would suggest that as the hour is late, my colleagues and I mull the matter over between ourselves and deliver our view in the morning."

Denis Gaunt had to return his file to the clerk from records. When he turned around, Sam McCready was gone. He had slipped away almost as Edwards finished speaking. Gaunt traced him ten minutes later to his office.

McCready was still in shirtsleeves, his creased cotton jacket over a chair, puttering about. Two cardboard wine crates stood on the floor.

"What are you doing?" asked Gaunt.

"Clearing out my bits and bobs."

"You're crazy," said Gaunt. "I think we may have cracked it. Not Edwards, of course, but the two controllers."

McCready straightened up and looked at the two boxes. "Not a lot, really, for thirty years," he murmured.

"Sam, it's not over yet. They could change their minds."

McCready turned and gripped Gaunt by his upper arms. "Denis, you're a great guy. You did a good job in there. And I'm going to ask the chief to let you take over the desk. But you have to learn which side of the sky the sun rises. It's over. Verdict and sentence were handed down weeks ago, in another office, by another man."

Denis Gaunt sat down miserably in his boss's chair. "Then what the hell was it all for?"

"The hell it was for was this: Because I care about this Service, and because they're getting it wrong. Because there's a bloody dangerous world out there, and it's not getting less dangerous, but more so. And because idiots like Edwards are going to be left looking after the security of this old country that I happen to love, and that frightens the hell out of me. I knew I couldn't change anything in that hearing, but I wanted to make them squirm. Sorry, Denis. I should have told you."

Denis Gaunt looked as if he were attending a funeral. "The chief will give you a farewell party."

"No party. I can't stand cheap sparkling wine. Plays merry hell with my gut. So does Edwards' being nice to me. Walk me down to the main door?"

Down the corridor to the lift, on the ride to the ground floor, across the tiled lobby, colleagues and secretaries called, "Hi, Sam." "Hallo, Sam." They did not say, Bye-bye, Sam, but it was what they meant. A few of the secretaries paused, as if they would like to straighten his tie one last time. He nodded and smiled and walked on.

The main door stood at the end of the tiled hall. Sam McCready pushed it open to the street. A wave of hot summer air blew in. He turned, reached into his breast pocket, and brought out an envelope.

"Give it to them, Denis. Tomorrow morning. It's what they want, after all."

Denis took it and stared at it. "You had it all the time," he said. "You wrote it days ago. You cunning old bastard!"

But he was talking to the closing door.

McCready turned right and ambled toward Westminster Bridge, half a mile away, his jacket over his shoulder. It was a hot June afternoon, one of those that made up the great heat wave of the summer of 1990.

It would be nice out at sea today, he thought, with the Channel bobbing bright and blue under the sun. Perhaps he should take that cottage in Devon, with his own boat in the harbor, after all.

Westminster Bridge rose before him. Across it the Houses of Parliament, whose freedoms and occasional foolishness he had spent thirty years trying to protect, towered against the blue sky.

Halfway across the bridge, a news vendor stood beside his stand with a pile of copies of the *Evening Standard*. A placard at his feet bore the words BUSH-GORBY—COLD WAR OVER—OFFICIAL. McCready stopped to buy a paper.

"Thank you, guv," said the news vendor. He gestured toward his placard. "All over, then, eh? All them international crises. Thing of the past."

"What a lovely idea," agreed McCready, and strolled on.

Four weeks later Saddam Hussein invaded Kuwait. Sam McCready heard the radio bulletin while fishing two miles off the Devon coast. He considered the news flash, then decided it was time to change his bait.

"When is the movie coming out?"

Frederick Forsyth has heard that question many times. Since 1973 a dozen of his novels and stories have been made into motion pictures,

Frederick Forsyth

including *The Odessa File, The Dogs of War,* and his first novel, *The Day of the Jackal.* But in the case of the stories that appear in *The Deceiver,* it was the other way around. "These were written initially as screenplays," Forsyth says. "Several years ago I was commissioned to devise, script, and produce six original thrillers for a British TV company." (American readers may be familiar with these productions, which aired on cable television's USA Network.) Forsyth later selected four of the stories and rewrote them to fit within the new framework that became *The Deceiver.*

Forsyth, a fifty-three-year-old British newspaperman turned novelist, agrees with his hero, Sam McCready, that espionage will continue to flourish long after the cold war is considered history. He also believes that the best of those he calls the thriller novelists won't be without subject matter in the years ahead. "Most spy writers rely on more than simple espionage for their inspiration," he notes. "And there is plenty of material—the rise of terrorism, hostage taking, and the ever explosive Middle East."

A farm in Hertfordshire, England, which Forsyth bought five years ago, is where he does much of his work. And despite all evidence to the contrary, Forsyth claims he is a "lazy" author. ("I'm the only writer I know who has raised indolence to an art form.") What, then, is his next project? He will say only that he's "mulling over an idea." But his many fans around the world—and filmmakers alike—are waiting eagerly.